SOOT

DAN VYLETA

WEIDENFELD & NICOLSON

First published in the US in 2019 by Doubleday
a division of Penguin Random House LLC, New York

First published in Great Britain in 2020 by Weidenfeld & Nicolson
This paperback edition published in 2021 by Weidenfeld & Nicolson
an imprint of the Orion Publishing Group Ltd
Carmelite House, 50 Victoria Embankment,
London EC4Y 0DZ

An Hachette UK Company

1 3 5 7 9 10 8 6 4 2

A CIP catalogue record for this book is available
from the British Library

ISBN (Mass Market Paperback) 978 1 4746 0096 5
ISBN (eBook) 978 0 2976 0997 1

Printed and bound in Great Britain by Clays Ltd, Elcograf, S.p.A.

www.orionbooks.co.uk
www.weidenfeldandnicolson.co.uk

For Lily and Ginger,

who have the biggest smiles in all of Ontario.

And for Boyd.

With love and thanks, old friend.

Dramatis Personae

SMOKE
OR,
THE HISTORY OF THE FIRST REVOLUTION:
A THEATRICAL CYCLE IN DRAMATIC DIALOGUE, MONOLOGUE, AND MIME

Thomas Argyle	An angry youth. Shot in the face and marked for life with a coal-dyed scar. Hero of the revolution.
Charlie Cooper	Thomas's friend. A sweet-tempered youth. It is he who convinces his friends to complete Lady Naylor's revolution.
Lady Naylor	A well-born revolutionary. Conceives the plan to change the world by dousing it in Smoke.
Livia Naylor	Lady Naylor's daughter. Vows to stop her mother, then helps fulfil her plan instead. A proud, wilful young woman.
Baron Naylor	Livia's father and a madman haunting his own attic. Former teacher to Renfrew.
Erasmus Renfrew	Master of Smoke and Ethics at Thomas and Charlie's school. A liberal who advocates rational progress and morality. Imprisons and tortures Charlie Cooper.

Eleanor Renfrew	Renfrew's niece. Subject to special disciplinary measures. Rescued by Charlie from her uncle's house.
Sebastian Aschenstaedt	Scientist and illegal immigrant to Britain. Assists Lady Naylor with the technical side of her revolution and procures Mowgli for her.
Mowgli	A child innocent of Smoke. Stolen from his jungle tribe, Smoke-infected to serve Lady Naylor's purpose, and burdened with a borrowed name.
Grendel	A man devoid of passions. Stopped smoking after a childhood illness. He adopts Mowgli and kills Julius by putting a bullet through his neck.
Julius Spencer	The issue of Lady Naylor's first marriage. Estranged from his mother, then befriended by her for tactical reasons. A villain. Also, a victim. Shoots Thomas, wounds Renfrew, and gives himself over to the Smoke. His carcass becomes the revolution's kindling.

OR,

THE HISTORY OF THE SECOND REVOLUTION:
A ROMANCE IN FIVE ACTS, INCLUDING AN OVERTURE AND NACHSPIEL

As above (barring the dead), and introducing:

B. A. Smith	A capitalist. The incarnation of the World Spirit (self-declared).
Balthazar Black	A playwright with a secret.
Etta May Maine	A member of Balthazar's troupe. A soothing influence.
Jagat Singh	A bicycle mechanic in the Raj who has read Marx and Lokmanya Tilak.
Godfrey Livingstone	A nihilist. Servant to the Lord Protector of Britain.

And many more!

OVERTURE

Darkness.

A match is struck, a candle lit. The light reveals a card table, a simple chair; a man, still young if no longer a youth. Gaunt, upright, tall. He places a book upon the table; fishes a stub of pencil from behind his ear; opens the book to a blank page; readies himself to write.

When he bends down over the book, the flame finds his hair and taps it for rich copper.

When we were young, the Smoke was simple. It was the physical manifestation of sin. It marked our bodies, left sooty shame on our linen. We lived in its shadow; were judged by it and praised for its absence; tasted it illicitly, like forbidden fruit. It structured society, aligned power with morals. Smoke was the central truth of our lives.

Then everything changed. You have heard the story: of the three spoilt brats who took it upon themselves to understand the Smoke. Thomas, Charlie, Livia—that's the order they always put us in, God knows why. We were young and had all the arrogance of youth. Smoke was our enemy then; by learning its truth, we thought we might defeat it.

We unchained it instead.

Oh, it wasn't an accident. We had a choice. We had learned something, you see, a secret well kept. Smoke was a disease, an infection of the organs. It came to us late in human history, in the 1600s, during that first great age of discovery. Some explorer must have brought it back; we still don't know from where. It infected the world—well nigh all of it—and retrospectively was named eternal, God's punishment for our Fall from Eden.

I still remember the shock of it. Smoke was a disease, an aberration. *It wasn't meant to be.* You would have thought it would have steeled our resolve to find a cure. But the more we looked for it, the more we realised something else, something subtle, no less shocking in its implication—that Smoke was a disease that made us more human, not less. It was a language of the body; a primitive tongue, animated by the deepest urges of the flesh. Ugly. Full of truth.

And of *potential.*

Imagine Smoke a whistle. All of our lives, we had been taught that the purpose of a whistle was to sound alarm. No, not just taught—we had been *trained* to it, like you can train a dog to bite all those who raise a stick, until every twitch of the arm caused our hackles to rise, our fur to bristle. Smoke was shrill to our ears. And then somebody came along and showed us *melody*. For there was music in the Smoke; a whole spectrum of emotion threading the raw need.

Lady Naylor taught us this—Livia's mother. She longed to teach the world. She showed us how to quicken the Soot locked within the soil, quicken it so thoroughly that it was like an orchestra rising out of the land itself: ugly and harsh in one place; playful, quiet, beautiful in another. She wished to reinfect the world. Retrain it, too, to this music of the body.

There was a hitch to this. Lady Naylor was a villain. To achieve what she wanted, she stole a child. We christened him Mowgli, after Kipling's hero. He came from South America, we were told, from a tribe of innocents deep within the jungle who had never been infected by the Smoke. She had him stolen and crated like an animal, then infected him deliberately once he was in her grasp. She needed his blood at the moment of change, while the disease spread through his resisting body, realigning his organs, changing him. A man called Aschenstaedt helped her, a scientist and engineer: it was his ingenuity that found the child. Aschenstaedt—and Grendel: a man incapable of Smoke, who traded his loyalty for milady's promise that his wife and he could keep the child and raise him as their own. As for Thomas, Livia, and me—we were a mere nuisance in their plan, a complication. They bamboozled us with half-truths; manipulated us; thought us misdirected and defeated.

And still we stopped them on the brink.

I repeat: we stopped them. The world need not have changed. The Smoke could have remained simple.

It was I who suggested we fulfil milady's plan.

And so I, too, am a villain: not just for the consequences of our actions (for we woke something unimagined in the land, a devil quick and ravenous) but for making use of that poor child's blood. Just like milady, I made a means of him who had been so terribly abused. Milady's son—dead of a gunshot, consumed by darkest Smoke—served us as kindling. One can hardly think of a darker conception, an uglier way of birthing a new world.

Two moments stay with me, after all these years. Both are laced with regret. The first is Grendel, lifting Mowgli onto his shoulders, carrying him home to his wife. I thought Grendel a monster at the time—a man who could not smoke; who seemed to know no love, no horror at himself. And yet he carried the child gently, lacing Mowgli's fingers under his chin. It was my companions and I who later failed to inquire after the safety of the boy. He was lost to history; to the chaos of the following years.

The second moment happened earlier and is unrelated, though it, too, centres on a child abused. Renfrew's cottage; his niece in harness. Her name was Eleanor. Renfrew had built a cage around her body so that it would straighten her soul. I did not see it then, but Renfrew was milady's mirror image: his whole life, too, was devoted to the Smoke. He, too, took an innocent and infected her with his obsession. I rescued the child only to abandon her on the school porter's—Cruikshank's—humble porch. It was he who cut her out of Renfrew's contraption. The *snip-snip* of his scissors: it worries my sleep.

Of Eleanor, too, I lost sight, though here at least I did inquire. Cruikshank left the island, I was told; the New World called him, as it called so many in those years. Of the girl I found no trace.

They say the Revolution eats its children.

Lately I have wondered if it is not the other way around.

ACT I

THE NEW WORLD

APRIL–MAY 1909

Laud we the gods;
And let our crooked smokes climb to their nostrils.

—WILLIAM SHAKESPEARE, *CYMBELINE*

[1]

They open with *The Lovers*.

It's a simple stage set. A bed just wide enough to suggest it serves marriage, not sleep. A vase with dried flowers; a garland on the wall. The bed is freshly made; in the air, drifting onstage from behind the curtain, Meister Lukas's ghostly countertenor. A wedding strain. It is enough to set the scene; the faint noise of guests leaving in the background.

The groom enters first. He is dressed in peasant finery, clean, God-fearing, and shabby. A young man, inexperienced and handsome. Two steps and he is at the bed. He stops before it, watches it as though it were a dog in a cage.

Sleeping.

Liable to wake.

The groom sits down on the starched sheet, keeping his weight in his thighs, so that only his buttocks brush the pert white linen. Again that long, suspicious look down the length of the bed, nervous and fretting. Then, for a moment as fleeting as a sneeze, some other note enters his gaze and one hand spreads on the pillow to a five-pointed star. And all at once the Smoke is there. It jumps from his mouth and hangs an inch off his chin, in the cone of light of a well-focussed lamp: hangs frothy, insubstantial, many-limbed.

Alive.

The groom sees it, claws at it, wishes to shove it back down his throat; leaps up, aghast, inspects the linen, and finds he has made a single crescent mark. A quarter buttock of Soot. His fingers trace it as they would a scar.

Then *she* is onstage. The bride. The audience have not seen her come on, transfixed as they are by the groom and allowing the light to guide their focus. That light flickers out now and a second comes alive, exquisitely timed; catches her wedding dress and makes a home in its starched cotton. She glows with her virginity, downstage, astride a low stool, tucked in behind a tiny dresser. On it stands a disk of mirror no bigger than her palm.

Oh, she is good tonight: so full of emotion that she is on the edge of Smoke—the audience can sense it, can smell it on the air—yet so terrified, so very meek and shy, as to make all thought of Smoke impossible. She shivers; tugs at her long, unadorned sleeves; crosses, uncrosses her legs (a murmur in the audience at this; a flicker of lust, disarmed by pity); watches the little mirror. The stagehand has positioned it well: it reflects back upstage to a second mirror, tall and rectangular like a doorway. A fluorescent glow spreads from this second mirror, cold, electrical, transforming it into a gateway to a ghostly realm. The bride's inner self. It is hemmed by a plain black lacquered frame.

Half the bride's face is visible on this cold slate serving up her soul: one eye, one ear, a twist of braid, and half of her delicate mouth. And next to this half-face—the laws of optics contracting the stage and folding space into a single frame—stands the bed, still unlit, a white rectangle, soft and hazy in its outlines. In its midst, just visible, like an inverted moon, is the crescent of Soot painted by her husband's buttock.

The bride rises, gets her dress tangled in the stool. It falls, impossibly loud, accentuated by an offstage cymbal. At the sound, the lights go up and her husband steps out of the shadows. They link hands, bride and groom; it feels daring in the sudden blaze of light. They smile. A sigh goes through the audience, of goodwill and relief. The two love each other.

All is well.

But for all their love the bed stands unmoved, unwelcoming; burdens them with its suggestion; expects them, lily-white, for an act that cannot but douse them in sin.

The lovers try a kiss. It is brief, chaste, smokeless. When the bride starts crying the audience sees it in the mirror: she has turned her back on them. The Smoke that has started to rise in the auditorium now reflects these tears. It speaks of old pain. There are many here who remember; living in a world where they were ashamed of their needs. Their wedding night. It played out differently for every couple (as awkwardness; as pain; as guilt). How often was it that the wedding sheets were burned? Not in ceremony or celebration but shamefacedly, by a husband crouching before the hearth in tears; by a wife shaken in her deepest sense of her own decency, transformed by marriage into a whore. And these two here, they are hopeless: pious and simple, brought up in a world where the inside of each bedroom in the village was whitewashed afresh during the weeks of Lent. Their bodies burning with love and need each for the other, they find themselves contracted to a sacred union that obliges them to a first coupling that must repudiate all lust. They walk to their bed like thieves, taking care to avoid the other's eyes.

(And then—as they stand before their marriage bed, shoulder to shoulder, hip to hip, not touching, not daring to scoot apart, unsure whether to sit or lie, to undress themselves or the other, fully or partially—just *then*, there is a pause, a hesitation, exterior to the play, like a hole within the fabric of the theatre. Within it, Balthazar can feel the audience like a living thing. It is there in its noise; in the web of its nascent Smoke. He stands at the threshold between stage and auditorium, hidden from the audience by a wooden screen. *Wait*, he signals to his actors and stagehands. Let frustration breed. Let them think you are lost out there, have forgotten your lines; or rather, that you have remembered yourselves: actors, not bride and groom. It will give you material that you can shape; Smoke-fabric you can weave. And then—three breaths, four—he gestures: *Now*.)

And so: a storm breaks. Meister Lukas again, raining down a barrel of peas onto a sheet of metal. Rain as loud and hard as hail. The large mirror turns window, shows a smear of cloud approaching in a moon-bright sky. It is a crude trick, a painted scroll that can be drawn across the screen, slowly changing the scenery, bringing the cloud closer along with its curtain of rain. Not just any rain: Smoke-rain, unmistakable now to those who have stood like these two, witnessing its first approach. Soon it fills the whole of the window and—a fine effect this, perfected after much trial—begins to patter as real water onto the stage at the bride's and groom's feet, then soaks their fronts, until that peasant shirt clings to his broad chest and her sodden dress discloses the woman underneath its virgin folds.

Next, the Smoke starts, pumped from beneath the stage through a crack in the floorboards, near enough the mirror-window so as to seem to blow in from outside. It isn't real Smoke but a chemical concoction. Harmless and scentless, it billows around bride and groom. They breathe it; she utters a moan; he turns to her, cradles her cheek in his palm, bends down to her in a kiss that is almost a bite (a touch too much perhaps, an actor getting in the way of the pure language of the gesture).

And just like that their own Smoke—real Smoke—leaps out of bride and groom, thick and many-hued. It is caught on the draught of two hand-operated fans and carries out into the audience in rich tendrils of emotion. The lights die, are cut off all at once; the bed squeaks, as the bride slams the groom's weight into its mattress.

Then: nothing. Not the sound of their lovemaking, which would push the scene into farce; no whispers or giggles or sweetly struck strings. Rather, a blank silence falls to be filled by the audience members themselves. The drama is theirs now, played out in their heads; on their skin, and in the air that binds them. It is guided by two well-positioned Shapers and contained by Etta May, the troupe's Soother who is also in charge of the bell. Ten seconds, Balthazar has instructed her, fifteen at most, and shorter if the Smoke starts to taste wrong.

Balthazar counts sixteen. Then the bell rings and light floods the room, thick with Smoke, already dispersing in the draught created by the redirected fans and hastily thrown-open windows. Its taste is lovely, the Smoke's, full of yearning and sadness and frisky, playful need. Ada and Victor—bride and groom—take their bows: his shirt is wide open and the hem of her skirt is in her hand, showing calf and knee. Balthazar snorts. It would be pointless to reprimand them. They are one now with the audience's Smoke. When they kiss, the applause carries envy but no resentment.

Victor's hand makes smudges on Ada's shapely bum.

[2]

They take a break. Not an intermission, just a few minutes for the last of the Smoke to disperse and the auditorium's air to clear. Best to paint new emotion on a clean slate.

While the stage set is being changed—the bed exchanged for the stylised prow of a ship; stool and dresser traded for a large, barnacle-studded tub filled with stinky brine—Etta May makes her way over to Balthazar. This irritates him. It is best if the Shapers and Soothers are not identified by the audience but merge with it. Balthazar does not look up as she steps behind the screen that shelters him; feels a stiffness come into his features. It turns his face into a stone, Etta May once told him. A brittle lump of flint: sheer and angular, barely troubled by a sculptor's hand; not enough skin for too much cheekbone; the slip of the chisel for a nose. Tarred, then dry-aged in a kiln. She herself is fleshy, closer to fifty than forty, cheeks florid like a baker's wife. In the heat of the room she had shed her cape, and her décolleté is heaving in her low-cut dress; her bosom Soot-flecked yet pale as yeasty uncooked dough.

"Don't scowl, Balthazar. Makes you look ugly. Scrunched like a hand puppet. A sour Negro Punch."

He flares his nostrils, already soothed, then makes a point of scowling more deeply. "You're leaving your post, Em. What do you want? Get fired?"

"Get a raise, more like."

Etta May smiles, fishes a cigarette from one rolled-up dress sleeve and lights it with a book of matches produced from out the other. Her movements are deliberate, exaggerated. Is she nervous? No: excited. Wishing to disclose her excitement and at the same time defer its explanation; build suspense. Balthazar makes a mental note of the gesture, of the pause it imposes. It will do well in a future play.

"There is someone here," Etta May says at last, blowing cigarette smoke past his face, then watching it curl and break up, so different in its movements from real Smoke it is like comparing water to quicksilver. "Someone unusual. In the audience."

"Who?"

"Can't tell, hon. Towards the back."

"A Spoiler?"

"No. More like the opposite." She hesitates. "Though that's not quite right either. Someone unusual. Potent. You may want to have a sniff around."

She takes another puff, passes over the cigarette, and smiles up at him in that way she has, at once sassy and maternal. Then she navigates her hips around the edge of the screen and back into the crowd. The cigarette she has left behind tastes of her lipstick and powder. Balthazar smokes it down to a stub. His eyes are on a crack in the screen and, beyond it, on the crowd.

There are perhaps sixty people in the hall. It could accommodate five times that number, but in a space like this, a market hall rich in brick and tile but poor in doors and windows, where the Smoke can rise but not disperse unless chased out by the action of some well-aimed fans, more would be dangerous, and greedy. Besides, there is no need. They can always put on more shows, raise the price of tickets. No matter how expensive they get, the performance is always sold out. Farmers paying in grain, in chickens, in pails of milk; trappers offering furs; shipping agents bringing silver, fabrics and spices, imported trinkets made of gold. The troupes that can do *this*, and do it safely, are few and far between. It is a question of material, and of personnel. All of it: his doing. Balthazar has written every gesture, scripted every burp of Smoke; has done the hiring, hand-picked every talent, from the actors to the stagehands and set painter, to those with whom he seeds the audience, orchestrating their response. You could say that he invented it. Smoke Theatre.

It is the art form of the age.

There are other companies, but his is the best: not just in the colonies, but anywhere Balthazar has been.

Anywhere it is allowed.

Shaper, Soother, Spoiler: these are theatre terms, specific to a practice not a decade old. Shapers are men and women one places in the crowd to guide its Smoke-response; actors whose disposition and training allow them to receive the stage emotion and magnify it. Soothers are sinkholes of a sort, slow and placid in their Smoke, and uncommonly kind in disposition. They walk the crowd looking for Spoilers: audience members whose Smoke is powerful and dangerous to the performance; who will take the love offered up by the play, or its grief, or its frustration, and have it feed their rage. It is a dangerous game, bringing scores of people together in an auditorium, dangerous, and rewarding.

It is a mystery to Balthazar how Aristotle could have written on catharsis, in an age long before Smoke.

[3]

The lights are dimmed, the stage made ready for the second piece. *Fishermen at Sea*. There will be words this time, and the emotional palette will centre on a forlorn sort of wonder. Four men, blown off-course in the dangerous waters between Norway and the English North, cod heavy in their holds; cold-chapped fingers and wind-blown faces; clutching tin cups of hot tea. Land is in sight. It starts in camaraderie, then; in the love working-men bear for each other when business is good and they have survived another day.

Then there comes a smear, staining the horizon, a sight familiar to many of the audience but new to the men: a strange, tinted fog that rises out of the cold of the land—out of the hills and rocks and sand-blown beaches of Northumbria—and slips into the Soot-thickened sea, igniting it until each swell rolls with a hazy halo and each trough fills crest-deep with a viscous mist. The sun rises, throws the fishermen's shadows towards the darkened water; a nice effect, crudely symbolic and pleasing to the eye. One after the other, the fishermen turn and show the audience their faces. Behind them, sunwards, the way to Norway lies clear. They consider it, unsettled by the blanket of Smoke that swaddles England; then turn their backs on sun and light and sail towards it all the same, for beyond the Smoke there lie their homes. As they enter the fog, one amongst the crew, the youngest, a Welshman, starts into song, singing shyly in his native tongue. The song's melody—thin, brittle, true—fills the room with trepidation and thin silvery Smoke. Out in the auditorium it turns a lighter shade yet, and is passed from row to row like a chalice of sugared wine. People weep in the full awareness that they are enjoying their tears.

It is a short play, good-natured and pleasing, connecting past and present, old and new. Saint John: a town of immigrants, hailing from England eight times out of ten. There isn't a tale as sweet as one of home. Balthazar has used it to open and close shows in the past. They have a repertoire of more than fifty now, all one-act pieces, not really plays so much as single scenes, situations, moments in time. Emotions given life; Smoke summoned and disseminated. But really they are all the one play, the only story the audience wants to see and hear. Their own story: Smoke's Second Coming. To England, to the colonies: everywhere it has reached.

The troupe has tried other stories. They have revived plays Balthazar found mouldering in private libraries and converted to the theatre of Smoke. People can be made to care about doomed, lovelorn Romeo, or about Vittoria Corombona, White Devil of Padua—but it is hard work. The time of kings and dukes; power struggles amongst princes; words written before the First Smoke: they all seem distant now, unconnected to the mystery that is the present. And then, too, when staging these old plays, one has to manage their crass violence. You cut out Lavinia's tongue onstage and the auditorium turns to tar. Anger and passion, secreted as outrage on four dozen skins. On a good night. On a bad night—the wrong audience, a Spoiler in the front row, angry with his lot—it turns to hunger and lust.

No, Smoke Theatre is at its best when it works quieter moments, and smaller emotions; when it captures doubt and tenderness, surprise and yearning, and leaves hatred to real life, where it breeds readily enough without Art's midwifery.

[4]

While the applause still lingers, and the sailors remain linked, arms thrown around each other's shoulders, a weeping scrum of men; while the buzzing ventilators stand inverted, bringing the audience's Smoke from spectators to actors rather than the other way around, thus forging a fresh link between stalls and stage; while the room is thick with memories and fellowship, and Sashinka, the players' cat, leaps to much hilarity onto the wooden rim of the brine-filled tub, sticking its arse in the air as it takes a deep sniff; while the room is thus self-occupied and happy, Balthazar does what he rarely thinks to do. He leaves the shelter of his screen and inserts his old, gaunt figure into the crowd. Flimsy though a barrier the screen may be, it is tall enough to encourage Smoke to pass around it, creating a pocket of almost clear air. In the crowd, Balthazar is exposed. The experience is immediate, like submerging in the sea. A loss of self; some inner fish waking, fanning its gills, like an atavism of the blood. Balthazar slips into the press, feeling his own Smoke leap in greeting, add its flavours to the mix. It is not aimless, this drifting and sharing of the self: Balthazar is looking for something, with his skin more than his eyes, an irregularity in the pulse of the crowd.

At first the only such irregularity he senses is Etta May, a quiet eddy in the current of emotion, offering repose. The two Shapers, Kolya and Pavla, are invisible to him, have blended seamlessly into the tide. Balthazar searches on, distracted now, temporarily relieved of the burden of being *alone*. He slows, tempted to linger in particular patches, constellations where his neighbours' Smoke is most in sympathy with his own wants. But enough is left of him—enough curiosity and self-regard; enough of his artist's sense of mission; enough discipline and force of will—to push on, ever deeper, towards the back of the room. Here: a man ripe with self-hate, temporarily at peace, disarmed by the festive goodwill of the room. There: a bent old grandmother of eighty receiving, in thin mauve billows, the raging appetites of adolescent flesh from a pink-cheeked schoolboy three steps to her left and trading them for memories of libidinal adventures half a century past (they both giggle where they stand). And then, his eyes closed now, reading the room only through his skin, Balthazar senses someone else, someone strange. Self-contained yet not a blank, shaping the Smoke in ways that are hard to make sense of. *Like a whale,* it comes to him. *Displacing half the ocean, yet trying not to move. Lest it crush the other fish.*

A talent, Etta May said.

Unusual.

Balthazar stops and opens his eyes, trying to identify who it is.

He is too late. Backstage, someone (Lukas? Edie?) has decided that it is time to open once more the market hall's ring of narrow windows, set high upon its tiled walls, and angle the fans so as to clear out the room. As the Smoke disperses, Ada's voice, surprisingly deep for her girlish looks, announces an intermission. It is too early for this: there were to be three little plays before the break. Balthazar realises it is his doing: he has abandoned his post, leaving the actors stranded without instructions. He turns, torn between the desire to reclaim control and to pinpoint the talent before all trace is gone. He has chased her to the far end of the hall, has formed an impression of who it might be. But now that the audience is in motion—heading outdoors, each taking the memory of their communion out into the street, where they will stand alone, divided by space and icy sea breeze, their hands thrust into pockets—now, caught in this steady flow of bodies, it is hard for Balthazar to make sure of his impression and harder yet to give chase. He is left with a guess, a glimpse. A girl not yet twenty. Straight auburn hair, touched by rust. A plump curve of cheek; a back held very straight.

Then she is swallowed by the crowd.

[5]

Eight plays in total; two intermissions. Two and a half hours of intense emotion. The room is painted by the time they leave, with patches of Soot like shadows cast and then discarded, stuck to tiles and dirty brick.

They finish with a traditional piece, one of many belonging to a cycle Balthazar has been working on, what he has come to think of as his life's work. The cycle is far from finished. One day he will perform all its plays in sequence, or perhaps in reverse. He has chosen a title and wants to publish the manuscript; has worked out a system of Smoke notation based around the symbols used in the choreography of dance. *The Rebels.* A running time of seven or eight hours, perhaps more. They will have to build a theatre especially, to handle the accumulation of Smoke: in North America, or on the Continent, or perhaps even in England, if politics and Gales permit. Tonight, though, the players will present the merest fragment. Act one, scene three. Balthazar wrote it many years ago, after his visit to the school. A pilgrimage, really, disappointing in its details. Few of the teachers remained; fewer yet deigned to talk to him. He had walked the grounds but received no access to the buildings.

It's a quiet scene, simple and clean. The stage set shows a dormitory, a little generic perhaps, a reflection of other schools visited, to which access was easier. A row of narrow beds and dressers. Some grass-stained rugby socks wilting on the floor. A stack of dog-eared schoolbooks, a blazer and tie tossed across the back of a chair. Daylight falls sickly through a window upstage left.

Two schoolboys run in, seventeen or thereabouts, one dressed in travelling clothes and holding a suitcase, the other in school uniform and cap. The casting was difficult. Most of the actors simply look too old and it was important to get the physical types right, familiar as they are from images and songs. In the end Balthazar settled on Ada and Geoffrey, their set painter. Ada has taken off the blond wig she wore earlier, as virgin bride, and her short hair has been hennaed until it shines in copper tones. Geoffrey looks much as he always does, intense and sullen. Two schoolboys, one a gentle redhead, the other dark and looking more like a butcher's apprentice than the son of the old nobility.

A murmur goes through the hall. The boys have been recognised. Here they are, in Saint John, New Brunswick, a town still halfway between civilisation and frontier. Shopkeepers, sea captains, the town doctor and his wife. Cowpokes, two or three natives, a gentleman dressed in his servant's clothes, worried for his reputation (or his laundry bill). One thousand miles and a revolution from the verdant fields of Oxfordshire. And yet: the boys have been recognised. Of course they have. In Britain, on the Continent, up and down the North American coasts: there is not a story more widely told than theirs. Balthazar has long puzzled over who took such care to spread it, put such colour in its details. He is a connoisseur of story, and this one, it has been *shaped*.

There is a sudden press as the audience rushes closer to the stage, as though for one mad moment they have come to believe the players have conjured the actual persons, enticed them to return. Thomas Argyle and Charlie Cooper. Balthazar knows some songs about them that, well sung, never fail to move him to tears; others that would make a madam blush. He would bet good money that the audience knows some songs, too.

Already, the auditorium is smoking. A curious flavour, of longing and wonder; twists of anger, of disappointed expectation. Onstage, the action is limited, deliberately contained. One boy showing the other around.

Charlie explains the workings of the school to the new arrival, who continues to hold the suitcase in one meaty fist. The words are almost incidental but set in blank verse all the same, to lift them from the realm of the banal to that of ritual. Charlie is asking why Thomas has arrived so late in the semester; is inviting him to choose his bed. It's a trivial moment, chosen precisely for its lack of drama, until, out of nowhere, Thomas steps close to Charlie, across five or six feet of space, and juts his chin into his face. Oh, how well Geoffrey has learned that step. "Walk like you are getting ready to beat him," Balthazar had instructed him. "Like you are stepping up to someone, willing to take his life." Geoffrey, it turns out, knows a thing or two about the intimacy of violence.

"What is it that awaits me here?" he asks of Charlie, flat and belligerent, blank verse be damned.

"Pain," answers Charlie. "Pain and friendship. But mostly pain." He reaches out and calmly, gently touches Thomas's cheek and ear. To the audience it is as though he marks the very spot where, much later, Thomas will be shot and scarred.

Then: a handshake as intense as a kiss. One clean thread of Smoke rising from their joint exhalation, seemingly too fine to have much sway over the crowd. But there is a final twist to the scene, a recent innovation that Balthazar has reserved for special nights. He sees Ada's eyes on him, sees the fist she has slipped into her pocket.

Do it, nods Balthazar. *They have been a good audience and the mood is right.* It is the final night in the Canadas and the tour will be done after New York. There is no need to husband their resources as stringently as before.

Ada reacts without seeming to react. Balthazar watches her pocket, sees her fist harden over the vial he knows is hidden there; fancies hearing it break, a sound like a fingernail tapping a glass.

The results are spectacular. It starts with the actors. They have entered well into the moment; have summoned emotions deep and pure. The vial's contents take care of the rest. They find their Smoke and, without visibly altering it, *electrify* it, giving it currency and charge. Soon the entire audience is weeping, hugging, shouting.

"Hear, hear," they shout (though there have been no speeches). "Revolution!" (though it has happened already, long ago, and a good half of them are unsure they like what it has brought). "Huzzah!" and "Hurray!" Some people are kissing, all sexes, young and old; a native trapper, black-eyed, weather-burned, and the old doctor's wife stand cheek to cheek. Balthazar signals for the fans to be turned on. Even so it takes half an hour for the crowd to calm down.

As the audience disperses, shy now, each unto themselves, avoiding further contact, Balthazar once again catches sight of the stiff-backed girl with auburn hair and full, round cheeks.

[6]

The girl with the auburn hair does not go home when the play finishes. She waits outside, in the shadow of the market hall, and watches the players spill out in a noisy gaggle. The tall man, the Negro, is amongst them, sour-faced and oddly regal. It is to him she wishes to speak. But she needs to find him on his own.

The actors head for their hotel. She has already learned that they are staying there and follows at a good distance. Inside, the waiting area of the lobby is split into half a dozen booths, each bordered by a parting wall: Smoke screens, guarding against indiscrete emotion. She sits in one of these booths and endures the concierge's gaze. Always now, there is the sense of being hunted. When he reaches for the telephone, she thinks it is to call the police.

The players have already gone to their rooms. She can hear them, shouting and laughing, somewhere deep in the hotel. Other guests come to complain about the noise. Once they quiet down she will get up and ask the concierge for the number of the Negro's room. The words arrange themselves within her with the staid formality that is her lot. She has no spontaneity, not when it comes to speaking. It is one of the things that make her stand apart. She rises and sees the concierge reach for his phone; sits down again and waits for the police.

The police do not come. Instead it is the Negro—the *director*—who descends the lobby stairs. He is wearing a flat cap and a herringbone coat; his steps are so long it is almost as though he's running. Everyone in the lobby stops to stare as he rushes out. It makes the girl feel a pang of sympathy for him. Here is another one who has been marked out.

Outside, the air carries snow. April the nineteenth, the Canadian seaboard. Her long johns itchy from six months' wear. She follows at a distance and watches the director retrace his earlier steps and let himself back into the market hall. An old man, thin as a rail. The dark face pruned under his cap.

Inside, he lights a lamp and steps onto the stage. She slips through the gates and, in the ring of light created by his lamp, watches him take stock of the props that stand still arranged for the final scene. It occurs to her that he is here to pack things up, but he sits down on one of the dormitory beds instead and sniffs the cold air. Instinctively, she mirrors him and flares her nostrils, takes in the stink of the market hall, sea fish and offal, the sweat of workingmen. It isn't so difficult to imagine into this smell something of school. Soiled laundry and digestive gases; clods of dirt clinging to rugby studs. If one cocks the head a little, one can almost hear it: the noise of boys charging down the corridor and down the steps. They never walked. As a child, their constant hurry was a puzzle to her, like the height of the moon. The bed the man sits on is the one that his play designated for Thomas. She quietly walks closer until she too reaches the stage. He has yet to notice her. His eyes are closed now, his bitter face un-pruned. An old man caught in reverie; stroking crumpled linen. Believing his own lies.

It makes her like him better than before.

"That's not what they looked like," she says into the silence. "The beds."

The words startle him. He leaps upright, the scowl returning to his features.

"You!" he exclaims. "The girl with the poker up her arse. Sneaking in here to steal!"

She does not respond at once but walks closer, pointing at the beds. "They weren't this narrow. And the backs were higher, you could prop up a pillow and read."

The man seems incredulous, as much at her words as at her manner of speaking. "How would you know?" he mutters, growing angry. Then: "How old are you, girl?"

She thinks about it, blinks, attempts humour. "Eighteen. But I have an old soul."

The director does not laugh.

The next moment she has thrown herself on her knees and bent forward, slipped her palm under the edge of the bed. "Here," she says. "That's where they carved in their initials. Come, you can feel for yourself."

She is unsurprised when he tells her to piss off.

[7]

She gets him to do it in the end, through obstinacy rather than any more words, waiting out his sourness until he slides onto one knee and bends down next to her, and allows his fingers to be guided by hers. She runs them across the unvarnished undercarriage of the bed, filling in with words that which is not there to be felt by their skin.

"The *T* first," she says, "big and bold, with a slant to the crossbar. The *A* much smaller, as if it didn't matter quite as much to him, or he was ashamed of it. And next to it, almost touching, two *C*s. The first jagged, two sides of a triangle; the second smoother, almost a curve. *TA, CC*, side by side. Like sweethearts."

As she speaks she pictures them, Charlie and Thomas, lying flat on their backs, passing a pocket knife back and forth, leaving their mark; pictures herself on the day of her discovery at a time when the school stood closed, abandoned. The old man next to her seems caught in his own yearnings; his fingers still laced with hers. Then he catches himself and shakes loose her touch so violently that his knuckles rattle on the wood.

"Nonsense," he barks at her. "Made-up crap. It's a boys' school. On the other side of the world. You weren't there!"

His Smoke blends anger, suspicion, hope. She takes it in and returns it to him, realigned in its components. His own hope, given back to him, appears to frighten him; or perhaps it is the strangeness he can sense within her. He rises up, looks down at her, still crouching at his feet.

"Who the hell are you?"

She looks up at the prune of his dark face and decides she does not trust him yet. There is some secret in his Smoke that she finds difficult to fathom.

So she says, "I was frightened tonight. At the performance. So many people in one room, shoving, talking, jostling for space up front. I haven't been in a room with more than a handful of people, not since the Second Smoke came. And even before, only in church. It's strange, isn't it? Most people *like* to Smoke now, at least some of the time. But we are afraid of crowds."

She pauses for breath and finally rises, dusting off her skirts.

"Tell me," she continues. "You must see lots of places. Is it like that everywhere?"

"You don't get around much, do you?"

"No," she says, and finds her voice free of resentment. "Since coming here, I haven't gone anywhere at all."

[8]

She sees him waver between his habit of sourness and the itch of his curiosity; the urge to know this awkward, pesky girl. She waits unmoving, long seconds that they share in silence, then prompts him gently with a question. It's a familiar question, one that has been asked a hundred thousand times across the world, whenever strangers meet.

"Ten years ago—when the Second Smoke came. Where were you?"

"*There.* England. You?"

"The same."

"Then you know all there is to know."

The old man stills himself and closes his eyes. His eyelids are lighter than the rest of his skin. When he speaks again, it has the precision of a recital. He must be recalling lines long committed to memory, something from one of his plays. He speaks them quickly, dryly, without pathos.

"It came like an infection," he says, "passed from body to body like the flu. The land itself had caught it; sweated, shivered, stank. Here and there it bled. England was first; then the Continent, raging north to south. The Atlantic proved no barrier. Ships brought it to the New World in random little bursts. Halifax. Montreal. Savannah. The Virginias, the Carolinas, then the cities by the lakes. The far west never caught. Then the Smoke ebbed and grew sluggish once more: everywhere but at the source. Within three months the Second Smoke was dead."

He opens his eyes and she nods her acknowledgment. It was how he said it was. She'd arrived here just when the Second Smoke had deadened. Normality soon returned. Officially, nothing had changed. Smoke was said to be what it had always been: a marker of sin. In territories like the Canadas, the same governor stayed in place, the same laws remained active. There was little news from Britain, not at first, but the Empire continued, like a chicken still running when its head has been chopped off.

It is running still.

And yet, nothing is the same. It's the people who have changed. They have tasted one another, *known* one another, high and low. Tinker, tailor, soldier. Beggar man, churchman, lord and lady: revealed in their needs. The Second Smoke coloured everything, down to the way people thought, how they prayed and raised their children. How they loved. There were new ways of speaking now: people said less, let their Smoke do the talking; or spoke one thing with their mouths and another with their skins. Smoke irony; Smoke humour. It is not a gift the girl has found within herself. Her Smoke is not that flighty.

"I was surprised by your play," she tells the old director now. "You made the audience create it as much as the actors. And there were so many shades of Smoke . . . Back when I was little, all Smoke seemed to be made of anger. Or of greed." She pauses, then carries on in her awkward way. "Tell me: what has changed?"

"What now?" he sneers. "You want to talk philosophy? Smoke episte-mology, eh? Who knows, girl! Some say it's the Smoke itself that's changed; others that it changed us, in our heads and down in our livers. What do I care? It feeds me well, the Smoke. It pairs well with stage lighting and mirrors."

But the girl does not believe him. The old man's relationship to Smoke runs deeper than that.

"You have a secret," she says abruptly. "What you did at the end, the scene with Charlie and Thomas. You released something. The Smoke was different then. Quicker, suppler. *Alive.*"

He recoils at the comment; a puff of anger jumping from his skin. She sniffs it, takes it in her blood; tastes again that strangeness she found hard to fathom.

All at once she knows what it is.

"There's another secret," she continues, not without wonder. "You are different from others."

He hides behind his anger. "How very perceptive of you! I'm the grand-son of a slave. People say it does not matter anymore. That everyone's black now, much of the time. But at night they still scrub themselves white." He spreads out his hands in front of her, flips them from the pallor of his palms to the blue-black of their backs.

The girl simply shakes her head. "No, not that. Something else. It's there in your Smoke. A kind of anger." And adds softly, wishing to be kind to him: "You're not a man."

"What, I'm the devil now?"

But she won't be put off. "Why do it?" she asks, genuinely at a loss. "Why be angry with your body? And live your life in britches?"

"I'll live my life any goddam way I please."

The girl can accept this. "Do your actors know?"

"You think you can travel with people for months and years and they don't know how you piss?"

His Smoke is coming thick now. It rages at the girl. She stands calmly in its fury, takes it in, then returns it as something both gentler and more complex. It is like she is holding up a mirror and showing him a better ver-sion of himself. Herself.

Whatever it is the director wishes to be.

When it is over, and Soot falls around them in the lamplight, the girl reaches across the space that separates them and touches one wrinkled black hand.

I trust you, the gesture says.

But she does not say it.

[9]

They are interrupted. It is a middle-aged man who announces himself with a cough, born of an actual cold by the sounds of it but now used strategically. He is dressed rather formally in a tailed topcoat and dark trousers. A fur hat frames a clean-shaven face so stiff with cold there is little life to his features.

"Hullo! Master Balthazar? I hope I am not intruding. I made inquiries at the hotel. One of the—ah—actors said I was likely to find you here."

He pauses, stares up at them upon the stage, and at the haze of Soot still riding on the air. His eyes first on the director, then on her.

"I'm Walton. The—ah—mayor, if you please. Though don't be alarmed. This visit is entirely informal."

Again he looks over at the girl. She shies under his gaze; does not know where to look. The director notices her discomfort.

"Mayor Walton! What an unexpected pleasure. I read your attack on the theatre in the local rag this morning. I note there was no attempt to stop our performances, though, not after the local burghers went out of their way to offer me this market hall as a suitable venue. I suppose your governor wanted one thing, and your townsmen another. Well, let us step into my office."

The girl watches the old director—*Balthazar!*—climb down from the stage and lead the man over to the screen. He has a stool there, offers it to the mayor, then stands towering over him in a twisted stoop. There they talk for some few minutes, too low for the girl to hear. Throughout the talk, the man keeps craning his neck around the screen to peer at her. There is a question in his eyes.

She turns her back and pretends she does not know the answer.

Before long their business is concluded. The director walks the mayor to the end of the market hall, then shuts the gate behind him.

"What did he want?" she asks.

"Somebody told him we had been to England recently. Recently? It's been almost a year! He asked me for my 'assessment' of the situation 'over there.' That man is a cretin. But even he is smart enough not to trust the official news."

"What did you tell him?"

He smiles, pleased with himself. "That the rumours are false, but also true. That the government is back in charge and also failing. That the Second Smoke has died, and yet haunts the land in Gales. That the country is at war, but nobody's fighting. It'll keep him up all night."

"He kept looking at me."

"Of course he did. An old stick like me and a young thing like you, holding hands in a cloud of Soot. It's more excitement than he's had in years."

"No, it's not that. He recognised me. There's a description. Maybe even a picture, it gets sent everywhere. He will go home now and think on it. And tomorrow he will start asking questions and learn that he's not the only one who's noticed me. The day after, he'll make a phone call. And then he'll arrest me and ship me home."

"Arrest you? What nonsense!" There is conviction to his dismissal but it lasts only a moment. Then she sees him recall to himself her oddity and her rummaging through his Smoke; her repeated refusal to give him her name.

"Who are you?"

"Eleanor. Eleanor Cruikshank."

Cruikshank. He must recognise the name. The school's erstwhile porter. In the stories, he is little more than a buffoon.

"You mean *that* Cruikshank? I did not know he had a daughter . . ."

Then he finally understands. The wonder of it uncreases his whole face. He steps back and stares at her: at her hips, her back, her chest. It isn't lechery that drives him and she does not shrink from his scrutiny. He is picturing a metal corset encasing her trunk, imprinting its stiffness upon her spine; a steel dial rising from her chest, inviting self-correction.

"Eleanor! Renfrew's little niece . . ."

She nods. "It's my uncle—Cruikshank said he'll never stop looking for me. Now that he's found me, he will want me back."

[10]

Balthazar starts packing up his props.

She had hoped for more: sympathy, an invitation; advice on how to disappear. She's placed her secret in his hands, has used a name her foster father told her to banish from all memory. "Hamilton"—that is what they lived under; a name she has recently paid to have chiselled into stone. But the old director seems to have lost all interest. He has withdrawn into himself; is cursing as he drags the beds clanging off the stage.

"Bloody stagehands said they would be here by now. I will dock their pay!"

She watches him quietly and realises that she herself must voice her petition. But her boldness has left her; the mayor took it out with him, back to his house, where he will lie in bed trying to put a name to her face.

What she asks is:

"How do you do it?"

"Do what?"

"The last part of the play."

"The scene with the two boys? I've done a lot of research."

"Not that. I mean the Smoke you released. It was . . . like it was in those first days. Like being out in a Gale."

"When have you last been in a Gale, Eleanor Crǔikshank?"

She shakes her head.

"Then what do you know? Now, if you will excuse me, I have work to do."

[11]

She leaves him, exits the market hall then wanders aimlessly into the cold of the street. They built it grandly, in grey slabs of stone. The sea is so near, even the snowflakes seem to smell of salt.

Balthazar comes running after her. Later, it will cheer her to think about his haste. He skids on the icy cobbles and nearly breaks his neck. She bends to retrieve his flat cap for him.

"Cruikshank's conked it, I suppose," he says as he snatches it back.

"Yes. Two weeks ago."

She wonders how callous she must sound, answering so calmly the calculated brutality of Balthazar's question. The dead man raised and protected her; she loved him much like a father. And yet he always remained "Cruikshank" to her, querulous and palsied. He gave her practice in dealing with the sour-tongued.

Balthazar thinks long and hard before making his offer.

"We sail tomorrow," he says at last. "For New York City. I could pass you off as one of the players. My Meister Lukas is good at forging paperwork."

When she does not respond, he starts swearing at her.

"Jesus Christ, girl, isn't that why you came to me? To charm me? To convince me to get you out of town? All right, so you've won, I'm offering passage. What now, am I not asking nicely enough? Or is New York not good enough for you?"

She pays no attention to his anger, skin-deep, free of Smoke.

"What made up your mind?" she asks.

"Nothing. You are amusing, that's all. And you have talent."

"Talent? At what?"

Balthazar ignores this, waves his hand in front of him like a magician, conjuring reasons.

"You met Charlie Cooper. If the story is true."

She nods to say it is.

His face unknots. "What was he like?"

"I only met him the once." Then she adds, speaking so quickly it outraces her need to parse her own words: "He rescued me, you know. Like a knight."

He seems delighted at the word. "A knight! So you're in love with him! Well, why not, half the world is, after all. And the other two? Thomas and Livia. Did you meet *them*?"

"No. Have you?"

"I went looking for them." He spits, dark on trampled snow. "They did not *receive*. Come now, better you sleep in the hotel tonight."

Later he asks,

"Why are you smiling?"

"Cruikshank always said I'd run away with the circus."

[12]

They leave town with the afternoon tide. The *Elsinore,* originally out of Denmark. The captain wants to know why it makes Balthazar laugh.

That night he stands on deck with Etta May and watches the black swell.

"Is the girl all settled in?" he asks.

"Tuckered out and sleeping. I gave her the top bunk."

"Good. It's better not to talk to her too much. It's like going ten rounds with a prizefighter. Exhausting." He flashes his teeth. "What do you make of her, Em?"

"Odd bird. Lonely. And her Smoke . . . I am a little scared of her." She lights a cigarette, shields it from the breeze. "You know she's a risk. For the troupe. For you."

"It'll be all right, once we are back in American waters." He sees Etta May smirk at the yearning in his words. "What now? So I'm sick of the stink of Empire. And of its reach."

"And yet you dream of England." She shakes her head, openly laughing at him now. "You know they say the Company owns half of Manhattan."

"So what?"

"Where the Company is, hon, the Empire is not far."

EXCERPT FROM "THE COMING OF THE PROPHETS," FROM
P. SAUNDERS, *A POPULAR HISTORY OF THE UNITED STATES OF
AMERICA FROM THE FOUNDATION OF THE COLONIES TO THE
ARRIVAL OF THE SECOND SMOKE, WRITTEN TO EDUCATE, AMAZE,
AND BEGUILE, WITH AN INTRODUCTION AND POSTSCRIPT BY CLAY
WARREN, ESQ., AND NUMEROUS ILLUSTRATIONS BY D. B. HYDE.*
BOSTON: JAMES B. WHITE & SONS, MCMVI.

While it is not the customary function of the Historian to commemorate acts and events that are as recent—and remain as starkly imprinted on the popular memory—as the devilish scenes occasioned by the arrival, by sea, on our national shores of that scourge popularly known as the "Second Smoke," the confusions pertaining to said events leave me little choice but to devote this final chapter of my History to their clarification. The precise circumstances that led to the generation or summons of this Second Smoke cannot detain us here. These happened far beyond our borders and remain shrouded in obscurity; doubtless the proliferation of vulgar ballads touching on the subject has done more to occlude than to clarify said circumstances. What can be established with good certainty is the date of arrival of that first group of unfortunates who had contracted this physical and moral malaise and, through a process of constant reinfection, contrived to sustain it during their nine days' voyage from Liverpool to the southern part of the Virginias aboard a Quaker steamer named the *Endeavour*. What scenes of violence and debauchery were witnessed by this ship as it crossed the icy wastes of the Atlantic, we can only imagine. Its landing, however, is well attested.

Behold, then, the sixth of February 1899: on a cold, misty morning, still half shrouded by dusk, a transatlantic steamer makes its way through the calm waters of the majestic roadstead known as Hamptons Roads to enter, without either seeking or being granted authorisation by the authorities of our proud and sovereign Nation, the mouth of the James River. There, possessing no knowledge of the depth of the river bed and sailing at a speed ill-judged for inland waters, the ship soon runs aground upon a sandbank. In a manner oddly shambling and disorganised, the lifeboats are lowered into the shallow waters. One hundred and one passengers—men and women both—disembark the ship to find space upon these lifeboats, the plume of their madness rising from the gunwales and thickening the morning mist. Some Negro farmhands who live near the riverbank behold their slow approach and note how haphazard is the rowing, how distracted the crew. It is as though these strangers are intoxicated. Some are singing, others clinging to each other like scared children; others yet appear to be copulating in plain view of their peers. Struck by this sight, the farmhands descend to the strip of beach that flanks the riverbank to offer aid to the shipwrecked. Once arrived, they pause at some distance from the strangers' Smoke, offended in their Christian consciences by its unrepentant bloom. Then the Smoke performs a feat no Smoke has yet been observed to do. It leaps at them across many yards of bank; plucks the very Soot from their work clothes, resurrecting yesterday's sins. As though mesmerised, the farmhands join those they came to rescue, drowning in the self-same madness that was brought ashore. Only a single youth of fifteen, whose lame leg and cautious nature kept him some ten steps behind his companions, escapes. He runs away, to safety. By the midafternoon he can be found drinking and spreading his story at a Negro establishment three leagues to the west.

And so our National Virtue was lost.

It took four days for the news to spread to Richmond, two more to verify its truth. The newspaperman at the *Richmond Enquirer* settled on the term "carrier" for those infected by the Second Smoke and issued a grave warning to city authorities. At this time another name—ignorant and blasphemous—had already spread amongst the rural Negro populace, inflected by their ill-digested knowledge of the Bible and its warning of apocalypse. "Prophets," they called them, "pilgrims," making the long voyage, spreading a new evangelism. There was a rumour of a mob of them marching upon Richmond. A telegram was sent to alert the state and federal authorities, urging them to close all harbours; in Richmond itself the militia was armed, the city closed to strangers, guards placed on all roads.

Richmond fell within twenty-four hours. By the end of the week, there were reports of new "pilgrims" landing on our shores. Smugglers helped them; self-declared revolutionaries; Negro fishermen bamboozled by the rumours of this new church of the Smoke. The arriving ships were fired on by our valiant navy, were sunk in our bays. Outlandish tales abounded, of single pilgrims swimming ashore from cannon-pitted hulls, then moving inland across the vast plains of the Americas, there to set ablaze whole cities. A shaven-headed child of six put paid to Charleston; a nursing mother infected Baltimore, walking bared down to her waist; a blind priest on a snow-white ass rode out of the Pennsylvania woods into a Pittsburgh factory, corrupting it to the last man. Congress declared a state of national emergency; the Democratic senator John F. Calhoun of Tennessee made the case that the landings by foreign citizens amounted to invasion and urged the president and Congress to consider a formal declaration of war. It was as though the first trumpet had sounded. Across the land, Christian men begged the Lord to be forgiven for their sins . . .

[1]

Fits you like a glove, boychik. No, look, you have to tie it at the waist. And now pull down the shirt. There—a Hindoo houseboy if ever I saw one! And look how the colour complements your skin. It's good cotton, that, soft as soft."

"Enough, old man, you're making me blush."

The boy is very appealing. Irresistible, even. That broad, dark-hued face, the slender lips, the small sharp nose: handsome, yes, but above all *mobile*, changeable, and (when caught unawares, unguarded, unprepared) surprisingly vacant. His body, too, is tidy, limber, well proportioned; unfixed in its mannerisms, eager for a role. The boy is a blank into which you insert your longings. It must work magic on the girls. Only that's something he does not do. *Intimacy.* And, of course, none of it is real. The first time Riedl realised this, it damn near broke his heart.

Which isn't to say Riedl is quite himself when dealing with the boy either. The boy is a customer, after all. A business associate. A fellow rogue. There are rules that govern their interaction, scripted into their relative positions of seller and buyer. The boy understands this better than anyone, embodies it to a frightening degree. It is Riedl who slips up and becomes familial; imposes on that mobile face the features of a never-born son.

"Just what are you up to, boychik?" Riedl asks now, growing angry at his own foolishness and ramping up his inner yid. "One of the Company warehouses, is that it? Or one of their ships? Be careful who you meddle with! You're not the first who thought he could grow rich on their fat. All swimming in the Hudson now, kiddo. Feeding the fish."

The boy takes up his change of mood, stops admiring himself in Riedl's mirror, deflects his anger into banter.

"I'm no *kid*."

"What, a man now? *Herrgott,* don't you even move like one of them darkies, though! Been studying, eh? Do that head waggle again. Perfect. And
that shit-eating grin. Very good. It'll fool any white man. You just hope
you don't run into the real thing. They'll be like the rest of us. We know
our own."

"I have no 'own,' Riedl."

"Oh, a poor little orphan, are we? All alone in the wide world, not a
people to our name. That's how you haggle. Next it'll be, 'I'll pay tomorrow,
Sahib, here's a nickel for my pledge.'"

"And who else is going to rent these rags from you? Look here, there's a
tear right above the kidney, along with a nice big stain. Got this from the
morgue, did you, you cheap kike?"

"Rags, Neel? *Rent?!* Not buy, he says, but *rent*! Take them off this second, you *schmutzig* little mongrel, or by God I'll put another tear into that
fabric."

Neel. That's the name they have agreed upon, Riedl and the boy. Nil,
actually, but it has lengthened with use.

"What do I call you?" Riedl asked him the first time they did business.

"Whatever you will."

"What are you, some kind of walking mystery? A no-name, a *niemand,*
a snot-nosed little nil?"

"Nil," said the boy, a curl in his lip like sour milk. "That rather has a ring."

He's been Neel to Riedl ever since.

[2]

It takes them another half hour to settle on the price. It is Riedl who is
reluctant to see him go. The pawnbroker senses an impatience in the boy
that is unlike him, who gives so little away. He must be off on a job. Something unusual, and dangerous. Something that *matters* to him.

"The Spires!" it comes to Riedl. "Chaim says he has seen you hanging
about the Spires. Watching. Talking to people at the docks."

Riedl gets animated, afraid for the boy; starts lecturing him.

"These are serious people, boyo. Secretive. I ask you: what sort of outfit
schleps its entire workforce over from the other end of the world when
there are a thousand coolies you could hire right here on the spot? They
like their privacy, see, and here you want to go and pry. And anyway, why

break in there? There's no money in the Spires. Just papers. It's where they do their orders and accounts. Don't be a *yonts*."

The boy listens unmoved, still caught in the half-smile of their banter. Then something raw rises out of him, something rare and unmediated, climbing up his throat. Or perhaps it is just that Nil has learned that pain, too, can be a mask, and that all the best lies start in truth.

"Home," he says. "I am looking for home." And he touches Riedl's hand. It's a squeeze not a shake (and what a calculated little gesture this is, forging a bond both binding and false). Next Nil runs off, the bundle of new clothes rolled under one arm. At the end of the alley, where he thinks he is no longer watched, his posture changes along with his gait, and he wrests new features from the mobile musculature of his face. Then he is lost from view, Third and Bowery, merging with the downtown crowd.

[3]

New York, né New Amsterdam. A city built to resist that paramount truth of cities: that crowds breed vice. Cities lend themselves to industry, and to sin. The Old World has long accepted this equation and written its cities over to workers and paupers. The respectable live in the fresh air of the hills. In the New World, where cities were built from scratch, a variety of models were trialled, though few as successfully as this. New York—the peninsula of Manhattan—is a network of villages separated by moats. Uptown, north of the mile-deep park that bisects the city east to west like a belt of grass and shrub, lies a world of villas surrounded by generous grounds: a New World Oxford built on a New World scale. North of these there are woods dotted with estates too grand for either Oxford: old Dutch money building a Protestant's idea of a palace. Farther north yet sits the rough little shantytown that is Yonkers: a paper mill, a general store, and a whorehouse, greasy with its own Soot. Beyond are homesteads and emptiness.

Downtown is a different story. South of Central Park, the city is dominated by four-block neighbourhoods separated by block-wide gaps of empty space. "Air shafts," "commons," "moats," these go by many names, though locals most often refer to them as "scars." Some are grass-covered and used for husbandry; some choked with shrubs and trees. Some are garbage pits; some sports fields; some are battlegrounds upon which annual war is waged, between Chinatown and Little Germany, between the thugs of Chelsea and the thugs from the meatpacking factories living in its flank. Each neighbourhood carries its own shroud of Smoke; in strong winds—in winter storms—they mingle, carry lust and violence from east to west. In the humid lull of summer, when the heat saps all strength and appetites grow indolent, truces appear as people creep from their brick houses and factories to seek air and shade within the neutral ground of the scars.

That's how it was and how it is again. Only the memory remains: of the year of the Second Smoke. It came to New York late. Quarantine kept it at bay; the necessities of trade smuggled it in. Whoever it was that walked the Second Smoke into the city—whether it came by cart, by sea, or steamed down the East River—it took New York in a matter of days. A few neighbourhoods—Murray Hill, Gas House—defended their scars by force of weapon. It was hopeless: a chance gust, an inflection of the wind, would transform defender into prophet. Once in the Soot-soaked streets, the bricks themselves would spread the Smoke's message. The deep blank of Central Park halted it until servants sneaked south to visit family, then carried it back into the pantries of the wealthy. It moved north. Yonkers caught like a match. Only the great emptiness of the woods beyond it proved an effective barrier. Much of New England remained clear.

It did not last, of course. The Second Smoke burned itself out. Normality returned: the rule of law, reinforced by money and arms. But like everywhere else, the memory lingers, of those months of *communion,* of passion and blood. Even now people will pass each other, in the width of an avenue or on the narrowness of a shared landing, and there will flicker between them the recognition that once they *knew* one another. That strange erosion of all thresholds; the immediacy of need and desire; skin speaking to skin. Some long for it now, preach ideologies of Smoke; stand on street corners, half naked, guttering like greasy candles. Many others have left the city. It is not easy, living with the shamelessness of the past. As people leave, others enter, fleeing their own revelations, seeking dissolution in the crowd. Manhattan, a holding cell for transients, absorbing strangers like the sea absorbs the rain. Nil is its perfect disciple: a man-boy without past or allegiance, changeable down to his very soul; angry and hungry and full of pluck.

[4]

Nothing, Nought, *Nil*—he has adopted the brisk version of the name, prefers it over others for the limited dialogue he holds with himself. Around town he is known by many names, as Maka and Mani; Fernando and Vikram; Carlito, Mohammed, Ezekiel, and Joe. He passes as Mexican, Red Indian, Hindustani; as an Eskimo, an Arab, a Negro half-breed who has ironed the kink out of his hair. As anything and everything—only never as white. It is all that holds him together: a palimpsest of names and the dark hue of his skin, a reddish brown, stretched over a facial geometry he has never found mirrored in anyone else. For it is true what Riedl said. He is an orphan; a man without people, without past. Stolen from his parents at an age that left him with few memories; used for an experiment that failed its progenitor; then raised by a man who did not teach him how to love (his foster mother succumbed to illness while he was still very young). He had a name, growing up, borrowed from a storybook, and a dream of revenge. When this failed, he left his second homeland and became a traveller, an imposter, a thief.

A man without a face.

For this is what life is to him: the donning of masks—of words and temperaments and Smoke—each adopted to suit a given situation, each day an angry reinvention of the self. His transformations are not a lie, exactly, for behind them he finds nothing, a void. When on his own he finds himself reduced to a vacant kind of fury from which he escapes only through sleep. Nil takes care to spend very little time alone with himself, awake.

How much better then to have a plan.

This one starts in an experiment of architecture. It is like a beacon of the future. For in the southernmost tip of Manhattan, flush with the docklands at the mouth of the East River, something new is being built, a cluster of buildings that reach twenty, thirty storeys into the sky. *The Spires*. Only one Spire has been completed at this point, but the others are to follow the same outline. The first few floors are given over to garages, workshops, and clerical offices, many of which are connected to the business of the nearby docks. The middle floors stand empty. In fact, it is wrong to think of them as floors at all: they are windowless pockets of pure space, vertical scars, bridged by enclosed stairwells and the metal skeleton of elevator shafts. Above, where the city's Smoke is dispersed by the wind, are the offices proper, separated from the city streets by a wall of air and money. The Company men come here from their uptown houses by boat; are delivered to harbour berths for which they hold thousand-year leases.

Like the members of a particular subspecies of bird, the participants in this daily migration all look the same. They wear dark suits and hats, bowlers for the most part, invariably black. They carry umbrellas and satchels;

starched collars spill from the tops of their lapels. There is to them no overt sign of wealth other than the gleam of the occasional watch chain, rich solid gold. All of them are men. It might as well be a monastery they are hurrying to—for hurry they do, as though fleeing their home lives for the rigours of work, only to rush home again at the end of the day to submit to the necessities of sleep and nutrication.

There is one other kind of person who can be seen entering and leaving this new constellation of buildings. These, too, are all men. But where the Company men wear black, these men sport loose, colourful shirts that fall to midthigh, and their heads are covered by cloth wrappings or brimless round caps rather than hats. They, too, hurry to and from the building, but it is a different sort of hurry, born from outer circumstance rather than inner compulsion: someone *is hurrying* them. They carry no satchels but parcels, boxes, papers, tools. Some are armed: with pistols or with slender, machine-tooled clubs. When out of earshot of their masters, they chatter with one another in two or three different tongues; gossip and joke and saw the air with gestures borne from another shore.

One more thing. Every one of them, from doorman to manservant, handyman to cleaner, soldier to messenger, bears a skin the colour of coffee, some watery and as though yellowed, some tempered with rich cream, some as black as the dregs at the bottom of your cup.

[5]

All this Nil knows from watching; from walking the neighbourhood and talking to tradesmen; from drinking with clerks and shadowing Company men all the way back to their homes; from bribing their maids and charming their daughters; from stealing a satchel and reading through the mail. If asked the value of all this information, he would but shrug; likewise in response to any query about the details of his plan. An *intention,* really, more than a plan; a thing whose shape must never be spelled out.

It is now six weeks old, ripened in some part of him that he takes care not to interrogate and fuelled by a motivation he would be hard-pressed to name. The hope for wealth, naturally, some discovery that will help him fill his belly for a month or six. But there is more to it, an anger and a yearning, tied up with the Company flag. The sun never sets on the Company's holdings. It trades in spices, in opium, in gemstones, in cloth. In knowledge, too. The Company is not who ordered him stolen from his parents, but he who did may well be working for it now. It employs geographers, mapmakers, explorers. Somewhere in Nil there slumbers the thought that the Company must know where he is from.

If there is no plan, articulated and committed to paper, there is nonetheless a sense of system, of steps that have to be taken in deliberate order to secure success. Nil follows them with a relentless focus that brooks no hesitation or doubt. First, he retires to the lodgings he rents in a boarding-house south of Houston. It is a luxury, this, securing a whole room rather than merely a bed, but Nil did not query the expense, just as he did not begrudge the price for the new and well-spun cotton cloth he unpacks once the door is closed behind him and secured with a nail and hook. He has identified, in his observation of the buildings, five separate styles of turban amongst the Company servants and has paid a man on the East Side docks to show him how to tie the one most frequently employed. Now, in the squalid room, in front of a square of looking glass he counts as one of his few permanent belongings, Nil tries to imitate the man's deft movements. It is a process of wrapping and unwrapping, trial and error, that he performs with an animal patience, neither smoking nor swearing nor breaking for food, for close to three hours until a tight high-crowned turban is firmly in place.

Next he dons Riedl's garments and combines them with a hip-length waistcoat he has acquired from a clothes and rags vendor in Chinatown; changes his shoes for the kind of leather loafer he has seen Hindustani men wear. It is still only early afternoon by the time he finishes his preparations, and without pause or another glance at the mirror he steps out the door. A moment later he is in the street, then amongst the shrubs and rubbish of the scar. By the time he emerges on the other side, his gait and posture have adjusted to the role, and he strides purposefully southwards, every inch a Company serf.

[6]

It is a question of timing. The afternoon mail arrives between three and four in the afternoon. The mailmen are couriers really, part of an internal Company network spanning the world. They come by boat, always in twos, their bags bulging with letters and parcels. The men are uniformed and well-known to the doorman, who will wave them straight around the back. That's where the drivers, errand boys, and lowest order of clerks dwell, sealed off from the building's higher levels. It is the *back door*: tempting, ill-guarded, the only place people of Nil's colour may pass.

But it is not the way in.

All that connects it to the top of the building, Nil has learned through bribes and careful probing, is a small service elevator in which letters and parcels may be sent up. It will not admit a body even as small and flexible as Nil's and, at any rate, is operated strictly from above. There is also a connecting door that provides access to the main stairwell, but this is bolted from the far side. In short: the back door is barred.

Which only leaves the front.

Here the security arrangements take a rather different shape. All there is is a single doorman, sitting stiffly on a little stool just outside the main gate. The men who walk past him show no badges or papers, and rarely acknowledge the guard by more than a nod. For the longest time this puzzled Nil, until he came to the grudging conclusion that the doorman simply recognised each of the hundreds of people passing his post. Indeed, whenever a newcomer seeks admittance, he must be accompanied by older hands, never fewer than three, who make a point of stopping in front of the doorman so that the old man can scrutinise the new man before stepping aside.

Nil has watched this doorman very closely. He must be sixty-five, perhaps seventy years old; is rake-thin and holds himself very straight; has a long grey beard, knotted under the chin, a saffron-coloured turban, and a uniform of light beige. Twice each day he is spelled from his duties for a precise hour by a man emerging from the nearby guard hut who is similar in aspect but twenty years younger: a relative, perhaps even a son. The younger man does not have the older man's certainty, squints and glowers at anyone walking up to his gate, and at times can be heard to inquire about a name or to exchange a few words with his employers. He is nervous, uncomfortable, hard to predict. He will not do.

The older man then, the afternoon mail. A question of timing: when the mail boat has docked and the two mailmen are walking quickly towards the building; not so close upon their heels as to encourage their noticing, turning to him, hailing him in the singsong of their speech, but close enough for their proximity to suggest their shared origin and purpose; while the sun beats down and the hum of the generators fills the air with a tension almost tactile—

Now.

Nil steps out onto the paved, barren killing zone of a square that surrounds the base of the building and begins walking to its front gate.

[7]

He walks quickly, loosely, a man with a task to perform and no weight on his mind. Nil does not slow when the doorman takes longer than usual to direct the couriers to the back; takes in the swirling pattern of the marble steps, the sight lines of the twin lions squatting to either side of them, cast in pigeon-soiled concrete, maned heads heavy on front paws; is conscious of the heat and the length of his shadow, keeping pace with him to his flank.

The old man turns before Nil has reached the top, caught in the process of resettling on his stool. His umbrella is in his dark hand, spread against the fierce May sun. It is an interesting touch, that, an eccentricity running against the grain of his spare, military bearing, and it made Nil like the old man from the first. He will trick him from *there*, this place of sympathy and warmth, where lies feel like kindness and are easy to dispense. Not that it will show on his face, this kindness. Nil's manner is brisk, bored, haughty. In his hand he carries a prop.

"Special courier, personal delivery, Mr. Smith, twenty-three."

He gives to the speech just a touch of the accent he has studied, a matter of running the words into each other and shifting their music, so light it is barely there at all. The old man, already in the process of waving him around to the back entrance, stops, folds down the umbrella, then stretches out his unencumbered hands to take receipt of the slender envelope Nil holds out to him.

It comes down to this rectangle of paper then: to its handwritten address and the red wax mark that seals its flap. There are only three types of servant ever admitted to the front of the building. The first are cleaners, closely supervised, who come at eleven each night, and are publicly searched on exit out into the square. The second are valets or personal secretaries who shadow their employer. The third—and there have been only a handful of these in all the weeks of watching—the third are mailmen of a special sort, bringing missives too sensitive or too urgent to be entrusted to the mailroom.

The old man holds the envelope very close to his face. Nil has watched him do this before. He would bet good money that the man cannot read.

But he is an expert in other things, in types of ink and seal wax; in how dirty or clean an envelope can be expected to be; in the idiosyncrasies—the slant, the symmetry, the preponderance of flourishes—of Company pen hands practised in the art of address.

"Smith, twenty-three," Nil repeats into this scrutiny, with the impatience of a bored man. In truth, he is not worried about the inspection. The envelope is real, the seal repaired by an expert forger with a special skill for wax. The Company is very careful about who and what is allowed to enter the building. It is much less careful with what goes out with its trash. It was a simple matter of finding the dustman who holds the contract; a trifling bribe to be permitted to riffle through his bins. Two weeks of patient rooting produced this prize. A name and a monogrammed seal. *Alexander Smith, Esquire.* It was considerably more difficult to find out any information about this Smith. A newcomer, that's all Nil has learned; import and export, come in from abroad. That and his address. The twenty-third floor.

An office at the top.

And still the old man won't let Nil pass. His gaze has dropped from the envelope onto Nil himself. Something about his clothes appears to irritate him, some nuance in the combination of trousers, long shirt, waistcoat, and turban that snags on his mind. *We know our own,* it flashes through Nil in a wave of anger. He pours it into his most clipped delivery, the English of a butler addressing a scullery boy, filled with a consciousness of relative status that would make his master blush.

"Stop jabbering, man," he snaps into the question—in Hindustani, Urdu, some other far-off tongue—the guard directs at him. "I must deliver this promptly, yes? So kindly let me through."

Still the doorman hesitates. His skin is so dark, even his lips appear black, his tongue and gums a shock of pink as he bends it around unfamiliar words.

"Where from?"

"What do you mean, where am I from? Overseas. The Bristol Station. Come now—Smith, the new man, twenty-three. Kindly step out of my way."

The old man blinks and does not respond.

Nil expected this, has counted on it in fact. For he knows the old man's secret, has lip-read it across fifteen yards of empty square in the many hours of quiet watching. When addressed by a Company man, no matter by whom and with what words, he always answers with one and the same phrase; if questioned further he smiles and bends into a bow. The man knows no English but pretends he does.

Now he's wounded in his pride.

"Where from?" the doorman asks again, torn between his suspicion and his reluctance to reveal his ignorance.

"Bristol," Nil answers once more. "*England*, you clod, England. A government communiqué."

He can see the man has understood but one word of his answer, but it is the one word that can explain all strangeness in this world, even incongruities of dress.

England.

The Isle of Smoke.

Nil digs in his pocket, frowning as though finally cottoning on to the reason for the man's resistance; finds some coppers, and shoves them carelessly into his hand. The old man, in turn, drops the coins in shock at the thought of him, a Company employee and guardian of its most sacred gates, being mistaken for a mere flunky holding out for a tip. Nil is past him by the time he speaks again, standing very erect now and hiding the spilled change under the heel of his boot.

"Good day!" he barks after Nil. "Elevator right."

"Yes, yes, I know." Nil does not break stride.

[8]

There are two elevators, facing off across the expanse of a marble-floored hall. The hall itself is shockingly empty but for the statue of an elephant, eight feet high. Three figures sit astride: a scrawny, seminaked native, straddling the beast's broad neck and holding the reins; above him, in a contrivance half viewing platform, half sedan chair, an armed officer in a wide-brimmed, tropical helmet; and, next to him, a burgher in a suit and top hat, his nose buried in a long-stemmed flower. The whole thing is cast in bronze. Nil passes in its shadow and veers right. He has never ridden an elevator before.

It is two dozen steps to the open cage. He can see a uniformed boy standing on the threshold, but for now his eyes are busy with other details. Two elevator shafts, ornate wrought iron; set back and flanking them, two mahogany doors. The door on the left is bolted and must lead to the back of the building; the one on the right stands open on the lit radiance of a stairwell. It's another way up, for those unafraid of exercise.

Another way out.

Nil reaches the elevator and steps inside without hesitation, not looking at the boy.

"Floor twenty-three," he says, and tries hard not to wince as the cage door is pulled shut.

A moment later they are in motion, the building's innards sliding past the ornamentations of the latticed iron door. They pass a parqueted corridor, empty of people, then reenter semidarkness as the elevator car bores itself through the concrete ceiling; then another strip of light, an inch wide and growing, revealing first the worn leather heels of a man's lace-up boot, then the hem and crease of his trouser leg and the dance of his coat-tails as he rushes past. Each grinding yard is accompanied by the creak of a metal rope and the humming of a generator; and by tremours too subtle for the eye that appear to reside entirely in Nil's bones and joints.

Two more floors and the shaft opens up around them into an enormous cavity of pure space. Glass-brick windows, long and narrow, bleed a yellowed light; raw brick faces them at twenty yards' remove, threaded with cabling and metal pipes; the smell is of emptiness, carbolic, rot. *The scar*, it shoots through Nil. *Seven storeys of nothingness.* In the eerie half-dark, he hears the flap of agitated wings. As though in answer he hears the boy next to him say, *"Aaja! Aaja kabootar!"* gently calling to the noise. But when Nil turns to him, the boy's eyes are on him, Nil, and are burning with a curiosity so undisguised it is akin to Smoke.

"Aap kahan ke ho?"

Throughout the ascent, Nil has been agonisingly conscious of the slender figure beside him but has avoided a direct look. Now he appraises the boy in full. It is as though he is staring in a mirror. They could be brothers; have the same age and the same slim build, accentuated, in the case of the elevator boy, by the high-waisted scarlet uniform he is made to wear. True, the boy's skin tone is darker than Nil's, the down on his cheeks and upper lip thicker, his cheekbones not as high nor his face as flat.

Still.

"Aap kahan ke ho?" the elevator boy asks again, then shifts tack. *"Too-saan khodroon aye hoo?"*

Something about his voice and intonation—awkward, less confident—alerts Nil to the fact that the boy has switched languages. He grimaces, cheerful despite his frustration, and tries again, in yet another tongue: *"Enkey irunthu vantheenga?"* He changes languages twice more before, bemused, undiminished in his curiosity, he arrives at: "Please, sir, where are you from, sir?" and then, pulling at the little lever that his left hand has never ceased to hold, brings the cage to a sudden stop.

They turn to fully face each other; lace a hand each through the lattice of the door; bounce and quiver, suspended in the void. They are high off the floor now, two-thirds of their way through the expanse of this vertical scar. Some instinct warns Nil not to adopt the hauteur that got him past the doorman. He feels his face relax, his eyes soften, a looseness wash through his limbs; sheds half a dozen years through the unclenching of his jaw. In a moment they are no longer employees, separated by rank, authority, and paycheque, but just two brown boys in a white man's cage.

Dangling like bait.

"England," Nil says, hearing in that one word the patterns of his childhood speech, acquired in that great wasteland that had once been the city of London, along with something more recent, an adjustment made to his vowels in response to the tones of New York. It is the closest he has to an authentic tongue.

"No. I mean, where from originally?"

Without breaking eye contact, the youth taps a finger against Nil's cheek, his skin. The gesture is as artless as the curiosity it stems from; is trusting and human, free of all guile.

"England," Nil says again, half startled by his own honesty. "I was raised there. Before that, I don't know."

The boy nods, sympathetically, and as though it explains some strangeness about Nil for which he had been unable to account.

"A courier?" he asks.

"Yes. An urgent package. Direct delivery. For Mr. Smith."

"Smith-ya! The new broom!"

Nil is unfamiliar with the expression and wonders where the elevator boy has acquired it. He also wonders what his employers make of him. Does he change his nature with every customer, efface himself as Nil would? Or is there something in his down-cheeked innocence that charms even these men? Again the silence around them is harried by the flapping of wings. This time the sound is accompanied by an odd throaty purr.

"Pigeons," the elevator boy proclaims. "Nobody knows how, but they find their way in. One of the air vents, perhaps."

He beckons Nil closer until they both press their faces against the metal lattice of the door; points downwards to their feet. The unfinished brick floor is dotted with feathers, bird crap, and carcasses: small dirty bodies, rotting in the dust.

"Once inside, they do not know how to leave again. On Saturday mornings, I get out of the cage and collect the bodies. I am told to put down poison. And disinfectant powder against the smell." He wrinkles his nose, lowers his voice. "Sometimes I put out food instead."

His simplicity frightens Nil. How is it that this stranger can take him in his confidence, based solely on the shade of their skins? Is it a trick, a test? Or is it genuine, a leap of faith unfathomable to Nil, demanding a reciprocity that Nil is unable to provide? His uncertainty is such that it translates into a scrap of Smoke, very faint, darting from his lips. The elevator boy leans forward, almost as though to kiss him, inhales it through the mouth. Whatever it is he tastes in Nil's Smoke, it prompts a hardening of features: not in anger against Nil but against something more abstract: himself, his uniform, this void between two worlds, ripe with carbolic and death. And just like that he turns, tilts the lever, and sends the cage back into its flight.

Unsettled, Nil feels the urge to speak to the boy, place a hand upon his shoulder, shake his hand. He does none of these things. In a trice, a hole in the ceiling swallows them, sends them through a slice of concrete and steel. Next comes a corridor, marbled again, lined with doors. The pattern repeats, three times, five, ten, each corridor identical. Only twice do they see people, once a crowd of six waiting for the elevator to stop (the boy bows to them, makes a gesture promising his swift return), then two men in hushed conversation at the end of the hall. And still the floors keep slipping past. Against his better judgement, Nil feels compelled to reenter into conversation. He casts around for something that will return the elevator's boy cheer. But all he manages is:

"This Mr. Smith—what is he like?"

His companion frowns, a little sulky now, then replies with a waggle of the head. Nil has practised the movement and mirrors it. All at once they both burst into laughter. They swallow it when their heads push into another zone of light.

"A bad one then," Nil whispers when the ceiling has once again claimed them to the waist.

"Bad?" repeats the elevator boy mischievously, then offers the Company slogan. "Englishmen don't smoke." And he sticks a tongue in the pocket of his cheek, signifying sweets; a touch of Smoke rising from him, light as steam, carrying more wonder than bitterness at how the world is carved up.

"Twenty-three, sir," he announces as they emerge on the topmost corridor, his English suddenly lilting, cumbersome, and formal. "Mr. Smith's office is just down the corridor. Next to the stairwell, sir." There is something knowing and playful to his offer of this final piece of information that should worry Nil but strangely does not. He has been recognised for what he is: a rogue, an intruder. And received some kind of blessing.

"Much obliged," he returns, very sternly, and holds the boy's eye. It takes an effort not to smile.

But the moment Nil steps past the opened cage door onto the hard marble of the corridor he already knows that this—this playing at friendship, at kinship, at rebellion against the world—was just another role, adopted with the ease and conviction of any other. Another self rises in him without hesitation. He hears but does not turn for the elevator's departure; walks down the empty corridor with quick-footed confidence, sees the door marked MR. B. A. SMITH in pencilled letters that contrasts rudely with the golden name plates all around, and next to it an unmarked door. A moment later, unseen and lithe, he is through and in the unlit stairwell, leading down twenty-three flights back into the city and its Smoke. But he walks up, not down. The roof has always been his destination. It is early yet, the final few hours of the afternoon, the building bustling with life.

Nil needs quiet to ply his trade.

[9]

He does not get far. In fact, Nil barely makes it onto the first landing, ten or twelve steps up from where he started, before the door behind him opens and, a moment later, radiant light fills the stairwell from its depths to the very top, as forty-six bulbs on twenty-three landings flicker to life. All instincts urge him towards flight. Instead, Nil crouches down, flattens his breath, fights down his Smoke as though swallowing his rising gorge. The soft sound of a step on the landing beneath him, a second, a third. Then a shout. It takes a split second to register that it comes not from inside the stairwell but from beyond the still-closing door; that it is directed at the stranger beneath Nil and not at himself. A split second: time enough for muscles to clench and unclench, bowel-deep; for the body to pucker, arsehole to throat.

"Smith. Smith! A word."

The stranger beneath Nil stops, waits. But he makes no motion to leave the stairwell and reenter the corridor. The door, arrested in its closing, is pulled fully open. When even that does not elicit a response, there rises the sound of a second man stepping onto the bare landing. The door behind him does not close. Nil pictures it: a man standing on the threshold, one foot in, the other out, wedging open the door with the flesh of his rump.

"There you are. Taking the stairs! It's extraordinary."

If a voice could wear a bowler hat and a starched shirt, it would be this. To Nil it echoes an English that surrounded him but once in his life. It is the language of the old elite; of country manors and boarding schools; of abduction, rubber masks, and pain. He winces to feel the smear of Smoke that dribbles out of him like snot; prays its stench won't reach.

"Twenty-three floors, Mr. Braithwaite. Subtract four for the clerical levels, seven for the mid-building scar. That leaves twelve. Each with what, a score of offices? Add secretaries and flunkies. Hundreds of people. Two elevators! The architect should be hanged. As should anyone who approved the plans."

Unlike his interlocutor's, Smith's voice is hard to place, a patchwork of accents and intonations, unabashed by their incongruity. A man from everywhere, the new broom.

Amused at the world.

"The newer designs are based on six elevator shafts. Once they are finished, we shall commission the addition of—"

Braithwaite's voice cuts off, presumably in reaction to some gesture of Smith's. Even without seeing the action, crouching on concrete, sucking on his Smoke eight feet above, Nil registers its rudeness and Smith's interlocutor's shock.

"What is it you want, Braithwaite? I've a long walk ahead."

"But where on earth are you going?"

"To the theatre."

"The theatre?"

"Indeed. There's a troupe newly arrived in town. I have heard some interesting things about them. A new kind of show. I don't imagine it would be to your taste, however."

A pause, a dismissal really, and the shuffle of feet as Smith descends a few more steps. He condescends to stop when Braithwaite speaks again.

"I had hoped to discuss matters," he announces, then adds when this elicits no answer, "I trust you have found suitable accommodation, Smith?

There is a house to let a street over from my own. I can make inquiries on your behalf."

"A house? No need. I won't be staying for much longer. To be honest, I am enjoying sleeping in the office. Very considerate of Cockburn to leave behind a sofa. It's surprisingly comfortable. I imagine he must have been partial to the odd kip himself."

Again the steps resume; again they are halted by Braithwaite's well-modulated voice, now soured by spite.

"I hear you have decorated."

"I moved a few things around." For the first time Smith's voice loses its virile cheer and hints at frustration if not quite anger. "Why spend all this energy on resentment, Braithwaite? So the board of governors saw fit to have me look into your shop. It's a temporary assignment. I will be gone again, chances are quite soon. Then you can tell yourself that I am just another new man without breeding or substance. We rise quickly, and we fall. And who knows, you may even be right. Now if you will excuse me, I will take my constitutional. Rough on the old knees, but it does wonders for my digestion. At least there's a toilet on every floor! Though the plumbing is a little suspect. Here we are, ruling half the world, and we can't build a pipe big enough to flush a turd. It does make you think. À bientôt, Master Braithwaite, servus. We can talk tomorrow."

In the moments that follow—as Smith clatters down the stairs, loudly and energetically, and Braithwaite opens wide the door so he can close it again with exaggerated calm—Nil dares a look over the bannister. Of Braithwaite he sees only a trouser leg, black, and the tails of a heavy top-coat, made of sturdy wool and twenty years out of style. Of Smith, the bald dome of a head, framed by a crescent of thick gold-blond hair and broad, flaring whiskers; a muscular corpulence in crumpled white linen. Then Smith stops, listens, pushes his head into the stairwell and cranes his neck. By then Nil is crouching on concrete again, chest heaving, bowels in a fist. A moment later, Smith's steps resume.

Downwards. He is still heading down.

Nil waits until he can no longer hear them, then waits five minutes more.

[10]

The roof is cold and cluttered like a farmer's barn. Bulbous water tanks rise from spindly metal legs in an arrangement that lacks all symmetry. A dozen platforms vie to be the building's summit, are interconnected by a system of steel ladders. Clusters of chimneys rise like mushrooms. There are dense networks of pipes and cables bolted into walls and floors; bricks, girders, buckets, and cement bags stacked into odd corners; coils of wire, plaster, cans of oil and paint. Above all, there is the wind, snatching at Nil's loose clothes, threatening to unravel the turban on his head.

He crouches, inches from the edge. Beneath him cascades the building's roof that, seen from below, slopes sharply to a point. From above it is a cruder thinning, more akin to a steep flight of steps, tapering to this flattened summit. Beyond the roofline lies the city. With no one to witness him, it does no harm to gape.

A peninsula like a cow's blunt tongue, flaring at the root. Smoke fogs it to the fifth or sixth storey. Church spires and factory chimneys puncture this haze, as do the tops of the grain elevators on the East Side docks. Downtown is a grid of scars, carving up the city Smoke like a system of trenches, their borders diffuse but easy to trace. To the north lies the park that splits Manhattan like a girdle; to the west, behind the stubby, trestled fingers of half-built towers, stretch the bay's brackish waters, black with oil spills, refuse, Soot. And New Jersey: a factory seafront choking on its Smoke.

Nil takes it all in, his hands numbing with the firmness of their grip. He is buoyant with fear, king of the world. A natural urge pries him loose from his awe. He pisses a yellow stream into the wind and shakes with giggles. The sun begins to dip and sits bloodied in the city's haze; the building's shadow a long black spar beneath his feet; a storm front blowing in upon the drama of its drumroll. Nil sits and hugs his knees into his chest, goosebumped with excitement and the rising breeze.

Soon, the Company men begin to leave. He sees the steam barges make their way to the docks, watches the stream of minute figures emerge from the bottom of the building, bowlered, clad in black. Victorian crows, overdressed for this New World spring. It makes Nil think about Smith, the man in light linen; makes him smile a little at the thought of these men pressed cheek to jowl in their too-small elevator, the boy amongst them, jammed tight between their armpits and elbows, one hand on his controls. Then Nil reminds himself that Smith will return—that he sleeps in the building—and that he better be gone when he does.

Darkness falls quickly, a clap of the hands. Inside the stairwell, it is so total that Nil feels compelled to slide down on his bottom, step by step. The landing seems vast to his reaching hands; the door not quite where he remembers. He tries the handle (nervously; might it be locked?) and is alarmed when light flares through the gap and sends its warning beacon against balustrade and wall. The corridor beyond is as he left it; its lamps— milky spheres suspended from ornamental chains—remain undimmed.

But all is quiet.

Nil waits and listens; steps through onto the marble, now every inch the thief.

[11]

Smith's room. What else? He had planned on making a quick survey of all the offices, to identify the richest pickings. His encounter with Smith has changed this. He is the "new man"; disliked yet important enough that he can afford to be. There may be more powerful men on this hallway, but none of them, Nil wagers, dares to shed his starched collar and trade it for a linen suit, or feels secure enough in his position to disgrace himself through the plebeian act of taking the stairs. Smith's room then: but a step from the stairs. A polished oak door.

It has no lock.

Inside rules a strange mixture of opulence and devastation. Smith has not so much "decorated" as torn through its furnishings. The books have been cleared off their shelves and stacked into towers or simply thrown onto corner mounds to make space for boxes and files, ribbon-tied piles of papers. Smith has taken down all the pictures and leaned them carelessly against the side of the desk. The wallpaper must have displeased him, for he has torn down much of it and covered other sections with a dazzling variety of maps, rudely nailed into the wall. The desk itself is tidy, organised. A gramophone balances on the windowsill, its flared horn pointing at the back of the office chair. In one corner, a large sofa has been made up into a bed. Shirts and underwear litter the floor; a washbowl of stale grey water balances on a heavy-limbed armchair; the chamber pot next to it has been emptied but not cleaned. The whole room is massive, dishevelled, bent to one man's unforgiving habits. A tub of beard oil, though sealed, spreads its musky sweetness through the air.

All this Nil has witnessed from the door, letting the hallway's lights illuminate the scene. He now closes it, walks soundless across the softness of the oriental carpets; heads to the windows, shuts the blinds, then turns on the desk lamp, moving as simply and swiftly as though he were walking in his own room.

A detail catches his attention. It rises from the ornamental chest that serves as bedside table to the sofa: a framed photograph, conspicuous because it has been perched atop another, folded facedown in a neat pantomime of usurpation. It shows a woman and a boy, presumably Smith Junior, eight years old, his father's bulk echoed in puppy fat. The woman is thin and careworn. She does not condescend to smile.

And next to her, as though cause and object of her sternness, there rises a glass casement, lead-bottomed and nearly a foot in height. Inside resides a beetle on a spit. A nail really, seven inches long and slender, entering the beetle's body at its sloping bottom, where winged back meets segmented belly, and emerging on the far side in between mandibles long and spiky like a crown of thorns. But what a beetle! Palm-sized, spread-winged, horned legs splayed and resting on the walls of its glass cage. Armoured in dull black. Its single mark of colour is the coarse speck of fur that sprouts underneath the triangular head, wasp yellow. A warning: the crescent shape much like a mouth. Frowning.

Nil starts. Stares from woman and child to beetle and back; expects a sudden wiggle of its legs. What disturbs him is not the thing itself but the monstrous nature of the juxtaposition. What breed of man travels the world with a picture of a family and the armoured husk of an exotic bug; feels compelled to position them side by side, within easy reach for night-time contemplation, for tender greetings at the start of each fresh day?

But there is more to it yet. It comes with a delay, has to be unearthed, as though with a shovel. First, a word rises to his mind, his lips. "N'tib." Nil says it and says it again, his mouth recalling a position, a movement of the tongue not needed for any English word.

"N'tib."

He does not know what it means.

Once spoken, the word cannot be forgotten; wakes something in his chest. It stirs in him, childhood-deep. The time before memory: his stomach heaving, his vision blurred. The glass casement, snatched up, won't open in his clumsy hands; slips, rolls on the soft of the carpet. He chases it, genuflecting, to the foot of the sofa; wrestles with the glued-on lid; and shatters the glass not with his right hand's clawing but the pressure of his left hand's grip: blood pooling between skin and insect fur as he pulls the beetle off its spit and cradles it against his cheek.

[12]

He must have smoked. He did not notice it, but the cuts on his hands are clogged with Soot, the beetle in his hands dusted with spent emotion. Nil himself feels brittle, used up.

Habit inserts itself into the hollowness of the moment. He rises and, this monstrous piece of childhood still cupped against his chest, starts making an inventory of valuables within the room. There is money in the desk drawer, coins and banknotes in a range of currencies that Nil stuffs into a pouch sewn into the inside of his trousers. The paperweight is made of gilded brass, the picture frame of solid silver. But Nil's heart is not in it, is pounding in his chest, hounded by the thought that the vermin and he once shared the same forest floor. Something less than a memory: his crouching amongst ferns, watching a black scuttle. He cannot dispel it, opens desk drawers without looking at their contents, shuffles through letters he is too shaken to read.

Then a new detail registers on his burglar's eye, an incongruity. There is a built-in closet in the room, marked by a narrow door. He was going to have a look through it as a matter of course but judged it to hold no special promise. Now Nil sees that it is padlocked. It is a flimsy lock, just good enough to keep out the cleaner, but a lock nonetheless. Its brackets have been crudely—recently—installed.

Nil walks over at once. One hand does not suffice to pick the lock, so he places the beetle on the thick carpet, then opens the door in a matter of seconds. Inside the closet, he finds an overcoat and a wide-brimmed hat made of pig's leather; a rifle case, a worsted suit, a belt with cartridges and holstered pistols; a stack of paintings wrapped in newspapers and cloth. On the floor, half hidden behind a pair of stout boots, there sits something very much like a cake tin or a metal hatbox. The lid is screwed on and perforated by a dozen pinpricks, each like a pockmark on the polish of the lid.

Pinpricks.

Breathing holes.

Gingerly, his hands suddenly clumsy, tongue twisting around a single, awkward word, Nil reaches for the box. He finds it light though clearly not empty, a lump of weight at its base. Too cautious to open the lid, he pulls the box out of the closet and places it on the carpet; kneels down and presses his ear, his cheek, to its top. Nothing: the metal cool against his skin, the ridges of the pinholes like a rash of burrs upon his cheek. It is only when Nil lifts up the box—carefully, keeping the box level as though it were filled with water; the lid still safely in its place—and places his ear to the smoothness of its bottom that he makes it out: a sudden burst of little taps as six horned feet drum their pattern into the tin. And for the first time since entering the building, Nil is afraid. Afraid not of the box and its contents but of being caught; of losing this singular key to the mystery of his origins and reverting forever to the boy who has neither home nor nature, who is nothing but the sum of his needs.

He rises, clutching the box, and forgets about everything but the need to leave. A minute later he is walking down the stairs: is walking, not running, because he must not stumble and cannot afford to exhaust his breath. Twenty-three floors, he counts them by the landings, notes the transition when he must be passing the blank of the scar, with its rot and carbolic and milky light. On the ground floor, Nil ignores the locked and guarded front entrance and chooses instead the door separating the entrance hall from the back of the building, bolted against entry but not exit. Ten minutes later, he slips out the window of a cluttered communal office whose heavy window grille can be unscrewed from the inside. As the quality of air changes, the tin stirs in his hands: a sudden, panicked pulse. Nil listens, strokes the lid, catching a finger on a breathing hole; elicits an answering tremour, a tattoo. He walks briskly, clutching the box tightly to his chest.

It is as though he is carrying his heart.

<u>Gale</u> (also: "Smoke winds"; "emotional weather"):
A surviving fragment of Second Smoke, crisscrossing the land. It can be
tinted or almost clear but even then is visible as a *density* within the air.
A Gale's prevailing temper varies according to the quality of the Soot
feeding it. Sites of grave crime or suffering, when quickened, produce
angry ("salty") Gales that can precipitate violence in those caught up in
them. The greater frequency of Gales in the North as opposed to the South
may be attributed to the historically greater proportion of workingmen
and -women in the North; since workers' lives were, at the time of
oppression, blighted by immeasurably greater suffering than the soft lives
of the privileged, the Soot deposits of the North are darker and more
plentiful, providing the Gales with greater resources of fuel. Gales have
been reported in Ireland, Germany, France, the Netherlands, Belgium,
Scandinavia, Russia, the Baltics, though not generally farther south than
the Alps. No fresh reports of Gales beyond the British Isles have been
received in several years.
See also *Storm; Gale Chaser.*

<u>Storm</u> (also: "Black Storm"; "Black Gale"):
Southern propaganda term for a particularly ill-tempered Gale blamed for
all manner of mischief.
See also *Gale.*

[1]

They have put up the tent at the southern edge of Central Park. The Big Scar, that's what people here call it. It's an old English circus tent, dating from a time when theatre was forbidden but the display of animals was not. When the sun hits the fabric you can still smell them, the lions and tigers and dancing bears: rising like ghosts, like yesterday's farts; urine, musk, and fur. Two weeks in the city and the sun has been out every day. It is as hot as if it were August. This is New York: a furnace full of strangers, vivid with stinks.

Eleanor fell in love with it at once.

It is for her a moment of unprecedented freedom. Already Saint John— her home for so many years—feels distant; already the fear of discovery, grown unbearable in the weeks after Cruikshank's death, has fallen away and been dismissed as overwrought. Cruikshank told her they were hunted; that her uncle's reach went far; that her papers would not bear official scrutiny. Here, in the city, anonymised, the fears feel far-fetched. How easy after all was her escape! Balthazar clapped his hands like a magician. And there she was, absorbed into his troupe.

She has met them all, of course: tall, quick-witted Victor who hides a rash of pimples underneath his stage paint; and beautiful Ada, so flighty she talks and smokes in one incessant tide. Kolya and Pavla, the Shapers, who spend all their free time bent over a game of chess. Edie and Tomaso, stagehands and mechanicals. Geoffrey, the set painter who plays Thomas in the final scene: a squat, quiet bruiser of a boy, his clothes so dirty they hang stiff from his frame. Peter, Yves, and handsome David, whom she first knew as make-believe fishermen singing a humble welcome to the Smoke; Greta Silvana Nemec, from Montreal via Budapest and Prague, who insists on her full name and is too important to speak to Eleanor for any length of time; and Meister Lukas who has a Chinese face to go with his German name and is so very shy he daren't look her in the eye. They are all sequestered in the same once-grand, now-shabby hotel near the Great Scar where they live with the intimacy of family, or of soldiers at war.

All the same, a certain distance governs their and Eleanor's relations. Eleanor lives with the players but does not quite belong to them; has been welcomed but not assimilated. She is what she has always been: an awkward girl, living at the margins of other people's lives, her only role within the troupe the passing out of flyers around town.

The flyers are Balthazar's design. COME AND SEE SMOKE'S PLAYERS, they read, NOW PERFORMING A NEW PROGRAMME OF PLAYS AND TABLEAUX. BUY A TICKET AND BE AMAZED. At their bottom, a pencil scrawl discloses their location and exhorts visitors to COME BRING YOUR SINS.

"Where shall I put these?" she asked when Balthazar handed them over to her along with a pot of glue and a coarse brush.

"Everywhere, Miss Cruikshank. Try not to get yourself killed."

[2]

And so she walks the city every day, from the edge of the Big Scar to the southern tip of the peninsula where a group of towers rise like fingers, up above the haze. The city is paved, hard on her feet; laid out in endless rulered lines. She learns its geography, each clutch of city blocks a little nation bounded by wasteland or a strip of orchard, by piles of rubbish or barley fields, by shade trees planted in long tidy rows. Eleanor sticks flyers to walls, lampposts, and shop doors; passes them out to butchers, grocers, and tobacconists; is offered tea and schnapps and still-warm oxblood; is propositioned, chased, or cheered by men and women of all colours and all creeds.

Wherever she goes, she hears things, reads things. Politics, gossip, sex. That in New England, where the Second Smoke never reached, there are Puritan villages where man and wife sleep in separate buildings and visit only once a month. That the United States is fragmented, united only by name; that a second civil war is looming and the dollar not worth shit. That China has thrown all foreigners out of its ports and Switzerland has banned the use of sweets upon pain of death. She sees her first motorcar and watches men ride through the skies in a balloon; listens to musicians on street corners playing a music of such abandon that people dance smoking in the street; walks under a garland of roasted ducks in Chinatown, strung up above the street to absorb a seasoning of Soot; and is chased by dog packs through the withered scrubland of a scar.

But no matter how far Eleanor wanders or how absorbed she becomes in the spectacle of the city, in the hot hours of the afternoon, halfway between noon and dusk, she embarks on the long walk back to the players' tent. Nightfall marks the rise of the curtain. In a city without public clocks it is the most sensible of conventions. Besides, Balthazar likes the dark. Unlike the sun, stage light is something he can shape. When the audience is admitted and the lamps are lit; when the hush falls over the public and the tent fills with the pre-Smoke of expectation; when a single beam picks out an actor or an object, transforming them from something everyday into a receptacle brimful with revelation—Eleanor is *there*, tucked in amongst the crowd.

She knows most of the repertoire by now, knows the actors' gestures, the props and bits of stage magic. It does not seem to matter. The experience is new every time, the Smoke ever shifting, a matter of the actors' moods, the make-up of the audience, the air pressure and the phase of the moon. People come from all over the city and beyond: a group of railway workers from Pennsylvania who stay three nights though they have money for only a single show; a perfumed uptown dandy with a made-up crest pinned to his cravat; a Boston magistrate's widow, travelling with two young Poles, each (it is said) a husband to her on alternate days; a towering Jew, sweating in his heavy hat of sable furs. Eleanor mingles Smoke with all of them, is soiled by some and ennobled by others, samples emotions far from her ken. The theatre absorbs her in its drama and its crowd; returns her to a sense of self seeded by the ghosts of others.

And how different they seem to her, these others, when they spill through the tent flaps at the end of the show: no longer strangers but relations, each as though chasing their own shadow, splayed huge and nebulous by the stage lights at their backs.

"Rushing home like they left porridge on the hob," Balthazar scoffs. "Hoping they will remember who they are. That their wallpaper, the neighbour's snore, will remind them."

"Don't laugh," Eleanor hears Etta May scold him. "You have no right. It's you who makes them lose themselves."

"What, I am a thief now? A will-o'-the-wisp? Leading people onto treacherous ground."

"A coward," she scolds, "always hiding behind your screen. You are the boy who never plays but thinks he knows the rules."

He spits and calls her names. "Minx," "cretin," "pan guts." "More arse on you than brains, and a mouth bigger than either."

For all his sour words, Balthazar's Smoke is hesitant and mild.

[3]

One detail has changed about the performances. They no longer finish in a fever. Whatever it was that Balthazar did to provide current, *conductivity*, to the Smoke released in the players' final scene, he now omits. At first Eleanor felt a sharp stab of loss at this omission, complained of it to an unmoved Balthazar. The alternate ending is not without pleasure, however. It leaves the auditorium trading in a light, subtle Smoke carrying flavours of a kind commonly obscured by stronger passions. It is a hushed, prayerful mood that spreads: each sense straining for the Smoke, the connection to the others gentle, light as silk. Something else, too. Eleanor has noticed that there are, in these final moments, points of density within the crowd, places where a single person becomes the centre of gravity within their corner of the room; has noticed, too, that she is one such centre. Afterwards—when the players have taken their applause, and the fans have been turned on, dispersing the last of the Smoke—it has become common for people to walk up to her, to touch her sleeve, her hand. Women curtsy; men slip off their caps and stand kneading them between their hands. Eleanor receives these tributes impassively, unsurprised and a little resentful. She has always been different.

It troubles her.

[4]

She takes her trouble to Etta May. She could talk to Balthazar, of course, but his manner with her retains an edge of hostility. It is as though he is angry at something that she is making him do. She and Etta May have a simpler relationship. They became acquainted on the boat journey where they shared a minuscule cabin, a space confined enough to dream each other's sleeping Smoke. A woman half flirt, half matron; her speech slow and honeyed, like she's savouring each word. She hails from Virginia, Balthazar told Eleanor when first introducing them. "Smell it? Her people's perfume: tobacco and nostalgia, for when they had slaves." The two like each other, Eleanor has gathered, and express it through the trading of unkind truths.

Etta May likes to sit outside after a performance, even in the downpours that often follow upon the heat of the day, on a folding chair placed underneath a mighty beech some dozen yards from the tent. When Eleanor comes to her, she fetches a second chair, sets it up so they sit side by side. An audience for crickets. Storm clouds on the dark horizon; moonlight slipping through the web of branches; a fox loping past them left to right.

For the longest time they simply sit. Etta May does not push for conversation, is patient, placid, waiting for rain; Eleanor awkward, precise, stockpiling words. At last Eleanor breaks the silence and describes it: the odd conviction that she has been accumulating *followers* at the end of each play; the shy obeisance paid to her by men and women twice her age.

Etta May absorbs it matter-of-factly; shifts her big rump in her chair.

"They come to you to be blessed, do they? Well, why not? Sometimes I feel like getting a blessing from you myself!" She pauses to retrieve a cigarette from her sleeve, lights it, then speaks through a wreath of smoke. "You take their pain away, girl, their anger. It curls out of them, all their nastiness, right into you and there it stays. What comes back out is lighter, kinder. The parts of themselves they *like*."

"You're a Soother, Em. Isn't that what you do?"

Etta May snorts at the suggestion. "I am merely slow to rouse. Sluggish Smoke—it calms things down, dampens them. And the Shapers are different, too. They are *actors*, see; they step into an emotion and broadcast it, making sure it dominates. But you don't *act*. It's quite the opposite. I have never met anyone quite so still."

When Eleanor does not respond, the big woman leans closer and touches Eleanor's shoulder as though testing her solidity.

"Balthazar says your uncle kept you in some kind of machine. It punished you when you smoked."

"It didn't. It taught me to punish myself."

"And now he's looking for you. What does he want?"

"Cruikshank said that I hurt his pride. That I was his vision for the future but I ran away instead."

"And what do *you* say?"

Eleanor considers the answer, considers it deeply.

"I think that he wants me back because he loves me. And once he has me, he will want to use me. Only I don't know how." She rushes the next words, willing them out. "I have a dream sometimes that I am pregnant by my uncle. It's growing in me, tailed and scaly. Holding a ledger to its breast. It frightens me, Em. It frightens me like nothing else in the world."

"Frightens you? Well, you sure scare the daylights out of the rest of us! Balthazar most of all. He says you make him feel *flimsy*." Etta May smiles, reaches over and pats Eleanor's knee in a maternal gesture, the stub of her cigarette wedged between soft knuckles. "It must be strange, being like that. Lonely. Like being the biggest fish in the pond. Some new kind nobody's ever seen, a catfish maybe, sitting there on the muddy floor, huge and unmoving. All the others watching it from the corner of one eye."

Eleanor blinks away the remark. She asks, "What's wrong with me, Etta May? Why can't I be normal?"

"Wrong, hon? Nothing. You have talent, that's all. Why do you think Balthazar is so interested in you? Oh, he is interested in your story, naturally. You met Charlie Cooper. One of The Three. You're an eyewitness, someone who can help him write his grand history of Smoke. If that's all there was to it, he'd ask his questions and be done with you. After all, you are a member of the audience. Not one of us. That's how he sees the world: players and spectators, never the twain shall meet. But you have *talent*. Balthazar respects talent."

Eleanor has heard the phrases before. "Talented Smokers." "Talented Smoke." The theatre people seem to prize nothing more highly.

"Talent for what?"

"Ah, there's the rub. Balthazar isn't sure. It sits in his craw." Etta May smiles but her eyes remain serious. "Whatever it is, hon, it's too big for the theatre. It does not *do* make-believe. And so Balthazar ain't sure that he can use you. You see, he's an artist, down to his bones. He only has time for people he can use."

They listen to the rain for some moments before Eleanor objects.

"*He* is a *she*, Em."

"And what if he is? It's easier, running a business, if you are a man. Always travelling, negotiating; bargaining with other men." Etta May stubs out the cigarette against her chair, fishes a fresh one from out her sleeve. "Second Smoke or not. The world has not changed that much in ten years."

Eleanor does not believe her. "It's more than an act."

"More? Why, of course. Don't you see what happens onstage, honey? You don the costume. And become what you play."

Eleanor distrusts the answer, senses denial underneath. She pictures it, putting on breeches, boots, and cap; tying her breasts down to preserve the clean lines of her buttoned coat.

"I am not like that," she says at last. "I'd just be a girl dressing up."

"That's just it—why you don't fit with us. You have no need to play at things. If someone scares you, you just take their Smoke and pay them back in kindness." Etta May looks over at Eleanor, still with that same gentle smile, still serious underneath. "Where does it go, all the hate that you absorb?"

Eleanor finds she knows the answer. "There's a tower, inside me—that's how I picture it. A high, narrow tower, like a grain silo or a smokestack, only it's made of steel."

"A smokestack, ha! Well, if you ever decide to let off steam, hon, do let me know. Now there's something I would pay to see."

[5]

For a full two weeks then, Eleanor Renfrew walks Manhattan every day and surrenders to the stage at night. And finds that she is happy. More than that: she's in love. It's the magic of the theatre. Etta May tells her they break hearts wherever they go.

Then something changes.

It is the start of the third week of the players' residence; the sixteenth show that Eleanor has seen. There is *someone* in the audience: a tremble in the Smoke. He's a large man, fleshy, not fat; his face bluff and big-featured, his skin fair and ruddy; the head bald, the cheeks framed by two thick wedges of whisker, a sun-drenched yellow, corn in a summer field. A man close to forty; in the prime of his life. Cheerful, sanguine, well contented in his vigour and his health. He dives into the audience's Smoke with the relish of a swimmer; adds his own appetites without hesitation or shame.

And then he cuts out.

They are less than a third through the evening's performance, not long before the first intermission. The players are staging a comic scene in which a maidservant and mistress undergo a series of inversions as, for the first time in their lives, they breathe each other's sins and see themselves reflected in the other. Two women; a chair; a sheepskin rug; a hairbrush;

and a sumptuous pair of pink culottes—these are the only things upon the stage. The audience lurches from Schadenfreude to the gentler need for reconciliation: between haughty missus and saucy maid; between masters and men. There is a moment before the stranger's withdrawal, when—for a heartbeat; the length of a wanton thought—something new crawls out of him, coarser, deeper than what he has thus far shown. A few of his neighbours take it up, corrode it into lust, vainglory, vanity: emotions unbecoming to the moment. Etta May notices. She sidles closer to the group, her body straining anger from the air; plump cheeks shiny with dark Soot. The next moment the man has shut off his Smoke. He makes a movement—digs in his pocket, manipulating something there. Then he is gone. His face, his bearing, does not change: the same toothy smile, eyes focussed on the stage. But his body has withdrawn from all communion, stands singular, the Smoke surrounding him now dead against his skin.

For those who surround him, the change is subtle, a pebble thrown into the sea. All the same, Eleanor feels it at once. She sees Ada and Greta Silvana notice it, too, and hesitate upon the stage; sees Balthazar peek around his screen, one eye and a sliver of black forehead, eloquent in their scowl.

Then the room catches itself: torn threads of Smoke are reconnected, between players and audience, front row and back, all now bypassing the man. The play carries on. It has incorporated the disruption, woven the unease into the fabric of emotion that it spins. Soon the auditorium is once again immersed, laughs in voice and Smoke as mistress and maid each thrust a leg into voluminous pink knickers and stand conjoined, grown together hip to hip.

Not so Eleanor. Though she continues to feel the play in her body, trading Smoke with her neighbours mechanically, the way one can eat without tasting the food, her attention is focussed on the hulking figure of the man. He remains where he was, immersed in the crowd but separate now, as though he were watching from the confines of a glass box. What strikes her most of all is that his focus and demeanour are unaltered: the same self-congratulatory cheerfulness he has displayed all along. Then the man catches her eyes on him, across the mass of bodies and the haze. A pale gaze, his; the blink of eyelids thickly framed in yellow lashes; the purse of wet lips. There is no hint of recognition.

It does not matter. Eleanor knows why he is here.

The Smoke that escapes her stirs a note of trepidation into the scene's finale, souring its cheer.

[6]

She hears Balthazar and Etta May argue about the man during the intermission. They are standing huddled in the shelter of his screen; heads
thrown together like conspirators.

"Don't let him back in the tent," she hears him say.

"He's paid for a ticket, Balthazar."

"I don't care. Return his money. Tell Geoffrey not to let him through the
doors."

"You want to risk a fistfight, just to keep him out? I had a good look at
him. He's not the type to go without a fuss."

"Sweets!" Balthazar rages. "In my theatre! He stands in the audience
sucking sweets!"

"It was impressive, though, wasn't it? The way he just turned himself
off. Must have stuffed his cheeks with a good dozen. A rich man! At least
we are costing him dear." Then: "Why do it? Why come and then not let
yourself feel? What is he—some uptown Puritan curious about our shop?"

"Curious, no. His type, they always come with a plan."

[7]

Eleanor does not return to the show after the intermission. Her instinct is
to run, far away, be lost in the city and its crowd. But the idea of the man
haunts her and bids her linger outside the tent trying to catch a glimpse of
him. She sees him but once, in the bustle that follows a riotous retelling of
"Little Red Riding Hood," in which, under the influence of Smoke, granny,
wolf, and girl gradually change positions until predator turns to pup and
infirm victim into hunter: sees the stranger shouting, finger-whistling, and
applauding, in tune with his neighbours' noise yet deaf to their bodies'
song drifting idle past his numb and deadened skin.

After the show, Balthazar finds Eleanor wandering listlessly along the
threshold of light thrown by the big tent's lamps. He pauses, studies her,
invites her out to dinner.

"Something decent for a change. Just us two; tête-à-tête."

She suspects at once he means to say good-bye.

[8]

They find a restaurant not far from the Big Scar, order veal and greens, sit poking at them with tin forks. Balthazar seems about to start into conversation several times, then gags himself by shoving a piece of meat into his mouth.

"Ada told me you will soon be heading to England," Eleanor says at last, and watches him swallow the "you" along with the veal.

"Actors! Bloody gossips, the lot of them."

"It's true, isn't it?"

"If I can find a ship that will take us. Without bankrupting us, that is."

Why go there? she wants to ask. The one place where—surely—theatre is forbidden. Where Gales still rage. The isle of madness. Of strife.

But whatever it is in her that ties her tongue and sifts her words until they betray no hint of inner turmoil intervenes, so that all that comes out is:

"They won't let you play. *He* won't."

They: His Majesty's government. *He:* Renfrew, doctor philosophiae; MP. Lately Duke of Marlborough. Prime Minister. Chairman of the Executive Committee. "The Lord Protector of the Realm."

"Half an arse-cheek of one island," Balthazar scoffs, meat in his teeth. "Hardly a *realm*." He swallows, chokes, coughs up grizzle. "A half-gut Cromwell! What of him, girl? He and his Parliament, they hide down in the South. We're heading north."

"To Minetowns."

"So you know something about English politics after all. Yes, Minetowns. I have a standing invitation. We have been there before. Besides . . . I have some business to attend to, over there."

For once her words outrace that semblance of composure. "Can I come?" she pleads, Smoke on her breath.

Balthazar smells it and puckers his lips, a connoisseur tasting wine.

"You tell me," he responds without rancour. "There was a man at the play today—I think he was looking for you. Just how badly does your uncle want you back?"

[9]

They return to the hotel. It's Meister Lukas who waits for them in the lobby. He is a fine-featured man, dark slanting eyes hemmed in by cheekbones, the nose small and flat; is shy to the point of girlishness. When he told Eleanor that his native city of Tsingtao looks just like Prussia, he spoke from behind a shielding hand, its back and fingers dusted with a hundred birthmarks, pinprick-small. Now that he is agitated, the shyness gives way to high-pitched babble. It isn't so much that he has lost his English but has superimposed it with tonalities imported from his mother tongue. "Thief," he keeps on saying. "Nasty bloody thief," the only words intelligible in this torrent, and two fine fingers become pincers tugging with delicate urgency at Balthazar's sleeve.

They take the stairs at a run. If the foyer retains a veneer of grandeur, the stairwell and corridors attest neglect. Soot and mould complicate the pattern of the wallpaper that is bubbling with humidity; the carpets are at one and the same time threadbare and as though bloated with grime; half the lightbulbs blown within old chandeliers long plundered of their crystal.

The players are all housed on the same corridor. In the absence of any other hotel guests billeted here, the hallway has become a common area where actors and stagehands will mill at all hours of the day and night, often in states of considerable undress. So it is a surprise to find the place abandoned; its doors standing wide open as though it has been fled. Meister Lukas does not stop until they have arrived at a particular door, also open, its handle broken along with the lock.

Balthazar's door.

One glance is enough to ascertain he has been robbed.

[10]

The thief remains in the hotel. This is the chief piece of intelligence Meister Lukas manages to impart. It is the only one that matters. Everything else can wait. If Meister Lukas led them this far by tugging at Balthazar's sleeve, it is now his own shirt-tail that is taken hold of.

"Go on, faster," the old director keeps shouting at his back, though it is he himself who has trouble keeping up. Eleanor is hard on his heels. They chase up a stairwell, down a corridor, up another flight of stairs. The hotel changes around them as they ascend, becomes better appointed. Six floors in total. Street Smoke rarely rises this high. Whatever luxury suites this run-down establishment may retain, they will be located here, at the top.

At last they arrive. Another bend of the corridor, a miniature foyer, partly furnished with armchairs, and there they are: the players. At first glance one might think them simply transplanted, from one hallway to another, by a windfall in their monetary fortunes, their routines unchanged. As on any other night they are indifferent to modesty and stand around in all manners of dress, some still in costume, some in nightclothes, curlers in their hair; others stripped to their undergarments, battling the heat.

But rather than the usual milling and gossiping, the nail-filing, mending, and ironing, the clusters of twos and threes, the arguments and the peals of laughter coming from the washroom around the corner, they stand silent, packed into a mob—an *audience*—in a ring outside a door. When Baltha-zar pushes his way through, Eleanor in tow, they part willingly enough, relieved that someone is taking charge. Etta May is there, wrapped in a bathrobe, a cigarette stuck in the corner of her mouth.

"He took your travelling chest, Balthazar. Kicked down the door and placed it on one shoulder, cool as you like. And then he went up to the reception and demanded their best room."

"Who, goddammit?"

"That man. The one from the audience. Gold mutton chops."

[11]

There is not much more Etta May can tell him. He showed up downstairs in the hotel an hour and a half ago and asked which room was the direc-tor's. He asked politely, mopping his forehead, complaining about the heat. Etta May told him Balthazar was out; that he could slip a note under the door if he liked. The man appeared to think on it. Next they knew, he had broken the lock.

And then? They followed him, a gaggle of goslings, jabbering at his back. Complained to the hotel staff; threatened him with the authorities. Only it seemed better not to rush into things where the authorities were con-cerned. David was dispatched to go find Balthazar, Meister Lukas to wait for him in the lobby. The rest of them laid siege at the door. They knocked and knocked until the man yelled to keep down the noise. Since then they have not heard a thing.

"Why did you not break down the door?"

"He can't escape, Balthazar. It's the sixth floor. And the fire escape is rusted through, we checked."

"He has my papers! My plays. *Everything*."

Balthazar makes to say more but chokes on his own Smoke. He begins hammering on the door and kicking it with one foot. "Open up, you bastard," he keeps shouting, tugging and pushing at the brass knob so that the door buckles under his force.

Almost at once a sound answers him from the depths of the room beyond the door. It is faint yet clearly audible, like a stage effect carefully managed in its volume. A splash; the rush of water down a risen body; the flat slap of a wet foot hitting tile. A moment later the latch is thrown back on the lock and the door pulled open. Beyond stands the naked bulk of the stranger, a rectangle of terry towel thrown across one freckled shoulder, water pooling at his feet.

"Ah, at last! The director. I was just cooling off. Come in, make yourself at home. Only, enough of the banging. It gets on my nerves."

And with that he turns his back on them, returns into the room. A grunt as he throws himself into a chair: the chair's grunt, not his, leather stretching under naked arse.

His broad smile splits him open chop to chop.

[12]

At first Eleanor thinks Balthazar will simply launch himself at the naked man. His fists are clenched, wrinkly black skin stretched taut and pale across the knuckles; his whole gaunt figure liveried in viscous Smoke. But he hesitates, stands arrested on the threshold, one foot in, the other out, confused, intimidated by the coolness of this man. His eyes search out Eleanor's. It is her fault, this.

She must know what to do.

The stranger meanwhile sits, unmoved in his hale humour; picks Balthazar's Soot off his bath-damp thighs. Now he rises and commences the process of towelling himself dry.

He makes quite a production of it, starts with his domed head, then his armpits, thinly studded with reddish-blond hair; moves to his shoulders and flanks, then bends to rub dry his calves and feet. At last he straightens, attempts to wrap the towel around his thickset waist but finds he can only just knot the top corner, the towel gaping over smooth, pale flesh. The man laughs.

"Some hotel, eh? All this talk about the 'best suite in the house' and then they give you a towel that won't even cover your bits. A scratchy little rag it is, too. Too many washes in lye." He rolls his shoulders, rubs his palms dry on his chest. "And you should see the bathtub! What grime—unspeakable! Like something in a French *chambre d'hôte*. If it hadn't been so infernally hot . . . But come in, stop dithering, we have to talk. Only close the door. I am sick of the gawking. There is a good man."

This much Balthazar does: enter, close the door behind. He drags Eleanor inside with him. She is willing, can sense his thought. *The man wants her; it's why he's here.* The stranger registers her entry without comment.

The room is a reception room of sort, part of a suite of three. The brass bulk of a bathtub is visible through the doorway on the right; the bedroom lies straight ahead. The reception room itself is surprisingly small and overfurnished with a set of sofas flanking a too-large desk and heavy chair. Balthazar's travelling chest adds to the clutter, stands metal-studded, massive, at the centre of the room. The parquet floor is scuffed where the stranger rudely dropped its bulk.

The chest's owner has yet to speak. Balthazar stands motionless, his anger long arrested, drifting as dust upon the air; dark eyes riveted upon the stranger's form. Eleanor, too, is staring and has done so through the long procedure of the towelling off: at his bulk, his nudity. Even now her eyes remain glued to the abundance of his flesh. She has slipped into the corner, to one side of him, faces his flank; sees above all the muscular hollow of the man's spine; the clotted scrawl of veins blooming black upon his hip; the play of sinew in his short, thick neck. Her fascination is not prurient, nor yet steeped in disgust; is shameless, smokeless, held by the man's freckled paleness, the sheer mechanical vigour of his movements.

The man, for his part, delights in their attention.

At long last Balthazar shakes off his wonder. The next moment he has stepped forward, reached for the handle of his chest, and dragged it, trembling, a foot towards the door.

"No."

The man says it calmly, points with his hand to the desk, where between a decanter of hotel port and the man's discarded stockings, lies the black bulk of a revolver. He does not move towards it or in any way betray his intention of taking hold of the gun; stands not much closer to it, in fact, than Balthazar himself. His confidence is total.

"All I want, my good man, is a conversation. To conduct business. Yes, of course, I stole your treasure chest. I am a thief, a rotter, whatever you will. You will note, however, that I have waited for you to arrive before opening it. Now that you are here, we will have a look through. You dislike this but have no means of avoiding it. So why not give in with good grace?"

He pauses there, extends a palm in invitation to sit. Three breaths and Balthazar accepts it: drops the chest with a loud *clang*, prunes his face, spits a slug of Soot upon the oriental rug, then lowers his lanky frame into the sofa's leather.

"There," the stranger nods, sitting down on the chair across. "'It's always worthwhile speaking to an intelligent man.'"

Balthazar hears the phrase, and frowns. "That's from Dostoevsky. *The Brothers Karamazov*. Smerdyakov talking to Ivan."

"Then you have read it! You read Russian? Or has someone done a translation? It's a splendid chapter, is it not?"

"One murderer talking to another."

"Murderers, yes," smiles the man. "But also: brothers."

[13]

The man begins with an introduction. Because, as he says, names make for kinship amongst men.

"Hard for a soldier to shoot those who have a name. Unless they are family, of course. We kill strangers and those we love.

"And so," he continues, "Smith, Bedrich Alexander, at your service. Well, Schmidt, actually, but try making your way as 'Schmidt.' Not in East India, nor in Cairo, let alone in Bristol or New York. So plain Alex Smith." He salaams playfully, touching sternum, lips, and forehead. "And you are who, exactly? I heard your actors refer to you as 'Balthazar.' A nom de plume, I take it. One of the three wise men. Ambitious! Balthazar what?"

"Balthazar Black."

"Oh, very good! A Mr. Black then, meeting a Mr. Smith. This will be a very English conversation. We should call down for tea.

"Now, Mr. Black, I enjoyed the performance earlier today. It is a remarkable thing, your theatre. A new art form, the summation of a whole era. I had been looking forward to coming for the whole of the past week—I even prepared for it, one might say, cleansing my palate. And when the curtain rose . . . my heart leapt, I swear, just like a little boy's.

"Only, there was something missing. I have a report you see, that reached me all the way from the Canadas. I'm a busy man, and much as I love cultural endeavours, I might not have dropped my work and come, had it not been for this report. It discussed your show's ending. The final cadence, so to speak. A *freeing* of the Smoke—something like a miniature Gale. There was nothing like that today."

Balthazar does not speak for the longest time. When he does, his voice is full of fear.

"Did the Company send you? What do they care about my theatre?" Then, his eyes on Eleanor; resentment, accusation, in his Smoke: "It's Renfrew, isn't it? But this isn't his turf!"

"Sent me? *Renfrew?!*" The man guffaws. "Let's just say I am here on private business of my own."

[14]

It registers in Eleanor's heart as a curious stitch of disappointment, underneath the relief. The stranger is not here because of her. Her uncle has not sent him. She is not *wanted*. All of Smith's interest lies in Balthazar's travelling chest at his feet.

He begins to unpack it. He does so deftly, neither careless with the objects he uncovers nor handling them with false reverence: makes a pile of books; another of notes, letters, and loose papers; a third of objects, trinkets, souvenirs, many of which are wrapped in newspaper to protect them against breakage. Amongst the latter counts a wooden cigar box with an intricate-looking lock. Smith studies this lock, then raises the box to his ear; rattles it very gently, then places it on the chair by his side. He stands bent over his task, legs straight, towel tight over his buttocks. With every movement, the quiver of his stomach. Gristle, not fat, moving ponderously. The pale skin is marbled with dark veins.

He takes up the papers next, finds a sheaf of maps, opens each atop the other.

"Weather maps," he mutters at one point, not expecting any answer. "Gales; marked with dates and durations. You are looking for patterns! An interesting hobby.

"And hello, what is this? A cast list? No. Witnesses! You are searching them out, are you? All the people who were involved in the Second Coming. A historian, are you? An admirable pursuit, if fruitless. My interest is for the future.

"And here: playbills for all of your shows. How sentimental of you to keep them all. But my, you have travelled! A wise man indeed. And this? Drafts, I take it. Future work. A curious method of notation. Well, I suppose it all makes sense once you put it on the stage.

"Next up: bookkeeping, accounts. Very meticulous. But my, is that what you charge? I'm in the wrong racket! Your actors' wages are quite paltry by comparison. Not a union man then! Oh no, don't blush, you have my support, we businessmen must stand as one."

Balthazar will not be drawn by any of these remarks, sits stiffly, his face ashen under the darkness of his skin. Time and again his eyes roam to the pistol on the writing desk. They do not remain there. Eleanor can see him consider and dismiss his options. He cannot fight. Nor can he leave. His life's work is spread on the floor in front of him.

He must have it back.

Smith presses on, relentless.

"Here then, your correspondence. This pile here is private. Fan letters, solicitations, declarations of love. Will you smell this perfume! And here the business letters. Contracts, invitations. Minetowns? How interesting. Courageous even. But I don't suppose you lack for pebbles, Mr. Black.

"Then here: an envelope full of photographic prints. How curious! Did someone really think to take pictures on that fateful morning? And look what he trained his camera on! Hmm, I better put these here aside. Like you, I have a taste for this sort of thing.

"And that concludes our initial inventory, Mr. Black. And returns us to the cigar case. Locked. It would be a shame to break its contents in the attempt to force the lock. You won't help me? Ah, just look at that scowl! Well then, let's risk it. Here we go, just a little jimmy with the penknife and voilà, it's open. Just like a jewellery box: a row of little hollows, in purple velvet no less! Very neat work. Custom-built to hold—what exactly? Vials! But only one vial is left. And how delicate it is: shaped like little hourglasses, so they can be snapped in half. Are you keeping this one for the grand finale? Or perhaps you have decided that New Yorkers are too volatile. You never know what you might release!

"Well then, that's all. Another question or two and I'll be on my way. But first, let us conclude the purchase. These photos here, the vial, and your weather maps, from curiosity if nothing else. Are American dollars acceptable? Here"—he fishes his pocketbook from out the jacket that lies crumpled on the floor, counts out a number of paper bills, makes a stack of them on the desk—"that should cover it, wouldn't you say?"

Balthazar sits still, eyes roaming between Smith, the papers, the gun.

"Piss off!" he manages at last. "My things are not for sale."

"Ah, Mr. Black. In my experience people who use that phrase are simply bargaining for more. But I forgot you are a theatre man and accustomed to melodrama. Forget all that. This is business. Remember your accounts."

And just like that Smith shrugs off his earlier good humour, his garrulousness and zest for life: shrugs them off regretfully but without hesitation, leaving an entirely practical man behind. He reopens his pocketbook, places four more bills on the desk, considers the pile, then takes one bill back.

"There—everything within reason."

He shoves the photographs and maps into a yellowed envelope embossed with the hotel's name, places the vial back in the cigar box, then reaches for the gun, not threateningly, but merely as a man collecting his things.

"And now that the purchase is concluded, Mr. Black, let us have a quick few words about this vial. I am interested, of course, in the locations and method of your harvesting. I note you are returning to England. I assume it's to restock. Does Minetowns produce the contents or do you have to head into the wilderness? Don't tell me you just stand in the open with a jar and lid, hoping for a Gale!"

[15]

Balthazar will ignite. Eleanor can feel it in her pores. Already his Smoke has begun to creep treacly down his shoulders and arms; is curling tendrils deep into the room. Eleanor does not flinch from their touch. She opens herself up, in fact, and feels her body probed by outrage. By instinct—with a deftness intimating *talent*—she sifts the Smoke and finds beneath the current sense of violation the traces of another rage, old yet ever present, born of a lifelong struggle between anatomy and soul, between performance and being; all this, along with a deep disgust (panicked, fierce: a cornered rat) at his own malleability, the insatiable hunger to be *liked*. An old man, Balthazar, crisscrossed by life's scars. Two more breaths and he will blow; paint the room black.

Eleanor knows it and watches Smith observe it; watches him play with the gun on the desk, mechanically, spinning it with quick flicks of his fingers against barrel and butt. She herself remains ignored: a bystander; a child at a meeting of adults. Redundant, harmless.

Forgotten.

She takes a step. Perhaps it looks to Smith like she is trying to put distance between herself and Balthazar, afraid of his explosion. Perhaps she is simply not important enough to command his attention. A dimple-cheeked girl of eighteen. She takes another half step, then reaches, not at all fast, for the desk. The next moment she holds the gun. Her hand touched his, Smith's, for the briefest of instances. A warm hand, mobile, gilded in ginger fuzz. Closing too late to capture hers.

She stands out of reach and levels the gun. Balthazar is shocked out of his anger, a drain plug pulled within his liver's blood. She sees him shift upon the sofa.

Smith does not move.

"You won't use it," he says calmly. "You don't even know how."

She cocks the hammer. Not her first gun, this. They owned one, Cruikshank and she, in the first few years after running away. Cruikshank made her do target practice. She was a child then, the hammer difficult to shift. It moves easily now.

"You won't use it," Smith says again, looking at her as though for the first time, giving her his full concentration. "It was very brave of you," he decides. "More than brave. Efficient. Like you have picked guns out of people's hands all your life. But you won't shoot."

Eleanor looks into herself and decides that he is right. Again she acts immediately but without haste. Haste, she knows, would make her clumsy. She opens the door without turning around to face it, feels rather than sees the players fight for balance where they stood, ears pressed against wood. Meister Lukas is there, Victor, Etta May. She ignores them, reaches through their throng and finds Geoffrey lumbering against the far wall. Without face paint and wig, he does not look much as she imagines the young Thomas did: is too old, for one thing, too thick-necked; looks bored and dim-witted, stands curled into his slouch. And yet there is something to his line of chin that makes plausible his casting. He accepts the gun without comment; takes a bead on Smith with one closed eye.

"I won't shoot, Mr. Schmidt. But Geoffrey here will."

"Will he? This oaf? Yes, I suppose he might."

[16]

For ten breaths things teeter on the brink. Geoffrey does not move or talk, stands arm outstretched, finger on the trigger. Smith just sits, thighs bulging from his towel, rubbing a hand up and down the back of his thick neck. *Thinking*. Balthazar has leapt up but stands uncertain, aware that any movement now may lead to murder, his body still metabolising its rage.

A fool tips the balance: a fool in a dinner jacket and pomaded hair. They can hear him from far off, running down the corridor and calling a name:

a harbinger of comedy. "Smith, sir," he keeps calling, very purely, in the high, light tenor of a former choirboy. Then he rounds the corner and barges into their constellation. In his haste he proves oblivious to nudity, and guns.

"Smith, sir! But there you are, thank God. You were impossible to find!"

Only now that his addressee fails to rise or greet him does the newcomer hesitate and look around. Geoffrey's gun has lowered in surprise and is now pointing at somewhere between Smith's privates and his still-wet feet. The other players form a semicircle in the corridor, Eleanor amongst them. It is to her that the man attempts to doff the hat he is not wearing; to the others he offers a quick smile. Then his urgency takes over and he pivots back to the one he was seeking.

"I've been looking everywhere for you! They told me you had gone to the theatre—no address, not even the name of the troupe! I chased a taxi-cab all across town only to arrive at an empty tent. The boy guarding it would not talk to me and his dog almost ate me. I was reduced to asking random passers-by about your whereabouts. Not a soul had seen you. At last someone directed me to where the theatre people make their lodgings. I thought perhaps one of them had noticed you and knew where you had gone. A desperate undertaking! And then they tell me you took a room!"

He delivers all this at an enormous pace, speaking with both mouth and hands, making an *Odyssey* of his chase and lanky perseverance, Smith his Ithaca to which he has been longing to return. When the latter does little to acknowledge his valour, the man steps closer yet, announcing first that "Braithwaite sent me," his voice so loud it is as though he wishes to inform the gathered company, then bending to Smith's ear and whispering a message betwixt his cupped and well-scrubbed hands. Even so the words are audible to all.

"There has been a break-in. A thief! At the office!"

Smith does not react at once, runs a finger across the hotel envelope he filled with Balthazar's belongings, plays with its flap.

"Yates, is it? Accounting?"

"Yes, sir. I happened to return to the office late. When I saw what happened, I called Mr. Braithwaite at once. On the telephone."

"Very good, Yates. Are you armed?"

"Armed?"

"Do you carry a weapon? A sidearm."

"Good God, no, sir." Yates looks up, prompted by a fresh idea, a bloom of pink in each cheek. "Are you being robbed?"

[17]

Yates's absurd query creates a momentary lull, what theatre people like to call a "beat." One of the players—Ada? Greta Silvana?—can be heard to giggle; another shifts their stance with an audible crack of the spine. Into this lull, this *gap*, Smith inserts himself, takes charge.

"So, Yates. The offices were broken into. Why come to me?"

Again Yates bends down, again makes a conch of his two palms. For once his voice drops, so the answer is inaudible. Smith rises with it, bends for his underpants, his shirt, his socks.

"What did they take?"

Once more the accountant attempts to sidle closer and win a perch at Smith's ear. But Smith has had enough.

"Just tell me, you fool."

"Well, sir, we are not sure. The desk drawer was open. Some papers are in disarray."

"That is all?"

"Yes, all. Well, and the closet lock has been picked."

It is this last bit that rids them of Smith. Eleanor can see an urgency creep into his movements that was absent up until now. He pulls on his clothes, slips into his coat. One last time his hand hesitates over the envelope and the vial, but Geoffrey's gun remains cocked, the stagehand's glower unchanged. Smith shrugs and reaches for his money instead. His good-bye belongs to Balthazar.

"Hide if you like," he says without anger. "I can always find you."

On the way out, he stops near Eleanor, sniffs her like a dog. "A strange one, you are! I should have paid attention. Next time, I will make sure we are introduced."

And then he is gone, still buttoning his cuffs and trailing Yates who, for all his lanky height, has to match his superior's intent stride with something closer to a run.

He leaves behind the smell of his pomade.

[18]

They speak later. Balthazar needs time to recollect himself. Eleanor knows this with a certainty she would marvel at, were it not a familiar kind of knowledge. One becomes attuned to people, once one has drunk deep within their Smoke. Eleanor more so than most.

So she watches him repack his travelling chest, then shout at Geoffrey and David for bumping it into the narrow stairwell walls when carrying it back down. The moment the chest is in his room, Balthazar turns away; offers no announcement, no speech or plan, just the slamming of his door. Eleanor returns there in the early hours of the morning and is unsurprised when her own sleeplessness is mirrored in a slip of light leaking out his room. She knocks, receives no answer, knocks again, then pushes down on the broken handle. Balthazar sits on a stool wedged between desk and bed of his tiny room. There is fresh Soot on his clothes, his face, the walls. The whites of his eyes look curdled.

"There," he says. "The hero of the hour. Coming to gloat."

She expected his sourness and is unsurprised to see him pour his relief into spite. She saw him stripped and helpless. It is a hard thing to forgive.

"He wasn't here for me," she says rather carefully, sits down on the bed. "I did not expect that."

"You weren't recognised after all. That mayor's ogle in Saint John: all he saw was a girl. Smitten with your curves! Or if he did recognise you, it's not Smith who got his letter."

She nods, works on the next sentence till it says what she means. "Still, you could have sold me to him. A bargain: me for the photos and the vial. I have value for one such as Smith. It might have worked."

Balthazar flinches, caught in a thought. "Don't think I didn't consider it, girl. Don't ever think that. I only protect my own." He blows his nose in his hand, stares at the Soot-black snot.

"There would have been no point to it," he continues at length. "He would have wanted everything. You *and* my papers. His kind always does."

"What next then?"

"Next? Next we go into hiding. New York's finished for us. Take the next ship to England. Smith won't be welcome in the North."

She nods, sits there, thinks the next part, does not speak it out loud.

Please, she thinks. *Take me along.*

Why say it? Balthazar already knows.

[19]

They look through the photos in the pale light of dawn. The ones Smith wanted to take. Balthazar has kept them out, spread them side by side upon his desk. Four of them show the same scene from different perspectives. Panoramas of London, taken from elevated vantage points within the city. The darkness of the Thames. Struck like a heavenly spear into its flank: a column of pure black.

"What's that?" Eleanor asks.

"A mystery. These were taken on the morning of the Second Smoke. They lit the fuse *here*"—Balthazar indicates a section of town not far from the river—"but this column rises all the way over *there*."

"It's a Storm, isn't it?"

"Yes. The first Storm. Some say the only true Storm there's ever been."

"And who is this?" Eleanor points to the fifth photo, which shows a boy, out of focus, glowering darkly at the lens. In black and white it is hard to gauge his skin colour. He may simply be dirty. But his face is unusual; the hair clipped as though against lice.

"That? Someone the world has half forgotten."

"A beggar child?"

"The boy from the jungle. Lady Naylor's sacrificial lamb."

Interview with an eyewitness, SAMUEL HERBERT VAUGHAN, now a Company employee, in February 1906, in the Company concession in Maccau, where said eyewitness works as a bookkeeper and resides.

Q: For the record, state your name and age.

A: Samuel Herbert Vaughan, thirty-three.

Q: You have stated in informal conversation that you were an eyewitness to a Black Storm while residing in Britain in 1899. Is this correct?

A: Yes, it is.

Q: Where and when did you witness the Storm?

A: *Then* . . . when the Second Smoke was first set off. In London, in '99.

Q: Can you recall the precise date?

A: The date? It was *then,* I tell you—the day they set it off! When the river came alive with Smoke. When we all went a little mad.

Q: Tell me what you saw.

A: It's like I said. I was in the streets that morning, part of a group of gentlemen engineers who had volunteered to improve London's sanitary conditions. We rode in a coach, it was dawn, the streets still empty, as Smoke-free as London ever got. We crossed the bridge at Blackfriars. Then the coachman stopped. We yelled for him to continue but he wouldn't: stood on the box, staring down into the waters. We craned our necks out the windows to see; stepped out onto the street . . .

Q: And? Continue.

A: But you know all this! The river had come alive . . . all the Soot trapped in the water and the river bed. We saw Smoke rising out of it, schillering. Colours we had never seen—not in the Smoke. Like an oil slick come alive. Beautiful, I suppose; moving like a living thing. Then it spread to the bridge, the streets. It quickened the muck in the alleys, the dirt in the houses. Some people ran from it, but it was faster than legs. Then we started smoking ourselves. It was like having a dozen people inside your skin. All their *wants*. And yours, too, mixed in with them. Anger, sure, and fear. But all these other things, too. The men I was with, my colleagues and friends—we could not bear to look one another in the eye, *afterwards*. But neither did we want to part. Like family—too close to be able to stand each other, too close to let each other go.

Q: And this was the Storm?

A: No, no. This was the Smoke, the Second Smoke.

Q: What about the Storm then?

A: There was a plume. A plume on the horizon, like from a fire, black as black. We saw it even before the Second Smoke had jumped up at us; while we stood there, gawping on the bridge.

Q: A plume? Where was this, exactly?

A: Downriver. East, I suppose. Quite a ways.

Q: What did you do?

A: We went to look. It wasn't a decision any one of us made. We simply went—Smoke-tied, moving as one. Some of us were crying; others were stopping to fight, or to . . . You see, many were shedding their clothes, that morning, though it was cold. Lust has a strong hold on the blood. But so does curiosity; it runs deep, that, a burning need to see. It kept us moving towards the plume. We were like kittens, chasing a twitching piece of yarn.

Q: And did you catch it?

A: No, thank God. We were too slow. We got close enough to hear the screams, though. Close enough to see them—the dead and the dying, all knotted together. Like they had tried to eat their way into each other. Stuck together by blood and Soot.

Q: What then?

A: Nothing. We got scared. Best cure for curiosity there is.

Q: And the Storm?

A: We saw the plume racing away from us. Like a wildfire, though the wind was blowing in our faces. It leapt and pounced. We ran the other way.

NOTE: File 13452/1905 was requested on 17 November 1908 by the Colonial Office in Bombay. Permission was granted and copy dispatched by Company courier.

[1]

He shares his room with the beetle.

Nil had meant to move out of the room by now, had planned to leave it right after the heist, from caution as well as thrift. The beetle has kept him there. Once he had brought the tin to his room he felt compelled to open it. Ten long minutes until the thing deigned to move. He wouldn't touch it—not yet—and was consumed by the fear that it was dead. Then a twitch of pincer, a sudden scuttle that saw it collide with the tin wall. He would leave the boardinghouse at dawn, Nil swore to himself, and spent the rest of the night stoppering up the room's every hole and crack, using his clothes largely, undressed by his need. Then he released the beetle, tipping the tin gently on its side. What he wanted was to see it move; imagine a forest floor upon which their paths would cross. He watched it lying prone with his chest pressed into the dirty floor; stretched a hand to it only to withdraw it whenever the beetle drew near. By midafternoon they touched. By evening Nil had lifted the beetle onto his skin, felt the dance of six hooked feet needle and explore him. A slow walk across his ribcage's undulating plain; pincers probing the soft of his throat.

It was then that Nil wept.

It has been two days now. Nil has not eaten, has not left the room other than to run to the dirty washroom at the end of the corridor to fetch a tumbler of fresh water. He spends his time watching the beetle, touching it; loses whole hours to some strange state of pure being that knows no thought or memory; is startled by the dark of nightfall and—moments later—by the feeble entry of the morning sun through the dust-clotted glass of the room's little window; by the growl of his stomach and the salt of his tears flavouring his upper lip. Now and again he thinks he can smell trees, the rot of vegetation; can hear the cry of a bird that lives high within the canopy, its plumage green and gold. He takes off his trousers and lies stark naked, thinking, *This is how I'm meant to live.* His body, unwashed and starving, begins to take on an urgent smell. The beetle grows bolder and makes a home of his cupped hands.

If it were human, they'd be moving towards vows.

[2]

Love is not without anxieties. The beetle won't feed. At the bottom of the tin there is some remnant of vegetable matter—grass? the stalks of some flower?—too dry to easily identify and glued into a tangle by the grit of Soot. If it was put there for food, little enough is left that the beetle shows no interest in it. Nil scrambles and finds an apple core amongst his refuse and some porridge oats spilled under the bed by a previous inhabitant; finds mouse droppings and the mouldy remnant of an ancient spud. The beetle spurns all of these; squats in the dirt in its black armour; walks patterns across his skin and floor. Nil decides to run out to the grocer's, terrified of being burgled, too scared to take along the beetle lest he lose it or be mugged. He returns with cabbage, carrots, potatoes caked in earth. The beetle ignores them. Nil hunts for spiders, woodlice, flies; offers their carcasses, then offers them legless and alive: they bend their crippled bodies like knuckles upon the concave pallor of a saucer. But the beetle is indifferent to sacrifice. By the third day of foraging for food, Nil is again in tears, of frustration this time, of raw, parental fear.

How long does it take for a beetle to starve?

[3]

It is this thought that decides him into action. He must learn more about beetles, seek advice on their diet and needs. The first challenge is to find a way to carry it around with him. The tin is too conspicuous to carry, too large for his knapsack. Nil acquires a wooden box with a simple lock, drills holes in it, transfers the vegetational mess and sits the beetle in a bed of rags; then he walks slowly without moving his torso, the canvas bag strapped to his front, supporting the box with the cradle of his arms like a woman bracing her pregnancy.

He heads to Riedl's shop. Riedl is a scholar of sorts. His area of expertise is the materiality of life. He is a pawnbroker and fence; deals in watches, jewellery, and table silver; surgeon's knives, captain's sextants, brass trombones; in sweets, opium, cocaine, and hashish; sells lapdogs stolen from uptown manors; lizards, songbirds, pure-bred cats. His whole livelihood depends on knowing the value, the nature, of things. To encounter an object and not be able to name its price would be a humiliation to Riedl, a challenge to his place in life. And if Riedl knows the value of the beetle, perhaps he can also tell Nil how to keep it alive.

Nil is spotted from afar. One of the neighbourhood urchins hails him, then takes off running to Riedl's shop. When the same urchin darts from Riedl's doorway even before Nil has reached it, and dashes down the side alley, something shifts in Nil and he enters Riedl's shop on his guard.

"The boychik!" the old Jew greets him, with evident warmth. "Coming to brag of his latest exploits. So you survived your caper, did you? But look how dirty you are. And skinny! Careful, boy, you have to eat."

Nil just stands there, aware of Riedl's eyes on his knapsack, unwilling—unable—to slip into his usual persona around the man.

"Go on," the pawnbroker continues. "Don't be shy now. Show me what treasures you have brought."

"They didn't tell you?"

"Didn't tell me? Who? You are coming to sell, no? Mind, I am low on cash right now, it won't be very much."

Nil thinks about how long it will take the urchin to run from Riedl's shop to the nearest telephone, wonders which number he has been instructed to call. There is a booth in a drugstore at the edge of the nearest scar. A minute to ask for the extension; another to explain his purpose. Then what? That man, Smith, will have a coach at his disposal, or perhaps an automobile. Five minutes to leave the summit of his Spire, more if the elevators are backed up. Ten more to race here through the crowded streets.

It gives Nil a little bit of time.

"Go on, sit down, boychik, you are making me jumpy. Take off a load."

Nil ignores the pawnbroker, makes sure there is no weapon on Riedl and none in his reach. Then he opens the knapsack and carefully pulls out the box.

"There! He wants to sell after all. But, *gevalt,* what a face you are making. Sit, boy, let me make tea. Then you can show me what you have."

But Riedl is far too excited to go to the rear of his shop to put on the kettle and far too keen not to let Nil out of sight. Nil, for his part, keeps his eyes on Riedl's face as he opens the wooden box. Immediately it is clear to him that the pawnbroker does not know what he is looking at. He closes the box before Riedl can come any closer, shoves it back into his bag.

"So they didn't tell you."

Riedl does not respond. He digs in a desk drawer, withdraws a bundle of money. "Here, boychik. Fifty dollars. A fortune!"

Nil ignores him, tries to estimate how much time has passed. "Do you ever deal in bugs?" he asks abruptly.

Riedl stands waving the money.

"Bugs? You mean insects? Only in silkworms. A long time ago. And some scorpions once. For a collector." He pauses, reaches back in the drawer. "One hundred then. Go on, see reason. What is it you want with such vermin?"

"How did you feed them? Your silkworms?"

"Mulberry leaves. I had to import them, very pricey. And for the scorpions, mice. It made a terrible mess." He pauses, pulls a cudgel out of the drawer, kept there in case of thieves, stands sad and quiet for a moment before putting it back and digging up more money instead. "A hundred and fifty, boy. Two hundred! It's all I have."

But Nil is already leaving. In the doorway he turns. "Tell me one thing, Riedl. Were you eager to help him? Did they have to beat you, or were you simply bought?"

The old man cringes, walks over to Nil, beseeches him. "Come now, don't be a fool. You've got yourself in trouble. And what good is a bug to you? Come, take the money. I will tell them you sold it for twenty, they won't bother you then. It's better that way."

Nil wants to shake off the pawnbroker, call him a bloodsucker, a filthy kike, but there is something to his appeal that gives him pause. *So all the while when I was playing at being your friend,* he thinks, *you went and believed me. You haggled and swore and you believed me all the same.*

And now you feel guilty.

"I must know where the beetle is from, Riedl. And I must keep it alive."

Riedl nods, though it is clear he has no answer to these needs; runs back to the desk, grabs a wad of money, shoves it at Nil.

"He'll find you. 'Mr. Smith,' he called himself. He's got the whole city looking for you. You saw the boy racing in here. I tried to tell him to wait. 'I will talk sense into Nil,' I said, 'there is no need in going running to this

Smith.' But that man bought him, soul and all. He might have bought half the town."

When Nil accepts the money, the pawnbroker seizes hold of his arm and stoops down low.

"Go on, hit me, I deserve it. And then I can say I tried to hold you and you put up a fight."

Nil does not move. "Tell me who can help me," he says. "You know everyone in this town."

Riedl shakes his head, continuing to present the exposed back of his neck, imploring Nil to hit him, to kick him, to give him a bloody nose.

Then he grows quiet.

"Try the Chinese. Ha Xin's Exotic Spices. They trade in the strangest things. Only be careful, they're gonifs, part of a tong. But they have no love for any Smith."

[4]

Nil learns two things from the Chinese. The first is that they don't recognise the beetle but do recognise the plant matter it was bedded in. He has not presented them with the live insect, of course, but with a drawing, having laboured for several hours to capture its every detail with coloured pencils he acquired from a specialist shop at surprising expense. The bedding of straw or stalks he brought along only as an afterthought, scraping them into a pouch. The elderly man he deals with—the spice trader—picks up a single stalk and brings it to his lips; chews a strand, then spits it on the floor; picks out the remnant of a ghostly petal, spreads it carefully upon his fine-boned palm.

"What is it?" Nil asks when he does not comment.

"The root of the Company's wealth," the man replies in excellent English. "All the way from India."

Nil studies the shreds of plant with new reverence. "Can you sell me any? Can anyone in New York?"

The Chinese does not reply. There is no need. The flower grows only in Hindustan; its export is forbidden. The Chinese government would pay much for a parcel of seeds.

"Where do you have it from?" the trader asks instead.

"I found it."

"Of course. Let me know if you find any more."

They attempt to look up the beetle in a book. That's the second thing Nil learns: that there exist books full of pictures of insects. They have to send for the book and for a man who is an expert in such matters, a tiny, cheerful fellow of thirty or thirty-five with a waist-long queue and not a word of English to his name. The book itself is large-leafed and leather-bound, each page showing drawings of insects of such proficiency they make a mockery of Nil's crude sketch. The drawings are systematic, showing top and side views, drawing attention to the legs, the head, the segmentation of the belly. Here and there a beetle is cut in half, splaying it open into a colourful system of tunnels and caverns, maw to arse. There are close-ups of legs and mandibles, of eggs, cocoons, and grubs. Nil's beetle is not in the book. The scholar spends considerable time on his search, leafing back and forth between three separate sections, tracing the outline of Nil's drawing with short, tapered fingers, pointing out various similarities between one insect and another, some of them obvious, others hard to spot: the colour and configuration of legs and joints; the shape of the thorax; the ruff of fur at throat and head. At long last he leans back, scribbles some characters on a slip of paper, offers it to Nil.

"What's that?"

The question sets off a consultation between the spice trader and the scholar, requiring several back and forths.

"It's the beetle's name. Not its precise name, but its family name. He says beetles come in families, just like anything else." The old man shrugs. "It costs twenty dollars."

"Will you translate it for me?"

"I cannot. He says it is a scientific name. A transcription into our system of writing. I don't understand it."

"Then it's useless to me."

"Yes, of course."

The man bows. He can see Nil's need and simply waits him out, pouring tea for himself, drinking it in short, precise sips.

"It isn't worth twenty dollars."

Again the man bows, takes the scrap of paper, crumples it up. It's only after Nil places the money on the counter that the old man orders the scholar to write out the characters once more. He does so, larger this time, with more flourish, embarrassed perhaps by the stupendous price, then passes over the paper with a bow.

"He thinks you must be a prince," smiles the old man.

"Why?"

"Only a prince would pay good silver to know the name of the cricket that he loves."

[5]

An hour later Nil can be found crossing the Big Scar. It would take a keen eye to recognise him. He has shaken off the two children the Chinese sent to follow him; secured new lodgings; has washed and cropped his hair close to the skull and donned a cap and woollen suit. A starched button-on collar is riding loose around his scrawny neck. It gives him that fresh-off-the-boat look, an immigrant dressed in his Sunday best in honour of the city, shorn in quarantine against the spread of lice. An upright sort of lad: button-eyed, decent, and hungry, quietly pining for some lunch. The private policemen who patrol the Big Scar on the lookout for riffraff don't give him a second glance.

As Nil crosses the great open space that cuts Manhattan in two, the scar changes around him. At its southern edge, it is a scruffy affair, Soot-blighted and pockmarked with rubbish. Towards its northern end it grows verdant and manicured, dotted with shade trees. Beyond lies a chessboard grid of leafy avenues; front lawns guarded by ornamental metal fencing, their artistry and whimsy masking fear. Many of the houses are new. Uptown burned during the Second Smoke.

Nil walks ten blocks, passes a field now used for baseball: knickerbock-ered youths stand pelting balls into each other's mitts. There used to be a public library here, albeit public only to the rich. It, too, burned in the riots. Whatever books survived have been moved to a newly built structure, which hulks amongst the uptown houses looking more like a fortress than a temple of learning, despite the sandstone, the decorative carvings, the portico and pillars that mark its gate. A philanthropist's name is engraved into its stone. Nil reaches into his bag and dons a pair of wire-rimmed spectacles. This, and a change of posture, and he is a student, or perhaps a house tutor of exotic origin, who is making his first pilgrimage to this, one of the wonders of the world. The New York Metropolitan Museum of Art and Natural History. He takes off his cap in reverence and enters as one would a church.

[6]

It is a risk, this. If Smith has gone to the trouble of hunting down Riedl, he must prize the beetle. The Company has a large network at its disposal: employees, business partners, friends within the civic government. Their description of Nil may be vague, but they know his age, his build, his shade of skin. The question is simply whether Smith has anticipated this move: that his thief will seek for answers in this place. As Nil approaches the front desk, the clerk's face betrays no suspicion. He simply looks Nil over and *places* him before adopting a demeanour in equal parts helpful and patronising.

"What are we looking for, young man?"

Nil stops his gawking at the opulent ceiling; crumples his cap against his chest in his excitement; speaks quickly and almost in a whisper. "Is it true that the building holds ancient Egyptian sarcophagi and that these can be viewed by the public?"

"Indeed it is."

"And how much might it cost to view these?"

The man smiles at so much self-abasing awe; collects the dollar entry fee with good-natured condescension and hesitates a moment only when noticing the dirt under Nil's fingernails.

"West wing, ground floor," he says. "Follow the signs to Egyptology. And be sure not to touch anything, if you please."

There is no inconspicuous way of inquiring about books featuring bugs. So Nil goes roaming, spending just enough time in each room not to mark himself out by his disinterest. On the second floor of the west wing he stumbles on stuffed animals; moves past governesses with well-dressed cohorts of young girls and boys staring at panoramas staged in a series of glassed booths: a lion, crouching; a rearing bear; a white-bellied ray skewered by a long harpoon; a (carved? stuffed?) Eskimo skinning a humongous seal. At the far end, in a room less popular with the public, the walls are lined with display cases full of smaller vermin: lizards in one case, spiders in the next, locusts in a third, along with a photograph of a flying swarm, black and ominous like a cloud of Smoke.

Two cases on he finds them. Beetles. The initial pang of excitement quickly gives way to disappointment. There are perhaps three dozen insects on display here, pinned to a board by fine, long needles under a banner that reads COLEOPTERA. Some schiller in vibrant colours; others are stripy like Humbug mints; some have horns or pincers serrated like saws, have their wings spread under shields of horn or sit impaled upon their spikes with the fissured solidity of flint. But ugly or pretty, tiny or monstrous, they all are just this: curiosities, ornaments, pests, devoid of meaning, the fern-rustle of *home*.

"Pretty, aren't they?"

Nil has not heard the guard approach. A tall man, a Negro, light of skin.

"They're my favourites. Them and the locusts. Strange things—like they come from the moon. A thousand varieties, all different. Praise the Lord, I suppose."

Nil nods, smiles. All he wants is to avoid being remarkable, memorable. But it is already too late. The guard has remarked upon him; has picked him out as different and extended to him a solidarity rooted in their shared complexion.

Nil turns to leave.

Then he stops. "A thousand varieties? You mean there are more here than just these?"

"Why yes. Cases and cases."

"Where can I find them?"

The guard points to a closed door at the end of the hall.

"In the Mendel Library. Members only, I'm afraid. Are you with the university? You will have to ask one of your professors for a letter of introduction. I am sure it can be arranged."

"Oh, I am certain it can."

[7]

The museum closes at seven. Nil finds a broom closet to hide in. How much of his life has been filled with this, waiting in dark places, still, encoffined, until it is time again to move?

Like a beetle in a box.

He has learned to shut himself off: no thoughts, no memories, just the hollow void of the wait. Time passes to the rhythm of noises drifting dully through the walls; to the sour pangs of hunger climbing up from his stomach into the dryness of his throat. At last Nil emerges, probing the darkness with his ears. Then he moves, one hand on the wall. He has made sure to memorise the way.

The Mendel Library is unlocked. A square room, not overly large, with a single long desk at the centre. It is flanked by chairs on either side, each workplace marked by a reading lamp with a coloured-glass shade, poison green. There are three walls of bookshelves, floor to ceiling, and a ladder on wheels so one can reach the top shelves. The fourth wall is made up of deep drawers to the height of Nil's chest. Above them hangs a row of windows like dark paintings in heavy lead frames.

Nil tries the books first. This is what brought him here, the Chinese scholar's volume, those vivid renderings of pincers, hooked legs, overlapping plates of armour made of coloured horn. He finds the relevant section on the bookshelf and is once again plunged into the miraculous abundance of shape and shade nestling between its covers. He fetches down volume after volume, turns their pages with reverence, haste, and greed. Then the overviews are exhausted and more specialist works displace illustrations with text. No doubt one of these volumes contains the secret of how to satiate one's beetle; it will yield to a week's study, or perhaps as little as a day's. But there are guards in the building and the lamp he's lit may show under the door. Nil needs instant wisdom: a revelation. Above all he must not be caught.

The drawers then. He knows what to expect and yet is awed by what he finds: whole flotillas of beetles, each impaled upon a nail; hovering inch-high above the white rectangle of felt that lines the drawer's base. Next to each nail, a series of words, the beetles' awkward, many-syllabled names along with the place where they were harvested.

Passalus interruptus, Bocas del Toro, Panama.

Phalacrognathus muelleri fuscomicans, New Guinea (Vogelkop Peninsula).

Dynastes hercules hercules, Boiling Lake, Dominica.

Ataenius strigatus, Georgian Bay, Upper Canada.

There are many hundreds in all.

Nil works quickly, pulling out each drawer in turn and perusing its contents with one intent glance. He knows he will recognise the beetle instantly, by the mark on its throat but more so by something less tangible: a tug at his sinews, at the tangle of tendrils that suspends us in this world.

The nineteenth drawer sports a gap, a blank spot, within the formation of floating beetles. Nil's eye registers it but fails to attach any meaning. It is later, when, without transition, the drawers begin to display plants not beetles—wrinkled, miserable husks pressed flat under a plate of glass as wide as the drawer—that this blank spot taunts him and makes him wonder whether a beetle—*his* beetle—slipped off its nail and lies crumpled in the drawer's corner. He retraces his search, relocates the nineteenth drawer, but again finds only a blank spot, marked by a tiny hole where a nail had punctured the felt lining. There used to be a name next to this hole but it, too, has been excised, the glued-down tag ripped out. Only one corner remains, spelling out half a country: "azil." It is a conjecture—a leap, made bold by his sense of persecution—but it seems impossible not to see in this puncture mark the action of his enemy; not to picture Smith's fingernail peeling away that name tag and his slipping the beetle in his pocket so he can carry it home and mount it for his private viewing pleasure. In his frustration Nil pulls another beetle husk off its nail; snaps it in half between his fingers and stares at the desiccated porousness that forms its centre, before crushing it to dust.

[8]

Plants, though.

Flowers.

The realisation floods the hollow of Nil's disappointment and returns him to the search. He devotes himself to a new set of drawers, yanks them open with urgent impatience, and discovers an entire section of wall devoted to tulips, another to roses; to twisting, faded orchids whose gaping petals and jutting protrusions seem nothing short of obscene.

And here, near the bottom of the second to last section, in an unlocked room of a labyrinthine building open to the public, at the back of a drawer scrutinised by some scholar maybe once a year, labelled in Latin, dried like summer hay and pressed flat as a coin by the weight of the glass heaved upon it, lies the treasure of the Empire, *Papaver fuliginosa richteria,* in full glorious bloom. The Smoke Poppy. Its grey-black petals look as though they are woven from dusk.

Nil steals it without hesitation. It takes some doing; the glass plate is heavy and fixed on with metal brackets. But he is buoyant now, careless of the noise, and soon picks the flower with a steady hand. Then he removes all trace he has ever been in the room, picking up insect legs from the smooth parquet floor, forcing his hands to patience against the shiver of his skin. A yank on a desk lamp's fine-linked brass chain, a game of cat and mouse with the night guards on duty, the long journey back to his downtown hovel: and all the while a humming in his limbs, the certainty that, tonight, the beetle will feed.

[9]

Only it won't.

The boardinghouse he has moved to lies quiet around him. Somewhere at the edge of his hearing he listens to a lovers' quarrel, the timbres of anger and jealousy giving way to cautious reconciliation. Midnight gone, one, two. He tries to woo the beetle yet again; smooths out his wrinkled piece of paper with its Chinese symbols that, for all he knows, instruct any readers to kill him on sight.

"Here, see. This is your name. And this here is your food."

He does not know at what point during the night he had started speaking to the beetle. It never answers back; crawls over to the flower now, inspects it once more with its feet and pincers, and does not deign to eat. By three or four it has stopped moving, reacts only when Nil reaches in its box and picks it up. He quickly places it back. The beetle is starving, conserving energy by playing dead. Nil shuts the box and feels . . . *something*.

Grief.

For the first time in an age he thinks about his late London mother and about his foster father, too, and wonders whether he is still alive.

[10]

He goes looking for Smith. Of course he does. Smith is the only one who *knows*.

Nil arrives at the base of the Spire just before dawn, cranes his neck, and is rewarded by the glow of a window near the top. Smith, rising early; performing his morning ablutions, no doubt, curling his whiskers before the glass. An hour later the first employees arrive, menials mostly, heading straight to the building's back. The doorman has manned his post by now and Nil makes sure to avoid his line of sight. Two elevator boys arrive in close succession, easily recognised by the colour of their uniforms. Neither is the boy Nil spoke to. He has a brief vision of his body lying crumpled amongst the poisoned pigeons of the building's central hollow, then dismisses it as fanciful. The elevator boy will be in some private prison somewhere, awaiting transport or a noose; or sunk in the muck of the river bed, weighted down by a stone. Nil wonders what someone like Smith might do to you to make you talk.

It isn't until late evening that Smith finally emerges. Nil is ravenous by now, tired out by the heat; has finished the flask of water he brought and eaten the small wedge of bread. For a moment he is alarmed that the Company man will simply hail a cab, making him hard to shadow. But it seems he likes his exercise. They walk for almost forty minutes, stopping only when Smith spots a candy store open late into the day and acquires a paper parcel of liquorice from which he snacks as he moves on. At last, he crosses the road, rings a bell in a nondescript building and is let in. The next moment he has charged through its entrance and is gone.

Nil gives him ten minutes. He has no plan of action, only his needs: for the beetle to live; for him to know himself, to undo his christenings, unnaught his name. And at the same time the memory of the elevator boy dances before him, the face so similar to his own, picked to whispers by Nil's fears. Ten minutes in which to speculate whether it is a mistress Smith is visiting; a tailor; an opium den. Then he steps up to the door, presses the third button from the top, and hears the answering *click* of the lock. The concierge is Soot-smeared and reading a magazine; one look at Nil and he points him to the backyard.

Nil traverses the hall obediently, trying to parse the smells and decor. Sweat, he decides, burnt dust and metal; the smell of wet cloth. A brothel, a laundry? The stairwell is bare but for its metal railing, the walls flaking old paint. Above his head he can hear the shuffle of feet, the grunting of men. The courtyard is cramped, the back building residential, its windows disclosing housewives bent over dish-filled sinks and men in armchairs perusing the day's news. In the front wing large, metal-framed windows are lit but the glass is milked with white paint. The shadows that pass behind are hard to make sense of. There is a servant's entrance with a separate stairwell; two men are perched not far from it, dressed in white cottons like cooks. They are chatting, passing a cigarette back and forth.

Nil ignores them and heads up the back stairwell. Two floors up he draws the momentary attention of a fat man burdened by an armload of limp towels, who stares at Nil's shorn head and thick suit, then dismisses him from his mind. Nil squeezes past him, sees a hall open up before him, thirty feet squared under a vaulting ceiling. The smells are vivid now, layers of sweat, of leather and Smoke. And of men. Some are on mats, flat on the ground, or squatting, or tumbling across the floor. Others lift dumbbells and sand-filled leather balls, or spin their bodies in mad circles around the pivot of a metal bar. Here a leather-covered box, raised on four legs, serves as a launch pad for a queue of men who vault over it in a variety of manners, headfirst, feetfirst, split-legged and upside down. Elsewhere two men are locked in combat, one astride the other's back like coupling toads, their bodies slick with sooty sweat.

Then, from a doorway opposite, Smith enters the gymnasium in white knee-length shorts and a cotton singlet. His forearms are rich in golden fuzz. Smith leaps up to two rings suspended from the ceiling by leather straps; grows red and bug-eyed as he pulls himself up by the strength of his arms. Aloft, his tremour travelling up and down the straps bolted into the ceiling, he pauses, lifts his legs; he huffs and puffs, and looks like nothing so much as a shitting pug near torn asunder by the strain of his excretion. And yet Nil cannot help but be awed by the man's raw strength that now sees him slowly spread his arms until he has pinned himself into a self-inflicted crucifixion before dropping heavily back onto the floor; the rings swinging in erratic circles high above his head.

I must go hide, it shoots through Nil as his mark picks himself off the ground to dip his fists in a bucket of chalk. *He will know me by my colour.*

But in truth the room is filled with all manner of men, not all of them white. Some are dressed in their workday clothes shorn only of their jackets and shoes. Others stand stripped to underwear so threadbare they are hardly dressed at all. There is such a hubbub here, such a chaos of activity, so viscous a stink, that his shorn little immigrant's face peeking out of his too-big collar is but another oddity in a room bereft of order.

Still, it will not do to be incautious. As Smith approaches a wooden rack to perform various types of callisthenics, Nil drifts out through a door on his right into a warren of hallways. There are further, smaller gyms: one a boxing ring, the windows wide open and fans running to disperse the Smoke seeping out of the two bloodied men within; another lined with heavy dumbbells and cracked mirrors, where the stink of sweat and man stands so heavy it seems fused into the very mortar of the unpainted walls.

Nil moves on, only half conscious of what he is looking for until he finds it: a small, tiled room lined with benches and narrow wooden cupboards, each with its own lock. Smith entered the building in his linen suit, a satchel clutched under one arm; leaped onto the rings in a singlet and shorts. One of these cupboards holds his belongings. Only a handful are closed, locked; the others stand open and empty. It will be a trifle to pick these few locks; find and search Smith's pockets and his satchel; see what he can learn. A trifle—were it not for the fact that Nil is not alone.

The man is slight, grey-faced and bent; is dressed in a cotton shirt and flannel trousers, holds a jacket folded in his lap. Patches of sweat have collected in his armpits. Indeed, the room is hot and damp with the mist of the steam room next door; it crawls in through a vent's iron grille, plunges the air into a haze and feeds a vivid mould that blooms like moss upon the grouting. Nil nods to the stranger, fades through the door, continues his survey of the premises. Farther down the hall he finds a second changing room, this one devoid of lockers, adjacent to a row of showers, their drains clogged with hair and lint and standing inch-deep under dirty water; finds a toilet, a cleaning cupboard, a plunge pool filled with ice-cold water; finds a front desk from behind which a corpulent woman stares at him until he produces twenty cents and drops them on her counter, whereupon she offers him a towel and a locker room key. In the gym Smith is now hanging by his bent knees from an iron bar. His singlet has ridden up and reveals on his flank and hip a tangle of lines, some dark, some fading into pallor, like a clot of veins risen to the surface of his flesh.

On Nil's second pass the sweaty little man still sits amongst the lockers and has been joined by a younger man who is changing back into his clothes; on the third (Nil has passed the time by watching the boxing, enjoying the cool of the fans that push the men's anger through the open windows out into the yard) he sees Smith waddle into the unoccupied steam room and close the door. In the locker room next door, the bent little man now sits alone. He raises his chin to Nil as he enters, offers his face up to the light.

"Don't be frightened," he says with a voice and accent like he's talking around a pebble tucked under his tongue, "all it is, I'm blind."

The eyes are not blanks but spheres of rot: they hold a pulpy darkness that seems to extend all the way through the eyeballs. It is as though two sponges have been dunked in muck, then encased in globes of glass.

"Please, young man, sit. This is the third time you have come here, I recognise your stride. I suppose I put you off."

Nil does not answer, stands quietly, thinks of Smith next door, sitting naked in that wooden box of a room: he can hear him humming through the wall, or perhaps it is the pipes that carry it, an Irish ditty, Nil has heard it around town. He steps past the blind man, sits down in the corner, fingers the first of the locks.

"You will ask yourself why they look like that. You see, it happened ten years ago, ten and a half. Yes, *then*. Somehow or other, I got Smoke in my eyes." The man laughs quietly to himself, resumes his former position, bent forward on the bench, his jacket lying folded in his lap. His voice is soft, a gentle chewing at the words. The first locker opens under Nil's fingers, but the clothes inside are not Smith's.

"And what is a blind man doing in a gymnasium, you may well ask! I often ask it myself. It's the humidity, I think, good for my joints. And then I like the baths. I am Hungarian, you see, from Budapest. The baths are in my blood. For a nickel they let me sit here all day, next to the steam room. Out of the way. Only I mustn't talk to the customers!" He laughs again, that same quiet, moist cackling, intimate and quite insane.

"But it's hard being quiet all day. You see, I have a secret, a wonderful secret, and there's nothing like a secret for making a man want to talk. It's this: I used to be famous. An inventor! Creating things that must not be. I was wanted by the secret police. They caught me once; asked me to work for them. An odd invitation, signed with a hammer." Here he wiggles fingers that are grotesquely swollen at the knuckles, then slips them back onto his folded jacket. "But I will shut my mouth now, I can tell you are listening to someone else."

Indeed, Nil is. Sometime in between working open the second locker (no luck) and moving on to the third, he has heard a knock on the nearby door. Smith's singing has stopped and Nil can hear the rhythm, if not the actual words, of an exchange of greetings. He rises, drawn to pipes that climb the wall here; steps up onto the bench and moves his head closer, chasing a whisper. The blind man reacts to Nil's movement by scooting down the bench until he sits right at his feet. He reaches up with his hand, gently tapping one of the hot pipes. Nil leans forward and feels as though he is pressing an ear against the heat of an iron. There, in the pipe, he hears the rumble of Smith's voice.

". . . feared you hadn't received my telegram. But here you are, very punctual. Why not strip? There is a locker next door. No? Well, it's your laundry bill. Go on, take the jacket off at least. You look like a prune."

Whoever has entered the steam room speaks in a voice that, although no quieter, is hard to catch. The only word Nil is sure of is "odd." Smith responds with his everywhere English, tinny in the pipe.

"You disapprove? What, too public? What could be more private than a building-full of random, sweaty men. Or is it too plebeian for you? We are safe here from my colleagues, at least." Smith pauses, grows quieter, business-like. "Go on, give me the news."

Again Nil cannot make out the answer. The blind man at his feet can. He mouths it, has mouthed Smith's words, too, a moist shaping of the lips. *I haven't found him,* he mouths.

The pipe responds.

"No trace at all?"

"Oh, I found his trace. Found where he lived, talked to four or five people who know him. But what good is that?" Somehow the blind man contrives to channel the man's emotion, blasé and tired, unless it is his own contribution to the words. Nil has inched closer to him, stands stooped between hot duct and wet mouth.

"Did he talk to anyone?"

"That man Riedl. And one of the tongs. I think they tried to tail him themselves but he gave them the slip."

"He tried to sell to them?"

"I don't know. You won't tell me what he stole, and the Chinamen don't discourse with my kind. All I can tell you is that he made them curious."

Smith's answer carries his frustration. "I wonder what he's up to, our thief. I doubt it's a ransom; he'd have been in touch by now." Then he reverts to more neutral tones. "How about the players?"

"Oh, I found them. Spread across three hotels; lying low. Here are the addresses."

"Leave them with my towel. Is the girl still with them?"

"Yes."

"Good. And their plans?"

"They've secured a berth to Liverpool. Leaving in three days. It's all in my notes."

"Three days, eh? Well, if you can't find the thief and since we don't know what he's planning . . . Better to act than to sit on my hands, you see. Time may turn out to be of the essence; and the girl is a stroke of luck . . . Do me a favour and let my ship know; quietly that is. The *Hyperion,* a Captain Pratt—tell him to get ready. But now you pull a face!"

"I am a Pinkerton agent, not an errand boy," whispers the blind man, his mouth sour and dank. A moment later the man next door has reconsidered. Nil wonders what happened in that moment. Did Smith make a show of displeasure, of money, of rage?

"Very well, Mr. Smith. Pratt, the *Hyperion,* on the q.t. I'll add it to the bill. Your work is done here then?"

"Ah, now you want gossip! The agency likes to be informed, is that it? Well, why not. Yes, I'm done. There's nothing wrong with Braithwaite's books. He's losing money as honestly as the next man. Ah, look at you crease your brow! You ask for gossip and now you think I'm being disloyal. What a funny parcel of values you run around with. Look here: you can hold faith with an idea. With destiny. With a wife, even. But with a company, bah! That's feudalism, man. Next you'll ask me to fall on my knee and kiss a ring."

Nil tries to picture the man thus addressed, sweating and taunted, but all he can see is the Hungarian's mouth.

"You're not afraid to tell me all this?"

"Afraid? Who are you going to tell? Braithwaite? The board of governors? Am I to be like the man who tries to hold in his fart when he's having lunch with the poor relations? It's *his* lunch, they are there for *his* money, and he's to protect them from his stink? But look, now I've insulted you. You are a Pinkerton agent, not a poor relation. A proud man, only here you have sweated right through your clothes. You know what, you should strike out on your own. Found your own agency. Call it Pride and Principle, Private Investigators. Then you can tell people like me to go to hell."

[11]

Next he knows, Nil hears the opening and closing of a door. He has but a moment to leap down from the bench and bury his face in the towel he's been given. Nil hears footsteps racing past. Perhaps it is the man's anger that saves him from discovery. A professional snoop, too hot, too baited by Smith, to give them any thought: a blind eccentric and a brown-skinned stranger, bent low over the bench, towelling off.

The moment the Pinkerton man is gone, Nil drops the towel and starts picking the next lock. Who can say how much longer Smith will soak in heat, now that his business is concluded? Nil is in luck: the next cupboard holds Smith's clothes and satchel. He moves very quickly now, reaches into his own knapsack to withdraw the perforated wooden box and places it without hesitation into the depths of Smith's bag. He will feel its weight and notice it at once. And the beetle will live. Then Nil replaces the satchel in the locker, relocks the simple mechanism without trouble. Perhaps he is distracted by the sense of loss that jumps up at him the way the ground leaps at a falling man: Nil does not notice the blind man's movement until he holds him by the wrist and hand. Those broken, arthritic fingers, strong as ropes. The voice remains quiet. His words are hard things on which he sucks, not bites, to save his teeth.

"Are you a thief?" the man asks.

Nil cringes, tugs at his wrist; is afraid of making a racket, of being caught by Smith. He calms himself, considers the man, identifies his need.

"I'm like you," Nil says, says it with a touch of Smoke that passes like currency between their palms. "All alone."

The blind man nods, holds on to Nil; rot in his eyes. "When it first happened, for the first month or two . . . I continued seeing. Things were just like they'd always seemed, vivid and real. But everything I saw was from the past." He shudders, stands up, face-to-face with Nil. "Now I am used to the void."

And then the blind man kisses him, not at all lewdly, a quick, wet-lipped kiss on the ridge of his cheek. Nil runs away the moment he releases his hand.

[12]

The *Hyperion*. Captain Pratt. It takes repeat visits to convince him to hire Nil; false letters of reference; and a ship's boy lost to the pleasures of the city thanks to a laudanum-laced drink. In the end this young lad who presents himself twice a day is simply too accommodating, too keen to see Albion, too amusing, quick-witted, good-humoured, and earnest, and too darn cheap for Pratt to hold out any longer.

"Cabin boy," he decides, "and general factotum. I'll work your fingers to the bone.

"Neel what?" the captain adds as he draws up the contract.

"Niemand."

"*K-n-e-e-m-a-n-d,*" Pratt spells out laboriously. "From where?"

"Dutch Antilles."

"Well, get ready, Dutch boy, we sail in the morn."

Back in the boardinghouse Nil lies flat on his back and whispers a word. "N'tib."

Eyes closed, he can feel the scuttle of legs upon his naked chest.

Dear Sirs,

I am writing in response to your request, dated 27 March 1909, to clarify the plant source and chemical nature of the Smoke suppressants known under the unfortunate tag of "sweets." As you requested, I shall endeavour to do so in layman's terms.

I must start by pointing out that, as you yourself acknowledge in your letter, our knowledge of the organic source of sweets is limited to little more than hearsay rather than being based on any systematic research. The plant that is understood to be the primary ingredient in the manufacture of sweets—*Papaver fuliginosa richteria,* colloquially known as the "Black Poppy" or "Smoke Poppy"—does not grow in North America. The Company embargoes its export from India (to which it is presumed to be native), and to my knowledge neither seed nor live specimen exists on American soil. The industrial and chemical processes by which flower is turned into sweet is an even more tightly guarded secret; again the Company holds a complete monopoly on this knowledge and it is reported that the Indian factories resemble fortresses in which workers are sequestered like slaves.

What we do hold here in our plant collection at Harvard is a single pressed and dried flower; a second such flower is kept in New York City's new Metropolitan Museum. From the morphological features of the plant it is evident that it is not a true *Papaver* at all but rather some broadly related genus, or a subspecies of *Papaver* that was arrived at through hybridisation. In its dried state it is impossible to speculate about its soil requirements; reports from visitors to Bihar who have seen the poppy plantations from afar allude to peculiar modes of fertilisation and to the quick exhaustion of the soil in which this pseudo-poppy is grown. The dried specimen does suggest that the plant is sufficiently poppy-like as to support reports that the harvest of the active ingredient for sweets involves the tapping of ripe seedpods and the extraction of their latex.

Our understanding of the biological operation of sweets is somewhat more advanced than that of their manufacture. The sweet does not operate merely by absorbing the Smoke generated by a given organism into its physical substance. In other words, it is not simply a sponge soaking up the unseemly vapours exuded by the body before they can cause public remark (though it is true, of course, that the sweet turns black during its use, just as a sponge would turn black if it were used to mop up tar, suggesting that this physical absorption plays some part in the process). Chiefly, though, sweets are not sponges but drugs, which is to say they work directly upon the chemistry of our bodies. As we slip a sweet into our mouths, our saliva begins to dissolve it. The sweet enters our bloodstream and organs, suppressing the affective response of he who consumes it, making him incapable of experiencing strong emotion.

I should also add that according to a well-regarded theory by our respected French colleague, Louis Radot of the Sorbonne, the process used in the manufacture of so-called Smoke cigarettes—i.e., dispensers of Smoke based upon dark Soot that is temporarily and briefly "quickened" (i.e., reanimated)—also depends on the self-same flower. According to Radot, the substance that allows for the limited and ephemeral reanimation of the cigarette's Soot appears to be derived not from the latex won from the seedpod but from the processing of the petals (or perhaps of the stems) in some unknown way. It is entirely possible that different subspecies of *P. fuliginosa*—or flowers of different sexes—are used for the two processes. In the absence of any research into the pseudo-poppy's reproductive cycles, we are in the realm of pure speculation.

Allow me to conclude by stating that it would be a violation of my conscience, and of my duties as a citizen, were I not to give voice to my personal feelings about the proposed new laws governing the import of sweets. While, as a man of science, I have nothing but admiration for a world in which dissolute passions are replaced by dispassionate reason, I cannot, as a lover of virtue, advocate the legalisation and state-approved trade of a substance that places us in moral as well as financial hock to an entity such as the Company, which knows neither nation nor creed and exists simply to further its own profits.

Sincerely yours,
Sereno Lunqueer Bolander
Amos Eaton Chair of Botany, Harvard University

[1]

Smith takes them by the easiest of means.

The players board their ship one blustery morning. It is a midsized steamer carrying cargo along with a small number of passengers; the prow very high and painted a deep oxblood red. One after another they walk across the quivering gangway, then settle into their lodgings. When the ship casts off the quay they think themselves free. The open ocean lies ahead. Then the pilot ship stops its engines and strands them halfway out the harbour. A second, smaller steamer pulls alongside and soon a single skiff is rowed across. Between the two sailors manning its oars stands a single passenger, one foot on the gunwale, looking like a painting of Columbus. He must have bribed the pilot. Perhaps, thinks Eleanor, he has bribed all pilots of all ships heading for the high seas. But no, this is no speculative visit: Smith knows they are there. Balthazar sees him only when the Company man is already clambering up the lowered ladder and runs back to his cabin at once. Within a minute, Smith follows, one hand clamped onto the crown of his hat. Its brim is flapping in the wind.

Eleanor cannot say she is surprised when, soon after, he presents himself at the door of the cabin she shares with Etta May.

"Miss Renfrew," Smith says very simply. His hat is in his hands now, his bald pate flushed and sweaty. "Let's go."

Etta May makes a movement as though to shield Eleanor with her bulk. But the cabin is so small that she inadvertently shoulders Eleanor forward, trapping her between two mighty pairs of bosoms, Smith's and her own. Eleanor turns, hugs the Soother, then reaches past her for the handle of her suitcase, still unpacked. Up on deck Balthazar stands remonstrating, unspooling coils of Smoke into the wind.

"This is illegal, Smith! Kidnapping and theft. The captain will arrest you."

But there is a gun in Smith's belt and no real fight in Balthazar's stark features. Eleanor wonders for a moment whether the old man sold her out. The Smoke whipping past her carries shame within its anger; seagulls snatch at its grit as it turns to Soot in the warm air. She reaches out to the old player with both her hands and tugs herself close, so they stand nose to nose.

"You should have stayed in Saint John," he says into the wind. "I'll write a play for you." It is as though he has already consigned her to the dead.

She kisses him all the same.

For an instant, while climbing down into the rowing boat, Eleanor contemplates throwing herself in the sea. Perhaps she can swim back to shore and seek shelter in the law. Balthazar is right, after all: Smith has no legal authority over her; the Company holds no special powers in the United States. But the act seems so desperate, the sea so very black and cold, that she hesitates. A moment later her feet touch the floor of the boat and one of the sailors helps her in. Smith follows, rump first, surprisingly nimble on the ladder. Arrived, he sits down and shakes his big head.

"The old fool threw his last vial out the window. He made sure I saw it— all out of spite! Well, at least I got the photographs before he could chuck them, too. And you."

Her heart sinks at the words. "How did you find me out?"

"Oh, very simply. I was intrigued after we met. You seemed unusual. *Remarkable.* So I made inquiries. A few telegraphs to our men in Canada— that's all it took. It turns out the mayor there had recognised you. He was about to write to your uncle. I told him not to bother."

Within twenty pulls on the oars, they are alongside Smith's Company steamer and Smith is helping her up the ladder, apologising quite earnestly as he pushes her up by her backside. Across the black water she can see the players, lined up on deck. Etta May is waving, Balthazar scowling, Ada dabbing at her tears. But it is shy Meister Lukas, stumbling late onto the scene, who is inconsolable, hiding his face behind his fine-boned hands, a tangle of Smoke whipping out of him, crimson and tan, infecting the others until they all stand racked by sobs.

"Love," observes Smith, evidently moved. "Did you know?"

She shakes her head.

"Too bad," says Smith. "He should've told you. It's a waste to love in silence."

And then he holds open the door and ushers Eleanor to her cabin belowdecks.

[2]

Smith locks her in. This is no more than Eleanor expected, though her captor apologises profusely and promises he will release her the moment they are "shot of land." She reviews her feelings, finds dread inside herself, and the bud of excitement.

England.

Her uncle.

It's like when a death is announced. There is a longing to run to it and *see*.

Midafternoon Smith releases her and invites her to stretch her legs. "Have a look around the ship," he says affably. "I trust you will find it to your liking."

Indeed it is a handsome vessel, small and well proportioned, with an air of luxury about its wooden panelling and polished brass fixtures. The crew comes from all corners of the world and sports all shades of skin: from the freckled pallor of an Irish deckhand to the blue-black of the cook and the parchment hues of the Malay entrusted with the rudder. Eleanor notes this variety with interest: it suggests the steamer is chartered rather than being Company-owned. She is the only woman on board.

At the tip of the ship's bow, leaning into the railing and struggling against nausea, she can see the players' ship on the horizon, perhaps a half mile ahead, dipping and rising on the roll of the sea.

Smith finds her there an hour or two later, still leaning against the railing, her stomach climbing into her throat, and invites her to join him for dinner. She attempts to demur, citing her sickness, but he promises a tonic "that will set you straight very quickly": his brow furrowed in concern; golden whiskers harried by the breeze. Eleanor finds she is interested in him, intrigued. She is used to finding a distance between herself and the outside world, imposed by her awkwardness, by that strangeness in her soul that marked her out to Balthazar. Smith appears genuinely oblivious to it. She, for her part, finds herself unable to get any clear sense of the man. For all his verbosity and indiscretions, he stands hidden behind the pallor of his skin; disinclined to speak in blood and vapours.

Englishmen don't smoke.

But then: Smith isn't English.

[3]

Dinner is already on the table when they enter Smith's suite. The main cabin is filled with bags and cases, the latter tied down lest they shift in a storm. A desk is laden with papers and what appears to be picture frames, wrapped in brown paper. Through a narrow door one can see his bedroom with its simple bunk. Out in the living area, the table is screwed into the floor.

While Eleanor sits, Smith fusses over the "tonic," which turns out to be largely concocted from brandy and some herbal additive that leaves a bitter flavour on her tongue. She drinks it obediently and notes a slight settling of the stomach. Even so, she declines the bread and cold cuts on offer and winces when Smith bites into a pickled gherkin and fills the air with the tang of its brine. He eats, licks his fingertips clean, dabs at his lips with the thick of his napkin. His eyes are shrewd on her, patient. It is for her to speak.

She does so at last.

"What now, Mr. Smith?" she asks in her even, rehearsed manner. "Now that you have me, what will you do with me?"

"Do? Oh, nothing very ghastly. Nothing at all, as a matter of fact. You're an asset, that's all."

"Like a thing, you mean."

He shrugs. "Like a house, or a horse, or a piece of art. Like this ship and its crew."

"And when we get to England, you will cash me in."

"In a sense. You are a gift—my letter of introduction. A rather fortuitous one to boot. But come, are you really so offended by the laws of trade? Here, try the wine. It's Portuguese. They line the barrels with Soot they harvest from brothels. No, really! They say it adds something. And who knows, perhaps it does at that." He drinks, smacks his lips, smiles. "Now tell me something. Something about yourself. How does it feel, being Miss Renfrew? The girl who grew up in a harness. Does your uncle want you back so he can punish you, or is it to keep you safe from future sin?"

Smith is asking, not heckling, his voice neither mocking nor condescending but perfectly in earnest, a curious man unabashed by his will to know. And so the emotion that rises in Eleanor is not directed at him but elsewhere, rises from the chest, from the very place, in fact, where she once wore a dial that would allow her to constrict her ribs and contain her evil by means of her pain. She does not suppress the feeling but lets it emerge in a faint frothy twist that drops from her lips like a hiccup and makes its way across the table. Smith notes and inhales it; wipes at the little stain it leaves on his starched tablecloth. But it seems to provide him with no answer, leaves him entirely unmoved, a tone-deaf man shrugging off Chopin as a tinkle of notes.

"If he punishes me," she says at last, "it will be from love. That's the worst part of it, don't you think?" Then: "They say my uncle has gone mad, Mr. Smith. Is it true?"

Smith snorts. "Madmen don't run companies, Miss Renfrew. Not well, that is. And your uncle came from nowhere to become something very like a king."

"A country isn't a company."

"Is it not? I suppose there is a difference. Countries get bogged down in their myth of themselves, in traditions and genealogies. But despite all that . . . You see, the laws of nature still apply." He sighs, with satisfaction not regret; doles out a spoonful of rice pudding for himself, then smothers it in custard. "Have you heard of a chap called Hegel, Miss Renfrew? His march of the World Spirit? No, I suppose he's long gone out of fashion. Hegel writes of moments of historical crisis. When one epoch transforms into another, transforms under the weight of its own contradictions. We are on one such *seam*. But what it takes, you see, is for one man to shoulder the World Spirit, to become its incarnation. A *hero*. Hegel thought Napoleon . . . But what did Napoleon do other than fire some cannons and redraw some borders?"

Smith pauses, shovels some rice pudding into his mouth, and for a moment he is just like a child, fuelled by sugar and alive to an idea. "So here we are, teetering on the threshold. The Age of Sin is almost over. The Second Smoke was its last hurrah."

"Then what comes next? After sin?"

"Rationality," answers Smith, growing more thoughtful with the answer. "The end of all illusions. Of sentimentality. When all the veils are torn asunder and we see things clearly, for the first time in all of history."

"And my uncle? Is he one of those heroes who will deliver this new age?"

"Your uncle? Good God, no! He is a regression. History's blind alley. A champion of the past.

"You know," he continues after a moment's silence. "It is curious. The path of history runs counter to my deepest inclinations. I felt it in that theatre of yours: the temptation to let go. Dissolve in passion. In the crowd. It's so much harder to be all alone, sealed up in your skin like stuffing in a goose."

"Poor you," whispers Eleanor. "You want to revel in life. But you have to host the World Spirit instead."

To her surprise it draws a giggle from Smith, then a full-throated laugh.

"Now you are sneering at me! But go on, I deserve it. It's this blasted Portuguese wine. And my joy in having escaped Braithwaite's accounts—a pox on them, eh? But go on, try the pud. The cook here, he puts cinnamon and raisins in it, then boils it in coconut milk. You won't believe how good it is until you try."

[4]

Smith rings a bell. It is an electrical bell, set into the wall behind him; he has to lean back in his chair and stretch in order to reach it. A moment later the door opens and in comes the cabin boy and sets to clearing up. He does so deftly, carrying out the crockery and serving dishes, then offering tea. He is a young man, about Eleanor's age, with the caramel hue of a mulatto and a soft lilt to his English; is handsome, loose-jointed, bright in his smile.

Eager to please.

Eleanor tries not to stare at him. Smith, for his part, ignores him other than requesting a cup of black coffee. A few minutes later the Company man has shifted to the armchair and kicked off his boots, pulled a blanket over his lap and reached for a stack of newspapers.

"Yesterday's news. Last month's, actually. These here are from the Continent, and those are from the Americas. And here's a little rag we print in Bombay to prove to ourselves we are beacons of enlightenment! No British papers, alas, though I've heard Minetowns is trying to set up a press. Well, good luck to them, though I fear it'll be called something dispiritingly worthy like *The Worker*, or *The Sentinel*. Or *Truth*, God help us!"

"May I be excused?"

"Of course! By all means. Stay awhile, though, the evenings on a ship are dreadfully dull. And once you are alone in your cabin you will remember all of a sudden that you are seasick and groan away until dawn. Have a look through my books if you like. There's even some of the old World Spirit somewhere, if you care to dig him out from this mess."

So Eleanor stays, not wishing to give Smith the impression of undue haste, though her stomach won't countenance any actual reading. With Smith's permission she walks over to the desk instead and studies the pictures that lie there, unwrapping those that remain wrapped. Some are paintings, evidently old, looking barren without the context of their frames. Others are photographs, mounted on cardboard; others yet maps, drawings, printed illustrations. They show ships and athletes; half-naked men from distant countries; animals and insects drawn in coloured inks; a woman stark naked wearing a strange metal mask; anatomical sketches of internal organs; a pebbled beach covered in a thousand starfish, black as tar: are so varied, in fact, that it is difficult to get any sense where Smith's interests lie. He, for his part, moves from newspaper to newspaper, reading very quickly, and sipping his coffee. One of his socks has a hole, and his big toe peeks out from under the blanket, wiggling a little from time to time. The domesticity of the moment chokes Eleanor and makes her think first of Cruikshank, then of her uncle, reading in his armchair while she tidied the house; the fire blazing, fighting their cottage's perpetual chill. Renfrew, too, needed many a sock darning.

Eleanor digs with renewed purpose within the piles of objects and papers upon the desk, wondering whether it is possible Smith has been careless about where he put his gun; then stops when she finds his eyes on her. And what would she do with a gun, on a ship in the mid-Atlantic, her friends lost to the line of the horizon? She turns abruptly, bids Smith good night, then takes her reawakened nausea into the hallway outside Smith's cabin, where she bends and retches. Three steps ahead, Smith's cabin boy darts across the corridor with two nimble steps; she calls but he appears not to hear. Back in her cabin, Eleanor accedes to her nausea, curls around it as one would around a pet. One hour, she promises herself, two at most. Then she will get up.

There is something she must do.

[5]

It proves a difficult task. Not only does the sickness remain in her bones and force her to lean on the corridor walls like a drunk; and not only is there a new tremour to the sea, the swell choppier, its intervals shorter, less predictable—she also has no idea where the cabin boy is to be found. At least there is some small amount of light: every five or six steps, a lamp is affixed to the ceiling, giving off a flickering amber glow in which the corridor's angles twist and rearrange themselves.

Her assumption, based on very little, is that the servant cannot be lodged very far from his master: it took him but a moment to respond to Smith's bell. But as she follows the passage to Smith's cabin, moving from stern to bow and up a level, she sees any number of doors, all of them closed. She carries on, then stops when she glimpses movement in the semidarkness ahead. It takes a moment for Eleanor to understand that she witnessed, in the unsteady light, the opening and closing of Smith's door; and the darting of a shadow, from out in the hallway into the cabin: a movement so quick and soundless that it seemed but part of the ship's roll, a trick of the quivering bulbs that shuffle shadows with every dip and rise. The door is firmly closed now: is plated in metal, cold to her touch. It has no external lock, hence no keyhole through which one might spy; discloses no noise when she presses her ear to its cool surface.

The handle gives without hesitation, and for all its weight the door swings easily on well-oiled hinges. She opens it just wide enough to admit her face. Some of the corridor's light pours in around her, mingles with the moonlight admitted by two portholes on her right. A cluttered room crosshatched by double shadows; the smell of rice pudding still sickly in the air. There is no intruder, no sign of anything being out of place. The door to the interior cabin that houses Smith's bed is closed.

The sea helps her. Eleanor remains at the door, patient, sure of what she has seen. The sea rises, falls, a pulse that travels from the soft of her knees to the pit of her stomach and drains the blood from her head. The resulting sickness drops her to her haunches. Thus: a change of viewing angle, the room transformed into a fresh array of shadows. Next a lateral wave hits their starboard side, then drops them in the hole of its deep valley. It shakes her, makes her fight for balance, both knees dropping to the ground.

It has the same effect on the cabin boy.

At her lowered vantage point she finds herself at one height with him: he is crouching in between the table and a travel chest, his hands hanging loose between thighs. It is one of these hands that the sea forces into action. Even in his loss of balance, he is graceful: pushing a single palm against the table leg to catch his weight, and turning one foot beneath his buttock to realign his inner centre. But, minimal or not, the movement has made him visible. Eleanor has *seen*. He knows it, too. They squat eye to eye across the distance of a dozen feet. Then he comes to a decision and rises without haste. A finger to his lips: that's all he does to acknowledge her. No waving her away or beckoning her closer; no whisper across the room or angry mime to go piss off and shut the door. Eleanor understands him completely. He has been caught. Nothing he does now will change this fact. She is not in his power and will do as she will do. So he might as well carry on with his work.

He has done this before.

This is the main thought she has as she watches him search the room, unhurriedly and in total silence. He examines all the closed containers first; opens chests and boxes, runs quick fingers through the contents. Whatever it is he is looking for is not there. Next, he turns to the pile of objects on the table. The pictures draw his interest, just as they did Eleanor's. There is a difference: one picture, framed, arrests him, brings a stiffness to his back. She wonders how much of it he can see in the weak light. Just as she thinks this, he walks it across to the porthole, lets the moon fall on its glass. A clear night outside, no waver to the silver glow; just the ceaseless meter of the sea, rehearsing its own vastness. He stands as though petrified, out of rhythm with this movement, made clumsy by what he beholds.

It is now she moves. Rising to her feet brings renewed sickness, a thick, furry lump that has to be swallowed down like medicine and leaves her mouth scoured by its acids. No matter, she will share her sour breath. She almost falls just before she reaches him, stumbles over a book discarded on the floor and loses her balance. He catches her before her fall can make any noise, catches her by the armpit and pulls her up against his frame. Almost an embrace, one-armed, his other burdened by the picture. The moon sits on his face, and she can see that he is angry. It's *him*, the child from Balthazar's photograph. She was not certain when she first saw him, or rather she was but dismissed the thought, dismissed the similarity between this young man's face and that eight-year-old boy's. The bones were the same but the expression would not fit; where the child had been hostile, the cabin boy was cheerful, servile, free of anger.

Now that the hostility has returned to the face there can be no doubt. His Smoke confirms it: the merest flicker of it, escaping his lips while his face is close. Eleanor ignores the anger and finds, underneath, an ache, childish in its forlorn magnitude, grown spiky from going unanswered for too long. She turns her back into his chest, wraps herself into him as into a blanket, then reaches a hand for the picture he is holding, and takes hold of the right side even as he keeps his grip on the left. Again she can taste Smoke on him, contained but vicious, crawling down the nape of her neck. But he controls himself for the sake of silence and even agrees to shift with her, in a back-to-front dance, so as to improve the angle of the light. Together, they study the picture. Eleanor's skin is clammy with her sickness and his heat.

It's a triptych of sketches, mounted side by side. She saw them earlier but attached to them no more importance than to any of the other pictures Smith had accumulated; less perhaps, for the drawings are small and faint with age, and look as though torn from a notebook not much larger than her palm. Now she studies them again. Two details, flanking a panoramic scene. At the centre, a group of men in a jungle clearing; tree trunks in the background, a tangle of hanging roots and vines, a giant fern spreading itself like a fountain. The floor of the clearing is filled with a curious flower, the same flower that is held aloft with a collector's pleasure by the white man in the foreground. He wears baggy breeches stuffed into calf-high boots and a ruffled shirt, dark with his sweat; long flowing hair under a wide-brimmed hat. The flower itself is also the subject of the left-most drawing. It looks something like a mixture of a poppy and a tulip, with a large, fleshy head. Back in the main drawing, standing to the man's right and arrested in a constellation whose symmetry suggests deliberate arrangement rather than chance, is a group of natives.

It is here that the thief's interest is directed. He could not give a fig about the white explorer, shows no interest in his horticultural pride, and feasts instead on the sight of the savages. For savage they look, men naked but for what appears to be bird beaks strapped to their privates. They are thin, brown-skinned, fine-boned; wear feathers in their hair.

Dress them in shirt and waistcoat and they'd look just like him: the youth whose heat pours itself into Eleanor's skin.

Several of these men wear jewellery around their necks. Because of the smallness of the figures, it is difficult to make it out in detail. The artist has addressed this problem by providing a third drawing. On the right panel, sketched very carefully, in finely shaded hues, stands a single native, rendered much bigger and in such a manner that the edge of the notebook cuts him in half: his left arm is missing as well as one leg, though both eyes have made it onto the picture. And thus it is as though he is peeking around the corner of the page the way one can peek into a window, curious at what lies inside.

Peeking at *them*.

This man, too, is wearing a necklace made of vine. On it—its horned back ornamented with precious stones; its legs and pincers rendered repeatedly, once in sharp outline, then as a series of ghostly echoes in what Eleanor realises with a stab of shock must be the artist's strategy of suggesting movement—hangs a large black beetle. Alive and *wriggling*.

It takes the thief a while to tear himself loose; costs him a wisp of Smoke that curls across her sight line. Then he steps past her, wrenching the picture out of her grasp, and replaces it silently within the pile of others. He allows himself a single angry glower at her, then turns away; resumes his earlier search, running fingers across the backs of books and furnishings, *looking*.

The tuffet draws his interest; Smith rested his feet on it before. He removes the top cushion, finds within it a panel-covered cavity and removes the lid. Then he kneels, bends his head inside. Eleanor draws close again, crouches beside him, but his shadow obscures what he has found. There is a kind of reverence suggested by his posture: bent low, skinny bottom up, head thrown down into the cavity's darkness. If there was anger in him before, there is nothing now: blankness, serenity. For a moment she thinks she can see something move in the depths of the secret compartment, but it is hard to be sure. The next moment the youth has replaced the lid and the top cushion and stood up. His hand shoots out, grabs her wrist, grabs it painfully. He pulls her out of the cabin, halts to softly close the door. Then he turns to her.

There is much in his face: hostility, curiosity, the imploration that she not return and rummage out the secret of the tuffet, nor raise the alarm and betray his intrusion to Smith. A mobile face, his, auditioning expressions; a storm of Smoke underneath. His hand is crushing her wrist.

"Don't."

It's all he manages to say—all his sentences start there. It is clear to Eleanor that he does not know what to say next: not to her, this awkward silent girl who stands too straight before his wayward face and hidden anger. He releases her arm without another word, walks off, rushing now, away from her.

"He knows who you are," she whispers after him. "Smith knows. You must be very careful," she whispers. "Mowgli."

This stops him briefly in his tracks.

Then he breaks into a run.

[6]

She looks for Mowgli the next day. She wants to warn him and something more: meet him, talk to him, make friends. They started something last night: negotiations, conspiracy, a bond. Then he crushed her wrist. It is sore this morning, will show bruises by the evening. Smith keeps to himself, though he makes sure to offer her breakfast; spends his day immersed in newspapers and ledgers. Outside, the horizon is clear of any ships; a cordon of sea birds strung along their wake, picking off the spill of their refuse.

Mowgli avoids her. She finds him twice: once in the corridor, balancing trays of dirty dishes, which he wields like a snowplough to push her out of his path; once on deck when he hastens away as though responding to an urgent summons. Both times his face displays that same harassed mobility. He does not know in which aspect to meet her.

So he flees her instead.

Midafternoon Smith requests Eleanor's company for tea. He drinks it strong, from a double-spouted urn that he refers to as a samovar. Alongside the tea, Mowgli serves a plate of jam-daubed cakes and a bowl of whipped cream; distributes napkins and saucers, every inch the cabin boy. Eleanor makes sure he is still in the room when she asks her question.

"Where are the things, Mr. Smith, that you stole from Balthazar? The weather maps? And the photographs?"

Smith looks at her, amused. "Stole? I bought them! Rather dearly, as a matter of fact. They'll be somewhere in my travelling chest."

When Mowgli is gone—Smith makes sure of it by leaving open the door; watches him walk the length of the corridor and ascend the stairs—his expression changes and he leans forward conspiratorially, somehow quite pleased with himself.

"So you recognised him, too! Why else ask that question? It was only during dinner last night that it occurred to me that you will have seen his picture." He slaps his thigh with pleasure, leans closer yet, spilling tea into his saucer. "And did you tell him? No, don't answer, you are bound to lie. Well, it'll slip out sooner or later, I suppose. I swear I did not sleep a wink all night. I thought if you'd told him he might take it in his head to murder me. But of course he can't. He has *questions*. Otherwise why take the risk and come to me like this? But how patient he is, how professional! When the captain told me he'd hired a new cabin boy, a first-rate lad, and introduced me, I almost didn't believe my eyes. In fact, I wasn't sure until I got the photograph back. But it's there, isn't it, written in his bones?"

Eleanor watches Smith stopper his enthusiasm with a cake: he stuffs it in whole, then chases crumbs along his chin with his fingertips and tongue.

"Why do this?" she asks, and finds that she is angry. "Why play with him? Is he an asset, too?"

"An asset? Why yes! He *knows* things. As a matter of fact, he'd make a good assistant. An apprentice, even. He's got pebbles, that boy. And he is *adaptable*. I'm rather impressed by him."

"You will hurt him!"

"Hurt? Why would I? Ah, you mean his poor tender soul. Don't you worry, I rather suspect he has no soul that could be violated. As I said: he is adaptable. A nonperson, almost. Or rather, he can be anyone he wants. Your Mr. Black would love him."

Smith pauses, swivels his head to make sure Mowgli has not returned to eavesdrop in the corridor, then parts with another of his secrets.

"He broke in here. Sometime last night, while I was in there, two steps away, listening for him. But I heard nothing. He's a professional, I tell you. It took me half the morning to ascertain he'd really been at all."

"What did he want?"

"I have something he covets but dare not steal. A conundrum! So he's stuck with me."

"Then you wanted him to break in. You counted on it. You laid out things for him to find."

Smith looks over to her, surprised, shapes his lips into a whistle, thick and round and smeared in icing sugar.

"Very clever, Miss Renfrew! Are you guessing? Or perhaps you had a look around as well! Are you, too, a thief?"

He stabs an accusing finger at her, more playfully than in earnest. Playful or not: her Smoke is in the air. A catfish, Etta May called her, lying buried in the river mud, scaring the other fish with its inertia. Well, the thick mud just twitched. It passes through Smith like it never happened, a drum roll past a deaf man. He picks a flake of Soot off the jam, eats another cake.

"Enough," he says, "I'll grow fat. Here, you have one, they're made of buckwheat and a pound of butter, simply delicious."

[7]

Over dinner, Smith lectures her on the history of the Company. Mowgli is there, serving. It makes Eleanor wonder whether he is speaking as much for his benefit as hers; if he is instructing Mowgli somehow, whom he has picked as an apprentice and a toy. Perhaps Smith simply wants to talk.

If his purpose is instruction, however, Smith proves himself a terrible teacher. He drinks heavily and has little sense of system, reeling off dates and incidences that mean little to Eleanor and jumping countries and centuries at the blink of an eye. Thus one minute he rehearses the Company's foundation ("Adventurers, they were, visionaries even. The dawn of a new century will have inspired them—the year reads sixteen hundred and finds a bunch of half-broke merchants with a dream. And what balls! After all, the Smoke first appeared just a couple decades later. Imagine it, pressing on, even while half the world plunged into war; Europe burning, and here they trade in indigo, spices, tea!"). The next minute he has turned to the topic of the Company's emasculation, its loss of direction and "virility" ("I blame Pitt, I do, though I suppose it started earlier than him. Government supervision, bah! Protectionism, that's what it was, making sure the Company could not fail. And then they had the gall to fight two wars over opium in the name of *free trade*. Besides, did you know that we caused the American Revolution? No, no, it's quite true. The Tea Act! The Crown's attempt to keep the Company from bankruptcy by giving it special customs status. Next thing they knew Boston was up in arms!").

What he returns to time and again is the Indian Mutiny and the Company trade in flowers. "The government said they had to *nationalise* the Company because of its mismanagement of the mutiny. Too many atrocities, too much bad press. Nonsense! The truth is, the revenues from the cotton and silk trades were drying up; the saltpetre mines were not half as profitable as they had been; even the opium trade into China had become difficult. But flowers! There is no end of money to be made in flowers. It's the most valuable crop ever harvested! Of course, the government wanted to *nationalise* their trade. How often is it that you spot a golden goose?

"And so the Company had to go. It was carved up, actually, the Crown selling off its monopolies one by one. The Flower Bill, it was called. It was passed quietly, without fuss, by special committee! The public hardly noticed: as far as they were concerned the black poppy did not exist. Oh, the *Times* wrote a few little articles, referring to 'new regulations pertaining to the import of Indian goods, specifically items of horticulture.' Items of horticulture indeed! Behind that pretty little phrase lay Empire's great secret: that it was financed by sweets. And by cigarettes, only that came a little later and was pursued even more quietly.

"And so, ten years ago, everything was going smoothly: the Company was dead, a few old families were elbowing all rivals out of the business, and a rich vein of wealth was pumping from the Raj straight into your quaint little island. Export, my dear; Britain was keeping half the world in sweets, even as it shut its borders and kept all innovation out."

"Until the Second Smoke."

"Hah! Here I am babbling away and you tell me to cut to the chase. Your uncle's flesh and blood indeed! And look how straight you sit! Like you're standing on tiptoe with a noose around your neck . . . But you are quite right, the Second Smoke changed everything. That schoolboy revolution! It plunged Britain into chaos. Parliament disbanded, the civil service paralysed, the Queen old and dying. From one week to the next all central authority had disappeared and all sweet production had stopped.

"The funny thing is that the chaos spread even to the places where the Second Smoke didn't. India stayed free of it. All we received over there was a handful of telegraphs from the Continent. Chinese whispers, more rumour than truth. Then: long weeks of nothing! No mail, no fresh orders, no trade. You imagine it: a whole infrastructure of merchants and agents, half of them members of the aristocracy, third sons and disreputable cousins; the whole bloody bureaucracy of the Raj—and none of them have a clue what to do! Half of them run scared and decide to return to Albion, where they get swallowed up by history. The others sit on warehouses full of flowers, unsure what to do with them. China might want them, but China must not learn the secret of their cultivation, let alone how to brew them into sweets. The Continent, meanwhile, is having its own apotheosis with Smoke: their economies, too, have collapsed. All this and a horde of natives surrounding us, minding our children, cooking our food; cottoning on that something is wrong! And every little maharajah asking, 'Why is there no news from Europe? Why are your soldiers not getting paid?' Twitching for independence. So our good Englishmen do what Englishmen do best: they sit tight and try to tell their darkies all is well; take laudanum; make speeches in clubs.

"But then something interesting happens. Private entrepreneurs step in. Some of them are minor government officials, wasting away in their posts and finding in themselves the pluck to set up on their own. Others are more colourful than that: plantation owners, local rajas, third-generation colonial coffee merchants who don't mind so much that the periphery has suddenly turned into the centre. And so a quiet takeover begins. Families are bought out for a pittance; import and export licences are redrafted; a lot of farmland changes hands. Oh, some money is stolen, some documents are forged, here and there some people are killed. The cat's away, after all: England's smoking like a chimney, and colonial governance is overwhelmed, the law courts clogged with cases and open to bribery. It's a moment of pure Darwinism; the laws of the market playing themselves out.

"And so a score of new companies are formed. Half of them don't know what they are doing and are soon defunct. Some of the others band together, then begin to swallow up the rest. Within five or six years the game's played and there's a new monopoly. They revive the old flag, resume close diplomatic ties to the new British government, and even adopt the old name. United Company of Merchants of England Trading to the East Indies. Unimaginative, really. Worse: *nostalgic*. And more than half of its leadership is just that: backwards-looking, dreaming of yesteryear, appealing to the remnants of the old order. Looking to turn back the clock.

"But there are others there, too. Adventurers, visionaries. Men of the future! The true heirs of the Company's founders. Sitting on the board of governors, looking for openings. Biding their time. There is no great rush, you see. History is on their side."

Smith leans back, as though exhausted by his long discourse, and for a moment sits turned inward, thoughtful, even grave. Then he remembers himself and gives an ironic little bow.

"Now you know who I am, my dear. Feel free to laugh, of course."

Laugh Eleanor does not. She studies Smith's face instead, those bluff, ruddy features, bracketed by whiskers.

"How do you know I won't tell my uncle? That you are an *adventurer*? A man who scorns good order."

"Oh, he already knows. He's a prude, a Puritan, a maniac of morals. But he knows which way the wind is blowing. And besides, I'm the Company's emissary to his little court. Bringing home his beloved niece. So what can he do but deal with me?" Smith smiles complacently, pats his stomach. "Now how about some pudding, my dear? Cabin boy, go ask the chef to steam the spotted dick. There. Let's have some port while we wait."

While Smith busies himself with opening the wine, she risks a look and catches Mowgli halfway out the door. He, too, has tilted his face to look at her, the certainties of the cabin boy replaced by doubt.

[8]

He comes to her that night. She has been sleeping; when she wakes— because he touched her? because he made a noise?—he is standing in her room. The door was not locked. On entering, he has kept it open a crack, letting in some little light: enough to be sure of his presence but not enough to read his face. Eleanor sits up in bed, gathering the blanket to her chin, not scared but somehow worried what her nightshirt might reveal.

"What did you mean last night?" he asks, his handsome face twisted, anger on his breath. "He knows who I am."

"He has a photograph of you as a child. He recognised you the moment he met you. And he knows you broke into his room. He arranged it for you. He told me so himself."

Mowgli stiffens, makes fists. She sees him only in silhouette. She would like to touch him but is afraid he would bolt.

"Who are you?" he asks.

"Eleanor. Eleanor Renfrew. My uncle is the Lord Protector."

He shakes his head impatiently. This much he already knew. He must have figured it out from snatches of overheard conversation.

"Smith took me prisoner," she says. "You and I are on the same side."

But the boy is doubtful. "Smith talks to you," he objects. "He must trust you."

"It's what he does: talk. It's from a kind of loneliness, I think. He suppresses his Smoke. He suppresses his very *sense* of it. Then he talks away the fact that he's all alone." She had not articulated the thought to herself before but knows at once that she believes it; that it has grown in her all day. It springs out of her with the awkward precision that is her lot. "That and it proves to himself how important he is, how careless of betrayal. The World Spirit moves in him—he really must believe it."

He does not respond at once. Slight as he is, his body seems to fill the room; his anger and his youth. Before she knows it, a wisp of her Smoke reaches out to him; she sniffs it along with him, blushes at how simple, how shameless, is its invitation.

"Sit down if you like," she says, pointing to the end of her bed. She says it both to cover her embarrassment and to put him at ease, he who shivers like an animal, ready to pounce or run. "Please, Mowgli."

He snorts, starts smoking, then contains himself. "Don't use that name."

"Which then?"

"Nil."

"All right then. Nil." And when he does not respond, does not sit, but simply stands there, shivering, fighting with himself over something she cannot fathom, she adds, adds it in a whisper, bashful over what she's asking: "Smoke, Nil, please do. Or else I won't know you."

He stays another minute or two, not smoking, thinking, tasting the invitation rising out of her body.

Then he turns and runs away.

[9]

Whatever it was he smelled within her Smoke, however it was that she scared him, it keeps Mowgli away for two days. They pass the time by playing hide-and-seek across Smith's dining table while the Company man imparts one-sided lessons on the laws of rational exchange. Then Mowgli is back, standing in her cabin. She wakes to his presence without fear or surprise. He has closed the door this time and lit a lamp. There are pictures in his hands.

"I went back to his quarters," he states without greeting. "I found the photo you mentioned. He had left it out for me to find."

He passes over to her the image of his childhood self, smileless and sallow-skinned. She looks from the picture to him and back, finds the same bitterness in the angle of his chin.

"Aschenstaedt must have taken this. The man who had me stolen. From *Brazil*." He says the word like he has never before pronounced it out loud. "Before I left England, I spent three months trying to find him."

"To ask him where you—?"

"That. And to kill him." Mowgli pauses, remembers himself; places before her the other pictures he is holding. "I also took these."

She does not need to look to know they are the drawings that they viewed together in the dark, plundered from their frame. It runs through her that he brought them to her to *share;* that they are something he cannot live with alone.

"You grew up in this place. In the jungle; amongst these men."

"Yes."

"How much do you remember?"

He shivers a little, grows tight-lipped and grim. "Nothing. Emotions, images."

He points to the beetle hanging off the naked man's neck, points to its horned wings, open like eyelids above the soft of its back.

"I know that it's alive. He wears it while it lives. He and it, they are . . ." He struggles, pauses.

"Man and dog?"

"Man and soul."

She nods as though she can make sense of the answer, urges him on. Something in their situation (she in her bed, sheets tucked against her chest; he at the bedside, twitchy on his feet) suggests a role to him, something that will hide him from her even as he probes his own past. His face unclenches; he grows softer somehow, wrinkles his nose and flashes a smile, shifts his weight from foot to foot like a helpless, hapless child. It hurts her a little, this transformation, places a distance between them that was not there a moment before. Her interest in him does not run to the maternal.

All the same, she plays along.

"What else do you remember, Nil?"

"A song," he answers, willing now. Perhaps the role is for himself, not her; helps him stare into the empty cavern of his memory with something other than despair. "About how the sky fell onto the earth a thousand years ago. Before the Smoke.",

"Like the Fall, you mean. The expulsion from Eden."

"You aren't listening. *Before the Smoke*. We had a word for it, see, in our native tongue. And yet I was stolen because I was an *innocent*. That's how the story goes, does it not? They took me from my smokeless people; they kept me masked on the voyage to England, where they infected me and waited for my organs to change."

He twists his face and swallows down Smoke, a child no longer.

"Smith must know where these pictures were drawn. But he likes his secrets. There's a section of the hold I have not yet got to. The lock is very good."

"You could ask him. He is waiting for you to come to him and ask."

"Maybe he is. But he'll feed me crumbs, never the loaf." He begins picking up the pictures he laid out for her to look at, then hesitates and shyly takes her hand. The gesture is strategic: a kind of lie. She knows it as surely as she knows her own skin; the odd little divot left in her breastbone from the pressure of her harness's screw.

"You mustn't trifle with me," she says, considering his hand. "I am a catfish. A monster. I swallow other fish whole."

It chases him just as quickly as did her Smoke.

[10]

It is the midmorning of the seventh day on the ocean. Nobody has announced it but they must be drawing close to England. Their destination, Eleanor understands, is the Bristol Channel. Her uncle's hold is strongest in the southwest.

As morning dips into noon, a ship is sighted off the port side. She sees it early on: a speck of metal silhouetted against a wall of cloud. It soon draws nearer. Eleanor watches it breathless, only half aware of the commotion around her, sailors swearing, passing around binoculars, rushing to their posts. The sun finds colour in the ship's bow, the dark flush of oxblood. Three chimneys, their plumes scattered by winds. The players' ship. In her excitement, Eleanor pictures Balthazar standing in the wedge of bow, a white scarf flapping from his scrawny neck. Any moment now, they will hoist a pirate's flag and demand the return of Smith's prisoner.

It is a chase now. The captain of her own ship has long adjusted its rudder and is plotting a parallel course. Behind the two vessels, a storm is brewing. It is as though a curtain has been drawn across the horizon, fusing sky and sea. The players could not have asked for a more dramatic stage. Eleanor smiles and shivers in the rising breeze; spreads herself out against it, making a flag of her flapping coat.

Then Smith is by her side.

"You better go downstairs."

She makes to respond but is flustered by his appearance. Smith is dressed from head to foot in sailor's oils and armed with two revolvers stuck into his waistband. A cartridge belt is slung across his chest.

It is as though he were going to war.

"So you really want to shoot it out? Or will you hold a barrel to my head while you negotiate a price with Balthazar?"

"Your head? Balthazar? You silly child, do you really think that ship is coming to save you? They are running for their lives. As are we."

He makes to rush away, hesitates, digs in his pocket and shoves a little bottle in her hand.

"Go, lock yourself in, block off the vents. Take a swig of this, if you like. It's laudanum. Who knows, perhaps you can sleep through the worst. Well then, *bon chance,* Miss Renfrew, it's been a pleasure. I shall see you *après la guerre.*"

The last thing she sees of him is a nest of broken veins, more black than blue, charging out his shirt collar up into his golden crest of hair.

Then Eleanor turns and fixes fresh eyes upon the storm.

[11]

A moment later she has rushed belowdecks. Smith's cabin, not her own. She tears through the piles upon his table, scattering pictures, books, and papers; dismisses the three-volume Hegel and that dark strip of beach overgrown with starfish, the anatomical sketches of the liver, each piece of tissue labelled in neat Latin. At last she finds the picture she wants. She falls on the way to the porthole, rips her stocking and scuffs her knee, a sticky warmth as blood soaks into wool. The window looks to port, she has to stand at a sharp angle to make out the centre of the storm. It is much closer now, is rushing in upon them; towers like a wall behind the players' ship, darker, *denser,* than the sea beneath. She raises the picture she is holding, studies it, then returns her gaze onto the steamer, sharply outlined by the afternoon sun. It does not take long. Little by little the ship is drawn into the wall of darkness, looking tiny by comparison, a fleck of oxblood and a thin plume of steam. Then it is gone—*ingested*—and Mowgli is in the cabin, a crowbar slung across one shoulder.

He looks distracted, distraught; opens the tuffet; rummages through the compartment beneath its cushion and comes up empty-handed, at a loss.

"I finally managed to break into the secret part of the hold," he mutters, not so much to her as to the room, as though making himself heard against the clamour of his thoughts. "Everybody's busy on deck, so I nipped down under. Some lock, that."

He drops the crowbar, makes a fist, then sticks up his little finger, bends it lightly at the knuckle.

"Like that, pale and tender, like candle wax before it has set; buried in cases full of straw. Grubs; maggots—whatever the word is. And I remember a whole forest of such fruit, bulging from the underside of leaves. Like tumours. He must have ten thousand down there, sleeping away in their little coffins."

He looks over at her, appealing for something—help, reassurance, support—and is met by her indifference. She has no time for childhood reminiscence. A storm has eaten her friends.

"Here," she says, not looking at Mowgli, "come and see."

He steps over sulkily. She positions him, tilts his chin to the right angle. He struggles, does not like to be touched.

"What? Bad weather. This is a well-appointed ship. I am sure we will be just fine."

She raises her arm, points at the heart of the storm, at that dense mass of cloud made solid upon the plane of sunlit water, cutting in half the world. There, stitched into the fabric of its *density*, towers a strip of unrelenting darkness, black, not grey. It is as though a strip of sky has been tarred before it was painted, and its blackness is now bleeding through the dye.

"What is it?"

She frowns, shoves the photograph into his hands. London, ten years ago. A pillar like a black spear thrown from the heavens deep into the earth; the Thames a greasy ribbon, unspooling itself behind.

Mowgli stares at the photograph; looks back out the window, where the same pillar stands shrouded amongst clouds.

"A Black Storm? But that's impossible. Not out at sea. Not *now*."

Eleanor does not argue with him. They both were *there*, in Britain, at the time. They heard the rumours, saw the refugees. The Storms rose up in the south and swept the land, not always moving with the wind. One took care of Cambridge, Ely, the Norfolk coast. Another swept Stafford off the map.

"Did you see the other ship?" she asks. "My friends are on it. The Storm has caught them."

"Then they are dead."

Mowgli says it so simply, so starkly, that anger curls out of her and straight into his skin. He bristles, then is made to gorge upon her grief; chokes on the force of her emotion. A twist at her breast, at that invisible key still jutting from the bone, and Eleanor shuts herself off, releasing him from her anguish.

"It's closing fast now," she says, sounding as sober and cool as the man who raised her in his image. "It'll have us very soon. Smith must pass out his sweets. They might help protect us, if only for a moment or two."

"He doesn't have any. Unless he keeps them in his inner cabin. But there are none in the hold. I have seen Smoke masks"—here Mowgli gestures to the trunks and cases behind them—"but only two." He walks over to them, digs through them, comes up empty. "They are gone."

Eleanor thinks it through.

"The captain and the chief engineer. That's whom he's given them to. So they keep the ship going, no matter what."

"And he himself?"

"He protects himself. I don't know how."

"And us?"

She shrugs, turns to the window, almost pressing her face against the glass. In a moment Mowgli is next to her, a little taller, his chin to her cheekbone.

Together they watch the Storm steal up onto their wake.

[12]

It starts with darkness and the sudden buckling of the world, deprived of any stable up and down. This is the outer edge of the Storm, delivering a premature dusk and heavy seas; the crazed howl of its gale. Metal pops all around them as the ship turns tin can, thin-skinned and hollow. Eleanor draws to the door, looks out into the hallway: sees the bulbs swing in their casements, the swill of water racing to each trough dug by the boiling sea; hears the ocean crash onto the deck above, then pour spumous down the hatches. Soon something else begins to register on her, a kind of scent evaluated by her skin and lungs and the organs of digestion, not yet visible upon the air. *The ship is burning,* it comes to her, but she at once corrects the thought. *The sailors are burning.* They have entered the black of the Storm.

When the first of the screaming starts up on deck, she comes to a decision. Eleanor closes then locks the door.

Mowgli tries to stop her.

"Let me leave first," he says. "Then you can lock it.

"It's a Black Storm," he continues, "and I am knit from anger. When it gets me, you don't want me around."

She pushes him out of the way; is aware of a tattoo of steps, charging down the corridor outside.

"Show me what you were looking for, Mowgli. There, in the tuffet. I want to see."

"I will hurt you," he insists, his mobile face grown stark. *Like a child at a funeral.* Outside, something, *someone,* throws his weight against the door, then buckles it with heavy blows. A thread of darkness slips through the seal of its metal lips, tentacular and probing. The screaming is now very loud.

"Show me," she repeats. "He must have put it in his bedroom. It's too late now anyway. We can no longer get out."

[13]

The door to Smith's inner cabin is locked. Mowgli tests it, then bends for his crowbar. While he heaves away at the lock, the door behind them throbs with metronomic violence. Is it one man or many beating his flesh bloody on its metal? The Malay, the handsome Irishman with his sunburn and his freckles? Or the dark-skinned cook whose lower lip looks swollen as though stung? The blows are spongy, dull, are edged with screams. The mind plays tricks: amongst the roar of sea and wind there is no scope to hear the breaking of small bones. And yet Eleanor does and winces and is scared.

For now the bolt she has slid into its place is holding fast. But the door itself has begun to warp, in grim copy to the one Mowgli is wedging open with the bar. Through the gap, a frothy darkness pours itself into the room. It comes from above, too, through the latticed mouth of a ventilation pipe; lowers itself on silky threads, then hangs twitching, fish-hooked in midair. Soon a halo of filth surrounds them, lapping at their skin; tars their lips and stains their eyes. The Storm is no longer *out there* but has slipped into their blood. She sees it in Mowgli's face and movements, in the way he wrenches the crowbar so hard that the metal cuts his palms.

She, too, catches it: the dark weight of anger; feels it ripple through her, scalp to sole. She opens herself, accepts it; locks it in the depth of her: there, in that same tall tower, slim and steely like a grain silo, that she has been slowly filling with such rotten wheat from the tender years of childhood so that now it stands pert and pressurised by its own fermentations. And in the same breath, as naturally as a flutter of the eyelids, she locks up Mowgli's rage, too, and passes back a kinder Smoke, seasoned not with anger but with want.

He receives it with a shudder.

"How . . . ?" he begins, aroused and unbelieving.

"Talent," she answers. "A gift. Quick now, or I must burst."

He nods, wrenches at the crowbar, and forces their way into the other room.

[14]

Smith's inner sanctum. A bed, a stool, a mound of underwear and socks; the sheets sweat-rank with bad dreams. They have closed the door and wedged it shut, but the lock is bust now and the whole door crooked in its frame. Outside, the blows upon the outer cabin door have ceased. Perhaps its assailants have beaten themselves dead upon its bulk; perhaps their truce of rage has ruptured and they have fallen one upon the other like mating spiders woken to their hunger halfway through the act. No doubt the Storm will find Eleanor and Mowgli, too, here amongst Smith's unwashed linens. But for now the air around them is unshrouded by anger, and their feelings remain their own. They stand and breathe; have clasped each other's hands in fear.

But Mowgli soon has need for his, and haste. He stoops, digs around the night table and its clutter, the knotted linen on the bed. He retrieves a syringe from the hollow of the pillow, its plunger down and the needle suppurating from its tip. It has drawn a dun and wayward circle into the white cotton.

Mowgli flings the syringe away, drops to all fours, searching the floor now, and with a yelp retrieves a little box stuffed with rotting stalks of flowers. Bedded on it, a matchbox Snow White in black plate, lies the oozing carcass of a beetle.

But wait, it isn't quite dead. Transferred to Mowgli's palm, the monstrous insects stirs to life; twitches a leg and spreads the twin horned covers on its back to reveal two sticky wings. From its rump the thing leaks a clear liquid, too thick to suggest blood. The keening that fills the room is the boy's, not the beetle's: love and worry rising out of him like morning fog.

Even so, his fingers move. Eleanor is not sure he is conscious of their action. They dip their tips into the beetle's juices, rise up to his lips and gums. There is something habitual to the motion, a tang of ritual, the smoothness and precision of signation.

Next she knows his hand is on her lips.

"Let me," he says, looking confused, as though he has only just woken to the strangeness of his act and the breath-warmed moisture on his fingers.

He makes to say more, then simply slips a thumb between her upper lip and teeth, anoints her gums. The beetle's ooze tastes richly of compost. Her tongue touches his thumbnail as it dives beneath it to the wet, private cavern of her jaw. It isn't how she pictured it: her first kiss. There is a little plop when he withdraws his digit overhastily, a thread of spittle dangling between lip and skin that almost makes her laugh.

"What is it? What will it do?"

"I don't know." He shakes his head in frustration, gestures vaguely at the air. "I remember . . . It's a kind of blessing, I think. It wards off evil. We did it for the sick and dead. So it's fitting, isn't it?"

She looks up around herself and sees the Storm has encroached upon their sanctuary, curling past the cracks in the doorframe and dropping from the ceiling, smuggled in by hidden vents. Up above she can hear gunshots, first one, then three in quick succession, and she has a vision of Smith holding off the sailors as they attempt to take control of the bridge. Somewhere beneath them, the engine is still chugging; perhaps the machinist remains, feeding the furnace through a madness held in check only by the thin filter of his Smoke mask. Mowgli returns the beetle to its box. He closes it, then slips it gently between bed frame and mattress, where it will be cushioned from their rage.

"We are trapped here," he says. "I must leave you and you must lock yourself in. Or else I will end up killing you."

She pretends to consider it.

"I can't," she says at last. "This lock is broken. And if you open the outer door, the sailors might force their way in. So we are stuck together."

"Then tie me. My hands and feet."

She refuses. "You'll be helpless. Once it gets too much for me, *I* might kill *you*."

"You might," he answers very simply. "But we cannot both be tied."

Smith's room holds his leather braces and a number of straps used to secure his trunks. She ties Mowgli's ankles to the legs of the metal cot that is itself screwed deep into the floor; ties his wrists together, then secures them to a strap she loops around his waist.

"Too tight?"

"Fine."

"And now?"

"Now we wait. It's almost here."

They watch the Smoke thicken: silken threads combining to finger-thick tendrils, mucinous streams sliding across floor and wall, an odd intelligence to their viscous probing. Without a word, Eleanor sits down behind Mowgli, leans her back against his, spine rubbing onto spine. He tilts his head back, opens his mouth, his pulse beating in her ear.

"Are you scared?" she asks.

In answer he starts talking, speaking of himself for perhaps the first time in years, rushing the words, trying to outrace the rage before it wins his tongue, telling her his nameless life and about the strange black beetle that he loves. Eleanor closes her eyes and listens.

On her skin gooseflesh soon spreads like a rash.

The news reaches me as I am sitting down to dinner. My man brings it, furtively, to this my cell that I have chosen as my home. "A Storm," he says, "was spotted out at sea." He says it calmly and composedly, though no Storm has been spotted for many years, and only once was a Storm ever reported to cross water, hopping fishing vessels in its leap from Northumberland to Norway, where it found Bergen ready to be put to waste. "Originating where?" I ask, and he shakes his head to say he does not know. "There were Gales along the coast this morning . . ." he goes on, only to trail off again. A Gale is no Storm, whatever some people may say.

"Who spotted it?" I ask.

"Fishermen."

"Were they caught by the Storm?"

"No. But they saw a ship in trouble. Further out to sea. Some say there was more than one."

It takes days for the news to solidify. The ships caught up in the Storm keep multiplying. First it is one, then two, then three. The first ship draws the lion's share of interest. "It's in one piece," I am told. And later: "There are survivors." And later yet: "The Lord Protector's niece is on that ship. It was she who . . ." But here my otherwise calm servant and spy loses his composure and is at a loss for words. "The sailors say she saved the ship," he tries at last.

"How?"

"Somehow."

Updates arrive twice a day. The vessel is a Company charter; the Lord Protector has sent a tug; the ship is already in harbour; there was a hush amongst the sailors when Miss Renfrew disembarked upon the pier. Afraid that his poor powers of eloquence will not do justice to the scene, my man brings a charcoal drawing on a piece of sailcloth, made by one of the survivors during the hours when they drifted at sea, or so he has been told. It is smudged but nonetheless evocative; shows a listing, broken ship. On its deck a handful of sailors stand muffled in bandages, with broken limbs and bashed-in mugs. Their heads are all turned towards a single point; their eyes drawn overlarge, dilated by reverence or awe. It is the girl they are looking at, chubby-cheeked and unremarkable, her spine so painfully straight one would pay her to slouch. A dark-skinned youth looks shifty by her side.

"Who is he?"

"Nobody. A servant," says my man, who has spent all his life taking orders.

There is a final figure in the drawing, standing in isolation from this beatific scene. The Company man, presumably: fire-scorched, the right cheek blistered, a munitions belt splitting his large gut. A fleshy man holding his cigar as if he were weighing his own penis; disgruntled, perhaps, at being so ignored.

"I paid for the picture," my man says now. It is my cue to reimburse him for his grave expense. I do, then put the drawing away. The scene holds little interest for me. Nor does the news of a second ship, farther north, nor of a third—not, that is, until something else attaches itself to the latter, a port of origin. Bombay, India. Headed here, to this castle on the Bristol Channel. The rumours report it to be sunk at sea; then unsink it some days later and beach it instead upon the Welsh shore; only to fling it upon rocks and sink it once more. Nobody can explain how it is that it missed the channel and sailed past us instead into the Irish Sea.

A Storm, out to sea; an Indian merchantman, cargo unknown.

I have long hoped for a message from Hindustan; have dispatched a man there—a rather different kind of servant—and waited for word. Did he send me a signal in the shape of a Storm? It's possible, after all. My man is marked, in more senses than one.

He has always had a sense for the dramatic.

The light dims. The room, small enough for a prison cell, sumptuous enough for a manor house study, shrinks to the size of a spotlight. In its gilded disk sits milady, now still writing, now folding up the paper and slipping it inside her bodice. The chair she sits on is high-backed and solid, suggesting the proud discomfort of a throne. Milady's gaze is trained into the void beyond the light, where the audience cowers in long rows. A steely gaze, unwavering. Brave is the patron who dares to move, or cough.

Then: a shiver in the floorboards, a rumble deep beneath the seats; releasing the tension; promising change. In answer to an unseen engine's groan, the stage begins to slowly spin upon a central axis, until the patterned wall of milady's room forms a tidy parting line between two equal halves of stage. On the left: the throne and its occupant, now in aquiline profile. The lights dim on this portion of the stage only to rise on the other side. Here then—on the right, the stage's East—emerges a fresh scene, also in profile. It's an oriental cityscape, marked by a dusty street and an imitation palm tree; by the flat roofline and dirty whitewash of a building overhung by the sign of a red bicycle. A man stands underneath the sign, dark-haired, European, his face paint so thick, it drains all expression from his features. He stands motionless, neck craned upwards towards the sign.

The next moment, a child runs onto the stage from the no-space that is offstage right, a boy in a knee-length orange shirt without collar or buttons, and a prayer mark on his brown-skinned forehead. Strapped to his chest he carries a calendar, outlandish in size, its topmost leaf showing nothing but the name of the month.

The child stops in his tracks; looks around; screws up his eyes to penetrate the gloom that shields the audience. Now he turns, studies the man underneath the sign; saunters over to the parting line dividing right from left and cranes his neck around to see. Satisfied, he faces the audience once more and, in an exaggerated gesture, thumbs at the dark side of the stage, then taps his chest, where MAY is written in black figures. He tears off the page and blows his nose on it, revealing APRIL; mimes wiping his arse with that, revealing MARCH. A nod and stamp of the feet confirms the month. Then the boy runs over to the frozen European and gives his sleeve a playful tug before skipping off the stage.

The tug sets things in motion. The man unfreezes; swivels his head; steps closer to the painted door. One hand finds the doorknob; the other makes to knock.

As the lights are cut, a sound fills the darkness: the marching of boots in tidy unison, as of soldiers making their rounds.

ACT II

EMPIRE

MARCH–MAY 1909

One day the god Shiva teased his wife, the goddess Parvati, about her dark skin. He called her Kali—"Black-One"— and said that her dark body against his white body was like a black snake coiled around a pale sandalwood tree.

PADMA PURANA

[1]

The bicycle seller expected soldiers to come for him, a group of four at least, shouting and brandishing guns, led by a middle-aged sergeant too fat for his khakis. But the man who steps into his workshop just as evening turns into night is young, slim, un-uniformed; is quiet, unarmed, and alone. There is something wrong with his face. It is covered in grease paint mimicking the colour of skin. Dust sticks to it, giving it a texture at once mottled and oddly smooth, like the skin of a burn victim. At the hairline and neck, the paint stops abruptly and reveals fair, sunburned skin. The man's clothes are dirty and ragged. He looks like a vagrant, one of those broken, down-at-heel sahibs adrift in this Empire-after-Empire: penniless, addicted to opium or alcohol, left behind by the changes of the past ten years. When he speaks, though, his is the voice of a prince.

"I am looking for a Mr. Jagat Singh," he announces in the sort of accent that distinguishes generals from subalterns, and Company Mughals from common shopkeepers. "Are you he?"

Defiance rises in Singh with the alacrity of heartburn. He has been waiting for his arrest since dawn. "What is wrong with your face?" he asks.

The stranger responds to his rudeness without rancour. "Scars. A disfigurement. Are you Mr. Singh?"

Gunshots sound in the street outside, interrupting their conversation. The shots set off dogs; into their bark, a woman screams. Or perhaps it is a child.

The stranger does not flinch at the noise. "What's going on out there?" he asks.

"That's what tyranny sounds like! Fool soldiers firing fool guns, to remind themselves they are not scared." Singh is no longer in control of his anger, a lick of Smoke pouring out with the words.

Then he catches sight of the stranger's expression.

"You really don't know, do you? It's retaliation. Some boys threw a bomb into the coach of the Company magistrate at Muzaffarpur. The news reached us this morning. Now your lot are combing the streets for 'terrorists.'"

"And will they find such terrorists?"

"They will find men who are sick of Company rule."

"Yes, I imagine they will."

The man looks around and finds amongst the clutter of the workshop a low stool that Singh uses when repairing bicycles. He draws it closer and then sits down on it, placing his hands on his knees.

He wants to show me that he is harmless, it flashes through Singh. There is a tension to the stranger's body that suggests the opposite.

"Who are you?"

"A traveller."

"A Company man?"

The stranger shakes his head. "All I want is to ask you some questions. Your name was mentioned to me in connection with . . ." Here he pauses, as heavy footsteps can be heard passing in the street. ". . . in connection with a business venture mounted out of Bombay. My understanding is that the people involved came here to speak to you."

"Who are you?" Singh demands again, stepping closer and towering over the sitting man. "Who sent you here?"

The man looks up with his calm, young-old eyes. *Judging him.* Singh bristles at the gaze. He wonders whether he could overpower the stranger. Singh is in his early forties now but still much stronger than his slight frame suggests. *If I fight him, I will have to kill him.* The thought frightens Singh. But not as much as the stranger's words.

"When I came in just now, you thought I'd come to arrest you. Even now, you half think it. I thought it was idle fear, a tradesman's panic about soldiers—but you don't seem the type. No, you thought I'd come to arrest you because you are worthy of arrest. You have something to hide. What are you, Mr. Singh? A terrorist, a freedom fighter? Are you building bombs there in your backyard?"

The stranger looks up at him, at his face, then at the hand that is slowly folding itself into a fist and rising up as though of its own accord. Any second now and it will hail down, consequences be damned.

"I am asking, Mr. Singh, because where I am from, I am known as a terrorist myself."

The stranger's sleeve comes up and wipes at the paint that covers his cheek and temple. A mark emerges, somewhere between ink blot and tattoo, written deep into his skin and charging up from cheekbone to temple and ear, where his longish hair hides a furrow raked into his skull and the missing half of his mutilated ear. It is said a rifle bullet dug that furrow; that coal dust dyed the wound. Mr. Singh stares at the mark; touches it with his left hand while the right remains in a fist high above his head.

His wife finds them thus, her husband's fingers in another man's curls, a wisp of Smoke connecting them like lovers.

"Who is this?" she asks, bemusement cutting through her fear.

"Change," answers her husband in a voice so soft it is as though he is afraid of disturbing the air. His fingers are still probing the mark. "Please, Gods, let it be change."

[2]

They retire to the back of the house to have tea. If the workshop was cluttered, the living quarters are pristine. Clothbound books line the shelves, framed maps the walls. A servant is clattering around the nearby kitchen, but Mrs. Singh sees to the tea herself, serving it in the English style from a china pot whose elegant spout is only slightly chipped.

"Sugar, sir?"

Her husband frowns at the word. None of his family must kowtow to the white man, whoever he may be. Mrs. Singh catches her husband's look and adds:

"What shall we call you?"

"My travel papers make me out as one Thomas Payne."

"Mr. Pain then. How do you do? Sugar?"

"One, thank you."

"You are welcome."

They sit in awkward silence for some minutes, drinking tea. It has been months since Thomas has had any that was not spiced and over-sugared, but the drawing room stiffness makes it difficult to savour the taste.

"You are Brahmin?" he asks to ask something, trying to square the bourgeois tidiness surrounding him with the work apron still strapped to Mr. Singh's front.

"We are Marxists. Caste is a prison from which India must free itself."

"Sikhs," adds Mrs. Singh, more gently. "But as my husband says, we are not religious." Her bindi rises on her forehead with her smile.

"*India*," echoes Thomas. "You are the first people I have met who call it that. 'Bengal.' 'Bihar.' 'Hindustan,' now and again. Never 'India.'"

"A nation needs a name," replies Mr. Singh. "Otherwise it cannot wake up to its nationhood." His eyes flash with the pleasure of instructing an Englishman in such simple truths.

They have some food. The servant brings it in, a corpulent woman well past middle age whose open stare makes Thomas hide his mark under the palm of one hand. The food itself is spicy and meatless, its strong flavours clashing with the tea that's cooling in their cups. Mr. Singh has changed into a clean chemise; it makes him look younger, as though he's taken off a piece of armour and, with it, some of the defensiveness it implies. He leaves it to his wife to lead the conversation. Thomas, aware of his need to win her trust, answers thoughtfully, in detail.

"Have you been here long, Mr. Pain? In this India of ours?"

"What is it now? The beginning of March? I landed in late December. In Pondicherry."

"That's French territory, is it not?"

"Yes. It seemed safer that way—their custom controls are less obsessive. It took me some weeks to find a way of crossing into the British parts of the country."

"And then you headed north?"

"North and west, at first. There was a man I wanted to see in Bombay: a horse veterinarian who used to work for the army and is now looking after the racing stables of some very prominent Company men. His name had been given to me as someone who was very well informed. It was he who put me on your husband's trail."

The last words silence Mrs. Singh for a moment, and she looks down at her plate, frowning. When she resumes her questioning, it is not with the inquiry Thomas expected.

"You must tell us what happened. In England. The New Smoking. If you are really who . . . You see, all we know is whispers, gossip—"

She breaks off, strangely agitated, rises and walks over to the bookshelf to fetch a large-format scrapbook. It takes her but a moment to find the place she is looking for. A newspaper front page is preserved there, marked as a "*Calcutta Express* Special Report." Thomas takes a note of the date.

"This was distributed free of charge. In Bengal, Bihar, Rajasthan—

throughout the whole colony perhaps. Illustrated editions, so that even the illiterate could see."

Thomas studies the page. It is a collage of images artfully arranged so that one grows into the other without obscuring it. It is a shock to see England again, evoked in vivid details by this unknown draughtsman's skill, through cobblestones and architecture, background shrubs and blank white skin. The page is dominated by the picture of a prone woman in a torn dress crossing her arms to protect the nudity of her chest. She is a beauty, long-limbed and slender; the dress very tight around the waist and spilling alabaster calves from its dirtied hem. Her eyes are long-lashed, closed; the chin raised upon a long white stem of neck; the mouth open in a scream that shows a row of perfect teeth. Two demon men stand close to the prone woman, their features distorted, Smoke curling from their workingmen's clothes.

Above their heads a row of crosses rises to line a muddy road. Children and animals are nailed to their wood. Next to them stand the ruins of a noble city: roofs burned, windows smashed, brick house-fronts blackened by fire and Soot. Beneath it, there marches an armed mob in the cloud of their dark wrath. "Britain Engulfed by Murder," Thomas reads: large angry letters. "Outrage." "Crucifixion." "Cambridge Destroyed." "Wild Mobs Rule the Land."

Thomas turns the page and finds another newspaper cutting, dated a half year later. On it there is the picture of a coronation: a young handsome prince astride a splendid throne, receiving his crown from the hands of a robed bishop. "Order Restored: Monarchs across Europe Hail Edward VII." In lips and jawline, in the clear-eyed kindness of his ink-drawn eyes, this freshly baked king has something of Charlie. It starts an ache in Thomas: for his friend and green hedges; for a world of cravats that he used to despise. He turns back to the horror of the first page; is startled again by the picture's skill at focussing his gaze on the half-exposed flesh of this unknown woman, arms crossed over bare breasts. It is hard not to feel outraged for her; hard, too, not to wish she would drop her hands.

"They tried to scare you," Thomas says at last. "They must have been afraid that our revolution would spread. Only, then someone realised that it is dangerous to tell people that the centre has collapsed. So six months later, you got a new king in a starched white tailcoat. Time to get back in the poppy fields. Resume business."

"Is it true?" presses Mrs. Singh.

"There is no king. The old queen is dead, the crown prince—lost. Gone mad say some; a born-again democrat, others. You've been living in a fiction of Empire."

"But the New Smoking? The stories say you yourself were the one who . . . You and your friends. Was it like the picture? Murder? Fire? *Rape?*"

Her gaze is frank and implacable. Thomas meets it grimly, from habit not inclination.

"It is always best to grow a lie from the seed of truth, Mrs. Singh. If you will excuse me for a moment, I must wash my hands."

[3]

When Thomas returns, Mr. Singh is alone. "My wife is seeing to your room for tonight," he says in response to Thomas's questioning glance. "She sent the servant home. The curfew is about to start."

"I have upset her."

"Not upset—*disappointed*." Mr. Singh smiles when Thomas winces at the word. "All we know of you are stories. 'The man with the mark.' 'The New Smoking.' Private conversations overheard by servants in Company villas and counting houses; letters read illicitly by pleasure boys and civil servants. Seasoned by fabulation, then passed on to relatives in town and country, all in a great big swirl of fear and hope. And here you walk into our humble house, dusty like a village mongrel. We yearn for truth. But when we ask it, you equivocate."

Mr. Singh takes a breath, his manner stern now, hostile.

He was struck by wonder, it comes to Thomas, *back there in his shop, when he first saw my mark.*

Now he regrets his weakness.

"I must press you for an answer, sir," Mr. Singh resumes, wielding the foreign honorific like a weapon. "Why are you here?"

"To ask for your help."

Thomas holds up his hand before Singh can bristle over yet another evasion; moves his chair closer, leans in eye to eye. *Smoking distance.* In the new age—up in Minetowns and across the "Free North"—this is the distance of truth and intimacy. *Half a foot for the truth; a full yard for lying.* The North is full of little homilies like that.

"Listen. The Britain I come from is splintered. There are those who want to turn back the clock of history and those who embrace the changes brought on by . . . what was released, ten years ago. We are divided by ideology, geography, money. There is talk of war.

"Some months ago, an old . . . acquaintance . . . asked me to visit her. I had not seen her since back *then* and was inclined never to see her again, but her letter convinced me to go. You see, she is rich and well connected—on both sides of the great divide. Especially when it comes to money; the world of finance. She had noticed something, something that disturbed her: the Company—someone *within* the Company—was quietly spending a good bit of money on something that did not make any sense. They were trying to trace a shipment—something secret, undeclared—that was imported into England some ten years ago. In the winter of 1898: just weeks before Livia, Charlie, and I set off what is now known as the Second Smoke. Whoever it is that is interested in this information, they have been spending a fortune to locate the shipment's point of origin. My acquaintance concluded that it was . . . *important*. 'World-changing' was the phrase she used. She urged me to look into it. The trail led here, to India."

Thomas pauses, aware of Singh's frown.

"That's it? You left your home and friends over a rumour to do with investments and imports? While your country is on the brink of civil war. You will excuse me, sir, if I state that it does not sound very credible."

Thomas nods, conceding the point. His throat is dry. Cold tea sits in a cup by his elbow. But he reaches not for the cup but for the scrapbook Mrs. Singh left open on the table. The coronation looks up at him. He flicks the page, to outrage and atrocity.

"It goes back to what your wife asked—about what happened, back then. You will know the outlines. We called to life the Soot; made Smoke subtle. The earth itself came alive. After some weeks it grew weaker, more sporadic. Soon things returned to how they had been, more or less. You could say that things had worked as planned.

"But there was something else, too, on that first day in London. A black plume, like a gash in the sky. Like the darkness behind a painted world whose canvas has been ripped."

Thomas pauses, his voice failing him; plants a finger onto the newspaper page, onto the crucified children, the burning embers of Cambridge.

"It moved like a blade. There were no witnesses to its passage; just the dead. People who saw it from afar soon had a name for it: the Black Storm. We did not know if there was one or many.

"For the longest time, I thought the Storm and the Second Smoke were the same thing, two sides of the self-same coin. After all, some outbreaks of Second Smoke were rather dark, feeding on pain embedded in the land or finding dark Smokers. Ugly things happen in such 'Gales'; impossible things, animal truths that afterwards one is ashamed to name.

"Only the Black Storm did not *feed* on the land, it scorched it. And its evil was *pure:* a distillation of hate. I told myself that Julius must have caused it: that his body—the body of the boy I had killed with my own fists—had turned into a wraith. That he was stalking the land. Taking revenge."

"You blamed yourself." Singh seems surprised by this thought, envious almost. It is as though he thinks guilt an emotion whose luxury one may sample only after one's battles have been won. "But now you think it wasn't Julius. That the cause was something else. Something new. An import, from overseas."

"I don't know, Mr. Singh. I have come all the way to India just to answer that question."

[4]

They sit in silence for a moment. Then Mr. Singh gets up abruptly, disappears into the living room, and returns with a bottle of Scotch and, somewhat quaintly, a box of digestive biscuits that he presents with great ceremony. Soon they sit, whisky in teacups, savouring the ancient biscuits, despite the mouldy dampness that clings to them.

"So what do you think it was," asks Mr. Singh, "this mysterious colonial import that you are chasing?" His tone is light, but Thomas can see that his interest has shifted, grown personal.

"I had a theory. You see, back in the time of the First Smoke there was a lot of money in sin. Cigarettes—you may have heard of them. The rulers of Britain had grown so good at being free of affect that they had to ingest other people's passions for a taste of *fun.* Cigarettes were based on very dark Soot, harvested in the most infernal places. Prisons, madhouses, execution yards. I came to think that maybe someone had set up a *factory* somewhere. A place where chance harvest was replaced by active creation."

"A production plant of sin! What a precise definition of our colony." Mr. Singh barks out a laugh and nearly chokes himself on his biscuit. "Did you picture giant torture chambers? Or some synthetic mode of production? Sterile vats and native engineers, stirring the soup, as it were?"

Thomas shrugs. "I don't know what I pictured. I just tried to make sense of it. Of the Storm's darkness. Of its *hate*. In the Britain I grew up in, vice was something for the cities. People produced it. So that's what I pictured: a factory compound in one of your metropolises; abandoned, now that the price of sin has plummeted.

"When I got to Bombay, however, and people made inquiries for me about who was spending what money, all this turned out to be nonsense. Someone was putting an expedition together. Adventurers, mercenaries, mountaineers. Maps; experimental new equipment for high-altitude climbing. They were headed to the mountains. North, that is. Apparently there had been an earlier expedition, eleven or so years ago. Now they were retracing its steps. But they were not heading there directly. Something was missing, some piece of information. They were looking for someone, a Hindustani. He used to be in the colonial service; a surveyor and cartographer in the western Himalayas. But then he quit his job rather suddenly, and disappeared." Thomas pauses, his eyes on the maps gracing the walls. "They spent a fortune to trace you here, Mr. Singh. I need to know what they did once they found you."

Still Singh hesitates, his fingers around his glass. His demeanour is cool, withdrawn. Above it, though, diffused in the whisky fumes, there is the scent of his anger, his not-yet-Smoke. Thomas feels it fan his own impatience.

"They did come here, didn't they? A group of Englishmen? I need to know, Mr. Singh. I cannot leave here until I do."

"Yes, they came. Three and a half weeks ago."

"How many?"

"Six. No, seven, though one stayed outside. Keeping guard. Only one talked. A Mr. Watts."

"What did he want? Maps?"

"Maps, yes. Of the Nepalese Himalayas. The Gandaki section—"

"Nepal! But the kingdom is closed. No white man may enter. Do such maps even exist?"

Singh shrugs. Thomas can see he's lying. No, not lying. Sifting his words. Holding back.

"When I was a younger man, I spent some time in that region. Very few people have, you see—other than the locals. They knew this and asked me whether I had records from that time. I denied it. 'Come, man,' this Watts kept on saying, 'don't be stubborn.' He was very insistent—just the way you are. He offered me money, first a little, then a lot. 'Why sell bicycles? You are no tradesman.' When I continued to deny having any records, they searched my house. Top to bottom. I had kept a few crude maps, for nostalgia's sake, in my private notes. They found them and stole them. When they left, Watts petted my cheek, like a dog. 'Sly little Arab,' he said. Then they went."

Singh finishes his whisky, then rises, wiping crumbs off his lap.

"It is time to retire," he says, his voice firm. "We can speak more over breakfast. Before you are on your way."

Thomas's breath is dark with his frustration.

But he obeys.

[5]

The guest room is a small high-ceilinged room, its walls painted bright saffron. A narrow army cot serves for a guest bed. There is no furniture other than a low rattan table, fraying at the edges. But the bedsheets are pristine starched cotton, and the carafe of water that has been placed near the bed is made of cut glass. A piece of soap has been placed on his pillow as a gift.

Thomas has only just started to undress, when he hears steps outside.

"Thomas-babu?" Mrs. Singh's melodious voice floats through the curtain that serves as a partition. "Are you decent?"

Thomas smiles at this version of his name and quickly does up his shirt. "Yes, come in."

Mrs. Singh steps through, then makes to draw the curtain behind herself before thinking better of it. There are proprieties to observe.

"I just wanted to ask whether you have everything you need."

The question is so obviously disingenuous that Thomas does not bother answering. He looks at her and she meets his gaze with a boldness that makes him think of Livia. Her bindi shines on her forehead like a third eye.

"You eavesdropped," he ventures. "You heard everything your husband and I said."

Mrs. Singh nods. "It is terrible to be nosy, isn't it? Mr. Singh, he always chides me. 'Keep your nose out,' he says. But he does not really mind."

"If you heard us then you know that he is lying."

She does not answer at once but simply looks at him, her eyes on his scar and his mark.

"You must think of what you are doing to him, Thomas-babu! Here you are: a hero from a sacred song. Like Arjuna. Or Mangal Pandey. My husband is very excited. And so he scolds himself for his excitement. After all, he is a serious man; committed to his cause. You confuse him."

"I will leave tomorrow. Then he can return to his revolution. Perhaps he can be convinced to draw me a map that will show me where those men are heading."

But Mrs. Singh's face tells him it won't be as simple as that. It might have been, had she not chosen to come here and ask after his needs.

"Will you tell me what else happened?" he continues. "When those men came here. Your husband is omitting something, something vital."

Mrs. Singh hesitates. It is clear she came here with the express purpose of answering this very question. But the repercussions weigh on her, or perhaps it is her conscience. Thomas reaches out instinctively but then lets drop his hand before it has touched her. Mrs. Singh may not appreciate being touched. He is a foreigner, a man in his bedchamber, his shirt open at the chest. He has no caste.

"Please," he says, and she sniffs at the haze that accompanies the word with interest.

"The men who came to see my husband—they were not just asking for maps. They wanted Mr. Singh to go with them. To lead them where they want to go."

"He was to act as a guide? Because he knows the region?"

"Not just the region, Thomas-babu. He knows the place. My husband was there."

"Where?" he begins to ask. Then it dawns on him what Mrs. Singh is telling him. "Eleven years ago: the first time someone went up into those mountains! The expedition whose steps this new one is retracing—they went to Nepal and found something there. Something they brought back and shipped to England. *And your husband was there!*"

Thomas pauses, breathless; thinks it through. He pictures this Watts coming to the house, trying to cajole Singh into his service.

"I am surprised they did not force him to come along."

"They tried. First, they offered money; then they threatened him; then they beat him. One of them suggested dragging him along in chains. But what good is a guide who wishes to mislead you? Then they found the maps and notes. They are very detailed, you see. They took every scrap of paper they could find. Next I thought they would kill us. Not as a punishment but to erase any trace that they had come. I heard them talk about it. In the end they decided it would leave a bigger trace than if they just went."

Thomas nods. "Yes, that makes sense. If the Company soldiers stationed here found you dead, there'd have been an investigation. This Watts is with the Company but his isn't a Company venture. They are trying to keep it secret. This was when? Three, four weeks ago? What happened next?"

"Mr. Singh was very angry."

"Because they stole from him and beat him?"

"Yes. But also—because part of him *wanted* to go. You see, they were tempting him. They are going climbing. High, high up—perhaps as high as anyone has ever climbed. My husband, he loves the mountains. He may love them more than he loves me. More than the revolution! But he has sworn never to help the sahibs again."

She falls silent at a noise, somewhere in the house, then turns back to him. It occurs to Thomas that surely Mr. Singh must know that she is here, talking to him. Did he send her? But no, she is too independent for that, too intelligent to be a mere messenger. He must respect her too much to interfere. It makes Thomas like the man, despite his prickliness.

"They were tempting him," Mrs. Singh resumes. "They didn't even know it. If they had, then perhaps they would have succeeded. And now, *you* are tempting him. After all, you are just like them. Another sahib with a mission. You, too, will want him to come with you. Already it is eating at his heart."

She waggles her head, a movement Thomas has learned can mean a number of things: approval, acquiescence, acceptance, doubt. Mrs. Singh's husband is not to be changed. Then something new occurs to her and she produces from some fold in her clothing a piece of paper not much bigger than a palm.

"There is something else," she explains. "One of them came back. I think he felt ashamed, at being a thief. He wanted to pay us. He had not many rupees, so he gave us this. My husband tore it up at once."

She hands Thomas a cheque, preprinted by a Bombay bank, now crumpled and ripped into two halves. Sum and signature are in a different pen, a different hand.

"Twenty pounds sterling. A large sum of money. But not so big that it would raise questions. They must carry a whole stack of these, presigned; good as cash."

He is about to hand back the cheque, then glances again at the scrawl of the signature, deciphering the bold double loop of two Os.

"Cooper," he reads.

If Mrs. Singh notices his sudden pallor she does not comment. She may have little practice in interpreting the quirks of pale pink flesh.

[6]

Mrs. Singh wants to go. She has been here long enough, with this stranger in his bedroom; has said what she came to say. Thomas sees all this and yet he stops her; moves around her, to the curtain, blocking off retreat.

"Why tell me all this?" he asks.

"Because my husband wanted to tell you but he would not allow himself to. So I betray him." Again that waggle of the head: mischievous, amused. "Are you married, Thomas-babu?"

The question returns the blood into his cheeks. "Not married—not exactly. But something like that."

"Then you understand."

He shakes his head. "It's different. The Second Smoke took care of all our secrets. Back home, the unsaid drifts on the air. It may be that your way is better after all."

This surprises her; enough so that her eyebrows arch up and her full lips shape a laugh. "Ah, Thomas-babu! Are you sure you are who you say you are?"

"Why do you ask?"

"Because in the stories, you're different. Always angry! You walk through the world with a snarl." She shapes it with her mouth, this snarl, then looks him in the eye: a searching look, as direct as a man's. "Are the stories wrong?"

"Some of them are."

Thomas pauses, aware that this is a nonanswer, designed to hide him from her scrutiny and judgement. Mrs. Singh has fed and clothed him. She made him the gift of a secret.

She deserves better than that.

"All that happened more than ten years ago, Mrs. Singh. I was a boy then." It comes out stiffly, at once pompous and unfeeling, a plaster cast of a phrase. "I have endeavoured to change, Mrs. Singh. You see, all that anger—it came at a price."

"You regret it then? What you did with your friends? Letting the genie out of its bottle?"

"I regret those who died."

"That is good," she replies. And adds, still in the same light, beautiful tones: "We will regret the dead, too, I believe, once it is over and our country is free."

It is only now that Thomas understands that Mrs. Singh is a revolutionary, too.

[7]

Mr. Singh wakes Thomas before dawn.

"Come," he says. The voice is not so much gruff as actively hostile. "Dress."

"Your wife spoke to you."

"Yes. She . . . *confessed*." Singh's lip curls over the word. As Thomas wraps a piece of cotton around his head to hide his mark, he wonders what school chaplain or teacher introduced Singh to the word and forever soured its flavour.

They leave the house through the back door. It is the coolest part of the night, and though the temperature may still equate to a northern English summer's day, Thomas shivers. Mr. Singh walks quickly, furtively, keeping to the shadows. The curfew has not been lifted yet.

"Where are we going?" Thomas asks.

Singh shushes him, runs across an intersection into the shadow of a building, then gestures impatiently for Thomas to follow.

It occurs to Thomas that Singh is leading him to his arrest; that somewhere in his head he has discovered some advantage in giving Thomas up to the authorities. Or perhaps he is jealous. He caught his wife flirting with the sahib. It's nonsense, of course, but people kill each other over nonsense all the time.

All the same, Thomas follows without hesitation. Singh is the link: between the men he is chasing and the thing that happened ten years ago. Without him, Thomas will never learn what it is that really transpired on the banks of the Thames. What he is culpable of. Sometimes he feels he never left school: that dentist's chair in Renfrew's office, where master and pupil peeled back layers of guilt as though they were divesting an onion of its skins—he is sitting in it still. One more peel (two at the utmost) and there'll be no onion left.

Soon it is evident that Singh is leading him not to the town's centre with its governmental buildings and the ugly bulk of a garrison, but to its outskirts. Here the houses are little more than mud huts, leaning on each other, some growing second storeys like boils. Filth lines the alleyways; semiferal dogs lie nose to tail in complex constellations and raise their heads at their approach. The imprint of Empire is weaker here; soldiers are only rarely dispatched to patrol its streets. Singh walks more openly now, if still with a fast, harried gait. He stops before a doorless gateway, as unadorned as all the others. Inside, the sweet smell of coconut pervades, the tang of rotting flowers. In a rough alcove, hewn into the mud, Ganesha hulks cross-legged on his giant mouse. Various offerings lie scattered at his feet.

"A shrine?" Thomas asks, but receives no answer. Instead, Singh steps through a curtain hidden in the gloom into an adjacent room, so small as to be little more than an alcove itself. A lamp has been left here; Singh strikes a match from the box he has brought but finds it won't light. Each fresh attempt reveals a flash of picture. It has been painted in brilliant colours onto a whitewashed section of wall.

At last the lamp is lit, the flame unsteady yet. Its flicker gives life to the figures depicted on the wall. There is a circle of three, bending towards a fourth. The prone one is rendered in black, lying on a curl of dark water. The girl is standing by his head, a companion to either side. Her hair is pale ochre and hangs down to her waist. On her left, a crimson-headed youth, a bowl of water in his hand. On her right, a featureless figure, dark-haired, the side of his face marked by a blotch of dark blue. He is holding a bowl of blood. Four figures, united in puja. Above their heads a storm cloud pelts black rain.

"Our paupers, the casteless, the despised: they come here and pray. The nation means nothing to them; 'home rule' is a term they don't understand. But they have heard a whisper: that the Smoke both sahibs and Brahmin have told them to despise is a weapon; that Kali will dance when the land is dunked in black. Look . . ." Here Singh bends down and lifts a little earthenware plate heaped with dark-grey flower petals, as delicate as moth wings. "From the black poppy fields. They risk their lives stealing them. They chew them, you see: they come here and pray and chew and dream of darkness brought to them by a half-god with white skin."

Thomas hears all this obliquely, as though at a distance. His eyes are on the figures on the wall. In truth, Ramsbottom, the Bombay veterinarian, told him about places like this. But he was not prepared for the raw power of this crude painting. It is as though one of his dreams has been snatched across five thousand miles to be etched onto this miserable wall.

"And what do you dream of, Mr. Singh?" he asks at last, distractedly, aware that the man expects it.

"Order! Trains. Telephones. Sanitation. A government plan against poverty and another against caste discrimination. Religious integration. The national seizure of the poppy fields. If a free India can produce sweets, then we will earn the respect of the whole world. And its credit!"

Singh pauses, as though exhausted by his list of dreams, then rouses himself to new energy.

"Have you come here for this, sir?" He jabs a finger at the wall. "My father once told me that every white man wants to be Jesus."

"Nailed to the cross?"

"Adored! Immortal."

Thomas turns to hide his bitter smile, lest it be misunderstood. It brings his focus back to the painting. As though by itself his finger rises, stops a half inch from the figure whose hair is rendered in a shade of ochre pale as straw.

"What do they call her?"

Singh snorts, then consents to answer. "In Bengali? '*Dumar mar*'—'Mother of Smoke.'"

"And him?"

"Fire-Hair."

"And this bruiser here? The one with the blue mark?"

"Full-Angry." As he says it, dour Mr. Singh surprises himself with something like amusement. His voice takes on a stronger lilt, the English of servants in Mr. Kipling's colourful books. "Maximum raging."

The smile they share is like Smoke, thinks Thomas: a bond forged of flesh not words.

"I am here, Mr. Singh, to find Watts's expedition and to understand what it is he is after. That is all. Once I know, I will return to the tepid skies of England."

Singh studies him and at length extends his hand. They shake like two clubmen who have agreed upon a bet: solemnly, taking pleasure in the formality. Thomas makes his plea while the other man's hand is still in his.

"Will you draw me a map of the place they are heading? And will you tell me what you saw when you first went there?"

Singh answers by freeing himself and leading Thomas back out into the street. Dawn is about to break. Far away, in town, a cannon shot sounds, signalling the end of the curfew. They walk quickly, side by side, as the town wakes around them to the sound of people hawking up their night-time phlegm. Back at the house, Singh stops Thomas by a tug at his sleeve as they enter the workshop.

"I will come with you," he announces. "You will never find them without my help." And then he adds, before Thomas can object or thank him. "It's a printing press, not a bomb. The thing I am hiding. Why I was afraid of arrest. I have been publishing a newsletter."

"Praising telephones, trains, and home rule."

"Why yes, sir," says Singh with a cheerfulness that becomes him. "And wishing the sahibs all to hell."

ENGLISH-LANGUAGE NURSERY RHYME OVERHEARD IN SOUTH
BENGAL, AS SUNG BY TWO NATIVE GIRLS PLAYING A VERSION
OF THE "CLAPPING GAME," FROM ANNA MCINTYRE (ED.),
*AN INDIAN TREASURE CHEST: COLLECTED FOLKTALES AND
IDIOMS OF THE RAJ, IN ENGLISH, HINDI, AND BENGALI.*
CALCUTTA: T. HENDERSON PRESS, MCMVIII.

Fair-face
White-face
Whisker-face
Prune

Rifle, trifle
Toffee, tiffin
Pud-ding
Spoon

Poppy-field
Train-track
Te-le-phone
Loom

Merchant
Vicar
Soldier
Boom!

There were four of them, each of them the son of a most noble house. They knew each other from school—one of those great public schools that so often feature in our children's books, where English boys learn the rules of rugby, cricket, and fair play. They were princes of Empire, you see, waiting for their turn at the mighty wheel of rule; but very young still, almost boys, sowing their wild oats out here in our Raj, where sins of youth are easily hidden. Their passion was not for women, however, nor for arak, nor for betting on horses—it was the mountains that had stolen their hearts. They had climbed, they later told me, all the peaks of Scotland, and had even obtained special permission to spend a summer in the Alps at a time when Europe was off-limits for most Britons. Now they were making forays into the western Himalayas and the Zanskar mountains, staying in the wilderness for weeks at a time.

"I met them in Kashmir. They had just arrived in the region and were looking for a guide. I was, at the time, a proud and faithful servant of the Crown. The British had educated me, albeit by the proxy of a swarthy Tamil schoolmaster who wore tails even in the most sweltering heat and spent his pennies on tinned English cheese imported from Devon. I went on to university in Calcutta, on an imperial scholarship no less, after which our kind rulers provided me with a position as imperial surveyor and cartographer which sent me into the remotest mountain regions of our northern border, with the task of creating topographical maps of military accuracy. In short, the Queen herself was kindly paying me to travel, to imbibe clean mountain air, and to climb!

"I, too, had long caught the climbing bug, you see. I had grown up in Mandi in the northern Punjab and, as a child, had stumbled on an illustrated book in the town library extolling the fortitude of British explorers. Of the many exploits celebrated there, none enthralled me as much as a short chapter devoted to those determined to 'ascend higher than any living man had ascended before and plant the British flag upon peaks that touch the very firmament.' I did not know what a firmament was, but there were mountains at our doorstep, and an officers' mountaineering club at the local garrison that would from time to time employ natives to carry loads for them. I presented myself to the club secretary on the day of my fourteenth birthday and impressed him with my English and my enthusiasm for his fatherland. By the time I left for university, I was an accomplished mountaineer and it was this, along with my university qualification and references, that helped me secure the position.

"Thus, when our four adventurers asked for a guide to take them into the Kashmiri wilderness, it was only natural that people would mention this mountain-mad Sikh known for his exquisite coloured maps and sincere devotion to the Empire. They sought me out and arranged, without the slightest bit of fuss, three months' paid holiday for me, so that I could show them some of my favourite routes and climbs. This alone should have told me something about the power these young men commanded and the reach of their connections. But I was young and flattered and rather in awe of them, and eager to be of service.

"We spent ten weeks in the mountains, supported by half a dozen porters whom I commandeered with the smug arrogance of the white man's favourite pet. Of course, I did not see it like that then. The foursome treated me courteously, even respectfully, and I had fallen in love with the thought that the higher one climbed, the more one could strip away all outward difference, so that on the highest peaks, on the rooftops of this world, I, too, would become an Englishman, smokeless and pale. Once, during a snowstorm that found us halfway up a mountainside, I slipped and fell into a crevasse, and it was only the quick action of one of my companions that saved me. This pleased me more than even the opportunity of saving his life would have done, for he risked much by not cutting the rope that fastened me to him and held me in an exhausted embrace once he had hauled me back across the lip of the crevasse. 'Rum luck,' he muttered, his lips inches from mine, and, 'Nothing broken, eh? Splendid!' For a long time after, these seemed to me the best, the noblest phrases in the whole world.

"I have not told you yet their names. They were Percy; Hounslow; Wyatt; Tulkinghorne. Hounslow was the one who saved me: a shy, pale, girlish man with a very beautiful voice and an uncommon ability to endure physical suffering. Wyatt was tall, wiry, quiet; with an odd and slightly sinister intensity that animated his every movement. He was the only one of the four who would allow himself to smoke from time to time, or at least would allow himself to do so in front of us natives. Tulkinghorne was garrulous, sociable, fond of food. He, too, might have smoked, but I could smell sweets on him quite often, even up at fifteen thousand feet where the air seemed too thin to sustain any passion other than the will to climb. Percy was their leader: not by rank or election but by an inner aristocracy that made him better complexioned and straighter-limbed than his companions; more cautious with his words; wider-ranging—deeper—in his thoughts. A man born aloof because he is better made than anyone else. There was a melancholy to him, and a quiet self-conviction. He and I were the strongest climbers of the lot.

"The season ended, the monsoons came. I returned to my position, consisting of desk work in this portion of the year, though not before my companions had bid me a warm good-bye and showered me with little gifts. It was seven months before I heard from them next. I had expected—or at any rate hoped—to receive a letter announcing a repeat of our exploits in the coming climbing season. What I received instead was a summons, reaching me via telegraph, to present myself at the Palace Hotel in Lucknow on such-and-such a date. My absence had already been cleared with my superiors, I was told. I was to bring climbing gear and cartography materials and would be reimbursed for the train. The telegram—curt even by the standards of that mode of communication—was signed by Percy. It bypassed the formality that was my consent.

"I went, of course. To tell the truth, by the time I had boarded the train, I had forgotten whatever slight offense I may have taken or dismissed it as inconsequential. I arrived wearing my best suit and hat and carrying with me a case filled with my climbing clothes and mapmaking materials. During the packing process it had struck me as strange that I had not been asked to bring any actual maps with me. At the hotel I was greeted by a porter and shown to a room in that part of the hotel that was reserved for native guests. I should have resented this perhaps, but the hotel's entrance hall was so overwhelming in its splendour that I followed the boy gawking like a village fool. On my bed lay a copy of the *Times of London*, only a few weeks out of date and still quite crisp in the fold. I handled it like a relic and read it religiously, assuming that it had been placed there by one of my travel companions because it contained a clue as to their intentions. It was only later that I learned that the hotel routinely collected and ironed newspapers that had been cast aside by the better sort of guest and turned them into welcoming presents for the likes of me.

"I met my companions at dinner that evening, a meal that they irritatingly and inaccurately referred to as 'tiffin.' They were in a buoyant, celebratory mood. Tulkinghorne and Hounslow were already quite drunk and continued to drink throughout the meal. Wyatt's intensity, too, was leavened by both joy and gin, though he remained reticent, observant, quiet. Only Percy was entirely sober and dignified, though he made sure not to dampen the others' spirits. It was he who explained the reason for their celebrations. After months of lobbying they had finally secured all the paperwork they had been waiting for; their expedition had been given the go-ahead.

"'Paperwork?' I remember asking. 'Expedition to where?'

"'Nepal. The central Himalaya. We will climb mountains no white man has set foot on before!'

"In his dignified excitement he seemed to include me in that designation and I felt a strange mixture of resentment and pride.

"'Look here, Singh, it is good that you've come. The viceroy wants you to make maps of the area—accurate, professional maps—only we can't be seen to be doing so; His Highness the King of the Gorkha would not approve.' And, indulging in a moment of boasting not at all typical for him, he added: 'My cousin is the British representative in Kathmandu; he interceded for us.'

"'Are we explorers then, or spies?'

"The table went quiet when I asked the question.

"'Explorers,' Percy at once assured me. 'But we must document our journey for posterity. We shall publish a book. One day, your maps will be pored over by every English schoolboy, Singh. We rather thought you would jump at the chance.'

"They excused themselves after coffee and promised we would discuss all the details in the coming days and weeks. That night, I gathered, they were going out to celebrate. There was a furtive, adolescent excitement about this excursion that suggested to me a visit to a brothel or some similar act of debauchery. Tulkinghorne drank off his brandy, dug in his pocket, and produced a cigarette that he offered for me to sniff. It did not smell of tobacco. He winked, stuck the cigarette rakishly behind his ear, and said, 'Englishmen don't smoke, Singh. Only once in a while—they bloody well want to!' Percy alone shot me a parting glance as they walked out of the hotel's dining room, communicating both an apology towards me and indulgence towards his friends. Some ritual of bonding had to be performed.

"Several weeks later we set off for the Nepalese border. The king did not want us anywhere near his capital, and so the Central Himal had been suggested as the realm of our exploration. We only had very crude maps of this area and no real idea what to expect. In truth there was no reason to believe that these mountains were any more interesting or spectacular than the giants of the western Himalayas, of which we had been able to summit only the tiniest of fractions. The allure lay simply in the unknown. When we crossed the border, a military band played on the Indian side, and a regiment of soldiers welcomed us on the other. We were escorted to the foothills of the Himalayas the way a pupil is marched to the headmaster by a kindly teacher, lending him strength on this slow march towards punishment or praise, and making sure he does not escape. Once in the foothills, though, they set us free. We hired porters and guides, bought provisions, and headed for the highland.

"It was, truth be told, a rather arduous journey. The highland villages that we slept in were unspeakably squalid; and the porters, less trained in regarding the sahibs as gods, were cantankerous and slow, interested only in their wages. Only two or three men who hailed from the mountains rather than the hills—Buddhists, with dark, sunken almond eyes and big cheeks burned near black by the mountain sun—seemed to comprehend our fascination with climbing. Though I could communicate with them only in gestures and a handful of words where my rusty Hindi coincided with whatever language it was they spoke, they helped us immeasurably in setting a route. We walked along a deep gorge cut by a raging river. It split the mountains in two, forming a trench so deep its bottom was a ribbon of white water, spuming over rocks. Rope bridges crisscrossed the gorge wherever it narrowed, swinging perilously when the wind caught them. Below was a world of jungle and water; above us a world of rock and ice.

"The expedition was not doing well. Too late did we discover that to travel somewhere without a definite plan meant to flounder, to waste time, to be morally eroded by indecision. If my companions had set off filled with boisterous confidence, they were subdued now, and irritable. In all their previous exploits, they had always tested their mettle in known landscapes, taking advantage of good maps and chasing a particular peak. Here, surrounded by some of the highest mountains anyone had ever seen, they found themselves at a loss. Percy, keen to fight this malaise of indecision, soon set his sights on a giant that my crude triangulation suggested was more than twenty-six thousand feet in altitude. Nobody, of course, had ever climbed as high as that, but Percy argued that even the attempt would be invaluable for science, for we should learn, firsthand, the effects of oxygen deprivation on the human organism. In his heart of hearts, perhaps, he believed that any mountain would yield under sheer force of his will, and that he was destined to be the first man to stand with his feet on earth and his head up in the stars.

"It came to naught. We hiked to the foot of the mountain, then spent an exhausting two weeks studying it from every angle only to conclude that any attempt at ascent was suicide. Frustrated, we turned back.

"To the east, on the far side of the gorge, there was another giant that, from the peak of some of the higher hills, we had already marked from afar. This mountain, too, towered over its companions and reached for the very sky. Broad-browed, *massive,* it formed the central piece of a range that appeared to form a semicircle around a hidden valley. When we asked the highland men about access to this valley, they at once informed us that it was inaccessible. There was something to the haste of their answer that made us suspicious. We pressed them, offering them food, then money, and at long last learned that there existed a secret pass but that the valley was off-limits; that the mountain was a pregnant goddess grown sick in her womb; that any attempt to climb her was sheer folly. Under no circumstances were we to go there. Nobody would guide us. We would incur the mountain's curse.

"We set off at once, of course. What self-respecting Englishman does not at once start running at the merest mention of a curse? Running towards it, that is: his tongue hanging out like a dog's. I was as bad as my companions. There must be gold in those mountains; a lost civilisation; El Dorado, displaced from the jungles of the Americas and hidden behind superstitious myth. It took further bribes and threats to get even one of the men to take us to the unmarked goat pass that offered the only way into the hidden valley. He came with us as far as the foot of the path.

"'The snows will come soon,' he warned us.

"'Not yet, not yet,' we dismissed him. And, carrying all our own equipment for the first time since we entered Nepal, we set off, singing a stately Purcell hymn, I recall, that Tulkinghorne had provided with rather more earthy lyrics: four sahibs, and the spiritual mongrel that was I, half servant, half companion, singing loudest of them all.

"We ran into trouble almost at once. It was overcast, the high pass so snow-mired that it was almost impossible to traverse. Near its summit, Hounslow started growing sick. I don't know if it was the altitude that had crept into his blood or some infection or other; or if his mind had simply started to unknit. He grew weak, disorientated; wandered aimlessly, and started speaking to himself. At times he would stop in his tracks and, bending over, listen to the whistling of his lungs for long minutes at a time; would laugh or start babbling; or lie down and bury his face in the dirt. Eventually, he stopped walking altogether.

"By then, the pass had led us down into another river gorge, so narrow and sunless that it lay entirely barren. According to the highland man's crude map, the valley opened near its mouth. We were within a few leagues of this opening when Hounslow, midstride, lay down flat on the ground and closed his eyes. He was not asleep but refused to answer any questions; moaned pitiably when we tried to shift him. Smoke would drift up from him, but even this was listless, weak. The man was spent.

"We could not leave him in the wilderness. Percy ordered Tulkinghorne to stay with him while the rest of us pushed on. Tulkinghorne refused. Why should he, a white man, play nursemaid and forgo his shot at glory if there was a golliwog ready at hand? It was not the crudeness of his question that shocked me but the coolness of Percy's response: the feat of their ascent would be diminished in value if they could not also produce a good map or at least an evocative artistic impression of the secret valley they were about to enter. None of the Englishmen had any artistic talent; while I had completed many a pencil sketch of the ridge outlines and mountain aspects, along with some topographical drawings of the land we had covered. In short, Percy agreed that Tulkinghorne had a right to the climb by virtue of his race; but my expertise was functionally more important. In their protracted argument neither of them as much as looked at me.

"And still Tulkinghorne refused to stay. To my surprise it was Wyatt who formulated a compromise. Since we were only a few miles to the valley, we would carry Hounslow to its edge. There, I would have leisure to sketch the area and visually document my companions' ascent from below, while at the same time looking after Hounslow's needs. I was tempted to object—I was by far the stronger climber than Tulkinghorne and would be missed on the mountainside—but a look from Percy shut me up.

"It took us two or three hours to reach the great plateau encircled by a wall of ice and rock. It was a broken, barren landscape, full of puddles of water and giant boulders, a rubble field of the gods. Ahead stood the giant that had roused Percy's imagination. Up close, the mountain's sheer size was overwhelming. I saw at once that it would be near impossible to summit it: its ridge lines were too long and broken to offer a plausible route. The air was so thin even down there in the valley that it felt like we were breathing through straws, laboriously sucking at oxygen that was not there. Up high, the body would simply begin to die.

"There was a more direct route up. Flowing down the face of the mountain like a great white road was the icy tongue of a glacier. Ahead, on the plateau, one could see where its blunt end had displaced earth and rock: it had churned the earth and was cleaving it, inch by inch, through the sheer weight of its frozen motion. Avalanche lines marked the glacier's flanks, where great cornices of snow had broken off the rock above and showered down. Near the peak, the glacier seemed to fold itself under a massive, sickle-shaped ridge, like a tear tucked into its duct, grown plump and pendulous with its slow grief.

"Percy, Wyatt, and Tulkinghorne left me the next morning. A climb like the one they had in mind takes weeks of preparation: the area needs to be scouted, various routes assessed; the lower portions of the route have to be secured with ropes. But a sort of madness had taken hold of my companions, a greed for some measure of success, which led them to disregard the most elementary rules of mountaineering. Time was running out. Soon the monsoon snows would clog up the pass we had traversed and strand us here. The only plausible route was the glacier, though it meant gambling against the risk of avalanche. In the morning light, the glacial tongue looked dull and devoid of contours, a blank within the landscape, like a spot of blindness in your vision that grows larger the closer you approach.

"The three friends headed towards it like condemned men rushing to their fate, each man walking for himself, his chin tucked, head bowed down against the wind. I watched them all morning. At my feet, Hounslow lay delirious, now quiet and shut-in, now raving in his high, melodic voice. I offered him food but he would not eat. From the way he moved I wondered whether he was paralysed in his left arm and leg. At dusk, I dragged him into my tent and hugged him like a wife, trying to warm him while he twitched and jabbered through the night.

"They started climbing early the next morning. I could see them quite clearly, though by now they were little more than specks of colour against the glacier's great white void. At times, their progress seemed steady, even rapid. Then some topographical feature, invisible at this distance, would stop them in their tracks for hours, before their steady progress resumed. At nightfall, I saw them put up their tent. A light flickered—they will have tried to melt some snow, so they could drink—carving them out of the gloom: three figures, a scrap of fabric like a lampshade, the shoal of ice upon which they seemed adrift, ahead and above, castaways on an ocean of night.

"The next morning, clouds sat low in the valley, hiding the mountain. When they finally lifted, I could not immediately see the climbers. I had not heard any avalanches or ice falls—the noise would have been deafening— so I assumed they were simply hidden by a fold within the rock. It was only when the angle of the late-afternoon sun turned the glacier into pure clear ice that I saw something I could not at once make sense of. High up, in that transparent frozen river, there hung a gossamer thread of something dark, leading from the surface down inside the glacier like a broken vein. Was it a flaw within the ice? A rope dangling deep into a crevasse? A frozen trail of blood? The last thought seemed so outlandish that I dismissed it at once. Nonetheless, the story of the goddess's sick womb rose up in me unbidden and took some effort to suppress. Then the sun dropped behind the mountains at my back and the glacier transformed once more into a dull white blank. That night, no light illuminated the mountainside. Whatever shoal my companions had drifted on had sunk.

"By the start of the third day, it was clear to me that all three of them were dead. There was no sign of them on the mountain. My thoughts turned to the practical problem of how I would manage to carry Hounslow to safety. I considered turning my backpack into a sort of harness in which the sick man could sit but at once realised that I would quite simply not manage. My options were simple. I could either stay with him and hope for a partial recovery, or abandon him to death.

"It is odd and perhaps telling that in the two days that followed my every thought was dedicated to this decision rather than to the death of three men who, for a long time, had been to me something very close to friends. Perhaps I shut out any grief from the necessity of staying focussed on the task of survival. Or perhaps I felt a certain satisfaction at the accident that had befallen the three men, for I had been sorely slighted in my pride. I cannot be sure. What I do know is that I lingered. Hounslow, I was certain, would not recover. But somehow I could not accept this and waited by his side, forcing water on him every few hours and trying to feed him soup. An unpleasant smell was rising from him at this point, as of rotting fruit. I held my nose and nursed him and told myself that I must let him go.

"On the morning of the sixth day since our arrival in the valley, I was finally willing to leave. As I surveyed the cirque of mountains one last time, I saw a figure traversing the valley, already halfway between the glacier and myself. It walked unsteadily but with determined step; would stop and kneel at the puddles of black water dotting the landscape and lower its face to drink only to rise again and stumble on. I set off at once to meet whoever it was, not so much overjoyed as awed by his appearance, but lost sight of him in the boulder-strewn land. After two or three hours, I gave it up and returned to my camp, only to find that the figure, too, had almost reached it.

"I was unsurprised to see that it was Percy. Perhaps I had recognised his gait, or some detail of his clothing; perhaps I simply had a superstitious faith in his superiority over the other men. I ran towards him, my arms spread out in an unconscious gesture of embrace. Percy walked with a rucksack heavy on his back; his face was frostbitten and dark. His own arms did not rise towards me—perhaps he was too tired—and his broken lips shaped no greeting. We walked side by side back into camp. There, I made tea and gave him some of the dried meat we had been living on. He ate and drank greedily, then crawled into my tent to sleep.

" 'Wyatt?' I asked him, though I already knew the answer. 'Tulking-horne?'

"Percy paused, his legs still outside, the rest of him in the gloom of the tent. After a minute or more—long enough that I thought he had fallen asleep—his snort of laughter reached me, made ugly by the dryness of his mouth and throat.

" 'Three men went up the mountain, Singh. Only one came down.'

"I noticed that he had taken his rucksack with him into the tent and lay with his arms wrapped awkwardly around it.

"We spent one more day in the valley, so that Percy could regain some modicum of strength. He barely spoke to me all day and grew attentive to my own prattle only once, when I explained to him my anxiety about Hounslow. Now that there were two of us, we might be able to get him out, but it would mean abandoning virtually all of our gear and taking nothing along other than some food and water. Percy did not interrupt me, but once I had finished, he said simply: 'We will leave him behind.'

"'We cannot,' I protested. Then, surprising myself by the strength of my feeling: 'I won't.'

"This time Percy did not reply. I made preparations, throwing away all that was nonessential of my gear and eyeing curiously the bag that Percy had kept close to him ever since returning. It wasn't as bulky as it had been when he set off up the mountain but seemed to contain some considerable weight. It was inconceivable that in his state he would be able to carry both this bag and help me with Hounslow, for whom I had constructed a stretcher from tent fabric and poles.

"The problem had resolved itself by morning. Hounslow was dead. It was I who found him: not in his tent, but some fifteen steps beyond it, though he had long since lost the ability to walk. His skin and clothes were covered in fine yellow Soot. There was something about the position of the body—the outstretched arms, the tucked-up legs—as well as bruising on his cheek and neck that suggested violence. Of course it was possible that he had crawled there then experienced some sort of seizure, and thrashed around in such a manner as to injure himself before passing out and dying. But the marks in the dust around him implied a body that had been dragged. What shocked me most, I suppose, was not the thought that Percy had murdered his boyhood friend but that he placed so little value on my opinion that he had not bothered to mask his tracks more effectively.

"We did not bury Hounslow, nor did I confront Percy. Was it fear that restrained me, or the servility that had been bred into me from the day I was born? Englishmen don't smoke. Indeed I could find no spot on Percy's clothing. Perhaps he had done his deed naked, or fortified by sweets. Perhaps Hounslow's dying anguish simply roused no passion in him at all. That morning, at any rate, he simply shouldered his heavy rucksack and bid me take the lead. I obliged and led him back across the already snow-mired pass. He remained weak from his ordeal but kept pace well enough. Now and again I caught him watching me, weighing me up. I wondered then whether he still had his pistol, or whether he had lost it during the ascent.

"Ten days or so later, we recrossed the border into India. This time there was no brass band to greet us. Percy commandeered horses the moment we came across our first military patrol, and asked directions to the closest town with a train stop and a telegraph line. We spoke little throughout this period. The generous, sensitive leader of men I had once known and deeply admired was quite gone. He had been replaced by a haughty, nervous, calculating man who observed me like I was an insect. But perhaps it was I who had changed and not him; it was as though my entire upbringing was slowly being cut away from me like a skin I had outgrown. Soon now, it would be time for me to moult.

"In Gorakhpur, on the afternoon before he was to take a specially commissioned train first to Lucknow then on to Bombay, Percy asked me to meet with him early the next day, so he could bid me good-bye and 'settle up with me for my loyal service.' I understood at once that he wished to murder me. That night, I noticed a guard outside my door. It wasn't a regular serviceman or sepoy, but rather a fellow guest in civilian clothing whose manner and language suggested a harmless Muslim trader in horses—had it not been for the way he left his own door ajar and monitored each of my movements.

"Unsurprised by any of this, growing angrier, more jaded by the hour, I waited until midnight before approaching the little window I had made a show of opening hours before. My guard did not monitor it, for there was a sheer fifteen-foot drop outside, and another man stationed at street level. But it was not the street to which I headed but the roof. A man without my climbing experience would have stood no chance at all. I, however, leapt up the wall of the house like a goat, slippery though it was from the constant rains. Once arrived, I ran from roof to roof until the rooflines got so low that I could reach the ground with the smallest of hops.

"I left the town long before our dawn meeting and headed not home but to a village in the southern Punjab where I had distant relatives. There, in the poverty and grime of my great-aunt's yard, my rebirth was completed and the revolutionary born. I listened to the stories of the villagers, about the grandfathers executed in the Great Mutiny, and the mothers and sisters who died in British segregation camps during the Pune plague epidemic, died of shame, that is, having been strip-searched in their own homes and carted off like animals. There, too, I found a little library of secret texts and read the theories of Marx and Herder, of Bakunin, Tilak, and Kaka Baptista. For a while, I even changed my name.

"Then the news came to us, of a great change across the ocean, of Britain going up in Smoke. We missed the moment to rise then: we waited and we blinked, and when our eyes were open again, the Empire was back, only its titles and leaders had changed. The Company owned us; religion and caste divided us; illiteracy and ignorance condemned us to be slaves.

"As for Percy, I heard nothing further. He sailed to England, I assumed, hugging his rucksack and whatever it was he'd carried down the mountain. From the way he cradled it, you might have thought he carried down a lover or a friend.

"I can only hope that he is dead."

Holtby House, the ninth of October.

Dear Miss,

I opened your letter which was addresst to the Relatives of Mr. Philip Percy.
No Relatives live here now. Their house has been ceased by Law and it is now
home to twenty families, all honest faulk. The others said don't answer the
letter, but with your currier waiting for answer and offring money I see no
harm in it. I was the cook when the Percys still lived here, before. Young Mr.
Philip returned here from travels just before the 2nd Smoke. He was mighty
changed. We servents were not allowed to speak to him because he was
melankly. When the Smoke came, he hung himself by his Necktie. That is
all I know. I hope your currier will now give me the coins he promised.

Yours faithfully,
Marie McMurtry
Holtby House

[Postscript is Soot-smudged and illegible.]

[1]

Mr. Singh does not finish telling Thomas the story of the first expedition until the morning they see the mountains for the first time. He rations it out deliberately, retracing its outlines over and over again, filling in details, correcting little slips of memory, so that the story, too, becomes a kind of companion, slow of foot and somewhat lumbering, relaxing into itself only in the evenings, when camp has been made. Whenever Thomas wants to rush it along, Singh simply ignores him. The two have developed a comfort with one another that is not to be confused with friendship. Singh distrusts Englishmen, not so much temperamentally as by profession. Since the day of their meeting, they have not shared any Smoke.

Their progress is steady. First, they travel by train across the Bihari border, then by bicycle across the great plain of the poppy plantations. This year's crop is coming into bloom; soon their seedpods will be bled, their latex processed. The fields stretch out in slender pools like winter lochs, black to the eye. In between this web of dark pools lie vast stretches of yellowed wasteland, marking previous years' fields. The poppy leeches the ground and leaves it barren. The plain is slowly being turned to dust. The great processing plants to which the spring harvest will be shipped lie many hundred miles to the south, factory fortresses under constant guard. Up here, the fields are patrolled by platoons of Company soldiers. They move from village to village, requisitioning food and board, restless and ravenous like itinerant kings.

As much as it is possible, the two cyclists keep well away from the fields. Even so they cannot avoid scrutiny altogether and, halfway across the plain, they are confronted by a mounted platoon of sepoys, guns strapped to their shoulders. The one white man amongst them, the officer, is a boy of nineteen with fat, sunburned cheeks and a moustache like the curl of a pen. Thomas talks to him only, ignoring his dust-plastered men, and watches the young officer's manner change no sooner have they exchanged their "how do you dos." The Company man inquires politely after their identities and purpose of travel, then quickly shifts to small talk.

"Do you require an escort?" he asks when they have exhausted the weather ("infernally hot"), the deficiencies of the local beer ("like spinsters' piss"), and the disgusting lack of "turn" in the Lucknow wicket that rewards fast bowling over finesse. "Or horses, perhaps?"

"It shan't be necessary, thank you. The bicycles are easier to take along on the train."

The officer lingers a moment longer, flustered by his inability to find the right parting words—heartfelt but not overly emotional, and appropriate to the witnessing ears of his subalterns—then simply shakes Thomas's hand and remounts. As the soldiers move out of sight, Singh lets out a nervous laugh.

"Thomas-ji! I thought we were done for, I really did. No travel papers, no reason to be here, so close to the fields, and your face paint dripping down your cheek. But he did not even want to see your passport! All you had to say was 'Company business; no grave secret here but a little sensitive all the same.' He simply took your word for it!"

Thomas's reply is terse. "It's *how* I said it. My whole country is built on this, placing a man the moment he opens his mouth."

Thinking: *We wear our accents like spoken marks of caste.*

[2]

And everywhere they go—on the roads with their English way signs; in the gestures of ablution the casteless perform when bursting into Smoke, marrying Hindu supplication with the sign of the cross; in abject villages that have not seen an English face in years but fly a bleached Company banner over the local revenue collector's hut—Empire is there: squatting on the land like one of those long-limbed insects that spends its life walking the surface of a vast and murky pond, spread-legged, busy, ignorant of the rich life gathering beneath its feet. It carries guns and money, but above all it is armed with an idea: that of good and evil, high and low, as it finds it written on the skin, both in complexion and in Smoke. Smoke came to India only a few years after the British; Empire and Smoke are fused at the hip. What then is Empire? A mercantile scheme hiding behind a messianic whisper.

The rule of starched shirts.

As they pass through yet another village and are beseeched by beggars and petitioners, are greeted by landowners and sized up by sullen youths, Thomas formulates the thought out loud.

Singh resists it.

"Starched shirts? Starched kurtas, starched dhotis," he intones grimly and somewhat didactically, as though quoting from a book. "We collaborated with the British: our Walīs and maharajas did, our priests and merchants, the rich and the educated. Smoke and Empire did for them what it did for your own rulers: confirm them in their specialness." He pauses, places an accusatory finger on his own chest. "As it did for myself."

Thomas lets him savour his moment of self-denunciation. He is all too familiar with its pain, its secret pleasure.

"Jagat," he says at last, using for the first time this intimate form of address. "Please be careful with your anger. It will swallow you up."

Singh waggles his head in ironic agreement. "Yessir. Say—are you some kind of expert on the subject?"

The smile they share is like a secret pact.

[3]

Two days later the fields and villages stop and they enter a heavily forested area, half jungle, half swamp. The paths grow smaller and smaller until they are forced to dismount and leave their bicycles behind. Singh keeps consulting one of the maps he has brought. On occasion he will stop and listen, raising his hand in warning.

"What is it? Border guards?"

"Tiger. These jungles are famous for them."

"You are having me on." When Singh does not reply, Thomas adds: "How far to the border?"

"We crossed some hours ago. Welcome to Nepal, Sahib."

"I thought Nepal meant mountains."

"Yes, mountains. First jungle, then hills, then at last . . . Do you know what a yak is, Thomas-ji? Or a thar?"

"No."

"How about a yeti?"

"No."

"Ah, what wonders you shall see, Sahib! Unless you get eaten by a tiger first, of course."

[4]

The "hills" turn out to be steep, overgrown cliffs that rise, so Singh tells him, to close to six thousand feet. Despite this, foliage covers them all the way to the top. Here and there, the local peasants have contrived to hew terraced rice fields into the terrain. Singh charges up the slope as though he is walking in the plain. Thomas huffs and puffs behind.

When they meet the first locals, Singh relates to them the agreed-upon story. He and the sahib are part of the expedition that passed through a few weeks previously. The men are traders and speak passable Hindi as well as their caste tongue. They have heard of the white men's trek into the mountains and of the special permission they hold from the king. It does not occur to them to ask for paperwork—who can say whether they can read, and if so in what languages?—and rather than sending for the nearest military garrison, they instead confirm Singh's map, taking comfort in the level of detail the strangers possess about the terrain and about the expedition they are chasing. They also agree to reprovision them, albeit at a price that Singh haggles over for a good hour.

"You are their first white man," he tells Thomas, amused. "And already they know it is their sacred duty to rip you off."

[5]

A few days later they finally catch sight of the mountains. The weather has been overcast, the air thick and hazy. But that morning they wake to brilliant sunshine, and when, at midday, they claim the next hilltop, there they are, walling off the horizon.

The sight stops Thomas in his tracks; silences him, his eyes on the rock face, the snowcapped peaks, yoking earth to sky. The wind is blowing ice off the tops, unfurling it in thin, long banners. Thomas turns his head east and west but finds no gap in the jagged wall. The whole world ends here. He tries to speak but finds his mouth is dry. *Awe:* the sensation of standing face-to-face with divinity. The Smoke that seeps out of him is a colour he has never seen before.

When he can speak again, he asks, "Which one is ours?"

"That one, over there."

Singh has to guide Thomas's outstretched finger with his own, direct his line of sight.

"Are you sure? It does not seem so very big. This one's bigger."

"That's because it's closer to us," Singh replies, a little scornful, and adds, as though the information will help Thomas assemble a sense of scale, "The snowline is at sixteen and a half thousand feet. That's where the real climbing starts."

As they eat their lunch, sitting shoulder to shoulder, facing the mountains, Singh tells the last of his long story. He tells of Hounslow's death and Percy's betrayal, of his flight to the Punjabi village and his growing hatred for the Empire—but his face is full of laughter, his eyes wet not with hate but with joy.

"What is it?" Thomas asks, unnerved.

"Nothing. I'm happy. I'm home."

And, mechanically, he, the revolutionary Marxist, performs the gesture of ablution as a jet of blue Smoke squirts from his open collar, placing raw yearning in that "home."

[6]

Soon it is as though Thomas is walking inside Singh's tale. It is all just as he has described. *There*—bounding the horizon—are the mountains, swallowing the morning and afternoon sun. *Here* is that deep canyon cut by the glacial river below, the rope bridges that bind the two cliffsides at a preposterous height. They pass through a series of squalid villages; are beset by local children who will follow them for hours at a time. When they cross the gorge on one of the bridges, walking gingerly and holding on to the guide rope for dear life, the children run after them laughing, showering them with greetings and questions, with laughter and pine cones, setting the bridge swinging from side to side.

It is only when Thomas and his guide veer onto the goat pass that is to take them to the hidden valley that the children finally melt away. They see their first thar, standing high on a wall that seems too sheer to offer footing, chewing some shrub and watching them from afar. As they near the high point of the pass—trudging through snow for the first time in their travels—Thomas becomes aware of a weakness inside him, a dizziness and disorientation. His breath is a whistle in his lungs. His legs are made of lead.

"The altitude," Singh explains. "It has slipped into your blood."

"Does one die from it?" Thomas asks, only half jesting.

"Some grow accustomed. Some do not." Singh shrugs as though the price asked by the mountains is not for him to haggle over. "Come now, carry on. This is not a good place to rest."

[7]

They make it over the pass and into a lifeless gorge filled only with rock and dust. The mountains crowd around them now; the high valley they are seeking must be near. They rest for a day, making sure to remain in the shadow of rocks in case the expedition has posted sentries. By now, they have found their first traces of the men who came before: food tins; the carcasses of two butchered thars; an empty cannister topped by a valve that provides no clue as to what it once contained. The words COOPER EXPEDITIONS are stencilled on its base.

The two men pass the time dozing, sharing memories: of family life, of youth. The one thing they don't address is what awaits them in the valley—what it is they came here to do. The landscape dwarfs them, leeches significance out of their plans and resolutions. It would be easy to acquiesce in obliteration. Lammergeier circle high above. The mountain Buddhists, Singh has told him, cut their dead to pieces and feed them to the birds. Thomas entertains the thought until he dozes off and sees himself with a knife bent over Charlie. Peeling back that freckled face. It jolts him to his feet.

"Let's go," he wakes Singh. "We've wasted enough time."

"It's the middle of the night."

"The moon's out. We can see just fine. And won't be visible ourselves."

It is only when they are back on the trail that Thomas notices his dizziness has passed.

[8]

The expedition camp is placed at the far end of the plateau, near the glacier's base. They see it first by its own lights: petroleum lamps blinking on in tents, turning them into lanterns. The moon is gone, but dawn is slowly creeping into the valley. For now the mountains are a starless darkness reaching high into the sky. When the first light comes, it flows in weak and sickly around this wall of mountains. It is all just as Singh has described it: here, the wide, barren plain dotted by waterholes and rocks; there, the great cirque of mountains, impossible in their magnitude. Up close, their relative scale can at last be discerned. One towers above all others: Percy's mountain; now theirs. The glacial tongue pours down its face like a frozen river. In the weak morning light, its white is dull, impenetrable; the colour of blindness. Down in the valley, churned earth marks the glacier's end. Beyond it stands a field of tents. Thomas counts more than two dozen. He wonders how many men share each tent.

"Did the villagers say how many porters the sahibs hired?"

"'Many, many.' They hired mountain people, mostly; they sent for them from up in the north. They and the hill men don't really talk."

"They must be paying them well if they are here despite the mountain's 'curse.' What are those animals over there that look like woolly cows?"

"I told you that you would see yaks. They must have used them for transport."

"This many people need a lot of food. They must have a team of hunters that head back into the gorge periodically."

"Then we aren't safe where we are." Singh studies the terrain. "Over there, between those rocks. We will be hard to see there."

They move towards the spot Singh has indicated. Its twin boulders hide them from two sides but also make it hard for them to observe the camp. Thomas is about to suggest they move closer when Singh produces a pair of binoculars. He helps Thomas clamber to the top of the larger of the two boulders, then shoots up effortlessly himself. There they lie flat on their stomachs, taking it in turns to study the expedition camp through the binoculars.

"I count seven, no, eight Englishmen. And some thirty porters. And look, Singh, there are people on the mountain—they have built a smaller camp higher up. There's a rope and pulley system connecting the two."

"It's not a climbing party. It's an army. Laying siege. Hewing a bloody staircase into the mountain." Singh seems to think this is unsporting.

"Can you see where they are climbing? Are they here for the summit?"

"Hard to say. They have put in fixed ropes in the difficult places, and ladders. And I think that's a third camp, over there. And look, beneath that sickle ridge—they have marked something with a flag. A crevasse, maybe."

Thomas lets his naked eye roam up the mountainside and finds the great sickle shape Singh is indicating. "How high is that?"

"Hard to say from here. Twenty-one, twenty-two thousand feet? Maybe more."

The numbers seem impossible. "Has anyone ever climbed that high?"

Singh waggles his head. "Climb, yes. But not *work*. I think they have some sort of tool up there. I can see the blink of something made of metal—something substantial. Imagine carrying that up! And there are men working there now—they must have slept on the mountain. Ah, they are heading down."

[9]

In the course of the day it is becoming increasingly obvious that the men who slept beneath the sickle ridge are not only coming down but are carrying something, something important. Whatever it is, it is not particularly large—the size of an adult torso perhaps—and has been wrapped into some kind of sheeting, before being strapped with ropes to a climber's back. Climbers from the lower camp struggle up to meet the man thus burdened and take the parcel off him. Two or three times they load it onto a sort of sled—something like a wheelbarrow without wheels—and lower it on a rope down a particularly steep passage. The climbers are struggling, taking frequent breaks; one man has lain down in the snow and is not getting up.

And still their precious treasure is threading its way down the mountain. Soon, it is in reach of the first of the pulley systems set up between the various camps. Through the binoculars Thomas can see the man receiving the wrapped parcel quite clearly. Bundled into layers of scarfs and hats though he is, there can be no doubt that he is an Englishman. It's in the quality of his movements; in his bulky boots and the many layers of chequered tweed; in the flash of blond beard that emerges when he pulls aside his scarf to shout something. When his companions squat to rest, he alone sits on his rump. One has to go halfway around the world to learn that something as natural as the act of sitting is not natural at all but bred into us from childhood. Thomas learned it aboard a long procession of third-class train carriages on his way up the subcontinent, pretending to be an English pauper; he sat in the filth while everyone else squatted on their haunches, ringing him, watching his cowled and painted face, tasting his Smoke.

Midday—the binoculars still clutched to his face—Thomas drifts off into a kind of half sleep. It's the altitude perhaps, or the memory of the long journey from Pondicherry across much of Hindustan; that half-pleasant, half-panicked feeling of being lost, adrift, unknown and unknowing. There are dreams that are like that, but dreams are not dusty; do not humiliate you with diarrhoea; nor speak at you in half a dozen different tongues. In dreams, old loved ones come to visit you, along with old enemies. In dreams you are never that *alone*.

When Thomas comes to the sun is dipping in the west. His first sensation is one of brightness; the haze has lifted, and light has filled the valley from behind. The binoculars are still in his fist and a mighty wind is roaring down the mountains. Singh is standing next to him, high up on the rock.

It's this last fact that fully shocks Thomas awake. He looks up, sees Singh leaning hard into the wind. His scarf has unfurled and flies out behind him like a flag, or a leash against which he strains. Thomas shouts at him, cursing his incaution, worried that they will be spotted with him standing thus exposed. Then Thomas catches sight of what brought Singh to his feet. A moment later, he, too, stands up and leans his weight into the wind.

Ahead, the mountain has transformed under the angle of the sun. Its soft outlines have been given lineament and focus, its ridges and cracks been chiselled in by light and shade; the sickle ridge high on its flank freshly scored and festooned in boils of ice. The ice itself has grown translucent and glows in shades of green and blue.

Lower down, the bulk of the glacier, too, is soaking up the sun. Where before it was uniform and dull, a blank within the folds of rock, it now flows luminous and contoured, broken into waves and jagged shards at its peripheries and bulging into convex smoothness at the centre like a single drop of water of astounding depth.

But within this smoothness, suspended in the centre of this *depth*, the sun finds something else: a dark web of roots threading the whole glacier. It is a capillary system drawn by a fine-nibbed pen, forked and re-forked a thousand times near the glacier's rounded base, but fusing and thickening on its journey upwards towards the narrow of the glacier's neck, until its myriad branches resolve themselves into a single vein of black that—at the foot of that sickle ridge—pours itself past the smooth lip of a crevasse, down into the ice and rock.

It is like an interior organ, Thomas thinks, *a heart or a lung, threaded in veins, inked in by cancer,* and at once vows never to eat offal again. He listens for it but cannot hear the mountain's heartbeat, the taking in of its breath. The locals warned Singh, all those years ago. The mountain is sick: down in its womb.

He had not considered that it might be giving birth.

Thomas shakes off the thought and forces himself back into a crouch, then reaches up and tugs Singh down beside him. The binoculars are back on his eyes. It seems they have not been noticed. The whole camp is on their feet, facing the glacier; in dread, not in prayer. The nameless thing they hauled down the mountain must have reached them by now, but Thomas can see no sign of cheer or celebration. An eerie silence reigns: the wind would carry any voices but only carries its own rage.

Then the sun slips behind the western peaks and dullness returns to the valley. The men in the camp return to their chores. Dinner is being cooked.

"Where are you going?" Singh asks, when he sees Thomas slide down the rock and prepare to set off.

"There—into the camp. It'll be dark soon. A good time to snoop around."

"That's madness. We must be patient. Observe from afar."

"Haven't you heard, Mr. Singh? Patience is not my strong suit." Thomas waits until Singh has slid down next to him before he resumes. "They brought something down that mountain, Jagat. I need to know what it is."

[10]

He waits until the last of the tent lights has been extinguished before stealing into the camp. Singh has come with him: up to a point. There is no sense in them both risking detection. It might be close to midnight. The moon has risen, its light softened by wispy clouds. The wind masks all sound. It is seeded with a smell both sour and human, the urgent tang of the latrines.

Thomas slips into the camp. At first, he keeps to the periphery, hiding behind boulders, bolting from shadow to shadow in a hunched-over sprint. It is no use, though: if Thomas wants to set eyes on the canvas-wrapped thing the men brought down from the mountain, he will have to enter the circle of tents itself. Once he does so, any movement that is not natural will itself be suspicious. So he straightens and slows, convincing himself that he will be little more than an outline, a human shape, indistinguishable from any other. A man answering the call of nature. Only he is walking away from the latrines.

There is an order to the camp: the porters' tents stand huddled together, filling three-quarters of the site. Then there is a gap of five or six yards that separates them from the Englishmen's tents. These stand at a greater distance from each other—habit, Thomas surmises; his race's inbred fear of proximity. It is towards them that Thomas is heading.

The wind tugs at him, now that he is erect; bulks up his jacket and tears at his hood. It carries the chill of the glacier. He wonders whether the men left their haul in a tent dedicated to storage, or if one of them took it with him, into his private quarters. The latter seems more likely: one does not leave treasure lying about unguarded. Thomas draws nearer to the tents and considers how much he will see if he sticks his head through their flaps. He steps up to the closest one and tries to calm his pulse. If the man inside is awake, he might see Thomas now, a denser darkness against the canopy of canvas. Thomas counts to five, expecting a shout.

It comes: not from inside the tent but from behind, a half-gagged exclamation launched across distance; plum of accent and annoyed.

"Miller! Where have you been? We've been waiting for a quarter hour. Watts has it in for you as it is." Then, more gently, but also sounding from much closer: "Has your stomach been bothering you?"

Thomas acts by instinct. He nods acquiescence, his chin tucked into his scarf; half turns, more with the body than with the face, and from the corner of his eye catches sight of a silhouette standing at four or five paces in the dark. The head is misshapen, bulbous, droops into a bulky, tin-shaped snout. Eyes like black saucers. It's a monster—or else . . .

"Now where's your Smoke mask, man?" the muffled voice inquires, back to being annoyed. "Go get it, you lazy sod. And your doctor's bag. What, are you drunk again?"

It gives Thomas no choice. He turns his back on the silhouette and undoes the tent flap, ducks inside.

"I'll go tell the others that you're on your way," the voice outside announces. "Hurry, will you? We've already fetched that Ajeeba fellow. We had to gag him—he's delirious with fever. God, what a beastly business all this is!"

Thomas, still crouching in the entrance, does not reply. Inside the spacious, man-high tent, illuminated by the wash of moonlight let in through the open flap, lies the dark bulk of a man. His left hand is wrapped around a bottle perched on his hip.

[11]

The man must be sleeping or, better yet, have drunkenly passed out. He does not twitch on Thomas's entrance and his shallow breathing does not change. And yet Thomas has the eerie sensation that the man's eyes are wide open in the darkness. Thomas lowers himself to his knees next to his bulk, careful not to touch him. Something rattles under his left hand and, by touch, Thomas makes out the bulky shape of a photographic camera. His right hand touches a pile of books, many of them open and stacked on top one another. Hanging from the tentpole like a discarded face droops the unmistakable shape of a Smoke mask. Thomas reaches for it carefully, but even so he cannot avoid shaking the pole a little as he takes the mask off its hook. The man's voice erupts at once, as though triggered by the push of a button. It is quiet, slurred, resentful.

"Is that you, Greene? Tell Watts he can stuff it. I'm not coming. Had myself a little party, see. Celebrating our success."

Thomas hears rather than sees the bottle being raised; then the urgent swallow that follows. A cough sounds, a retching; spit on the tent floor.

"Pass me the cannister. By your knee, man. Yes, there's a darling."

Without looking up, Thomas fumbles around himself and hands the heavy metal tin over to the prone man. It is the same design as the cannister they found in the gorge leading to the high plateau; as Thomas passes it over, his hand can feel the stencilled ridges of the letters at its bottom. COOPER. The unspoken name fuels him with anger. The question he asks slips out in lieu of Smoke.

"What's going on, Miller?"

If the man notices the whisper is not Greene's, he does not comment. Instead he places the little spout growing out of the side of the cannister into his mouth and fumbles with the valve on top. A hiss sounds. The stranger inhales, slowly and deeply, then moves his mouth off the spout and closes the valve.

"Don't say you haven't tried it," he chuckles. "Who knew you could get drunk on air! It helps if you combine it with gin, naturally." His fingers search his pockets, then dig underneath his sleeping bag. "Do you have any cigarettes left?"

Thomas shakes his head, *No,* while slipping the Smoke mask over his face. All of a sudden, a hand has snuck around his elbow, tugging him down. He falls next to the drunk man, stares at him through the thick glass of the mask's twin lenses, the proboscis jammed between their chins.

"Stay, have a drink with me. To hell with Watts! To hell with this whole venture!" And, flicking from confidence to suspicion in the blink of a glassy eye: "Why take my mask? And this jacket—I have not seen it before. Who are you? A newbie? Some sort of reenforcement? Did Watts whistle for you?"

Thomas tries to free himself but the man holds him close, struggles with him like a wrestler.

"He will send some of us back to Bombay, is that it? Deliver the goods, while he keeps digging for more. He needs fresh hands! But how did he send for you then? Or did you grow out the dirt?"

At last the man relents and lets him go. Thomas quickly gets to his feet, stands hunched under the tent flap, breathing hard within the mask, his mouth filled with the stench of rubber.

"Go!" says the man. "Stand in for me, if you like. The good doctor. Attending the experiment—as a man of science, right?" The drunk fumbles, finds the cannister again, sucks on tinned air. "Say, you're not the devil by any chance? Not our sort of devil, naturally—one of *theirs*. A proper little juju swine. Like they have in their temples, eight arms and tusks, eh? Though your English sounds proper Oxford. A 'varsity devil, who would have thought?" He coughs, splutters, digs in his pocket. "Say, man, do you have a cigarette for me?"

The man's still talking when Thomas walks away.

[12]

He finds the other Englishmen with some difficulty. They are half a mile from the camp, in the shadow of a ten-foot wall of ice that marks the end of the glacier. Whatever it is they are doing, they have already started, having concluded perhaps that the tardy Dr. Miller would not come. There is a jerky haste to their movements; the nervous need to *get done*. That these men are acting in secret from their porters cannot be in doubt: Thomas watched the site before he snuck in, and even so he did not see any hint of their preparations. No light was struck, and the exit from their tents was accomplished at least as stealthily as Thomas's own approach. They became visible only when they reached the snow, the result of an avalanche that spilled all the way into the valley.

Thomas's boots crunch as he approaches, announcing him from afar. He stops when he has neared to thirty or so paces. He sees them more clearly now, dark shapes against the snow's faint glow. A woodcut of a scene:

seven men, standing in a circle; Smoke masks robbing them of human traits. There is an eighth man lying prone within their midst; next to him, still wrapped in sheeting, is the secret fruit plucked from out the mountain at great height.

A few heads turn at Thomas's approach, then refocus on the task at hand. The sheeting is removed, not entirely but enough so that some part of the thing lies exposed to the sky. There is a jerkiness to the movements of the Smoke-masked men that contrasts oddly with the object's stillness. A lump of black; rock or maybe coal, absorbing the moonlight in mineral indifference.

The man who lies prone upon a stretcher alone is unmasked. He is a native, one of the expedition's porters: his dress says so; his set-back eyes, guarded by burned watermelon cheeks. One of his legs is splintered; there's also a bandage wound around his head. Another detail: his mouth has been gagged. Without seeing his eyes, it is impossible to know his fear— impossible, that is, until a spout of sulphur Smoke escapes his gag and groin and stains the snow. The circle almost breaks apart; not from disgust at his Smoke but from something more pressing. Heads swivel, watch the lump of black. It is as though the men are waiting for it to explode.

What happens next happens quickly, with Thomas still in slow approach. One of the Englishmen pushes the stretcher closer to the *thing*, then pulls the injured man into a sitting position and gives him a hand drill. Ajeeba, that's what Greene called him. Perhaps it is Greene himself who is steadying him by the armpits. Not Watts. Watts is the man next to him, Thomas decides: the man barking orders. *The expedition's leader. Taking the lead.* A short, broad-shouldered man. His stance so wide it is as though he's modelling for his own statue.

With gestures, Greene (if it is Greene) bids the injured man to drill into the lump. When the man won't, Greene looks to Watts (if it is Watts), who pulls a handgun from his pocket and places it to the injured man's head. Ajeeba works the crank. The drill sinks in: an inch, two inches, three. It is soft, this rock. At last the drill has penetrated to its hilt; it gets snagged inside so that its crank won't turn either one way or the other. The circle of men sees it and seems relieved: stand straighter, less tense. Two or three had pulled out their own pistols when Watts produced his. Now they let them dangle from their wrists.

Thomas watches all this and takes another step towards them. The ground is uneven, the snow hiding rocks.

A new experiment. While Greene continues to support Ajeeba's back and weight, Watts puts down his pistol, ungloves his hand, and reaches carefully for the bandages at the injured man's shin. Thomas wonders whether his task is distasteful to him, or pleasurable. For now, Watts does not smoke.

The gloveless hand has found what it is looking for. A ripple runs through Watts's back, of muscle and weight applied to the man's splintered wound. In reply, Ajeeba's body jerks. He cannot scream his pain: a gag is in the way. His body screams for him: thick, treacly Smoke, wasp-jacketed yellow and black. It spreads like ground fog, covers the men's boots, laps at the black lump from which the drill protrudes like a metal bristle. Still Watts's hand is buried in the man's bandages; still the weight of his squat body is pushed downwards, into the wound. The Smoke darkens, thickens, hides the man from view. Then there is the sudden jerk of violent motion, of Ajeeba's body yanking itself from Watts's grip and throwing itself forward. The next moment, the Smoke has stopped; it drops as Soot all around the scene, marking a circle. At its centre lies Ajeeba, his head resting, facedown, upon the hard pillow of dark rock, the drill's handle bent aside by the force of his motion; the drill bit snapped off at the base and protruding between ear and neck.

The black snow all around him masks the flow of blood.

[13]

Greene and Watts slide the man's body off the drill, then wrap the rock back into sheeting. Then two of the other men pick it up, somewhat gingerly, and the whole group of seven walks towards Thomas. He remains a dozen paces from the scene, rooted to the spot. His clothes, he is aware, are as though tarred from the inside and crunch when he moves. *Impotent anger.* A younger Thomas would have converted it to action; would have raced to Ajeeba's rescue and no doubt gotten himself caught in the process. The older Thomas is more prudent; more practised at turning anger on himself. That and he was scared—he might as well admit it. Scared of that black lump now being tidied away, like a family heirloom in between official viewings; making its way towards him, swinging weightily between two sideways-moving men.

Watts makes sure he is in easy earshot of Thomas before issuing orders. He slips up his mask just far enough to free his mouth. None of the men seem eager to remove their masks. *They are hiding their faces. Hiding their shame.* As is Thomas himself.

To the two who carry the rock, Watts says: "Well, chaps, that was ugly, but we learned what we needed to learn. It's safe to transport. You two will set off with it tomorrow. Take ten of the porters and two of the yaks and send them back to us once you reach the border. Don't tell anyone anything until you reach Bombay and talk to our people there; I suppose they'll have a ship waiting. Tell them there's more on the way. They can wait for it or send this first delivery ahead, just as they please. That's all, really. And—let's keep it on ice for as long as we can, shall we? That's how we found it, after all. We haven't tested what happens to it in heat."

To the other men, Watts adds: "The rest of us will stay until we can harvest a second, larger section. We'd be fools not to, with all the pain it was to get the blasted winch up there. Get some sleep, and at dawn send some natives ahead to restock the upper camps with provisions to get us ready for the next push. Let's hope the weather holds, eh, chaps?"

And to him, Thomas, Watts says the following: "Thank you for joining us, Doctor. Greene here tells us you were indisposed but I think we all know what kept you. For a medical man, you really are awfully squeamish. Well, you can pull your weight now. Bury the body, will you, and make sure it cannot be found. We will have to come up with some kind of story about his disappearance. Desertion, I suppose. Though it may give some of the others ideas."

And, stepping closer, and speaking much lower, Watts adds: "Get a grip on yourself, man. You are drunk and your clothes look like castoffs you found at the bottom of your backpack. You don't even look like yourself! Show some pride, what! Or do you think this is easy on any of us?"

They leave him then, there in the black snow, a procession of men walking away in the moonlight. Soon they have blended in the night. Thomas looks after them, struck by the fact that, up close, Watts's voice was hesitant and humane, and his cheeks strewn thick with boyish pimples.

[14]

Thomas leaves the body where it is, though he steps close enough to learn that Watts or Greene or someone else closed the man's eyelids over the dead stare. He cannot afford the time for a burial. When the real Miller sobers up, Watts will learn there was an imposter in the camp, an Englishman. There will be a search. Time is running out.

Thomas returns to where he left Singh, at the camp's western periphery.

By the time he finds him in the shadow of a mighty boulder, Thomas's mind is made up.

"We must climb," he says. "Now. I need to see it for myself."

Singh is incredulous. "Now? They will see us when the morning comes."

"We can hide, wait until there are others on the mountain. From down here, it will be hard to say who is who."

"And up there? You don't know what you are asking. You don't climb."

"You said it yourself, Singh. They've cut a staircase into the mountain. Put ropes in all the difficult spots."

Singh makes to argue then stops himself. The moon is setting. Even so there is some light by which to see. Starlight: the great, misty smear of the Milky Way. Up here, the sky seems to have shed its lid.

"That tent over there," Singh says at last. "That's where they keep all the spare equipment. I had a look before. They have some interesting innovations. Things I have not seen before. Iron spikes for the feet. Short-handled pickaxes, so you can hold one in each hand. A new kind of climbing harness."

"They have air, too. Compressed air." Thomas describes the cannister and Miller's use thereof.

"Imagine the cost of all this," Singh says, almost reverently. Then: "If we get caught . . . or the weather changes. If a serac breaks off, or a cornice . . ."

"Then I will have a lot of explaining to do to Mrs. Singh," answers Thomas, which is his way of saying, *Your blood will be on my head.* Ezekiel. His school's old vicar, Swinburne, was fond of quoting the passage. He might have been surprised that so disappointing a pupil as Thomas would find occasion to recall it, here amongst the eternal ice.

DEFINITIONS: A Smoke Mask (otherwise known as a György respirator) is a tightly fitting full-facial mask, made of Indian rubber or leather, with inset glass goggles, that protects the face from immediate contact with Smoke, while a coal filter located in the "snout" of the mask physically binds Smoke and prevents inhalation. Its primary use is to prevent & delay infection by Smoke and maintain discipline in combat situations or when exposed to so-called Gales. The filters quickly become overwhelmed and have to be replaced after every serious exposure to Smoke. The original mask was designed by Lazlo György (1848–?), a Hungarian inventor. György was put under arrest by his own government in 1895 or 1896; he is presumed dead. The Company now holds the international patent on the Smoke Mask (Patent No. 205/D/441).

NEW REGULATIONS (1/1/1908): Smoke Masks are to be considered mandatory standard issue for Company soldiers & security guards. Their cost (Company rates) is to be deducted in increments from their wages during their first year of service. Regular practice of martial drills while wearing the Smoke Masks is mandatory and to be performed twice a year. Experience shows that only a small minority of men can get sufficiently used to the mask to wear it for much longer than an hour, and that strenuous exercise while wearing the mask is physically challenging due to insufficient airflow.

MANUFACTURE: Below, please find detailed technical drawings based on the model of Smoke Mask produced in our Calcutta factories (the so-called Indian Cut). Note the innovations of the buckle system (figs. 7A and B). A lighter, more elegant but less efficient version is manufactured in our Paris factory for export to Britain ("French Cut," figs. 11–13).

[1]

First they turn into thieves, taking what they need from out the explorers' equipment tent and distributing it across two bags.

Then they start climbing.

Singh takes the lead. His backpack is by far the heavier; two brackets studded with iron prongs are tied to its top. These are designed to be strapped to one's boots and provide grip on the ice. For now, they lend a hedgehog's prickliness to Singh's dark outline. The moon is long gone, clouds are gathering above the valley. Even so, there is a glow to the glacial ice that makes it navigable.

The expedition porters have hewn steps into the ice wall marking the beginning of the glacier; the first few yards of climbing are as easy as climbing a flight of uneven stairs. Then they belong to the mountain, their world reduced to the visible yard or two ahead. Their path is made obvious by the trampled-down snow. When they reach a first vertical wall, they find fixed ropes and footholds that have been screwed into the ice. Time passes to the sound of their breathing, the squeak of compacted snow. Thomas finds it a thoughtless time, literally so. All of his focus is poured into setting foot before foot. At difficult sections, he follows Singh's gestures of instruction without question or hesitation. They do not speak. There is no need to. Life is breathing; is placing one's toes; is keeping up with the shadow walking in front of you.

It is easy to see why you might fall in love with climbing.

[2]

At dawn, they stop in the lee of a giant lump of ice. So focussed was Thomas on the sheer mechanics of movement that he did not register the gradual change of light. Now he blinks and stands in daylight. Singh reaches into his backpack and fishes out two pairs of tinted eyeglasses. They have leather blinkers attached to their sides.

"Here, put this on. We mustn't grow snow-blind."

He offers Thomas some dried meat and makes sure he drinks. "Not too much. Water is precious up here."

"What about all the snow?"

"You cannot drink snow, not in quantity. And it takes a lot of effort to melt it."

"We should push on."

"Let's rest a few minutes. They can't see us here. It's the last peace we might have."

As it turns out they cannot see much of the camp either. Fog sits down in the valley, though above them the sky remains clear. Looking carefully, one can make out the outlines of the tents. A fire is burning—a glow in the mist—but it's hard to tell rocks from people.

"The weather is helping us," he observes to Singh. "It'll hide us from pursuit."

"For now. It might decide to kill us later on."

"You have a sour disposition, Jagat."

They sit and try to spot movement in the camp. Thomas is waiting for a shout to go up as Ajeeba's body is found or Dr. Miller relates the story of his encounter. But there is no sign of alarm. Did one of the snow leopards Singh has scared him with climb down off the mountain to make off with the corpse? Has Miller held his peace, unsure whether the apparition visiting his tent had been real? Or has Watts simply decided to keep quiet about the news so as not to alarm the porters?

Within half an hour the fog has thickened to such a degree that the camp becomes entirely invisible.

"Let's push on," says Singh, then grows concerned when he sees Thomas wobble on his feet.

"It's nothing," Thomas reassures him. "Dead leg. Or rather, dead foot."

"You must move your toes when you rest. Make fists of them. Same with your fingers. And keep your nose covered, Sahib! Or it'll simply freeze off."

[3]

They carry on climbing. Gradually, Thomas becomes aware of how thin the air has already become. His heart is pounding in his ears. At steeper sections, each step takes four, five, six breaths. Soon it is ten breaths, twelve. Singh notices his struggling and works one of the metal cannisters out of his backpack. Thomas tries to open the valve but cannot manage either with his gloves on or with them off: his fingers are clumsy with cold and the cannister sucks out all the sensation left in them. Singh has to do it for him; he feeds Thomas air, like a babe from a bottle. It's an odd taste, metallic, but a dozen breaths help calm him sufficiently that Thomas nods for Singh to carry on.

Whatever strength was lent him dissipates fast. Stubbornness takes its place. Singh has roped them together, and Thomas's only goal becomes to maintain some little slack between their moving bodies. The condensation between his mouth and his scarf has long frozen, gluing wool to beard. He cannot remember when he last shaved. Livia hated him with a beard, Charlie less so. For the stretch of an hour, he becomes convinced they are climbing behind him, tied to him by the same rope.

"Stop tarrying, goddammit," he grumbles at them, and hears Livia's snort, Charlie's bright laughter. "Bloody slackers."

But when he looks behind him, there is nothing but ice.

[4]

They reach the first of the expedition's upper camps. It consists of two tents, their sides billowing in the breeze; a petroleum burner and some saucepans; and a small stash of food. Thomas tries to estimate what time it is but finds it difficult. There are clouds above them too now, hiding the sun, and dark spots dance before his eyes.

"We will rest," Singh decides. "You are done in." He, too, sounds weary.

Thomas does not object. He shelters in one of the tents and crawls into his sleeping bag. He tries to sleep, but his head is pounding and his lungs cannot get enough air. It is like drowning very slowly; a whistle sounding deep inside him. Livia is lying right behind him, whispering something he cannot hear. Even here her hair smells good, like tinned peaches.

Singh shakes Thomas out of his unsleeping trance with a cup of hot, sweetened tea. He has melted a saucepan of snow on top of the burner and melts some more when Thomas bolts the hot drink, scalding his gums. After three cups, some strength returns to him and he eats the food that Singh offers, then finally falls asleep.

Later—impossible to tell how much later, other than there remains some evening light—Thomas rolls out of his tent to answer a call of nature. The wind whips at him, relentless, and as he turns and buttons himself he nearly collides with Singh. Like Thomas he has not undressed even inside the tent. For some reason, fresh frost rims the scarf that is pulled across Singh's face.

Thomas is about to push past, when the figure reaches up to free his mouth. The lips and teeth that are revealed are not Singh's. The shock of it makes Thomas stumble, lays him flat out on his rump. Now, seated, other details strike his air-starved brain. The man is shorter; the hat he wears a different shape. His tinted glasses make it impossible to read the man's eyes. The stranger reaches down to grab him. Thomas bats away the hands with desperate force.

"Sahib . . . what wrong?"

Again the hands reach down. This time Thomas lets them; feels the stranger haul him to his feet. Standing close once more, Thomas stares at the man, his mind reeling, spooked.

"Sahib—how you get ahead?"

Can it be that the man confuses him for someone down below? *We all look the same to him,* it flashes in Thomas. *A white, bearded face, half hidden in hat and scarf.* He recalls Ramsbottom, the Bombay horse vet, telling him that some Company Moghuls struggled to tell apart their own servants. "We fingerprint them when they enter the Company's service. It's what it was invented for—to tell one darkie from another. Now I hear in Europe they use it for crooks."

"Sahib . . . ?"

Thomas starts to speak, breaks off, coughs; he is looking for the tones of Empire. "Never mind how I got ahead. I set off early. In the night."

The man accepts that, ungloves a hand and takes off his tinted glasses. The eyes behind are deep-set slits, the cheeks burned black by sun and frost.

"Weather bad," the stranger says now, and points into the cloud and wind. "Soon more bad."

"Yes, I know." Thomas stares past the man, down the mountain. The visibility is poor now. He cannot see anyone else.

"Are others coming?"

"Five more. Long way behind. I fast climbing." His face beams with pride. "I bring air, Sahib." He shakes his backpack and produces the clink of metal on metal. "Air. Petroleum. Sugar."

"Well done. Leave the provisions here and go back down. Tell the others to turn around and wait until the weather clears. Do you understand?"

The porter nods, puts his backpack down, unpacks much of its contents, then shoulders it again.

"Good. Go back. Wait."

The man's manner has something both pleased and avuncular. The white men are fools and do not respect the weather. This one has more sense than most. Or does he? "You come, Sahib?"

"Soon. I will return very soon. Look, I have a porter here to help me." Thomas points at the sleeping shape of Singh, back in the tent. Through the half-open flap, one can make out the bottom of his sleeping bag. "Go ahead now, don't worry. You have done well."

Once the man is gone, Thomas wakes Singh and tells him about their visitor. The Sikh listens with his eyes to the sky, studying the weather.

"If a storm is coming—"

"We can't turn back. We won't have another chance."

Singh grimaces. "You don't know how many dead mountaineers have spoken those words." He hesitates, weighing their options. "Let us sleep some more. It will be dark soon. We will see what the weather does over-night."

[5]

They return to the tent, roll close to each other, for warmth. There is no real sleep at this altitude, just dreams. Each breath a slow dying. And they will climb higher yet. Thomas listens to the wind and Singh's breathing and knows that behind him, at the end of the tent, Livia is brushing her hair.

"I wish we had chocolate," he says to her once, very quietly, and: "Your mother wrote. She says she must see us."

"*You* go see her. The truth is that you want to leave. Just like Charlie."

He turns to protest and in his dream she is there, her eyes hidden behind tinted glasses, her face so close they nearly touch.

Her kiss heaps Soot into the pocket between lips and teeth.

Thomas leaves it there till morning, sucking on it like on a gone-off sweet.

[6]

It is still dark when Singh shakes him conscious. The Sikh is already in his boots and is repacking the two backpacks, finding space for the porter's provisions. Snow is melting in a saucepan.

"The wind has dropped off a little. If we want to risk it, we better go now."

Thomas at once starts lacing up his boots, then accepts a cup of very sweet tea.

"How many hours to the third camp?"

But Singh does not know.

They return to climbing. There is a moment, when dawn breaks, that Thomas is struck afresh by the majesty of the mountain face above them, by the purity of this world of rock and ice. But soon his vision shrinks once more to that narrow tunnel straight ahead. Each step has to be placed, each movement fought for, his body heavy and, increasingly, cold. He does not notice the passage of time or the gradual change of weather; is surprised to look up and see snowflakes fly at him sideways with the malice of hail. Soon the storm cocoons them, two men tied together by a rope. The rest of the world has ceased to exist. In the shelter of a ledge, they drink some sweetened water while the wind screams around them like a living thing. Singh's left side is covered in frozen snow; his scarf, hat, and glasses have fused.

"Can we make it?" Thomas shouts into his ear.

"Better to go up now than down," Singh returns. "We must be close."

In the endless hours that follow, however, it becomes increasingly clear that this is a dangerous misjudgement. The terrain is steep now, their strength waning. Fixed ropes and footholds still guide them along but often have to be worked free from the fresh snow. The ropes are frozen hard. Every step is pain.

When the accident comes, it unfolds with the slow inevitability of nightmares. They have just negotiated a desperately steep ledge and Thomas lies panting on a comparatively flat section some ten or twelve steps past its rim, trying to regain his strength. Singh yells at him to keep on going. Cursing the man, Thomas rises, slips, and—unworried yet—tries to catch his weight on his arms, the ice axe dangling useless from its wrist strap. The ground betrays him, gives no purchase, and suddenly he is sliding, shooting ever faster towards the edge. A moment later he goes across: the sickening weightlessness of free fall. The world is white around him. He sees no bottom to the drop.

The rope breaks his fall harshly, the straps of his harness cutting into his hips. Thomas flips upside down and hangs dangling over the blank abyss, the storm tearing at him and turning his body into a pendulum. Thomas screams then—sound and Smoke—and in response he falls some two or three more yards, before the rope interrupts his fall once more. For a split second of dark suspicion, he pictures Singh above with his knife's edge to the cord that ties them. Then Thomas realises what strain his body must be putting on the man above.

He tries to still himself against the wind, puts his hands to the rope and slowly pulls himself upright. The rock face is a yard or so away; he reaches for it with a foot, then with the ice axe whose grip he regains; hooks the guide rope and draws himself closer. Soon he can rest some of his weight on an iron spoke driven deep into the ice here; feels Singh above respond and pull in the slack. Step by step he works himself back into the world of the living: the ledge above is his horizon line, the pain in his fingers, his legs, a welcome spur. Up at the top, a hand reaches for him and hauls him over. They collapse on top of each other.

"Rum luck," it pours out of Singh, echoing the poor dead Hounslow, "splendid," and he drenches Thomas in his Smoke. It's *first* Smoke, this, crude and unmodulated, full of triumph, resentment, fear. Thomas's body responds. It, too, lacks subtlety. There is a comfort to the very coarseness of the exchange. Thomas has never grown comfortable with the ease with which those raised upon the Second Smoke communicate their moods and wants. He, the tales' great Smoker, the revolution's angry man, continues to make his home in self-repression and the sudden eruptions of emotion fed by the simplest, deepest sources of the self. They speak, body to body, high up on the mountain: the wind making a flag from out their Smoke, snowflakes laden with dark Soot. It lasts but a moment. Then Singh remembers himself. He has let a sahib creep into his heart, *his skin,* before.

It is his duty not to let it happen again.

"Get up, you fool!" he insists, though he himself is still sitting. "We will freeze if we don't move."

A little later, he exchanges the rope that ties them for a different one, in case it has been damaged by the fall.

[7]

It's dark by the time they find the last of the camps, a single tent, somewhat larger in its dimensions and very carefully tied down. Snow has blown into a wall on one side and threatens to flatten it. The tentpoles bend; the canvas billows in the wind. They crawl inside without speaking. Fatigue has long turned into something else, simpler in its outlines. The body's slow dying.

Thomas walked on only from stubbornness, from spite; half accepting the inevitable, clinging hard to the "not yet." His feet have no sensation, and they lie head to sole, massaging each other's toes because it hurts too much to touch one's own. When sensation returns, the pain is unspeakable, and yet their bodies are too tired to convert it into Smoke.

There is food in the tent, saucepans and a burner; tea, sugar, additional sleeping bags. The exhaustion is total but it proves hard to eat, to sleep. The body craves and won't be satisfied. Air helps them, pours breathfuls of strength into their limbs, their thoughts. At some point in the night, they sit up shoulder to shoulder and pass a cannister back and forth as one would a cigarette, or a bottle of liquor: Singh on Thomas's right, Charlie on his left.

"Why did you come here?" the latter asks, in his kind, frank manner. "Is it from guilt? Are you trying to die?"

Thomas does not answer; he accepts the cannister and sucks on air.

"And you, Charlie? Why did you go? You did not even leave a note."

"I told Livia I'd be going. I don't like writing notes."

Singh stirs next to him, inhales the last of the oxygen, then opens a new cannister.

"Are you dreaming of home?" he asks.

"Dreaming? No. You?"

"I dream of Mrs. Singh."

"Have you been married long?"

"We met in the village I told you about. Where I studied Marx. She, too, was studying. We argued about everything—revolution, the nation-state, the Indian way. We were married that winter."

"What is her first name? Mrs. Singh's?"

Singh makes to speak, falls silent, passes the cannister. "We cannot be friends, Sahib," he says, firmly if a little mournfully. "It is better not to pretend it."

Thomas returns to talking to Charlie.

"Did you ever find your angel?" he asks. "Did he have wings?"

But Charlie is tired now and will no longer answer. Outside the wind howls and makes a bellows of their tent.

[8]

The storm finally blows itself out midmorning. They crawl their way from the half-collapsed tent, stare up the mountainside. For now, the sky remains dull, the light subdued. Somewhere near must stand the machine they spotted from below, and the cut in rock and ice that is their destination. But try as they might, they cannot see it. Fresh snow covers everything. The guide ropes lie buried in it; and in the dull light none of the black veins they saw snaking up the glacier are visible.

They have to break a fresh trail. It takes hours to locate the guide ropes in the hip-deep snow, and each yard gained swallows a thousand breaths. By midday, the sun has burned away all cloud. It is now Thomas notices he is no longer wearing his glasses. He has no memory of taking them off and cannot find them in his pockets. Perhaps he left them in the tent that morning. It is a sign of Singh's tiredness that he does not notice. The stark light gives fresh contour to the landscape. It helps them perceive a bulge in the snow, not ten steps from them, that soon discloses a complex winch system somehow bolted into the ice. A chain stretches from it into the snow. They follow it, breaking through the icy crust, and are led to the lip of a crevasse, into which the chain disappears. The cut is perhaps five feet wide and as much as sixty feet long, if masked by the fresh snow: it has blown across it and partially frozen, half closing the thin, long mouth of the crevasse.

Exhausted but also exhilarated by the discovery, Thomas and Singh lie down flat on their bellies and stare into the darkness below. The first few yards are found by the sun and shine in bright azure: pure ice, reflecting the colours of a tropical lagoon. Then the hole angles away into darkness. The chain hangs slack into the pit.

"What do you smell?" Singh asks, inhaling, his face hanging over the lip.

"Nothing," Thomas replies. Then he changes his mind. "Mushrooms."

"Mushrooms?"

"Yes."

"So do I."

They smile at the absurdity of the thought, but a hint of fear creeps into that smile.

"The chain . . . ?"

"Yes. We might be able to get the winch going. Then we can see where it leads."

[9]

It takes them an hour to beat the ice off the winch mechanism and then another twenty minutes to realise that, while there exists a mechanical crank, the main power supply comes in the form of three backpack-sized batteries marked with the name EDISON. The thought of carrying these, or any part of the winch up here, troubles Thomas; it points not just to money but to a relentless will fuelling the whole operation from afar; a will indifferent to difficulty and intolerant of failure. Watts is but an agent of this will. Thomas wonders who is the principal.

They pull at the chunky lever and are rewarded by the slow gyration of the central drum, slowly hauling in the chain. There is a lot of it, the drum growing thicker by the yard, until a large metal hook emerges. This, in turn, holds something like a playground swing suspended at its corners by four thinner chains and anchored in the hook. Thomas understands its purpose at once.

"It's an elevator. Like a miner's cage—only this is for one person at a time." And before Singh can take in the implications, Thomas adds: "I am going down. You must operate the winch."

"You can barely walk."

"I won't have to. All I need is to sit."

Their preparations don't take a moment. Thomas walks over to the swing, tests its solidity, then places it so it is just poised over the crevasse. He gets on it, feeling more alive than he has in days, basking in the sun reflecting off the ice. In an afterthought, he ties his harness onto the swing's chain.

It is now Singh notices Thomas is not wearing glasses.

"Where are they, what have you done with them?" he chides, clearly upset. "Here, you must take mine."

"No need, Singh. I am going underground. I would not be able to see in them below."

"When you return."

"When I return, Singh. When we are finished here. When you tell me Mrs. Singh's Christian name."

"Christian, Sahib?"

"You know what I mean."

[10]

He goes below, shielding his eyes against the fantastic glare produced by the pure ice, then, sliding down on an ice shelf that tilts some thirty or forty degrees downwards, into soft shadow. Soon he is under the ice. The light follows him, flooding around his body, the ceiling glowing white and arching. He smells mushroom and rot; blood, too, his nostrils torn and clotted by the altitude. Above, Singh has arrested the chain; too early, thinks Thomas, the swing dancing, spinning in thin air.

He stares down into the gloom. Beneath his dangling feet, the crevasse widens into a pocket of air. The light from above cuts a swathe into it. The spin of the swing makes it hard to see what it reveals. A pattern, a darkness; something mottled on the icy wall. The winch unwinds once more and he plunges farther, into open space. A renewed stop sends the swing into wild gyrations; Thomas holds on to the chain with clumsy mitts and prays that he won't fall.

"Slowly," he shouts up, though he knows he won't be heard. "Get me closer. I can't see."

And he can't—not clearly—not until the mountain itself turns on its lights and the whole of the glacier becomes a paper lantern. The sun must enter it from a dozen places; surface fissures focussing the light. The rays converge here, in this great chamber. Thomas spins and dances at the heart of this great lamp.

He understands two things: that this is the quarter hour or so of magic light, when the sun dips low but has not yet disappeared behind the mountain range to the west; and that the light, impossibly bright, reflected over and over by the smooth ice walls, will burn his eyes as though he were staring at the sun itself. His first action then, by instinct, is to screw shut his eyes with those same tired muscles that have held them scrunched into slits for much of the day. It takes several moments to master the instinct; to smooth out that face and force open the eyelids. What choice does he have? He has come this far.

He has to look.

What he sees defies his sense of scale. If the glacier looked like an organ— a lung or womb—from afar, he is now inside it, swinging in a cavity of pure white light. Black veins thread the ice: buried too deep to be visible at any other time of day, opaque like frozen Smoke. They thicken and converge, grow solid down there at the bottom of the hole beneath Thomas's feet. There, growing out of the icy floor beneath, is a black boil, bulbous and well rooted, its outline visible deep down into the ice for it alone binds the stark sunlight: a breach within the mirror surface of the chamber, an ink stain risen on a twist of blotting paper, up towards the open air. The ink-well underneath is ocean-deep.

Thomas rests his eyes upon this darkness, trying—failing—to gauge its depth. The mountain itself seems to rest on it, its growth into the glacier but an outcrop, a reaching forth towards the surface, the way a spire hungers for the sky. *It's like a buried cathedral,* it comes to him, *like a stranger's dark faith. Welling up to us from the centre of the earth.*

He hushes himself, up there in the air above it, as though afraid to wake it by his motion.

The expedition members were less cautious than Thomas. Down by the black boil that pierces the ice sits a second mechanical device, powered by gas cannisters, and resting on a sort of tripod. Its disk-shaped saw blade is the only part that is at once recognisable. A cutting machine. And staring into the darkness of the boil, Thomas soon locates the machine's bite: a notch within the light-absorbing blackness, more cubical in shape perhaps than the rock he saw down in the camp suggested. The first sample: hauled down the mountain and on its way to Britain, if Watts stuck to his plan. A white chalk line luridly denotes a second, much larger chunk.

And still Thomas hovers in midair, the chain above unmoving. He looks up only to be struck sightless by the glare above; trains his eyes back down upon the darkness, then slowly lets them climb the walls of this cavity turned lamp. For there is something stranger yet than that vast, weird blackness underneath. A rash has grown upon the smoothness of the glowing ice around him, translucent grey in shade and far more textured than the veins that thread the glacier. From where Thomas is hanging, this rash is hard to make sense of, hard even to see.

So he swings to it, kicking out with his legs and feet as though he were six again and dangling from a rope swing under a willow branch, building momentum, back and forth. Soon the chain is creaking and his arc brings him ever closer to the wall above his head. He reaches with one hand, both to catch himself should he have misjudged his momentum and to touch, perchance catch hold of, that strange growth. His gloved fingers are too clumsy to make any purchase. On the next pass the glove is in between his teeth, the fingers bare, looking very pale and bony in the light. He sees the growth more clearly now, a network of lichen from which rises a carpet of tiny, hooded mushrooms, glassy grey, a yellow pinprick at the centre of their mantles. His fingers touch and sink into the eerie warmth of something living, growing on the ice. He tries to pinch off a stem but fails to hold on to it, swings once more, determined to hold on this time, when— mid-arc—he is hauled up.

The shortened line costs him his balance; he crashes into a bit of wall and spins widely, almost falling off the swing. Next thing he knows he has entered the searing light of the entrance to the cavern. He slides up its bottleneck with his eyes held shut and emerges back into the wind. His glove is still in his mouth.

He starts shouting no sooner has he spat it out, his eyes still shut against the light.

"Lower me back down, Singh. I wasn't done."

Then he dares a look and sees the reason for his sudden extraction.

Jagat Singh is no longer in control of the electric winch.

[11]

The man who holds Singh at gunpoint and has taken over control of the winch is English, or at any rate white. One can see this by his moustache, whose red-blond hair shines through the ice that covers it. He is also clearly so exhausted he can barely stand. He does not speak but merely gestures Thomas off the swing. Just as he does so, the light changes: the sun has dipped beneath the mountains in the west. A welcome dullness reasserts itself.

Thomas climbs off the swing and approaches. Singh is sitting down, not far from the winch and in the man's flank. The latter divides his time now, pointing his gun first at one then the other of his prisoners. His hand is shivering. Thomas does the math and realises that he must have set off after them in the middle of the storm; that he gained on them despite it all. Presumably he did not climb alone. Perhaps the others did not make it, or else they will be following soon. His pace must have been inhuman.

"Watts sent you," he says to the stranger now. "When the porters told him there was someone on the mountain. You are his strongest climber."

The stranger does not answer. Everything in his stance suggests a man spent. Everything other than the gun.

"What do we do now? Look at you, you can barely hold the metal in this cold. Your fingers must be frozen to it. Put the gun away and we will talk. What's your name?"

The man's focus is bound now, by Thomas and his words. He is too exhausted to notice Singh stirring in his flank.

"Have you eaten? We have food. Maybe some tea, even; we can melt water."

Thomas cannot see his eyes, or his face: everything is covered by hat, glasses, and scarf. Only the upper lip twitches under that moustache. Copper, actually, not red-blond. Charlie's colour.

"What are you planning on doing with the thing below . . . ?" Thomas continues, gently now, only to break off when Singh hits the stranger over the head with the flat of his ice axe. "You did not have to hit him that hard."

They kneel down together, remove the man's glasses, his hat.

"Look, he is bleeding. We must get him to the tent below, or else he will freeze to death."

Thomas does not put into words how relieved he is that the man looks nothing like Charlie. He buries his ice axe in the gears and levers of the winch, kicks its batteries into the crevasse. Then they drag the unconscious stranger down to the closest of the camps.

[12]

They spend the night lying stretched out, three men in a tent, a bandage around the stranger's head and his hands tied very loosely, more to mark his imprisonment than to enforce it. If his companions show up, the situation will soon be reversed. There is nothing that can be done about this fact.

As they lie there, while the stranger remains unconscious or is faking sleep, Thomas and Jagat talk. Their fatigue is now such that they drift off between words only to recover themselves some minutes later and resume. Neither sleep nor the waking world will have them anymore. They inhabit the half-life of the in-between.

"A cathedral," Singh says now, perhaps for the fourth or fifth time. "Mushrooms on its walls! How can that be?"

Thomas's response is a whisper that follows ten minutes later. They lie so close, they share each other's breaths.

"Whatever it is, it's something new, unheard of. Something outside nature." Then: "The snake, the apple. Lucifer falling from the heavens. Shiva dancing the destruction of the world."

"Fairy tales," says the Marxist.

"Fairy tales transcribing something. Something unspeakable. Something *wrong*."

Singh does not reply; he lies breathing in the dark. Perhaps they both drift off at last, for there is light on the tent wall when Singh speaks again.

"What do they want it for, this unspeakable thing?"

"I don't know. For money, I suppose. In the end, they always want money."

"What now? We go back down? Evade the searchers? Tell the world?"

"I've gone blind," Thomas answers softly, though he suspects Singh already knows. "All I see is white. You must go down alone. I will wait for them and look after our patient. I think you cracked his skull."

"They will kill you," Singh objects.

"I doubt that. Not here, not on their own authority."

"And they will catch me."

"They mustn't. I think whoever climbed up with him did not make it. Or they turned around. So you have a little time. You may be able to hide somewhere, farther down, and wait until the next lot are past you. Slip through. There is such confusion up here. Or you can use the night to find a fresh way down."

Singh wags his head, sceptical, thinking. Then he starts packing his things.

"I'll go." Singh bends to the bandaged man, checks his breathing. "Don't let him die."

"I won't."

There is no need to mention Hounslow. His ghost is in the tent with them.

They do not touch each other in parting. And Thomas never does learn Mrs. Singh's name.

Excavation delayed (sabotage). Winch broken.

Arrested today a known terrorist and traitor to the British Crown and Company. Right to fair trial as imperial subject was asserted and accepted.

The man is snow-blind and has three frostbitten toes.

A taciturn man, this Watts. Punctilious. Onstage he looks small and unimposing. He pockets his diary, puts away his pen and ink, then folds up his travelling writing desk with a precision that goes beyond the merely soldierly. A frightened man, making a ritual of the few things he does control. Behind him rises a tent, dark green against the blank white wall that delimits the stage and suggests glacial isolation. Inside the tent, a shadow can be seen bending over a second shadow stretched out low upon a camp bed.

The first of these shadows—the upright one—now emerges from the tent. He is taller than Watts, looser in his movements, and is dressed in a surgeon's apron that is spotted with bright blood. His hand cups something, black and red; at Watts's inquiring glance, the surgeon walks over and shoves the contents roughly into Watts's palm. Watts inspects them and, alarmed and disgusted, at once lets them drop: black toes raining down onto the stage, where they lie, curled and stubby, like sausage ends; discarded meat. We cannot see Watts's eyes. Both men are wearing snow goggles.

The audience sits darkly mirrored in their lenses.

NORTH AND SOUTH

Wherever the poor rule, that is democracy.

—ARISTOTLE, *POLITICS*

[1]

The Miners rescue the players as an afterthought.

They find them strung out on the tidal current like bait upon a fishing line, sitting in their broken boats half filled with water, their clothes soaked and icy, full of horror at themselves. Etta May. Greta Silvana. Geoffrey. Ada has a raking wound across her cheek, three ragged lines; she must have put them there herself. David bit his lower lip to shreds and stands swollen-mouthed, silent. Meister Lukas won't stop crying. The tear ducts are so sooty, it runs out of him all black.

One of their rescuers—a man wearing oilskins and a woollen hat—asks them how it is that they survived. Balthazar notes the accent despite himself, the compression of vowels, that odd songlike intonation, the hint of a roll about the *r*. Liverpool. More than anything else it tells him they have arrived. England. Miners' Country. Well north of Renfrew's lands.

He tells the man that when the Storm overtook the ship, the players climbed into the lifeboats and strung them out on ropes behind the main bulk of the ship in order to contain infection. A person a boat: they each met the Storm in isolation.

Private little hells.

They tied themselves to the seats with crafty knots that enraged fingers would not easily unpick to curb the impulse for self-destruction; sat, life jackets bulky against their chests, waiting for the wall of black.

Half the boats flipped or sank and, anyway, there weren't enough to go around. Those whom they had locked into their cabins drowned when the ship ran ashore and split its hull upon a rock. The machinist, God bless him, had barricaded himself in the engine room and continued shovelling coal. He kept the ship going: not fast enough to outrun the Storm but fast enough to hurl it ashore. He, too, will have drowned.

The man listens to Balthazar for a minute or two, then walks off. He is too busy to indulge in story. There is work to be done elsewhere on this rocky beach. They are salvaging the ship itself, not looking for survivors so much as keen to strip it for its iron, its generators and engine, the fine brass fittings and the goods within its hold. The hull is too far split to give any hope that it will ever sail again; and thus welders swarm it, cutting off pieces and loading them onto a fleet of trawlers. Everything they touch is covered in an oily blanket of Soot, sticky and cloying like coagulated milk. Seagulls swoop, looking for pickings, and get caught in this tar-skin; they scream their seagull screams and have to be cut out or killed to restore peace.

Those men who finish their shift return to shore tired, stomping through the black foam clogging up the shoreline in their knee-high boots. And as they unpack their lunch boxes and flasks, they curse the South as though it was Parliament that had belched north all this darkness with the express purpose of soiling their beaches and spoiling their fishing grounds; of drowning all the herring in their filth. The next moment—in the same breath almost, not quite crossing themselves, but touching the temple and the tip of one ear, the food as yet untasted—they whisper a quick blessing.

We thank the Smoke.

It almost makes Balthazar laugh.

[2]

They feed them meat broth and bread. The broth is thin and the bread stale. Minetowns remain poor, it appears; half the people there were hungry last time Balthazar went. The Miners chat with Ada a little, for bloodied or not, the girl's pretty; to Geoffrey, who looks like one of them and can speak the blunt, hard language of a workingman. Balthazar they avoid, though they are polite enough. Here they are, a mining people with a hundred years of darkness in their blood, building a secular religion out of Smoke: hesitant around a Negro.

They'll crap their pants when they figure out he is a lass.

They remain on the beach, within three miles of where the players spilled onto the shore. Riders have arrived, from the "capital," as they proudly say. Members of the Workers' Council. They have abolished all titles, live without king or priest or minister, stand, as Balthazar has heard them say, "strong and equal before the Smoke." And yet a wave of awe goes through the crowd when it is passed around that it is Livia who has arrived, Livia and Francis Mosley, the mining foreman's son who became one of the architects of their republic. Balthazar throngs with the rest of them to catch a glimpse of his heroes and sees them from afar: she, short and scrawny, but with a sense of bearing that resides in the cool high tilt of head and chin; he, moustachioed and soft-eyed, an ornamental smudge of Soot spilling out of his cap, down his temple and ear, the so-called Mark of Thomas.

They fend off the crowd, move through it, towards the carcass of the ship; can be seen questioning the man who organised the salvage effort. At another time, Balthazar would not hesitate and follow them down onto the dirty beach, for a chance to question and study those who are the subject of his plays. Above all *her*: Livia, Smoke's Mother Mary, the apex of his Trinity. But he is tired and his breathing hurts: one of his ribs, it may be broken; his plays and notes are drowned and lost; half his players dead; his theatre in tatters—and all that comes to him, all that jumps into his head, are the witless songs and dirty stories that cast her lewdly as cog and pivot of her dual lovers' needs and make orgies of that adolescent feast of love. It's the pornographic version of the Trinity, and there's not a schoolboy in Britain who cannot sketch one of its constellations.

So he sits down again, having sprung up in that moment of excitement that greeted their arrival; huddles in his blanket and sits there listless till a stranger tells him it is time to move. Where? Inland. This is Gale country. The people here are eager to get back to town.

As for the two riders, they have already left, taking some men along and heading down the coast.

[3]

A girl stops them three or four hours into their march. She is a preacher, it seems, sent out to spread her holy writ. A bird, some kind of swallow, sits on her shoulder, then flies up and circles, lands on a shrub and chirps away, beholden to its human friend. Saint Francis had the knack, they say. The girl is dressed in friar's rags.

She does not have much of a voice. How could she? She is skinny as a twig, thirteen years old, half frozen in the drizzle. Balthazar hears the people around him mutter as they slow and round her like a rock.

"How do they live?" one says. "They do not work, they seek no shelter. What on earth do they eat?"

"Some say each other!"

"Poor thing, look how cold she is. Not one of ours, though. And Lord knows we have enough mouths to feed."

The crowd's mutters almost drown her out. But then, as the comments die down, her thin litany makes itself heard by sheer persistence.

"We are Smoke-borne," she says, or rather chants, the smile tainted by scurvy. "We walk the hills, we chase the Gales. All hail the Angel of the North."

Balthazar watches a figure leave the crowd and slip a crust of bread into the girl's hand. He, too, digs through his pockets but finds that he has eaten all he was given. The girl accepts the handout and turns around to go God knows where. Something medieval clings to her, otherworldly, as though she were a sprite or fairy stranded in this age of steamboats and the telephone. Balthazar watches her until someone takes his arm and gently pulls him along. It is Etta May.

"That girl is starving," he protests, as if it were she who is withholding the child's food.

"She does not want our help," Etta May says, and her voice, American, southern, and kind, saves him somehow, delivers Balthazar from the horrors of the Storm so that for the first time since landing he seems to feel his skin and feet and knows that he is cold and sad and full of fear before his Smoke.

"One of the Miners told me that there is a movement," Etta May carries on, "with some sort of leader, far in the north. Mostly children, no older than ten, eleven, twelve."

"A religion?"

"Something like that." She looks behind her where the girl can be seen trudging off. "You need a new notebook, Balthazar. You'll want to put her in a play."

But the thought of scripting Smoke frightens him, and so he turns away and quickly trudges on.

[4]

The news reaches them just as they are entering Minetowns. Balthazar cannot say whether it comes from the city ahead and arrived by telephone or telegraph, or whether riders bring it from the open country at their side. A second ship, they hear, was caught in the Storm. Unlike the players' vessel, it was pushed south and was salvaged by the pretender's government. Here, too, there were survivors. The image of Eleanor, stiff-backed and awkward, flashes through Balthazar, but he at once suppresses it and consigns her to the place he keeps his dead. It is too much to hope.

All the same, there is a special timbre to the news, a pitch of excitement in the manner it runs through the column of returning men and mules and wagons that remains unexplained until an hour later, when the players have been lodged in a cramped little cottage in Toptown that has been standing empty since its family "upped and left."

"Left where?"

"South. He was *gentry*. Came here looking for 'freedom,' he said, far away from the fetters of his noble birth. Six whole years he worked the coalface, took a wife and all, ate bread in the fat months and starved in the lean, happy as a pig in shit. Then they had young 'uns, a daughter and a son. It's the son that changed his mind, that chubby little 'eir. Now he's back in his manor house, I expect, poring over the fam'ly tree and teaching the little ones which fork goes with the game and which with the cheese. Good riddance, eh?"

The tall, matronly woman explaining this to Balthazar snorts and breathes a twist of Smoke into his face to underline her words: scorn and amusement, finely mixed.

"Here are some blankets, pet, here some tallow candles, and here's a bucket of coal. Toilet's out in the yard, just follow the smell. If you hear the watchtower bell, head for the shaft over there. Or else you can sit tight and brave it. Some do."

"The Gales have been light then?"

"Some light, some salty, but nothing very dark." She shrugs. "You do wonder sometimes. What's the point of revolution if we're going to hide from it like moles?"

Balthazar watches her leave, then runs out after her, into the muddy street. The cottages stand shoulder to shoulder, like a wall.

"We heard there was news," he calls to her. "About a second ship."

"Why yes," she laughs, "the great miracle! It spreads fast, don't it? I expect they're already busy drawing a picture, for our *Illustrated News*. 'The Girl Who Calmed the Blackest Storm.' Soothed the waves, turned water to wine then walked on it, Hosanna and Hail Charlie. She'll have a ripped, wet blouse and long, flowing hair.

"For a godless people," she adds, scratching her rump through the many layers of skirt she is wearing, "we are awful keen on our saints."

It is how Balthazar learns that Eleanor has survived.

[5]

Toptown.

There had been a city between these hills before, squalid and vice-ridden, a cluster of mines and textile mills, and a great ironworks into which young lads were sent to grow old and mean in half the time conventionally allotted to such alchemy; a paper mill, too, stinking up the valley and choking the river fish in its refuse. The Second Smoke emptied the city and sent its workers into the hills and fields: first for bacchanalia best enjoyed in a pastoral setting; later in the desperate search for food. But they came back, organised themselves, and seized the factories from their erstwhile owners—in the name of the people. Minetowns was born: an entity somewhere between an ideal, a city-state, and a political movement. Self-determined, nonhierarchical, communal. Governed by that mysterious entity, the Consensus of Smoke—and by the bureaucrats who sprouted from its soil like mushrooms. A dysfunctional sort of place, no doubt, but no more so than any other polity you care to name. Filled with story and song, much of it newly composed and rather coarse.

Build it and they will come. And come they did. The working classes first of all, drifting here from Liverpool, Sheffield, and Manchester; from Newcastle, Grimsby, Scunthorpe, and Hull. Londoners, too, walking tall, made proud by the knowledge that the revolution started with them, down in the Big Smoke, that greatest of all ratholes, and bringing with them the joys of their rhyming slang.

People from other walks of life soon followed these workers, many of them displaced from the South, some running from the Second Smoke, others chasing it like lovers. By the time they arrived all were sworn converts to its truth—apart from the cadgers, that is, and the curious, and the many spies who were sent to them by Parliament only to be sniffed out by the rotten flavour of their Smokes.

And so the city grew. At first the existing housing stock was filled. It remains distinctive by the square grey stones used in its construction;

stones mined from these very hills, blending into the colour of the land. Then a brickworks was opened and added bright, glazed scarlet to the city's hues. Unlike the natural stone, Soot was found to cling to brick with a rain-defying obstinacy that soon turned the houses reddish black. And thus they stand, some ten or twenty thousand terraced houses, cheek to jowl in tidy rows, their front doors opening straight unto their living rooms, trailing lean rectangles of yard at their narrow backs.

There would have been space in the valley, initially at least, to build houses standing by themselves, four solid walls and a little square of fenced garden to separate them off. But the Miners do not believe in separation: one is to share one's Smoke—or at any rate one's noise, which drifts unhindered through the thin dividing walls. *Isolation* is frowned upon; it reeks of the old ways, of secrecy and social ambition; of "having lost the run of oneself," as the many Irish in town like to put it in their brogue.

Or so the Miners say in public. In the privacy of their homes many are known to close their windows and lock their doors to ensure some separation from their neighbours. "Smoke softly," a saying goes, and "Not every fart needs to be shared." The tension between public mores and private inclination is a well-known topos and the subject of much local humour. Say what you want about the Miners, but they are always game for a laugh.

"Miners"—the word has stuck though coal is no longer the main business in town and only a small proportion of citizens are employed in its harvest. The old ironworks has long reopened and great smelting cauldrons can be seen steaming in its yard; it is now ringed by a slew of factories dedicated to the shaping of steel into machinery, engines, tools, and guns. The textile mills are spinning wool again and there are farmers grazing sheep up on the hills; and families of fishermen whose fathers and sons—and some daughters, too, for the Miners have some fresh ideas in this respect—toil on trawlers off the coast and return but once in eight days, to spend Smokeday under their own roofs.

Climbing the hills that ring the city, one can see its whole layout: the factories not separate, but rising right out of the midst of residential housing and bordering on shops, schools, and a dozen tiny commons, populated by communal goats and pigs, semiferal and living off the city's trash. Concentration, *density,* is everything: the Miners huddle together as though for warmth. Dotted around the city, clearly visible by the latticed towers that straddle them, are the mineshafts. Some are there to access still-profitable coalfaces, and shifts of workers can be seen making their way to them three times a day. Others are mere transport hubs to the city beneath their feet. Toptown is but the peak of the iceberg: if not by size then by significance. Downtown remains a mystery to Balthazar: he has been to Minetowns before, has brought his theatre here and performed several pieces for the workers to good acclaim. But he has yet to be granted permission to enter down below. He is not a citizen, you see, nor is he grown from worker stock. Minetowns knows no hierarchy, but it would be foolish to think everyone is worth the same. He is a stranger, an out-of-towner; has not toiled or yet been *tasted,* and there are limits to the welcome for those who don't belong.

[6]

Etta May was right: Balthazar needs a new notebook. Not to commence upon a *project*—he is not ready for that yet. The Storm remains potent in his blood and feeds a quiet terror about shaping Smoke upon a stage. But he is unused to living with thoughts and observations resounding in his mind without the relief afforded by placing them upon the page. It's why other people marry: for companionship, for dialogue, to be heard and recorded, to talk themselves out. Balthazar has no taste for matrimony. Hence: a notebook. Bound virgin paper he can spoil.

Acquiring this notebook puts him to considerable trouble. He has lost his money and anyway much of the economy is run through an opaque system of vouchers and goods stamps, or is conducted by direct exchange. The Workers' Council has issued him and the other survivors of the wreck—six players, two sailors, and a handful of other passengers—food stamps. But it might be construed as an insult to Minetowns' hospitality were he to trade these away. And so Balthazar goes looking for someone willing to exchange paper for some hours of his labour. He does so furtively, for there is a man living here in Toptown he is not keen to meet: a business acquaintance whose goods Balthazar no longer desires and at any rate cannot afford. A man trading in Gales.

It takes Balthazar several days of looking. His players are no help to him. Etta May is lending a hand at the communal kitchen and is as cheerful as ever, her only complaint the absence of spices in the civic larder. Ada has taken up with a blacksmith's apprentice, handsome as the devil and engaged for "civil marriage" to another woman who is already said to be sharpening her knives. Meister Lukas remains haunted by the version of himself he met during the Storm: he is not sleeping and barely eating, refuses to leave the bed. Geoffrey and David, too, remain unnerved and idle: they mope about the street in search of alcohol in a manner that predicts trouble. Greta Sylvana, meanwhile, has disappeared and is rumoured to have left for the South on a stolen mule. This last item of news surprises Balthazar less than the sudden encounter with Sashinka, the players' cat, whom he finds stretched out upon his bed one evening, belly up and legs akimbo, the long fur of its stomach matted with Soot.

"So you made it," Balthazar murmurs gently. "I did not see you on the beach and thought you drowned."

He spends the night lying wedged between the wall and the edge of the bed, disinclined to shift the cat and somehow irrationally afraid it will abandon him. But in the morning, it is still there, toying with a mouse it has caught but seems uninterested in eating.

On the fourth day in Toptown, Balthazar finally gets his chance to acquire some paper when one of the neighbours requires help unblocking the sewage pipe connecting his outhouse to the civic grid. The man—a greengrocer—has some old order books he is willing to trade. They spend the whole day standing shoulder to shoulder, shovelling first dirt then shit. As they finish up and cart the last of the mud and excrement away, the greengrocer tells him a joke made up half of words and half of Smoke that has Balthazar still laughing when he returns home and finds, in place of the cat, a lad of fourteen or fifteen, ordering him in a rehearsed little speech to make himself available on the morrow, to present himself to the Workers' Council. The boy is shy and nervous and unable to provide any details. All he has to add to the message, twice repeated, is "We thank the Smoke," before running back out into the street.

It does not matter. The Workers' Council, in the morning.

Balthazar is going down into the coal.

[7]

They send a pretty young thing to fetch him, what Geoffrey or David might fondly call a "skirt." She arrives in an odd assemblage of heavy workman's boots and riding trousers bulging loosely at the thighs but clinging tightly to the rump; a collarless shirt spotted with coal dust and Soot; a hunting cap that spills her fiery hair; and a schoolboyish leather satchel strapped to her narrow back. It's the face that is pleasing: a full mouth and freckles; large, red-lashed eyes; an upturned nose that gives her a guileless air.

The Miners are fond of hand-shaking and so Balthazar extends his, only to have it seized and the young woman link herself into his elbow.

"Miss—?" he inquires.

"Teddy," she says, firmly and naturally, in the accent of someone well born. "This is Minetowns. We use first names here."

"Teddy," he smiles, charmed despite his natural gruffness. "From Theodora?"

"Ursula. *Ursus,* see. Latin for 'bear.' Hence: Teddy. A family joke."

She walks while she chatters, leading him through the puddle-strewn street as though they are promenading, calling out greetings to some of the Miners around.

"Have you been in the elevators before?"

"No."

"Oh, it's a thrill! Only I hope you haven't eaten yet. Some people find it upsetting. For the stomach. No, you haven't? Marvellous! We can find something for you down below."

Within minutes they have arrived at a mineshaft and hear the whirring of the wheel high above, then see the hole spit up a cage.

"I have gone down a thousand times, but it still gives me goose bumps. You see, he described it to me, their own journey down. Fugitives, in the middle of the night! Listening to the singing of that wire. He is most particular about that sound! Like a knife on a stone, he always says, but somehow pretty, too."

She pauses, looks up into Balthazar's puzzled face.

"He," she laughs. "Charlie—my brother. He must have told me the story a hundred times."

[8]

If the purpose of their trip is to present him to the Workers' Council, they appear to be in no great hurry. Rather young Miss Cooper seems intent on showing off the place and giving him a tour. They exit the cage on the very first level and enter a warren of buttressed tunnels. Everything is brightly lit by electric lights; some of the tunnel walls have been bricked and even plastered, others remain lined by raw stone. There are tracks for a train system and a network of internal elevators; a bustle of people here, rushing from one place to another; a moist stillness there, water running down the walls.

In places the tunnels widen into pockets of space, low-ceilinged and segmented by a dozen metal pillars. Their purpose is varied: one will be filled with mining equipment, carts, and pit ponies, the next will feature shopping stalls selling anything from cold cuts to underwear. There are barbers and knife sharpeners, cobblers and a haberdashery; a pub filled with people drinking pints and playing cards; a coffeehouse in which a poet-singer stands drunkenly upon a table, declaiming his coarse verse. Above it all sounds the wheeze of the ventilation system, congested and regular like an asthmatic's snore.

True to her word, Miss Cooper stops at one of the stalls and acquires some sandwiches—cheese and sour pickle—which they eat perching on some packing crates and wash down with two pints of murky ale. The young woman sits unselfconsciously, her legs crossed in front of her, and eats with great relish. It is only her hands—the way she holds the sandwich between three fingers of each hand with her little fingers stretched out taut—that betray that she was bred for a different sort of luncheon. Balthazar notes it and commits it to memory so he can transfer it to his notebook later on.

"Come," she says, drinking the last of her ale. "Let's carry on. Oh, it's such a joy to share all this with you—an artist! But look, I am quite tipsy now, you better hold me by the hand."

And then, in a sweet-scented whisper, close to his ear:

"Is it true what some people say? That you are a woman really, dressed up as a man? Well, I would never have guessed! Of course, there are many here who do the same. Cut their hair and all! But then they still put a little Soot in their lashes and wear their caps *just so*." She laughs, pouts her lips, lays a hand upon his shoulder. "Still, things are changing fast. We do have women on the Council now. *Equality*, they say. There was a declaration! *Man is a universal creature. We Miners recognise no sex.* We even voted on it and it carried in the Smoke! But you just ask the women who it is that cleans the house when they get home. No, don't laugh, it's not funny, though maybe it is! But quick now, the Council will be waiting and there's one more thing I must show you, it's ever so wonderful. Don't worry, it isn't far."

[9]

Despite this announcement, it turns out to be a long walk, following a series of tunnels big enough to accommodate a whole mob of people but curiously deserted at this hour of the day. They take some ramps and stairs, always leading up. Balthazar has the feeling that they must be near the surface and have moved beyond the limits of the upper town, perhaps as far as the hills. There are a number of underground apartments in this area, Miss Cooper explains, still in the same breathless, confidential way. Some have their own light shafts: systems of mirrors, trapping the sun and whisking it down into lush living rooms.

"For Council members," she confides, "though officially they are given out by lot."

She shrugs, unfazed by this evidence of corruption; drags him on, leading him by his hand like a dawdling child.

They arrive. She makes him close his eyes before they enter, and so the first he knows of the place is the smell of fresh air, dropping down from above. She leads him on, reprimanding him whenever he is tempted to risk a squint. A large, unbroken space, the floor hard and smooth underfoot. A feeling stirs in Balthazar, familiar from a thousand rehearsals, of walking out onto a stage. But this stage is slanting downwards, very gently, as though for drainage. It is like walking in a giant tub.

It takes some thirty steps before it levels off.

"Here we are," Miss Cooper—Teddy—says at last. "Ekklesia. Is it not the most wonderful place on earth?"

Balthazar opens his eyes. It's a giant bowl, carved into the rock and opening above into a natural valley, so steep-sided as to form a funnel straight into the earth. The sun sits on one of the hillcrests, high above; a circle of sky overhead; the eerie feeling of being trapped deep within a giant well. Here, at the bottom, the space is the size of a village square and more or less round. The floor slants towards the centre. At the periphery, stalls have been erected, consisting of little more than wooden footboards and iron frames that are sunk into the rock: fifteen, twenty levels, each new circle several feet higher than the last. He imagines these stalls packed with people. Along with the floor space at the bottom, the bowl may be big enough to accommodate the adult population of the town.

"Ekklesia? From the Greek, I suppose. You hold meetings here?"

"Meetings, announcements, sport. It's where we achieve Consensus, a few times each year."

It takes him a moment to wrest meaning from this awkward little phrase.

"You mean you smoke down here?" he asks, unbelieving. "The whole bloody town? That's insane."

She laughs, snatches the hand that she has only just released, tugs at it.

"I knew you would love it. But come. The Council meets not far from here. They will be wondering where you are."

Before they have taken more than a half dozen steps, she stops once more, digs in her little satchel, which has rested unmolested on her back all this time as though its main function were for its straps to accentuate her breasts, and produces a small brown paper parcel.

"Here. They won't let me come into the chamber with you and I have been meaning to give you this. It's a rarity, you know. It has only been out a week and it is entirely sold out!"

[10]

And so Balthazar enters the meeting chamber of the Workers' Council distracted, clutching the little parcel whose wrapper he has ripped open on the short walk from the public meeting hall to this murky, low-ceilinged room deeper underground. It's a book, bound in thick cardboard, unadorned on the outside. He has not had time to open its covers.

Miss Cooper delivered him to the door but did not enter. She has no status in the Council. And so he stands alone, like a priest before his congregation, or a culprit before a court: rows of benches starting some five steps from him and forming a three-rowed U, its mouth open towards him. Everything about the room is dim and somehow squalid: the ceiling very low and buttressed not by metal struts but crooked pieces of timber; the benches themselves roughly tailored and evidently uncomfortable. The only light is provided by the Council Members' mining lamps, the traditional safety design, burning in low blue flames. There are gaps amongst the seats, but even so there must be fifty people in the room, filling it with their heat and slowly fouling the air.

Balthazar, the theatre man, understands at once the symbolism of this stage set; understands that everything—the squalor, the lamps, the sheer coal walls that will bind any Smoke before it can infect—is a reference and reenactment of that first meeting room, where the miners forged a secret union and learned to speak up for their rights: there, in some other hole deep in the ground in Nottinghamshire, far to the south.

A man rises. He is seated at the back, Balthazar notes, near the centre of the U. The Mark of Thomas sits dark on his weather-beaten face: at his temple and the tip of the ear.

"Thy name?" he asks, flat Yorkshire vowels and all the gruffness of a factory foreman. "For th' record."

"Balthazar Black."

"Tha have been summoned to give witness about the storm that sank thy ship. Art tha willing?"

Balthazar hesitates. He is a director not a player and as such resentful of being asked to *perform*. Besides, he is not sure he is ready for it yet. Putting words to the Storm. It is the first step towards staging it.

"I will write you a report," he hazards. "Then you can ask me questions about details."

This causes a titter, of irritation if not outrage.

"We do not accept written testimony in this chamber. Only the living word speaks true."

"Well, ask then," Balthazar snaps back, then immediately regrets his tone. He is a guest here and dependent on the goodwill of this Council. The book in his hand suddenly feels awkward, as out of place as a hunting crop or crucifix, and he slips it quickly in the pocket of his coat.

[11]

And so Balthazar recounts the coming of the Storm. He starts slowly, haltingly, sulkily; knows he is speaking too low; is interrupted by shouts to "speak up, friend," "put your back into it." Before long, the story begins to absorb him and brings back moments, sights, he has suppressed. Smoke soon pours out of him, at first thinly, like watery gruel, then in a sudden billow from the white palms of his hands, and he smells in himself the frightened old woman he has never wanted to be. A council member stands up at this point, dips his hands into a bucket standing to one side; throws some coal dust into his Smoke before it can reach the benches, then quickly disperses it with a handheld fan, aware of the dangers of explosion.

The man has reason to dip his hands twice more before the tale is finished.

When he is done, the Council sits in silence for a moment. Then a young man rises from one of the benches on Balthazar's left. He wears no Mark of Thomas; rather his whole face is blacked out with coal dust and Soot, and a leather cap is covering his head.

"Thanking you for your tale, brother," he says, and says it somehow sneeringly, the voice full of superiority and distrust. "You say it was a Storm, a Black Storm, that found you out on the sea. But we all know that that's impossible. Black Storms are the propaganda of the South. Now I'm not calling you a liar, brother—I understand you are a theatre man and that a bit of embellishment is part of the trade. But why not say it was a Gale, blowing out to sea, that had picked up a little filth along the way? After all, here you are, in one piece and survived."

A murmur follows these words: of approval from the other black-faced men surrounding him, of anger at the other bend of the U, to Balthazar's right, where shirts tend to be cleaner and are at times adorned with collars; where hats and caps have been taken off and faces are scrubbed and lightly painted with the Mark.

The same old Yorkshire backbencher who started the proceedings quiets both sides by hammering his fist against the bench.

"Let him answer the question. 'Tis fair."

Balthazar faces them. He can read doubt in half the room. They must have reports of what the hull looked like, caked in Soot. But even so. Ten years of living with emotional weather have impressed on them its rules. Gales turn dark when they ignite violence within people and spread it down the line; turn darker yet when they dig out from the soil—from the depths of a disused well, from a place of execution or an old battlefield— deposits of black Soot accumulated there and quicken it into fresh life. Some Gales bring lust and orgy; drunken joy and folly. Some bring pub brawls, knife fights, and self-loathing. But even these can be withstood and moderated; can be soothed by a happy Smoker just as they are darkened by one raging or abused.

The Black Storm was nothing like that.

"It ate us," Balthazar says now. "We ran away and missed the bulk of it and still it ate us. It was pure rage. Like something injected in your blood; taking possession. An anger so total it seemed to belong to someone else." He turns to the young Council member on his left. "I'd hate to think my friends were killed by propaganda from the South."

There is much murmur to his response, and further questions, but Balthazar is increasingly monosyllabic in his answers, is tired, hollow, spent. It is as though he has relived it. Perhaps it means that he is free to shed its memory; cut it out of his flesh and remand it to his notes.

Soon after, he is dismissed. As he leaves, the Miners all reach for their lamps and douse them. They will debate his interview in darkness.

[12]

He expects Miss Cooper to be waiting for him outside but instead finds a child of eight or nine, rather shy, who in a tongue-tied sort of way asks him to follow. They walk a fair bit, Balthazar slow now, and unable to get any answers out of the child, other than that her "Pa" wants to see him. At last they arrive at a door and enter without knocking into a family apartment full of noise and cooking smells. It must be one of the luxury apartments Miss Cooper talked about, for there is natural light in the room leaking from a hole in the ceiling, along with the scent of rain. Four further children are running around, playing train, with the eldest the engine, and the youngest toddling at the back. Toys litter the ground; there is a sofa made up as a bed, a dining table, a door to another room.

"Pa! 'E's here," his guide yells at this door without bothering to walk near it. A moment later Francis Mosley steps into the room, closely followed by Livia. The smell of boiling turnips follows them.

Balthazar saw them on the day of the rescue, but he was cold then and they were far away. Up close, he is handsome, if careworn; is tall and rangy, thick brown moustaches framing his mouth. Livia looks even smaller than on the beach, the plain clothes hanging off her skinny frame. What beauty she has resides in her hair and fine-boned features: elfin running to gaunt. There is no Mark on her temple and her skin is scrupulously scrubbed.

Francis greets him with a handshake; Livia with a nod. Neither invites him to sit.

"You spoke to the Council," she says at last. Even more so than Miss Cooper's, her voice is pure aristocrat. It has the effect of making the room look tiny and poor.

"Yes, they grilled me."

"Don't worry, I won't ask you to repeat yourself. I had someone taking notes for me."

She lets the words sink in, her disregard for the chamber's interdiction on written records, then walks over to a chair and sits down, straight-backed and prim. The two men remain standing.

"You have heard about the other ship caught up in the Storm? The one carrying someone who is said to have soothed the Storm. A saint."

He nods.

"And do you believe the story? They say it was Renfrew's daughter who saved the ship."

"His niece. Eleanor. A remarkable girl."

"Then you have met her. How interesting."

But even as she says it, Balthazar can see that Livia is unengaged in the topic, finds only trifling significance in Miss Renfrew's sudden rise to fame. She is not why Balthazar is here.

"There was a third ship," Livia carries on. "We found it shortly after we found you. A Company vessel, we think, hailing from India, not the Americas, run aground on the Welsh coast. A ghost ship, not a soul on board. The insides were as though lacquered and overgrown with a strange black fungus. It had a *feeling* about it. A rather nasty kind of feeling. It might have been salvageable but we left it to be smashed up by the tide. The Council was upset. The ship was valuable and I didn't have authority."

She says all this flatly, unemotionally, studying his face for a reaction. But both her fists are clenched. Little fists. Like a sparrow girding for war.

"What exactly did it look like, Balthazar? The Storm you saw."

"A black spar. Like a cut in the sky. Like the one *you* saw in London, ten years ago."

"How would you know what I saw?"

"Because I had pictures. Photographs. Taken on the morning when the first Storm was set off."

"Photographs! How curious. But then, Aschenstaedt had a camera. Perhaps they are his." She pauses, looks at him. "There hasn't been a Storm in nearly ten years. And now one rages out to sea. Why there? Why now?"

Balthazar tries to understand what she wants of him, parses her words, her questioning look.

A Company vessel. From India.

A Storm out to sea.

All at once he grasps her point.

"You think it started on that ship! The one whose insides were 'as though lacquered'! But how . . . ?"

She shrugs and lowers her gaze, disappointed. "I don't know. And I can see that you don't either. It was worth finding out whether by chance you might. But no, I suppose you are no more than what you claim to be. A playwright, not a politician. Nor an emissary."

When she continues, her voice is unchanged, but Balthazar can see her interest in him is diminished. He stands unconnected to the great things that are afoot.

Which is not to say he cannot be used.

"I have a commission for you, Balthazar. This is a town of workers and you have been idle. I want you to ply your trade."

For a moment Balthazar stands reeling with the speed of his devaluation. Then the implications of this new request become clear to him.

"A performance? Impossible! I have lost all my notes and most of my players. And those I have are frightened. The Storm hurt—"

"Some activity will do you all good. And you can always find new players. There's no shortage of people here happy to shirk their work in the factory in order to strut around and talk for a living. Just look at our esteemed Council members. Besides, we don't want your old material but something new. Something suited to our people here. Something that will make them feel good about themselves. Build hope." She delivers all this rather coldly, dismissively, her hands back in fists.

"You want me to write propaganda plays."

"Ah, here it is, that prissy bourgeois scruple that our angry young men so like to shout about. *Propaganda*. Are you worried it will violate your artistic soul?"

For a moment he thinks she will laugh at him or spit at his feet. But she is too self-possessed for that. Too noble.

"Write something that matters to people. Something that helps them hold their heads up high. Something that smells of the brickyard or the sausage factory."

Balthazar thinks about it. "Or else you will have us starve."

"Or else no more free lunch. Is that so very cruel?"

[13]

It is Francis who dissolves the tension of the moment by inviting Balthazar to join them for some food. He has been silent all through their conversation, impassive. Now he bids Balthazar sit at the dinner table and gathers the many children together who squeeze onto a bench. The next moment a plump, handsome woman appears with a steaming pot of soup and begins ladling out bowls.

"Mary, this is Balthazar, a playwright. Balthazar, Mary."

The young woman stares hard at him as she passes over the food bowl. "Is that Soot on your face and hands or just the colour you are?" she asks briskly.

"Skin," he answers.

"Good. I like clean hands at the table. Here, have some bread. There's no butter. And if some busybody asks, up above the coal"—here she cocks her chin to the ceiling, denoting the whole of Toptown—"I'm the wife and she's our guest and that's all there's to say about that."

Balthazar sees Livia squirm at her words, not so much at the insinuation as at the coarseness of the woman.

Again Francis takes it upon himself to mediate.

"You see, Balthazar, our people love a bit of gossip. Two women under one roof! We are a revolutionary society, of course. But awfully conservative for all that."

He shrugs, bows his head before the food, puts a finger to his Mark.

"We thank the Smoke," he intones, quite sincerely, sitting here in his fortress made of coal. "Please don't be bashful. Tuck in."

And so Balthazar eats, thinking of another rumour he has heard Topside and scanning the children's faces, studying their features for Livia's, or Charlie's or Thomas's, whom he knows from a hundred bad drawings but has never met. If their winter of love bore fruit, it is not so far-fetched to imagine the child here, mixed in with these others, anonymous. But the children all look different to him, each capable of having all sorts of parentage, and besides he is not afforded much time for his scrutiny. No sooner has Balthazar finished his bowl than Livia rises and leads him to the door.

"Francis will see you out," she announces, "while we women clear up. But what's this, sticking out your pocket?"

Balthazar stares at her confused, then fingers his coat pocket and finds the cardboard binding of a book. "I don't know. Miss Cooper gave it to me, as a present. I have had no time to look at it."

At the mention of Miss Cooper, something runs through Livia's features, too quickly to be parsed.

"Well then, have a look."

Balthazar opens the binding and finds a roughly printed frontispiece and title page declaiming the book to be *A History of Minetowns*, dedicated to "The Miners' Revolutionary Struggle." It is written by someone identified only by a nom de plume and a crudely drawn tool.

"Who the hell is 'Shovel'?" he asks.

Francis makes to answer but Livia shushes him.

"We are all of us Shovel."

He accepts this, leafs through the book, finding pages upon pages of closely printed text, interspersed with illustrations. Whole sections of narrative appear to be rendered as sequential sketches in little panels across the page. He looks more closely and realises these wordless sections capture life within a Gale, or on other occasions when the town gives itself over to the Smoke while congregating in Ekklesia. The pictures are at once simple and masterly: eschew realism for something more direct and vital. The prose, by contrast, is turgid, overdetailed, dense with statistics and subclauses. The wonder at all this must show on Balthazar's face. Livia misinterprets it.

"You laugh," she says. "You find it ridiculous, our Minetowns. Workers playing at being rulers. Costumes and symbols, like children at a mummery."

Balthazar is quick to shake his head. "No, I admire it. But I find it filled with contradiction."

"Oh, it is. We are caught between the original union's ideal—of darkness, smokelessness; of speaking reason in the void, each man and woman reduced to his or her voice—and that thing that we released: communion, the sharing of desires, of sins and dreams. But tell me a city that is not built on contradiction!"

She pauses, draws herself up, five foot three and towering before him, her accent clipped and precise.

"Do you think Robespierre liked his revolution at the end, Balthazar? Did he look out the window and swoon over the guillotine? Do you know what I think? That all he needed was just a little more time. But the people lost faith, and so they got Napoleon and another bloody king."

Now it is Balthazar's turn to grow irate. "It is said your mother was fond of talking about Robespierre."

"Mother?" she scoffs, Smoke on her breath. "You bloody poets! Always pretending you were *there*. Write me a play, Balthazar, and keep Mother out of it."

[14]

Write me a play. He mulls it over for the next few days until the ration cards run out, then sends down a message that he accepts the commission. Oh, he will write Miss Livia a play. A play for all of Minetowns, to be performed at Ekklesia. And for it to be the play he wants—a play for Shovel to include in the next edition of his history—Balthazar is in need of a little stage magic. And thus, on the eighth day in Minetowns, his recently acquired notebooks already filling up with ideas, Balthazar goes looking for the very man he has so studiously been trying to avoid.

NORTHERN JOKE

q: How many southerners does it take to change a lightbulb?

a: One. But afterwards it takes six inspectors to establish if the man had impure thoughts while screwing it into its socket. *(suggestive Smoke for emphasis of punch line)*

SOUTHERN JOKE

q: How many northeners does it take to change a lightbulb?

a: What's a lightbulb?

[1]

Eleanor Renfrew, Shy Madonna of the Storm, newly returned to the country of her birth, her chin and forehead in pimpled revolt against its island dampness, stands before a mirror flaring her mouth like a horse. Horses do it to enhance their sense of smell, Cruikshank once explained to her: peel back their meaty lips like the skin of a banana to expose the bony pallor of their gums. And so Eleanor, too, now sees fit to flay the outer layers of her mouth. She uses her fingers to pin the upper lip against the base of her small nose; pins the lower lip against the little valley between chin and mouth. The mirror watches her transformation: sees a child making faces, scaring herself with the monsters sculpted from her pliant flesh; then finds in her gaze no gleeful sense of play but the sober focus of a medical exam. She bends closer; raises her chin; *looks*.

Much of what she is searching for is gone. The black forked lightning that patterned the roof of her mouth has faded. Nor is she peeing black any longer, the urine collecting thick and oddly scentless on the enamelled bottom of the chamber pot. But here, in the pale pink of her gums, some threads of it can still be seen. Mowgli's touch.

The beetle's mark.

She would like to ask him whether he, too, stared in trepidation at the black leaving his body, but their conversation—terse, frustrated, conducted by means of scraps of paper pushed under the door of this, her prison—does not extend to micturition. They survived the Storm together, flooded one another with their anger. Now distance governs their relations, a distance not imposed simply by the lock upon her door. Eleanor has thought much of late about the wedding night scene that opens so many of Balthazar's shows. He should write another scene, showing bride and groom at breakfast on the morning when the Second Smoke had gone.

Avoiding each other's eyes.

She finds it easy to forget that Balthazar is dead.

[2]

If it is a cell she is inhabiting, she can reassure herself with the fact that everyone else here is in one, too. The building was purpose-built, thrown up with a speed that speaks volumes for the will of its master. It is the seat of Renfrew's government, his Parliament and royal court, but what one sees from the outside is functional and drab: a cluster of three-storey buildings, long and low like barracks, forming a five-pronged star; a squat tower at the hub; the windows small and uniform. There is a parliamentary chamber somewhere inside the structure, but most of the space is taken up by identical square rooms, built for single habitation. Pentonville: that's one of the names for the building, after the prison used as its architectural model, the first British penitentiary to isolate its prisoners in individual cells. Smith told her this, back on the ship. He told her other names, too. The Commons. Borstal. Penitentiary. The School; the Workhouse; the Nunnery.

The Silent Keep.

Here families are not allowed. Each body has a cell here and all private life is reduced to desk, bed, and chair.

No man is an island.

Except here.

[3]

A prison then: a locked door. Through it comes but a single visitor, at time-tabled intervals, to see to her needs. He is a servant, hard-faced and old, with lank grey hair and a spare, compact body oddly younger than his features. A dangerous man. The notion formed in Eleanor's head on their first meeting and won't be dislodged, though he has done nothing but bring her food and clean out her chamber pot, and dismiss all her questions with a dead-eyed stare. She listens for his steps at breakfast, lunchtime, and dinner; catches them seldom. The servant walks softly. He has not offered her his name.

There are other communications she holds with the outside world. There is a window, for one, that she can open and lean out of, craning her neck to scrutinise the drab flank of the building. Pigeons visit her there; they must roost in the rafters above. In front of her there is a flat ridge of barren land that drops away steeply into the Bristol Channel. They are quite near its tip, but even so it must be several miles to the Welsh coast. In the water, far enough out not to be stranded by low tide, lie anchored some twenty ships, few of them seaworthy and none under steam. Figures can be seen swarming their decks, too far away to observe in detail, though the breeze carries their sounds. The impression is one of overcrowding and misery. A haze of Smoke surrounds each ship and shifts only in high winds. Around the ships the sea is dark with their effluvia.

These, she learned from Smith when they were tugged into harbour, are prison ships. Those convicted of crimes against the order of the state are incarcerated there: women on one ship and men on the others. They eat what they catch, plus some small ration of bread and vegetables rowed out to them twice a week. It cannot be coincidence that the ships are anchored here, in plain sight of the worthy parliamentarians. They are stark reminders of the price of disorder, both political and of the soul. Eleanor has watched them for a week now. She wonders why the birds and fish keep coming to their hulls where so many of their brethren have been hooked and eaten by those who hunger inside; wonders, too, what bloody slop is dumped into the sea each morning to draw the black fins of a hundred sharks.

She wonders what the damned do with their dead.

[4]

If Eleanor has made a habit of watching the prison ships—from pity and boredom, and to read their darkness as a primer to her uncle's soul—her interest today is more urgent and specific. She woke this morning to find a fresh message underneath her door. Mowgli's missives: twists of paper, covered in pencil and folded in half. Every night she deposits her own, hoping Mowgli will retrieve the note before the servant brings her breakfast; will herself search the gap beneath the door a hundred times each day for news from the world beyond. If her questions are detailed and wide-ranging, his answers are short and incomplete. She asked Mowgli why he does not visit her; pick the lock as surely he can. He did not respond. She has sensed him there, late in the night, lying on the threshold of her door, listening for her breathing. But when she herself lay down on the floor and whispered his name through the gap, there had been no answer; just another scrawled pronouncement waiting for her in the hour before dawn.

As a result, her grasp of the events beyond her cell is limited to isolated facts. She knows that Smith is in negotiations with her uncle; that he pursued Company business at first but has now changed tack and requested private meetings; that Smith, for reasons of his own, has retained Mowgli as his servant and in this function has allowed him to accompany him on many of his engagements; and that Mowgli is playing along with this in the hope of learning more about his origin and the secret of the beetle. She has learned, too, that her uncle is "thin, sick-looking"; that as recently as a few weeks ago the King, long gone into hiding, has been deposed in absentia; that Parliament is made up of an odd coalition of aristocrats, capitalists, churchmen, and lawyers, as well as a handful of commoners yearning for the stability of the old status quo.

"Some here wear powdered wigs," Mowgli has written, "others wear Smoke masks. There are no women in this keep."

It is too thin a fabric, too colourless and torn, for Eleanor to shape into reality. The cell, the servant, the black of her pee: these have weight. Everything else is hearsay. Voiceless whispers in a boyish hand.

Until today. The promise of something different, definite and concrete. A jagged piece, ripped from the corner of a book, the pencil fighting to be visible above the printed ink. "Noon excursion," the message reads. "Smith + Renfrew. Going out to the ships."

Finally, then. An *event*. A chance to see her uncle for herself, however much from a distance; to glean some firsthand knowledge of the workings of this place. Judging by the sun, noon is still some hours away. So she studies her gums and paces; opens the window, leans out, watches pigeons mill above her head.

[5]

At long last, a procession of coaches appears on the little road that winds itself towards a rocky beach and jetty. They divulge a dozen figures. The soldiers are marked by the rifles that are strapped to their shoulders. Eleanor can make out Smith by his bulk and the golden glow of his whiskers; makes out Mowgli by the swarthiness of his skin. The servant is there, the one who serves her food, recognisable by the tidiness of his movements. He is attending yet another man, hunched and haggard and wrapped into a coat despite the mildness of the weather.

She thought she would recognise him by his walk or the way he has of holding his head, but what she sees down by the pier is the figure of a stranger, shrunken and diminished, his identity disclosed only by the deference paid to him by all the others. Then, as he laboriously climbs into a rowing boat, he makes a private little movement: both hands digging underneath the coat to smooth down his shirt, making sure its skirts remain safely tucked within his trousers. Her own hands mirror the gesture and find in it a gateway to her childhood. It is he, Renfrew, master of this building and ruler of this kingdom: her strict, unsmiling uncle who would sit with her and read when she was lying sick with measles or with mumps.

The next moment he has seated himself and turned up his overcoat's collar, and the similarity is gone. He reverts to what he was before: a stranger of great prominence, a sick man shivering in the warm spring breeze.

The oarsmen take him out to sea.

[6]

The ships stink.

They stink of sewage and fish guts; of seaweed, Smoke, and unwashed bodies; of the rotting basking shark that dangles from a hook at the rear of the closest ship and attracts to it a swarm of seabirds and a maelstrom of dark circling shapes just beneath the surface of the water. With each stroke of the oar, the stink grows stronger. Nil finds himself puckering his nostrils and breathing only through the mouth. The soldier in front of him does much the same. He has risen, stands legs spread at the bow of the boat, and has cocked his gun. What he is aiming at, Nil cannot tell.

As for the prisoners, they have begun to cluster ever more thickly on the decks ahead to watch their slow approach; watch in silence, for the most part, jostling for space. There is a familiar tenor to their stare. Not fear, not anger. Hunger: that hollow-cheeked greed. Many of these men are armed with clubs or nails or a shard of glass picked from a broken bottle. Few are smoking as of yet.

Behind Nil, sitting with his back to the prison ships if occasionally turning for a look, Smith is chattering away at Dr. Renfrew. That's what Smith calls him. Not "Lord Protector," not "sire," nor even "sir." Plain Dr. Renfrew. Nil took it for insolence until Smith explained it was Company policy. Renfrew's precise rank and legal status are a matter of debate. His academic honours are not.

"Do they not try to swim to freedom? It does not seem a very long distance. Though I suppose there are tidal currents to negotiate and the water is rather cold."

Smith's voice: as hale and affable as ever, speaking loudly into the breeze. He has brought along a little wooden suitcase that Nil was asked to carry for him and is now using for a seat. A rolled-up umbrella is strapped to its top and is tangling up Nil's legs.

"One of them will try, on occasion. We have soldiers on watch."

Dr. Renfrew. Speaking with distaste or perhaps boredom; the voice crisper than the shrunken body would suggest.

"They shoot them, I suppose."

"They fish them out, cut their knee tendons, and return them to the ship."

"Ah."

Five more strokes of the oars and they draw alongside the nearest ship. The soldiers are nervous. They don't wear uniforms other than a blue armband on which yellow lines mark their rank. Perhaps, thinks Nil, Renfrew is short on money and would rather spend it on arms. Or else he is making a point. His is a citizen army. Which, turned around, would mean that there are no civilians, no bystanders. Renfrew is waging a war in which everyone is involved, body and soul. He himself is wearing a dinner jacket and tie, and a lamb's wool greatcoat tied at the waist. Nil is at a loss how to square the dinner party clothes with the pinched Puritan face.

They have brought their own ladder: a six-foot wood-and-iron structure that bends into a U at the top. It was rowed over by the second boat and is now hooked over the ship's railing. The first soldier soon ascends. The other soldiers are nervous, watching their comrade climb the rungs. It requires both his hands, which means he cannot hold a gun. As he reaches the railing, he draws a pistol from his belt and shouts at the men on top to step back. Five further soldiers soon follow him up. Only then does their own rowboat moor at the bottom of the ladder. Renfrew's servant is the next one up. Then his master. He shivers like a leaf while climbing up the ladder, his shrunken body lost in his too-big coat. Smith and Nil make up the rear. Nil pulls up the suitcase with the help of a rope.

The deck is shiny with fish scales, grease, Soot: specks of silver, rainbow puddles, and dark muck. The soldiers have cleared a crescent of space by the side of the railing; are standing, twitchy, rifles pointing into the crowd. Now that Nil can see them more clearly, the prisoners look more pitiful than he expected. Starved peasants, tradesmen, petty thieves: most as shrunken and sickly as the man who condemned them to their fate.

There can be no doubt that they have recognised Renfrew. Their eyes are on him, some in deference, some in anger. A few of the prisoners have fallen to their knees but are still holding on to their clubs.

It strikes Nil what a risk Renfrew is taking by coming here in person. Smith will have insisted, no doubt, and clubs and glass shards are no match for rifles. Even so, the Lord Protector must have great courage. And be desperate. Negotiations, Nil understands, have not gone well. The Company sells Renfrew all manner of things: food, fuel, textiles, drugs. Sweets. But Renfrew is out of money and the Company's line of credit is stretched to a point "where our risk assessors advise against further extension." Nil chewed on this phrase of Smith's awhile before he understood it. "Risk assessment" is a term from the insurance business, which Nil understands is a form of gambling. The Company is staking a bet on Renfrew. The potential gains are good but the fear of losses very real. Renfrew might lose; might die and his debts not be recognised by his successors. Nil wonders whether the Company has another Smith, sent north, selling the Miners goods against a similar line of credit. But no, it is said the Miners do not deal with Capital. Which may be the only reason the Company condescends to contemplate further loans to Renfrew at all.

For a moment, all is static, like a tableau: the soldiers standing with rifles cocked, bayonets mounted on the barrels; the press of prisoners, made impassive by their ignorance about the purpose of this visit. Then Smith takes charge. He turns, says something to one of the soldiers, who in turn whistles down to one of his mates remaining with the boats. It appears that other than the ladder, the second boat carried two stools, a small table-top, and a sawhorse that can serve as its base. These are quickly hoisted onto deck and then assembled. Smith takes a seat on one of the stools and gestures to Renfrew to join him. The Lord Protector does but only after whispering an order to his servant. At his gesture, with a haste that speaks of relief, the soldiers open a knapsack they have brought, distribute what is inside, and quickly slip it over their heads.

Smoke masks.

The smooth leather skulls, brass-rimmed goggles, and dangling snouts lend the men something insectoid and strange. Their humanity has fled. Renfrew's servant, too, dons a mask, then offers another to his master. Renfrew shakes his head. Unsurprised, the servant then offers it to Nil. He sees it and recoils against the railing, retching up Smoke from deep within his throat; stands for a moment in the swell-rocked darkness of another ship, eight years old and treated like a monster. His Smoke is caught by the breeze. It whips towards the prisoners; spreads from skin to skin like the spark of a flame in a summer-parched forest, kindling fear of execution. Soldiers' guns are pointing at their chests.

But it is not for the purposes of killing that Smith has mounted this venture. He bends instead to retrieve his little suitcase; lifts it to the table and opens it wide. There are plates inside—bone china—bottles, crystal glasses, and a silver chandelier, all safely strapped into lined cavities. Also: a ham, a jar of mustard; a grilled kidney wrapped in paper; roast beef, already sliced; a jar of pickles, an assemblage of pork pies, a dozen boiled eggs. He puts these out as though he were at a picnic, licks clean his fingers, stuffs a napkin behind his collar. The umbrella he bids a soldier hold, to serve as a parasol. It is true, the day is uncommonly bright.

The prisoners smoke. They smoke from hunger, from outrage, from humiliation. Soot soon spices the food. It does not halt Smith's relish. He eats with his fingers, ignoring the silver cutlery, dabbing rolled-up slices of roast beef in mustard, cramming them whole into his cheek. Renfrew sits across from him, not eating, shivering, pale; fighting his body's response with nothing but his will.

Just as it seems that the crowd's Smoke has reached a tipping point where even the guns won't prevent a riot, Smith rises. The napkin he has stuck into his collar flaps in the breeze. He pulls it out and, still chewing, shoulders in amongst the soldiers' half circle so that he can address the crowd.

"Hungry?" he says, not jeering but as though he genuinely wants to know. "Fancy a luncheon with the Lord Protector? Well, I say, I will fight you for the privilege."

Without further ado he begins to strip, taking off his shirt and climbing out of his trousers, which leaves him in a one-piece cotton undergarment, starched and white, clinging disagreeably tight to his bulky form. He's kept on his footwear, which turns out to be soft wrestling boots laced up well beyond his ankles. The prisoners watch him with curiosity and distrust; their Smoke has lightened, is carrying new flavours, not excluding hope.

"Well then," says Smith. "Pick your champion. If he wins, you all eat."

A murmur goes through the throng. There must be social structure to the ship—a king of rogues, a ruling council, gangs locked in rivalry and feud—but no one takes charge. Most of the prisoners seem unfit for fighting, and unschooled. Only here and there does the stance of a man suggest an acquaintance with violence, handed out and received. After a few moments, a man shoulders through. His thinness cannot quite disguise the size of his frame. What muscle remains on him resides in his powerful legs and the sunburned stump of a squat neck. He does not strip but simply rolls up his sleeves. His hands are the size of spades.

Smith sizes him up and nods.

"Look here, soldiers, give us some space."

[7]

They fight in the no-man's-land between the muzzles of the soldiers' rifles and the press of the crowd. A circle has formed between these two groups, not quite closed but familiar enough from schoolyard brawls. At the centre, the two combatants stand, legs spread, hunched forward, their wrists tied together by a two-yard length of rope. Immediately it is obvious that both men have wrestled before: they tug at the rope, trying to pull one another off-balance; watch their distance and make sudden, controlled lunges for each other's legs. Nil, observing the fight from the railing he has climbed to see over the top of the crowd, is transported back to the New York gym: the spectacle of Smith crucifying himself high in the air between two swinging rings and forcing his big body into slow gyrations. Now he leaps forward, takes hold of his opponent's thigh, slams him hard into the decking, only to receive his opponent's knee into his groin.

They tumble across the ground. The prisoner comes out on top, his big hands spread across Smith's face, fingers probing for his mouth, his eyes, something to hook and pop. Smith twists onto his belly, stabs an elbow into the man's ribs, grunts when a fist rains down onto his neck. Already the prisoner is smoking, the purple froth of triumph and hate. The crowd catches it and, on a turn of the breeze, feeds it back to their champion. He's got hold of Smith's whiskers now and is slamming his head against the deck. Blood squirts from a cut near the eye. The crowd roars and smokes.

Then Smith makes his move. He must have been preparing for it all this time, so smoothly does it come off; must have wriggled into position even while being beaten, taking advantage of his opponent's rage and attendant sloppiness of technique. He pushes with one arm, twists, rolls; heaves his opponent off his back and in the same smooth movement rolls on top of him, the rope looped around the prisoner's neck and one of the man's legs so bent between his own that it seems it must break. The next moment it does: pops at the knee, so that calf and thigh no longer align. At the same time the rope turned noose tightens, cutting off the man's scream. The eyes soon bulge within their sockets.

If the man smoked before, he is now burning. Hurt and panic pour out of him, yellow and black, snake their way into the crowd. For a moment, it seems certain they will charge and a massacre will ensue. But something stalls them: takes the sting out of their anger, transforming it to fear.

Smith.

It's nothing that he's said or done. Rather it's his very muteness that hushes them so, the muteness of his skin. It isn't *catching*. Smith is smeared with his opponent's Soot; is bloodied, coughing, retching in the fog of raw emotion; strains, grotesque and murderous, in his too-tight, one-piece toddler's suit—but his skin exudes not the faintest wisp of Smoke. The man beneath him is now nearing death, his face dark and swollen, the eyes glossy and distended like boiled eggs trapped under the pressure of a fork. Then Smith relents; rises and, filled with the heat of his victory, thumps his Soot-black chest; stalks up and down before the hushing mob like a farm-yard rooster and subjects them to his crow; then shoulders his way back through the soldiers and towards Renfrew, raining sweat and blood down on the sitting man, his mouth wide open to show it isn't hiding sweets.

"There—this is how you'll win your war!"

The Lord Protector looks up at him, dabs away the sweat and blood, then rises to return to the boats.

[8]

It is an orderly retreat. First Renfrew and his personal servant; then Smith, still breathing heavily, who has climbed back into his trousers but has yet to button up his shirt; then Nil and the soldiers, one by one. They leave behind the little table and the stools. The moment the last soldier has climbed onto the ladder, Nil expects to hear a roar, a charge, the noise of people fighting over food. But there is no immediate sound and within four strokes of the oars they are out of earshot. Soon the cluster of people on deck are too far away to interpret with certainty their movement. The soldiers have ripped off their Smoke masks by now, half suffocated by their charcoal filters. When Nil turns from the ships to a sweating Smith, he finds him calmed and fully dressed, studying Renfrew. Nil expects a look of satisfaction, a salesman's joy at a pitch well made. What he finds instead in Smith's gaze is an expression so new to those bluff features that it takes all the way to shore until Nil has made sense of it. Disappointment. Doubt. A sulk, even—a child getting the wrong present at Christmas. Chin jutting, the eyes soft and moist, his tongue overactive in the pocket of one cheek.

The boat bumps quietly into the side of the jetty. With the help of his servant, the Lord Protector rises, steps onto dry land, and walks his invalid walk back up to his Keep.

[9]

Renfrew has another offer.

This is the thought that Smith returns to, again and again, as he stands in his little broom cupboard of a room, stooping over a ceramic basin filled with water. He has taken off all his clothing other than his underpants and is in the process of sponging himself down with a wet washcloth that covers his right hand like a mitt. Dyspepsia constrains his movements, the result of exercise on a full stomach. It is calmed by sips of milk straight from the bottle, only to flare up again with sudden vengeance. When he washes the swollen bruise along the left side of his ribs it is not the pain but the sudden uprush of acids that makes him crumple to the floor. Plain floorboards, no carpet, not a cushion in the room. No comfort, no vanities. He even had to send for a mirror from his ship. It is in this that he watches himself now.

Smith's body is a curious thing these days, the fatty tissues of his stomach, flank, and back marbled by black lines. These are not unlike veins but finer and many-branched, clustering most thickly near liver, kidneys, and heart. His flesh has always been quite pale and smooth and the contrast is not unpleasing. His neck is affected but not yet his throat and face. He does not fear the moment: he has seen photographs of New Zealand aboriginals and admired the virile charm of their darkly patterned cheeks. But it will be best if his business is concluded before such a transformation. Smith is too much a realist not to understand that Renfrew may balk at negotiating with a man who has black tendrils growing in his face.

Which brings his thoughts back to the Lord Protector and their lunchtime excursion. Well, of course his performance had been theatrical, even melodramatic. Nor had it been strictly necessary. Had he, Smith, not survived a Black Storm and come to Renfrew's shore in a ship repainted in Soot? But it seemed important to have Renfrew see for himself and, in doing so, shed all possible doubt. Smith had had the idea no sooner than he saw the prison ships moored out in the channel: Smoke-shrouded and isolated, they made for the perfect site for a demonstration. The slow approach by sea, the precautions, the Smoke masks and guns—they all just added to the drama. As for the picnic, did not each bite and swallow prove his cheeks were not hiding any sweets?

And then the match. Smith did not enjoy it as much as he once might have. Perhaps this was due to the constraints of the occasion, or the fact that much of the joy he used to feel resided in the mingling of Smokes. Perhaps, too—and this is a troubling thought for Smith, for it suggests a future reduced in possibilities—prolonged exposure to the beetle's spore dulls the passions to some degree. But even so he imagines it was easy to see that he fought his opponent not like a eunuch or machine, sapped in his affects by the refined juices of the Smoke Poppy, but like a man: self-contained—*complete*—in anger, vainglory, and triumph. The prisoners certainly had seen it and had hushed. And Renfrew? The Lord Protector had simply sat there, pale and shivering, trying not to smoke. Like a man clenching himself against a bout of diarrhoea, too proud to use the crapper that's but three steps away. It was unfathomable.

Unless, that is, Renfrew has another offer, which is to say there is another player in this game of buy and sell.

Smith would dearly like to know who.

He had pictured it all quite differently, starting with their arrival. Smith had not envisioned them limping into harbour, most of the crew dead, the ship listing with engine damage, Eleanor treated as some kind of saviour even though it had been he, locked in on the bridge, who had defended the rudder and guided them through the Storm. Someone had seen her emerge from belowdecks, leading Mowgli by the hand; the Storm buffeting her, flooding her with hatred, then pouring back out of her body *cleansed*. It was nonsense, of course, a fairy story; they had left the thick of the Storm by then, and in any case, all the witnesses were off their heads. But that's what the sailors told the fishing boat that met them near the coast. The fishermen turned it into gospel by the time they reached shore. By now the story had the girl standing in the prow all through the Storm, piloting them to safety; a halo over her streaming hair. The Shy Madonna. She was welcomed like a victorious general, whisked to Pentonville in a coach. Smith was allowed to accompany her only as an afterthought; the poor relation cadging a ride.

No, what Smith had envisioned was presenting Eleanor as an opening present; unveiling her, as it were, to a disbelieving uncle, rattled for once in that famous composure, *receptive* to Smith's influence. Then the demonstration, followed by disbelief and excitement; an eager bid for his goods. Instead Renfrew had smiled. Not a superior smile, the smile of someone who wanted to appear unimpressed, but rather a cold, calculating, rational smile that took the measure of Smith's miracle and put it to a use beyond Smith's ken.

It is precisely this—the thought that he is shut out; that History has spurned him and he is to be but the bridesmaid at another's wedding—that fills Smith with despair. Moved, he walks to the desk and, still clad only in his underwear, composes a sentimental letter to his wife and son that he will post when he has occasion. Then he dresses, combs his whiskers and crest of yellow hair, and steps out into the corridor in order to find Renfrew and talk to him man-to-man.

[10]

Smith does not meet a great many people on the way to Renfrew's chamber. Two or three servants, running errands for their masters. A group of dandies in brushed velvet dinner jackets, wearing embroidered Smoke masks tucked into their belts. Three workmen charged with examining all the coal filters that can be slid in front of the windows in the event of a Gale. Then he reaches the Lord Protector's door. There is a guard outside, armed with a pistol. His hand is on the holster as he sees Smith approach.

Beyond the door lies an ordinary cell no different from all the other rooms in the building. Despite its sparse furnishings it feels crowded. There is a narrow bed and an equally narrow desk; a wardrobe and two plain wooden chairs. Renfrew's servant is there, one Godfrey Livingstone, smelling as always of sweets. He, too, carries a pistol at his belt. Unlike the guard outside, he looks like a man who enjoys its use.

As for the Lord Protector himself, he does not rise from behind his desk when Smith enters. He looks shrivelled, ill. Rumour has it that, ten years ago, the doctors had to remove much of his lower intestine. He is said to be living on a diet of gruel that runs through him like water. Nobody ever actually sees him eat. The desk in front of him is strewn with little squares of papers, wrinkled as though they have been crumpled, and covered in dense writing. The telephone that hulks amongst them is dusty with disuse.

"Mr. Smith."

"Dr. Renfrew. I came to discuss business."

"Yes, of course. Sit."

Smith settles himself deliberately. The chair is hard, uncomfortable; his big thighs overhang it on both sides.

"I am displeased," Renfrew opens flatly. "Wrestling is illegal. It's a Minetowns aberration that encourages needless Smoke. When the story spreads, people will say I have grown lax with the law."

When the story spreads, there will be a queue of people making propositions to Smith. Already the place must be abuzz with rumours. Smith knows this and has considered the potential of coming to an agreement with some other party. Renfrew has enemies, those who would unseat him. But his authority runs deep, and his opposition is divided. Months of infighting would ensue, with uncertain results.

"You understand what I am offering, Dr. Renfrew? It does not bind the Smoke, the way sweets do, sapping a man's passions. One simply stops smoking." And then, more passionately: "I have brought you a cure, Dr. Renfrew. An end to the Smoke! So stop acting coy."

"Oh, I quite understand. You have found a way of making evil invisible. The body ceases to speak. All our moral corruption is to remain hidden, shut up within the flesh. You are *privatising* vice—but I see that my words amuse you. You find my views outdated. The concerns of another age."

Smith does not respond at once; wriggles his arse upon the chair, looking for comfort. Then he tries another tack.

"All I am saying is that you must be practical, Dr. Renfrew. The nation's broken. All you hold is the south and west. You have forged a coalition and are assembling an army, but it is unable to fight a war. If you march it on the North, it will get caught in a Gale. The next thing you know half your soldiers will have defected to the Miners. You can supply them with sweets, of course—or you could, if you had the money—but the effects are weak and, when it comes down to it, few men can kill without anger. As for the Smoke masks, you saw your soldiers today. Gasping for air after standing still for a quarter hour. No, your army cannot march in masks. And it certainly cannot fight in them." He waits a beat, lets it sink in. "I can solve all that."

"That's it then, your offer. A drug that enables us to march on the North. And to fight: with *passion*. The Miners will crawl underground, of course, into their tunnels. Then years of siege, while you bleed us dry selling us your product. No doubt my successors will sue for peace the moment I drop dead. And by the end we'll live in a world where we have given up on fighting evil. We will simply hide it within our breasts." Renfrew sighs, wearied by the exertion of talking. A sip of water steadies him. "What is it, your magical substance? A new distillation process of the same old flower? No, if that were the case, my Company sources would have told me about it. Something else then. A synthetic product? Or something you found? My sources say you like to travel."

Smith's answer is blunt. "There is no pressing need for you to know."

"Is there not? I could order your stores seized, Mr. Smith. You are a guest upon my soil."

"The stores are Company-owned, standing on land ceded to us by your government. Which would make any seizure an act of war. You cannot afford war with the Company, Dr. Renfrew. It keeps your kingdom in grain. You would starve without us."

"You are not the Company, Mr. Smith." But even as he says it, Smith can see that Renfrew concedes the point. He finds a clean sheaf of paper, uncaps a fountain pen. "Your price? How much will it cost me to inoculate my army against Smoke?"

Smith does not hesitate. "The city of London and its surrounding lands. From Edgware to Croydon, from Hounslow to Deptford, along with exclusive rights to the River Thames. Not a lease, mind, but permanent ownership. It's worthless to you as it is, a stretch of wasteland, picked over by vagrants. I will rebuild the city, turn it into a thriving heart of commerce."

"You want to be paid in land. I suppose every carpetbagger secretly yearns to be a king." Renfrew pauses, recaps the pen. "Very well, I will consider it."

This angers Smith. He sees no reason to hide it.

"Don't think too long, Dr. Renfrew, or the North will march on you. They have figured out a way to bottle Gales. They may use them as a weapon."

For once Renfrew looks startled. "What do you mean?"

"Just what I said. While I was in New York, I came across a rumour, about a theatre group whose performances summoned the Second Smoke. A miniature Gale. Not all their performances, mind, but only some, here and there. Like they were trying out some new technique. So I made a point of looking up their director."

"His name?"

"Balthazar Black. Don't bother looking for him. He and his men died in the Storm."

But Renfrew's face tells him they did not.

"He's alive?"

"There are reports," Renfrew concedes, "that Mr. Black is in Minetowns."
So you have spies there. How very interesting.

Smith looks again at the little squares of paper scattered on Renfrew's
desk and wonders what has crumpled them so. There are, now that he
comes to think of it, an awful lot of pigeons about the place.

"Tell me more," Renfrew says now, "about these bottled Gales. Do you
have a sample?"

"No. By the time I spoke to Mr. Black they had all been used up."

"So it might just be a rumour. People getting excited about a theatre act."

"Oh, it is no rumour. I talked to Black myself. He was heading back to
Minetowns to replenish his supplies. I tell you, the Miners are developing
a weapon, something that takes ordinary Smoke and makes it volatile. Go
ask your niece. She was a part of Mr. Black's little troupe. It's where I found
her."

[11]

The servant fetches Eleanor at the hour of her dinner. When he comes in,
she assumes it is simply to put down her tray of food and water. But he
stands empty-handed, the door wide open at his back. A hand gesture,
curt, impatient—that's all she receives by way of invitation. *Uncle wants to
see me.* Up close, the servant's breath is rich with sweet.

Twenty steps, a flight of stairs, another thirty steps. Empty tracks of
corridor, not a soul about. A single soldier, guarding an unadorned door,
straightening when he catches sight of them. Curiosity is written in his features as he watches her approach in the floor-length shift she was given to
replace her Soot-spoilt clothing. The guard steps aside; the servant opens
the door. And just like that they are reunited, uncle and niece. He rises to
greet her with a kiss.

"Eleanor."

"Uncle."

"God, how you've grown! Already a woman. And pretty!"

He is not at all how she'd imagined him. Thinner, older. Diminished.

But it's not this that gives her pause.

"You frown, my dear. Have I grown so very old?"

"No," she answers, hesitates. "I did not think that you would dress like
this."

"Like what?"

"The dinner jacket. It suits you. It looks expensive. Like you are going to a ball."

The remark amuses him. And something else: a glitter behind the eyes. She remembers it from childhood, when she did something well or said something clever. A flash of pride.

"Ah, well, what did you expect, a hair shirt and a smock? You see, what happened was that no sooner had we created some semblance of order—reassembled Parliament, organised food distributions and an agricultural quota, set up shelters against Gales—all the young gentlemen at once went to Paris. Literally all! And when they returned after a month of debauchery they all came dressed in dapper suits. *Le dernier cri.* Some even brought back their own tailors. I resisted, of course—it seemed insultingly frivolous; we were fighting for our lives, the country was in tatters, famine and disease—but then it occurred to me that it was a simple way of finding acceptance. Dr. Renfrew, that dry old stick, wearing the latest rags. It appeased those who eyed me with suspicion and helped me build bridges with my onetime enemies." He pauses, smiles. "You see, my dear, I am quite changed. I have grown practical. But please, take a seat. I apologise for the chair. It's like an instrument of torture."

If she did not expect her uncle's slim-framed elegance, neither did she expect his fussing, offering to send for tea, closing the window against the draught. Only then does he assume the pinched, precise manner familiar to her from childhood. He dons it like a pair of gloves: it will help protect his delicate hands.

"I would like you to tell me," he says without further preamble, "what happened on the ship."

"You already know. There was a Black Storm."

"Yes, I interrogated the surviving sailors." He pauses, makes a point of finding her eye. "But I want to hear it from you."

She tells him. She omits Mowgli, the beetle, the hour spent in Smith's cabin; tells him instead about the Storm's slow approach, the dun wall spanning the horizon; about the other ship being swallowed up within its darkness; about Smith defending the bridge with his gun.

"A cloud of pure hatred," she explains, "turning everyone into a beast."

"Yet here you are, healthy and unmarked. People are telling stories about you. How you soothed the waters and repelled the winds. Like a magician." He pauses, paces awkwardly, his legs stiff and body clenched, then slumps onto his chair. "Did Smith give you something? A drug, an injection? Some kind of sweet?"

"No."

"Then you weren't . . . *immune*?"

"No."

"Smith was. Or so he has me believe."

She does not react, unsure of what her uncle knows and what to entrust him with. All through the years of her flight with Cruikshank she feared him. The old man had been convinced that Renfrew's agents were looking for her, to bring her home, punish her, resume her moral education. That Renfrew had an inkling of her nature—her *talent*—and wanted it to put it to use. Now all she sees is a grey-faced man in nicely tailored clothes; a blackguard for a servant.

"Come, dear," he says now, "the stories have their root in something. Tell me what happened."

What happened. The Smoke reached for them, her and Mowgli, cowering in Smith's cabin. For a few minutes, they did not feel it and she was aware of her wonder at the fact; the beetle's taste upon her lip. Perhaps it bought them time; perhaps every minute's respite carried them out from the dark heart of the Storm and into its peripheries. She remembers the engine still chugging deep within the hull; the ship hurtling itself against the sea. Then madness: things pouring out of their bodies too raw and ugly to acknowledge, Mowgli thrashing in his bonds. So she *did* something; an exercise of talent. Took in the darkness, transformed it; gave back something of herself. Then she walked outside, out onto the deck, where men were screaming, fighting, dying of their rage. She stood amongst them until the skies had cleared. They said to her later that it looked as though she'd drunk them clean.

"I swallowed the Storm," she says to her uncle.

"I think," she says, "it is inside me still."

[12]

He curls his lip. He does not believe her. Perhaps he wishes to; wishes it very much even, to believe this girl he helped create; wants to ponder with her the potentialities implicit to her miracle. But Renfrew's a practical man now; he has talked to Smith. There are other questions pressing on his mind.

Her relief is so visceral, it takes effort not to wreathe it in Smoke.

"Tell me," her uncle says, "about this theatre troupe I have been hearing about. Smith says you had joined a group of players. Over there, in the New World. I did not know you could act."

"I can't. I saw them in Saint John and they took me with them, to New York. I handed out leaflets, put posters up on walls."

"Smoke Theatre," says Renfrew. "I need not tell you that the very thought is distasteful to me. Think carefully now. I have had a report that their performances made use of something, a sort of trick. Making the Smoke volatile. Like it was *then*." (A hand on his midriff as he says it, on those missing yards of gut beneath his ivory-buttoned shirt, torn out by Julius's dog, the stories say, and cauterised by Soot.)

"Smith told you."

"Naturally. Is it true?"

"Yes. I witnessed it once."

"Was it like a Gale?"

"It was beautiful," she says, and a ring of Smoke comes out with the word, hangs in the air between then, then falls upon his desk and leaves an iodine stain amongst his many letters.

Her uncle does not stir. He wants to know: "How was it generated?"

"A vial. Ask Smith. He, too, came running, asking questions, wondering how he could steal the miracle and turn it into cash."

"Then you don't know."

"You will have to ask the players. Only they are at the bottom of the sea."

"How petulant you have grown, Eleanor, how bold. You used to be such a timid little thing. You will forgive me for saying I rather preferred you as you were."

He frowns, bends down to his papers, pretending to read. Minutes pass, his fingers smoothing letters. When he speaks again, his voice lacks all inflection or affect. A dead voice. It may be the voice he uses to make confession to himself.

"Have you ever been tempted, Eleanor? No, perhaps not. Not truly. I used to imagine it very simply, the devil showing up with an offer, reading the weakness of your heart. Not literally the devil, of course, but someone more mundane. A woman with a smile; perfume on her throat. But it's much cleverer than that. It comes in pieces, often quite by chance. You are given a scrap of metal here, a trinket there; a pin, a screw, a bullet; a silver hammer, tiny like a toy. And before you know it, you have assembled a gun, cocked and loaded, with just the right heft. And, of course, your cause is just. It would be different if you found evil lurking in your heart. It'd give you pause." He smiles, wanly, without humour. "I am dying, Eleanor; starving to death, little by little, ounce by ounce. It's as though I am eating myself. And when I die this country will fall into disorder. I am running out of time." He rises, pushing himself up with his arms. "Enough of this. We shall speak more tomorrow. Livingstone will escort you back."

But before she can so much as move or say good-bye, her uncle carries on, still in the same flat tones, like a puppet winding down its clockwork, a puppet with a cold.

"I received a telephone call this morning. There is only one line—the Company put it in. The only place I am connected to is some office of theirs in Cherbourg: my single window onto the world. I pick up and am told that Thomas Argyle has been captured. In India. When I ask for particulars, the man tells me it is all he knows." He pauses. "If it's true, they will ship him here. Do you know how it makes me feel?"

"Triumphant?"

"Tired. If it's true I must try to have him strangled before he reaches this shore. It's like I said, dear niece. I have grown practical. I will see you in the morning."

[13]

Livingstone walks behind her; soft, weightless steps. He unlocks the door to her cell, then enters after her, watches her notice the box upon her bed. All at once his evil is palpable, filling the room: a hard-faced man in need of a haircut. She recoils by instinct and watches him follow, penning her in between bed and wall.

"You drank the Black Storm." His voice is flat, quiet, confident. It's not unlike his master's. "I find that hard to believe."

His fingers dig around the inside of his mouth and retrieve five, six, seven sweets, some dark and opaque, others still clear. It is as though he's removed a stopper from a tub. Smoke pours out of him, from the palms of his hands and the back of his collar, in intense, pressured jets. She meets them without moving, takes them in; returns a curl of sadness and disgust that puckers the man's face. Hastily turning away from her, he shoves the sweets back in his mouth, then scrubs his hands clean in her washbowl. A moment later he is gone and she is alone, lifting the lid off the box.

Dear Sir,

As instructed, we made a survey of London and surrounding areas. The primary object of our mission—to wit: to identify the point of origin of the first Black Storm as described by various stories and witness statements—has been a failure. No definite point of origin could be ascertained. Without a map or a more detailed witness statement, I believe any such search to be doomed to failure. As instructed we also searched the sewage system built in the closing years of the 1800s under the architectural guidance of the traitor Sebastian Aschenstaedt (also known as Ashton). Here we were successful in identifying a chamber with pool-like receptacles that broadly matches the description disseminated in (illegal) songs and stories. The place was rat-infested and abandoned. We did not encounter any Gales in the sewers or anywhere else in London. We abandoned our search when our food supplies ran out. There is nowhere in London that would have allowed us to replenish them.

Signed: Captain Peter Goodfellow; sent by military courier.

[Filed together with nearly identical report of a repeat mission from 3 June 1908, also signed by Goodfellow.]

[1]

The longer he stays in Minetowns, the more attention Balthazar is paying to the way people dress.

There are codes and fashions. Leather caps are favoured by those the Miners call "Commissars." Most of these are not city officials but simple busybodies and enthusiasts, fanatics of the Smoke. The cap must not be clean but rather stiff and shiny with Soot so as to appear almost lacquered. A cotton suit, a wide leather belt, and bulky worker's boots complete the outfit. These are the vanguard of Minetowns, guarding against "pretentiousness" and "bourgeoisification." Many of the city intellectuals and former members of the gentry are attracted to their ranks. They spend much of their time composing panegyrics to the simplicity of the Miner. Those Commissars who are elected onto the Council blacken their faces with Soot.

At the opposite end of the ideological spectrum are those collectively referred to as the "Foremen." Many of these used to think of themselves as skilled labourers before the Second Smoke; were lathe operators or textile cutters, engine technicians and welders. They dress in wool, wear donkey jackets and brimmed hats with little trinkets thrust into their headbands. Above all they are recognisable because of their advocacy of soap; some go so far as to scrub down their house walls once a week. The women may wear skirts or trousers and hold much respect within this community—it is from here rather than from amongst the Commissars that the push for the integration of married women into the workforce was first made. A type of bonnet goes with this brand of politics, and a particular variation of the Mark of Thomas: finer, more ornamental, dyed with rouge.

There are other groups. Proclaimers, who remain Topside during Gales and spurn Downtowners as retrograde sceptics of the Smoke. Dark Miners, who only rarely venture out from underground, and favour the rational darkness provided by their coal-dusted existences. Shock Workers in colour-coded coveralls, whose exploits in the factories are broadcast like sports results and celebrated across town; Mutes, who make little use of the spoken word and attempt to communicate only in Smoke. There is a loose alliance of forces arguing for decisive preemptive aggression towards the South, and a loose alliance of others advocating a more defensive stance and even peaceful coexistence with Renfrew's de facto republic.

Minetowns has politics and codes it with cloth.

He cannot help but think that all these dress codes would make lovely costumes.

[2]

Balthazar is working on his play. He has a simple concept: a collection of scenes from everyday life, depicting different social groups within Minetowns. A comedy of manners, played out in Smoke and mime. Ekklesia seems too big a stage for long oration. What he pictures for the grand finale is something unprecedented: a whole city laughing at itself. Laughing in Smoke, rainbow billows rising from the hole in the ground that is its sacred meeting place as though from a giant chimney; the sheep grazing in the hills looking on confused as they are bathed in many-hued Soot. Balthazar hopes it will dye their wool for good. He wants a miracle; an event so remarkable, Shovel will have to put it in the next edition of his book. To achieve it, he requires Smoke so supple and quick, it will race from skin to skin like a hummingbird darting between flowers; a Smoke so subtle, it will carry emotion notes normally drowned out by the dross of everyday life.

In short, he will need a little help.

Balthazar spent his first week here avoiding the man who sold him the vials that can quicken the Smoke. It's why he came to Minetowns in the first place: to stock up. The last time he was here, he did not really know what he was buying. *Farts in a glass,* he remembers thinking. *I'm being had like a fenland virgin.* But there was just enough in the man's manner to convince him that the bottle he bought was filled with something more than air; and even to keep his promise not to sample its goods till he was a day's ride hence. Balthazar should have returned then, and bargained for more, but his ship was sailing and, truth be told, he was a little afraid. A Gale in a bottle. It wasn't just Renfrew's government that might decide that knowledge of such a thing was reason to throw you in gaol.

But now that Balthazar is looking for his seller, he cannot find him. Balthazar asks around. He does not know the man's name but remembers the house; knocks on the door but learns only that he has moved. He works in the sausage factory, Balthazar is told, but when Balthazar asks there, he finds the man has changed jobs. At least Balthazar learns his name. Martin. Miners don't like to use last names but, like everyone else, they have need to distinguish one Martin from another. This one is Martin from Spennymoor, recently of Red Brick Lane.

When they say it like that, they make him sound like a prince.

[3]

He finds him at last. Martin from Spennymoor, recently of Red Brick Lane, has moved a half mile from town, into a shed cresting a hill. Martin is in the field behind the shed, looking after his goats. It looks like the sausage factory worker is making cheese for a living now; the money can't be good, but his skin is ruddy from sun and wind. Even so there is a sadness that clings to the spare little man. No sooner has he seen Balthazar than he invites him into his home. Balthazar takes it for hospitality but at once revises his opinion. They are up in the hills, out of scrutiny of town. Even so, Martin is nervous about being seen with the playwright.

They talk over mugs of hot water; Minetowns is out of tea. The man knows why Balthazar is here, of course, and it is not long before he leans forward and explains in urgent whispers that he's afraid that he "cannot help"; that he has "nothing" and, in fact, "never had anything"; and that even if he did have something at some point, "it was only that one time"—all the while looking about himself as though expecting a spy to be lurking in a corner. Balthazar takes it for sales strategy and makes sure to prune his face.

"Come off it, Martin. You know yourself you sold me a bottle. 'The Breath of a Gale'—you'd even given it a name! I paid you in cloth, good tweed that I was using for costumes. Look at your breeches, they are cut from my wool." He pauses, sips at the water, burns his lip. "And now I'm back to buy more."

"I'm telling you, I've got none to sell. I only had the bottle quite by chance."

"I find that hard to believe."

The man falls silent, brow furrowed in thinking; gets up, decided, and throws open the door as though getting ready to throw Balthazar out; then closes it again and returns to his chair; sits dumb and rooted, chewing on a thought. Balthazar looks from him to the narrow camp bed, the clumsy attempts to make homely this miserable little shed.

"You are alone," he says, quietly, sensing the man's loneliness, his need to talk. "Last time I came you lived in a house. There was a boy. And a wife. You were wearing mourning; your father had died."

Balthazar hesitates over the next part, aware that it is important he gets the words right.

"Do you want to tell me what went wrong?"

Martin starts, smokes: anger and need. He rises a moment later, still drifting between these two poles, then slumps back into his chair.

"Our Sammy," he says. "He left us."

"Your son died."

"No, no. He ran away."

"Where?"

"Where they all run, all the little bairns. North to their Angel and his fool religion where they freeze and starve."

[4]

It is not the first time little Sammy has run away.

They call them Smoke Children, the boys and girls who leave to live amongst the Gales. It all started two or three years ago, with a rumour. A children's crusade, is how the rumour ran, like in the Middle Ages, only they are not marching on anything, just walking in the countryside, without apparent aim. A ragtag mob with no permanent abode. Always on the move, living off the land. Like locusts, say those who know their Bible and are put in mind of plagues. There is some sort of leader, a prophet who calls himself the Angel of the North. He's sending out child preachers, to spread the word, or perhaps he doesn't send them and they simply take it upon themselves to go looking for converts. They find them across the whole of the North. Children as young as seven or eight. Many are orphans; others are running from parents too liberal with the rod. Others yet are happy, loving, loved.

Little Sammy first left when he was nine. It was summer, long days and warm. He finished his porridge in the morning; left a drawing: himself, walking up a hill, a winged creature up on top, bathed in its Smoke. Martin went after him but could not find him. Four weeks later, the boy returned, bringing with him a glass bottle. It was filled, Sammy explained—after he had received and recovered from a hiding—"with the living spirit of communion." He said it very proudly, as though he knew what it meant. The boy had taken it into his head that he would open it, in the centre of Minetowns, and release whatever was inside. Naturally, his parents took the bottle away from him.

"I nearly threw it away, I did, carried it out onto the moor and buried it. But Pa was dying and I didn't want to leave his side. So I just locked it away."

"But surely you must have tried it out? After all, it might just have been air. Child's play, some foolish game."

Martin starts denying it, then stops himself short. Balthazar can see joy in him now, the joy of unburdening to someone other than his goats.

"I tried it just the once. Pa was going fast. Coal on the lung, struggling to breathe. We sat at his bed, my boy and I. This was just after he'd come back, when we didn't yet know about the bottle. Then the boy dug in his knapsack and pulled it out. I thought it was gin at first, then realised it was empty. He opened the stopper, just for a moment, and then we just sat there, on the sickbed, holding hands. The things that crawled out of Pa!" He shakes his head at the memory, fights off a smile, his eyes wet and cheeks very pale. "Frisky, he was, like a lad of fourteen. On his deathbed! Then the pain came and we felt that, too: his anger at the pain. And our fear at his dying, and all the anger I held for his leaving Mam—all of it standing in the room like a ghost." He pulls up his snot, wipes his mouth with the back of one hand then waves it about as though dispersing the memory in the room. "I opened the window then. Couldn't take any more. Took the bottle away and hid it out of reach of the bairn."

[5]

Now that his tale is told, Martin wants Balthazar to leave. It shows in his body, the way he has sat back on his chair when before he was leaning forward; shoulders squared, the teacup now a barrier between him and his guest. Balthazar does not stir. He has questions and knows Martin will answer them. The man has put his faith in Balthazar; entrusted him with the pain of his loss. It *binds* them together. Not like Smoke, thinks Balthazar, with its knotted tendrils of emotion. More like a ledger listing credit and debt.

"Why not give it to the Council?" he asks. "You must have realised the bottle was important. Valuable. They'd have taken it off your hands."

"I thought about it. But who can say what they would've done? Might have made my son a hero, or thrown him out of town. And they certainly wouldn't have paid us. No, I just locked it away in a box. Tried to forget about it. And then you came along with your players, and I thought here's a man who'll make it disappear."

"And pay."

Balthazar tries to think himself into the man's situation. Being handed a miracle; something unheard of. Hiding it, hoping only that it'll go away. Afraid he might be held responsible; the father dying in his bed upstairs.

"How did your son get the bottle? How was it . . . *harvested*?"

"Don't know."

"You didn't ask? How can that possibly be?"

But Martin has turned stubborn and won't say. Balthazar waits five breaths before changing tack.

"And Sammy's back with the Smoke Children now? Where are they?"

"Who knows? Scotland, some say, up in the tip, though I wonder why they'd go there. No Gales that far north, or so people say."

Balthazar thinks back to the beggar child they met on their march from coast to town. What did she say again?

"They chase the Gales," he says out loud.

"So everybody says. Christ knows what the hell it means."

[6]

And that's all Balthazar gets from Martin. He is what he is: a little man hiding from history. Now he fears for his boy. His wife, he explains, went looking for him and has been gone nigh on two months.

"And you?"

"Someone's got to look after what we have."

Martin colours with his answer, then stands up with a puff of Smoke. Balthazar rises with him, sniffing the air; finds something in it that rattles him.

"You're afraid. It's not the journey; not even of the Gales or the fear of losing property. You're afraid of your own child."

Martin starts, makes to deny it, forms a fist.

"What do you know?" he barks, anger winning out. "It isn't just our Sammy but all of them. The children born in the Second Smoke. They are *different*." He spits onto the well-scrubbed floor of his hut, watches it sizzle and smoke like a piece of burnt bacon dropped from a pan. "Everything's changed. Sometimes I wish things would go back to how they were before."

"Leave then. Head south."

"And live with the Idlers?"

He says it with disbelief rather than distaste; it is not so much that the notion is unpalatable as that it is *unthinkable*. Balthazar is not surprised. Everywhere he's gone in Minetowns the same shorthand rules, the world reduced to simple terms, Miners and Idlers; the North, the South. The South is a bogeyman, the world of pampered toffs. This is a split land, hollowed out, stuck in the past.

Balthazar misses New York.

[7]

There won't be any vials then. Balthazar tells himself that it does not matter; that it is even better without, more honest. All the same he frets about the work. What if the scenes are too small, too intimate for the size of the stage? How to control the Smoke of so many people with no Shapers and a single Soother in Etta May?

All week long, he runs around making arrangements. He needs to have stage props built and find a better rehearsal space; must train three helpers from scratch; requires two new actors, people who can step into emotion as though into a pair of shoes. Everywhere he goes with his requests there is the same mix of bemusement, interest, scepticism. The Miners like theatre; but the moment they hear the work is commissioned, they grow suspicious. They want entertainment, not education.

Balthazar talks to factory workers, shopkeepers, washerwomen. He notices things: takes *note* of them, pencil ever at the ready. The factories are like fiefdoms, competing for output, for workers, for reputation; even for allotment produce grown in their yards. Some are men only; others employ both sexes, women in coveralls smelting iron ore. Downtown is where the black market has made its home, nestled up to the Council in more ways than one. Toptown children run in the streets unspeaking, conjoined by clouds of Smoke; mothers watch them, afraid that they will leave.

For the hills, and the Angel of the North. Balthazar wants to stage him and wonders if he has wings.

He notices something else. Wherever he goes he seems to come across young Miss Cooper. She is everywhere: at the brickwork's kitchen, doling out cabbage soup; joking with the metal workers on their way to their shift; trading gossip with the milk woman at dawn. Time and again he sees her at the dovecot at the edge of town, laughing with the pigeon fanciers; sees her with her hands around a prize bird, making cooing noises to the animal, her full mouth screwed into a raspberry purse. And increasingly, too, he sees her with Meister Lukas, drawing him out of his melancholy, walking with him hand in hand, innocently that is, more like a girl than a woman, though sometimes her hand will brush his leg or, leaning over while they picnic sitting on a little wall, her breast will crush itself into his upper arm, just for a moment, while she reaches for the salt shaker on his side of the wall. Balthazar notes it, studies the pigeons.

He wonders: are they flying north or south?

[8]

Balthazar talks to Meister Lukas. They have been working all morning on some details of the lighting arrangements, talking about sight lines, shadows, wattages, bulbs. Lukas is attentive if passive. He is wearing his work face, clear-eyed, not given to movement; asks precise questions in the lilting English that is his. Balthazar looks at him and realises how little he knows about his employee. Meister Lukas's hometown in China became a German colony when he was still little more than a boy; he apprenticed himself to a Lutheran engineer, adopted a new name, and was taken to Germany. The Second Smoke will have found him there, in Dresden, where (he once told Balthazar) he was such a curiosity that children would follow him around in the streets. When Balthazar met him, he was in Hamburg, working for a shipyard. Meister Lukas came to a performance; stayed afterwards and started talking about how the ventilation fans were set at the wrong angles, and how the sound effects were poor. They have never talked politics, or family, or love. Now Meister Lukas wears the Mark of Thomas at his temple; blinks, fans out his fingers; sketches a calculation in the air.

"I will need another helper," he decides. "Maybe two."

"I will find someone."

"It's in the budget?"

"There is no budget." After a pause: "We could ask Miss Cooper. She seems the helpful kind."

Meister Lukas blushes at that. No, it's more than a blush. It's irritation, his boss meddling in private affairs.

"You like her," Balthazar says, just to fill the silence. It seems to prolong it instead. "It's none of my business." Then: "Maybe she's got a motive, you see. She might not be as innocent as all that."

Lukas's face does not change but his nostrils bleed a tiny slug of Smoke. "Nonsense," he says, certain and curt. "I have tasted her."

Balthazar snorts at that, makes to argue, stops himself. What he says instead is "What do you two talk about? You do talk, don't you? Not just smooch."

It comes out lightly, playfully, and wins a little smile from Meister Lukas.

"This and that. She is curious about China. And the Storm. And she loves the theatre."

He pauses and Balthazar waits him out, smiling, encouraging him, feeling false.

"She has been asking me about the vials," Meister Lukas admits at last in a tone overeager to allay suspicion. "She had already heard about them. Perhaps you mentioned something to her."

"What have you told her?"

"Nothing." A hesitation. "This and that."

"Everything then."

"What was there to tell? You never told us where you had them from. I just told her when we first used one. And how they worked in a performance. It's hardly a secret."

Balthazar nods, acknowledging the point. "She has another man, you know. One of the pigeon fanciers. Big fella."

"So what? She told me herself. He's only a friend."

"And you? I thought you were in love with Eleanor. Two days weeping on the ship! Whatever happened to that?"

Lukas looks back at him coldly, the Mark on his temple making him look bolder somehow, more rakish.

"Eleanor isn't here." And more quietly, a moment later: "Is it true that she survived?"

"Ask Miss Cooper. She makes a point of being very well informed."

[9]

Etta May comes to him within the hour, her hands planted on her fleshy hips, all in a lather to tell him off.

"You big bully!" she opens, Virginia cadences, slowed down for emphasis. "Why be so hard on the boy?"

"Meister Lukas? He's what—twenty-two, twenty-three? Hardly a boy." He flashes her his best-pruned scowl. "You think the 'Meister' is an actual title or just an affectation? I suppose there must be a piece of paper: with gold trim and a big German seal. Though he does seem a little young for a 'Meister.'"

But Etta May will not be sidetracked.

"Why interrogate him like that? Like he's done something wrong. So he found himself some consolation, after the horror of the Storm. It's perfectly normal. And why not Miss Cooper? She's pretty. She has . . . *attributes*."

"You have attributes," he answers crudely, cupping his own chest.

"So I do! And who is to say I have not found myself a sweetheart too?"

Balthazar laughs, then realises Etta May is not entirely joking. He chews on the notion, dissects it. What he finds underneath is this:

"You like them, these people."

It comes out more incredulous than he means it.

"They have my sympathies. It's difficult, starting history from zero; wiping out a thousand years of prejudice. So, of course, they messed it up. But the heart's in the right place. And they know how to laugh, down from their livers and Smoke." She pauses, looks him over. "I thought you of all people would appreciate that."

"If they wanted to restart history, they would have done better to move. Get away from this mire; start out somewhere fresh."

"What, in the New World? You like it better there, eh? Home of the free and all. Oh, you're right, we got the better end of the deal. Secondhand Second Smoke: a torch rather than the whole bloody bonfire. Just enough revolution to set the country free from its stuffiness, without tearing it all down. And you like New York. The capital of Capital; where money is more important than Smoke." She snorts, real anger on her breath. "I am not sure it suits you, old woman; nor the colour of your skin. Money or no money, you go down south where I'm from, you'll still be the nigger director who has to leave the room while your plays are being staged. We don't mix our Smoke with just any old coon."

"I didn't know you were a wit, Etta May. And *political*."

"What a contrary old sourpuss you are, Balthazar Black! It might do you good to put skirts on, once in a while. It unclenches you, honey: feeling the wind between your legs."

And she storms off, hiking up her own skirt to well above the knee, as though there were a puddle to negotiate, ankle-deep and clogged with mud.

[10]

And so Balthazar finds himself shunned. Not that he is banned from his own rehearsals, or that the actors won't talk to him. But word has spread that he is "in a mood." Where he was his players' companion before, he is now their employer, no longer included in their jokes and banter, their repartee of Smoke. Even the cat has abandoned him and taken up with the milkman who lives across the street.

Balthazar does not mind, of course. He's got work to do and is glad not to be distracted; was never truly one of *them*. Only sometimes does he get lonely; sits sulking in his room, rewriting scenes or composing bitter little sonnets about the futility of change. The writing is poor, the consolation slight. Balthazar is bored. And so he starts watching young Miss Cooper.

As hobbies go, it is more riveting than some.

For Miss Cooper makes an interesting study. For instance, there is the simple fact that she has no work yet seems flush in tokens, enough so to be liberal with gifts. Then, too, her movements follow no known schedule, with only a handful of fixed points to her day: Meister Lukas (though his star is already waning), the dovecot, a tailor's shop, a warehouse, Downtown. Ideologically, Miss Cooper is a strong advocate of Smoke, but it is rare to see her smoke herself. She smiles instead, touches people, above all men; touches them as though by accident or from spontaneous bursts of affection. When she does answer someone's banter with her Smoke, it is light, tinged with flirtation and caprice. There is an air of the ingenue around Miss Cooper; of simplicity and sex. Even those people who dislike her—older women, mostly, matrons with sons to protect—think her a ninny gifted with charm and a fabulous arse.

Balthazar does not make the same mistake.

All the same, he is surprised to find she has noticed his watching, and—having noticed it—come to conclusions of her own.

[11]

She comes to him late one night while he is sitting over his notes. He thought the house door locked but there she is, already standing in his room, unannounced and spreading scent.

"Here you are!" she greets him warmly. "Lukas told me you had shut yourself in. He said you are sulking. And will you look at all these notes!"

Lukas. No "Meister" to her. Balthazar turns over his notebook and papers, watches her step to the window and close it. Something about her attire is different. The coat is heavier than seems necessary for the relative warmth of the evening; the riding boots too formal for a stroll. She looks as though she is getting ready to travel. But what sort of person travels at night?

"You are a spy, Miss Cooper, aren't you?"

"Teddy, please." She hops up to sit on the desk in front of him, dislodging notes; touches his forearm in her winning way. "You know yourself that spying is impossible. We live in the Smoke here and the Smoke does not lie. Everybody knows that much."

She smiles, aware of the absurdity of telling a theatre man that all Smoke is true. All it takes is a moment's conviction; spotting the emotion within oneself, in a gesture or smile, then dredging it up from the deep. It is a lying to oneself. Some people have a talent for it.

"And who do you think I am spying for, Balthazar?"

"I don't know. Renfrew? Your brother? Your pigeons fly south. Does the Miner who collects the notes know who they are from? No, I imagine he doesn't. He's just happy you pat his cheeks."

She raises an eyebrow at that, mimes slapping her own rump, more cheeky than saucy, the hand fine-boned, white, and small. Balthazar is dried up and old. Even so he feels her charm.

"So what are you up to, Miss Cooper? You've been interrogating Meister Lukas about the vials—you must have realised you'd get nothing out of me. What do you want with them?"

She shrugs, picks through his notes, with the insolence of a little girl winding up her favourite uncle.

"I found your supplier, Balthazar. Out in the hills with his goats. He's lonely. Missing his wife." She scoots off the table, leans her hip against his chair. "Let's trade answers. What I want to know is do you really have no vials left?"

"I don't."

"And do you know how it was done? The bottling I mean. You can't just stand in a Gale with an empty jar."

"I don't know."

She accepts this without showing any disappointment. "Your turn then."

"Where do the pigeons carry their messages?"

"South."

"To Renfrew?"

"To a Mr. Livingstone, mostly. But yes, some I suppose end up with Dr. Renfrew. But look at you frown!"

"So you're a liar. A traitor. You live with these people and don't believe a thing."

"Believe?" She brightens at the word; wanders over to his bedside and starts picking through his things.

"Have you read Pascal, Balthazar?" she asks, becomes distracted, mouthing a line from a scene he has worked on and discarded: *For in thy Smoke I find myself lost,* he can read it off her lips.

"Pascal? You mean his wager? Yes, I have, as a matter of fact. It's better to gamble on God's existence than not to; if you have faith and are wrong, nothing much happens; but if you don't and God turns out to exist, you've pissed away paradise. I always thought it a rather silly argument; something that might appeal to a banker. Or a fraud."

"That's because you haven't read to the end! His point is merely that it would be *reasonable* to believe. Pascal understands perfectly well that in itself this does not change anything. To actually start believing you have to *act*. Pray, attend service, hang the cross on your wall. You have to write faith into the practice of your life; and do so even though you don't *actually* believe, at least not yet. Do this for a year, or three, or ten. 'Custom, without violence, without argument, will make you believe. It is custom that makes men Christians; custom that makes them Turks.' I am paraphrasing it rather badly. Pascal's French is very nice."

"What is your point, *Teddy*?"

"My point, Balthazar, is that you asked me what I *believe,* which is a very Minetowns sort of question, for above all it's important to believe very passionately here, more passionately than the next man. And yet I am telling you, nobody here *believes,* or if so it's only from habit. It's all a big lie; *make*-belief. And your beloved Livia is the biggest liar of all." She stands up from the bed, saunters closer, playful and girlish, trading secrets.

"I hear she told you about the *third* ship. The one they believe started the Storm."

Balthazar bristles. "How can you possibly know what she told me?"

Miss Cooper smiles, leans close, whispers in his ear. "Did she also tell you they *found* something on that ship? They salvaged it and brought it back and hid it down the mine, without telling the Council. And just today I heard another story: that she goes to look at it. A black piece of rock. She *talks* to it, like they are sweethearts. They say it reminds her of Thomas."

She studies him, sees that all this is news for him, and, pleased by his ignorance, shrugs and turns away.

"The stories people will make up to pass the time! What about you then, Mister-Mistress Black? What is your story? Where did you read Pascal, and learn to write like that? And when did you put on breeches? Oh, come now, tell me, whyever not?"

Balthazar hesitates. A part of him wants to shake his fist at her, or call her names. But he does not want her to leave. God help him, but he *likes* pretty Miss Cooper. Worse yet: he wants to be liked by her.

"I worked in the kitchens of an Oxford college," he says at last. "When I was a young thing, young and handsome. A don there took an interest."

Miss Cooper laughs: *warmly,* even now that she is mocking him. "Don't tell me. He read to you in bed!"

"He had an extensive library. Including a secret shelf of illegal books. Theatre plays, Dekker, Marlowe, Shakespeare. It's surprising in how many plays a woman puts on trousers, and is remade."

"So you stored up that lesson, for later when you were old and pruned."

He shakes his head, annoyed by her at last, at her presumption that she can guess his life even before it's been told. All at once her charm has worn thin.

"Your kind will never understand what the Second Smoke meant for the likes of me. Or for these Miners."

She smiles at his reprimand, though he can see she is stung.

"I don't know, Balthazar. Half of the Miners seem about ready to return to the tried and true. People like structure. And food. And the old custom runs deep. As for me, do you know what I miss, Balthazar? A really good bath. With a maid topping it up every quarter hour. And a white fluffy towel that's soft and new and radiantly clean."

It strikes him now that she has washed. There is no Soot on her at all.

"Your brother must hate you, Miss Cooper."

"My brother ran away from here two years ago. You know why nobody here talks about him? They are afraid he got fed up with it all and headed home to our family pile."

[12]

The next morning, Miss Cooper has gone from Minetowns.

The moment he has verified it, Balthazar feels relieved. He had little stomach for turning her in. By midday it has become a rumour, by evening it is a truth. Miss Cooper has left after a lovers' tiff. Miss Cooper has gone to find her missing brother. Miss Cooper has remembered her aristocratic roots and gone to join the enemy; "good riddance to bad rubbish." People are upset: grim faces around the dovecot, a weepy-eyed Meister Lukas screwing up his lighting cues. But life goes on.

Nobody connects Balthazar to Miss Cooper's departure. Or so Balthazar thinks until he receives a summons. Downtown wants him: Livia. It's the same boy delivering the message as the first time Balthazar was fetched, although this time he also serves as guide; an unresponsive fellow, if lively and imaginative in the Smoke that wells out of him when Balthazar tells him to stop picking his nose.

They take the elevator, descend into the cool of the mineshafts. A long, confusing trek through semidarkness, passing costermongers, workers, councilmen heading to a meeting. Then: Ekklesia, that giant hollow in the ground. Balthazar has clamoured for access for days but none has been given. Now he is surprised to find some of his stage props have already been transported here. Livia sits in the stalls, near the stage, and rises when he enters. Again, that same wonder: how short she is, how haughty.

How pleasing it would be to make her smile.

She is irked, though, the "Little Mother of the Smoke," and sees no need to hide it. Not from Balthazar at any rate.

"I am told you scared off Teddy," she greets him, sending the boy away with a wave of her hand. "Whatever for?"

Balthazar matches her for sourness. "I merely asked if she was a spy. I think her disappearance has answered that question. For all you know, I might have saved your republic. If I were you I would have a talk with the pigeon fanciers. She was sending messages."

"Of course she was sending messages, Balthazar. She's with the Company. The pigeons are how she conducts business."

Minetowns has no truck with the Company. Balthazar swallows the words before he can speak them. Why make an even bigger fool of himself?

Livia, meanwhile, has descended and joined him on the stage.

"She was an 'unofficial liaison.' The Coopers have been involved in the East Indian trade for generations. They lost their hold in the revolution, but she has managed to carve out a new stake."

She pauses, holds Balthazar's gaze.

"You disapprove."

"You are lying to your own people."

"And what would you have us do? Minetowns needs sugar, saltpetre, salt. Our hospital needs morphine. Last winter we were short on grain. So we deal with the Company and they, of course, spy on us. And yes, I expect they will be selling their information to Renfrew." She grows quieter, makes fists of her hands; looks bitter, weary, wise. "It has its uses, this indiscretion. It's a way of talking to him; a line of communication, indirect, deniable. It's not good for us, being so very sundered. North and South."

"What if I tell the people? Put it right here, on the stage, where everyone can see. Lady Livia, whispering secrets across the big divide. I'll stage it in a big old bed, you and Renfrew, pillow talking, your naked feet poking out from under the bedding."

She snorts at the image. "Do! They won't believe you. Or maybe they will and throw me out of town. Exile. It doesn't sound so bad."

Her weariness leeches the anger out of him, disarms it like a sweet. He wants to do something: touch her, vow that he will keep her secret, share a secret of his own. But she has already turned away from him, is studying the tiered and sloping walls of the crude amphitheatre; shivers, then retches up a little puff of Smoke and watches it rise towards the sky.

"Do you know why the decision was taken that the Council meet in the coal, rather than Topside? We didn't start down here. In the beginning we met on shop floors, or on the village green, a ring of people around an empty centre, speakers rising, addressing each other above the din of too many voices, speaking their minds. Most just came to listen. Some few put themselves forward. To *lead*. Sometimes it felt like every village bully saw his chance.

"But here is the thing. The bullies soon learned that the Smoke gave them away. The tactics of before didn't work anymore. Big words, shouting, waving your fists and strutting like a cock—it all comes to naught if your Smoke is thin and empty. The Second Smoke opened our eyes, taught us *nuance*. People learned to taste the depth of you; swished you in their mouths like a sip of wine. And so the bullies got together and decided that it was better to hold the meetings in a place where the old rules apply. Down in the coal it's like it was before. He who shouts loudest wins."

Balthazar listens to this, thinks about the rules of his theatre, and of that strange sense of awakening that came with the Second Smoke.

"Strong Smoke does not make someone a leader," he objects. "You might just be angry. Or an arsehole."

"Yes. But an arsehole with *presence*." Livia laughs, a startling sound, lovely and young. "Thomas would like that—he'd say it's like a summary of his soul. But it's not all anger, is it? Or lust, or domination? That's what we learned, if we learned anything at all. And why we are here." She points upwards, towards the town. "But you are right, Balthazar. Maybe the Smoke *is* just another kind of shouting: one person imposing himself on others. Perhaps democracy would work best if nobody talked to each other at all. Let's build small huts a dozen miles apart and communicate by letter."

Balthazar listens and says nothing. He is thinking of Eleanor; wondering what would happen if she took it in her mind to *shout*. Not democracy, no. Epiphany perhaps, or maybe slavery.

It is hard to say.

[13]

And thus they make friends, Livia and he, or seem to for a moment: stand in comfortable silence, here, at the bottom of this well.

Then Livia asks: "Are you ready with the play?"

Immediately, he is irritated. "Ready? We only just got started rehearsing. We need another week at least."

"Oh, we need it earlier than that. Things are difficult at the moment. Minetowns needs something—to bring us together. This coming Smoke-day, when everyone's off work. That gives you three more days."

She waves away his protest, won't even consider it. Instead she asks: "When can you send me a copy of the script?"

He bristles at that. "Why, so you can censor it and ensure it's patriotic?"

"So I know what it is about. I want to have flyers printed, distribute them in the factories."

He frowns, still suspicious. "It's about a people trying to adjust to their own revolution. Many fail. A comedy, naturally."

"Fail to adjust? You should stage Mother! When the Smoke turned volatile, she was triumphant. And, of course, she must be the only person in the world who actually made money on the Second Smoke. But then, after a few years of things not working, and all decorum going to the dogs, she got tired of the squalor and—"

But Livia stops herself short when she sees Francis rushing through the entrance to Ekklesia. He is flushed and carrying a letter.

"There you are, Livia! This just arrived for you. I thought you'd want it at once. It's from *him*."

"From whom?" she asks, running to him, suddenly girlish, and rips it open. Her face lights up as she reads it, utterly disarmed.

"How did we get this?" she begins to ask. Then she remembers Balthazar is there. "That will be all. Come back whenever you like and bring your players. Three days. I will see to the flyers. Only excuse us now, we have work to do."

"I am not your servant, Lady Naylor."

This stops her short, her joy spoiling on her face. *Like milk.* It should soften Balthazar. Pride eggs him on instead.

"I heard you are talking to a rock. Cuddling up to it even. A black rock. You lied about it to your Council."

She stiffens. Haughtiness is a posture: a toss of the hair, an angle of the head.

A chill in the voice.

"What a little busybody you turn out to be, Mr. Black. Remember that you are a guest here. Useful, for the moment. Until you are not."

"You were mouthing off about your mother, just now. What a bitch, a hypocrite, she is," he counters, trying to hurt her. "I thought I would like you, Livia. No, not like. Admire. But you are just . . ." He trails off, unsure where he is going

"Ordinary? Petty? Full of bile? I was a schoolgirl who happened to change history. *Ordinary people.* I thought that was what your theatre was all about. But I don't suppose that means you actually have to like them. At night you dream of heroes. Just like everybody else."

[14]

They work day and night, trying to get ready. In a sense it helps to heal the rift with his players. He hears them say, "He's always been pissy before a show." Making excuses for him. Welcoming him back.

On their first trip Downtown, Balthazar tries to gauge the players' reaction to this world cut out of coal. Most of them are too busy with the play to pay it much attention, other than Ada who complains that she is suffocating down there. Balthazar assumes she is claustrophobic until she tells him she cannot tolerate the thought of being unable to reach others with her Smoke.

"Like being alone in the world," she says, "like loving someone without kissing," all the while touching him, confiding, daughter to mother, niece to uncle, vulnerable and shy.

They get it done, or most of it anyway. Ekklesia is transformed. At the back, near the entrance, something like a living room: an armchair, a sofa and carpet, a clothes rack full of costumes. They could wall this off, turn it into backstage, a secret place where props can be prepared and costume changes can take place. But Balthazar wants this performance to be transparent, the tricks of theatre visible to all; the line between actor and role porous like a sieve. Onstage, near the seating, they have installed a ring of mechanical ventilators alongside a ring of lights. "We won't be able to light faces," Meister Lukas complains, and, "The wiring won't cope," but there is no way to update the electrical system nor any place amongst the stalls to anchor lights. A clear evening will help them. Balthazar is unsure how the show will work in heavy rain.

Then another complication. Livia sends word that they have to share the stage: the evening will start with wrestling matches, as is traditional. Balthazar rages at this, fears that he will lose the daylight hours and that the audience's energy will be spent before his actors take the stage. Livia ignores his tantrum, and, anyway, the flyers have been distributed, are crudely printed but illustrated with a rare sense of energy. Shovel's work. On the morn of Smokeday, the whole town is abuzz with expectation. Balthazar frets, rehearses, shouts at actors; has an upset stomach; swears and mutters prayers; prunes his face and underneath it all is happy, for he loves the theatre like nothing else in life.

[15]

Dusk. Too many people, filling a hole in the ground: tier by tier, standing in rows three or four deep, their feet in kicking distance of the necks and heads beneath them, boots at the base of their skulls. Balthazar sees Ekklesia fill up, this inverted tower built into the earth, and feels its danger. A density like this, already smouldering a little wherever a foot treads onto foot, or a shoulder pushes into shoulder; where a handsome youth cocks an eyebrow at a wife or daughter; where flesh presses onto flesh. Each tier has ushers, holding buckets full of coal dust to douse sudden fires. Balthazar's job will be to set them: the right ones in the right order, controlling their spread and reach.

"It's crazy," he says to Etta May. "It'll be a riot. Blood on our hands."

"You want to cancel?"

"No."

"Then shut up and watch the wrestling, hon. You are making me nervous with your pacing."

The wrestling starts without announcement or ceremony. There is a man who manages the pairings. He has set up a blackboard and is taking names down in chalk. Most of the combatants come in pairs: they have long agreed to fight, for fun or to settle grudges; from the simple need to see which of them will win. There are factory workers who fight in their work coveralls and shopkeepers who strip down to their underwear, darned and splattered in Soot; potato farmers who wear home-made gym shorts and colourful jerseys, their faces adorned in Soot and paint. Masks are popular, as are pictures painted on chest or back, showing Charlie or the stylised figure of Thomas, boxing gloves weighing down his arms; or the husk of a blackened Julius, thorn-crowned like Jesus, and nailed to a charred cross. A woman welder fights masked but otherwise stark naked, her bulky body covered in a thick layer of grease; a middle-aged schoolteacher who has been blind from birth jams the blacked-out goggles of a Smoke mask down over his face before climbing in the ring.

The last of the bouts is fought by torchlight: two scrawny brothers, made timid by the fear of hurting one another until one suddenly charges and slams the other hard into the ground before hugging him fiercely in tearful apology. There are whistles and jibes; then a small commotion as, from the entrance behind the stage, Livia enters and finds a space within the lower stalls where people scoot apart for her.

Then the torches are doused and the roar of cheers and whistles stops. Silence falls, eerie in the company of thousands, the hush of expectation. Everyone's waiting.

Smoke Theatre is next.

[16]

They open with a simple two-person scene. A living room, suggested by a chair and a table; man and wife. Ada plays the husband: Balthazar needed a face and skin that suggested aristocracy, the pampered softness of a life of ease. She carries it well: has slicked down her short hair and changed her posture. When she speaks, the words carry the slurry, nasal vowels of the gentry. "Minetowns," she declares, making it sound like she is at a club dinner, sharing a witticism from the *Times,* "is the very seat of culture." She is wearing a shirt and waistcoat as she says it, workingman's garb if somewhat too clean, and no trousers. The tight cotton of her long johns are Soot-blackened on her too-round rump.

The person she is addressing—the wife—is an amateur player, a brick-yard worker much older and broader than Ada. Balthazar cast her for her physicality only to find that she has talent. She is standing at the table, ironing her husband's trousers, pockmarks painted onto her face. In the corner, uncommented on, unconnected to the scene, stands a sofa with two Commissars on it, sitting stiffly, watching, taking notes.

And so it goes: Ada stands, makes speeches, espousing the virtues of Minetowns, her "patria late acquired, but all the more loved. I wish Papa could see how well I'm getting on." Every line or so, she interrupts herself to curtly instruct the wife how she wants them, the trousers, pleated crisp and turned up at the bottom (the wife is not doing it right). Mostly, Ada picks at her underwear: at the arse, principally, or at the front where a sock forms a generous bulge: peels the cotton back an inch to shake herself loose. She would be a happy man, her movements make it clear, an idealist even, a Shock Worker and leader of the Council—if only her linen were not so damn itchy from the Soot.

The scene ends with the wife helping her husband into his trousers, but-toning his fly; Ada looking down at her, eyebrow cocked and naughty. And all of a sudden—as the wife is kneeling there before her slender hand-some lord, her fingers on his crotch—an erotic charge transforms the little farce. The brickyard worker responds to Ada's playful twist of Smoke with a sudden plume of raw desire. It jumps out of her at mouth and lap; is unscripted, *real,* at once moving and joyously frisky. The two Commissars who have been scowling at each other on the sofa catch it at once. In a moment of lovely improvisation, they drop their notebooks and lean in to kiss. The mechanical ventilator spreads their joy up into the stalls. A riot of laughter follows, of smooching and giggles and lust, as roving hands are slapped and encouraged; flesh is squeezed and held. The ushers have hardly any work to do.

"We got lucky," Balthazar mutters to Etta May. "Saved by a workingwoman's marvel at lily-white skin."

"Stop griping, old man, and listen to the laughter! You've just put a pulse in a whole city's loins."

[17]

Things go downhill from here. The reformed aristocrat with itchy undies is followed by the two Commissars trying to outbid each other with their ideological purity while throwing fistfuls of coal dust at an old miner every time "Granddad" tries to open his mouth; by the wife who berates her burgher husband for not smoking enough in public, all the while fending off his lewd advances and telling him to behave. It is not that the audience is not alert to the ironies depicted, or fails to recognise the types. But they do not enter into communion, sit fragmented, smoking different colours in different parts of the stalls, passing on not the emotion of the play but Chinese whispers, echoes and distortions without rhythm or coherence. Perhaps the space is quite simply too big, the audience too divided into camps; their own smoking too habitual to surrender to the show.

"Excuses," Balthazar rages at himself. "The material is no good."

He watches it all with dispassionate horror. His plays have never failed before.

When the players arrive at the scene that exposes Minetowns' fear of its own children, fights break out high in the tiers and boos become audible (though there are cheers, too, and laughter, and some Smoke so expressive it wafts back onstage and transforms the play). Balthazar signals to end the scene and axes three others, skipping forward to the final piece.

They wait a moment for the Smoke to thin within the crowd, then Meister Lukas splits the darkened stage with a single tongue of light. A lone actor walks out in it, carrying a basketful of clothes. It is hard to say whether it is a man or woman. Balthazar has picked a beardless young man, big-hipped and plump, who works as an iron smelter. The man understood at once what he was talking about. Now he stands in his everyday work clothes and begins to undress.

It is a simple idea, the culmination of the evening's logic. He strips, reaches into the basket he brought, and puts on a costume: becomes a Dark Miner; a butch woman Commissar; a moustachioed Shock Worker celebrity; a foreman's bourgeois wife. And as he stands there changing over and over, cycling through the whole range of Minetowns' fashion, transforming from man to woman over and over again, his movements become quicker, more agitated, lost between his roles.

The scene is meant to resolve itself in a joke: the actor finds a Puritan's black hat and coat in the box and dons it: becomes a southerner, a revanchist and Renfrewite, and skips happily—whistling—off the stage.

But as it turns out the Puritan costume is missing from the basket; Meister Lukas's mistake, it will turn out later, caused by the haste of moving the scene forward in its sequence. And thus something remarkable happens. The actor searches frantically for the costume that is not there. If his earlier agitation was mere mummery, he now grows genuinely distressed, an amateur betrayed by the professionals who lured him onstage. He stands arrested between costume changes, half woman, half man, no longer acting but himself. And then, his Smoke pouring out of him (or *her*?) in pure thick billows, he strips off all that remains upon his body, strips stark naked in the glare of Meister Lukas's lights, hiding his sex in the cup of his two hands and staring boldly, blindly, into the light.

His fatty skin throws folds upon the hairless chest.

The ventilators catch the Smoke, carry it upwards, to the silenced crowd. It isn't a pleasant Smoke: proud but also upsetting, flavoured with a question so existential that most of the Miners shrink from its disquiet and search instead for someone to blame. Soon boos ring through Ekklesia, carrying dark billows of ill will; people rise and want to leave, shouldering friends and comrades aside; others stand and block the exits, rooted to the spot by their own doubts.

It feels like the beginning of a riot.

Down below, in the darkness of the stage, stands Balthazar, two steps from the actor but beyond the strip of light. Black, smoking tears are running down his face. Etta May is there, soothing him, one hand upon his back.

"Not everything can be a hit, hon."

But it isn't that. The scene is the most personal thing he has ever staged. Balthazar sees himself in that wide-hipped, breastless figure with the too-round limbs, his skin turned ebony with Soot; sees himself exposed—

caught between the sexes—while ten thousand people boo and jeer and wish above all not to know.

"We must douse him," Etta May urges. "Or else there will be violence. They'll charge the stage."

"Let them charge."

Slowly, not knowing his own intention, Balthazar steps into the light next to the actor and begins unbuttoning his shirt.

[18]

When silence falls like the drop of an axe, he thinks it originates in him, in the shock of his bared chest. *Wait until I get my pants off,* it flashes through him, grim and irreverent, eyes blinded by the light.

Then a child steps up and takes his hand.

She comes from behind, not from the crowd whose voice has been so suddenly smothered, and brings along another stranger. In the glare of the stage lights, his hair burns like fire on his head.

"Hullo," says Charlie Cooper to the silenced crowd, sounding like a toff and rebel all at once. "I'm sorry to interrupt."

He pauses, looks down upon the girl, his cheeks hollow under a thick beard.

"This here is little Mary from Butterwick. She brings a message from your children. From the Angel of the North."

And as she steps farther out into the light, fists on hips and scrawny in her filthy dress, Charlie draws back into the shadows and gives his body over to the brutal rattle of a sick man's cough, almost drowning out the child.

All my life I dreamt of a Republic of Virtue built upon the principles of reason and restraint. The passions could be mastered: through the power of will; through habituation. A good life—a good state—could be erected upon this mastery, a return to Eden. In this great endeavour, I believed Smoke to be our friend and guide, for it showed us when we erred. I enlisted science, that child of reason, and devised methods to tame the animal inside us. I placed childhood in a corrective harness; studied the rules of heredity and selection of species and came to believe that across the generations, the lustful and vicious could be bred out of our race—by edict, if necessary. In my vision, the distortions of social privilege would wither away alongside our base nature. To learn restraint meant to become rational; and to be rational meant to be successful, and to be unimpressed by pomp and empty titles. Thus a natural meritocracy would triumph and we would live as God intended us, both kind and free.

Then came the moral catastrophe that was the Second Smoke. It brought something worse than immorality and violence—something worse than copulation, merrymaking, murder, rape. It brought a lie and spread it on the air like so much poison. It convinced our people that restraint was undesirable; that reason dehumanised us; that the ordered soul was sick and starved by self-negation. Compared to this lie's ravages, the Storms themselves were nothing—all they did was kill.

And so I did what few men do within their lifetimes. I changed my mind. And found my way back to God—not to the Deist First Mover that had for so long been in my arid prayers but to the God of the Jews, terrible in His aspect. Man must relearn what it means to fear. The Republic of Virtue will rise only out of abject terror—Louis Antoine de Saint-Just, my fellow dreamer of a better world, was not such a fool after all. We will have reason and merit. But first there must be war.

I have no illusions that what I am about to do is a grave crime. The sacking of Jericho was a grave crime—every man and woman killed, every child and animal slaughtered, all but a single harlot left to mock the dead. The killing of Jesus was likewise a grave crime—the cross and the nails, the kiss and the spear. It was the price that was paid for resurrection.

I must be our age's Judas.

My tree stands withered, waiting, a coil of blue intestine for a noose.

[1]

Nil watches her from afar. In the corridor, or walking in the courtyard arm in arm with her uncle, while Renfrew is out on his daily constitutional. Nil has not spoken to Eleanor in days, nor passed a single note. Not *since*. Smith has been keeping him busy. Running errands, spying. It has made it easy to pretend he has not had time.

Today, though: the hour of dinner. He knows she is in her room. The same dreary cell, on a hallway otherwise near-abandoned; the only light a window at its far end, narrow like an arrow slit. He approaches the door, hesitates. There was a time when he might have picked the lock but was afraid to speak to her. No, not afraid. *Ashamed.* In the days after the Storm, it seemed easier to stick to notes.

Now the door is no longer locked.

He knocks: softly, as on the door of an infirmary. Wary of troubling the sick. Eleanor answers almost at once, swings open the door, happy to see him.

"Come in!"

He steps in only far enough so he can close the door behind himself. She keeps distance, moves a step for each of his.

"I was hoping you would come."

He notes how pale she is; how much her face has thinned. A role suggests itself, of *friend*. He resists it, this easy slipping into pattern; repeating phrases, gestures, learned from watching others show concern.

"Why?" he says at last, anger curling out of him. "I don't understand it."

She backs away from his Smoke. Her movements are awkward, even stiffer than before, her torso made bulky by ribs of steel. A wind-up key grows from her chest.

"I'm back in harness, Mowgli. Broken like a horse."

[2]

She explains it to him. How she went to talk to her uncle and afterwards found a box in her room. "Like a present, though it wasn't wrapped." It was not the old harness but a new contraption, refined in its design. And it fit very well. Her uncle must have had it built to her size.

"I thought he had changed," she explains, "and in a way he has. He's grown cruel in his righteousness. Where before he wanted to correct, he now wants to punish. Only he won't admit it to himself." She sits down on her bed, painfully upright from the waist up. "He was so nice to me when we first talked."

"Take it off!" rages Nil. "Throw it out the window, run away. Fuck your uncle."

She smiles at the obscenity, smiles at him, his childishness, his seeping anger.

"There was a note in the box, Mowgli. If I don't wear it—if I smoke or don't obey—he will kill one of the prisoners on one of those ships. A life for each smear of Soot he finds upon my linen. If I run, he will kill them all." She pauses, watches him take it in. "It's not just cruelty, you see. With Uncle, everything has purpose. He says I have a reputation—because of the Storm. There are rumours about what happened on the ship. Now he makes a point of walking around with me, loyal and tamed. I've become a part of his authority, rather than a challenge. And look"—she brushes her hand down the lush fabric of her skirt—"he's given me dresses to wear. Silk and lace and thick white petticoats. And he in his dinner jacket. Like we are going dancing at a ball."

Nil nods, as though it makes sense to him; his skin is crawling with her calm. He is at the door before he notices he's fleeing. She watches him; controlled in her sadness. It makes him want to run all the more.

"What will you do, Eleanor?"

"He's planning something, Mowgli. Something monstrous. I will stop him."

"How?"

When she does not answer, he makes himself step back into the room.

"Smith is part of this," he ventures.

"Yes."

"But there's someone else. Someone new."

"So I have heard. Have you seen her?"

"From afar," he answers, too quickly, as though she's caught him at some indiscretion. "The only woman in this whole big place. She's hard to miss."

"The only woman?" echoes Eleanor. "No, not quite."

[3]

He stays another few minutes. In a sense it is easier, talking to her, now that she is *bound*. On the ship, during the Storm, she saw him as though naked: all the sickness of his soul dredged out of him, joining the Storm's anger. For a moment he felt her, too, stripped to her failings, a helpless rage as deep as his. Then something else rose in her, like a whale from the deep. She ate it, her own darkness, then watched him (watched his ugliness: *dressed* while he lay *bared*) with the terrible indecency of a surgeon studying the broken body of his patient. Then she ate his darkness, too, leaving only their shared wants.

He has avoided being alone in a room with her since.

Now, though, with Eleanor locked away within that harness, Nil's very gorge rising with the violence it implies, his sense of shame has lifted. Eleanor has seen him naked. But now her eyes have been gouged out.

God help him, but it makes him feel safe.

"Smith says Miss Cooper has come here from Minetowns," Nil tells her now. "She is a Company woman, he says, only she's playing some game of her own. Just like Smith. He's desperate to find out what on earth it is that she is selling, and for what price."

"Whatever it is," Eleanor replies, "it comes from India. Uncle has been talking about shipments. The first was lost at sea. The second—I think he's waiting for news that it has sailed."

"What sort of shipment?"

"I don't know. But the ships are hers, I think—Miss Cooper's. And they have captured Thomas Argyle, and are shipping him back, too." She pauses briefly, studies him. Nil isn't sure what emotion she finds written on his face. "And there is something else yet. Uncle has been seeking information on someone, far in the North. Someone he calls the Angel. He wants to know where he is. Does Smith know about this?"

"I haven't heard him mention it. He is in an odd mood. Buoyant one moment, and half in despair the next. Bustling about, writing letters, disappearing into the Company storehouse for hours at a time. At night he stays up and reads Hegel."

"And the beetle?"

"He keeps it hidden in a box." Nil hesitates, tries to put into words a recent observation. "Something's wrong at the storehouse. Smith is nervous. Perhaps he thinks Renfrew wants to rob him, I don't know."

They go on like that, comparing notes, filling one another in: standing in the middle of the room, two yards apart, conspirators not friends. Then Eleanor kicks him out.

"Livingstone will be here soon to fetch me. Uncle is making a habit of it. Inviting me for an evening drink."

"Stop calling him that. It sounds like you like him. He's a bastard. He's making you wear that thing."

"Oh, he's family," she replies, calmly, without bile. "He made me the monster I am."

[4]

Livingstone arrives within ten minutes of Mowgli's leaving. Ten minutes within which she struggles to contain herself: turns the wheel upon her chest, to trap her grief. They did not touch, even in parting. She had not known how much she'd want to. Now steel ribs make literal her heartache.

Then Livingstone is there with his breath of sweet. He leads her wordlessly. Her uncle's study has been tidied, the desk pushed into a corner to make space for a card table set with a teapot, cakes, three cups and plates. He watches her gaze at the third cup.

"Miss Cooper," he explains. "She's fashionably late."

Indeed she makes them wait another quarter hour. Eleanor has not seen her before, though she arrived at the Keep three or four days ago. She enters in a dress that makes Eleanor's own look tasteless and overelaborate, the pretensions of another era: sleek and high-buttoned if very tight at waist and chest. The hair is pinned up but a strand has escaped; curls fetchingly down to one shoulder.

"Lord Protector Renfrew," she greets Eleanor's uncle warmly. "And this, no doubt, is your famous niece—Minetowns is all abuzz with her story! But why put her in that awful thing? It's frighteningly medieval. And will you look at these cakes! Perfectly ruinous for my waistline! Where do you get your marzipan in this day and age?"

And truly, Miss Cooper is charming: not at all affected, but rather chirpy, funny, at ease with herself. She eats with great relish, and laughs at the icing sugar that ends up on the tip of her nose. She grows more serious when Renfrew leads the conversation to business matters.

"I hear there's trouble in India, Lady Cooper."

"There's always trouble in India, Dr. Renfrew. *You* would be cantankerous if you went there. It's just too bloody hot."

"Still, I have had a report of popular unrest. And your ship remains in harbour. It appears the harbour master is not granting it leave. A Company man, no less. Internal conflicts, is what I hear. Factions and power struggles. I do not much care for these reports."

"You worry too much, Dr. Renfrew. And look, we are boring your niece. Why don't we discuss these matters later? In private?"

"You need not worry about my niece. She has my complete faith. And you no doubt have her fullest attention. Is that not so, Eleanor?"

Eleanor hesitates, looks back and forth between the two of them: the former scholarship student who has risen to be king; and the daughter of a noble house who is rebuilding its fortunes. The Puritan and the flirt.

"I do not know why I am here," she says quietly. Then she asks, still in a tone so direct it brings a little pout of displeasure to Miss Cooper's charming face, "I would like to know where your brother is."

"And what is your interest in Charles?"

Eleanor pauses, fights down emotion, locks it in with a quarter turn of the wheel. "He helped me when I was a child. He helped me escape."

"Why yes, of course. So the story is true! The snow, the escape across the roof—it would make a lovely children's book, I've often thought. That was the night of your . . . injury, Dr. Renfrew, was it not? Charles rescued your niece while you were being attacked by Julius Spencer." She beams at them both, something dangerous mixed in with her charm. "Well, Eleanor, I imagine you must have been a little bit in love with Charles ever since. What a disappointment then that he has become such a rover. My mother and I felt we had no choice but to disinherit him. On grounds of insanity, actually—oh, it's not as far-fetched as it sounds. He has become a sort of mystic, a holy fool. Left his beloved mistress—there are rumours of a child, though it may just as well be the other one's—and took off to *commune* with Gales. Or so I have heard. Much the same is being said about our dear lost King, of course—and chances are *he* is rotting away in one of the Keep's dungeons, while the Lord Protector here decides whether he can still be useful or not . . ."

Miss Cooper trails off, ignoring Renfrew's denial. Her focus remains on Eleanor. Eleanor returns her gaze.

"Where is Charlie?"

"Stubborn! Ah well, you are in luck, my dear. As a matter of fact, a little bird told me only this morning that he has returned to Minetowns. Apparently, he has been living with an encampment of runaway children. They are starving, the dear little mites, so he has come to Minetowns to appeal for food.

"I was going to mention it to your uncle," Miss Cooper finishes, and reaches for another little pastry. "It might be of *strategic* interest. Dr. Renfrew, I am bursting with all this food. Why don't you and I take a little walk in the fresh air? Then we can continue talking business, just us two."

[5]

It leaves Eleanor alone with Livingstone. She knows the old servant relishes these moments: his darkness muffled by the sweets that he is constantly replacing; her horror at him hidden in the depths of her by a painful act of will. Like sharing one's room with a snake; watching it sleep, curled up underneath the chair. The man is clearing up around her, arranging the dirty cups and plates upon a tray. Soft, fluid movements. When he speaks there is the same bland fluidity. As though a voice is but a tool, like a hand, or a knife.

"You don't know why you are here."

It takes Eleanor a split second to realise that these are her own words, echoed back at her. It strikes her that far from being oblivious to all that goes on in Renfrew's study, Livingstone is always listening, recording, turning things over in his mind.

"He needs a witness," he continues. "A conscience. He is afraid of what he is about to do."

"I won't absolve him."

"Of course not," says Livingstone. "He wants punishment, not . . . the other thing."

He picks up one of the cups, holds it up to the light. The china is so fine, it seems translucent. A smear of lipstick is visible upon its rim.

"He used to speak to *me*," Livingstone carries on. "He would stand here, his back to me, and address the window. Talking to God, I suppose. But God is only a story, and I was *there*, right behind him. But now he has you."

His voice is quiet, his breath sweet. Eleanor cannot tell whether he is jealous of her usurpation. For all she knows he is relieved; or planning her murder as he speaks.

"Where did he come by you?" she asks.

"You mean, why does he tolerate me?"

"Yes."

"Because he's righteous, and I'm a villain?"

She recalls their encounter on the day she found the harness: spitting his sweets into his open palm; trying to tar her in his Smoke.

"You're ugly inside."

Livingstone seems amused by this: the ghost of a smile on his placid features. He is still holding the china cup. *In a moment he will smash it,* she thinks. *Crush it in his fist.* But Livingstone merely runs a fingernail over the lipstick, scraping it off.

"I was your uncle's nurse. It's true. After he was attacked, they sent to Oxford, to a famous surgeon. I was the man's coachman. And assisted in the operation. There was nobody else, you see, and I didn't mind the blood. What a way to meet a man: my fist inside his stomach, pinching close arteries; his guts around my wrist.

"The surgeon left me with him when he had to go, promising he'd send help. But it wasn't a nurse that came; it was the Second Smoke. So we smoked together, your uncle and I. You would have thought we were burning alive.

"I think it saved him; he was bleeding again, but all the fresh Soot must have plugged the wound. We painted his sickroom black. And found something, in the depths of each other. Kinship. You see, he and I are just the same; down in the depths of us, in our livers. So now he keeps me around and I carry his knife for him, his whip. I smoke for him, even. Together we are the most feared man in Britain."

He says it stolidly, not as a boast but as a matter of fact, then raises his lipstick-stained finger and sniffs at it with great intensity, as though sniffing the woman who wore it, rooting her out. It could not be more indecent if he attached his nose to Miss Cooper's rump.

"But you needn't worry, Miss Renfrew. You'll have your uncle to yourself. I am going away soon. On a mission to the North. I am to find an angel—imagine that."

They say no more until Renfrew returns. Miss Cooper is no longer with him. The walk has winded her uncle and he sits down heavily upon the bed.

"Escort Eleanor back to her rooms, Godfrey. And fetch me Smith. Tell him no more excuses. We require a sample of his wares."

"You mean *I* am to sample it."

"Yes."

"As preparation for the journey?"

"Yes."

"Good," says Godfrey Livingstone. "All these sweets are rotting my teeth."

[6]

Smith is in a flap. It shows in his attire as much as in the state of his room. The latter is a mess of maps, notes, letters, and books; of laundry, bedding, half-eaten meals. The man himself is thinning, his lustrous whiskers uncombed, bristling on his cheeks. Food stains down his shirtfronts; his collars soiled with sweat. Much of the time, when Nil comes to call on him, all Smith is wearing are his bathrobe and stockings; meaty toes showing in their holes. Today, though, he is dressed to go out in a double-breasted chequered suit. The fabric is expensive but rumpled; the shirtfront unironed, the bow tie askew.

"There!" he greets Nil. "I was waiting for you." Smith waves him closer with something of his usual ebullience, bends down to him across the barrier of his stomach. "It's time for action. We have been given an ultimatum."

We.

Nil and Smith.

It is not quite as absurd as it sounds.

Indeed, it has become increasingly difficult for Nil to define his relationship to the Company man. In principle, of course, it is unchanged. Smith has the beetle. It is there, in the room, in a bolted metal chest too heavy to lift by oneself, secured with a lock too complex even for Nil's skill. Smith has the key: not just to this chest and the storehouses kept by the Company not far from the Keep, but to Nil's past, to the boy they called Mowgli whose real name is forever lost. And so he remains, chained by his need for answers and by the complex feelings that bind him to Eleanor.

In principle, then, Smith is an enemy or rather a *mark,* someone to be tricked and robbed. The fact that Smith knows very well that he is a mark— that Nil wishes only to steal from him and that his servility is feigned— does not change this, only complicates it. But of late Smith's conversation with Nil has been increasingly intimate. He has been sharing his thoughts and memories with remarkable freedom, to the point where Smith will read out his letters to his wife and child, or confide his doubts about his place in history, or confess to the social rancour he feels towards the members of the high aristocracy who "infest" the Keep and Company alike.

The truth is the man is isolated. Sure, there are about a dozen Company clerks who administer and guard the nearby storehouse. But they are men with limited horizons who are visibly discomfited by Smith's manner. In the Keep, too, there are men who grow sick of its austerity and go in search of diversion in nearby villages—but these do not invite Smith to come along; nor would he want to risk a prolonged absence from his chamber.

And thus he talks and shares himself with words, this man cut off from Smoke. Nil plays his role, insinuating himself: has become confidant, valet, protégé. It is in the nature of the deception that he struggles to distinguish between the role and his true feelings.

I will know when I betray him.

There is a surprising sting to the thought.

[7]

The ultimatum, then. Smith has been challenged to provide a sample of his "cure," or, if he won't submit it for study, to inoculate a volunteer. Or else the deal is off.

Nil listens to this unmoved.

"Do it then. Did you really think he would buy it without testing it?" And then Nil adds, secure enough in Smith's need for him to prod him in his tender spot, "Renfrew's been seeing Miss Cooper. Long, intimate meetings. Perhaps he's trying to decide who has the better product. Or who asks the cheaper price."

Product. That's what Smith has been calling Miss Cooper's secret. He has been frantic in his attempts to find out what it is. Now, though, he barely reacts to the words but rather studies Nil. A thought runs through his features, a weighing of risks. Then Smith snorts and rises, decided: a man with more pluck than patience. Turns, walks over to the heavy metal box, digs out a key chain from his pocket and sets about opening a complex series of locks. A moment later the beetle is in Smith's hands. He passes it over like a relic, cupped hand to cupped hand. The dance of feet on Nil's palm; emotion welling up in him, a physical thing, pouring red and lilac from his throat. Smith sniffs at it with his usual obtuseness. Even so, his eyes are moist with the moment.

"I need to know, Mowgli," he says into red mist, "how much you remember of your past."

[8]

Smith offers to answer some questions first. He unrolls a colourful map of Brazil and points to a patch of inland jungle: his fingers denoting an area so large it would take a lifetime to explore it. "Eleven, twelve years ago, there was a rumour that there existed a tribe, deep in the forest, that did not smoke. Sebastian Aschenstaedt heard it and sent a man to fetch him an exemplar, making sure not to infect it in the process. They captured *you*."

"I know this."

"Yes, of course. How about this then: Aschenstaedt's was not the first expedition to find your people."

"Impossible. If someone had found us before, we would have been infected."

"Not if it happened *before* the Smoke."

Nil ponders this. "When?"

"The early sixteen hundreds. An explorer by the name of João Vasconcelos. A Portuguese."

"He made the drawings I found on the ship!"

"Yes. I was wondering whether you would recognise your birthplace. And react to it; spill the beans on your memories. Oh, it was done in the spirit of play, largely. After all, I had not counted on your being there. But when you showed up on the ship, I at once saw the value of what you might remember!"

Smith beams at his own far-sightedness, and from the sheer joy that here they are, Company mogul and thief, their heads thrown together like two boys playing marbles.

"On the picture you can see the natives wearing beetles. Like jewellery. He collected some specimens, Vasconcelos did: a handful of villagers, several dozen beetles. And plants, a whole range of plants, including a most curious flower that was like nothing he had seen before. Then they fought their way back through the jungle, all the way to the coast, and boarded their little fleet of ships, the *São Martinho*, the *São Pedro*, and the *Madre de Deus*. And headed home, to Porto."

With these words and the vision of the three ships crossing the black ocean, something falls into place in Nil, a truth both momentous and simple.

"They brought the Smoke."

Smith smiles, excited by his own telling. "The crew on two of the ships soon developed a strange fever. It was, Vasconcelos writes, as though their insides were regrowing themselves. Some had a curious rash here, above their livers, 'black and speckled, fading after two or three days.' Most of the infected crew died. Those who did not recovered but started 'emitting a pungent, many-hued fume.' Soon both ships were down to a skeleton crew of Smokers."

"And Vasconcelos?"

"This is where it gets interesting. The disease started on the *São Pedro*. A few days later the *São Martinho* reported its first case. The sailors had no grasp of the laws of infection, of course, but even so they were careful not to mingle crews: no boat went across from one ship to the other, all communication was by flag signal or else shouted across a twenty-yard gap in calm seas. Naturally, Vasconcelos expected to receive a report of the sickness being spotted on the *Madre de Deus:* he had the crew assembled twice a day and examined for symptoms. But the strange fact of the matter was that not one of them grew sick.

"As they were drawing towards Porto, he came to the difficult decision to order the other two captains to turn around and head for an isolated island. The devil had touched them; they must not be allowed to land. The other captains—both new in their posts, having replaced the dead incumbents—refused. Vasconcelos decided he must sink the other ships and ordered his crew to fire on them. A naval battle ensued, just a few leagues off the Iberian coast. He sank the *São Martinho* and damaged the second ship, but took heavy damage to his sails himself. Vasconcelos watched the *São Pedro* escape. In a few days it would be home.

"Afraid of what might await a crew associated with this new plague that had been carried into Porto by its sister ship, Vasconcelos patched his sails and made south for Madeira. They only stayed long enough to resupply and complete the most urgent repairs. He was nervous the illness would show itself within his crew, or that their stories would spread in town and lead to their arrest. Vasconcelos decided it was best to disappear somewhere far away; a safe haven, under Portuguese control, where a merchant-explorer like himself could quickly blend in. Soon the *Madre de Deus* sailed again, heading south and around the Cape of Good Hope. They were headed for Goa."

"India!"

Nil looks up at Smith's flushed, expectant face; picks through the details of his story, pieces it together. At length he asks:

"What cargo did the *Madre de Deus* carry?"

"Clever boy! Yes indeed; what did one ship carry that the others did not? Well, they had split the spoils. The *Martinho* and *Pedro* were carrying precious metals and minerals; seeds, exotic feathers, a pair of captured jaguars, two dozen exotic birds, and and and. But the things they had taken from your birthplace—the natives, the beetles, the strange, dark-petalled flowers—those were all on board the *Madre de Deus.*"

"And did they make it to Goa?"

"Barely. They had escaped one disease but got ravaged by others. Scurvy, dysentery, influenza—it's hard to make sense of the notebooks. What is clear is that he arrived with barely enough men to sail the bloody ship. Vasconcelos's cargo had no commercial value and he had very limited resources. He seems to have settled in the hills: a small house lent to him by a distant relative who had business interests in Goa. The natives all died, he writes, as did the beetles. But Vasconcelos planted a little garden. The flowers he had brought did not take to the soil, not until he bred in a strand of a local flower. The hybrid plant did better, though it seemed to suck all nutrients out of the ground within a few growth cycles. He completed his travel journals, drank a lot of brandy, and went a little mad. But his garden survived. It was not until much later that his flower's properties were discovered. And later still until it was given a common name."

"The 'Smoke Poppy.' So it isn't Indian at all."

"Not originally."

"And you found the Portuguese's notebooks!"

"I did. As well as a specimen beetle, remarkably preserved, that had made its way all the way from Goa to the Metropolitan Museum in New York City. But this was later, after my own expedition. Initially, I had little interest in bugs. I was looking for the ur-poppy. The original flower. I thought perhaps it was more potent. A super-poppy. Hence, a business opportunity."

"And?"

Smith smiles. "Your turn, Mowgli. We are trading, after all. Like for like. Tell me what you know."

And Nil would like to trade, is desperate for information; is willing at this moment to strike any bargain with this man if it but solved the riddle of who he is. He stands, groping around the dark cave of his memory. Smoke soon sketches his frustration.

"I can't remember. Help me—I need more."

Smith leans close, plucks the beetle from Nil's palms that all this time has sat twitching in their cup. "Are you playing games with me, boy?"

Nil shakes his head, feels a connection break with the removal of the beetle; a loss of identity, an *un-belonging*, as though Smith had taken a sponge and used it to erase his face. "Please," he begs, humiliated, lost.

"Did you notice how plump it has grown since our crossing?" Smith returns unheeding, the beetle between his forefinger and thumb. "I thought I had killed it. But it fed on the Storm."

[9]

Smith takes Nil to the storehouse. He does so reluctantly: Nil can see the risk of it written into the flush of the man's face. Nil, for his part, follows him eagerly, his obedience more than mere expedience. It is only when he imagines Eleanor watching them from her narrow window, Nil chasing Smith's coat-tails as a duckling chases its mother, that a pang of shame runs through him.

The storehouse is a compound, actually: walled and gated, dogs barking in the inner yard. Smith is known at the gatehouse, but even so he has to sign a number of forms before he is allowed entry. Only then is he presented with a key that the clerk recovers from a strongbox behind him and let through the reinforced door. Nil enters without any additional precautions. It has often struck him that in the world of the rich, a flunky is no person at all.

They cross the yard, dogs barking at them from behind wire fences; unlock the door to a low, barrack-style building with a second interior gatehouse and a second guard. Again Smith has to sign. Then they enter the warehouse proper. It is a wide-open space lit by sparse electric lighting. Massive crates are stacked on top of each other, creating corridors within the single enormous room. Here and there the gap is wider, marking a thoroughfare, a route through which goods can be moved. The crates themselves are chalk-marked and studded with customs seals. The Company logo is everywhere.

"We are no longer in England," Smith comments as they walk the length of the building. "This place lies outside Renfrew's jurisdiction."

Deep in the building they come upon a lift. It is a crude thing, its chains and gears exposed to the air, the cage itself unornamented steel. They enter and stand side by side, the cage a-quiver with their weight. A memory rises up in Nil, of the elevator boy in New York and his realm of dead pigeons. He recalls the fleeting feeling of companionship, of twinning: a doubled Nil, half servant, half thief. Now he stands next to the man who will have beaten a statement out of the elevator boy, then punished him for his disloyalty. Smith's hand hesitates over the buttons. A soft hand; fine golden fuzz along the knuckles; each fingernail topped by a white crescent moon.

"You must not tell a soul what I will show you," he says. "Remember, boy. I'm your only link home."

[10]

There are two subterranean storeys. The first replicates the warehouse space above. The crates here are smaller both in number and volume, and are clustered near the lift shaft. Beyond lies the mouldy emptiness of a cavern.

They walk out into this emptiness, segmented only by brick buttresses at every eight or nine yards. Above them run electrical cables; weak bulbs dangling from the ceiling creating islands of light. Deep in one corner, well masked within the floor, lies a trapdoor. Smith unlocks it with a key he produces from a chain around his neck. There's no lift this time but a steel ladder; next to it a pulley system designed to lower goods. Smith hesitates, then descends first. When Nil follows him, he finds the Company man waiting at the bottom, his hand shoved deep into his coat. Its pocket might be big enough to hide a gun.

Ahead of them is another storeroom, much smaller than the warehouse above, if still sizable. It is empty apart from a handful of crates. Nil has seen them before, down in the hold of the ship: broke the lock that protected them not an hour before they were taken by the Storm. Now Smith walks over to the closest of these crates; drops to a knee and opens it wide. The insides are packed with straw. Nestled into the straw, Nil knows, lie pale, translucent grubs, fine black patterns running through their midst. He touched them, back on the ship, felt them curl under his fingers; remembered jungle fronds strewn with them as though with swollen raindrops.

Now he again approaches the crate and kneels down next to Smith; reaches in to part the straw. The grubs are not there. He searches carefully, the straw no longer golden but smeared with Storm Soot. It must have crept its way inside through minute cracks. After a minute's groping, Smith's hand takes hold of his and guides it to the crate's inner sidewall. There they jut like boils out of the Soot-soaked wood: no longer pale, no longer grubs, but shrouded in cocoons, black and spongy—fungal—to the touch.

"They have turned into pupae," Smith mutters, his voice subdued. Church whispers from one votary to another. "An entomologist—a bug man—told me they might do this. *'Might,'* he stressed, and gave me a long lecture on the varied life cycles of vermin. That's the problem with experts. You ask a simple question and you get a thousand 'mights.' Hard to do business based on that."

But Nil is not listening, is touching the cocoons, stroking them, remembering this very touch and with it a place, a chant.

"Now watch!" Smith continues, oblivious to epiphany, and draws a syringe out of his pocket. He attaches a needle, plunges it into one of the cocoons, draws back the plunger. Pale, viscous liquid fills the glass chamber.

"It looks just the same," he carries on. "Bug snot. But I tried it on one of the clerks here and it has no effect whatsoever. A dark rash for a day or two. Otherwise, nothing. And of course it kills the bloody thing."

Smith yanks loose the cocoon he has just milked, rips it open between his thumbs, reveals a half-formed, flesh-pale thing more worm than beetle, then wipes his fingers on the crate.

Nils says nothing, his breath caught in his throat, his skin goosefleshed at Smith's action. "Violation," "sacrilege": he has to cast around for the words. What presents itself instead is a sound, a sequence of syllables, so very far from English that his tongue is unable to shape them. A ghost within his thought.

"Don't do that," he manages weakly, touches the smear of gunk left on the wood, then lifts his finger to his lip: a moment of childhood residing in the gesture that he cannot otherwise recall. Smith sees it and grows excited; rises, towers over him who remains prostrate on his knees.

"There—you remember something, boy! Tell me. Show me how I get them to hatch. If you do—you will be rich! The richest man in the world. After me, of course."

Indeed Nil does remember *something*: not as Smith imagines it, in chunks of information that could be listed and bartered with, but in dislocated fragments. A pattern of light within the canopy; the echo of a distant chant. The croak of a black-patterned frog. Rainwater and rot; the smell of fallen leaves transforming into soil. But Smith won't wait and let Nil sink into this smell. He wants something immediate, concrete. Nil struggles to lay hold of it.

"There was a place," he says at last. "Far from the village, a day's walk, more. A valley, round like a cup."

"And?"

"I don't know. Black ferns. Birds and insects that were different from the forest. We sang and danced and touched the beetles."

"Cultic rituals! Describe them to me."

But Nil is stuck, words welling up in him that he does not know and cannot pronounce.

"A valley," he says again. "An outcrop in the middle, covered in black moss." Then the words spilling out without definite meaning: "We hail the rock."

"A rock? Where—under the moss? How big?"

But Nil can only shrug. It is all he knows.

Smith studies him, greedy for more but not unsympathetic to his plight.

"Your people must have gone there to collect beetles. Strange insect life indeed! A place where things grow wonky. And then? Think, boy! They must have harvested the spore. How did they do it? Did they collect grubs and farm the beetle? To immunise the tribe?"

At this Nil shakes his head. His certainty is guided by logic, not memory. "No, we had no need for that. We don't smoke, remember? We don't have the *organs*. The Portuguese sailors—the sickness you describe, their blood rebelling against change . . . That only happened to me here. In London."

Smith accepts this; straightens, his hand moving once again into the depths of his pocket. Perhaps he has just remembered what Nil is: a spy, a witness. One who has no knowledge to trade. What better place to murder someone than this hidden tomb? Nil shivers and speaks, turning assumptions into truths.

"It's too cold for them down here. They need more heat. And they need to feed."

"Yes. But what? The beetles seem to munch on Soot and poppies, as long as the Soot is very black and the poppies reasonably fresh."

"They cocooned in the Storm. They *ate* it."

"You mean they need another!"

Nil wonders at this.

"I don't know," he says at length. "They only hatch in the valley of the rock."

[11]

They return to Smith's room. The reverse journey through the warehouse. Outside, mist has rolled in off the sea, and with it a springtime chill. When they arrive, Smith locks the door, then proceeds to once again unearth the beetle.

"Well, there's nothing for it. We only have one cow to milk."

He produces the syringe once more, makes to plunge it in the beetle's rump.

"Not like that! You will hurt it."

Bemused, Smith hands over the beetle. Nil holds it, expecting his hands to remember how to do this only to find that they don't. Still, that *connection*. It makes him feel whole. He takes the syringe, removes the needle, plunges the tapered end into the glands at the base of the beetle's abdomen. The spore pours out, viscous and murky.

"More," says Smith. "We need to give Renfrew as much as we can. It'll be a selling point. It mustn't wear off for several weeks."

Nil nods and accepts a second syringe. As he milks the beetle, it changes before him, growing paler, almost translucent. It becomes agitated, spreads out the horned back plates that cover its wings. Nil removes the syringe.

"Enough."

Smith agrees. The beetle's health is paramount. He combines the harvest in a single glass tube, holds it up to the light. Observed closely, a dark web can be seen hanging in the thick of its gloop.

"There! That's more than enough. You know, in the beginning I was very careful. Two drops, that's all I ever took. I ingested it at first, before risking injections. It would last a day, three days, five. Then on the ship, I panicked."

He pauses. Regret colours his voice. "Now I don't think I will ever smoke again." He shrugs, smiles away his regret, strokes his whiskers. "Tomorrow then. Another demonstration! A bluff of sorts.

"You know, my boy," he adds not without affection. "There's nothing quite so joyful as pulling off a really good bluff."

[12]

Early morning. An exchange before witnesses. Eleanor is there; Livingstone, Smith, Mowgli. And Uncle, of course: they are in his chambers. There is tea but nobody is drinking it. Smith is studying the paperwork, a legal deed, then requests a map of London.

"It's not much," he complains. "Not even half the city. Chances are I will go and find everything has long burned down."

"It's an opening payment. And it gives you control of the river."

"There won't be any legal problems?"

"The public has appropriated the whole of the city; I asked Parliament to ratify the seizure."

"And you are the 'public,' so it's yours to give out." Smith nods, satisfied, and hands the paper back for signature.

"You first, Mr. Smith. Please proceed with the inoculation."

"Will you yourself . . ."

"We will try it on my manservant here."

"This brute? Your name? Livingstone? Well, Master Livingstone, would you kindly drop your trousers. With apologies to Miss Renfrew."

For all his cool, Smith's hand shakes a little as he produces a full syringe from his pocket and plunges its needle into Livingstone's buttock. Eleanor notices it and she is sure her uncle does, too. Livingstone does up his breeches, rubs his rump.

"When does it take effect?"

"At once. There will be some . . . discolouration. Do not be alarmed, it is perfectly natural."

Livingstone nods, takes up a teacup, starts spitting sweets into it. Eleanor watches Renfrew watch him with disgust and fascination. His evil twin. When Livingstone is done it is to her he turns: he reaches out with one hand and starts stroking her cheek. Her uncle does not stop him. Instead he asks: "Is it working, Godfrey?"

Livingstone studies himself, his limbs and shirtfront; laughs with surprise and delight. "Yes, Lord Protector. It works!"

"And your affect is unsuppressed?"

"Rest assured," he answers quietly, still holding Eleanor's cheek, "that I am smoking on the inside."

"Very well. In that case, please let go of my niece. Thank you."

Renfrew turns without waiting to see if he's obeyed and signs the paper

Smith has laid out for him. His manservant lets go of Eleanor, though not before reaching for the screw on her chest and giving it a little turn.

"I think you will find you need it."

It draws a gasp of Smoke from Mowgli's throat.

Renfrew sees it and frowns in displeasure. Then he turns to Smith and orders inoculations for an army of three thousand men.

[13]

It takes but a few minutes for Smith and Renfrew to finalise terms. The price, Eleanor can see, has long since been agreed on. The only point of negotiation concerns delivery times. Renfrew wants the vaccine at once.

Smith demurs.

"I will have the supplies sent for, but it will be a few weeks. Surely, Dr. Renfrew, you did not expect me to take the risk of arriving with all my goods in hand?"

They agree at last and shake hands. Then Smith and Mowgli leave. She follows them out.

"I need air," she pleads.

Her uncle seems inclined to stop her, but he sees in her face the discomfort at Livingstone's presence. "Stay away from Smith," he says simply.

"I will."

He does not remind her that disobedience will be punished by the death of innocents. There is no need to. The prison ships are as visible from his window as they are from hers.

Out in the corridor, Smith and Mowgli are already out of sight. She catches up by accident not design, for they have stopped. It is Miss Cooper who has waylaid them. Eleanor, too, stops, and hears Miss Cooper invite Smith to her room, for "a chat and a cup of tea." The Company man accepts at once and offers her his arm.

"Only, leave your coolie here," Charlie's elegant sister adds. "I think we will have more fun without him. Don't you?"

This leaves Eleanor alone with Mowgli. An idea takes hold of her that she has entertained before but dismissed as unwise. Now she walks past Mowgli, stiff in her harness, and asks him to "follow me." He understands her meaning and hangs back ten, twenty, at times as much as thirty paces, seemingly on business of his own. They do not meet many people on their long walk through the Keep; those they do—aristocrats, petitioners, flunkies—take note of her, the Lord Protector's ward, but not of him, the Company man's servant, by now a familiar sight around the building. Soon they arrive in an isolated corner of the Keep: the top floor of the east wing. Here there is no foot traffic at all, nor any lodgers. Or rather: only one.

They stop at her door. Eleanor has been here before, trying to identify the room. She did not knock then but rather returned to her chamber, pondering the consequences of such a knock. Her uncle has not interdicted her coming here. In fact, it was he who alerted her to this lodger's presence in his realm; indulging in a rare moment of vanity, perhaps, unable to banish triumph from his voice. Nevertheless, he might disapprove of any visits. Eleanor looks into herself, checks her breathing, the rate of her heart. She must not sin. Virtue is a walling-in of doubt; a dis-involvement of one's self. Mowgli catches up with her, a question in his eyes. It is for him she found the door. He has a right to this meeting, more so than herself.

"Who?" he asks.

"You mustn't smoke on me," answers Eleanor, then swiftly raises a fist and raps the door.

[14]

Lady Naylor is surprised. It does not show in her bearing or her well-modulated voice, but a hint of colour has risen to her cheeks that are otherwise quite pale and somehow yellowed, as though she is suffering from some disease. Other than that she is just as beautiful as she is in the stories: near fifty perhaps, tall, straight-necked and angular, and dressed in an elegant gown of mauve. She recognises Eleanor at once—the tale of her harness must have made its way to her—then rests her eyes on Mowgli. There, too, recognition is instantaneous, along with a weighing, a judging of intent.

"How do you do?" she says at last, inviting them in. "I am afraid this is a rather squalid place in which to receive visitors. But do come in."

The squalid place is a room identical to all the others in the Keep, if much more lavishly furnished, and richly wallpapered in a pattern of purple and silver. Eleanor notes that Lady Naylor locks the door behind them and pockets the key.

"Then it's true what Uncle told me," Eleanor says with awkward directness. "You really aren't a prisoner. He says you came of your own free will."

"A prisoner? No, I am something a little more complex than that. And yes, I did come of my own free will. What was I to do? Sit in my dirty palace in Nottinghamshire? Or live in the North and pretend to be a proletarian? No, this is better. This way we keep an eye on each other, your uncle and I. He reads my mail and tells Parliament that I repent for my crimes; that I have thrown myself on his mercy—while I watch and listen and learn what I can. Did he tell you that he comes here quite often to chastise me? He is lonely, I believe. Though if I displease him, he will still put a bullet through my head. But sit, both of you, don't let's stand around like cattle. I really did not anticipate what damage my little revolution would wreak on simple courtesy and manners."

Lady Naylor gathers her skirt and settles herself in an upholstered armchair before gesturing to a little settee next to her. Eleanor follows her invitation, sitting awkwardly on the softness of the cushion. Mowgli remains standing with his back to the door, breathing hard through his mouth. The Smoke he is battling is colouring his lips.

"Will you look at him!" says Lady Naylor with a note of impatience. "Standing there dumb like a post. Did he tell you he came to see me before? Oh, he did. Three or four years ago, when he was still half a child. He crept into my house and surprised me in my bedroom. And it was the same thing then: he stared at me from a distance and did not say a word. He only had one question. *Where am I from?* And of course I didn't know, other than in the most general terms. That and I had laryngitis. I could hardly get a sound out. I thought he would murder me just for that." Lady Naylor purses her lips—disgust or mockery?—then returns her attention to Eleanor. "And you? I see you are disappointed. Am I grown old and ugly? Or do you find me compromised by my decisions?"

"Uncle says you made a lot of money out of the revolution. That for you it was speculation, more than anything."

"Money? Land, actually. Well, what was I to do? I knew it was coming, so I could either gain or lose on it. It hardly proves I am without ideals. But come, why are you here, other than to *inspect* me? And why bring this angry little man? He looks ready to soil my furnishings at the drop of a hat."

Indeed, why did Eleanor come? For help and information; in the hope of finding an ally in this place; to see another woman in an isolation ward for men. Because Lady Naylor *owes* Mowgli.

Only Lady Naylor does not seem aware of that fact.

"What is Uncle planning?" Eleanor asks. "Ursula Cooper. India. Smith. How does it all connect?"

[15]

Lady Naylor is remarkably well informed. She has, she explains, contacts within the old families that did not altogether wither away with the Second Smoke; links, also, to the scientific community on the Continent that bypass politics. A good number of those contacts and connections lead to elements within the Company and, hence, to India, the centre of the old imperial wealth.

In itself the size of Lady Naylor's network is unsurprising, a function of blood ties so ancient they override even her treason. What is more remarkable is that Lady Naylor appears so willing to share some portion of her knowledge. True, she is at one and the same time fishing for information herself, asking questions about Smith and Ursula Cooper, neither of whom she has met. But at the centre of her willingness to share lies something other than barter; it is as though she senses something about Eleanor and Mowgli that connects them to *change*. It strikes Eleanor that it is this the old revolutionary hungers for: not resolution, or polity, not even justice, but perpetual motion. Lady Naylor is bored. She was a player once, a lead.

Now she's sick of sitting in the wings.

This is the substance of what she tells them: Cooper and Smith represent different forces within the Company, forces that are defined by social class and ideology as well as by different sets of opportunity. Of Smith she knows little, other than that he is a "new man," his sudden rise to the inner circle of Company power based on a reputation of daring and the efficient ruthlessness with which he put down a peasant uprising in southern Bihar. Last she heard, he had turned his focus to South America under the banner of diversification.

Miss Cooper, on the other hand, is part of a recent reassertion of high aristocratic interest within the Company. The Coopers (that is, mother and daughter, not the disinherited elder son); an obscure wing of the Spencers; a few minor Hounslows; and two of the Collingwood brothers have all reasserted their ancestral claims on the Raj, using their wealth to buy up new land and expand poppy production. Of these, it was the intrepid Miss Cooper who started to ask questions about something she believed had been smuggled into the country some ten years ago—some kind of curiosity or *sample*. It appears it came from India and was brought in by a private citizen—the son of a noble house who had been travelling in the Raj. Whatever it was, Miss Cooper must have seen considerable value in it, because all of a sudden she was throwing money at a new pet project: an expedition, assembled in secret, with orders to secure a second such sample. It appears she was blessed with success. Her people found something—God knows where—and sent it back to these shores. Only this time, the sample did not arrive. A Gale caught the ship carrying it, as it was nearing the shore—a freak accident, created by an offshore wind—and the next moment the Gale had *transformed*. Transformed into a Storm, that is.

"The very Storm that caught you." Lady Naylor pauses, studies their reaction. "Well, we shall know more soon. I believe a third sample is being shipped from Bombay."

"Thomas Argyle is in India." Eleanor says it before she grasps her own implication: "Was he looking for the . . . sample?"

"Naturally. I sent him there. It's the last thing I did before my 'surrender' to your uncle. I needed someone clever and relentless, someone with a personal stake. The sample and the Storms are connected, I told him. By the time I added that a Cooper was involved, he was rearing to go. I may have omitted to say which one."

"He's been captured."

"So your uncle told me. He crowed about it, in his pinched and miserable way. Well, I am disappointed. I had better hopes for Thomas."

"Uncle will have him killed."

"I expect so. He is a danger to your uncle's interests. And a trial would give him a platform of sorts."

All at once, Mowgli is beside them. All this time, he has been standing in the corner, silent, staring; Eleanor conscious of his muffled anger, afraid that it would burst. Now he swoops down on Lady Naylor's armchair and puts a hand to her throat. For a moment Eleanor thinks that he will throttle her. But it is the *touch* he is after. His other hand is spread over Lady Naylor's head. Smoke pours out of his skin, straight into hers. Eleanor backs away from it, afraid that she will soil. Lady Naylor's face has lost some of its haughty composure; something is creeping out of her, yellow and sickly. Eleanor recalls the story of her mutilated liver—Lady Naylor's husband cut her open in an experiment to remove the organic source of Smoke—and connects it at once to her waxen sheen of skin. She is sick indeed.

Mowgli speaks. It is a voice Eleanor recognises from the Storm: very young and very angry, the eight-year-old boy who was caged like a beast, stupid with his grief.

"You—you *took* me," he says. "You don't even know from where . . . And here you sit . . . soft carpets and golden wallpaper"—this last bit despite the fact that the wallpaper is silver, with a purple pattern.

But even as he spits his confusion at her, Lady Naylor calms under his fingers; sits ups straighter; pushes him off her with one firm hand, his Soot a mask upon her face.

"What now—you would like me to apologise? Join the queue. They're *all* waiting for me to apologise—my daughter most of all, though she is a hero now, almost a saint! Have you noticed how they've all become heroes somehow: her, Thomas, that sweet wet dishrag that is Charlie? I am a mere footnote to their epic." She curls her lip, speaks as though she were at trial, the speech long prepared. "I was Prometheus, giving humanity fire! So what if I prefer wallpaper and carpets to spitting on the floor?"

"Was it worth it?" asks Eleanor, quiet in the face of Lady Naylor's fervour. "Giving humanity fire?"

"It did something. Cleared away some of the clutter, killed the old gods. But somehow their altars survived. We are living in a museum, Miss Renfrew; in an echo of things past. Here; up north; overseas."

"So what do you want?"

"What I have always wanted. To be free. If it takes another fire, I will light it myself." Lady Naylor rises and, pushing aside Mowgli, walks in two strides to the door. "Otherwise, it would have been better not to have started with this at all. I could have spent my whole life sleeping in a comfortable bed; fresh pastries for breakfast, and good Ceylon tea."

[16]

Back out in the corridor, it is Mowgli who leads, encrusted in his anger. Eleanor wishes to speak to him but she cannot risk their being seen together. An inverse procession, thirty steps apart, courtiers turning for her. He leads her to Smith's rooms and appears to own a key. She slips after him once she has confirmed the corridor is empty.

"Mowgli—" she starts, but he interrupts her.

"*Nil*. Nothing. No-One." His anger keeps her at four or five steps: the maximum distance the small room allows. He is digging in Smith's papers with an odd sense of proprietorship; it is with a pang she realises he is at home in here, in Smith's camp. At last he finds what he is looking for.

"There!"

He places the photo down on the floor, so they both can see it from opposite ends of the room. London. A dark pillar of Smoke connecting sky and Thames. The day of the Second Smoke.

"What?" she asks, though she already knows.

"The first *sample*," he says, "the thing from India. It caught. My blood was the spark, Julius Spencer's body the fuse. It quickened the Soot along the river's banks and started the Second Smoke. And then, downriver, *there*"—he points, stabs a finger at the photo from afar—"a Storm started."

"Then what—" she begins to ask, but the door opens.

Smith.

He is buoyant; a smudge of lipstick rides his cheek.

"Nil! And young Miss Renfrew! Arguing. And my dirty undies littering the floor!"

She runs away then, rounding him, emotion rising in her throat; her right hand busy at her breast-cage's wheel, doing its best to shut it in.

[17]

Mowgli comes to her one more time. It is early the next day. She has slept little, the harness intruding on her comfort; fog in the bay outside, the prison ships standing murky in their reek.

He starts speaking before he has as much as closed the door, his voice flat and fast.

"I told Smith everything. The expedition, the sample in London. It connected the dots for him. Now he wants to go and find it—with the help of the photographs! He thinks the pupae will hatch there. I am to come with him. As his *expert*. He has me figured out, you see. He says to me: 'You were not loved enough when you were small, and now you are seeking something, *approval*, only you don't know yourself that you are seeking it. All you know is that there is a hole, right in the middle of you, so big you are hardly there. All that's holding you together is your anger.' He says that if I come with him, I will discover myself. My past. Banish the anger; fill the hole."

Eleanor listens, watching Mowgli fidget. He is too agitated to stand still.

"Perhaps it is Smith who has the hole. Half his bluster is him convincing himself that he is real."

But Mowgli only half listens. "Smith killed the elevator boy. In New York. That's what I told him, to show I shan't trust him, not now, not ever. And it took him a full minute to understand what I was talking about. Then it came to him at last. 'Killed him?' he guffawed. 'It's the twentieth century! I paid him off.'"

Mowgli raises his palms—disarmed, unfit for resistance—then drops them again.

"Screw Smith," he says, quietly, even shyly. "Let's go to London, you and I. I can figure out how to break into the Company stores. We will steal the grubs and run off with them. Figure it all out. I am sick of people telling me who I am."

He reaches out a hand to her, touches the leather buckles that flank her harness. There are steel ribs and a padded corset separating his hand from her skin. Still, it's the closest they have been. Since the Storm.

She lingers in it for just a moment. Then she says: "Don't stand so close, Mowgli. My body . . . I . . . am attracted to you. And I mustn't be."

God help her, but it pleases her to see colour seep into his face.

"Come," he says again, though he is already retreating. "Us two. Please."

And she would like to tell him that she will come and fly with him; that together they will find all he seeks to know; that the knowledge that he wants is already there within the flavours of his Smoke and that, stripped naked both, she can show him the truth of himself and make him whole; or else that he should stay with her, and help her watch her uncle; that Livingstone is gone to learn how to bottle Gales and that Renfrew is all alone and that they can win the battle here, together. But her eyes find the prison ships drifting in the bay, and her ribs, expanded by emotion, dig painfully into their steel counterparts; and in Mowgli's face she finds a torn urgency that fears her presence as much as it craves it.

And so she says, "No," simply and firmly, and watches him leave with anger on his skin but no surprise. A flake of his Soot settles on her hand. She stares at it, then licks it; smothers herself with the quick turn of a wheel, and wonders, not for the first time, whether it is possible for the contraption to break her very spine.

[18]

She does not see Smith leave. The story he tells her uncle is that he, Smith, wants to inspect "his lands" while waiting for the shipment of the inoculant. On the morning he and Mowgli set off, Eleanor is disturbed by something unprecedented. There are noises in the corridor, voices, steps.

She opens the door and sees a throng of people, all walking in the same direction. Doors open to rooms she thought uninhabited: curious faces, inquiring what is going on. They, too, soon join the people passing, as does Eleanor. Three long hallways and two flights of stairs: she had not realised how close she lived to the chambers of Parliament. A plain door admits them. Beyond lies a great hall, tiered seating on both sides, plain wood like church pews. The left row of benches is entirely empty. It is reserved for the opposition. But in Renfrew's realm there is no opposition. Hence the absurd spectacle of a press of men occupying but half the room, even now, when Parliament is not in session and the Speaker's chair stands empty, as does the Lord Protector's seat.

Eleanor soon comes to realise people weren't summoned but merely drifted here, the only *public* space in the whole Keep. In its long corridors and narrow stairwells, there is no room for this, a *crowd*. She sees the sons of eminent aristocratic houses in their Parisian suits, jewel-encrusted Smoke masks tucked into their belts. She sees older men still dressed in the fashion of the mid-nineteenth century in which Britain was so long frozen by embargo: heavy, sombre suits with large cravats; or hunting tweeds with riding boots and chequered flat caps. She sees burghers in shirts worn thin by too many washings in lye; former liberals, copying her uncle in dress and hairstyle, starving themselves to match his gauntness. The buzz of talk is in the air, hushed yet excited, even afraid. The crowd quiets and parts wherever she treads; closes behind the tear she makes within its fabric, the conversation resuming once she has passed. She picks a man at random, a short, sweaty, rotund fellow mopping his forehead under a top hat made porous by moths.

"What?" she asks. "Is there some news?"

He hesitates but only for a moment, too excited to still his tongue.

"The Raj," he says. "India is in revolt! The poppy fields are burning. They say Bombay has gone up in flames."

What is the Smoke Poppy?
  – The sacred wealth of the Indian people.

Who controls the poppy fields and steals our wealth?
  – The Company.

What is to be done?
  – Seize control! Rise up against oppression! Burn this year's harvest!

*Today the fields will burn. Tomorrow, the Company lies bankrupt.
Home rule awaits.*

[1]

This is the revolution. Heat, fear, gunshots; the great roar of ten thousand feet running riot through the city streets. The bittersweet stench of burnt poppy, mixing with the tang of Smoke. The rains bind it, plaster the smell onto the walls. Bombay's burning—not in a single blazing wildfire but in a dozen managed fires: the Company warehouses, the police headquarters, the Central Post Office, the Empire Hotel, all reduced to rubble and ash. The Company's troops, British and native, have been mobilised, martial law has been declared. This morning, a machine gun was fired on civilians—old men, women, and children—drawing water from a city well; many jumped inside for cover and were drowned. Last night, a bomb was thrown into an army barracks where fresh recruits lay sleeping on their bunks; another into the stables of the Bombay Officers Club, ripping the legs off a dozen polo steeds. Drowned women and the scream of horses. From here on in, it will be a fight to the death.

And yet here they sit, Singh and his two companions, waiting, doing nothing, the sea breeze lively in their faces, distancing them from the city noise. They have found shelter in a customs building that has been abandoned by its officers, and are sitting on its flat roof, biding their time. Beneath them, the harbour lies tranquil. It is no coincidence, this. The movement, though no puppet master, is guiding the mob's fury, suggesting targets, theatres of action; creating pockets of comparative peace. The harbour has been designated one such pocket by special orders.

It shows on the waterfront below. The soldiers on duty are clustered around a single stretch of pier, a single ship. They, too, have special orders, two separate sets, with conflicting aims. One lot is here to guard what lies hidden in the ship's hold and prepare its departure; the other, to ensure the ship does not sail. Both sets of soldiers are a problem. Somehow, Singh and his comrades must board the ship.

They have come prepared, are wearing sailors' uniforms and have packed away their instruments in crates that are marked with the ship's name and adorned with the blood-red bloom of a customs seal. They also have a contact on board who is sworn to help them, and even some forged orders, though it is hard to know whether these will be believed. Moshin, the younger of his two companions, is growing impatient. He's been chewing paan and it is making him twitchy. "Let us go trying our luck," he says, not for the first time. His English is thick with Urdu.

"Not yet," repeats Singh, conscious that his own English must sound to him like the enemy's. "Those soldiers will be called for, sooner or later. They need the manpower in the city. You'll see."

To pass the time, he quotes Marx at them from memory, reciting it rhythmically, like a mantra.

"A spectre is haunting India," he says, "the spectre of home rule." And: "The Company has drowned the most heavenly ecstasies of religious fervour, of chivalrous enthusiasm, of philistine sentimentalism, in the icy water of egotistical calculation. It has resolved personal worth into exchange value, and in place of the numberless indefeasible chartered freedoms, it has set up that single, unconscionable freedom—Free Trade. For exploitation, veiled by religious and political illusions, it has substituted naked, shameless, direct, brutal exploitation."

Neither of his companions has much formal education, but even so the words seem to please them. "Company is bastard," Ashook, the elder of the two, agrees. He is from the south but has lived in Bombay since the age of ten or twelve, working at the chemical plant. It is for skills acquired there that he is here.

At last there is movement down below. A soldier comes running from the direction of the city, his uniform blood-smeared though he appears uninjured. He talks to the soldiers whose function it is to make sure the ship does not sail. The exchange is brief. Within minutes all but two men have joined the newcomer and are sprinting back to the city.

"Now?"

"Let us wait half an hour, Moshin. Right now they are riled up. Let them relax; get sleepy with the evening heat."

As Singh answers, he pulls a revolver from his pocket and checks its bullets. Violence won't get them where they need to go. Still, the weight of it reassures him.

[2]

Just as they are ready to descend from the customs building, there is a new development. The soldiers on the ship's side—the guards—walk down the gangplank connecting pier and decking. Singh assumes it is to talk to the soldiers who were left behind on the pier. Perhaps they want to ask them for cigarettes, or suggest a game of cards. Instead, they simply walk away without speaking to them, not running exactly but walking with an odd, furtive haste.

"Fresh orders?" Ashook wonders.

"I don't think so." Singh watches their trajectory, trying to fathom their destination. "I think they are deserting."

Even as he says it, the two remaining soldiers start talking animatedly to one another. Both of them are sepoys. The briefest of consultations appears to suffice: then they, too, are walking—now openly running—away from the harbour, heading not in the direction of the city centre but somewhere up the coast. It is hard not to see the hand of fate in this: the laws of historical materialism manifesting themselves in a single breathless moment.

"Let's go," says Singh. "Don't forget the crates."

Not five minutes later, they are on board.

[3]

Their man is there, as promised. He guides them to the entrance to the central hold, then closes the hatch behind them and stands guard outside. They climb down a steep iron staircase, deep into the ship. For a moment Singh is back on the mountain, descending alone, dodging the expedition porters, his feet and hands numb with cold. At the bottom they light an oil lamp and find themselves in a short corridor, acrid with the smell of rust. A second hatch bars their way.

"Let me go first," says Singh. And: "We don't know what state he is in."

He squeezes past his companions, tugs at the bolt that holds the hatch shut and realises too late that it is padlocked.

"Allow me, Singh-ji. I have the bolt cutter."

The honorific briefly angers Singh—"We are comrades, man!"—perhaps precisely because he has missed its usage. The next moment it is forgotten. He watches Moshin work the heavy bolt cutter, his muscles bulging in his sailor's shirt. At last the padlock falls and Singh once again storms forward and tugs at the heavy hatch. It swings open on well-oiled hinges.

Beyond lies a cube of space the size of a town square, an iron ceiling for a sky. It reeks of seawater and corrosion, of the ghost of opium and sweets. It is also almost entirely empty. The single piece of cargo that is stored here is encased by a strange kind of metal crate, half giant wardrobe, half machine: pipes, chemical tanks, and pressure valves grow out of its flank, like industrial warts. It stands more than twenty feet high. A loading hatch can be seen at the far wall, barred and bolted. It's a big hatch, but even so it is hard to see how so large an object as this strange crate-machine could have fit through it. They must have assembled it here.

A man is chained near it.

It's the kind of arrangement you might make for a yard dog that you wish to keep forever in ill temper. Six, seven yards of chain are anchored in a ring soldered right into the floor. The chain leads to a bracelet encircling the left ankle: again, it is soldered rather than just screwed in place. The man's hands are in iron cuffs that allow some limited movement. Enough to lift food to the mouth, or to loosen the cord about his trousers when he needs the privy. Not enough to wipe himself clean.

His face is hidden by a sack.

Singh curses and runs to him and tugs at the sacking. But it is sewn into place very cleverly around the neck, so that it won't easily come off. Singh puts his fingers into the small slit that's been left around the mouth and tries to tear the fabric. But the cut, too, has stitching running around its lip, making it impossible to tear. He digs through his pocket, disturbed by the man's passivity, and locates a knife. As he cuts the sacking he finds himself shaping soft cooing words—"It's me, it's me"—like a mother soothing her child. Moshin and Ashook seem embarrassed by this and are keeping their distance. Perhaps it is the man's smell that puts them off.

At last the sacking is cut open. Thomas Argyle looks thin, worn, dull. He has been drugged, Singh can see, with sweets and opium, suppressing his affect. His naked feet are clumsy on the metal floor. Three toes are missing, two on the left and one on the right. Singh sees it and holds up his two finger stumps; their upper digits sacrificed to the mountain and the cold. A belch of Smoke pours out of Singh's throat, surprising him by its density. Singh sniffs at it and wishes it were words. He wants to tell Thomas that he never left him. That he climbed down the mountain with luck and guile and left the valley to seek help for his frostbite. That, exhausted still, teetering under his bags of supplies, he returned to the mouth of the high pass a week later, waiting for a sign of the expedition. That he laughed for joy when it emerged and he spied Thomas, tied to a yak's back, his features hidden by a Smoke mask.

From then on, Singh watched over him—like a father; like a guardian angel from his strange English faith—on his travels from the Kingdom of the Gorkha all the way to Bombay. He walked the same paths, rode the same trains, stowed away in freight cars, playing hide-and-seek with the guards.

It was only at the Bombay station that he passed the vigil on to others. He had telephoned ahead, made contact with a friend he knew from the Punjab who in turn contacted a local cell of nationalists. They were at the station to wait for Thomas and follow him to the private villa whose premises provided his first prison; and also, separately, to follow the crate whose progress Singh had monitored along with his friend's. A crate very different from this current monstrosity, if large enough to make its transport difficult; a thing the yaks shied from and the porters were wary of; that crushed a man's leg when it slipped while they loaded it from a cart onto the first of the trains and that seeped black water as the straw-wrapped ice that formed a part of its contents gradually melted in the heat.

But Singh says none of this and simply stands at arm's length to Thomas; and a calculating part of him is grateful to the Englishman who decided to crop his friend's hair close to the skull. The mark shows vivid with no hair to hide it, from ear to temple to cheekbone. Behind Singh, Ashook and Moshin unpack the tools they have brought.

Singh interrupts them by asking if one of them carries water, then takes the tin flask from Ashook's hand and pours it over Thomas's face, before offering him a cup to drink. Gradually, Singh sees Thomas struggle up from the well of drugs and despondency. Intelligence returns to his eyes; some modicum of purpose.

"There is no key" is the first thing he says. "You will need a cutter. Something strong."

Singh hesitates before responding.

"We cannot free you." He wanted to say "will not," but the words stuck in his throat.

Thomas takes this in without reaction; makes to speak then grows distracted. "Do you hear it?" he asks. The next moment he scuttles away from Singh towards the crate-machine. The chain does not quite reach. Thomas strains against it, throws forward his hands, almost touching the metal side walls.

"There! A gurgling, and something like a knocking. It's the machine, Singh. It makes ice, somehow. Chemically. And the walls are lined with lead. I saw. They assembled it right here in front of me. Five engineers wearing Smoke masks. Scared."

This is not just opium and exhaustion, thinks Singh. *This is hysteria.*

Thomas returns to him, dragging his chain across the floor.

"I understand, Singh. You have a bomb. You are here to sink the ship. Do it!"

Singh shakes his head. At this Thomas grows agitated; his breath takes on the smell of Smoke but not its colour.

"But you must! You saw what was squatting in that mountain. Like a spider, spinning . . ." He trails off, tugs at his chain, gestures. "That guide they tortured—Ajeeba, they called him Ajeeba. I've been asking myself, why did he kill himself? He was in pain, yes—but to throw his head at the drill like that . . . Something answered his Smoke, something frightful. Watts saw it, too; why else this ice machine? I heard them talking, Singh. The first shipment—the first piece of rock—it did not make it."

Thomas breaks off, strains against the chain and the sweets within his system, looking for his anger.

"You must sink the ship, Singh. It's alive, you see." Here, he jerks his head at the ice machine and its contents. "That rock must never reach England."

"Yes, Sahib! It would be better to sink it in Bombay Harbour and let it blacken our seas. English shores must stay clean!"

[4]

Singh's rancour is short-lived. He forgives Thomas. After all, their difference is fundamental: they were born on different patches of dirt, one at the centre of power, the other in what was forced to serve as its periphery. Perhaps there are people more fluid in their loyalties, or more capable of seeing the world dispassionately, as a whole, beyond the ideologies of turf and mores. Singh does not have this luxury. First, they must set India free.

"Please understand the situation," he says to Thomas now, glad to be free of his scruples at last. "Bombay has risen. And not just Bombay: half the north. Every day new reports reach us. The poppy fields are burning. There are rumours running wild through every city and village. Rumours about a black god that the English have cut out of the mountain—or a demon. Rumours about you."

Singh pauses and thinks back to the first meeting he had with the local revolutionary cell. He told them about the rock within the mountain; about Thomas, masked and bound. The men were not interested. Nepal and mysticism: what did they have to do with home rule? In Thomas's presence, at least, they sensed something that they might be able to exploit. But how?

And even as they sat and dithered, haggling over strategy and theory, how action could best be made to conform to dialectics, a landslide started in the country. Perhaps Singh himself had caused it: by telling his story to the Nepalese villagers who saw to his injuries, and later to some people in Agra, where Watts and his team changed trains and rested for one night. Or perhaps the porters talked, those Watts had hired and then dismissed with stern warnings that he owned their silence. The masked Englishman; the demon from the mountain. Then the Company raised the taxes on salt; and, independently, onion prices soared as demand outstripped supply. The next anybody knew, mobs were running through the street. The revolution was happening, while the revolutionaries sat talking, making tea.

And still they were slow to seize the situation. Eight men, shut away in a back room, half of them in Western suits, the others in dhotis, kurtas, pyjamas, speaking in English because there was no other tongue they all held in common. Should they attempt to free Thomas and use him as a symbol, or keep their revolution native? Was the rock national property or an English abomination? They debated all night and in the end they voted. Singh, heavy-hearted, raised his hand for the winning proposal.

That was the day before yesterday.

"The Company is divided," Singh says now. "Those who paid for this"—he points at the ice machine, at Thomas's chain—"worked in secret but others have taken note. They are asking questions. Until they have answers, the ship does not have permission to sail." Singh pauses. "We will make sure it does."

At last Thomas understands. "You're sending the devil back to Britain. And me, too. You told me months ago—you have no need for a white saviour."

He shivers, tugs at his chain, peers past Singh into the gloom of the hold, where Ashook and Moshin have completed preparations. For the first time, he appears entirely rational.

"If that is so, Jagat, why did you come at all?"

Singh welcomes the question. "Do you know what 'propaganda' is, Thomas? It's a Company term. The newspapers you saw in my house, the ones that showed what happened in England in the Great Smoking. That's propaganda. It's a weapon used to wage war." He turns, points to the two men behind him, one of whom stands humped behind a wooden box erected on a tripod. "The country rose because of half a rumour. Imagine the effect of a few seconds of film of you, chained like a beast, aboard this English ship. We don't want you, Sahib. But we have use for your image."

[5]

They can't do it. The lighting conditions are too bad, the two gas lamps they brought barely adequate to see by but too weak for the camera's narrow lens.

They had anticipated this, of course, and Ashook has brought a rig of magnesium flash powder lamps for this very reason, imprinted with the stamp of the Bombay Chemical Works at which he worked until last week. Now, however, he hesitates. He must position and light them near Thomas, though not so near as to be visible in the camera's frame. Moshin is trying to direct Ashook into the required position, but the older man won't move. Stepping that close will bring him into the range demarcated by Thomas's chain.

"He's afraid of you!" Singh realises. "He's heard the stories. *Always angry. Maximum raging.* He's afraid you will throttle him alive."

Thomas does not react. He has withdrawn into himself once more and turned away from them, appears to be listening again for the gurgle of the icebox. Singh steps close enough to touch him, turns him slowly by the shoulder until they both face the camera.

"Will you let Ashook here close enough so he can light the flash lamps? And will you stand still, not moving too much, so the camera can get a clear image? Will you do that much for me and our cause?"

When no answer comes, Singh adds,

"A letter arrived for me yesterday. We burned down the Central Post Office, there is fighting in the street, and yet the local postman comes this morning and cheerfully delivers a letter, stamped with the picture of your dead queen. I open it, and it's from Isha."

"Who?"

"Isha," he repeats while Ashook gets ready to light the first lamp. "Mrs. Singh. She is coming here. She is coming, so we can fight side by side. Don't smile now, Sahib, that is very important! You are oppressed and tortured, remember? That's why we're here."

Seven seconds of flickering film. First we see a ship, under heavy arms. It is not the same ship that holds Thomas but this is immaterial; it is the nature of the cutting room to impose one reality onto another. The lens finds the twin flag of Company and Empire, hanging limply from the mast. Not far from it tilts the metal pipe of one of the cannons. The film wavers, intersperses a white frame. Then we are inside. At first there is darkness. Then a bright, pulsing light flares up to the frame's right. It gives movement to a scene that is very nearly static: a single man standing in cotton rags. For a moment—the camera has not yet found its focus—he appears to be smiling, laughing even, but then the face turns grim. He turns his head to half profile, showing off his mark. There it squats amongst his stubble, that coal-dust tattoo-scar that is his brand and stigma. He turns back and raises his chin, and all at once he is recognisable from all the stories: that pugilist's stance, that hard directness to the eyes, a habit of honesty, unflinching will. The chained hands only serve to emphasise his strength. Then he turns his back on the viewer, hunching his shoulders, dropping his head. Behind him hulks the machine. A trick of the wavering light makes eyes of its valves, a maw of its gas tank. At Thomas's feet there snakes a metal chain like an umbilical cord. It appears to connect him to the shadow of the monster.

Then comes nothing, the searing white blankness of empty frames, like a snow blindness that follows upon the witnessing of truth, like a baptism of light that follows upon darkness.

INTERMISSION

The film projector is wheeled out, the stage is swept. The laughter of actors sounds from the wings.

When the bell is rung to reassemble the audience, there's a new presence on the stage. It's a woman in her twenties dressed in a starched white shirt and greasy tails, a top hat on her close-cropped hair. She sits on a stool, unassuming; picks at a loose thread on her lapels; straightens the ruffles of her opulent shirt. Come to think of it, we have seen her before, prompting lines from the edge of the curtain, her whisper a pretty thing, melodious and quick.

A sign above her head pronounces her to be our Narrator. She seems too young to fill the role with any wisdom.

A miner's shovel lies discarded at her feet.

ACT IV

CHILDREN OF THE SMOKE

JUNE 1909

If we perceive History as this slaughter table on which the happiness of peoples, the wisdom of states, and the virtue of individuals have been sacrificed, this thought necessarily generates the question for whom or what, for which goal or end, these unspeakable sacrifices have been made.

Alexander the Great . . . Caesar . . . Napoleon . . . these are the great persons of history, whose particular purposes contain the essential purpose, that which is the will of the World Spirit. Insofar, they are to be called Heroes.

Nothing great has been achieved without passion . . .

—GEORG WILHELM FRIEDRICH HEGEL,
LECTURES ON THE PHILOSOPHY OF HISTORY

[1]

The night is clear and very still. The compartment soaks up this silence; grows strange upon its diet. Objects become unlike themselves; they appropriate sounds and arrogate motion; grow consciousness (and fangs). Two suitcases stacked one upon the other in the luggage rack, a glint of moonlight on their buckles; both breathing—snoring almost— dogs on a chain. A heavy leather coat drooping from its corner hanger, the flap of its buttoned pocket curled up into a sneer. Two pairs of boots forming chess games on the floor: a pawn lies sole-up, toppled, filthy; the bishop unlaced and drooping at the shaft.

Time whispers life into these details. Time is the scuttle of beetle legs against the inside of one's skull. Time is the passage of the moon in a large rectangle of window; the shift of shadow across the carpeted wedge of floor between two rows of seats. The upholstery smells of mothballs and wood polish; of mould and sweat and old cologne. On one side, two stock-inged feet peek out from a blanket; twitch then curl themselves around their owner's dream. The blanket groans in its sleep (dyspepsia, or gas?); the pillowcase gapes at the seam; like a Golem's forehead it is stamped with a letter, its laundry's cabbalistic mark.

Time is a thief rising from the bench opposite; rising so slowly, he is but another shadow moved on by the moon.

[2]

In plain prose: two men in a train compartment, stopped for the night. An *English* train—a rarity, almost an antique. Small for all that: two train cars and an engine; no longer under steam. Stopping where? At the edge of the world, or very nearly so. The proverbial *end of the line*. Fifty yards on, the tracks simply cease. Someone's made off with the sleepers, and also with the tracks themselves, melted them down perhaps, or used them to buttress their crumbling house. The great British railway system is flashing a gap-toothed smile these days; more of a grimace, truth be told. To the west of this particular gap lie the remains of what was once if not the heart of the nation then its guts. London. The Big Smoke, capital of factories, and of sin. Long may it rot.

Inside the train, one man is rising. A youth really, still in those difficult years wedged between boyhood and maturity, when thought has not yet frozen into habit, and one still wears one's skin a size too large. Rising so slowly, so silently, that the patience required must chew at his very soul. He plants his feet, leans forward, stoops; and with infinite care, half an inch at a time, withdraws a case from underneath his companion's seat. Then, reclaiming his seat, he pulls it onto his lap. Next you know, the youth has bent double upon the hinge of his waist and lain his own head onto the box within his lap, lain it sideways, one ear down. Listening. Even the moon holds its breath; bends down to him, straining for sound.

Then—nothing. Prayer silence: the snore of the suitcases, the blanket's digestive gurgle; the *tap-drip* of your heartbeat on the inside of your ear.

[3]

The box was the easy part. Now Nil needs the key. It is in Smith's trouser pocket; was kept on a chain around his neck until the Company man elected to shave this afternoon, right here in the compartment, despite the jolting of the train. Smith stuffed it in his pocket as he unfolded his razor and—red-throated and raw, bleeding from a dozen nicks—left it there when he was finished, afraid perhaps that it would chafe. Now the trousers are hooked from a peg by one of their belt loops, their legs trailing down to Smith's head. The latter is invisible, lies buried in shadow and a lumpy pillow overstuffed with down. All Nil can see of him is a curl of whisker, erect and frizzy as though charged with an electric current, rising up out of this down-padded pit. Smith's breathing is dislocated, everywhere at once. Sometimes he mutters in his sleep, isolated words, and these, too, seem to rise from the corners and fixtures rather than from his stretched-out, lumpen form. "Lemons"; "Caoutchouc"; "Never you mind"—the hat rack says it; the doorknob; the crates piled up in the corridor outside that are filled with half-formed beetles refusing to hatch.

Slowly, hardly seeming to move at all, Nil reaches for Smith's trousers.

He does so in a single fluid motion, graceful and natural, so that rather than him slowing, it is the moon that picks up speed within its rectangle of the window, and Nil's pulse becomes a telegrapher's finger, tapping out urgent Morse into the fold of skin where throat meets jaw. His fingers find the correct pocket; find the leather string attached to the key, then the key itself, tangled up into the knot of a well-used handkerchief. And—fluidly still and utterly silent, the trousers unmoved upon their hook—he withdraws the lot and draws it over to his side of the great divide.

Then he hesitates.

He could try to take both box and key and leave the compartment, though he knows for a fact that the door into the hallway squeaks; and that the second door, the door to the outside, is jammed and bolted and will require a kick to open. Or else—

Or else Nil could insert the key. Could turn it in the well-oiled lock. Swing open the lid on quiet hinges. Revel for but a moment in the touch of carapace and finger; then reach inside the lid, whose leather loops hold an array of glass syringes; withdraw one slender tube of glass and hold it up into the moonlight.

The beetle's spore comes slowly out of its gland. The insect scuttles in Nil's palm with an agitation he does not remember from milking it last. He pulls back the plunger—three drops, four, then five—and knows he's hurting the beetle now, must pinch it firmly between forefinger and thumb. Still he continues to draw the spore. He must get *enough*.

Satisfied at last, Nil lifts the syringe once more into the air. He watches moonlight break in its half-inch column of murky goo, then looks for a needle amongst the box's kit. And notices—the way we notice sudden danger: a tingle in the colon; a needle prick through both our lungs—that the curl of whisker no longer rises above the down pillow; that the head has turned; that from behind the curve of fleshy cheeks, two blue eyes stare out at him, their lashes coarse and pale like awns on winter rye.

"Good God," moans Smith, in genuine distress. "You move like treacle! All night long I've lain awake, wondering if you will kill me or simply rob me blind."

[4]

"So you want to be cured, eh? And after all, why not! But will you look at the beetle! It looks pale, and shrunk. All out of bug snot, I suppose. Remember, boy, we must be careful. This beetle is all we have."

Smith has snatched the box from Nil's lap; has yanked syringe and key from the boy's weak grasp. There was haste in these actions but no anger. Now Smith has calmed and sat up, his blanket spread over his legs, and is running his fingers' comb through his mottled crescent of hair.

"Well, if you want it so . . . I suppose it makes sense, given your past. I should have thought of it before."

Smith falls silent abruptly, turning over the thought. Within moments he comes to a decision: a salesman's smile at his own boldness.

"Go on then! Here, I will even do it myself. What, you don't want to now? Or are you afraid of dropping your pants? Let's put it in your shoulder then, it'll smart more but in the end it's all the same. Stubborn, what? And yet you have toiled all night, just for this."

Indeed, Nil has recoiled from Smith and drawn his knees up to his chest. His eyes are riveted to the syringe. He sees something there, a becoming, a path back to boyhood; it is hard to put into words. His longing is soured by suspicion.

He wants to know:

"Why help me?"

Smith purses his lips. "Let's just say because I can. So we are equal . . ." He breaks off, leaps from one thought to another. "Besides, it's no fun, doing it by yourself. Changing the world, I mean. History needs a witness, I suppose, though that's not quite it either. I always thought my son—but then, he's still half a babe. They are on Madeira, he and my wife. But I told you that already. At any rate . . . a partnership. So what do you say?"

Nil stares at Smith and says nothing.

I am being bought, it flashes through him. *I don't know why and what is the price.*

And almost immediately a second thought rises in him.

Go on then. Buy me.

He unbuttons his shirtfront, slips his shoulder out of the wide-open collar. There is something vile about the needle puncturing his flesh; the slow slide of the plunger; the gooey thread trailing from skin to needle as it pulls away.

"Done," says Smith, then more grandiosely: "The truth shall set you free."

They sit in silence for a moment while Nil rebuttons his shirt and Smith busies himself with putting away the syringe. When he has finished, he looks over at Nil with a strange kind of fondness, almost a joy.

"There you are. Yourself again! Uncluttered, unadulterated, private. You will miss it at times, the touch of others, right there in your skin, letting you know they are real. Solipsism—it's the price we pay. Never mind though, welcome to the future!" He chokes up, eyes brimming; guffaws at his own emotion. "But listen to me prattle while you sit silent as a fish. Go on, boy, try it; let yourself go. I know you have been holding yourself in."

Nil does not respond, sits quietly, contained in his slender frame. All the same Smith's words course through him, along with the spore. He pictures them sinking into his liver and lodging there, each syllable a little cyst, changing him back somehow, into who he was.

"How long will it last?" he asks.

"Ah, my friend, that is a question half the world will be asking itself once we are done. Do you know what a monopoly is? A monopoly is like having a tap. You choose when to turn it on. And when you do, money comes out, one pretty bill at a time."

[5]

Dawn breaks and Smith insists on callisthenics. He even talks Nil into joining in. Here they stand, at the edge of London; stripped to the waist, legs spread wide, making windmills of their arms. There is no need to feel embarrassed. They are quite alone. The clerk who rode down with them stayed behind in what remains of Windsor, where the Company maintains a warehouse and store. The engine driver, too, has been sent back; he will return every afternoon starting the day after tomorrow, to await news and act as a liaison. There are no farmers about: the country here is so Soot-soaked that it is hard to grow anything edible. To the west lies the city; clouds squat atop it, promising rain.

"How long did you live here?" Smith asks, as he leads them into a series of squats.

"Six years."

"With your foster parents?"

"With Grendel. Mum . . . my foster mother died within a year of the Second Smoke."

"And then? Where did you go?"

"I set off to find the ones who robbed me."

"You wanted information."

"That and also . . ."

"Revenge? Yes, of course! Though I can see from your face you didn't go through with it."

Smith falls silent as he drops to the ground and starts on a long series of push-ups, holding his hands very far apart, and planting his chin all the way into the ground on the way down. Once he is done with his exercises, he sighs happily, cleans his hands on a little towel he's tucked into his waistband, unzips and urinates happily into a nearby bush.

"Black piss," he mutters. "The world better get used to it. In a hundred years, they will have forgotten that we ever peed other than black."

Then he turns back to Nil, who sits exhausted on the ground.

"What will we find in London? Is it abandoned like people say?"

Nil shrugs. "Not entirely. But it's hard to grow food there. There are fish in the river; crabs and eels in its mud. The factories are all abandoned . . . You'll see." He pauses, looks up at Smith buttoning his shirt. "It's a good fifteen miles. How will we get there? Walk?"

"No. We can't leave the cases here."

"The grubs?"

"*Pupae*, my boy, *pupae*," says Smith, who has it from an expert whom he does not trust.

[6]

Nil has to repeat his question about their mode of transport before Smith consents to offer a reply. In the meantime, the Company man busies himself with getting dressed, putting on a double-breasted leather coat and buttoned leather gloves.

Satisfied in his attire, still fastening on a leather cap complete with chinstrap, he walks to the second train car and unlocks it; reaches inside and pulls down a wooden ramp before climbing in. Inside stand a number of wooden packing crates; some squat metal cannisters, tied down with thick belts; a trunk with a rifle case tied to its lid. And a large, four-wheeled something, protected by a tarp; gilded spokes winking at the light. Smith raises an eyebrow at Nil: the salesman is back and tempted to theatrics. The tarp flies off with a sharp little snap.

"Voilà!"

"A motorcar?"

"A motorcar, bah! A 1908 Stilson Six-Cylinder Company Special Edition. Sixty times the power of a horse! Let us roll it down the ramp and then load it. We'll need fuel, too, and provisions. And the rifle case, of course, and that box over there, it's full of ammunition. And here are goggles for the both of us; we will be going fast as the wind. Careful now, we don't want to scratch the finish. There you go, boy."

It is fair to say that Smith is enjoying himself.

[1]

On the coast of northern Wales, in the half-world between North and South, near the southernmost slopes of the mountains of Snowdonia whose snowy tops were spared the Second Smoke, on a pebble beach still rife with Gales, Godfrey Livingstone stands bargaining with a boy of sixteen for his services in reconnaissance. There's a gaggle of them, actually, a little gang of thieves, connected by a web of constant Smoke so light it is visible only where it brushes the walls of their shabby hut and dusts them with its colours. But it is only this one boy—the eldest, the tallest and fairest; the *leader*—to whom the old servant pays attention. The others are merely fingers on his hands (and sometimes knuckles to his fist). As for Livingstone, the boys find him odd but harmless. He does not smoke.

What danger can he harbour?

"Dive?" the boy asks. Livingstone notes his halting, lilting English. Since the Second Smoke, after many decades of being banned, Welsh has resurfaced in these parts from God only knows what hole. "Do you have any idea how cold the water is?"

"I'll pay."

"You have money then?"

The boy's question is not so much for the man he is bargaining with but for those who are massing at his back; a prod of the elbow by other means. Livingstone does not answer it at once.

"I understand you," he says at last. "We are much alike."

"Really?" A smile, dismissive, leering. "You sound rich to me. Fancy."

"I am a servant. I was a coach driver before then and a groom before that, and the assistant to a surgeon. The surgeon taught me how to read.

And to speak like him. He told me I should better myself. I was his pet. For a while I even took to it."

Again that leering look. Livingstone has just confessed to weakness.

"And before all that," he says into the boy's budding thought of violence, "I grew up an orphan. On the street. Terrified of everyone and everything. Of being *used*." Here Livingstone lowers his voice so that the boy has to bend close. "It's a strange thing, isn't it? The day you figure out that the best way not to be scared anymore is to become a terror yourself. And how difficult it is at first, finding that cruelty within yourself. It starts out almost as a chore. After a while, though, well . . ."

"You're talking nonsense."

The boy says it quickly. But there's a new timbre to the voice, a new tint to his Smoke. The others pick up on it, trained as they are in spotting weakness. Their leader has stumbled somehow.

He tries to catch himself. "About that money, man."

"A southern half crown.

"If you don't dive," Livingstone adds, "I swear to God I will skin you like a rabbit. And your little friends over there will laugh and hold the knife."

[2]

Before they enter the water, Livingstone has the boys recount once more what they have seen. It's been several weeks now and they hardly paid any attention even then; but young minds are impressionable and little things will leave their imprint, vivid like a line of poetry. There had been a Gale the night before, not dark but potent, catching them in their sleep: shared dreams and that strange quickening of all emotion; a sharing of the soul that left them frightened and ashamed. The next day the tide brought close the drifting shell of a ship; a steamer, large and very dark, as though painted in dull black; seagulls screeching at it as it ran aground upon a rock and lodged there. A dangerous place, that, rife with tidal currents pushing the sea around: there was not one fisherman who attempted salvage. Not until the Miners showed, on horseback, led by a woman and a man with a moustache. Livia and Francis: people who lived by first names, like children and kings. Cursed by some and admired by others; rumours of Minetowns orgies woven into the old songs. They wanted to see the ship and paid for it with promises of Minetowns steel.

There is always a madman who will risk his life for money. And so there was here: a Captain Fry, Edmund by Christian name, the part owner of a rusty little trawler amongst whose nets and tools the visitors were told to sit, arrayed in borrowed sailor's oils for the occasion, for the sea was moody and the wind on the rise. They chugged across to the grounded ship; transferred onto a rowing boat, and boarded. A half hour on board, then a quick return to beat the tide. Some say they carried a box off the boat, some say they did not: the boys do not know but look for clues within Livingstone's face, ready to vouch for either, depending on his needs. The very next day a storm struck and the hull was wrenched loose. It tore on the rock and sank, right *there* (five pointed fingers, all of them sure of the direction), and lies there now with its front chimney exposed at low tide. The boys have taken a boat out and looked down at the wreck. The mackerel own it now; the sea crabs and urchins. The water around it has stained a tarry black.

[3]

It is up to the leader to pick the divers. It leads to an argument and a bloody nose. In the end the boys he has chosen—the youngest two, one tall and gangly, the other a runt of thirteen—are more afraid of him than of the sea. Livingstone rows out with them on their little, leaking boat and watches the two strip naked, whilst another boy busies himself bailing the water. One of the boys lowers himself in by inches—feet, legs, hips, and shoulders—before letting go of the boat; the other simply leaps, arse-first, then comes up again gasping with the cold. On three they dive together: bubbles in the tarry sea.

The first time they dive, they don't stay down long. Yes, they say, the wreck is right there, just a few feet underwater; they can stand on the hull and breathe. Livingstone has asked for a full survey; he wants the captain's cabin and the hold explored in detail. Perhaps they cheat, perhaps they don't, but they dive six, seven, eight times, bringing reports of tarred walls and a thick spread of jet-black algae dancing on the current; of barnacles edged by a strange yellow fur. There are no bodies, no sign of the men who sailed the boat. The captain's cabin was ransacked, they say, its chests and drawers flung wide open, objects floating freely in its waters; the hold is dark and empty like a tomb. At long last Livingstone permits them to return. Their friend pulls them up over the gunwale. They have no towels and sit shivering, pressing their clothes against their bodies. The boat is still leaking; Livingstone's boots are wet up to the ankles. A drizzle starts. By comparison to the sea, the rain is warm as piss.

[4]

"So it appears Miss Naylor took it. Or else it consumed itself when it blew up."

"What exactly are you looking for?" asks the smaller of the two divers. The boy is dressed now but his lips and fingers remain blue with cold. There is so little meat on him, you would not give a farthing for his chances if he catches cold.

"There was something on that ship. A kind of bomb."

"You are looking for a bomb?"

"Actually, I am looking for a fuse." Livingstone pauses, thinks of the stories, how everything started with Lady Naylor's own search for a fuse. The irony does not displease him; history's wheel, iron-shod and all.

"Have you heard of a pied piper?" he carries on. "Someone up north who is collecting children. An Angel, he calls himself. Living amongst perpetual Gales? Has anybody come here, preaching his faith?"

But the boy is too busy with Livingstone's earlier words to give weight to his question.

"What does the South want with a bomb?"

"That's a rather dangerous question, wouldn't you say? And here you stand being inquisitive rather than getting warm. Mind, don't catch your death now."

It takes the boy a heartbeat to catch his meaning. Then he runs away into their hut.

[5]

Livingstone asks for dinner before he leaves. One of the boys makes it, fish soup and greens. He is a good cook, though there is little spice to the dish other than a bit of fermented seaweed he scoops from an old barrel. It lends the food an iodine tartness.

After the meal, the boys sit over mugs of hot water. There is, of course, no tea. Livingstone digs in his pocket and produces some lumps of sugar, with which he is well supplied. He has found that after years of sucking on sweets he cannot quite abide without. The boys stare at the scattered lumps and his gesture of welcome; then each scrambles for a piece. A contentment spreads through them, almost comical to behold. Next thing he knows, they surprise Livingstone by launching into song. It is one of those that tell of the coming of the Second Smoke: the one in which Julius is shot by Grendel; a sentimental variation Livingstone has not heard before. When they are finished, he clacks his tongue.

"So you, too, sing the songs and tell the stories?"

"You don't?"

"I live in the South. The songs are forbidden there. All the same, everyone knows them. Stories are like mice. They will crawl in through the smallest hole."

[6]

Before he leaves, Livingstone tells them of his fascination with the story about Julius visiting the farmer. The boys have not heard this one before, so Livingstone recounts it in full: how Charlie comes to the farmer, begging for food, and is given rotten potatoes; how Julius, hunting him, arrives soon after, already half mad with Smoke; how he gets his answers from the farmer without trouble, but rather than leaving at once, he lingers. How he makes the man cut off a finger; takes it away as a trophy and then, not ten steps hence, throws it in the shrubbery, like a child who badgered its parents for a toy and then ignores it once it is bought.

"That's what gets to me every time," Livingstone says, whispering now, the way one tells ghost stories, "precisely the fact that he threw away what he took. I always wonder whether the farmer saw it: his finger flying into the dirt. In one version of the story, he hangs himself from the gables the very next day."

He spreads his hand on the table whilst he whispers it, spreading it wide upon the wood; then scoops up the hand of the boy sitting across from him and flattens it out just the same, like a pale crab pinned down in the sand. The others make no move to help him. The boy whose hand is pinned has grown very pale.

"Which one?" he asks at last, Smoke pouring out of his rump and creeping up his back.

Livingstone studies the hand, touching each of its fingers with his own. Then he lets the boy go. "It's just a story."

The boy runs out of the hut and can be heard vomiting outside.

"Time to go, I suppose."

[7]

While he stands, saddling his horse and scribbling a note for one of the pigeons to carry south, the leader of the pack follows Livingstone outside. The old servant can sense him behind him, shuffling his feet and wrestling with a thought.

"You do not smoke," the boy says at last. There's complaint in his voice. Evil, for him, has always worn a plume.

In answer, Livingstone pulls up his shirt and lifts it clear at his back. The evening light catches the lines that swirl out of his waistband and snake up his spine and flank; like a twist of thistles growing in his skin. This frightens the boy further.

And yet: curiosity is a devil.

"What is it?" he asks.

"The future. The sign of those who will be spared."

"Spared?"

"When the reckoning comes and the rain falls black once more. A Storm is coming, boy, and it will cleanse the world for good."

"Cleanse it of what?"

Livingstone gives his master's answer.

"Corruption," he says. "The road to virtue is full of pain."

I t's good staging is what it is. A child petitions the masses. And of course she is small, thin, and red-cheeked; is speaking neck craned upward, as though from the bottom of the ocean; stage lights in her eyes, so that she cannot see. Little Mary from Butterwick, asking Minetowns for help. Asking for food. She does not say, 'Help us, we are starving,' it's more refined than that. 'If you have some little something you can spare,' et cetera. She's rehearsed it ahead of time—of course she has!—but it comes out nice and natural. Her voice so quiet everyone has to lean forward in the stalls.

"Only then the hecklers move in and drown her out, just as she tries to tell us something about the Angel being on the march. Oh, the pathos; the fear and anger, all very righteous. 'Where are they?' 'Where is my daughter?' 'My son?' 'I am his father, I have a right to know.' All of them shouting at once of course, spreading a Smoke of ill will, as though it is she, pretty little Mary, who has hidden their children away. Hidden them in her bonnet perhaps: any moment now they will leap onto the stage and search her head to toe.

"Then Charlie saves the day. He steps forward, into the light—and *coughs*. A proper stage cough, larger than life, it rattles him right down to the bones. Raises his handkerchief to his mouth. And as he charges forward in defence of little Mary, the handkerchief unfolds and hangs limp from his fingers, like a flag. It turns out he has new family colours: red spots on a field of white. The House of Consumption, well respected across the world. The light catches it just right.

"And then? Tears in the audience. Silence followed by fresh shouting. Exit stage right. Gossip for applause."

Etta May blows a raspberry. Back in New York, they call it a Bronx cheer.

"God, what a little drama queen you are when you are drunk, Balthazar. 'The House of Consumption'! Please! Besides, I was there, hon. I don't need your summary."

They are sitting in an ironworks foreman's living room. There are three tables packed into the stuffy little space, but they are the only customers. It's not a public house, exactly; Smoke is Minetowns' only legal drug. But there is always someone who will turn their potato ration into liquor, and the Council's been too busy lately to bother with Toptown civic regulations.

Balthazar reaches for the bottle and refills his glass. He tries to refill Etta's, too, then realises it remains untouched. Liquid and glass have the same colour. Both look like they could use a rinse.

"At least nobody's talking about the show."

"So that's what's eating you! Not that it's been a failure, mind, nor that half the world's seen you in your birthday suit, but simply that your play has been ignored. What a vain old cock you are." She studies him dispassionately, leaning her elbow on the table and her head on one palm. "Go back to work, Balthazar. You're tiresome when you're not scribbling away at something."

He drinks, shudders; reaches for tartness. But the words come out drink-slurred and weak. "Can't. My notebook's in Ekklesia. I left it behind after the show."

"So, go fetch it then. And for God's sake, stop drinking, old girl. It really doesn't do you any good."

[2]

It has been a week since Charlie's sudden appearance in Ekklesia. In its wake, there has indeed been much "gossip for applause." The evening itself finished with people charging the stage while the ushers showered them with coal dust, to quell their passions. Next anyone knew, Charlie and the little girl had been whisked away somewhere: to Livia's; to a special suite of guest rooms adjacent to the Council; to a prison built in secrecy even from the Council itself. In Toptown, crowds soon gathered outside the warehouses holding the city stores, some demanding the immediate release of "a third part of all food and other supplies in aid of our children"; others making sure that "not a scrap of food be stolen to fuel some fool crusade."

For despite the fact that everyone had heard the exact same version of Mary's plea, there exist a score of opinions on what precisely her words meant. Some see in her appearance little other than a new strategy of beggary, a way of "going after the whale, not the minnow"; others as clear evidence that the Angel is desperate and the children are starving to death. Ergo, the Angel must be denied, "to teach him a lesson"; or else indulged, "for we cannot eat whilst our children hunger."

One little "fact" excites passions most of all: the Angel is on the march! It's a pity, in retrospect, that they shut up the girl before she could tell them what the phrase means. Busybodies have long filled this gap in knowledge. The Angel is outside Glasgow, with an army of ten thousand mites. The Angel is in the Borders, heading for the coast, where a hundred ships have assembled to carry them to Norway, or Holland, or some mysterious island in the Baltic Sea. The Angel is in the Pennines, not at all with an army but with a pitiful gaggle of children, a dozen at most, all of them dying of disease. The Angel is a criminal, a crank, a "soft-brained messiah," "holy for all that."

A Parental Committee has been formed, made up not just of the actual parents of children who have followed the Angel's call but of all manner of persons, all of them pledging to "head out into the wilderness, and fetch back our babies once and for all." If only they knew where to go. Shovel, the anonymous author of the city's chronicle, pours oil on the fire by printing a flyer depicting, as from the point of view of a bird flying high above the city, a vast mob of Miners leaving the city, going west, even as the Angel's own mob enters it from the east. He's titled it "A Change of Guard." People read it and decide Shovel is a "wise man"; a "cynic"; a "blackguard and a shite."

As for Charlie himself, here the rumours are at their most heated. Charlie has been questioned—nay, interrogated!—by the Council and has refused to speak. Conversely, Charlie has addressed the Council and won them over, making everyone weep. Charlie and Livia are fighting, "almost at knife-point." Charlie and Livia are rutting like rabbits. He, Charlie himself, is the Angel and is trying to pull the wool over everybody's eyes. Charlie is an errand boy, a victim of the Angel's ruse; is a fanatic; is a saint and a fool.

Charlie is as good as dead.

It is only this last whisper, fuelled by the memory of his terrible cough, that has the power to silence the crowd. People will bow their heads and snatch their caps off their crowns whenever conversation turns to this;

touch their temples, tracing the Mark of Thomas, and ask the Smoke to keep Charlie safe.

As for Balthazar, he has spent much of the week in the blackest of funks. His play was a failure. Worse, it—*he*—is irrelevant. He is a stranger to the city, a spectator, uninvolved in its fate. Livia has not sent for him and has no reason to. It might be time to leave and rebuild his theatre abroad. If it weren't for a nagging truth. *The Angel is nigh.* He knows how to lure Gales into bottles.

It's a trick Balthazar wouldn't mind learning for himself.

[3]

Etta May is right about one thing, though: he is missing his work. In the past week, sober, hungover, and drunk, Balthazar has caught himself scratching words and stage designs into the dust on his windowpanes, or repeating to himself colourful lines overheard in the streets, trying to commit them to memory. *Corpse twitchings,* he tells himself. *The artist is restless even after the art has gone to shit.* Still, it is infuriating, not having his notebook by his side, and all the drinking does is give him a headache, and the runs.

And so Balthazar takes Etta May's advice and heads Downtown. He half expects to be told he has lost access, but nobody challenges him when he joins the queue for the lift, then climbs aboard the cage with a half dozen workmen heading down. They stand a little too close for comfort, Balthazar squeezed in in their midst, the men eyeing him up. They know who he is, of course. The playwright with tits. One of them is not content with stares and snorts his Smoke at Balthazar the moment the cage gathers speed; repulsion and scorn in a thick purple puff. His neighbour spits and tells the man to keep his stink to himself. Soon coal dust binds all bodily emissions and the mine's half-light makes Negroes of them all. Downtown welcomes Balthazar with the feeling he is unknown; safe. It's the first time he appreciates it for the sanctuary it is.

[4]

Ekklesia is much as he left it. Someone has picked up the costumes and props and put them in a box to one side; and the stage has been scrubbed with lye soap. The day is overcast and the light is murky. Perhaps that's why he does not notice Livia at once. It is only when he collects his notes, left undisturbed on a table near the door, the top page marked by drizzle and dew, and surveys the space in a silent good-bye, that he sees her, sitting high up in the stalls, her knees drawn up into her chest. Alone. He climbs up the steep staircase and walks over to her; the drop so sheer it gives him vertigo. She has seen him, of course, but does not acknowledge him until he is right next to her.

"May I?" he asks as he folds himself down next to her, feeling his age. "Where's Charlie?"

He expects something sharp in response, the haughty sourness he has met with before, but receives instead a little thread of Smoke, shy, young, and heartbroken. It is only now he sees that she's been crying. Awkwardly, he tries to comfort her, patting the back of her hand. Even that feels like an imposition. She tries to say something—thank him; assure him she is fine—and starts crying again; wipes at the snot stuck to her upper lip.

"How I'd longed for him to come! All these months, waiting for news. And then he does and he is sick. He didn't even want to kiss me. 'I don't know if I'm infectious,' he says." Livia blushes. "Listen to me. I sound like I am ten years old."

"Fourteen. Ten-year-olds don't care about kissing."

This makes her laugh. Smoke jumps out with the sound.

"So where is he?"

"Already gone. We couldn't get rid of him fast enough. Smuggled him out, actually, for the sake of public order. In a few days we will send some provisions after him, on the sly. In return, Charlie will try to convince those children who belong to Minetowns to return to their parents."

"The Council did this? But why?"

"Oh, for once the Council and I are in total agreement. What else can we do? He will split Minetowns, don't you see? Half the city will follow him— to rescue their children, or else to join them—and the other half will fight them over the food they will wish to take along. And just now we can't afford unrest. We have contracts to fulfil. Bricks and steel for wheat and gunpowder and American cotton. It's all disgustingly pedestrian."

Livia breaks off; makes fists of her hands; curls her lip.

"And perhaps I'm telling you all this because, deep down, I even want it to rip itself apart. Like a little girl who has spent all week making a doll's house and then kicks it over in one second because it isn't as nice as she had hoped."

Balthazar does not reply, and for a while they are content to sit and share the silence. A drizzle starts up. Within moments it is replaced by sunshine. The English spring; almost summer. Balthazar thinks back to snow in Saint John.

"I still don't understand it," he says at length. "Not this, I mean, but you. You, Thomas, and Charlie. Our Trinity. I always thought you would be together. Inseparable. What happened?"

It takes Livia a moment to rouse herself out of her silence.

"What do you think happened? We were like everyone else. We enjoyed our wedding. It's the after that turned out to be harder than we'd thought."

She looks over at him, appears to sense his frustration, his need.

"You really want to know, Balthazar. For your theatre? Or for yourself? No, don't answer, it does not matter." She sighs, looks up, speaks to the sky not him. "We stood on the riverbank, that morning, and walked into the Second Smoke. Holding hands. I remember the feeling: a mad joy rushing through my body. We did not walk, we skipped! The black plume of the Storm on the horizon; Smoke all around, in colours we had never seen. We breathed it in, became *connected*. God, it was intense: like being born again, rediscovering the world all over, the way it felt to others.

"It wasn't until a week or so later, when the Second Smoke had already grown more sporadic, that we first heard about the destruction wrought by the Storm. It missed us, thank God, danced its way through London, then headed north and east. When we heard the rumours, we looked for the path it had cut. We even followed it for a while. Thomas's idea. He felt himself responsible and needed to see the full extent of his guilt. Once we'd seen what was left of Cambridge even he'd had enough.

"After that we just kept walking. Weeks on the road: total chaos in the land, not a train running, not a soul working. And in every village and hamlet, every little town: a Grand Awakening. Priests taking off their vestments, shaken in their faith; farmers turned prophets, finding a new God. Stately homes burning wherever the servants found their betters hid small, dirty souls. Communes forming in one place, and people turning into hermits in another, looking for solitude high in the hills. Disease, too, and hunger. And words! Everybody was talking, trying to give meaning to what they'd seen! A thousand declarations—of freedom, self-rule, universal human rights. When news spread that the Queen had died, a thousand village halls voted to abolish monarchy all by themselves. Who'd known the country was so ready for a change?"

Livia breaks off, transported by her words despite herself.

"But you don't need me to tell you, Balthazar. You, too, were here."

Balthazar nods but does not elaborate. It is her story he craves. "What happened then? The three of you—where did you go?"

"Here. We helped found this, Minetowns, the city of the free. Took a cottage, played house for a while. I suppose it was just like any other marriage. Petty jealousies, ecstatic reconciliations. For a while it was . . . fun." She bites her lip, smiles. "Those dirty poets—the ones who made up songs about that part—they are not entirely wrong."

"But it did not stay . . . *fun*?"

"Thomas was riddled with guilt. With every report of the Storm springing up again—leaping the sea, putting waste to Norway and beyond—he became more convinced that we had made a mistake. *His* mistake. That's the thing about Thomas: if there is a weight to be carried, he wants to carry it alone. Charlie, meanwhile, had made a religion of the Gales. If only everyone communed and *knew* one another. He had a notion that you would never really hurt anyone you'd taken in your blood. In the end, he left. To walk the land. Chase Gales. Also, to leave us alone, Thomas and me. He had decided that we would be happier without him."

Balthazar ponders this, his head already composing a scene. Charlie packing his knapsack: all his clothes Soot-stiff, but folded neatly all the same.

"And were you? Happier?"

Livia hesitates over her answer. "Without Charlie . . . there was a lot of passion, not all of it good. We moved Downtown, trying to quiet ourselves and make a life in the shelter of the coal. For a while it almost worked. Then Mother got in touch by letter. She even used her old seal. She said she had grave news to impart. I told Thomas it was nonsense, a ploy. But Thomas insisted on going to see her. I think he just wanted to get away. Next I heard, he was bound for Hindustan. He sent me a two-line note."

"And the rumours about a child—"

Livia hushes him.

"Leave me some secrets, Balthazar. At least for today."

[5]

Their conversation seems to have run its course, yet neither of them moves. The sun remains out and directly overhead. It is warm all of a sudden, the light golden. Perhaps it is this that brings Balthazar's thoughts back to the Angel.

"Who is he?" he wants to know. "What is he up to?"

"That I don't know. All I can tell you is this: Charlie Cooper has his dream. 'Universal Communion.' The end of all strife. Perhaps the Angel, too, believes in this dream. He is waiting for Charlie in Cumbria. They are heading south: to convert it to the Smoke. And when they get there, Renfrew will kill them. It's as simple as that."

"Then you do not believe in Charlie's dream."

Livia snorts at that, replies with a question. "Have you been in many Gales, Balthazar?"

"Only during the Second Smoke."

"Did you like it?"

"Yes and no."

"Most people are afraid of losing themselves within a Gale; or of having their secrets exposed—the nasty little things they love, the pettiness with which they hate. But the biggest secret is this: that we are flimsy things, made up of air and need. Sometimes all a Gale leaves you with is just one little kernel that's unquestionably you. For Charlie that kernel is kindness. For me—pride. So how can I believe? I am too shabby for Charlie's dream." She pauses, looks over at Balthazar, half serious, half in play. "How about you, Miss Black? What would I find at the bottom of your Smoke?"

"Confusion. Vanity. Spite. A prune for a heart, and a soul as shallow as a pauper's grave."

Livia laughs at that, genuinely pleased with the answer; embraces him and kisses him on the cheek.

"I forgot to thank you for your play. That toff in his dirty underwear making speeches about democracy—it's been years since I've laughed like that!"

"Thank you." But even as he says it, he works himself out of her embrace; rises and turns to leave. "Good-bye, Livia."

"Where are you going, Balthazar?"

"I'm going after Charlie."

This stings her. "Why?"

"Curiosity. I hear the Angel works miracles." He wrinkles his nose over the silliness of the phrase. "Perhaps I want to learn to believe. Adieu."

When he reaches the stage at the bottom and looks back up into the stalls, Livia is still sitting there, alone in the bright almost-summer sun.

[1]

The maid is young, perhaps only a year or two older than Eleanor. It makes the approach simpler somehow. Eleanor waits in the corridor until the young woman steps out of the room she has been tidying and begins to lock the door. She looks up at the sound of Eleanor's steps, the key still in the lock. Then that familiar double take at the sight of the harness; a note of awe entering that plain young face. Renfrew has told Eleanor that the stories about her arrival have already adjusted; that she is now said to have worn the harness even then. There are even some who hold that it is more than just an apparatus; that it has grown into her flesh. In the chambermaid's eyes there is a simpler speculation. Here she is, face-to-face with Renfrew's ward.

She wants to know why.

Eleanor considered using a ruse to explain her request; some cover story that might fool the maid. But standing face-to-face with her—stepping closer now, so her words won't carry in the corridor—it does not seem right. You must choose whether to treat people as tools or as equals. Renfrew told her that—the old Renfrew. He said he had it from a man called Kant.

"I need to go in there," Eleanor says now. "I promise I shan't steal anything."

The maid blushes at this, confused and embarrassed. But her answer is firm. "I can't . . . You'll have to ask the mistress."

She is taller than Eleanor, her simple uniform hangs loose on her. Eleanor does not argue but reaches up with one hand, to cradle the girl's cheek; rises to tiptoe, brings her eyes level with hers.

"Please."

A curl of Smoke comes out with the word, travels from breath to breath: Eleanor's shame is in it, her worry that she will get the maid in trouble. But so is her need. The maid recoils, shocked at the strength of it, of the depths hiding in Eleanor's girlish frame. She does not hesitate but simply nods; reverses the action of the key and opens the door wide.

"Thank you," says Eleanor, no longer sure whether a ruse would not have been more honest. *I have talent,* she thinks. *I use it to frighten those who should be my peers.* "You can come back in half an hour and lock the door then."

[2]

Drab brick-and-mortar walls and the same narrow window. Miss Cooper's room is a cell like all the others, spartan and functional. Only her personal items provide a touch of colour, of femininity. There is a hairbrush with an ornate silver handle; a desk mirror and a second, larger looking glass that she has leaned against one wall; a rosewood writing case; a porcelain vase vivid with irises. The wardrobe is full of dresses in bold colours; a chest of drawers holds undergarments, white and stiff with starch. A row of little crystal bottles adorns the writing table. Eleanor bends to sniff at them and finds in them different accents of Miss Cooper's scent. Slung over the bed's footboard, recently straightened by the maid, is a pair of gloves made of such fine leather it has the weight of cloth.

Eleanor starts to search the room. It is the desk she searches first, then the travel chest whose lid proves to be unlocked. Papers interest her: correspondence, money orders, private notes. It is a shabby business, this riffling through another's affairs, but she performs it without impatience or guilt, reading every scrap of writing, making a note of every addressee and foreign stamp. A photograph—no, a daguerreotype—is buried amongst personal effects. It is a formal family portrait taken in a drawing room. Charlie and Ursula are perhaps fifteen and thirteen years of age, respectively. Their mother is plump and strikingly handsome, the father whippet-lean and heavily freckled. He died during the Second Smoke, Eleanor has heard, killed in a dispute by his own valet. The mother is alive and has a hand in the Cooper business; up until five minutes ago Eleanor had assumed she was planning a tranquil retirement at the Coopers' ancestral home in the West Country.

She replaces the photo, not without another look at a childish Charlie, whose nose seems too big for his boyish face; then resumes her study of some older telegrams that Miss Cooper has collected in the back of a pocketbook filled with dollar bills and Indian rupees. And as she stands there, wallet and money in her left hand, the papers in her right, the door swings open, and in a cloud of lace and perfume Ursula "Teddy" Cooper returns to her room.

[3]

She gives a little yelp of surprise, Miss Cooper does, and raises a mist of Smoke from ears and throat. Then she quickly regains her composure.

"Good God, but you scared me!" she exclaims, already herself again and charming-sweet. "I suppose I shall have to sack the maid. A nuisance, Miss Renfrew—do you have any idea how hard it is to convince any of the village girls to come and work in this place?"

Miss Cooper sits down on her bed—flops down, really—and unbuttons her coat.

"So are you here on orders of the Lord Protector or on your own account? Your own, I wager. Renfrew would not risk displeasing me, not at this juncture."

Eleanor has said nothing thus far; has hardly moved. Now she replaces the pocketbook in the travel case, then turns to Miss Cooper.

"If you tell my uncle, he will punish me by killing an innocent."

"Will he now? And will it have been Renfrew who has killed that innocent, or you—or I, as you imply? Or perhaps we will all be accomplices in murder. But come, why talk about death and killing, there's no need for any of that. Sit down, I beg you. There! Oh, but how stiffly you perch in that monstrous thing he's making you wear! And how pathetically your dress pokes out from under it—you're like Cinderella stuck inside a parrot cage."

For the moment, Miss Cooper appears to have quite forgotten that Eleanor is a spy and an intruder. Good nature comes easily to her, a family trait. In her, it sits side by side with something else, calculating and dispassionate, appraising the world for what it's worth.

"So tell me, Eleanor, what did you learn about me this morning? What were you hoping to find?"

Eleanor does not answer at once. In truth, there isn't much she has learned. Just this:

"You are leaving. You have sent for a ship. First it will collect your mother.

Then it will come for you. A fast ship. You're in a hurry to get away." Eleanor pauses, looks over at Miss Cooper's smiling face. "What is it you are selling Uncle? That's what I came here to find out. It's almost here, isn't it? It's why you are rushing off."

"So that's what you've pieced together! Not bad." Miss Cooper seems genuinely impressed. She sits forward and studies Eleanor, as though she were a mathematical problem, demanding subtle calculation. "Tell me, Eleanor, what do you think of your uncle these days? I need an honest answer, mind."

Eleanor's mind races back to a recent conversation. "Your uncle's a paper person," Lady Naylor had mocked. "All his ideas come from books. The one time he looked into a mirror, he found that he was ugly. And now—the mirror has to be destroyed!"

"He is sick," Eleanor says now.

"Yes, of course. He cannot digest. He's wasting away."

"No, it's not just his body. He . . . used to be a good man, in his way. Principled. Now he has convinced himself that principles can wait. Must wait. And at the same time, he knows he has *fallen*. So he must punish himself, just as much as he must win."

Miss Cooper nods. Eleanor's judgement tallies with her own.

"The thing I am selling him—how much do you know?"

"I know that it is evil."

"Evil! How laden a term. Let's say it is dangerous. Like a dragon—a sleeping dragon, all curled up into a little scaly knot. We found it in its mountain lair, on the other side of the world. Actually, it was Renfrew who first thought of it. You see, our dragon had a little brother—or perhaps something like a child, or even just a toe clipping. Eleven years ago, an expedition had stumbled on it and brought it to England. To Oxford initially, for scientific study—defying the embargo, the mavericks! But after only a few weeks, this little dragon was moved to London—not because it was judged dangerous, mind, but because it was judged to have commercial *value*. You see, the dragon's skin looked, in some respects, just like petrified Soot. Very, very pure Soot—the purest anyone had ever seen. A thousand times purer than the kind used in the manufacture of cigarettes. If it could be *quickened*—well, the market for cigarettes was booming just then. An Oxford college wasn't a place for a treasure like that. But the experiments proved futile; the baby dragon slept and slept. Until, that is, my brother and his two friends set off Lady Naylor's little bomb."

"It woke the dragon," replies Eleanor to Miss Cooper's expectant look. "And started the Black Storm."

"Bravo! That's just what your uncle concluded. The first thing he did was send some men to London to look for that toe clipping—the place where the first Storm originated. But they could not find it and he concluded it had been consumed. So he had his servant pick through what remains of the Bodleian in Oxford in search of some record of its origin. The trail led to the Raj. Renfrew has no influence there—he needed a partner. So we began to correspond. It's funny, isn't it? They used to be arch-enemies, my father and Renfrew, a Tory aristocrat and a liberal upstart. But the present age pays little heed to such niceties. We got into business easily enough, the Lord Protector and that little corner of the Company where we Coopers were making our mark. There! Does that answer your question?"

"It tells me why you are running. You sold Uncle a weapon. Now you are scared of it yourself."

"Scared"—Miss Cooper pulls a face at the word. "Well, perhaps I am at that. You see, all this time I thought Renfrew wanted the dragon simply as a threat: once woken, nobody will be able to control it, so I never dreamt he would want to wake it up. But as a threat, the ultimate weapon, buried deep in some coalmine perhaps, kept in reserve—it might prove a powerful tool. It could be used to bring the country in line; scare the North into submission.

"But something has changed. Smith, I suppose, and this talk of a 'cure'— I have heard the rumours, of course. Your arrival, too, the way you weathered the Storm. And then Renfrew is *mad:* you have said as much yourself. Hence Britain will burn, my dear. Either your uncle figures out how to start Gales and then lights the fire just where he wants it, or else a Gale will set the weapon off, sooner or later, quite by chance. I never dreamt how unstable it might be.

"And so I'm leaving. There's a whole world out there and half of it has never even heard of the Second Smoke. China is just getting an appetite for sweets and cigarettes. The India rubber trade out of South America is booming, and there are diamond mines in Africa that are just waiting to be dug up. Forget the Coopers of Somerset! What's a little plot of dirt if you can own the world?" Miss Cooper smiles at her own grandiloquence. "Of course, all this is just a story. There is no dragon, just a silly old rock."

She rises from the bed, walks slowly to the door, runs her fingers over the handle.

"All the same, there is a price for the story, Eleanor. I want reports. Everything your uncle says and does. Come by after breakfast each day. And in here, please take that dreaded thing off your back. We can talk dresses and hairstyles. And if you are good, I will even snatch you away with me, somewhere where Smoke is still Smoke, and servants are servants, and the sun always shines. Now wouldn't you just love that?"

[4]

Once she has been dismissed by Miss Cooper, Eleanor goes about her daily chores. She visits her uncle, tidies his room, bathes and dresses the hole in his stomach that has never quite healed. After that he takes time to further her education: a lecture on ancient history, some Greek and Latin declensions, then a conversation about a book of physics he has had her read. Next, Renfrew has her copy out some letters in her formal, large-lettered hand (his own is shaky these days, a nasty, slanted scrawl). "I am his nurse, his secretary, his student," Eleanor has explained to Lady Naylor. "I'm the new Livingstone."

"You are his Christ," Lady Naylor had answered. "How is it you don't know he wants to nail you to his cross?"

When she has completed the copying, they typically go for their afternoon walk, or attend a parliamentary session together, a hush falling over the room upon their entrance. The *Lord Protector and his ward:* they are a unit now, in the eyes of the world. Recently a young man has been invited up to Renfrew's study to make sketches for their portrait. Elsewhere in the Keep, Eleanor has caught glimpses of fops old and young wearing stylised harnesses over their dinner jackets like outsized waistcoats. Subjugation is the fashion; carries the promise of a country disciplined and standing tall.

Today, however, Renfrew and Eleanor eschew Parliament and keep their walk short. The portrait artist does not make an appearance. Her uncle is ornery. His stomach is troubling him. He is impatient for news. "Where is Smith?" he barks at the servant who is in charge of the pigeons that bring his twice-daily mail and who would be put to death if he dared read the crumpled missives.

"I am running out of time!" Renfrew complains to Eleanor later, pinch-faced, running a fever.

"Hush, Uncle," she says, and changes his dressing. "The wound is suppurating again. You really must rest."

Later that evening, once he has dismissed her and locked himself in, she leaves the Keep by the western gate and walks down to the little pier, to stare at the prison ships anchored in the bay. When a guard comes out of the little guard hut, she accepts his offer of a cup of tea and sits with him and his comrades, who stare at her in awe while she makes small talk in her awkward, abrupt way.

I am making friends of them, she thinks, *and am treating them as equals, so I can make tools of them when the time comes.*

[1]

There, *beta*, eat. No, don't speak, otherwise I must be fetching the hood. Are you liking it, is it toothsome? I asked the cook not to make it too spicy. It is for the prisoner, I tell him, his stomach cannot digest the spicy food. The cook, he tells me that he has food left over that he prepared for the other sahibs, it is very bland, he says, your Englishman will like it. But I say no, moong daal is better for him, he has suffered much and has a tender stomach. He is not ready for English meat. And here, drink some water. Go on, finish the bowl. It is important to drink. Are you needing the potty? No? We will leave the hood off for now, what do you say? Only don't speak, *beta*, the orders are very strict."

The old servant looking after Thomas likes to play the fool. He does so from habit, perhaps, as a mode of dealing with the sahibs; and from self-protection (one cannot hold responsible a fool). Two times a day, he comes to bring food and empty the chamber pot. It was he who, the evening after Singh's visit, found the torn piece of sacking that had served as a hood. Despite his constant reminders that Thomas must not speak—as though his words were spells that might entrance the servant into doing something bad—the old man has not replaced the hood; it is possible he has not reported the torn sacking to those who sail the ship. And sail it they do: the ship left harbour that very night. The shiver of the engine; the roll of the open ocean, so different from the subtle swell of port—they have started to grow into Thomas's body, are assimilating it into their rhythms, until one day the stillness of land will have become an alien thing, a disquiet to the blood. Land: England. *Home*. He'll be returning with a present. The ice machine gurgles half a yard beyond the reach of his chain.

Something about Thomas has changed these past few days since they have left Bombay. His food, though it retains the medicinal note of sweet, is no longer laced with opiates. His body is missing it: a fever has spread, along with nausea; there's an ache in his bones. But his head is working again for the first time since that nightmare journey down the mountain. They kept him masked and blindfolded so thoroughly that it was only when they put him in the first of his Bombay prisons that he learned for sure he was no longer blind. Now Thomas is chained, is filthy, is mollycoddled by a servant.

But at last he is awake.

[2]

He has nighttime visitors. The first time he wakes to them, he immediately asks himself if there have been other visitors before. The old man must have led them here: he is keeping them at a distance and whispering at them in one of India's many tongues. The men with him are merchant sailors not soldiers: their clothes say as much. They ask a few questions of the servant. Mostly they stare.

Thomas rises where he lies. This makes the old man nervous; he appeals to him with a look and puts his finger to his lips. Thomas obeys—he owes him this, at least, and at any rate he is not sure he can tell the men anything they don't already know. Chances are they have little English. They stare at the curio that is this living, breathing incarnation from some peasant story. Thomas lifts his chin into the lamplight so they can see more clearly the outline of his mark.

More men come the following night, and some repeat visitors the third. Thomas waits for them; there are other hours when he can sleep. One of the men, to the old servant's agitation, squats down within reach of Thomas's chain. He stares at him and winks—something, Thomas thinks, he must have seen Englishmen do because it looks too studied to be part of his normal repertoire of facial gestures. Is it mere idleness, the showing off of a new trick? Or does it have a purpose? Thomas winks back. This satisfies the man. He rises quickly while the old servant jabbers at his back. The next night there are no visitors, nor the night after. It does not matter. Bombay has risen. Singh must have had help when he came aboard the ship.

Thomas puts his hopes in that wink.

[3]

Three days later (Thomas counts them by his meals), there is a commotion on the ship. Few noises reach here, down in the hold, but even so he can make out faint shouts and sudden running across the ceiling above him. Minutes later, he hears the whip-crack of a single shot. More running, more shouts, then a silence followed by three further shots, spaced out at tidy intervals that bring to mind an execution.

Then nothing.

Into the quiet that follows the commotion, the icebox emits a sudden grunt. A hiss of gas follows, the stench of ammonium, the groan of steel. Underneath it is another sound that Thomas was aware of while doused with laudanum but has since dismissed as raving. The tap of a fingertip on a taut drumskin. Now he hears it again and tells himself it is nothing but his pulse.

[4]

The old man will no longer talk to him. When Thomas bombards him with questions, he picks up the piece of cloth he has threatened to use on him as a hood or gag. If he comes close, thinks Thomas, it would be an easy thing to overpower him. What then, however? The man holds no value to the captain; he has no keys, and anyway, Thomas's chains are soldered on, not locked.

Thomas falls silent and accepts the bowl of daal.

That evening, he notices a slick black condensation seeping from the corner of the icebox. Near the bottom, a metal seam has split, and its lips bulge outwards, curling away from that which they contain.

[5]

Thomas dreams. Charlie is there, Livia. Julius as he was after Grendel shot him, a brittle carapace of Soot. In his dream they put him in an ice machine, then hear him knocking at its inside walls. Charlie stoppers his ears. Livia pulls him down to sit with her on top of the box, the knocking rising up into their thighs like an evil, carnal pulse. She kisses him, greedily, her mouth in his mouth. When she leans back her tongue is long and black but for a yellow mark right at its tip.

He leaps up from his blanket and falls over his chain. The sound echoes in the empty hold. On his gums there is the bitter taste of Smoke the sweets in his blood were unable to suppress.

He lies in darkness and strokes the gaps between his toes.

When the servant finally comes and brings light, Thomas sees that a growth of lichen covers the icebox in a dense black fuzz. The metal is distended in places, bulging. Where box meets floor, a single tendril of the growth probes outwards, like the first crack in a sheet of ice. It points sideways, away from Thomas. All the same, he suddenly feels looked for, hunted. He scoots away from it, as far as the chain will allow.

"You must tell the captain," Thomas appeals to the servant. "The machine is broken. The rock is growing. Tell him there were mushrooms on that mountain! Tell him to come and see for himself."

The old man shushes him, first gently, then threatening him with hood and gag. But Thomas can see that he is shaken: not by the words so much as the sight of that black fungus. Before he leaves through the hatch at the far end of the hold, he turns to Thomas once more with his light shaking in his fist and says very quietly, "There was a mutiny some days ago. They shot three men. But I was loyal to my duty. It was I who warned the first mate."

Thomas looks back at him, aware of the question in the other man's gaze. "Did you know they would shoot them?"

The old man does not answer. What else does one do with mutineers?

It is not for Thomas to grant pardon. "You made your choice," he says. "Now I ask you to make another one."

[6]

The next day a different man comes to look after him. He seems disturbed to find Thomas unmasked, and does not react to any questions. The food is placed down and shoved near Thomas with a long-poled gaff hook, the chamber pot retrieved in the same manner. That day, the ship hits a storm and is tossed between waves. Seawater must pour over the deck high above Thomas's head, because after a few hours some little quantity has found its way into the hold through some flaw in the main hatch. With every new lurch, Thomas slides across the slick metal floor, working hard not to be swept towards the ice machine. In the end, he holds on to the chain's anchor point, wrapping the chain around his arms. He stays there until the storm relents and the servant brings again his light. The rock's fungal tendrils are everywhere now; one jagged shoot reaches close to Thomas's thigh. He recoils from it, smells the stench of sea rot filling the whole hold.

"Leave the light," he yells at the sailor.

To his surprise, the man does: far out of reach, near the doorway, he screws it into a designated place where it flickers away the hours.

The way the light throws Thomas's shadow, it merges with the hulk of ice machine and rock.

[7]

That night, he hears again that strange drumming in his blood. The fungus has reached the anchor point of the chain and is now working its way up towards him, link by link. On the icebox itself, a colony of tiny barnacles has taken residence, slick and black and adorned by a fine yellow stripe. A curl of fear escapes Thomas—he's been fasting, unable to keep down his sweet-laced food—and drifts towards the rock. Deep in his pulse, the rock appears to hum its answer.

"You are dreaming," Thomas mutters at the rock, in full consciousness that the thought is but a road to madness. For the first time in days he approaches the ice machine and finds that, bulging as it is, its sidewalls buckled in a dozen places, its valves and pipes sticking out like bristles at odd angles, he can now touch it. His hand reaches out but curls itself into a fist before it can make contact.

That night he dreams again of Livia and Charlie: Soot-faced, yellow anger in their eyes. They fight, or maybe they fuck, and when he wakes he finds that he is sobbing and a sea-slick black fungus has grown into the shallow wound cut by the manacle that connects his ankle to the now weed-heavy chain.

"Leave me alone," he shouts, but what good is it, speaking to a rock?

[1]

Londing looks different from up on high. The river is a curl of molten lead, its banks embroidered with Soot. In places—a river bend, a stagnant eddy—this Soot sparkles in rings of mineral colour like a petrified oil slick, violet, sulphur yellow, or rust red. Mostly it is mud-dark. The buildings, too, are marked by Soot to a height of twenty or twenty-five feet: a tide mark that runs across streets and courtyards, takes in churches, public buildings, hovels alike. The streets themselves stand empty. Where cobbled, grass and weeds have rutted them; where unpaved, they have been swallowed up by yellow shrub. Desert plants, that's what they seem like, these hardy, sickly-looking weeds that contrive to suck nutrition from the sooty soil. Here and there a patch of wildflowers has colonised a street, a yard, a patch of roof, and dyed it vivid like a stain. The only trees are the sycamores of ancient city squares, their roots anchored deep in better soil. These have spread their branches and stand triumphant in full leaf; have flung their young into the street, where saplings vie with cobbles and dream of turning city into wood. Foxes, wild dogs, feral cats live amongst the buildings and the sycamores' roots. They feed on the mice that breed in Soot-choked cellars. In the high grass crickets play their scratchy violins. To the east, above Limehouse and the docklands, the sky is thick with swooping birds; a haze on the horizon where one dares suspect the sea.

Of people, there are only limited signs. To the north, a few courtyards where cultivation has been attempted and tomato stalks stand staked and stunted in haphazard rows. To the west, a little tribe of London natives bastes a spitted badger in their rough-dug fire pit. South, on a bend of the river, a group of fishermen works the thigh-deep mud, digs up crayfish, cockles, barbed-faced bottom feeders whose very flesh carries the tang of Soot. But mostly the city stands empty. London's factories are closed, its people fled, whole neighbourhoods burned down to charred facades. Those who come soon learn that it is tough work squeezing food from out the broken city. What wealth there was, what food, has long been looted and consumed.

Nil knows all this as well as anyone: has spent his childhood fishing for eels amongst the river reeds, and stuffing them into a sack where they would knot and seethe until back home Grendel's knife would sheer off their heads (and even then their en-slimed tails would whip and curl within the sink). Nil has carried buckets from a well—a half mile there, a half mile back—to water spuds that came out dry and wrinkled, riddled by blight; has kept chickens that laid dun-shelled, blood-yolked eggs; and one hungry winter freed the dog he was tasked to kill and butcher, and served a meal of boiled nettles in its stead. It was then, too, that he first learned to pick locks, for the London of his childhood still held many a locked door: in factory offices and counting houses; on cabinets and post-office strong-boxes; in hidden-away apartments kept by rich folk who used to come to London for sin and play.

"You are thinking about the past, aren't you? Over there, where you keep looking. Is that your old neighbourhood?"

Smith's voice: intruding gently on the view. They are standing side by side on this rooftop made of pigeon-fouled tiles; the afternoon sun hot on their backs, sending their shadow across the precipice of the building. The Company man is holding binoculars, while Nil is in charge of the photographs and the map.

"Is he still there? Your foster father, I mean. If you like we can go and look."

Nil does not reply but studies the pictures.

"We are still too far west," he decides at length, "and too far from the river. There"—here he points to another building about a quarter mile from them that he knows to have once been a hotel—"we should climb up there and try again."

"Fine," says Smith.

It is only after they have descended and retrieved the car that it occurs to Nil that Smith is sulking, disgruntled at not having been taken into confidence concerning Nil's feelings for his past.

[2]

They have to climb to the tops of three more buildings until they see it. The hotel helps: the view from its rooftop aligns with one of the photographs so perfectly that Nil at once becomes convinced that it was taken from up there. But a single vantage point proves insufficient to get a fix on where the vortex of the Storm stood anchored, once upon a time. So they carry on looking, picking buildings for their height and climbing derelict staircases, hoping to catch sight of something, a sign, a clue.

What they find is a chalk mark. Black chalk, mind, marking the ground. It's not as obvious as it sounds. Everywhere you look the ground is dark with Soot and mud. But this mark is different: tar black, at times as much as fifty steps across, well defined at its borders. It does not respect the city's layout, will run down a thoroughfare for five, six hundred yards, then twist across the face of a building; mark its roofline and its yard; will split, double back on itself in an angry scrawl, write swirls and loops into the city. One sees it best where it crosses land that has long turned into wilderness, where grass and shrub have overgrown the stone. Here the mark is as though drawn with ink and cuts a swath through all the greenery. The effect is misleading: the mark came first, the plant life later. But nothing will grow upon the fatal stripe.

Nil sees it first: stretches out a finger and points, and street for street, bend for bend, traces its trajectory for as far as they can see, unspooling it in the air. They run to it, Smith huffing and puffing down the stairs despite all his gymnastics, and race into the street. Here, the Soot smudge is more subtle, its borders less clean. Nil stoops, digs his fingernail into the grit. It is mixed with dust and has been washed by a thousand rains. And yet there is a definite feel to it, fine-grained and somewhat oily. Rising, stepping back, he sees it stretch underfoot, binding the light of the sun. The mark of the Storm: a high road of hate.

All they need to do is follow it home.

[3]

It takes them all evening. The car is more encumbrance than help at this point. Every time the Storm's dark mark defies the city's layout of streets and alleys, courtyards and squares, and charges up a wall instead, leaping across rooftops, they have to circumnavigate along the roads available to them; then speed up and down the next street over, trying to relocate the track. Their search pushes them east and pens them ever closer to the river. Periodically, Smith will stop and consult his map of London, onto which he has drawn, in fire-red pencil, the borders of his claim.

"We remain on home soil," he decides afresh, ruddy-faced and beaming. "'Smithtown.' There are worse names for a district." Impulsively, he throws an arm around Nil's shoulders. "We are like Federmann or von Speyer. Like Humboldt—or Pizarro! Explorers! Conquerors! Looking for our pot of gold!" His eyes are moist behind the driving goggles; the hand that ruffles Nil's hair is gloved.

Nil is unsure how to respond to such effusion. It is not simply that he cannot calculate the best response. There is a knotting in his stomach that he cannot parse. The beetle is to blame: he had thought he would experience a sense of liberation after injecting himself with its spore. Indeed there has been some of that, the certainty that he can no longer be found out. But there is another, more complex side effect. His own emotions have become invisible to him.

Nil does not know what it is he feels.

In the face of Smith's expectant gaze, he opts for action.

"Quick now," he says. "It'll be dark before long."

As they drive on, Nil finds his heart is racing. Perhaps, then, he too is caught up in the excitement of the hunt.

[4]

The ribbon of black leads to the docks. They may be the very docks where Nil was smuggled into the country, drugged, encoffined in a rubber mask. He has no way of telling, no memory of this place. It is like a city unto itself, dead and enormous, and covered in black. There are stagnant rectangular pools, a hundred yards across, still spotted with abandoned ships, their mooring ropes arm-thick and groaning under the loads; twisted propellers, engine parts, nets, winches, chimneys, scattered like toys upon the wharf; shipyards, warehouses, customs buildings all facing the Thames. Everything—the pools, the ships, the wharf and buildings—is covered by a viscous blanket of tar-like Soot as though encased in inch-thick lacquer. The street itself is made smooth by it, and silent; their wheels leave tracks that do not break the surface and fade the moment they have passed. The air smells dead.

Before realising what he is doing, Nil starts scanning the ground for bones. The Storm's first victims. There must have been workers here, and shipping crews; warehouse staff and merchants checking on their stock. But ten years is a long time, for maggots, rats, and foxes; for city dogs and rot to do their work.

Or perhaps they are there, beneath the black. When they set down their feet, the ground is spongy, like tree sap or India rubber, like the meat of a mushroom, down at its stem. Nil turns to Smith and sees he has drawn his pistol and is stuffing whole boxes of cartridges into his coat pocket.

"This is it, boy! The epicentrum. We will have to search for it on foot."

They drive into a coach house whose gate is unlocked. Nothing stirs inside, not even rats. A row of coaches stands encased in tar like everything else. They leave the motorcar next to them; place a dust sheet on top, taking along only the most necessary items. The beetle scuttles in its cage when Nil lifts it off the seat. They will have to risk leaving the grubs. But he won't abandon the beetle, not even for a minute. In the stables next door, the stall gates have been broken open with great violence, and a leather harness swings empty from a blackened chain.

They set to exploring, splitting up at first to cover more ground but quickly reuniting, spooked by emptiness and expanse. The place is desolate, profoundly so: a barren heath of total black. The light is *wrong*, the failing sun swallowed by the ground: objects have contour but no shadow. It is as though they have left the world and are walking on the dark side of the moon. The water in the pools stands so thick that it seems solid; firm enough to walk on. There is a total absence of wind.

They drift away from the waterfront and nearer the shipyards and warehouses; are dwarfed by their scale. As they walk farther yet, past the beached carcass of a trawler, encased in perfect black, into the open yard of a large warehouse, the air grows full of swooping swallows, darting bat-like about their heads. Only they aren't swallows but a bird Nil has never before seen: more bulbous in the body, like a swollen, bent-winged tit, tar black but for a yellow mark along the wing. He walks through their flight as though through a cloud, puzzled at the sudden eruption of life in this waste. The beetle buzzes in its case within his fist.

Then: a voice from the rubble. Nil nearly jumps out of his skin. Its source is a man, so dirty he blends into the mound of blackened ship parts piled against the warehouse wall. He is singing, talking to himself: a butterfly net in one fist, dead birds strung upon a piece of yarn slung across his neck. It does not take much insight to know that he is mad.

Smith raises his pistol, then drops it again; looks back across the ground they have covered, to the coach house hiding his car and treasure, evidently deciding it is too far away for the man to have seen it. The stranger, for his part, takes their appearance in his stride. He continues singing and muttering, swings his net, Smoke rising out of him like the morning mist. After six or seven attempts he snatches a bird, midflight: reaches for it, then scoops it up in a well-practised manner, so as to arrest its wingbeat and the motion of its legs within a single fist. Only then does he deign to acknowledge his visitors' presence.

"Who are you?" he says. "Good evening!" It's an educated voice and somehow foreign; clipped and suspicious and a little off-key.

Smith looks at him, points to the ground, the warehouse, the docks, and the river; uses the hand that holds his gun. "I'm the owner. All this is mine."

"What, you're God then?"

The birdman seems sceptical yet willing to admit the possibility. He draws closer, unintimidated by the gun, holds out the bird in front of him.

"I've been studying the birds," he confides. "They're *infected,* you see. They've lost their sense of season."

"You are trespassing. I have a charter. A contract. Ratified by Parliament."

Nil studies the man's face, stung by its familiarity and his own sense of disquiet.

"Come," he says to Smith, who stands flustered and passive, uncharacteristically so. "Let's carry on. This man has lost his mind."

The stranger hears it, waggles his chin. He is wearing rags, extremely filthy, and is rail-thin. A top hat, brimless and almost comically tattered, is drawn low onto his brow.

"I have started eating them of late," he explains with great earnestness, as though the point must be established before any further conversation can take place. "I eat their little livers.

"I, too, am changing," he whispers with a wink and note of triumph. "Here, in my armpit, there is a growth of black and yellow, pert like a boil."

"Let's go," urges Nil, his senses crawling with the stranger's words, and this time succeeds in pulling Smith away.

They walk towards the warehouse entrance. Its gate is wide open, but try as they might Nil's eyes cannot penetrate the darkness inside. He feels rather than sees the cavernous space opening up in front of them, the air behind agitated by a thousand wingbeats. Then the birdman is next to them again. He has approached far too quietly, stands far too close.

"Then you are looking for it! Here, come. I will show you."

The man's hands twist absently, breaking the neck of the bird he is holding. He stuffs it in a pocket, disappears into the dark.

Again it is Smith who hesitates.

"Come," says Nil once more, and takes Smith by his unencumbered hand, the left. *I am No-One,* it comes to him somehow incoherently as though someone else is thinking the words. *My feelings are strangers to me.*

I will know them only in my actions.

"Come," he says a third time, and tugs at Smith's hand, as a nurse might guide the sick, or a son his old, befuddled father.

Together they enter the warehouse in search of the eye of a ten-year-old Storm.

[1]

They catch up with Charlie in less than two days. Perhaps it is his sickness that is slowing him down, or else it is Mary, whose little legs will only walk so fast; perhaps Charlie simply likes to take things slow. There he is on the hilltop, red hair catching the sun; the girl skipping next to him, chewing on a roll. Balthazar stops when they come into sight, a reverent shyness coming over him at which Etta May cannot help but smile.

"Starstruck old fool!" she chides him, then quickly squeezes his hand.

He squeezes back before remembering to scowl.

"What, another breather? Is your arse too big to drag up one more hill?" he vents, though it was he who stopped. "Or do you need to powder your nose again? Let's get to it then. Look, he has seen us, he's waving. God, see how skinny he is, how tall!"

[2]

Balthazar had wanted Etta May to come along. Of course he had. Not that he asked her; in fact he made a show of trying to dissuade her no sooner had he told her of his plans. But the old playwright is cracked and brittle these days, in need of support. As for Etta May, she had accepted the unspoken commission with good humour if no enthusiasm. Now—sitting around a campfire, singing songs with Charlie, the girl Mary curled into her lap—she is glad she came. It is Balthazar who sits apart, too tin-eared to join in, bursting with questions he has had no opportunity yet to ask. The night is cool but clear, the moon bright over gorse-covered moors and dry stone walls; sheep in the hills, their smell on the air.

"Say 'unicorn,'" whispers a sleepy Mary, fascinated by Etta's southern drawl.

"Yew-nicorn."

"Say 'doghouse.'"

"Dawg-howse."

"Say 'Maypole.' Say 'potty,' say 'uncle.' Say 'Butterwick,' 'pea soup and sausages.' Say 'I do love my cheese.'"

Etta May obliges and watches Mary smoke happiness into the sheep-scented night.

[3]

Balthazar gets a chance to ask his questions over the next few days. He and Charlie are walking ahead by some ten paces while Etta May and Mary follow behind. The girl has taken to Etta May and reaches for her with constant threads of Smoke. It teases the child out of Etta May, dares her to clamber onto boulders or pick flowers from the wayside; weave chains and crowns out of buttercups, then drop them with no sense of loss at the sight of some new wonder up ahead.

The little girl seems less sure about Balthazar and keeps her distance to him. At first Etta May assumes this shyness is the product of Mary not having seen black skin before, or perhaps her confusion about whether Balthazar is "a girl or a boy." But when she says as much, the girl shakes her head.

"What then? Why don't you like him?"

"He tastes sour," answers the girl rather seriously. "Like gooseberries and pickled fish."

"Gooseberries? Pickled fish? You mean his Smoke?" Etta May laughs at the thought. "And me? How do I taste?"

"You taste like Charlie."

"What does Charlie taste like?"

"Sugarplums." Then, cheeks dimpled with mischief: "Say 'sugarplum,' Auntie, say 'plum-plum-plum-plum.'"

[4]

When not talking to Mary, Etta May listens in on the conversation ahead. It is a one-sided affair, with Balthazar working his way through a long ream of questions about the past and Charlie answering them patiently and expansively, often with a storyteller's gift for detail. Nevertheless, Etta

May can sense the playwright's frustration mounting as the day wears on. It takes Etta May a while to figure out the reason. Balthazar is looking for *news*; some crucial detail that will overturn all his thinking on the coming of the Second Smoke and provide a new direction for his play. But Charlie's answers are familiar, not just in their outline but in their tenor and phrasing; in the perspective they inhabit. Late in the day, when they stop to make camp, she puts this impression into words.

"It was you," she says to Charlie. "You spread the story of the Second Smoke. You are the reason why we know so much."

He smiles at her, a little roguish, delighted by her surmise. "Yes, I did! I thought it was only fair. We opened Pandora's box, after all. People had a right to know what we did and why. So I started telling everyone I met all I could remember and asked people to pass it on. I did not compose the songs, though; someone else came up with that. And then they simply spread." He hums one of the best-known ditties. "Of course, people soon added variations. It's part of the joy of telling a tale, I suppose. Making it your own."

Etta May watches Balthazar's face shrivel up with this answer. Perhaps, she thinks, the playwright is shocked by Charlie's lack of care about felicity. If someone took such liberties with one of Balthazar's plays, there would be hell to pay.

"How about Shovel?" he asks. "The historian of Minetowns. Who is he?"

"That I don't know. Someone told me that he was a bricklayer, someone else a lathe operator, in the steelworks. And a third person told me that this same bricklayer or lathe operator, or what will you, is actually the Prince of Wales." Charlie laughs. "It's a thought, isn't it? The rightful heir to the throne, writing the chronicle of the first true democracy."

"It can't be. The writing is terrible. And the drawings are too good."

Charlie smiles at that. "You may be putting too much faith in the education of the old aristocracy, Balthazar. Believe you me, it wasn't all that. But look, there's a Gale on the horizon. Over there! I doubt we will catch it, it's too far away."

[5]

As they head farther west and north, the country gets hillier and hillier. Soon mountains rise from the horizon. Etta May has only a sketchy sense of the isle's geography and can do little with Mary's assertion that they are heading to the "Lakes." Behind them on the crest of the unpaved road she makes out a group of other travellers. They, too, may be heading to the Angel. When she asks Charlie who he is, Charlie simply tells her, "You will see."

Late that afternoon, they reach a crossroads marked by a wooden pole. Two horses have been tied to it, one saddled, the other serving as a pack-horse and laden with bags and a cage containing several pigeons. A man sits leaning against the pole, eating a hunk of cheese. He is slight and elderly, with stringy grey hair and a clean-shaven, somewhat haggard face. But when he rises to greet them his movement is smooth. His eyes, Etta May notices, rest on Charlie's hair.

[1]

At an unmarked crossroads deep in the Yorkshire Dales, unsure as to which road to pick, his pigeons restless in their cage upon the packing horse, Godfrey Livingstone sits, munching on a hunk of cheese, and studies the horizon. Gorse and dry stone walls; the bucolic whiff of sheep shit; the sky a latticework of cloud. Pretty, he supposes; desolate. He digs a coin out of his pocket, fixes on the fork ahead, flips it. A high arc from the tip of his thumb back into his palm; a little slap as coin hits skin. Tails means left. A dirt path still muddy with last night's rain. He shrugs, flips the coin once more, and at the high point of its flight, when the coin seems to pause for half a heartbeat in midair, suspended between rise and fall, he spies beneath its copper circle a group of travellers crossing the hilltop to the east. One look and he is decided; the toss ignored, the coin banished back into its pocket. A stroke of luck, the nudge of fate—who is he to scorn the stars? Livingstone stills himself and waits; hate coursing through him like a drug.

There are four of them, an incongruous group, walking with the certainty of those who know the way. An old Negro, exceedingly dark of skin, a flat cap pulled low onto his brow; a girl of ten, flush-cheeked under a crown of buttercups she has weaved together by the stem; a corpulent woman of forty-five, florid of face and dull of expression; and a young man with bright red hair and copper skin who stops high on the hillcrest to hand his thin frame over to a lung-deep cough. Livingstone watches them approach and takes their measure, starts packing away the hunk of cheese upon which he has lunched, only to unwrap it again and add to it a loaf of bread he bought three days ago from a farmhouse that he passed, and a fist-sized lump of sugar. He lays them out upon a handkerchief as offerings, or bait. As they come into hailing distance, the girl darts ahead: inspects the bread—the sugar—from five steps' distance, then runs close to Livingstone and reaches out to him with a mauve tendril of her Smoke. The touch goes unanswered. The girl is stumped by this, arrested in her step.

"Go on," he says to her, loud enough so that her companions will hear. "Eat your fill."

The girl continues eyeing him with some suspicion, more febrile Smoke wafting out of her and going unheeded by his skin. She runs back to the redhead, beckons him down onto one knee, then whispers something in his ear.

"She is scared," says Livingstone, "because I do not smoke. You see, I can't. It frightens people."

This stops both black man and fat woman in their tracks. It is the red-head alone who dares approach.

"Is it congenital?" he asks, as though inquiring of a lame man the reason for his limp.

"Yes," replies Livingstone. "Like Goodman Grendel in the stories. I am another one like he."

Then he pauses, as though a new thought has just occurred to him, though he is not actor enough to place wonder in his voice. "You are Char-lie Cooper, are you not?"

"So I am."

Livingstone taps his temple in greeting and supplication, the way he has seen farmers do at the mere mention of Cooper's name.

"I am looking for the Angel of the North," he explains just as flatly as he has spoken before, "but I fear I have lost my way. Do you know where he is?"

"You are in luck," says Cooper. And he adds, without trying to hide his scrutiny of Livingstone's pack horse, his pigeons and guns: "We are head-ing there ourselves. You can join us if you like."

[2]

And so Livingstone comes to travel with the enemy, leading his horse by its bridle and offering to load it with his companions' bags, an offer that they steadfastly refuse. It takes little art to figure them out. The Negro and the fat American belong together. He fancies himself some sort of historian or artist and spends his time peppering Charlie with questions; she is the maternal type, come along against the old man's express wish, and much to his relief. Livingstone beholds her fatty arms and neck and listens to her drawn-out vowels and has to remind himself that they do not necessarily mean that she is stupid. The girl—Mary—is lionising the woman and infecting her with childish pranks. On occasion, the girl's eyes will stop on him, Livingstone, cripple of the Smoke: incomprehension in her gaze, disgust and fear. The fat woman mirrors this childish gaze with something cooler. No, not so very stupid. At night he hears her whisper a warning into Charlie's ear.

Cooper then. He's more impressive a figure than the caricature Livingstone has sneered at this past decade. Older, for one, a man not a boy; more considered in his manner; less the silly puppy of the stories than a hermit lately emerged from his cave. Delighting in the sunlight. Good-natured, it is true, skilled at putting people at their ease. And disgustingly patient: short of breath as he is, his handkerchief heavy with expectorate, he will answer the Negro's questions for hours at a time, unfazed by his compulsive need for detail. Livingstone listens to the answers as he walks. They sketch the same old tale that half the world's been telling for ten years. At day's end, sitting around the campfire after a simple meal, Livingstone asks a question of his own.

"Would you do it again?" he asks. "Would you summon the Second Smoke?"

Charlie Cooper turns to study him. "I see you wish I hadn't."

Livingstone finds it hard not to be brusque. "Leave me out of it, Mr. Cooper. I want to know whether *you* wish you hadn't."

Charlie leans closer, an intensity to his kind features that is not much different from anger. "Doubt is just what I was once told Smoke is. It's a poison, a drug. Addictive, unruly. Self-destructive." He makes to place a hand on Livingstone's arm, then thinks better of it and merely brushes his sleeve. "It's best not to spread it."

They bed down not long after, Livingstone on the far side of the fire, a few steps from the others. *Doubt is a poison.* An intelligent answer, one Master Renfrew would appreciate.

Livingstone sleeps that night with one hand on his gun.

[3]

As they move from the barren high moors into the mountainous, slate-rich country of the Lakes, it soon becomes evident that they are not walking alone. Other travellers are moving ahead of them, and behind. Livingstone studies their movements from afar and comes to the startling conclusion that most of them are children. Here and there an adult will walk with them; a number of groups are accompanied by a cart. Cooper notices Livingstone's look.

"They are heading where we are heading."

"Why?"

"The Angel has called them to him. Just like you."

"Nobody's called me."

"And yet here you are. What do you want with the Angel?"

Livingstone has expected the question and prepared for it. Again his words are flat. He has little skill at dissimulation.

"I have heard it said that the Angel chases Gales. That he lives in the Smoke. Perhaps he knows how to cure me of my condition."

"You are lying," says Charlie Cooper, firmly but without aggression. "There is evil on your mind."

"If you believe that, why take me to him?"

"I rather walk beside you than have you at my back."

Cooper might have said more but interrupts himself; looks up at the horizon.

"Another Gale," he says, loud enough for all to hear. "There, over that hill, blowing towards us fast. Come, let us all hold hands."

[4]

It moves on them like a many-hued funnel of air, tall and slender like a maypole; makes their hair fly and frightens the pigeons, brings dust and sand along with its Smoke. The Gale swoops in from the west, moving along a path that defies wind direction and topography, feeding on some thread of Soot buried in the soil. One moment they stand in sunlight; then it pounces on them like the predator it is. The girl, Mary, catches first, a giggle on her lips. She explodes into bright colours: volatile Smoke, darting from her to the others, uniting them with one another and the Gale.

Together they burn.

Livingstone alone stands amongst them, spurned. The Smoke is scentless in his nose; the Gale an empty wind whose residue stains his clothing but leaves inviolate his soul. He watches the dance of colours; watches the girl's giggle mirrored on the thick lips of the Negro while her shoulders droop with the weight of his old-man defeats; watches a current pass between the fat woman and Charlie that forces from them a shared sob; feels the Gale deposit grit and Soot between his teeth and stares at it as unmoved as his horse.

Within minutes it is over. The Gale has passed on. It leaps in a giant stride to the group of children a half mile behind them and draws from them a high-pitched squeal. His companions stand shaken; unclasp their hands, rub Soot-encrusted eyes; study one another from the corners of their eyes. Livingstone has been in a Gale but three times in his life and associates their aftermath with a burning feeling of corruption; with humiliation and self-betrayal, and the fierce sting of shame. All the more surprised is he to see the old man flash a smile at the fat woman, and the little girl draw close to them and weave her fingers into the Negro's bony hand. They commence walking. Not one of them speaks. Cooper alone walks apart.

He is studying Livingstone's face.

"I pity you," he says at last.

"Because I cannot feel it?"

"Because you face alone all the ugliness within your soul, thinking that no one else could bear it. Always afraid that someone will find you out."

"So you think my soul is very ugly?"

"*You* think it. That is enough."

Livingstone laughs and flushes with anger. It is then he decides that, one of these days, he will cut Cooper's throat.

[5]

That evening they reach the shore of the most easterly of the Lakes. Windermere. In the failing light it shines like a shard of mirror, narrow and long. Many others are camped along its flank; they have lit campfires and can be heard singing, laughing in the quiet. A village lies some hours' walk ahead: slate houses, the hills full of grey-fleeced sheep.

Early the next morning, thinking himself unobserved, Livingstone scribbles a note upon a piece of rice paper and attaches it to the leg of one of his two remaining pigeons. The bird coos between his hands, then flaps away, heading south. He watches its flight. All at once the sky above the lake grows full of birds, swooping in a great flock down towards the water, then skimming its surface in playful dives. One bird darts close and alights upon the hand that only just released the pigeon, a swallow of some kind, its wings marked vivid yellow. Livingstone snatches for it, misses, has the bird circle around his head. Others join it, play a game of chase around the spare pole of his body, their wingbeat in his ear. Instinctively, his hands find his gun; take a bead upon the darting mass upon the water.

Then Charlie is there.

"Don't," he says. "It'll wake the whole valley."

"What are they?"

"Soot-swallows," says Charlie. "They're bunching. Like starlings in autumn."

"What does it mean?"

"It means the Angel is nigh."

[1]

"I hear you attended Parliament this morning."

"This morning, yesterday, the day before. Uncle wants me there. There is a dress I must wear: white muslin, cut very high at the neck. I sit beside him. I have no voting rights, of course, I'm merely his nurse. I must neither move nor speak."

"His nurse? His mascot, his monkey! His own little Virgin Mary! But what do you know, it's working. People here are starved for symbols. The North has its Trinity. Even an Angel in the hills! But down here there's nothing but edicts and admonishings. Your uncle understands this. So he carts you out, to add mystique. You provide him with a religious note— don't laugh, I'm serious. Besides, you must look very pretty in white. And all those parliamentarians are missing their mistresses. Some go as far as even to miss their wives. Half the Keep will be busy composing homilies to your virginal bosom. Two hundred humming cocks: and nobody must smoke!"

Eleanor is having tea with Lady Naylor. If she is shocked by the baroness's words, she does not show it. The harness gives her a similar carriage to the older woman's; both sit erect, holding the saucer in the left and the cup in the right. Real tea, too, though no cakes. Even Lady Naylor's reach cannot conjure butter and sugar. They make do with preserved cucumber on tidy triangles of bread.

"Does he know you are here?" Lady Naylor resumes the conversation.

"Not yet. I will tell him later."

"And why will you say you keep coming here?"

"For woman's company. It displeases him but he has not forbidden it yet. He will, sooner or later."

"Then this may be all we have. Well then, to business. What do you want from me, Eleanor?"

"I have been reading Uncle's correspondence. And Miss Cooper's. Now I need to write letters of my own. I assume you have a network of communications. Pigeons, perhaps, or some private mailman of your own? Someone you bribed? In any case, I wish to write to your daughter. Minetowns must be informed."

Lady Naylor looks at Eleanor, haughty and amused. "Let us say it can be arranged. What else?"

"I also need to communicate with Mowgli. I must keep him abreast of things. He's in London, with Smith."

"And how on earth am I to engineer that?"

But Eleanor has an answer ready. "You could buy off one of the Company clerks. Here, in the warehouse. They must know how to reach Smith."

Again that same haughty amusement. "How easily you dispatch of my wealth. Do you have any idea what it will cost? The Company prides itself on its employees' loyalty . . . And why should I do all this for you, my enemy's niece?"

"Because you want to, Lady Naylor. It's what you are after, isn't it—your name in the history books, your fingers on the wheels of change?"

"So that's how you see me! And how coolly you attest to me my own vanity! Perhaps there's something of your uncle in you after all."

"You will do it then?"

"Will I play or sit on the sidelines?" Lady Naylor snorts, most unladylike. "Here you are lining up your troops. Like a general moving armies around on his scale map. What an odd bird you are! And what is it you are hatching? There—you blush and hide behind your harness. All right then, I will buy you your clerk. Don't think I won't read your letters! What, you are leaving already? I see: my audience is finished, you have other business to attend to. You try my pride, girl."

Lady Naylor rises along with Eleanor, walks her to the door, stops her with a hand to her elbow, the touch too firm to be comforting.

"There's an easier way," the baroness says. "A cheaper way. You could kill him. The Lord Protector. From what I hear he has quite let down his guard."

Eleanor does not flinch from the suggestion. "I can't," she replies. "I care for him too much. Besides, Livingstone has his instructions. He will carry on no matter what."

Lady Naylor seems pleased with the answer. "Then you have considered it! Good. I'd have been rather disappointed if you hadn't!"

She bends closer to Eleanor, lowers her voice, her face playful and a little wicked: drawing room manners, built for gossip that the servants must not overhear. "Did you know Renfrew made a pass at me once? Oh, he did, though he would of course deny it. It was a week or two after I came here. He showed up with a 'reprimand': a formal document listing all my 'crimes.' He'd just had it endorsed by Parliament: came running fresh from his triumph, tail up and strutting.

"I swear he read it to me like a love letter; lingering on the words. And at the end we stood just like you and me right now. Smoke in his mouth! I could smell it, though he didn't show. 'If only . . .' he said, and for a moment we stood on some sort of precipice. And I thought to myself, if it happens, if I can seduce him or he me, I will be queen. Only I will have to kill him; or else he will kill me out of shame." She purses her lips, intense in her reminiscence. "Though, who can say whether his manhood is even in working order? After all, he is rather diminished, is he not?"

She lets go of Eleanor at last and unlocks the door for her.

"That shut you up, did it? Perhaps you are too innocent to hear about your uncle's privates. But no, it's not that. You are thinking. *Scheming.* Wondering whether you've done enough. Well, whatever it is you are hatching, I am yours. One of your little soldiers. From vanity and something more. Curiosity. I want to know how it ends. Have you ever been to a horse race, Eleanor? I have, when I was young, in France. There's a simple rule. It's terribly more exciting if you have put down money on one of the horses to win. Especially if it is a lot of money, and the horse is a drab little runt."

[2]

That same day, not an hour after meeting Lady Naylor, Eleanor presents herself to her uncle in his chamber. In her arms are her bed linen, her towels, her underwear. She piles them onto his desk and stands by as he picks over them, examining every inch. The shame of her used bloomers: it bothers her less than his gauntness, the shake that affects his knotty hands. His body is eating itself. Soon all that will be left will be his resentment, and his will.

He looks up at last, removes his reading glasses.

"Very good," he says, startling her by the warmth of his voice. "You have not sinned."

He consents to her helping him up and onto his bed; allows her to pile up pillows behind him so he is propped up.

"It is good you came to Parliament this morning," he continues, still in the same warm tones and as though she had had a choice in the matter. "You see, they need to be primed. In a few days, we must declare war. And ratify the use of . . . the new weapon. It all must come from the people's will." He shudders, points to the jug of water on his desk. "Would you mind?"

As Eleanor pours the water she considers her words. She could tell him that he himself is the first to see through his own deceit; that the people's will is a farce, as is his Parliament; that he is upholding it all not because he wants to elide responsibility but from some perverse remnant of his old liberal ideals that sit in his flesh like a stillborn child, right there in the hole left by his cut-out guts. But if she does so, he will feel the need to punish himself, and her. So she sits down instead on the edge of his bed and hands him the water glass; bends down to him and says to him with all the little love she can summon for this man who raised her like a father:

"The thing you are planning, Uncle—you mustn't do it."

He stiffens under the words, gets water down his windpipe, coughs as helplessly as a child. It would be easy to murder him now; she might be able to smother him with his own pillow. He shoves the glass at her while she stands nursing this thought. He rises weakly but only gets as far as the edge of the bed, sits doubled over like an old man, his feet looking for his slippers. But when he speaks his voice is terrible and firm.

"So you have figured it all out, my little niece!" He coughs again, spits on the ground, halts her when she moves to wipe it up. "I have no choice. The world needs a lesson before it will listen to duty." He looks up at her, searches her face. "Don't think you can stop it. It's already in motion. Like the blade of the guillotine, already released. Or is it that you are afraid? Don't be. You know Smith has a drug, a kind of vaccine. I expect it will be here soon. You will be the first to be injected. It will make you safe."

Tears spring into her eyes: at his insanity; at his twisted righteousness; at the care for her that runs through his words. She reaches for her harness, renews her diet of pain.

"Then you are not planning on injecting yourself, Uncle."

Renfrew does not answer. So long is the pause that she begins to think he has fallen in a stupor: bent forward on the edge of his thin-mattressed bed, staring at the gob of spit between his naked feet.

"Did you know we found the King?" he says all at once, as though it answers her question. "Two years ago. I don't know if you remember: when the Queen died, shortly after the Second Smoke broke out, the crown prince went missing; they crowned him in absentia. Rumour said he was surprised to find he was no better than his valet and changed clothes with him on the spot. There were all sorts of silly stories: that he went to the colonies. That he helped found Minetowns, anonymously, and worked as a bricklayer. That he had gone mad."

Renfrew laughs, a disconcerting sound, like a parrot mimicking human speech and emotion.

"But we found him. He had returned to one of the Crown's estates and lived off all the tinned food left in one of the cellars—he'd even grown quite fat. I thought we could use him, to legitimise the government, appease the royalists. But he was such a consummate fool! 'Let's make peace with Minetowns,' he said. 'Let's embrace the Smoke.' 'The whole world will hold hands,' et cetera, et cetera. He was worse than useless. A liability.

"Then some people got wind of our find. Soon there were rumours flying about. We had to act and quickly. Once you start thinking about it, there was only one course of action. Livingstone would have done it for me. He volunteered. But sometimes, a leader must . . . But it wasn't that. You see, something in me wanted to hold that gun."

He looks up at Eleanor, a pained, self-mocking expression in his lips; cocks his thumb and index finger like a child playing soldier and considers the weight of this imaginary weapon in his fist.

"Two shots, at the base of the skull. He cried while I did it, and shat his breeches. I did not smoke, not until two nights later, and then only in my dreams. Livingstone had to scrub the walls."

He drops the "gun," rises at last, wipes away the spit with the heel of his foot.

"It is the last time I showed."

Eleanor walks over to him, touches his shoulder with both pity and revulsion. "You don't want to be saved, Uncle."

He shakes off her touch. "I hate the Smoke. It's stronger than us. We must learn again to fear it."

Yet looking at him she knows he is already afraid.

[3]

Late that night, when Renfrew is in his bed, awake in the darkness (he has told Eleanor he no longer sleeps), and Lady Naylor presumably in hers, tucked into her blanket of pure down and reading some French romance she had sent from abroad, Eleanor Renfrew steals out of the Keep with the help of a guard. She has not bribed the guard, nor beguiled him, nor yet become his friend. Instead she has made a frightening discovery: that people are willing to follow her command. It is not that the man is simple enough to think she is on her uncle's business. She herself carries authority. It's her Smoke perhaps, sensed and potent even when it's shut away; or the story of the Storm. Her elevation courtesy of her uncle plays some part in it, too. She is the girl who sits in Parliament. The girl in white. When she asks the guard to unlock the door he does not hesitate.

The night is overcast, dark. She has been waiting for such a night. There is some little light from the Keep itself, from the curtainless windows and bare electric bulbs. It illuminates the path, the beach, the pier. The sea by contrast lies flat and black. The rowboat is where she has arranged for it to be, visible only when she is almost upon it; the two men aboard nervous but also keen to be of service. She notes with displeasure that they are heavily armed.

"Leave the guns here," she instructs, and the soldiers obey with only the slightest hesitation. They are violating direct orders; risking their lives. With them it was necessary to be more than an odd girl sanctified by story. She took off her harness, her garments, there in that little guard hut of theirs, once she had asked them to avert their eyes. Then, naked, covered only by a blanket she had stolen from a spare room and staring at their broad backs while they stood defying their instinct to turn and sneak a peek, she spoke to them in Smoke. It spoilt their clothes. It is just as well that Renfrew's army doesn't own uniforms. Later she washed in their tin basin, using the piece of lye soap Miss Cooper had gifted her, and slipped again into her clothes and steel-and-leather shell.

Now, too, she is wearing the harness like a snail carries its shelter. As oars split the calm waters, she once again peels out of it, slips off her clothes and wriggles into the shift she had begged the soldiers find for her. Sea-damp on her naked skin: she feels exposed, ashamed; alive, too, and not without a sense of sensual expectation. "Smoke is copulation," her uncle said to her recently, on one of the evenings when his body hurts and he grows fond of lecture. "We should look for it not in the livers but the loins." Smoke is sex; is prayer; is sin, or truth; is the raw and ugly of your blood. Three hundred years, an army of scholars, revolutionaries, moralists—and still everybody tries to stick a collar on it, leash it to their purpose.

One of the soldiers, the oarsman, pulls her out of contemplation. They have entered the perpetual haze that surrounds the prison ships. As he speaks, he stills his oars.

"Are you certain about this, ma'am? These people are criminals, savages. If they weren't when we put them on board, they sure are now."

She does not answer at once, imbibes the haze and *tastes* it.

"I am certain," she says. "That one over there. The women's ship. Draw close and hook in the ladder, then wait for me down here."

[1]

Deep in the earth of Minetowns, in a portion of the mine now long abandoned, in a room whose flawed and brittle coal seam was judged too much trouble to exploit, Livia Naylor sits staring at a piece of rock.

She sits on a dairy stool that she has brought here for such occasions; a miner's safety lamp for company, the light more blue than white. The rock itself is the size of a pumpkin and surprisingly light—Francis carried it here without much effort. She assumes that it was bigger before; that the Storm it fed ate away at its substance. It looks like coal, almost, but more crystalline. Dull, velvet black. Sometimes, when she sits here, she convinces herself that she can hear its pulse.

But Livia is not here for the rock. She merely needs a place to think. She has come here often, these past weeks, and more often yet since Charlie left. There is nobody who knows about this place; nobody who can disturb her or catch her in her tears. When the sheer walls of Ekklesia become too public; when the thought of sky above becomes an encumbrance rather than a pleasure; when councillors and Concerned Members of The Public haunt her looking for support and guidance, she comes here to bury herself with her grief. What she is grieving, Livia would be hard-pressed to say. *I am like a girl who hides herself deep in the cellar, then cries over being lonely.* The thought is followed by a hard, self-mocking laugh, her mother's. At least there's nobody here to catch her turning old and gaunt of heart.

[2]

"Here you are! I've been looking all over."

Nobody: Francis. The only initiate to her secret. How easy it is to treat those closest to us as though they were air.

He's walked softly down the mineshaft, has walked in darkness like the union men of old: not from any wish to surprise her but from a delicacy of feeling that is at the root of their long friendship. Francis does not like to impose. Now this squeamishness annoys her.

"What?"

"A letter for you."

"Can't it wait?"

"It's from the South. From Eleanor Renfrew. The Lord Protector's little saint."

She accepts the square of smoothed-out paper, notes its size and how crumpled it looks. "How did it get here?"

"Pigeon. It was brought to me by a man who confesses he has long served as your mother's mailman."

"My mother's! So she's in this, too. Have you read it?"

"Yes. I could not find you and needed to know if it was urgent. It's a warning and a request to enter into communication. Renfrew's starting a war. We will need to speak to the Council."

Francis summarises the letter's contents to her even as she reads. It almost makes her smile. He used to be so quiet. When they first met, he hardly spoke a word. "The Silent Miner"; soon the leader of the union, one of the architects of Minetowns. It took a lot of talk to build a city. "The Silent Gobshite," someone soon dubbed him. A young man, this "someone." Young men will say just about anything, just to prove they dare.

Livia is twenty-seven now and is starting to feel terribly old.

"It confirms some of the things we have been thinking. About the Indian ship and the rock. It's a weapon. A new rock is on its way; bigger and more potent. Eleanor writes that a Gale will spark it. But it appears Renfrew is considering another way. What Charlie told us about the Angel—Renfrew knows it, too." Francis pauses, stares at the rock. "Imagine if a Gale had caught us when we carried that thing here. We would have done Renfrew's work for him."

"I'd guessed it," says Livia. "Renfrew's plan—I'd guessed it all along. Do you know how? Ever since we found the rock, I have been hatching the same plan. Send the rock down to him somehow, right into his fortress. Hope for something to spark it at just the right moment—like it did on that ship. It's monstrous, of course, but that's not what stopped me. Too risky: that's what it came down to. And yet I could not leave it there, sunk in the sea. It's funny how if you find a bomb you can't help but bring it home. No, not *you*. I. You were against it."

"What about this cure she mentions? The inoculant?"

"Ah yes, Renfrew's trump card. He's found a way to light the world on fire again and watch it burn unsinged. It must confirm him in his sense that he's elect."

Francis nods, turns to leave, beckons for her to come along. "We must hurry, Livia. We need to send somebody to warn the Angel. And to stop this agent of Renfrew's."

"A messenger? Or an assassin?" She smiles at Francis's horror at the word, then stops him short in his response. "I will go. Today, this very hour."

Immediately Francis tells her that she can't. "It's impossible, Livia. People will hear and follow you. These are difficult times. Even now there are demonstrations, rumours that we are holding Charlie prisoner. The Council is being ignored, people say it's undemocratic. Every day people are leaving, for one reason or another, and half the factories are well below their production targets. If you go now—there may not be a Minetowns left for Renfrew to destroy."

"And still I will go." She looks over at him, summons that voice that she thinks of as her mother's, well shaped and superior and exquisitely cold. "Say it, Francis: I am a spoilt aristocrat. You always knew I would grow sick of this one day, pretending I was something else. Now the day has come."

But Francis won't hear of it; reaches for her wrists and holds them tight as though wishing to restrain her; whispers platitudes right in her face. "Don't go, Minetowns needs you." But his real meaning is not in his words but in his Smoke: blue and mauve, tinted by her safety light, expressive in his rich, moist curls. In the coal that surrounds them, Livia cannot smell or parse it. There is no need. She has long known that Francis loves her; knows that his wife knows it, too, and that Francis will never act upon his yearning; that his mute, one-sided love is just one more corner of confusion and complexity in a life already far too complex for her tastes.

"You should assemble the Council and read the letter to them." She extricates herself from Francis's grasp and begins to leave. Something stops her. A sound.

Francis's Smoke has reached the rock. It is *humming* in response.

They stand and listen to its song.

"What is it?" Francis asks once it has died down. "A plant? An animal?"

"I don't know, Francis. It's something we have no word for. Not yet."

[1]

Anew sound can be heard in London.

True, west of the city's geographical centre, in Westminster or Covent Garden, one would have to have sharp ears indeed to pick it up. Here, quiet rules in the abandoned squares where feral tabbies hunt amongst the roots of sycamores, with only breeze and leafy rustle for a soundscape (if one discounts the caws of squabbling crows).

But move east along the river's curl and there it begins, so softly at first that only a bat's or an owl's superior hearing can pick it up and parse it. Picture it: the tilting of two thin-skinned ears (vein-threaded, Gothic-arched, fur-haloed), or else the smooth, neck-twisting swivel of a soft-feathered head whose sulphur-yellow eyes rest all too round within that pancake of a face; then the flat, inscrutable stillness of animal contemplation. The bat refuses to be drawn. It does not lack for food: the summer's wet and warm, the midges make rich pickings all along the riverbank. The owl, however (hypothetical to this tale and hence compliant to its needs), overrules its sated stomach. Why? Curiosity. It is not just cats that are subject to its itch. How else to shed extraneous lives that have grown to be a burden?

The bird stirs. It stands for a moment on the edge of the hole that serves as its nesting ground, high up amongst the brick of an old factory smoke-stack, and—like a diver, a suicide—it lets itself fall. Within a yard of dead-drop, it has unfolded those wings that until then seemed like a solid part of its puffed-up, rotund body. Feathers spread and catch the air. The owl banks, gains height; flies east along the dark flow of the river. The moon is bright enough to furnish it with shadow. Rodents cower. A sharp-eyed fox, confused, pounces at the passing shade. Nearby, a mangy pack of dogs, as daft as they are hungry, let sound their inane barks.

The owl is heading for the docks. It is a wasteland, this, a barren desert, though all the same a flock of birds has picked it for a home and makes a living off the stringy parasitic lichen—indistinguishable from its host by all but botanist and sharp-beaked passerine—that is threaded through the Soot as mould runs through some pungent types of cheese. They are airborne now, these birds, swoop swallow-quick towards the owl, moving from dispersal to density like a hand forming a fist.

The owl halts, midflight, in defiance of that skinflint, physics: stands nailed into the wind, wings cocked, talons sprouting from its feathery culottes; ignores the dance of not-quite-swallows; listens for the siren song that called it forth. It's not much of a song, one must hasten to add, and certainly devoid of any melody: more like a cricket's strum or a fingernail's ceaseless picking at a drum skin, relentless—nay, *demented*—in its constancy. The sound is loud now, loud enough, perhaps, to be apprehended by a human ear; rings out above this ghost town that was once a bustling hub of international commerce, a place of work, tax, trade.

There are no humans to be seen.

The owl begins to circle, triangulating sound. Its face is a parabola collecting vibrations; its ears topographers. Within moments it has picked out the building that is the source of the low buzzing. A warehouse, richly painted in dull Soot, its gate closed but its many-paned windows studded with holes. They will serve as entries for our feathered burglar.

And enter it does, not in graceful flight but folded up into itself, stepping stiff-legged from outer window ledge to inner sill like a rheumy seaman wrapped for warmth into his coat, careful not to snag it on the jagged pieces of the broken pane. Inside, a simpler entrance at once suggests itself, for roof and wall are torn towards the far end of the building. It's not a hole so much as a cleft that runs from the foundation all the way into the roofline, there to gape up at the sky. The song, deafening now to the shy bird's ear, issues from the base of this cut. There used to be an office there, at the back of the building, separated from the warehouse proper by an internal wall. The wall is half fallen, the office full of its debris. What remains in one corner is an iron staircase—narrow, round—to the cellars underneath. The staircase, the cellar, the song: to the bird's avian brain they seem as one. It is the earth itself that's calling it, twisted metal for a tongue.

The owl's talons are not made for steps. There is no need, however. Whatever ripped open the roof also rent the floor in a toddler's version of a line, drawn with a pickaxe not a pencil. Light shines from underneath, lamplight, a type of illumination entirely foreign to the bird's experience whose London knows fire but not gas. And revealed by this light (a stooping bird; yellow eyes fastened to the crack in the floor; talons spread upon its Soot-baked surface): a square cell of a room, its walls so perfectly black they offer no reflection; its floor so filled with *something* that it covers every inch.

This *something* then: too dark to be water, too solid to be tar; too much a-tremour to be anything but alive. A writhing mass, an endless scuttle: black-horned, yellow-furred, jammed in carapace to carapace; rubbing barbed legs one against the other, bumping chitin antler into antler, drumming sticky wing-case against wing-case—and thus emitting a deep jungle buzzing, bass-low and disturbing, all through the hollow shell of once-proud London, claiming it now—forever—as its own.

The owl sees it, cocks its head, contemplates this overstocked and seething larder; hops from leg to leg in lieu of furrowing its brow; then spreads its wings and rises through the hole within the roof. It is flight in all the senses of the word, unseemly in its haste (were it the bat, not the owl, one would see need to make mention of hell).

A mile westward the sound grows faint once more and the owl's flight calmer. It cuts north and farther west and circles over Islington; makes a killing of a squirrel and flies the dangling carcass home. There, pulling at the stringy tissue of the squirrel's diaphragm, the owl feels safe again and—having (so to speak) changed into the comforts of pyjamas, pipe, and slippers—is quick to aphorize experience in much the same way that the ancients transposed slaughter into epic song.

Some food, it turns out, is simply too noisy to eat.

[2]

"How can they have grown so fast? It's unnatural!"

"They were hungry. Starving even. Then we finally found them food."

"And who knew they would breed? At this speed! We must have several thousand now. More, perhaps. And every time I look, yet more grubs and more bloody cocoons; fresh bugs hatching, all sticky with goo. And the noise! It's like living with a cicada in your ear. No, don't laugh, Nil, it really is too much."

Smith is unnerved. This surprises Nil. After all, there is money to be made from the beetles' fecundity, and this, their nursery, successful beyond all hope, represents the triumph of Smith's most daring plan. It may be that he is simply tired after their recent exertions. They have had little rest ever since finding it, the room that held the black rock, the epicentre of the Storm. The madman showed it to them, the madman with the familiar face. He bent down to the rip within the floor, genuflecting, leapt up again and ran off, jabbering about birds. Darkness was falling. They had to retrace their steps to the automobile and fetch lamps before they could study their find.

Their first reaction was one of disappointment: it seemed unspectacular, a few fist-sized lumps, piled like coals upon the naked floor. Only the hole above it gave them *weight*. That and the fact that it was hailed by the beetle in Nil's hand. It started buzzing. Freed, it charged the lumps and ate; turned plump and black in what seemed like seconds; then staggered away like a drunk. They worked long hours that night: brought the motorcar to the warehouse, unloaded the cases; detached with much care each single cocoon and stuck it to the pieces of rock until they ran out of space. Soon, the lumps looked like hedgehogs, bristling with quills.

Beautiful in their way.

Then exhaustion caught up with them. Smith slept sitting upright behind the wheel of his motorcar, which they had parked at the centre of the warehouse floor; Nil curled up on the back seat, dreaming of home. They missed the miracle of birth. By the next morning, the first of the beetles had already hatched from their cocoons.

"And have you noticed the yellow fur? I swear it's changing. Growing denser, and more yellow. On the beetle we brought it's a narrow crescent. But some of the new ones have a full tuft now, and in some of them it's growing from the joints of the legs. What does it mean? Ah, that smile again! The one that means 'I remember something, from *back then*.' Only when I ask it's all very vague. Heathen worship, ancient myths; the rhythms of a cultic dance. Rider Haggard stuff. You should write it up, boy. Throw in a half-naked blonde tied to a tree and it is bound to sell. It'll make you rich. But I forgot, you are already rich! Here, let's shake on it. My assistant and business partner: a pagan bug-lover and thief. Old Braithwaite would have a fit! To hell with him, I say. Money knows no creed."

They do shake hands and even linger for a moment, then laugh at their own foolishness. In truth they've been getting on splendidly: working contentedly side by side; sharing the tins of corned beef and potatoes that Smith had chosen for their main supplies; living an easy camp life of labour, food, and sleep. There is an animal power, Nil has discovered, to such proximity; to sticking one's fork into the self-same tin and falling asleep to another's sound of breathing; to forming a tribe. Without Smoke it is hard to say how deep this bond has grown.

[3]

The main work these days is the harvest. The beetles have to be milked. For this delicate process, the two business partners have fast evolved a precise method. Nil takes the lead: his hands are smaller, more dexterous; his touch gentler. The syringe has proven to be unnecessary. With the right touch, the right pressure, the gland that holds the beetle's spore can be expressed like a tube of paint. After some experimentation, they discovered that the easiest way of doing so is to slide the beetle along a flat, smooth surface. Smith's shaving mirror: it is his job to hold it, at just the right angle. Each beetle paints a line; five or six lines fill up the mirror; then his cutthroat scoops up the gooey liquid and transfers it to a lidded glass. The future of the world in jam jars: they have filled some three score thus far. Smith has brought a set of scales to weigh them once they are full. He labels them like a grocer.

"We need a brand name," he says, thoughtfully, "something catchy."

" 'Bug Shit.' "

Smith grins. "Nice but a little too blunt. It might work in Germany. For the United States we'll need something a little more grandiose. Like 'Liberty' or something. A touch of the Pilgrim Fathers."

" 'Deliverance.' "

"Perfect. You are a genius, you are."

[4]

Later they sit side by side in the warehouse dirt and smoke cigars. Smith has brought a gramophone. He's playing opera; some crooner called Caruso. Sitting close to it, the singing almost drowns out the beetles' drone. Next to them stands a packed crate full of jam jars: their first delivery for Renfrew. They are leaning against its back.

Smith is tired, happy, ruminative; hums along to the melody, slightly off-key.

"We will need to hire men soon," he says, abruptly. "Milkmaids, a foreman, guards. Turn this into a factory, with a production line and daily searches, so nobody can sneak off with our goods." He sighs. "It's inevitable, I suppose. But this here, this is what I like: the pioneering days. Getting your hands dirty, digging for gold.

"It's funny," he adds a moment later, wistful and serious. "I work for a future that takes away all the things I most enjoy. Ah well, it is what it is. History won't be denied."

He grinds the stump of the cigar into the ground, looks over at Nil, changes topic.

"I'm taking an awful risk. Leaving you here while I go deliver the crate to our men at the edge of the city."

"We can't leave the beetles. Not without guard."

"No. And I suppose you can't run away with them. Those pieces of rock are heavy like lead." Smith grimaces, puffs up his cheeks. "But it's worse than that . . . I trust you! God help me, but I really do."

His look is searching. Nil meets it without hesitation and finds that he is moved. Words fail him, so he reaches out a hand; places it briefly, awkwardly, on Smith's bulky shoulder. The Company man sits stiffly under the touch, his eyes brimming wet.

"There! As good as any contract."

He wipes at his eyes, blows his nose with gusto; leans over to the gramophone, cranks the handle, and puts the needle back to the beginning. When Smith settles back against the box, his mood has shifted yet again.

"You know, I have a theory about that rock of ours. Think about it: we know about two such objects. One lies there"—he gestures left—"deep in your Amazonian jungle. The other in the East, on the other side of the world! So, you have to ask yourself: how is that possible?"

Nil spoils Smith's dramatic pause by providing an answer.

"They fell from the sky."

Smith starts, then carries on, not exactly annoyed but deflated. "So you think so, too! Or is it something you remembered? One of your people's myths perhaps, yes? Well, let's say it fell from the sky then. A meteor, a burning piece of rock, plunging to the earth, who knows how many centuries ago. Only it wasn't made of ordinary stone . . . More like a coral perhaps, only harder. Or else it *was* stone, but locked within it, it carried something. A germ, or a bacillus, God knows—we'd have to ask some egghead expert and even then we wouldn't get a proper answer. Something alive, in any case. Something *foreign*. And here it finds itself, abroad. What next? War! That's what! That's Darwinism, isn't it? The rock's germs against ours, battling it out. 'Adaptations,' that's what Darwin calls it, things changing so they can survive in this new world, feed on the new food. All sped up a millionfold, I imagine: a strong stimulus calling for a strong response."

Nil listens to Smith, pictures it, the rock in the jungle: crushing a deep hole, burning the trees and plants. Then: a growth of ferns in the scorched earth, reclaiming ground. Making contact with the thing that came from the sky. Nil ponders it, feels his heart pound at the images he conjures, and decides to share a fraction of a recent dream.

"There is something I do remember. It's a myth, I suppose, or a song, only I dreamt it as a drawing. A stick man with a curl above his head. One of my people, smoking. In ancient times." Excitement takes hold of Nil, bids him jump to his feet. He starts pacing to Caruso. "Do you understand, Smith, what I am saying? We, too, *smoked*. Perhaps we were the first ones who ever did. The rock hit near us and it changed our organs. Not at once, I suppose, but eventually. After a hundred—or a thousand—generations. And then something else happened—another *adaptation*—and we stopped. And the next generation did not even grow them: the organs, the gland within the liver, whatever it is. We must have discovered the beetles and lived smokeless in its spore."

Smith's face, too, is flushed with the joy of discovery, of explanation. All the same, he raises an objection. "You told me you did not inject yourselves. You did not even harvest it, you say—'Deliverance.'"

Nil shrugs, pleading ignorance. He thinks of the sailors on the *Madre de Deus* who were kept free of infection merely from having a chestful of beetles in their hold. He does not say: perhaps it suffices to be around them; perhaps their spore is carried on the air. Smith might not like the implication.

Instead he says: "Those birds outside. The ones that look like swollen swallows. With a yellow mark on their wings."

"They, too, are changed, yes. And how quickly it must have happened! Perhaps they nested right here, or a flock passed just as the first Storm was released. I wager . . ."

But Smith falls silent as Nil whips around, a finger to his lips. He crouches, waits, then—with a sudden movement—yanks the gramophone needle off the record. In the relative silence that follows a footfall can be heard, behind them, where the warehouse wall is broken.

"Ah, our ghost!" exclaims Smith. "Still poking around. Hunting birds, I suppose. Even a ghost needs his dinner!"

He studies Nil, who is aware of the disgust showing on his own face.

"I have had a thought about our ghost," Smith continues. "Something about his accent. *Mitteleuropa*, eh? Ah, I can see you have had the same thought! And have you noticed that our photographs have gone missing? The ones that led us here. I've looked and looked but they are gone."

Nil does not reply at once. When he does, he has turned away, to keep his face hidden.

"I thought you would . . . get rid of him."

"Is that what you want? That I put a bullet through the man? I'd be safer, I suppose; keep him from filching anything else. But that's not why you want it."

"If he is who we think he is . . ."

"Yes, of course. He has much to answer for! Think about it, though—we would neither be here without him. We'd never even have met."

Nil does not reply. Smith accepts his silence. It is almost as though he is developing tact.

"In any case," he adds at last. "It's a good thing he's gone mad."

[5]

Smith leaves early the next day. He won't be gone long. Nil watches the motorcar drive off until it has disappeared from view, then waits a full hour in case Smith returns. Then, taking a single beetle with him—*his* beetle, the first—he leaves the warehouse himself and sets off, following the bank of the river, heading west. Within a few hours he has entered a neighbourhood he well remembers and finds the same half-burned house in which he spent his youth. He sneaks into the yard, looks up to the kitchen window. A potted geranium sits on the sill. Nil stands for a long time, considering that geranium. It's in full bloom: a well-watered, cared-for purple-blue. His mother's favourite colour. *Foster* mother's. He's been lost, all his life, in the gap between those two words.

Nil stands until, in the shifting light, he becomes aware of a shadow moving behind the kitchen window. Doing the dishes. It is strange how one can recognise someone by the rhythm with which they scrub. No, not just anyone. *Family.* Nil parses the word, curling his lips over it, and then ascends the stairs to his old flat to talk to a man who shares his name with a monster. A man who can *fuss* and *care* and *like*, but who does not know what it is to love.

[1]

Swooping birds and screaming children: the Angel's encampment is strung out along the southwestern tip of the lake, where fields give way to a little patch of woodland. The eastern shore in particular is far too steep for habitation, a wall of rock that defers dawn each morning, dying the waters with its shadow. The lake itself is perhaps three miles long but narrow; it has been scooped out of these hills with a sharp but slender tool. It's a desolate place far to the west of the region and retains a flavour of wilderness despite the occasional farm. Flare your nostrils and you can smell the Irish Sea.

At present, however, what blows towards the newcomers' faces (for the breeze is westerly, and stiff) is the smell of unwashed bodies. It turns out that children stink, thinks Etta May; not as badly as adults perhaps, and less of sweat than of badly wiped backside, but still strongly enough to scent the valley with their odour. There must be several hundred of them: not quite the "army" of the rumours but a considerable number, spread out across the shore and into the little wood. They are dressed in rags and self-fashioned ponchos; live in tents and under tarps; are filthy and skinny if not quite stunted. They shout and play and squabble, trade scraps of Smoke that snag on the visitors' skin and tug at them like fishing lines, in four directions all at once—at all but at the Smokeless One, whose infirmity earns stares wherever they pass.

They are walking in a row: Balthazar, Charlie hand in hand with little Mary, Etta May, and the lank-haired stranger. She keeps her eye on that one; turns frequently to reassure herself that he walks none too close. It is hard not to loathe him by instinct, for being something less than a man. Etta May—the Soother; the placid one, professionally slow in all her passions—feels her skin pucker with his presence. She berates herself a little and makes sure to avoid his touch. Above the grey-blue pebble of the lake, a cloud of birds is flying low, playing tag; batlike, erratic in its motion. "Soot-swallows"—that's what Charlie called them. Also: "Gale birds." Etta May has never seen them anywhere else before.

She looks over to Charlie and sees he, too, has been watching the birds.

"There're so many of them!" she marvels out loud. "Are they native to these lakes?"

"Not especially. As far as I know they have no fixed home. They fly with the Gales, see. It's what we Gale Chasers used to do: look out for the birds. It is one of the easiest ways of finding a Gale."

She shakes her head, uncomprehending. "But there is no Gale here now."

Charlie laughs. "You'll see. Ever wonder why there are so few Gales these days anywhere but in the North?"

Balthazar turns at these words, curious, but Charlie is far too delighted with his riddle to provide an answer.

"Not far now," he says. "I can see the Angel over there. Come, I'll introduce you."

[2]

There's a press of children that surrounds the Angel. If these are his courtiers, they appear singularly uninterested in paying court to him. Instead they are talking, playing, performing for one another. A group of girls is practicing cartwheels and headstands; another is immersed in a game of hopscotch crudely drawn into the dirt; next to them two boys compete for distance sending clumps of spit high into the wind. In fact, the only thing that differentiates these children from any of the others in the camp is that they stand more densely packed around a common centre obscured by their milling bodies.

They make way for Charlie, though, who is either greeted with a nonchalant nod or quickly, shyly hugged around waist or leg; is "hullo-ed" by a dozen different voices and, responding to the calls, must stop halfway to clear his lungs of cough. Recovered, he leads them through a final clot of children to a figure in an armchair. No, not a chair. A throne. Upholstered in a garish floral pattern, faded and mildewed, and decorated around the back and armrests with all manner of junk: mirrors and empty picture frames; wigs and belts; a fox stole and the bleached jaws of a fish. A cloud of birds surrounds it; squats on it; fouls it with its shit.

On this barbaric seat of office, his legs tucked up under him, and offering a blade of grass to a bird that has landed in his lap, there sits a boy. It is hard to guess his age: he might be thirteen and short for his age, or ten and chunky-limbed. Part of the difficulty comes from his face. There is something oddly puffy about the features, something far away about his narrow, slightly slanting eyes. The teeth sit very small in his wet smile.

"An idiot!" it escapes Balthazar. Etta May scalds him with a look and knows in her heart that she has thought the same word. Charlie appears unfazed; points to each of them in turn and utters their names, then, laughing, bends down to the child and greets him with a hug.

"His name is Timmy," he says happily, "Timmy Angel. That's how the whole nonsense got started."

"But all the talk about a new religion! A movement, a crusade: marching against Renfrew. He isn't leading anything—he's a simpleton!" Again it is Balthazar who speaks, in the full brutality of his disappointment. He stares at Charlie, Smoke in his voice. "You've been lying to us. It's you yourself who—"

He does not get further. The child—*Timmy*—leans forward, sniffs at Balthazar, and smiles, his big cheeks swallowing up his almond eyes. The next moment he starts smoking. It comes out of his mouth like laughter, spontaneous and willed all at once; is subtle in hue, almost colourless. The effect is immediate. It summons their Smoke like it is summoning their souls: does not impose a flavour but simply strips them naked in their passions and bids them mingle.

It happens very fast: passes through their group into the camp and travels up the valley, so quick and nimble as to make normal Smoke seem a crude, dark, turgid thing. Etta May feels Charlie's pride and hope and raging anger that he's soon to die of broken lungs; and, beneath all this, the boundless good nature that has made him something like a household saint. She feels Balthazar's confusion and vanity, his terror of ridicule and exposure, his angry marvel at this podgy child; feels Timmy himself, mischievous, happy, and painfully shy, a child who would rather watch than play. Then Mary is there, *right there in her skin*, full of rich delight that she has returned to this weightlessness of self, like a hooked minnow thrown back into the water where its school is painting shapes beneath the surface and accepts her back within its throng.

A Gale, it courses through Etta May. *He's laughed up a Gale. Pure as glass.*

The thought is so conscious that she knows it is already over. The Gale has passed. It has returned her to the sanctuary of her flesh. There's relief in the thought as well as regret.

The Gale leaves her with something else, too: a feeling of connection to every child and adult within the valley, as though she's been at a village dance and touched each villager's hand. The ugly and the fair. All around her the birds are singing their odd song. When she turns she sees they have left their play above throne and lake; have drawn close and formed a cloud upon him, the dead point of the Gale, the spare, aging body of the man who does not smoke; threaten to roost upon his brow.

When Timmy sees it, he claps his hands with raw delight.

[3]

"You don't like it."

Etta May had to go looking for Balthazar. Her friend and employer has withdrawn, up onto the flank of a hill, a half mile from the encampment. He sits in the wind-shadow of a boulder. A sheep stands nearby, chewing, huddled into its dirty fleece. They make a good pairing, director and sheep: the ceaseless motion of the jaw, working over the regurgitated cud, and the motionless man, withdrawn into himself.

"It's a good surprise, you must admit, Balthazar. We thought the Angel was following Gales. Catching them, maybe. But he actually *makes* them. Or, as Charlie has it, 'the Gales make a home in him.' He calls him a 'vector,' Charlie does. He says there used to be others, back in the early days. Some of those Pilgrims who carried the Second Smoke over the Atlantic . . . But they did not last; lost the knack. Not so our Angel: a little boy called Timmy. That part at least should make you laugh, hon."

She sits down next to him, uninvited; snuggles close with her hip and pushes him aside a little, so she, too, can lean against the boulder and enjoy its shelter from the breeze.

"But I can see it's making you dyspeptic—the camp, the Angel, everything. Idle Smoke. Nobody for you to boss around."

He grimaces at this, is drawn out of his silence at last.

"It's irresponsible," he rages. "They're only children—they can't live like this. What if they grow sick? Or starve?"

She sighs in her maternal way, and for the thousandth time since landing in Britain searches her pockets for a cigarette. There is none. She lost hers to the Storm. Minetowns had long run out of tobacco.

"The farmers bring food, Charlie says, and have done so all along their journey. Donations. I suppose they take in the sick ones, too. Most of these little ones are orphans. They have nowhere to go." She pauses, studies her old friend. "But it's not this that bothers you, is it: the poor bereaved parents and how will they live come winter? You're not that sentimental. Nor that practical."

He chews on this, prunes his face. How familiar she is with all his facial tics: the downturned lips, the way his nose wrinkles around his thoughts, the thick dark lids that come down to hide his eyes.

"It's changing them," Balthazar says at last. "This constant living in a Gale. It's like they are losing bits of themselves. Like they are growing together. Into a herd."

"I always thought you believed in the Smoke. In communion."

"In the theatre, yes, or in a church! But after the show is finished and the psalms are sung, we go home." Balthazar is earnest now, agitated. "We are built for solitude, Em. For hard borders between *you* and *me*."

"Says who, hon? It strikes me we are built for both."

"Then you *like* it? All this?"

The question coincides with a break in the clouds. All of a sudden rain falls, a hard, quick shower, ten steps to their left while sunlight fills the hillside on their right. It is so dramatic, so *theatrical,* that she cannot help but giggle. Balthazar fights it but succumbs. It is only when they have laughed themselves out that she returns to his question.

"It's Eden, I suppose. Have you noticed that there are no real fights? Some scuffles, but nothing very serious, and the other children soon prise them apart. They have lived in each other's skins—in their needs and wants. I suppose it makes a difference." Etta May sighs, wishes once more she had a cigarette there to help her think. "Only it's not for us, Balthazar. We are too old, see. Have you noticed that even Charlie keeps a little apart? He makes his camp on the other side of that hill. We are just not bred for this. But most of these children are right around ten, eleven years old. They are Smoke-born. It's the first thing they knew."

"You are telling me this camp is the future?"

"Who knows, Balthazar? Don't fret. The future, hon, it always looks ugly to us old farts."

[4]

They fall silent after that but remain on the hillside, enjoying each other's company and the warmth of the sun. But when the clouds begin to bunch once more and Balthazar starts getting up, she reaches out and stays him, her plump hand on his wrist. There is something else she wants to talk to Balthazar about. Something she wants him to do.

"What?" he asks.

"That man. The Smokeless One. Livingstone. The birds all flock to him, like he has birdseed in his blood. Little Timmy's taken a shine to him and now he sits there all day whispering into the child's ear. He's up to no good."

Balthazar's answer comes out quiet; cautious. "You can't know what he's up to, Em—he doesn't smoke. Perhaps he simply has an ugly mug."

Etta May waves away the objection. Her gut is her gut. "Talk to him, will you, Balthazar? Sound him out. Let him know we are keeping an eye on him."

Again Balthazar is careful in his answer. "Why me?" he asks.

"You are the one in britches."

Balthazar snorts, thinks. "I will talk to Charlie."

It is only then she understands his hesitation. Balthazar is afraid.

[5]

She has to do it herself then. It should not take much courage: it is not quite dark yet and Livingstone has made his camp within shouting distance of the Angel and his court. She will be well watched.

All the same, a dread overcomes Etta May as she approaches the man who is arranging his blankets and stirring his own private fire, then puts a pot of water on to boil. Birds perch all around him, move only when his feet or hands push them away. As she draws close, she is struck by the smoothness of his movements. It is as though his body belongs to a younger man. The face is lined and grey and inexpressive. He does not pause or greet her though she'd swear he's seen her from afar.

"Mr. Livingstone," she says at last.

He looks up but does not reply.

"A word if I may." She gathers herself, forces herself to step closer. "I would like to know what you are talking to the child about. To Timmy."

"Why don't you ask him?"

Livingstone's voice is flat, the rudeness of the answer purely in the words themselves. Etta May, by contrast, cannot hide her irritation.

"You know yourself he does not talk, Mr. Livingstone. He is a mute."

This seems to interest the man. He looks at her more fully, considers her.

"I think he can talk just fine. He just thinks that the Smoke is enough."

He smiles, a bland event, though not entirely free of humour. "You might say we are well matched. A mute who talks in Smoke, and a man who's deaf to it."

"You are up to something. Something bad."

He returns to his work. It is almost like she has not spoken at all.

"I will tell Timmy. I will warn him about you."

"Do," he says, bent over and not looking. "He won't listen to you. You do not matter to him. Nor to me."

For a moment she is lost for words. She feels her face flush at the direct-ness of his dismissal; feels diminished, six years old and without rights.

"That may be true, Mr. Livingstone, but we both know there's one person Timmy *will* listen to. And I will make sure they speak. Good night!"

She all but shakes her fist at the man, then marches off in rotund indigna-tion. Charlie is camped on the other side of the hill and it is too dark now to go find him. Never mind, she will warn him in the morning. Etta May returns to where Balthazar has built their tent, in a little clearing amongst the trees; beds herself down along his narrow shape, and hums a little song to herself that has ushered her to sleep for as long as she remembers.

She does not see, therefore, how the man who does not smoke sits hun-kered before his fire, chewing on her parting words; does not see him come to a decision. Nor does she see him rise in the darkest hour of the night and navigate the hill ridge by thin moonlight. Nor yet does she witness a great portion of the birds flocking 'round the man like an extension of his shadow abandon him and lake and campsite, and go flying out to sea, as though they have heard or seen or smelled something irresistible to their natures.

Livingstone ignores their flight and checks his pockets for a knife.

[1]

They have been warned not to sail too close to land. Should wind and weather give them no choice, they are to head for the shelter of the Irish coast rather than the Welsh or Cornish. The sailor need not be privy to the captain's orders to understand why. They are carrying a disease. Perhaps it is more accurate to say that they have become a disease. The ship's infected. Its very steel is riddled with the rot. Not that you could tell from afar, other than perhaps by the sheer density of barnacles threading the hull, right at the waterline, painting an outline of the hold. That and by their speed. Something's wrong with the engine. It started playing up mid-voyage and has been steadily growing worse. The machinists complain they cannot build pressure. The ship is limping to their destination.

Then, too, there is the anger. The crew has been issued sweets—an unheard-of luxury!—distributed afresh every morning to everyone on board, from cook to mate to cabin boy. It's like Captain's handing out gold. During the day it dulls their anger, culls the Smoke. At night, it finds them in their dreams: down in the crew quarters, where they sleep hammock to hammock. Those hammocks were white when they started out, freshly bleached and stiff with starch. Now they droop limp and black from their ropes, the fabric grown heavy from its patina of Soot. There is a rhythm to those dreams, a strange kind of drumming, like the ship's own heartbeat. Sailors wake, shrouded in Smoke, and shove the last of their sweets into their mouths. If they have them. If not, they get up to mischief. There have been suicides and knifings; two serious fires set by sailors belowdecks. Some say the engine is failing because a machinist took a hammer to its valves. They are a sickroom—a madhouse—sailing across half the world to deliver their sickness.

The sailor has often wondered what those who'll receive it have done to deserve such a gift.

[2]

Their self-imposed quarantine also extends to other ships. Whatever it is they meet, whether fishing boat or cargo steamer, they are under strict orders not to approach and warn them away with a complex series of signals painted onto the wind by their signalman's flags. This includes other Company vessels. Not long ago two Company ships came up on them from behind. They passed at a league's distance, going full steam. Only the captain and first mate command binoculars, but despite this the rumour spread amongst the crew that the ships' decks were packed with sepoy soldiers, "prow to stern." At the time, they were already nearing England; were too close to it, in fact, to make a riddle of the ships' destination. The sailor, a native of Surat, has pondered this fact. Soldiers, he knows, mean war, mean occupation. Someone's heel is being planted on the land. He surprises himself with a pang of pride at the thought that it should be the sahibs' soil and his brothers' heel. They used to whisper of such a thing when he was a child.

Now that they have limped past the narrows of Saint George's Channel, it is fishing vessels they meet and warn away, not Company steamers. The ship is listing a little, as though they are taking water; there are some who say that the thing in their hold has the power to change weight and unbalances them when it chooses to be heavy. The sailor does not believe this. He has gone to a city school and knows that physics are physics; that everything on earth is bound by rules. But he also has eyes in his head and has seen what he has seen.

He has gone down into the hold only once, on a dare. Most of the sailors have, at some point on the voyage, drawn by the same strange fascination that a sore holds for the sick. Few have made a habit of such visits. The old servant who looked after the prisoner has long been relieved of his duties. His immediate successor disappeared and is thought to have thrown himself into the sea. Now the cabin boy has taken over; it is said he has devised an ingenious way of feeding the prisoner without going near him, a matter of boathooks, ropes, and baskets.

For all that, the things he saw down in the hold did not fill the sailor with any immediate horror. There was the fungus he had heard of, black and thick like the carpets in rich men's houses; the tiny mushrooms growing out of floor and walls; islands of barnacles that wrinkled the inner hull, giving way in places to patches of oddly patterned clams, finger-long and feeding on God knew what.

There was the box-machine, too, its metal sides split and bulging, the top squeezed open from the inside, giving a glimpse of the black rock: distended, *growing*, absorbing the very steel into its substance and twisting the machine's pipes around until they pointed outwards like spikes.

And then, of course, there was their fabled ghost, haunting the hold with his foot tethered to the floor by a chain so overgrown it looked braided from seaweed; rail-thin, feverish, and heinously filthy, his face so Soot-plastered that he was as black as any southern Tamil come to Bombay to beg for work.

Thomas Argyle.

When the sailor first heard it was he, he felt the same thrill as all the other native sailors; the same thrill that led some to plot mutiny and saw them shot and ditched into the sea.

But seeing the prisoner's sorry state and watching him pace at the limits of his living tether; damp, dark Smoke rising out of his skin at every step; his closed lips humming a melody that captured the strange rhythms of the sailors' angry dreams—the thrill died away and was replaced by disgust and pity for this creature more beast than man.

The pacing stopped when, after a whole minute of the sailor's watching, the chained one suddenly became aware of the intrusion. He looked up then; looked at the sailor with eyes whose whites were threaded by a web of fine black veins; and tore aside the blanket into which he was wrapped. There, in his naked flank, on the same side as his tethered ankle, something wet glistened like a wound. The prisoner's hand went to it—perhaps, thought the sailor, he wished to beg for medical aid. The Soot-stained fingers searched the skin; reached *into* it, down below the bend of the lowest of the ribs. He plucked at himself and produced between thumb and forefinger a delicate stem, crested by the thin black hood of a forest mushroom, and tiny, dangling roots wet with the prisoner's blood. And as he stood, proffering it like a gift, a new expression came into the prisoner's face, and for the first time he looked human, full of horror at himself, the mouth a black-lipped oval shaping a silent plea for help.

The sailor turned, ducked through the hatch, and scrambled back up the steep steps. Halfway up he slipped upon a little crab, black-horned and yellow-patterned, its joints embroidered in thick fur. It cracked under his foot and took his balance. The sailor fell hard upon his hip and cut his chin on the sharp lip of a rung. Two fellow sailors had to drag him up, unconscious. He has limped on the left side ever since. If he'd broken his hip, he has heard the others joke, they would have fed him to the thing in the crate.

Tonight he dreams of this, his visit to the hold; wakes up smoking, cramming sweets into his mouth. Soothed, he nonetheless has trouble breathing, and rolls out of his hammock to trade the cabin for fresh air. Out on deck, the breeze is strong, the water choppy; and a hundred birds sit lined upon the railing, far too small to suggest gulls. He walks to them; sees that they are land birds and is momentarily cheered by the promise of earth and trees. Then one bird stirs and the moonlight finds a crest of yellow in its spread-out wings.

The sailor's charge sees the birds explode into a cloud, then resettle on the railing one by one. Twenty times they play this game, until, exhausted, the sailor settles on his haunches and is still. His cabinmates find him there at the change of the watch, slumped against a lifeboat, his hands in his shirt, searching his ribs and groin for telltale growths.

[1]

Charlie does not sleep that night, the night the birds fly to the ship, the night he is to be murdered. He lies halfway up the hill, alone, awake. Fretting.

Doubt is a poison, he's told Livingstone. He knows as much because he has long sampled it; decants it from its bottle from time to time to rub its stink into his gums.

This time it was Balthazar who'd loosened the cork for him: the look on the old man's face when he saw the camp of children and beheld the Angel. Charlie has been an icon to him, a thing from a story, a symbol of good. And here Charlie was, leading children into danger. They should be home with their mothers, or—if they had no mothers—in a Minetowns orphanage, to be raised on stale bread and homilies to labour. They might have gone hungry there, too. But at least they would have been safe.

And behind this simple doubt there lies another, ten years deep. Charlie set off the Second Smoke because he was angry with his father. His father never knew it; his own servant killed him, as though acting out Charlie's anger in proxy. Charlie has been told that there is a man in Vienna who claims that all sons wish to murder their fathers. And that it is those who succeed who are forever cursed.

The guilt and doubt should have turned him away from the Smoke, transformed him into its critic. Instead Charlie embraced it as his truth. For how could he forswear it? After all, it had shown him something, in those early days when the Smoke they had unleashed was so alive that it rewrote all the rules of being human. It wasn't that the Smoke was *good*. But it was honest. Complicated, messy, dirty. Compromised and compromising. Violent, tawdry, fickle. *Fun.*

He could not deny it, even as Storms carved death into the land.

So Charlie went chasing Gales. Oh, he did not go at once. First, he tried to help with Livia's project of building a new polity on the principles of liberty, equality, community. But Minetowns was riven by politics. It had grown half afraid of Smoke even as it worshipped it; pampered Charlie as a hero while mistrusting his temperament: in matters of policy, he cleaved too much to the middle road. To the south, Renfrew's power was rising; soon enough the wheel of history would turn and return them to an age where one tried to cut Smoke from one's flesh. Then, too, he wanted to give Livia and Thomas the privacy they yearned for but did not dare request. So he left; found Gales and fellow chasers; and gagged on his doubt whenever he came across Smoke's violence and those scarred by all the anger he had helped release.

And then he met Timmy. A child brought Charlie to him, a Smoke-born orphan girl, preaching the Angel's faith unbidden, begging for food. There he was, this little boy, living on an abandoned farm in an empty stretch of Scotland, breathing Gales into the air; birds and children swooping all around. Timmy reached out, held Charlie's hand.

He gave him hope.

No, more than hope. A vision, religious in magnitude, feverish in urgency. In this vision, Charlie saw the boy walk south, into Renfrew's lands, carrying his Gale: a thousand birds heralding his coming. He would unfurl the playful goodwill of his band of children; would spread it on his breath, converting the world to his promise: until the day that the Lord Protector himself would stand hand in hand with him, and cry. Renfrew spoke to Charlie once of his dream of a Republic of Virtue: a sinless world, achieved through careful rearing, breeding, self-denial. Here, against that, was a Republic of Play: borne on the pure breath of a little boy who seemed to live only to connect those around him. Charlie met Timmy and he started to dream of a world much better than the one he'd helped build down in Minetowns.

All children, except one, grow up.

He would have told all this to Balthazar, had Livingstone not come that night, carrying his darkness and his knife.

[2]

He hears him coming. Perhaps Livingstone's foot dislodges a stone, or perhaps he has slipped upon the heather and falls down to one knee. A soft sound in the dark: it is enough to rouse Charlie from his blanket. He sits up, stares into the night. There he is: a silhouette in the moonlight, cresting the rise, still fifteen steps away; his movements smooth, untroubled by exertion. Charlie recognises him at once. He does not need to see the blade to know the purpose of his coming.

Charlie acts at once (were Thomas here, he would be proud to see it). He rolls onto his stomach, reaches for his bag. There is a revolver there that he carries on all his travels. As Charlie digs for it amongst his underwear, he finds that he is angry with himself. After all, he'd known that Livingstone was up to no good. It was there in his eyes and too-many guns; in the way he sidled up to Timmy with his pocketful of sugar. The man meant violence: to someone, somewhere. It was just a matter of time.

The problem was, Charlie *knew* it—but he wasn't sure. Livingstone does not smoke. Charlie cannot *taste* him. He's come to rely on a world where we share our secrets like air.

Still, all is not lost. Charlie has seen him in time. Livingstone has his knife—Charlie can see it in his fist now as the man walks closer, unhurried. But Charlie has a gun. His fingers have found it, he is tugging it free from its wrapping in the bag. Charlie knows that it is loaded, that the mechanism is free of rust or dirt. All he needs to do is cock the hammer, pull the trigger. There is time for all that—five steps, perhaps six; time to aim and warn the man and then to shoot. Charlie knows it and is calm.

He is not afraid to kill.

Then he starts coughing. Consumption: he contracted it in Minetowns. By the time it was diagnosed, it did much to hasten his decision to leave. He did not wish for Thomas and Livia to know. The doctor recommended he seek out the mild climates of southern Europe. Charlie went to Scotland instead. He's found it a shameless disease, corroding his lungs, emaciating his body, bent on bringing up pieces of him, blood and gunk, as though to remind him that he is nothing but a wrap of meat. Now, too, it shakes his frame; shakes loose some little chunk of him and slips it bitter onto his tongue. Charlie tries to swallow it (he should have spat) and inhales it back instead.

When he tries to raise the still-uncocked gun, Livingstone is there, bent over him, turning Charlie's arm aside with one knee.

How helpless he is: coughing, retching, struggling for a sip of air. Charlie tosses, buckles in his blankets, a man drowning on himself. Then Livingstone reaches for him, not with his knife but with his open hands. He kneels down beside Charlie and lifts up his head; cradles him gently, his palms warm on Charlie's skin. Smoke hacks out of Charlie, giving material substance to his cough, now raw with panic, now full of fucking anger, the good lad sent raging at the last. The Smoke rises up and passes through Livingstone as it would through God inviolate.

Livingstone shifts his hands, supports Charlie's head with one and slips the other onto his mouth, light as a feather, weighing his every bark of failing breath. Charlie kicks and tries to punch him; tries to think of Livia, of Thomas; tries to make his peace with his father, and with that other Father in whom he does not know if he believes. All he wants to know is that he did right, ten years ago; some gentle voice to say, *All is well*.

As his body weakens, so does his anger. It mists the air around him, colourless, then condensates against his skin as Soot so pale, it bleaches his face into a mime's. One more puff of self-pity, one of fear.

Then comes a surprising calm.

[1]

To Parliament!

Her uncle has given her a new dress, for this, their special day. Its long, full skirts and tight, high-cut bodice are suggestive of a wedding gown, as is the sheer radiance of the white silk. The harness fits on top and is, strange to say, at once monstrous and not unbecoming: too bulky for a corset, it nonetheless accentuates her waist and hips, and makes her arms looks graceful and slender. Eleanor observes herself very closely in the small mirror of her cell. When Renfrew knocks, she is ready. He wears the same suit as ever, but the shirt is new and the cravat formal and black. He takes her arm like a gallant and together they march forth, to the parliamentary chamber, where they will take a seat, as is their custom, on one of the back benches, side by side.

The room is already packed, though the session is not to begin for another quarter hour. As always, the room is severely lopsided. Everyone is sitting on the right, with the opposition benches spurned by all and sundry, lest it suggest the existence of dissent. The Speaker alone sits separate, at the head of the room, and wears the wig of his office.

He is not the only one in costume. If there is no opposition, there is nonetheless faction—and fashion. The old high aristocracy attends, as is their wont, in clothes newly tailored to the exact specification of the clothes they wore ten years ago, which even then reflected an earlier age and was horribly out of step with Continental fashions. The simpler folk— merchants, capitalists, moneyed commoners—have adopted a more comfortable style of clothes, sombre and practical. The richer of these hold sweet boxes in their hands, gilded or jewel-encrusted, to remind their betters of their worth. Amongst the young generation—some the sons of former liberals; others members of the gentry full of scorn for their parents' ways—dandyism is the norm. Their suits are beautiful and formal; their shirts pearl-buttoned and ruffled at the chest; some have donned ornamental harnesses in tribute to Eleanor; many wear a Smoke mask either at their belts or on a strap around their necks. Fine leather gloves (in mauve or fawn or radiant white) complete the outfit.

Dandy or aristocrat, merchant or financier—they all have fallen silent on the Lord Protector's entry. Her uncle is not entirely without a sense of performance, Eleanor has found, and not opposed to accentuating his body's weakness on their slow approach to their seats. He will cast it off, later, and stun the chamber with his *willed* vitality: Eleanor has seen it before, and knows that he rules, in part, because of this strange mixture of mortality and vigour. Renfrew is at once temporary and irresistible; "the man of the moment." She understands that he has long eliminated anyone dangerous to his position.

Which makes this morning session pointless, of course, just as all parliamentary sessions are mere legalistic theatre, an empty forum. All the same, she senses her uncle's tension. He wants more from these men today than their formal approval. Today he will declare war: a war so total that it may kill half the island and grant him alone the power to determine who is saved. Eleanor does not know whether her uncle will care to mention that it will require that the nation put itself in hock to a Company maverick; or that the Storm released might jump the seas again and lay waste to half the world. Her uncle, she noticed, has been reading Paul of late, and Revelation.

The Rapture has been much on his mind.

[2]

Which explains, perhaps, why he is willing to veer from standard custom, and, once the hour has struck and the room has fallen painfully silent, in his quiet voice asks the Speaker whether, on this one occasion, he might address his fellow Members of Parliament from the floor rather than his seat on the bench. Permission granted, he gets up laboriously and climbs down the tiered seating until he has reached the floor, Eleanor helping him along. On their arrival, the Speaker vacates his chair so Eleanor can sit.

Now Renfrew alone stands tall in all the room and cherishes the silence.

He reaches into his pocket, brings out a little brass bell, rings it. The doors fly open; two servants carry in a heavy crate. It came the day before yesterday, by courier from Smith, and was stored in Renfrew's bedroom. He showed her the contents. The jam jars made both of them laugh: honest laughter, though she kept her hand on the harness, in case it should tip into passion. Renfrew has decanted one of the jars into a nobler vessel, a plain silver chalice, unconsecrated but suggesting liturgical gravity even so. It is this chalice a third servant now carries in and stands upon the little table behind which the Speaker ordinarily sits. A glass syringe is laid out beside it, on a thick cloth napkin of purest white. Renfrew reaches into another pocket, checks his pocket watch, looks up.

"Good morning, gentlemen," he says, as though only now becoming aware of the precise time of day. "I must beg you to indulge my eccentricities this morning. Today I wish to talk to you of war and peace. A final war, and a final peace. I took the floor just now to promise you a reckoning and a solution. We have been the victims of an act of terrorism, performed from spite and inexperience; from impatience at the pace of progress and youth's lack of moderation. For ten and a half years we have looked for a way of turning back the clock. We have not found such a way. The polity is broken; the disease of immorality is rife. Today I wish to suggest to you that we cast away the past and in a single leap move to a new, a higher age. Today I will show you how we can crush our enemies and lay the foundations for a Republic of Virtue. Today I will show you freedom; for an age chained to vice can never be free."

He stops there, makes a loose fist of one hand, and coughs in it softly. He has spoken emphatically but without raising his voice or flapping his arms. The cough takes the place of such gestures. Eleanor sees movement in the seats; eyes moistened by emotion. The room is *stirred*. A number of gentlemen check themselves for Smoke.

"If there is no objection, then allow me to begin."

[3]

Renfrew speaks at length. His explanations are detailed but at the same time manage to elide certain specifics. He uses the example of making a fire; explains that they have match, kindling, fuel, all at the ready; announces that they will raise "a great Storm," right there in the heart of Minetowns, that will burn away their enemy and forever lay a curse upon the Smoke.

The isle will be purified, the spectre of "Smoke socialism" banished for evermore. Once the Storm has passed, the rule of "scientific virtue" can be imposed and free commerce thrive.

The reaction is muted, twitchy. It is that word, "Storm," that makes the parliamentarians nervous. None of them has seen one; few people have, and lived. It is to these assembled nobles and princes of trade a thing of story, like the devil or the bubonic plague. But unlike devil or plague, they know its consequence firsthand. Cambridge is no more. Bedford and Ely are bald spots on the map. Half of York was *taken;* the other half abandoned, for people had no wish to live beside a grave. Norway's Bergen is a wasteland of black.

Renfrew is aware of the nervousness and allows it to grow. He pauses, looks over the tiers of parliamentarians, nods.

"I know," he says at length, "that you are worried. What if the wind turns and the Storm heads south? What if—like the sorcerer's apprentice—we wake a demon servant we can't stop?" He nods gravely, moistens his lips, picks up the syringe from the cloth napkin and dips its needle in the chalice. "It worried me, too, friends. Then I found an inoculant. A *cure,* gentlemen." He pulls up some liquid into the syringe, turns it, squeezes a drop past the needle's fine tip: half preacher, half surgeon. "Those who stand with us will be inviolate, while those who oppose us will perish. We alone will choose who has the right to build the future."

He beckons then to Eleanor, who has waited for his gesture. Demurely she rises and traverses the room. The dress is long and tight and awkward to walk in; the harness keeps her upper body perfectly straight. She walks up to his side, as he has instructed her to, and, her palms upturned, extends her naked wrists. Her uncle hesitates just a moment before taking hold of her left arm. She understands the hesitation. His dream is of a world of natural virtue; his niece in particular was to have goodness bred into her flesh. The inoculation is a violation of this; a temporary measure, while the world's slate is wiped clean. It bothers him.

Still he proceeds.

He draws her arm closer, lifts the syringe. Just in this moment, Eleanor surprises him with a movement. She steps closer and kisses his cheek.

Renfrew flinches. How long has it been since these cheeks have felt the imprint of another's lips? Most likely, he has not been kissed since childhood and then only by his nursemaid. His mother would not have been willing to put up with his infant Smoke. The kiss is like sticking a finger in the hole beside his navel.

It *hurts*.

All the same Renfrew plays along. The gesture suits the moment and there is a beautiful, formal chasteness to the kiss, a supplication that he can't resist. It is a good hurt, this, a fitting hurt, purifying, clean.

Until Eleanor smokes.

There is a trick to it. Her right arm has long dropped from its extended position back down to her side. A sewing needle lay hidden between her fingers. Now she pricks herself, a deep stitch, right into the flesh beneath her hip. The pain is immediate; Smoke in her mouth. She breathes it right onto her uncle's cheek.

Renfrew's self-control is absolute. His body knows what is happening long before he has *understood* it. It fights the intrusion with all the craft of discipline acquired through a lifetime. Eleanor twists the needle, digs it deeper. She is looking for something, buried deep. She pictures it: that sealed container (smooth-walled, metal-hard; a silo, a cage, a train engine boiler) where she has learned to trap her pain and rage since early childhood. She finds it at last; digs the needle into its steel wall. A single puncture; the pressure inside is such that it's enough. In a moment she is gushing black. Along with a cruelty grown fat feeding upon itself, a phrase wells up. She last heard it as a child, heard it rising through the floorboards, chanted over and over by the educated voice of Julius Spencer, while Spencer's dog was slipping teeth into the schoolmaster's gut. *Smoke for me, Master Renfrew.*

Smoke for me.

Her uncle makes one last attempt to escape. But by now her left arm has shed his grip and taken hold of his head, pressing his cheek firmly to her lips. And still Smoke pours from her half-open mouth. Into his skin she breathes it; her hand clinging to his beard, his jaw; his bony chest pressed into the hard front of her harness.

Then Renfrew breaks.

It happens first at the far side of his face, there between her fingers clamped into his skin. A sudden jet of black, thin and dense. It is as though she has shot him and the bullet has carried through. Then bullet turns whip, leaps away only to snap back onto itself, snakes around his neck and shoves its tip into his open mouth, right down his throat, all the way to his broken bowels.

Renfrew erupts. His own silo of pain has been breached. Together they burn, uncle and niece, set alight from groin to scalp, hurling their hate at the world.

It finds the parliamentarians. Some try to protect themselves: they shove sweets into their mouths, or pull their embroidered Smoke masks hastily over their faces. But there is not one who does not catch the Renfrews' stench. It creeps into their bodies, soils them inside out; exposes each to all and strips their Lord Protector naked, shames him in his frailty and doubt.

[4]

She won't allow it to go on for long. There is no need. Her uncle is finished. He will never again command these men. But now the Smoke is in the room it starts to feed on everybody's fear. A riot looms, a lynching. Renfrew's death is on the air.

To prevent it, Eleanor does the impossible. She *stoppers* herself. She seals the rend within the depths of her; pulls the needle from her flesh and drops it on the floor. Her Smoke continues unabated, but she has begun to shape it, refining her uncle's darkness into something subtler, spinning a finer yarn from his black wool. Her body filters the rage out of it; binds it in her flesh. One can see it in the colours. Renfrew's charcoal plume passes through her and emerges brightened, dyed. Soon the room's aggression becomes infused with purpose, its despair with defiance, even hope.

One by one the parliamentarians turn to her. All of them have long risen and invaded the valley between the twin rows of benches. Those who have donned masks remove them now; blackened lumps of sweets are spat carelessly upon the floor. They drink her in, this girl to whom the Smoke itself has bent both knees. She, too, turns to face them: blood on her hip, a bright red ring, encircled by Soot.

I am turning into a flag, she thinks giddily. *Now I must nail myself to a high pole.*

She begins to walk, a ritual measure to her step, the crowd of men parting on her approach. *Here comes the bride.* Behind her, a crack sounds. She turns to see that her uncle has hurled his temple at the edge of the lectern, splitting his scalp. Unconsciousness releases him from his Smoke. A black mist hovers, then rains down on him as Soot.

"Please," she says to one of the parliamentarians, a young dandy with long, sculpted hair. "Carry him to his chamber then go fetch Lady Naylor. She will look after him. Tell her I said so. Quick now, he is bleeding." And in that same quiet voice underwritten by the weight of her Smoke, she adds to two others, "Will you carry the crate for me? The one my uncle had brought in? I thank you."

Then she walks out of the chamber, trailing her Smoke, feeling like a fraud who tricks people by the sheer depth of her need. A bridal train of men follows her five steps behind.

They are heading to the pier.

[1]

"Home sweet home! God, I'm all out of puff—and all I did was drive! It's nerves, that's what it is. All the way back I kept asking myself: what if he's gone? Stuffed his pockets full of beetles and absconded. It drove me half insane. But here you are, sitting around and eating tinned meat. All is well? Good! Wait, I have brought you mail."

Smith is indeed "out of puff," or at any rate flushed and in a high state of excitement. He has found Nil at lunch; hovers around him, then squeezes him into an awkward embrace when he rises. They are in the upstairs part of the warehouse; one has to shout against the subterranean buzz. As Smith digs through his satchel, he continues talking, too excited to be mum.

"All's well at court, or so I am told. My clerks will have delivered the jars of spore by now. Apparently, our Lord Protector has called an extraordinary parliamentary meeting for this very morning."

He finds what he is looking for at last and pulls a sealed envelope from the satchel.

"There," Smith beams. "From your girlfriend. Please note that I have not opened it! I was sorely tempted. But then I thought it's bound to be love stuff. And besides, we are partners."

Nil receives the letter and opens it. He reads the single piece of paper enclosed therein, trying not to move his lips as he does so, then folds it back into its envelope and quickly shoves it in his pocket.

"Well, boy, what is it?"

Nil is thinking fast. "Nothing," he says. "Love stuff."

"I knew it! I wish you could see your face, boy. And they always say you darkies cannot blush."

[2]

Smith is hungry. He casts a cursory glance at the breeding room ("It's like a swimming pool full of bugs, isn't it?"), washes his hands in the rain barrel they have set up outside, then settles down onto a box next to Nil ("I see you have been collecting crates. Good thinking, boy, we will need to pack up more bug snot soon"). His table manners remain rustic. He picks the half-eaten tin of corned beef from off the floor and starts spooning it out with his fingers.

"God, but this is good!"

Other than his relish, Smith has also brought fresh provisions, including a basket of strawberries. It takes their explosion of flavour to jolt Nil out of his silence. His mind is racing; a half-formed plan disrupted by a page-long note.

"Did you hear anything else?" he asks abruptly. "From your clerks."

Smith shrugs. "Not much. I received a letter from Miss Cooper. She is leasing out Company sepoys to Renfrew—I'd been wondering where he was going to conjure an army from! God, that will have cost a pretty penny. As for herself, she is leaving the island just as soon as she has overseen their arrival. Running away. A cautious girl!"

Nil won't share Smith's smile. "She told you all this? Then you are . . . partners?"

Smith shakes his head. "No, not quite. There is mutual interest, see, but no trust. When I spoke to her in the Keep we kept dancing around one another, dropping hints. She told me she was selling Renfrew a weapon; and I hinted I had a new kind of sweet, only better. I even offered her a taste! You know what she said? 'I will try it once it is past the experimental stage.' Oh, she's pert, that girl!" He laughs, sees Nil's look, misinterprets it. "Now don't get ideas, boy. I'm a family man! I don't play around with girls. Still, there is something there: old money and new. A tacit alliance. A competition, too, of course."

Smith continues eating, first finishing the strawberries, then opening a tin of beans and wolfing it down, too.

"Travel," he beams. "Makes you hungry."

Nil, meanwhile, has stood up and started pacing. Eleanor's letter is working away in him. He speaks abruptly, incoherently. "You know he will start a Storm. Renfrew. Up north."

Smith nods. "And then invade it with inoculated sepoys. They'll be marching through a graveyard. Old Hegel's Slaughterhouse of History, eh? I never thought of it so literally."

"But the Storm won't stay north. It will spread. South. Perhaps across the sea."

"No doubt it will. And we—you and I—have a total monopoly on the one thing that provides shelter from it. It's a perfect economy."

A pause falls, filled by the strumming of beetles. There are moments, fleeting, eerie, when all of them seem to fall into rhythm, so it is as though there were only one beetle, moving its pincers, clapping its giant wings.

"We should go north, Smith. We should load up the beetles and go north." Nil feels his heart pound with the words. He hastens on before the Company man can reply. "It's good business, see. We can sell the inoculant to Minetowns. Renfrew won't like it, but what can he do, he needs it, too! We can make twice the money. It's a risk, sure, but a profitable one."

There is urgency in the words, in the look he flashes to Smith. *This is what it feels like to have hope.* It's not just that they can save people—that part of the idea is newly formed; is too young yet to have acquired any weight. It's the thought that they can do this together, Smith and he; that Nil will be spared a choice, an act.

Smith, for his part, has stopped eating. It's the idea that he's chewing now: quite literally so, his jaws moving, tongue busy amongst teeth.

"It's bold," he says at last. "Unprecedented. You and I, selling snake oil out of the back of our motorcar! Only our snake oil works and costs a fortune . . ." He laughs at the thought, delighted, then rises and starts pacing, rubbing the back of his neck with his palm. "Alas, it is too risky. The Workers' Council—they are slippery customers. They may decide to rob us and call it a 'redistribution of assets'—no really, they are pompous like that. And then Renfrew is not a man to trifle with. We are vulnerable. What are we, after all? A boy and a fat man, guarding a basement full of bugs. All we have to protect us is a contract. We better keep to it."

For a moment longer, businessman wrestles with adventurer. Then the latter surrenders.

"Good capital is conservative. It's how life is, Nil. At the very moment of success, one starts longing for the early weeks of struggle. You aren't mad at me, no? Good. Then let's shake on it, or better yet, embrace. There! Look, you've made me tear up with your idea! I better find my hanky."

And Nil hugs him back, resting his chin on the big man's shoulder, unprepared for the knot within his chest, trying in vain to unpick the strands of sorrow and guilt.

[3]

Later—though not very much later—Nil resumes their conversation.

"What next then? What will we do now?"

"Go back to milking beetles. Two of the clerks are coming soon, to help us, and I have written to friends in the Netherlands to send us five more, men personally loyal to me. One of them is a trained engineer, a Swiss chap, very clever. Perhaps he can build some kind of machine to help us with the work; mechanise the process. This was fun, but we are barons of industry, after all."

"When will they come?"

"The clerks? In a few days. It will take the others a week or two, I imagine. Once they are here, we—" Smith interrupts himself, whips around and scans the walls of the factory. "There, that sound. What was that?"

Nil does not look up. "Ghost."

Smith furrows his brow at that, then laughs. "Why yes! I had almost forgotten about him. You know, we really need to flush him out. We can't build a factory that's haunted. It's just not done."

[4]

Later yet—Smith sitting on the naked floor, leaning his back against a crate while reading a month-old international newspaper his clerks have given him, while Nil stands tall, hovering behind him, as though trying to read over his shoulder—Nil says softly,

"It's time you told me. Where I am from. You promised me."

Smith stops reading. From behind and above, all Nil sees of him is the bald red pate of his head and its frame of whiskers.

"You are right," Smith says at last. "But I don't think I brought a map of South America. It's not much use without a good map."

"Tell me what you remember," urges Nil. "You said you went there. Describe it to me."

And Smith, reluctantly, not turning around but speaking to the dark of the warehouse, starts telling his story. He describes the river first of all, "tea brown and as though rotting, like a flowing swamp"; the rusty steam tug that carried him and a native guide upriver, following the outlines of a hand-drawn seventeenth-century map. After weeks of travel, on ever narrower branches of the river, the tug deposited them on a shore and promised to wait for them there. He and his servant—"a boy just like you, a few years older perhaps, a line of fuzz above his lip"—worked their way inland, along a corridor of jungle just a little less densely overgrown than the rest, suggesting a path.

"It was machete work. People say the jungle there is 'fecund.' I tell you what it is—it is *obscene*. Anything will grow on anything. You wake up and have maggots burrowing under your skin, like you're already dead. Little flowers shooting out of your boot leather! You spit and it takes seed; grows fronds, or tentacles. And the creepy crawlies there! Simply disgusting.

"After a few days we met our first native tribe. We had gifts on us. Some cash, some glass beads and other junk. They were butt-naked—or very nearly so. Savages. But even they had already been touched by the white man. They asked for whiskey, will you believe it, whiskey and brandy. There was a caoutchouc farm just twenty miles from where we were hacking out path. *Cao-ochu*—'tree tears,' that's what my guide says it means. Mind, twenty miles in that jungle is like a different continent."

The tribe had heard about the people who do not smoke. They could make no sense of the lines and squiggles of the map Smith showed to them but described the way in terms of foliage and day walks.

On they travelled, ever deeper into the jungle. For the first few weeks, they saw some evidence of other tribes—shadows watching them from trees, too suspicious to approach—then no one. No-man's-land, the end of all paths. The jungle so dense that midday felt like dusk. The native guide cut himself on a thorn and developed a fever. He raved as he walked.

And still they carried on. A swampy creek, a little waterfall, served as points of orientation: they were marked on the map. Another day, Vasconcelos's map implied. Two at the most.

"I looked out for the flower, of course, the original Smoke Poppy. It's what I came for. But there were so many bloody flowers: growing from the soil, the tree bark; whole root systems floating in thin air. I collected some and threw them away again. I suppose I had pictured something different: a nice bouquet I could harvest, supplied with a nice Latin tag. By then we had almost run out of food and were starving ourselves, trying to make it last."

At last they found the village, or what remained of it. There might have been many huts once but the jungle had eaten them. There remained a clearing, now reduced to a crescent of beach by a stagnant pool of river water.

"We only noticed it had been a place of habitation because someone had drawn a picture on a man-high slab of stone. A stone! Nothing but soft soil around us for scores of miles. The picture itself was meaningless: abstract lines; triangles; waves. And something that looked like a bug.

"The village was not quite abandoned. They came out of the tree line that evening, attracted by the smell of our last tin of sardines. Three women, all past child-bearing age, tiny-framed like girls. They looked at us with stupid eyes, would not react to our gestures. I offered them a chunk of sardine but they simply stood there, vacant. I thought the jungle had rotted their brains until, all at once, one of the women stepped past the edge of light of our little campfire and squatted down in the darkness. She said a word, and the other women joined her. There was something to the way they moved. Haste but also something . . . *careful*. Reverent even. Like three nuns rushing into a church.

"We shone a light over to them. They were squatting very low, their faces pushed down low between their pointy knees. And there, in the midst of their little circle: a beetle. I realised at once I had seen it before. Those pictures in Vasconcelos's notebooks. I pushed them aside and scooped it up, ignored the women's yelling.

"Over the course of the next three days, still looking for the bloody flower, we found two further beetles. The women hovered about, at the periphery of our vision, but never came close again. God knows what they were eating. We left eventually, spooked, deflated, hungry. Two of the beetles disappeared one night—something scuttled up into our camp and ate them right through the little improvised cage we had built. The third, the plumpest and blackest, lived. On the ship home, it hatched a thousand little maggots. I almost threw them away, they looked so disgusting. Then I discovered the beetle leaked a curious liquid. I touched it, smelled it— *tasted* it."

Smith falls silent, reliving the moment, one finger raised before his face. It is a while before he speaks again.

"And that's all, really. I will show you the place on a map, if you like. But I'm afraid your people are dead. They survived their first encounter with Europeans but not the second. It was a disease, I suppose—Sebastian Aschenstaedt's hunters must have brought it to them. Influenza perhaps, or the measles; something nasty and everyday. Perhaps it did not kill all of them at once but only half. Enough so the village could not recover. I got there ten years after you were taken. Those three women were all that was left.

"It's almost funny, isn't it? We swapped diseases, your people and the white world. They gave us Smoke and we killed them off for it, three hundred years later."

He half turns, craning his neck, trying to catch Nil's eye. There is a perplexed look on his face as though he has only just discovered the moral import of this information, now, in this last phrase of his that came to him as a witticism, as something to say. Nil won't look at him. Smith, too, soon turns away once more.

"There is no home for you to return to. By now even those women will be gone."

It is just then, as he turns away and says it, that Nil swings and hits him with a brick. It's not because of what Smith has told him. Nil picked the brick the day before, while Smith was away; deposited it here, close at hand, amongst the clutter of the packing crates. At the time, Nil thought he would be heading west, not north, once *it was done;* and entertained the hope, half hidden from himself, that the brick might not find use.

The impact shocks him: the sound of brick on bone. Nor is he prepared for the blood. Smith's skin has split, near the crown of his head. It looks as though he has been scalped. The next moment, Nil is at Smith's side, trying to stem the bleeding with the skirt of his own shirt. His throat is thick, his hands clumsy. But, of course, he does not smoke.

Behind him, a shadow detaches itself from the depths of the warehouse rubble. Five steps and it bends down next to Nil, proffering its handkerchief and placing it on the wound.

"Here, let me." Grendel: Nil's foster father.

Recruited to help.

For a moment they play a game of tug-of-war for the privilege of being Smith's nurse. Then Nil gets a hold of himself and leaves the injured man to his foster father's care. Two bald men, both smokeless, one ruled by the rationality of money, the other ignorant of love and hate.

They should get on just fine.

"Let me bandage this properly and make him up a bed," says Grendel placidly. "Then I will help you fill up and load the crates."

He does just that, and within two hours Nil sits behind the wheel of the motorcar with a dozen crates strapped to its back, each spilling a droning hum that creeps into his pulse.

"There is another man here," Nil tells Grendel, to whom he has otherwise hardly spoken. It is an old wound that divides them, his foster mother's death. Grendel was lukewarm in his grief. It is a failing Nil finds himself unable to forgive.

"You already told me. The 'ghost.' I will be on guard for him."

"You don't understand. It's *him*. He's responsible . . . He killed my parents. My real parents."

"Yes, I heard what Mr. Smith said." Grendel nods; patience, kindness in his eyes. "Go now, Mowgli. You said you have a friend in need. That you must rescue her. You must not tarry. I will take care of things here."

Nil flinches but does not correct the use of his name. *Mowgli.* Perhaps it is time to own it again.

As he drives off it is not Grendel's voice that rings in his ears but Smith's, saying "boy" to him over and over, a word one uses for one's servant, never one's son.

[1]

Eleanor has hardly stepped on deck when it starts: a strumming in her feet. They are under steam. That itself is a minor miracle. The prison ships are decommissioned steamers; not wrecks, exactly, but ships no longer deemed seaworthy by their owners, a graveyard of broken parts. Some have breaches in their hulls, badly welded, and leak like rusty buckets. Others have been half gutted for parts and no longer have a rudder and propeller; are missing their chimneys and doors and half the bolts. Not one of the ships had a functioning engine.

Here is the thing, though, about broken-down machines: they all break different parts. By bringing them together in this bay—mooring them side by side—the possibility was created of finding spares for virtually any cog and piston. It is the sort of rubbish heap that would drive mad any respectable engineer. For a tinkerer, by contrast, it is paradise.

It was a woman who realised it first: Anne-Louise Dalabert, one of the prisoners on the floating prison reserved for her sex. She was, by any reckoning, a remarkable woman, of French nationality, hailing from Marseille. Her father was a shipyard worker who had dreamt of sending his son to university. But his wife was blessed only with daughters. When the youngest was born, and it became obvious there would not be any further children, her father began dressing her only in breeches. Louis, he called her, and spent his nights teaching her—and himself—mathematics. When she turned eighteen he sold all the furniture other than his bed, gave her the money and sent her off to Paris. Five years on and she'd become one of France's first female naval engineers.

It proved an empty title, for Anne-Louise could not find work, not in Marseille, not in La Rochelle, not in any of the northern ports. It was not that there were no posts for naval engineers. But when she walked in with her wide hips and cropped locks, the men just looked at her and dismissed her without a glance at her credentials. She found she was hungrier than her father, the simple stevedore, had ever been.

After the Second Smoke came across the Channel—preceded by some hours by a cloud of rumour very nearly as intoxicating as the real thing—Anne-Louise soon made up her mind to travel to England. She had understood that a revolution had begun that would turn it into a workers' state. She landed in Dover. Everyone she talked to—men and women with puzzled faces, forever scanning the land for the next Gale—told her to go north. Minetowns was no more than a thought, a dream, back then, but word had travelled. Something was happening in the factories of Manchester and Liverpool, down the mineshafts of County Durham. Anne-Louise wanted to be part of it.

She never found her revolution. Instead she found work: not up north but in the West Country, where the Second Smoke had made only limited inroads, and industry was continuing apace. The old order held fast but was not picky about who it hired. Some of her class anger left her when she was given a workshop to supervise and an advance on a week's wages. Coming from France, she was familiar with industrial techniques that had been illegal in Britain on account of the embargo. As such she was highly prized. For the first time since childhood, Anne-Louise ate well.

Then Renfrew's star started its slow ascent. In the year he was named Lord Protector, Anne-Louise was apprehended under suspicion of espionage and sedition. She had been making speeches about workers' pay. The trial was quick, the sentence brisk. The idea of the prison ship was new then: when they rowed her across, there were only three moored on the water, though their stink was already fouling up the bay.

Once on board, anger overwhelmed her. Anne-Louise lived like an animal for six months, fighting with the other prisoners over food and scraps of clothing. Then a Gale blew in. It intensified the inmates' anger. But it also revealed other passions. For the first time the prisoners apprehended each other as persons; for the brief spell of half an hour, they *knew* one another.

Afterwards, something shifted in Anne-Louise, subtly but comprehensively. She remembered hope. And, watching more and more ships being anchored side by side, she conceived a plan. It took several months to convince the other women to spare a little of their rations, each day, so they could trade and, through trade, escape. Trust was wanting, and more than once their entire stash of put-aside food disappeared, stolen by one of the women who had gorged herself until sick. So they started over. And made contact with the men.

They used the cover of night for their approach: sent a group of swimmers over to a single ship. They were older women, these first, carrying cudgels between their teeth in case they were attacked.

The first steps were the hardest, the men full of violence and suspicion. Then they realised they could sell off useless ship parts for good food. An economy sprang into being. Soon more than food was being traded: the sexes hungered for each other. Not all of it was pretty. There were marriages of sorts; two men were clubbed to death for attempting rape; a few of the women sold themselves and shared their profits with the ship. It was, in many ways, how it had been, in the mean streets of Marseille. Anne-Louise revelled in it. Here, under the Lord Protector's nose, they were creating *society*, were rutting and trading and manufacturing hope. At night they looked over to the lighted cells of the Silent Keep and bared their naked arses; peed across the railing amongst giggles and Smoke.

[2]

All this Eleanor had learned on her previous trip to the ship. She came that night from the need for finding allies; hoped to win over the desolate and dispossessed by argument and Smoke; had some vague dream, it is true, that one of these ships would carry her away when the time came, if little concrete sense of the practicalities involved.

What she found, to her surprise, was an escape attempt in waiting. The engine was only days away from being fixed; the women had already organised themselves into a crew and were running practice drills for the day of their escape. What they did not have was fuel. All the wood on board had long been cut into thin logs but would not suffice to put the engines under steam. They needed coal and had no place to get it.

Eleanor did. She had seen—had held and tidied away into its drawer— the order book her uncle used to authorise provisions for the prisoners. The order slips were sent to the Company clerk in charge of the stock-piles (the state's own supplies were long exhausted). The clerks, in turn, put together a cart with all the cargo and then handed it over to soldiers charged with its delivery. It was an easy thing to add a special order of coal to the delivery; her uncle was too sick to read over the details before sign-ing. This morning, the clerks had sent out three carts rather than one. It was not their place to question the Lord Protector's orders, nor was it the soldiers', who sent a stream of boats across with the provisions and won-dered idly at their weight. The provisions were received just as Parliament went into session: Eleanor caught a glimpse of the unloading as she was finishing getting dressed.

Now she climbs on deck. Anne-Louise rushes to her surrounded by a dozen other women. There is Smoke in the air, light and jubilant. A dozen rowboats are in the water, filled with parliamentarians, fishermen, soldiers. The decks of the other prison ships are packed with haggard men. All are staring over at her as she embraces the captain.

"Are we ready to sail?"

Anne-Louise nods. "All we are miss-ing are the skull and the crossbones," she says, her English elongated, impish, soft. "Where are we 'ead-ing?"

"North."

"*Bien.*"

[3]

They don't make it as far as the open sea.

The Bristol Channel is a narrow V, splitting England from Wales. An "az-crack," as Anne-Louise puts it cheerfully, softly, unwittingly turning Bristol into Britain's arsehole. Sailing south as they are, a string of boats seeing them off, the coast recedes on both sides and the waters grow chop-pier. The tide can be murder out here; it regularly pushes its weight into the river that feeds the narrow bay, reversing its flow. The tide is helping them now, though, is sucking them seawards, where three ships have moved into position to block their way.

All three are Company vessels: the flags striped red and white, with the Union Jack tucked into one corner. There are cannons aboard two of the ships; their muzzles have been brought into position. A warning shell splits sky then sea. On deck of the nearest ship a row of dark-skinned sail-ors cock guns in their general direction.

The third ship is different. Smaller; less obviously, less copiously armed. A pleasure yacht, almost, if somewhat too large for that. Eleanor is not surprised when a rowboat detaches itself and approaches. On board are two rowers and two soldiers, all wearing Smoke masks. The soldiers have attached bayonets to the tops of their rifles; bulky turbans hide their heads. Between them sits a daintier figure. A sunhat, its brim the size of a drinks tray. From underneath, a flash of colour, ginger and gold. The way it flies upon the breeze, the hair is freshly washed.

As the rowboat draws closer, the sunhat soon discloses a face. Miss Cooper is not wearing her Smoke mask; it dangles fetchingly by a strap from her long white neck, its snout-like filter curling against her chest. Once in hailing distance, Miss Cooper bids the rowers stop. She does not hail them, however, but simply gestures with one gloved hand. It's an invitation not an order. Given the circumstances it amounts to the same.

Eleanor won't heed Anne-Louise's protests and accepts at once. She unrolls a rope ladder over the railing, then commences on the descent. Near the bottom, a memory rises in her, of stepping into another boat, New York's coastline in the distance; Smith's hands helpful on her rump. This time gloved fingers merely brush her wrist to deliver her aboard. This time she is wearing a harness. It used to be an object of humiliation. Of late it has acquired a different feeling, as though she's grown a carapace or shell. It shields her, protects her, keeps enemies at bay. Down here, in this boat, surrounded by soldiers de-faced by their masks, it feels like she is safe.

Eleanor does not care to swallow the Smoke that slips out with her smile.

[4]

"So what is this—a gaolbreak or a coup? It rather looks like the latter. You betrayed him, did you? Stole his kingdom right from under his feet. And look what has hatched!" Miss Cooper's eyes run down Eleanor's blood- and Soot-stained dress as if it were the latest fashion. "Only I suppose it means your uncle will not pay what he owes me."

She turns around to where the Company ships hover under arms.

"I was going to hand them over to his command today. Shall I send them home? No, I think not. India might test their loyalties now that they have seen the seat of Empire and found it to be tatty. Better to send them north to Renfrew's lieutenant. He might answer for the debt."

Miss Cooper pauses again, studies the prison ship, the string of boats that make up its wake.

"Give me a good reason not to sink them where they float."

Eleanor thinks about it, opens her mouth. Smoke, not words, come pouring out of her. Miss Cooper quivers under it, slips sweets into her mouth. Her soldiers, Smoke-masked, turn to Eleanor with open threat.

"Stop it right now, your little trick. God, you are intoxicating, though. Minetowns would have made a goddess of you. You might even have dislodged the Council. But alas, Minetowns is not long for this world." Miss Cooper shrugs as if it had nothing to do with her, picks at the grains of Soot that have landed on her dress. "So where are you heading with this ragtag mob, if you don't mind my asking?"

"You know where. North. I will put a stop to your dragon."

"Will you now? Then you must have it—Smith's mystery inoculant. I am told there's been a delivery."

She leans forward and lowers her voice to a stage whisper, as if imparting a secret the help must not hear.

"India's in full rebellion, my dear. The Company's hanging by a thread. I imagine a drug like that will be worth a pretty penny over there just now."

Eleanor is incredulous. "But don't you want to stop it? You said it yourself: Uncle is sick. Your weapon will destroy half the island—perhaps all of it! This is your *home*."

"Home? It was before Charlie and his playmates mucked it all up. Now it will forever reek of mediocrity. I have decided to make a new home."

"In money."

Miss Cooper's pretty little face hardens. "Fetch it. I know what it looks like: one large packing crate full of jars. These two gentlemen here will help you. Fetch it or I will drown your little fleet right here in this bay."

[5]

It takes some doing, lowering the crate down onto the rowboat: a rope has to be found and someone skilled at making knots. Once on board, the thing proves heavy enough to unbalance the little boat: for a mad second Eleanor hopes that it will topple and sink it. But that, surely, would see them sunk, too. The women on the deck of the prison ship are cursing and yelling insults at the two Hindustani soldiers and the "aristo bitch" in the boat below. In truth, though, they are not fighting the exchange. A crate of gold would be a small price for freedom, and there is no reason to believe that the plain wooden box holds anything near as precious as gold.

Once it is loaded, Miss Cooper waves Eleanor down to her once more.

"Is that everything? The whole delivery, every last jar? I won't be cheated. Swear it by your uncle's life."

Again Eleanor breaks out in Smoke; again Miss Cooper sniffs her with displeasure.

"Don't bother swearing, I can smell it on you. God, how righteous you are! Your uncle's little girl indeed. So what now, you will go on empty-handed? You know, if you ask nicely, you can still come with me—it's not too late. We will cut you out of that ridiculous thing and find you a pretty new dress to wear. No?" For once Miss Cooper looks genuinely disgusted. "And here I was thinking I should leave you one little jar, so that at least *you* could live. But I can see it's gone to your head. Being Jeanne d'Arc. You cannot wait for the fire and the stake." Her gloved finger points up to the ship. "Do they know, Eleanor? Where you are leading them? Have you put it to their vote? Or are they just following because your Smoke makes a mighty stink." She drops her hand, dismissing her guest. "And you think I am the villain here."

[1]

On Livingstone's suggestion and with Livingstone's help, the Angel of the North has shifted his throne to the hilltop. There he sits, the backrest turned into the wind, its decorations flapping against soft upholstery.

Livingstone has given Timmy one of his guns, unloaded, and the Angel of the North spends much of the day taking a bead on things or simply sitting there, feet pulled up under his buttocks, admiring the revolver in his lap. Most of the children who make up his court have found it too exposed and windy up there, on the hillside, and so Timmy's entourage has thinned out considerably. There is a tall, surly chap of twelve who kicks about the ancient, deflated remnants of a football; and a group of three girls that has found a flat patch of heath and is engaged in an endless game of rope skipping, with two of the girls swinging the rope and the third standing between them performing a complex series of one- and two-legged hops whenever it scythes towards her feet.

Livingstone keeps a close eye on all of them; from habit, not because they represent any threat. In fact, he has insisted on moving up here for the sole purpose of watching. The view is magnificent. To the east he can see the whole of the lake: slate grey at dawn, the sliver of a fogged-up mirror; deep blue when the sun stands overhead at noon; purple-black in the fading light just before dark. Beyond the lake Livingstone can see a mile or two of the path that winds its way between the hilltops. It has been busy these past few days. More people keep arriving in the camp, both children and adults. Many climb the hillside upon first arrival, from curiosity or to beg blessing from the Angel. Livingstone's presence quickly convinces them to descend again down to the lakeshore, where no doubt they are regaled with rumours about Charlie's disappearance and dark mutterings against the smokeless monster living on the hill. There is unrest in the camp. Another day or two and there may be violence.

[2]

The monster and the Angel.

Livingstone can see the adults puzzled by their fast alliance, and shocked by Timmy's lack of worry over Charlie's disappearance. The other children, too, did not seem particularly upset; Charlie has been known to wander. When the fat woman openly accused Livingstone of foul play, craning her neck around his frame to lock eyes with Timmy, the child simply looked displeased at all the shouting, stoppered his ears and turned away. In the past two days, he has breathed but a single little Gale. It appears that Livingstone has tamed him. It's not just that the strange birds seem to like him as though they sense a kinship in his blood—though it is clear that Timmy is impressed by this and regards it as some sort of sign. There is something else. Livingstone has sugar. A whole box of it, large dark-brown lumps, spreading the smell of Caribbean cane. As it turns out, the Angel had never tasted sugar in his life. Not until Livingstone slipped him a nugget. Timmy took to it like a fish to water. Now he feeds out of old Livingstone's hand.

A shout goes up. Something has been found in the reeds at the far shore of the lake. Livingstone had expected it would be, sooner or later, though he'd hoped for more time. He raises the German-built binoculars that were hanging by a strap around his neck and studies the scene. The Negro is there and has waded into the water, as have some of the newcomers, and a crying child who stands submerged almost to her neck. Smoke is spreading, many-hued. It dances on the breeze. More people—children and adults, *pilgrims*—are racing towards the side of the lake.

Livingstone tilts the binoculars, his gaze following this stream of people backwards, away from the lakeshore and back to the path, then farther back to where the path threads itself through the hills until it becomes hidden by their folds. There is a rumour, carried into camp by some of the newcomers, that Livia Naylor is headed for them; and another rumour that half of Minetowns is following hard at her heels. He considers this, imagines them spread out in a line, stretching from Cumbria back into the heart of their republic, like a trail of powder one can light.

No, not *one*. Timmy.

Livingstone's Gale in a bottle.

Livingstone swivels, finds the seashore to the north and west. The binoculars contract the miles of distance and spread beaches at his feet. He leaps into the water, starts scanning the horizon. And there it is. Dark and steaming, too large for a fishing boat, too far yet to make out the name. A cloud of birds surrounds it like a haze.

Livingstone judges the distance and trajectory, follows it shoreward and finds the pier-bounded harbour that is its agreed-on destination. There have been no fresh instructions from the Keep. He did not expect any. Livingstone has sent the last of his pigeons, and Renfrew must have found a way to pass on his coordinates to the ship. Now that it is here, Livingstone knows exactly what to do.

"Come," he says to the child on the throne, holding out a lump of sugar to him. "Let's go to the seaside. We will ride. I have tethered the horses down there." He points to the west of the hill.

Timmy hesitates. He does not like leaving his throne even for a moment; will get up only to relieve himself, then squat furtively, five steps away, his eyes fastened on his seat of rule.

"Come," says Livingstone again. "I am running out of sugar. But there's a ship that's bringing more."

Timmy rises, decided; stuffs the proffered lump into his mouth and swallows it whole in a few short seconds. Then he takes Livingstone's hand with a natural trust that continues to startle the old servant. "Quick now!" he says, almost angrily, aware that there will be people coming up the hill very soon. Ten minutes later they are on horseback, Livingstone sitting behind Timmy, whose chunky frame was surprisingly heavy to lift into the saddle.

By evening, they are on the coast and the ship is close enough to make out its cannons. Livingstone waves, then lifts Timmy out of the saddle; searches his saddlebags and pulls out what he needs.

"Here," he says, "you must put this on. That ship there brings the future. The Heart of the Smoke. And you must breathe on it when the time comes. Not here but in Minetowns. We will travel there and bring peace. Don't be afraid now, it's only a mask. Here, take another chunk of sugar; you can eat it while I strap it on."

Livingstone does up the last buckle, then steps back. The Angel of the North stands gagged, a leather Smoke mask strapped over face. He's a weapon cocked and loaded, taking aim.

Behind the goggles, his almond eyes look out in trust and boundless wonder.

The first time they stage Charlie's death, they do so as a simple monologue. In total darkness, an actor sits upon the stage. As the lights gently rise during the course of his speech, we find he is a ghost, white-sheeted, and staring out through eyeholes cut just large enough to frame his frightened, long-lashed stare. At the end of the monologue, he reaches down and finds a bucket stored under the chair; he raises it above his head and douses himself in blood.

The audience grows angry and demands its money back.

They try variations: a red-haired actor, wearing a white suit; a pig's lung in the bucket, leaving vivid marks upon his shirt as he fishes it out and cradles it, then rips it into chunks of mottled meat that rain down between his fingers.

They stage it wordless, as a pantomime; then have two actors do the motions while a third barks out Charlie's monologue through a megaphone that changes his voice into that of a tin. They play it in wooden masks, like the Greeks are said to have done; then place an already murdered Charlie in the pond of reeds that served as his grave and have him tell his story quietly to the rotting carcass of a pike.

In the end they change the script. They cut all the words and have Charlie beaten bloody with a claw hammer. His head bursts open like a pumpkin under Livingstone's heavy swings, a fine effect, dependent on a prosthesis worn under the wig and careful lighting so as to hide the bulge.

There are shrieks when they try this, and vomiting; abuse from the critics; complaints in the papers; threats and condemnation. But the next day the auditorium is full again, as it is the day after that and the day after that, until one begins to suspect that half the crowd just comes to watch poor Charlie's head explode.

ACT V

BREACHINGS

JUNE 1909 TO EARLY 1910

Suppose everyone had a box with something in it: we call it a "beetle." No one can look into anyone else's box, and everyone says he knows what a beetle is only by looking at *his* beetle.

If a lion could speak, we couldn't understand him.

—LUDWIG WITTGENSTEIN,

PHILOSOPHICAL INVESTIGATIONS

Human beings fear nothing so much as being touched by something unknown.

—ELIAS CANETTI,

CROWDS AND POWER

[1]

Onstage, drawn in thick white chalk, the foreshortened outline of England. Distributed on this map are five actors, three of them moving very slowly towards the fourth and fifth, their steps slowed down, tiny and in rhythm, choreographed to coincide.

To the southwest, her feet just outside the boundary line marking solid ground, stands Eleanor, recognisable by her harness, a pirate's hat upon her brow. On a bright red string she pulls behind her a procession of toy boats made from wood and tin, gaily painted and strung out in a line, more rat's tail than retinue. At least one of the boats has turned over and is being dragged upside down.

East of her—which is to say stage right—an enormous crate strapped to his shoulders, walks a brown-skinned youth, Mowgli. He inches north wearing a leather cap and goggles; clutches the polished wooden wheel of a motorcar in one hand and, in the other, a large toddler's rattle whose droning buzz is the only sound that frames the scene.

North of him, there where the map narrows towards the neck that connects England to Scotland, halfway between east and west, walks Livia and, incarnate in her, Minetowns: a blond woman, petite, in rustic boots and aristocratic finery, holding a bucket of coal between her hands. She walks bent forward, as though into a wind, and her heavy boots leave clods of dirt in her wake.

And west of her, high on the coast, at the precise point where the trajectory of the three others must converge, stands a child in a leather Smoke mask. The Lakes are visible in chalky outline just to the right of his feet. Cardboard wings are attached to his back, snow white and ludicrous. One of the child's hands is raised, quite high, clutching the hand of someone much taller, though the figure itself is invisible to us.

And close to him, as yet beyond the line that demarks solid land and kingdom—which is to say still drifting upon coastal waters—stands a rock, jet black and sculpted, more like a curled turd than a menhir, an ugly, towering thing. A soldier guards it, turbaned, a rifle in his hands, his regiment already written off in the accounting books of its owners. He, too, does not move from his spot. His only action is to lift his rifle, very slowly, and to take aim, first at Minetowns, then at Eleanor and retinue, then, briefly and disturbingly, at the masked head of the boy, which is close enough to him that barrel touches leather-covered skull.

All this is quite unintelligible sitting close up in the stalls. Only up high, in the gods, where paupers stand pressed against a flimsy railing, does the map below unfold itself and geometry and geography become apparent. Thus, gods and paupers alone bear witness to the mincing plod of history: both hoot a little and are rowdy, impatient for what is soon to come.

[2]

It's nonsense, that—a fantasy, a lie. If it were true, the rich would buy up the theatre and close it down.

(Sisters)

[1]

Polly sees them first. She is hanging up the washing. Cotton knickers are flapping at her in the breeze. Her shout alerts her sister, Margaret, and sees her running from the kitchen. Together they clamber up the shoulder of the hill to its steepest point, where it drops away to the sea. It is neither high nor steep enough to be called a cliff, but its view is nonetheless commanding and the wind fierce. It makes banners of their skirts.

"More ships," says Polly, though her sister can see that for herself. Then, brow furrowed, she adds: "These don't carry soldiers."

"Fishing trawlers."

"Not that one. It looks more like a river barge. And those two are being rowed—they must be local." Polly lets her eyes travel back to the ship at the front. "The only reason they are keeping up with the convoy is because the steamer up front is going so slow."

"What's the flag they are flying?" asks her sister with screwed-up eyes. She has always been short-sighted. "Company again? Or the South?"

"Neither. It looks handmade. A white figure on a red field."

Polly does not say that the figure looks like she is wearing a dress; nor that her chest is sheathed in something black, suggesting both armour and breasts.

"Is it all right if I run down to the village, Maggie? Someone might know what is going on."

"We were going to fix the barn roof this afternoon."

"I can skip lunch and be back in an hour. Please, Maggie. I'm done with the washing and all."

"Run then. One hour. And don't tell Mother. She does not like it when you go to the village alone."

[2]

But it is more like three hours before Polly returns. By then, Mother is home, having inspected fields and livestock; her tall, sturdy figure is wedged into the narrow armchair, a cup of hot water warming her hands. Father has been gone for more than ten years now. He left during the Second Smoke; beguiled, says Mother, swept away by a Gale. Maggie says he ran off with another woman. Some of the villagers say he ran off with a man. It is their agreement to treat him as dead.

By long tradition it is Margaret's role to scold Polly. Mother conducts her, with looks and tilts of the head and twists of Smoke. Today, though, the accusations of tardiness and moral dissolution are perfunctory and overhasty. Maggie, too, wants to know. It bursts out of Polly soon enough: what Mrs. O'Shea said ("The Irish," scoffs Mother. "Always full of tales") and old Danny Jones; how the Stoney brothers, all three of them, have nicked their pa's boat and have set off after, while the Barrow twins are following overland; and how Mrs. Prescott has declared it all the devil's work and been dictating a sermon on the matter to their moonfaced vicar, twenty-two-year-old babe that he is.

"So what is it then?" interrupts Margaret. "A revolt, a pilgrimage, a war?"

Polly shrugs, flushes, cannot help smiling. "They say a girl is leading it. Your age, Maggie, imagine! She's Renfrew's secret daughter. They say he cut her heart out and replaced it with springs and cogs, so she does not need to sleep."

"Cut out her heart—will you listen to this nonsense? And where is she heading? Whose side is she on?"

Polly shrugs once more. "Nobody knows." Then, quietly, avoiding the gaze of Mother. "I want to go."

[3]

She won't be talked out of it. Polly can see that Margaret knows it; knew it from the moment she spelled out the thought. Even so they stay up half the night, arguing. Mother is silent through all of it as though indifferent, holding her mug of now-cold water. All she says, late that night, as she rises to go to bed, is "Run off then. Just like your father did."

At dawn, Polly is packed to leave. She has a knapsack full of food and blankets, a change of underwear, and a pair of shearing scissors that she thinks of as a weapon. Margaret watches her stuff them topmost, where she can reach them quickly if she must, and returns to the cottage. A moment later she re-emerges with Father's old rifle. In the early years, after the Second Smoke, it was all they had for protection against the violent gangs that then plagued the land.

"Here. It's loaded. And here are the shells we have left."

Margaret hands her four more cartridges and helps her strap the rifle to her back. This being accomplished, she lingers close, tugs at Polly's knapsack straps, straightening them.

"I, too, would go," she says suddenly, speaking hurriedly. Then: "Someone has to stay with Mother."

"I know."

"Be careful, Polly."

Polly smiles. "I won't be alone. There'll be people. Lots of people."

"Where there are people, there is Smoke."

Margaret says it as a warning, but her own skin carries envy not fear. It stains Polly's cheek when they kiss good-bye.

(Motorist)

[1]

It's a stroke of luck in the end that nobody's around. It's a market day, you see, and there is a travelling fair that's come to town. The only reason Loon's not there himself is because he's in disgrace and consequently barred from all outings. And after all, someone's got to look after the farm. It's *Luke*, actually; or Arseface, or Donkey, or "That daft naughty boy." Not that he is crazy, or ugly, or stupid. Naughty, yes; stubborn, too. Freckled and short. There is not a prank in the world Loon has not considered, or played.

The farm lies abandoned then, the weather rather fine; Loon on top of the barn roof, sunning his hide. The noise alerts him, a double buzzing: one mechanical, the other organic, a wasp's nest agitated by a prodding stick. Loon stands up, scans the road, watches the horseless coach roll up. It is not going very fast but is otherwise rather grand; the windshield mud-splattered and dusty, gleaming metal underneath. On the driver's side there sits an apparition clad in leather cap and goggles, so covered in dust it pours off him like Smoke when he stops the car and rises from out his seat. Behind him, stacked one upon the other and strapped down with heavy belts, is a tower of crates. The mechanical chugging has stopped but the organic buzz is loud. Loon has to shout his "Hullo!" to make himself heard.

He knows what it is, Loon does. A *motorcar*. The barber in town has a picture of a motorcar in the window of his store and has told Loon (who does not yet shave but makes the odd penny, sweeping up for the man) that his business has doubled since the picture's installation. "It's like displaying a picture of a half-naked woman," he said. "Nobody knows why, but everyone wants to have their whiskers trimmed by the man who holds such promise in his window."

Wondrous though the motorcar may be, Loon is even more impressed by the figure that peels itself out of goggles and cap. His skin is the same colour as the road dust. Stranger yet, he is young, just a few years older than Loon.

Loon walks to the edge of the barn roof, takes hold of the drainpipe, and swings himself down in an acrobatic manoeuvre perfected last summer.

"Welcome," he says impressively, "to Master Holland's dairy and farm. How may we be of service?"

The dark-skinned stranger smiles and shakes Loon's hand. His eyes, Loon notices, are calculating, shrewd.

[2]

It takes a minute or two for Loon to comprehend the bargain the man-boy is suggesting. This is not because he is speaking unclearly (though the stranger's accent is odd), but simply because the terms of exchange are surprising to Loon, even preposterous. Once he does understand, Loon agrees to them at once. After all, it is not his wagon, nor are they his horses. And Loon has always wanted to own a motorcar, even one that is out of fuel. No, not a motorcar. A 1908 Stilson Six-Cylinder Company Special Edition. Both boys can't stop grinning over the silliness of the phrase.

Part of the bargain is that Loon will help transfer the packing crates to the wagon and help secure them there. Though not particularly heavy, the size of the crates makes them awkward to handle and the buzzing that emanates from them is disconcerting. For half an hour of concentrated labour Loon holds his tongue. Then the questions spill out of him.

"Who are you?" he asks. "What's in the boxes? Where are you going?"

The stranger answers the last of these questions. "North."

"To Minetowns?"

"Maybe, I'm not sure." The stranger flashes a smile, toothy and forced. It is unclear to Loon which one of them it is trying to bamboozle. "I received a letter saying that someone's trying to destroy the world. But the details were a little hazy."

They talk some more. Loon wants to know why. Not the destroying the world bit—Loon takes that in his stride—but why the stranger's rushing towards disaster. In his experience, if someone yells "Danger!" it is best to run the other way.

The stranger considers this argument. "I'm going there to help someone. Save her, perhaps."

Loon gets it at once. "A girl! You're in love with her.

"Splendid," he adds, the way he has heard the farmer say the word when his wife announces the Sunday roast is done. "Now what's in the crates?"

[3]

The strange youth won't tell him, not right away; not when Loon asks again while harnessing the horses, nor yet when he helps him climb up onto the box. Then, leather reins already in his hands, the stranger pauses, and considers Loon. Loon holds his gaze and tries to decipher the cause of the sudden hesitation. He finds it hard to read the dark boy's features. All he knows is that the face is serious; concerned.

"What's your name?" the stranger asks.

"Luke," says Loon.

"How old are you?"

"Sixteen."

"Do you have a box or a cage or something like that? Something small?"

Loon thinks at once of Mistress Holland's pet finch, Albert.

"What if I do?"

"Fetch it, Luke."

Loon races inside the farmhouse. Once past the threshold he surprises himself by bursting into Smoke. He had not known just how excited he was and marvels at the fact that he should show *now*, inside, where his Soot will leave a mark on the freshly polished floorboards. The farmers are funny about Smoke. They live in border country here. The local lord has some sort of arrangement with the Lord Protector. Officially Smoke is a sign of sin, of commonness; there is a vicar who reminds them of this every Sunday. Unofficially, they have all smelt the vicar in a recent Gale; now the womenfolk can't look at him without either blushing or laughing. At any rate, the farmers don't approve of smoking indoors. They hold with it as they do with swearing, spitting, and other noxious habits: they are for the yard, the outhouse, the barn. They will query every speck of Soot.

Without slowing, Loon wafts at himself, almost tripping on the hallway rug. He races up the stairs and whisks cage and Albert off their perch on the mistress's windowsill. A moment later he is back in the yard, where his Smoke slows then stops as he approaches the wagon.

"Here you go. It's the mistress's pet bird."

"Let it fly."

Loon opens the cage door. Albert (who in truth seems much too large for the cage, or the cage much too small for him) does not stir. He must be shaken; complains, flutters and hops, then squats down again upon the cage floor the moment the earthquake has subsided. Loon fishes for him with his hand but cannot grab hold of him; cuts his wrist on the wire door. At long last, Albert emerges. He squeezes out, then at once attempts to return into his cage only to miss the small doorway. Next, he celebrates his freedom by flying headfirst into the farmhouse window across the yard.

"Ouch!" says Loon, uneasy now. "This better be good."

The strange boy walks around to the back of the cart, very carefully pulls a few nails from a crate so that the lid can be pulled back an inch or two, then reaches in and produces a fistful of wriggling legs and pincers.

"The cage, quick."

In a trice, three beetles are locked into the wire cage, their bodies just fat enough not to slip through the gaps. Loon raises the cage and studies the beasties. They are fist-big, ugly, made of shiny black horn. A thick shock of yellow fur bursts from the points where legs grow into belly, as though their entire bodies are stuffed with it. Loon yelps in surprise when the bugs split open their backs to reveal thin gossamer wings underneath the peeled-back armour; yelps yet again when they take sudden hops suggestive of aerial ambition.

"Keep them close at all times," the strange boy instructs Loon. "If something bad comes—you will know what I mean when you see it—take them out and . . . lick them. You have to breathe in their spore."

Loon wrinkles his nose in disgust, only half understanding what the stranger is saying. His eyes remain on the beetles and their ungainly leaps. "I've never seen a bug this big. Or this furry. Do they fly?"

The strange boy hesitates. "I can't remember."

He climbs back on the wagon, takes the reins, then quickly slips off his cap and goggles and passes them down.

"I won't need these now."

Then he is gone, taking his buzzing with him, down the long farmhouse driveway and left upon the open road, until he can no longer be heard or seen.

Loon, for his part, is sitting behind the wheel of his Stilson Six-Cylinder, wearing his goggles and cap, the beetles taking flea-hops in their cage upon the passenger seat. Loon wishes the barber were here, or maybe Betsy Summers from one farm over. She once told him that he might turn out to be quite handsome if only he consented to wash. They could lick beetles together, Betsy and he, and wait for the end of the world to come, from somewhere, up in the North.

(Materialist)

[1]

Now behave yourself, pet, it's time to get you powdered. It's carbolic, that's all it is, it'll stop you from stinking even worse. Wait, let me draw the curtains, no need for others to gawk. There, now let's get this cloth off of you. Poor thing, how swollen you are! Soaked like a sponge. Ready for the wringing.

"There, that'll do for the powder. Now let me comb your hair, there's a good boy. Such nice thick hair. A proper ginger, you are. My ma used to say it keeps on growing even after you've died, but that's nonsense, surely, old wives' tales. Well, now that you're presentable, here's the sheet again, let's wrap you up tight, so the flies can't get at you. All good and tucked in? Then I'll open the curtains, let the wind at you, and give my old nose a rest."

It's been two and a half days now. The curtains in question are not actually curtains at all but the canvas flaps of a covered wagon that Livia has commandeered and turned into a hearse. She commandeered the old woman, too, bossed and bullied her like a servant, though no bossing or bullying was necessary. After all, Old Granny Henderson agreed to the task without the slightest hesitation. The dead man needed someone: a watcher and keeper, a washer and witness. She was more than happy to serve.

Two and a half days: the body waterlogged and heavy, smelling of spoilt meat; a crowd of mourners around the wagon at all times, now silent, now singing vigils; one moment placid and numb, then breaking into sudden fumes of anger, fright, and grief. It was a procession, really, not a crowd, moving west then north, the two horses plodding, walking with the measured, shuffling gait of casket bearers, though no casket has of yet been made.

They reached the shore last night—a beach, yellow-tipped gorse giving way to coarse dark sand—then followed the coast up to a ghost town, its two curving piers stretched out into the sea like arms open for an embrace. Moored in the harbour basin shaped by this embrace float three ships flying the Company flag.

Rowboats have been going back and forth between these ships and the coast, transporting turbaned troops who fill the boardwalk and streets in oddly geometric patterns, marching two abreast, or four, or five; setting up tents in tidy lines, occupying houses row by tidy row. Clouds of black birds hover above the scene and roost upon the ship moored at the tip of the pier, where some repair work appears to be in operation. Welding torches and showers of sparks add their glow to the dull day; a black metal crane, bolted into the pier's stone, inclines its arm towards the scene. The shouts of workers give a semblance of life to the old harbour.

The town itself—once famous for its import of colonial tobacco, and consequently rich—was painted black ten years ago by the passage of a Storm, then saw half its structures stripped and pilfered for their roof tiles and stone. The few inhabitants who returned to live within this gap-bricked house of death have long joined the crowd of pilgrims on a hill just south of the harbour. With every hour, another handful arrives: from the town below the hill, from Minetowns and Cumbria, from the coastal villages south of here where people spied the passage of the ships. Men, women, children: spreading rumour and Smoke. The soldiers below are aware of this gathering; they have been busy building barricades. Cannons have been landed and brought into position; are manned at all times by teams of gunners. Day and night, gun muzzles and bayonets are pointed the pilgrims' way. It feels like the prelude to war. Before long there may be more bodies to wash and tend.

[2]

Of course it would be best to bury the dead. Livia won't hear of it.

"Not in this soil. We will bring him home."

Old Granny Henderson does not know where home is: not for Charlie. For herself, Minetowns would do. She has spent only the last six years of her life there, but it is the only place in the world she's ever felt free. If she falls here—is shot by one of these dark-skinned soldiers from the other side of the world, or speared by one of their blades—it is unlikely her bones will make it back. It does not much matter. Bones are dust; death is the end of all. "I am a materialist, I am," she says, proud of the word. Not that it keeps her from talking to a corpse.

She does it now, less from an innate need to talk than from a sense of loss at Charlie's death best expressed by scolding him.

"You made a right bollox of your dying," she mutters, some of her mother's Irish coming through in her voice. "Went too quickly and forgot to tell us why. Leave us a note next time, will you, pet? And if you could clear up what's going on 'round here while you are at it, we will be thanking you kindly."

In truth, rumour rules the camp. Everybody has a theory to impart. The soldiers below are Renfrew's doing, an invasion; these ships will be followed by two hundred more. Or: the government down south has abdicated, too far fallen into debt; the Company now owns the land and has come to milk it dry. Or yet: the Company is changing alliances. It has torn up its contracts with Renfrew and agreed to recognise Minetowns as the seat of the people's will. Livia was sent to welcome them; only she has grown distracted in her grief.

The only thing that's certain is that Charlie is dead.

But even here confusion has wormed its way into so simple a fact. It is easy to point the finger, of course—there is talk of a quiet stranger, a man who does not smoke—but the truth is that there is not a mark on the young man's body, neither wound nor bruise. He was found submerged amongst cattails and reeds. Stones were crammed into his pockets; his handkerchief spotted with his cough.

"Charlie Cooper would not suicide himself." So say the faithful.

"Who knows what sickness will do to a man?" So, the sceptics.

The children—those who lived there, amongst the Lakes, hungry, dirty ragamuffins that they were—simply huddled together in a cloud of Smoke. All but the child they call the Angel.

"Angel's flown," offered some wit. "Spread 'is wings and off 'e went."

Another: "He's been stolen, cooked, and eaten by that smokeless Jew."

"Jew, eh, my love? That's funny, that. Well, better they cry 'Jew' than 'darkie,' eh? Fewer of them around, just now."

And Granny Henderson adds, sitting high upon the wagon and surveying the scene, "It's funny what some people will come out with, pet, just because they're scared."

[3]

Livia comes. Bent and weak-eyed though she is, Granny Henderson sees her coming from afar. Livia walks under a cloud. Granny Henderson has never seen anyone grieve like that, with such concentrated fury, yet so contained and self-consuming. Her Smoke is close-knit, moist, a frightful stink; it creeps into your skin and makes you want to flay yourself. The crowd parts for her, oddly disgusted by the flavour of her grief.

"How is he?"

"About the same. What else?"

"Then make space, so I can climb up to you."

Granny Henderson leans back as Livia clambers up, away from her Smoke. Livia must have tried to douse herself recently: her face is smeared with coal dust. Together with her Soot it forms a shiny patina, leaving free only her mouth and eyes. It is as though she painted herself to mock that Negro who follows her around, looking drawn and constipated, grimly fond of the stone-hard weight inside his bowels (unless it's true what Granny's heard and *he* is a woman grown attached to britches, and short-cropped hair).

"Did you clean him?"

"Cleaned him, combed him, rubbed him down with disinfectant. For all the good it does."

"Leave me alone with him."

Granny Henderson sighs, rises, makes to climb down from the wagon. "He isn't going to come back, pet."

Livia does not respond.

"Them soldiers going to charge us?"

"They are unloading something. When they are done, then yes, perhaps."

"It might be an idea to get out of the way."

"Leave me alone with him," Livia says again, and this time Granny Henderson does, stepping off the box while Livia disappears inside the wagon.

"I'll be back in a quarter hour, pet," she calls up. "Just going to stretch my legs."

[4]

Dusk is falling. The camp has spread further since she last clambered down from the wagon. People are burning driftwood and twigs hacked out of coastal shrubs; are warming porridge oats or boiling water. Here and there a hare or squirrel has been caught and is now hissing fat into an open flame. Smoke, unwashed bodies, the nearby latrines: it's a heady mixture. If a Gale hits them now, who knows what will happen.

The old woman draws towards the edge of the slight hill, where it drops down to a ribbon of beach. The breeze is livelier here, the smells more subdued. Gulls ride the gusts, displaced from the harbour area by that strange flock of birds. The fleck of red upon their yellow beaks shines vivid like blood. As she stands there, two figures detach themselves from the camp and walk to join her. The fat American and the Negro: an unequal pair with an unequal gait; all the same joined at the hip. She has met them before, but they have hardly spoken; the gap separating their world and Granny Henderson's seems too large to bridge. Now, too, they exchange nothing more than a greeting and a handful of words about Livia and Charlie ("Yes, she is with him"; "Yes, he should be buried, and soon"). Then they fall silent and watch the strangely static flight of the gulls. It's like the birds have found perches on the wind. Yellow beaks, red flecks. A cry like a beggar's, drunk, needy, irate. There is comfort in standing like that, watching. The American woman has a nice feel to her, warm and soft like a down cushion. Her companion is rigid like a post.

Out to sea—sundown painting the horizon; a cloud bank pressing down its lid—a shape detaches itself from the play of current and squall. A ship, more drifting than steering, perilously close to the coast. Around it, like the debris from a shipwreck, a flotilla of smaller vessels: trawlers, sailboats, river punts. Low tide, the sand flat and dark.

At last the ship runs aground some three hundred yards south and people pour from it like rats from out a flooding basement. A gust catches them, sends long hair flying. Women, a band of women, perhaps fifty strong. They wade through waist-deep waters, skirts glued to their thighs. The one who leads them wears an upper suit of armour. She stands mirrored on the ship's crude flag.

"Who is that then?" asks Old Granny Henderson.

"Eleanor," answers the Negro.

All at once his features have smoothened; he has remembered how to smile.

"There," Granny Henderson will later tell her Charlie, "that's the face of a backed-up wench who at long last has taken a good shit."

It is not a landing then so much as a shipwreck. It wasn't the engineering that let them down but the scarcity of fuel. They simply ran out and ran aground. There was nothing for it but to walk to shore.

The water is cold on the skin; their wet skirts heavy once they reach dry land. A hundred campfires up the slope of a gentle hill; still enough daylight left to make out the people thronging towards them. The wind is coming from these people, from the north. Eleanor walks into it. It spreads her Smoke behind her like a cloak. Men and women drop into its shelter, children, too: parliamentarians and fishermen; prisoners; farmers and villagers. As she reaches the first of the fires, the Miners there soon join their march, as do the Angel's pilgrims. They smell the depth of her, her burning will, her reservoir of Smoke. Even Eleanor's doubt seems to comfort them, her reluctance, her unwillingness to lead. "It may be," said Anne-Louise upon climbing down from the ship—said it not without resentment—"it may be, we will follow you to the end of the world." The end of the world is a Storm of pure hate. Eleanor means to swallow it.

She is not sure she can.

Then Balthazar is there, in front of her, and Etta May: blocking her path. Eleanor cannot stop now for greetings or explanations, though her relief, her joy, runs like a shiver from her and on through the crowd, where people hug one another and share smiles, as though it is they who have been reunited with old friends.

"Eleanor!" Balthazar greets her, and in greeting, tries to stop her in her tracks.

"It must wait," she mouths, passing him.

"Charlie is dead."

He points towards a wagon, half a dozen steps adrift from all the many others. Then he, too, is downwind from Eleanor and party to her Smoke. He falls into step, as does Etta May. The direction has veered, some ten degrees. The wagon is now in the centre of her path.

[2]

She climbs up alone. The train of people that has followed her bunches then widens to a crescent. The wagon is its silent centre. Inside, Eleanor finds Livia and Charlie. Livia has exposed his head and is cradling it upon her lap. Bundles of men's clothes are strewn around her; letters and notes. Charlie's possessions. Livia must have been digging through them. Perhaps she is looking for a final word. Livia's Smoke is vile, a thing of hate; echoes the rot. Eleanor reaches to soothe it, but a look from Livia stops her. Livia does not want to be soothed. She looks just like the stories say she does, much more so than Charlie, who is unrecognisable now, except for the hair. Eleanor bends to touch it, then stops herself. She has no right to him. All he did was save her, when she was still a child.

"I am going now," Eleanor says. "To the soldiers and the rock."

"You will be shot."

"Perhaps."

"I will come, too."

Outside, through the canvas flaps of the wagon cover, the crowd catches her wind-borne grief and at once starts to weep. Eleanor turns, descends, walks on.

It is a weeping army she leads to war.

[3]

Livingstone has not been sleeping. There has been too much to do.

The cargo ship had trouble docking. It is listing, sinking in the harbour. Its captain is insane. The cargo itself has grown too large for the cargo hatch and has attached itself to the steel of the hull. Welders are needed, but only two of the crew have any idea how to wield a welding torch. They complain of a "ghost," a "wraith," living in the hold who has bitten through his chain, and insist on cutting the hull open from the outside. Hot white sparks and the groan of steel on steel: Livingstone is making them work night and day. Birds fly like bats all around, their ceaseless darting making everyone twitchy. A noise in the air that is not quite wingbeats. It's like the pier has its own pulse.

The Company ships bearing soldiers bring further uncertainty. A handful of white officers afraid of their own men: Livingstone does not need to taste their Smoke to know as much. Even so, the officers are reluctant to submit to Livingstone's will despite having written orders to do so, signed very prettily by Lady Ursula Cooper, Vice-President of Exports. Livingstone is too much the upstart, the servant; a man without rank or wealth. Smokeless, even his force can be denied. The officers dawdle over his orders. They treat him like a dog.

He's a dog then: a terrier, ragged and fierce. Forever rushing from one man to another, harrying them, pulling at coat-tails, at trouser cuffs, handing out samples of his bark, his bite. Dragging behind himself (a dog holding a leash!) the tied, gagged figure of a child.

Livingstone has not slept in three full days.

[4]

Along with the cargo and soldiers, the ships have brought news. News from the South, the Keep. Something has gone wrong there. The warships never reached their destination; they were turned back halfway down the Bristol Channel. Renfrew is "indisposed," Livingstone is told; "deposed," one of the officers tells him more bluntly. A girl in a corset has been chasing the warships, along with a fleet of rabble. She's done in her uncle and now she's here.

Not a single soldier has been inoculated.

It is this last part that changes things. Far from crushing Livingstone, it feeds a dream. It is a simple dream, a beautiful dream, of a world engulfed in Storm. He will be the only person to witness it. Only the thought of Smith rankles in him. Smith's cure may yet sabotage his dream. As such it has to be found and destroyed. Livingstone closes his eyes and sees himself walking a barren earth. He is king of a dead world.

He alone is saved.

And thus he does not mind being a terrier; does not mind the end of the world being mired in incompetence, in shouting, insubordination, and delays. Contentment is spreading through him, steady and certain. He is like a man nailing shut all doors and windows. The nails are rusty, the hammer has broken, the hands full of blisters. But no matter what, he will soon be alone, in darkness. There is nothing that can stop him now. The rock is here, the child is here; a crowd has been gathering, and there's a trickle of people that leads back into the very heart of the North. He has the pyre, the gasoline, the match. The Storm will know its road.

And so, Livingstone has already won. He does not need the rock out on the pier to set it off; does not need to place it on a cart and drive down the country road, through the throng of those who are afraid, until he stands above the mines. All that is mere aesthetics: making more perfect a moment that will be. Livingstone thinks of the song that they will sing of this in years to come. Then he realises that he is the only one who will ever sing it. It is so beautiful a thought, he shivers under it. His bladder tugs. He pisses pure black in a wide arc off the pier.

Five steps from him, the hull of the cargo ship at last gapes open like a burst conker. Livingstone buttons himself and gestures for a soldier to operate the crane. Another order is carried down the length of the pier and sees the parabolic mirror of the lighthouse come ablaze: it strafes them with its cone, finds first the crane, then the ship with its jagged hole. Two sailors are trying to attach something inside the hole to the large metal hook that swings from a rope leading back to the crane's arm and from there to the winch system at its base.

The leash tugs at him. Little Timmy has finally understood something; he's growing restless. All this time Livingstone has kept him close; tugged the child's clumsy fingers away from the buckles of the mask; kept his breath away from the rock. At first, he continued to feed the boy with sugar, held his hand. Then came minor tantrums, and the end of Livingstone's supplies. A leash, tied in a choke hold around the boy's throat, soon clarified the nature of their bond, as did the string around the boy's wrists: the child held out his arms, docile and stupid, and even now resists very rarely, trundling along with Livingstone like his shrunk, masked shadow. He's an imbecile, an idiot. And yet the eyes that stare back at Livingstone through the thick glass of the goggles carry an odd sort of understanding, along with a patience that is nauseating to Livingstone. Sometimes he fancies them both dead and drowned; water pressing against the inside of those goggles, his own movements weighted by the heft of the sea. Sometimes the dead man comes to him, too, and stops behind him out of sight. The rattle of his cough; his lips pursed (Livingstone can see them although his head is turned), planting a kiss right behind Livingstone's ear.

In Livingstone's hands, the leash stirs again and tugs him closer, to where the crane dips its arm down to the ship. Ropes have been wrapped around the cargo: he cannot see it yet, only the ropes extending like fishing lines, ready to be reeled in. There is a battle of inert mass against the clever physics of pulley, rope, and mechanical winch. Then—*like a fish from a barrel,* thinks Livingstone, *like a tooth yanked out upon a thread*—the rock bursts through the sundered hull and hangs above the pier. It is studded with sea life and the metal debris of some strange machine. Something rides it, on the far side of the rock, hiding behind its bulk; brings to mind a hermit crab, slinking back into its knotty mollusc shell. The crane groans—how heavy is it, this piece of pure black?—it heaves, shudders, the rope taut and still. Then something snaps. It's not the rope, but some rivet and crossbar, worn by rust and disuse. All at once the crane starts to bend, right in the middle, crumpling into itself and dipping both the tip of its arm and the cargo beneath the lip of the pier into the cold of the sea.

Livingstone sees it, tugs at the leash, and orders a hundred soldiers to man the rope and *heave.*

[5]

When a play is good, thinks Balthazar, *at the point of its climax, there is little to choose between an audience and a city mob.*

He is walking in a throng as he thinks it, is rubbing shoulders, sharing breaths; his step aligned with others'. Smoke surrounds him: his own, his peers'. Eleanor's. He can feel her in every pore of his skin, in the sweat of his neighbour, in the pale, frothy billows that come from the group of children walking just ahead. The crowd lives in it and through it; it is as though they are in the belly of a whale. It should be unbearable, but the whale is kind and (somehow) they belong. *Together.* It is only later that it will seem like a lie, like despotism, and the touch of others will once again be strange.

It is hard to estimate how many they are. Three hundred, four hundred? Perhaps it is twice that number. Their movement is slow, almost ritual. It is getting dark now and some people are holding lanterns or torches high above their heads. Some few carry weapons: sticks and clubs mostly, here and there a knife or a rusty old rifle. The hill slopes down towards the harbour with its twin piers. They reach the edge of the town proper: all at once there are cobbles underfoot. The smell of sea rot salts the air.

Balthazar is taller than most and can see ahead. Down here, in the trough, the harbour basin has become invisible but for the tips of the two lighthouses and the crane that rises near the one that's lit. Now the crane is being put in motion: it pivots its arm, the rope grows taut, it begins to haul. But there is a wall between the moving crowd and whatever it is hauling: built of rotten boats and timbers; of broken furniture that has stood moulding for ten years; of mattresses so eaten up by rats they seem like skeletons made up of rods and springs. From the hundred gaps within this makeshift barricade point gun rifles, and bayonets.

Eleanor leads them close until the front of the crowd is pressed against this deadly wall barring access to the harbour. Those behind her do not at once slow their momentum; it pushes the front row closer yet, bellies tempting mounted blades. The wind is still coming from the north; Eleanor's Smoke belongs to the crowd and not the soldiers. Even if it turned, it would be to no avail: the faces of the turbaned men are hidden by rubber masks; coal filters clean their breaths. The whale may sing, but these men won't hear its song.

Balthazar squeezes closer, aware of Etta May shadowing his movements. He sees the children sneak through the gaps in the crowd, drawing towards Eleanor. It puts them on the front lines. Soon their little bodies are pushed up against the guns. Five steps from Eleanor, just as tight against the barricades, Livia stands, spreading her own Smoke. The flavours that come from her carry pain and the promise of revenge: they spread through the crowd like a new idea, leave it uneasy, wavering between emotions; the wind fickle as it rises, half turns, ebbs.

Balthazar continues pushing forward, wriggling between strangers. Etta May's bulkier form has trouble following.

"Where are you going?" she calls to him.

"To her." He points to Eleanor, standing in her bride's dress, bloodied at the hip and cinched under the bulk of the harness. Close to her now, he feels the full weight of her *presence;* her doubt and burden part of its texture and its force.

"She does not need us, Balthazar."

He half turns, finds Etta May close, her hand slipping into his.

A shout goes up, not immediately intelligible, and all at once the ranks of soldiers at the barricades thin out as more than half turn to follow whatever order has been barked at them. The Smoke masks may obscure their faces, but there is no mistaking the hasty relief with which they turn and rush away. They don't want to be standing here, threatening children. Those few who remain look uncertain, forlorn behind the household rubbish that serves them as fortification. Eleanor looks straight at them, steps forward, and wriggles her harnessed body through a tiny gap. A dozen rifles swivel to her, quiver as they observe her progress. For a moment it looks like she will be stuck, become part of the wall. Then she is through. The moment when she might have been shot has passed. Others follow, more forcefully than her, shoving aside what she slipped through, creating a gap within the barricade. The soldiers stand back. Many lower their rifles; a few are absorbed into the throng.

Balthazar and Etta May are about to follow when they notice a splintering. A single figure, yellow-haired, walking under a dark cloud, slips sideways and finds another way through. She does not join the throng heading down the pier but rather runs across it to where its inner edge meets the harbour water and disappears from view.

"Livia!"

Without saying anything else, Etta May begins to follow her. Balthazar, still holding Em's hand, agrees at once. Whatever it is Eleanor is hoping to achieve, they can have no role in it. It's down to her talent. Livia, on the other hand, is armed with nothing but her anger. Her, they may be able to help.

A quick dash carries them across to the far side of the pier. There, a steep flight of steps leads down into the water, the lowest steps blackened by seaweed and tide. Livia is nowhere to be seen.

"There! She's swimming."

Indeed, just a few yards from them, near invisible in the black water, Balthazar spies Livia's pale face, upturned, surrounded by the ragged halo of her floating hair. She is on her back and kicking herself along with her legs, her naked toes breaking the surface. Her left arm rises in a backstroke. The right is held rigid and upwards, holding something small and heavy; making sure it does not get wet.

"Quick," says Etta May.

"I cannot swim."

This stops Em in her tracks. "You cannot swim? Oh, Balthazar, how come you are so badly equipped for life?"

Etta May lets go of his hand. She has kicked off her shoes and is ready to go on alone when he stops her.

"Over there—by the promenade. Rowboats. It'll be quicker than swimming."

A few minutes later, they have run down to the bollards that stud the promenade and commandeered a ten-foot boat. Livia is lost to sight in the shadow of the pier.

It is Etta May who takes the oars. As it turns out, Balthazar cannot row either.

[6]

The harbour water is cold. The shock of its touch helps cool Livia's anger. It might be a purely physical reaction: her skin puckers, her mouth clamps shut, her Smoke must squirm through contracted pores. The swimming, too, helps to cool her head, for it is hard work. She has kicked off her shoes but left on most of her clothing. It is tugging at her now, and her right arm is useless to her, her hand thrust up and occupied. She dug through Charlie's things—found abandoned on top of a hillside—not to find a lover's note or private diary (though the latter exists and tempted her with its secrets). She dug for what she knew Charlie carried on all his travels, because for all his goodness, Charlie was not a fool. She found the gun was oiled and loaded; no shot had been fired since it was last cleaned. It changed nothing. She knows he has been murdered and she has been told by whom. She is swimming down the length of the pier to shoot the man who killed the one who taught her what it means to love.

It is not a long swim, some two hundred and fifty yards at most. All the same, Livia is tired by the time she reaches the end of the pier. She can see the lighthouse rise above. The cone of its light focusses on a scene invisible to her from this angle. The hull of the Company cargo ship is close, smells of rust and sea rot. Between the darkness of the night and the shadow of pier and ship, Livia is reduced to groping about herself. She is looking for a staircase comparable to the one that led her into the water but finds none. The fear grips her that she will be thwarted by so stupid a detail. Then her left hand finds the icy rung of a metal ladder bolted into the side of the pier. Her feet feel for further rungs beneath the waterline; finding them, she heaves her body out of the water and tucks the gun behind her belt. Then she begins to climb.

Near the top she stops, then peeks over the lip of the wall, trying to get her bearings. The pier is narrower here than it is near the shore, but even so it remains some fifteen yards across. At its very end, where the pier's wrist grows into its fist, it widens again to accommodate the bulk of the lighthouse. Its light is misused, shining down at an acute angle. It cuts in two the pier and creates two unequal zones. A sliver of darkness gives way without transition to a glowing field of light.

The field of light holds a wealth of things. Half the cargo ship's hull is bathed in it. A rope threads towards it, also in the light, and is held by a row of some thirty Company soldiers who have dropped their rifles at their feet and are engaged in a silent tug-of-war. Moving towards them, no doubt blinded by the brightness that engulfs this section of the pier, is the throng of children, Miners, farmers. Eleanor is at the front, uniting them with the threads of her Smoke.

Straddling dark and light stands a twisted, broken crane. The rope heaved by the soldiers still threads through its winch, but its arm has collapsed, its engine blown. The edge of the light runs through it like a blade, as though *it* were the thing that cut it down.

A few steps from the crane, in the thin sliver of pier that rests in darkness, shielded from the approaching mob by the long row of heaving soldiers and the base of the broken crane, stands a spare old man with lanky hair holding a leash that ties to him a faceless child. How small he looks, how insignificant. A pinch-faced everyman in drab, worn clothing. She knows his name, has learned it from Balthazar, and from a letter sent to her by Eleanor.

Livingstone.

And right behind him, in that same thin strip of darkness; risen by another rung, so that both her elbows are now on the pier; her foot wrapped around a rung of the ladder to make sure she does not slip: Livia herself.

Livingstone's assassin.

It does not bother her that he will never know who killed him. It is the child—masked, tied, *leashed*—that causes her distress. He carries the echo of another boy, ten years ago, whom she and her friends failed to free. Instead they consented to his use. The shame pulses through her even now. It conjoins with her anger, her grief; her body warming, smoking once again, wet, greasy smears.

They make the gun very slippery to hold.

The shot is not an easy one. Tools and debris litter this portion of the pier. A crate obscures the man from the waist down and reduces the masked child to little more than its head. Livia could climb up higher, attempt to sneak closer to the man. If she thought it feasible, she would walk right up to him, and hold the muzzle against the scrawny bit of bone that connects head to neck. Just to make sure.

She does not think it feasible, though. If he notices her he will duck; use the child as a shield; order soldiers trained at shooting to rid him of this amateur. No, better to act now. Livia levels the gun, stretches her arm out as far as it will go. Soothes her breathing. Cocks the hammer (it takes surprising force to slip it back). Trembles.

Shoots.

The noise shocks her, the force of the gun leaping upwards in her hand. It nearly makes her drop the gun. Ahead, the reaction is delayed. One moment she thinks she has missed her target. Then he doubles over, cut down at the waist. Next to him, in the bright world of light, the soldiers' final heave catapults something over the lip of the pier. It is large—the size of a steam engine, of a factory furnace—and surrounded by a wide-meshed net; comes up suddenly like a cork out of its bottle and slithers across twenty feet of pier, the soldiers falling hard upon their rumps. It is as though its weight has suddenly changed.

Inside the netting, attached to that darkness that glistens like a fisher-man's catch—a ball of black fish stunned to find themselves in breathless air—something *moves*. It is ugly, toadlike, wriggling between catch and netting; seems grown into the darkness of the nameless *thing*, yet is inde-pendent of it, too; wriggles then presses its black face into the mesh of the coarse netting so that eyes and nose and mouth are cut apart and bulge from separate casements. A cry of fear flies out a blackened mouth; the gaping panic of a rope-framed eye.

Livia knows the eye, the mouth.

She drops the gun and runs towards the creature without thought.

[7]

Timothy Angel is not stupid. Not an idiot, nor even stunted, underdevel-oped, half grown, dim. Different, to be sure. So different, in fact, that he does not care to speak in sound. His words are breath and colour; like magic spells they tip you into a world that scorns our grammar, a world that jumbles pronouns, i-you-he-she-mine-yours-us. He may be saviour or devil. But stupid he is not.

There's another thing that we must understand. The Angel is shy and full of pity. He believes in love, in play, in fate and signs. Oh, he is not naïve. He knows we are made up of wants that fast turn ugly; are made up of pain and needs first learned when we were snatched from our mothers' wombs. That all our lives we struggle to reconnect. That's where his pity comes

in. A man was brought to him, a man cut off from all communion. A cripple. The birds picked him, just as they had picked Timmy himself (and
what choice does he have but to think himself *picked,* he who is different from everybody else? and who can blame him for reading the world
for signs of purpose, he who's been given a gift without instruction?).
This man was—to a boy for whom all hearts had always lain wide open,
flayed—inscrutable. How was he not to think him lonely, lost, and sad?

Then, too, there was relief in it: with this stranger alone, the Angel could
slip his wings and hang up his halo. In the man's condescension, Timmy
saw the reflection of the relationship of other adults to other children and
through it—strange, exotic—the siren song of the mundane.

And then of course there was the sugar. It would be remiss not to mention its allure. That first lump offered revelation, there behind the closed
door of his mouth: an intense and selfish sweetness spreading on his palate, in secret from everybody else. It was, to a boy for whom all love had
always been communal, something like a mother's secret bedside kiss. A
boy not yet eleven. Is one to call him imbecilic for succumbing to a childhood opiate that still beguiles so many an adult?

First came the pity then; the pity and the sugar. Then came the mask, the
heavy hand seizing hold of Timmy's shoulder. Later, the wrist ties and the
leash; the cryptic whispers about the Heart of the Smoke.

This violence has not cancelled Timmy's pity, nor eroded his conviction that he is where he is meant to be; that the leash does nothing but tie
him to his approaching purpose. But Timmy now assumes the man is bad.
Being alone, incapable of Smoke, he has no way of airing his own evil: of
expressing and sharing it, of seeing its fever spread to others to return to
him adulterated, strange. He cannot see himself; cannot taste his anger on
a stranger's skin and find in it some cause for self-forgiveness. As such, he
cannot be saved.

As though they, too, have come to realise this, the birds have abandoned
the man and made a residence of the sinking ship. There, Timmy's purpose
has acquired shape and mass and colour. When the rock first emerges,
yanked from the hull by the crane's might, it staggers Timmy by its scale.
Then the crane bends in two and the soldiers are called to drag it from
the water (soldiers masked as Timmy is; also straining at some too-tight
leash).

Following the soldiers and soon filling the whole length of the pier, but
separated from Livingstone and the boy by the taut rope and the row of
pulling soldiers, there comes a crowd: not a mere assemblage of people

but a creature many-hued and many-limbed, bound together by its central need. Its Smoke unites it the way an orchestra is united by a score.

It is this shared and unifying Smoke that rouses the child, wakes in him a longing. He yanks, he strains, he wants to join the crowd. There is a woman up front, with a breast of steel and leather and a wet white skirt. It is to her that Timmy strains. The leash chokes his breath and fills his eyes with tears beneath the thick glass of their goggles. He cannot get away.

Then comes the shot.

It happens in the same moment that the rock leaps from behind the lip of the pier; that the soldiers fall in one great row, so it is as though it is they who have been shot and the rock that is the shooter. The bullet's noise is twofold: a bang and a hornet whistle. It passes Timmy's ear so close, he can feel the heat of its hard flight. It hits a piece of the crane ahead, striking sparks, and dies.

A shock then: his body is taken by surprise. It reacts. The child swings around—towards the close flight of the bullet, though of course it is long gone. Torque comes into play. The child's feet become a pivot. His arms— tied wrist to elbow and awkwardly stretched in front of him—a pendulum. Imagine a hammer throw, all energy bundled into the double fist formed by Timmy's lashed-together hands. He does not mean to hit Livingstone but Livingstone is in the way. A child four and a half feet high: the fists rising from beneath the level of his waist to a point near the height of his shoulders. They collide with Livingstone at the rotation's apex; catch him tidily, slightly rising still, between the skinny prongs of his two thighs. Right in the groin.

It cuts the man in two; bends him double as though on a hinge.

Next he knows, Timmy's leash hangs free. The boy turns around and starts running: towards the leather-breasted woman and her Smoke. Half-way there, his run crisscrosses with another's, perpendicular to his, aiming for the black rock that glistens in its net. Timmy pays it no attention. He slips between the row of fallen soldiers, stumbling a little on the water-slick rope. Two more steps deliver him into the woman's arms. Tied though his wrists are, his fingers still jump up and reach for his mask's buckles.

Her hands meet his there.

[8]

Eleanor understands.

Walking down the pier, a crowd of hundreds at her back, she has watched Livingstone command the soldiers. Lined up, pulling at the rope, they formed a wall of bodies between her and him, but there were gaps enough to catch glimpses of her uncle's servant. She saw his haggard face and the leash held in his hand; caught sight of the child, trussed up and gagged within his mask; heard the shot and saw—in the very moment the soldiers tumbled to the ground—Livingstone, too, double over, felled by an accidental, guileless blow; and held out her arms in welcome when the little body raced across the twenty steps of pier.

She understands that this child must be the "trigger"; that it is he—or whatever it is he can do—that her uncle sent Livingstone to find. She surmises, too, that the mask was put there with good reason, that there are dangers to the child's clear breath. As the little boy in front of her tears clumsily at the mask's buckles, she understands therefore that his hands and action must be stopped. Her own hands rise for just this purpose: to wrestle free his stubby fingers and restrain them gently, to hold him close and tell him that he must not be freed.

For the world's sake, he must not.

Then she looks into his eyes.

They are goggle-drowned, distorted, pressed into clefts by the puffy skin surrounding them; are embrasures, not "windows to the soul," unlit, half hidden, thickly draped. Need spills out of them even so. Her fingers touch his, hold them between hers, then let go and assist him with the buckles.

The world might go to hell. But this child must be allowed to breathe.

A moment later the buckles are loose, the mask is off. Behind him, the soldiers have picked themselves up and are raising guns. A scream sounds to the left—Livia!—but she is hidden by the hulking rock. Livingstone is on hands and knees, vomiting bile.

So much is happening, so much that is important. But between her hands, Eleanor cradles a smile. An ugly child, fat-cheeked, puffy-skinned. Smiling ear to ear.

You are safe, she wants to say. Before she can do so, he has hugged her and breathed a Gale into her skin.

In a heartbeat, half the pier is in its grip.

[9]

Balthazar is trying not to shout at Etta May. It is not her fault that she finds the boat awkward to row; nor can she do anything about the funny currents that disturb the harbour water near the pier. All he knows is that they will come late: that Livia has long arrived at the bolted-in ladder that was her destination; that she has a gun and is aiming it; that he cannot help her in whatever it is that she has planned. When the gun goes off, Etta May has brought them close enough so he can hook an arm through the pier's iron ladder, then pull the boat alongside. By the time he laboriously scrambles up the rungs, Livia has already disappeared from view. He pulls himself over the lip of the pier, not standing up but remaining on all fours; finds Livia's gun by accident as one of his hands presses down on it.

The moment he gains his bearings is the moment Eleanor slips the Smoke mask off the Angel's head. Closer by, he sees Livingstone, retching. Much of his body is obscured by things littering the pier, but the head is clearly visible. Balthazar shudders and aims the gun. He is not thinking clearly. His fingers feel clumsy and cold. Behind Livingstone he sees the rock and, pressed into its flank, two figures. He does not know whether they are embracing or fighting.

Then the Gale erupts. It happens downwind from them and is recognisable by an eruption of colour within the crowd's Smoke. What was thin and stolid before now becomes nimble, many-hued, playful, thick. The wind direction holds, the soldiers remain free of it: are cocking guns, awaiting orders. Balthazar tries to concentrate on the man who might furnish one.

How hard can it be to squeeze a trigger?

Then he becomes aware of a movement in the Gale. The child, Timmy, dashing full-pelt towards the rock. His arms outstretched, palms open. Eleanor is following him but Balthazar can see that she won't catch him.

If his breath reaches the rock—

If the wind turns now, for even a moment—

Balthazar swears and turns around the gun, so that the muzzle is now pointed at the child.

How hard can it be to squeeze a trigger?

[10]

Livia tears at the netting that holds rock and Thomas. Black teeth; barnacles upon his temple; an oozing growth there in his flank—she can see, of course, that there's something wrong. Still she does her best to discount it. There are urgent needs driving her that have no patience with infirmity. Livia needs to tell Thomas about Charlie and that she slew his killer with a gun. She needs to hold him breast to breast; feel his weight on her; be held. This is no time for Thomas to be other than he was.

So she focusses on the netting, slack now that the tension of the rope is gone, pulling at it with her modest weight and growing vexed at Thomas's passivity. At last the net splits open on the sharp ridge of some piece of metal and falls down around his ankles in black loops. Her hands rush to him, then her lips. They taste seawater on him and sweat, and a rank strangeness that is not quite Soot. Thomas hangs limp in this embrace: his mouth wide open and his eyes still filled with morbid fear. It is not fear of her, or of the noise that fills the pier, but a sightless, inward sickness. He is a man sleepwalking in a private nightmare, a mountain tied onto his back. She sees it, screams despair at him (it sounds a little like wild laughter), then pulls him closer and lets her body tell him about Charlie's death.

Preoccupied as she is, she does not hear the patter of little feet nearby.

[11]

Three steps from the rock, Timmy slows. It is the size of a shed perhaps; taller. Mussels, seaweed cling to it. Metal pipes and jagged shards of iron hull. The rock itself is coal black, ink black, a bottomless hole: it swallows the lighthouse's light and reflects nothing back. Timmy hears a voice on the far side of the rock—anguish? laughter?—and half rounds it, a gust whipping at his face. The woman with the harness-chest is close behind him, but absorbed in his Gale-quickened Smoke, she falters and stops. There: he sees it now, the source of the strange laughter: a man and a woman. She is blond and tired and very pretty. He is dark and grown into the rock. Not literally—not *quite*—but things connect him (seaweed, stringy like webbing). More than that: the rock's grown into him. The woman is holding him; her Smoke is very dark. It decides Timmy. Frowning, a little anxious, arms held wide at shoulder height, he steps up to the rock and folds it in his Gale's embrace.

Somewhere close, he hears the thunderclap of a second gunshot.

[12]

Livingstone's still on the ground and retching when the child hugs the rock and goes up in Smoke.

No, that's wrong. He was already Smoke-wreathed, already the nexus of a Gale of volatile emotion. Now, he goes up in hate. Yes, that's what it is. His chubby little hands touch the rock and *wake it*. It's like touching a torch to an ocean of gas. All that is solid melts into air. A vortex forms, as yet narrow, unfurls itself three leagues high into the sky. The rock has found life. Through Timmy. *In* Timmy.

It is the most beautiful thing Livingstone has ever seen.

And as Timmy steps away: as he turns his back on the rock and looks over at Livingstone—his almond eyes black and shining, filled socket-full with burning pitch—Livingstone sees the heart of the Storm move with him as though the rock has moved into his flesh. And all at once a new vision arises in Livingstone, so clear and powerful it is as though he sees it on a postcard, nicely framed by a printed black border. It shows him holding the grip of a leash, twenty feet long, the burning child straining at its end; shows him walking this child-turned-Storm the length and breadth of Britain until the very earth is black and barren at his feet. At this vision, threading through the sickness resulting from the boy's low blow, a wash of warmth pours through Livingstone such as he has never felt before. He is transported. It is as though he is ten years old again, and gladly hates the whole wide world.

Then something hits him (a boot? a pickaxe?) and turns this warmth to screaming pain.

[13]

Balthazar must shoot the child to save the day. Balthazar cannot shoot the child. He cannot do it while Timmy is still running; cannot do it when he stops and hesitates; cannot do it still when his small hands dig into blackness and something horrible unfolds, here upon the pier. As Balthazar balks and quivers, Etta May's sturdy figure folds itself around him from behind, embracing him, guiding his arms. Together (Smoke-bound, her breath in the nape of his neck) they swivel the gun ten, fifteen degrees. Together they pull the trigger. The effect is like kicking a man who is crawling on his hands and knees. The bullet slams into Livingstone's spare body and sends it tumbling across the pier.

Then the Storm twists and spreads to them, and all they know is hate.

(Nurse I)

[1]

"**E**at your porridge, Lord Protector. Still sulking, are we? Or is it that you want to die? You keep an old woman guessing. Has that blow to the head finally robbed you of your wits, or are you simply holding your breath? Waiting for the end?"

Lady Naylor holds the laden spoon a moment longer to her patient's lips, then drops it in the bowl. It is unappetising stuff, oat porridge made with water. There has been no one to deliver milk or any other food since Eleanor left. The Silent Keep stands all but empty; a nunnery whose every nun has flown. She alone remains to raid the sad remnants of the larder. Lady Naylor does not cook. She has been eating the same damn gruel that Renfrew keeps rejecting.

"I should just smother you with a pillow," she says now, as she removes said item and shakes it out, trying to redistribute the sweat-clumped down. Then she slips it back under Renfrew's head. "But I suppose you have as much right as anyone to see how it ends."

She turns to the window of Renfrew's study, into which she has moved, an armchair serving her as bed. She could have ignored Eleanor's request and headed north, of course. Towards the action. But it has proved difficult to leave this man, her enemy, to starve. More difficult yet to kill him. It has trapped her here, that and Eleanor's words, which the young man who fetched her after delivering the unconscious Renfrew to his bed repeated like a mantra: "Tell Lady Naylor I said so." The nerve of the girl! It was really quite admirable. And so she has been stuck here, waiting for news. When she tried the telephone, she found the line had gone dead.

"How will we learn? I don't suppose anyone will send us a pigeon. For all we know it might already have happened. The Storm may be on its way to us. Or Eleanor, triumphant. Riding bareback on a snow-white mare."

She snorts, turns back to her patient and notices that his hands lie folded on his blanket, that his lips are shaping words. Lady Naylor hastens to him, bends her ear, but can hear nothing.

"What now? Do you need water? Or are you praying, perchance? And if so, for what? For Livingstone's triumph or Eleanor's survival? You know you cannot have both."

She receives no answer and is not sure whether the sick man can hear her; whether he is trapped in phantasms conjured by his deranged mind. The thought brings with it another; lures her back to another sickbed, another madman, more encrusted in Soot than this one. She hesitates, then slips in next to him, pushing him aside on the narrow bed. They end up in close proximity, shoulder overlapping shoulder. Up close, Renfrew's body carries an acrid smell.

"My husband died alone. Did you know that? They took him from our home—this was before the Second Smoke, after I had been declared an enemy of the state—and placed him in a 'hospital.' When I finally found him, he was long dead. I think he must have starved."

She reaches over to Renfrew, takes his hand; shyly almost, a debutante at a dance.

"You were his student, Lord Protector. I remember his bringing you home. Oh, I thought you rather handsome. A little common in your manners. But burning with a special sort of flame."

Lady Naylor smiles at the memory. Then a noise startles her, the shrill ring of a chime. It makes her drop Renfrew's hand, though she snatches it up again at once.

"God, your bloody clock! It catches me out every time."

She laughs, genuinely laughs, her head thrown back and baring teeth.

"And here I thought it was the end of the world."

[1]

S mith is making excuses. He remains pallet-bound, too dizzy to rise
for any length of time, and complaining of a continual headache. It
has not affected his ability to speak, though. In the absence of any bodily
movement, he seems to think it important to give his tongue a good work-
out.

Through these extended soliloquies, the topic of his discourse remains
remarkably static. Nil. How "he had no choice, if you think about it"; "and
of course, he must have been upset, I'd just told him about the destruction
of his people." "It does show pluck, though," he will add later, for the ump-
teenth time, as though shouting down a dissenting opinion at a debate.
"Not just pluck—proper balls. Entrepreneurial spirit! Of course, he is inexperienced. Liable to piss away a fortune. I tell you one thing, though: a man
of pluck will always find another opportunity. That's how we are made.
And for all we know, it is *he* who is doing History's bidding and I was
merely in the way." He seems to be under the impression that the boy has
stolen his beetles to sell their spore to the Miners in the North. Grendel has
not had the heart to tell him otherwise.

Indeed, Grendel has hardly said a word. Instead he has listened to hour
after hour of declamatory nonsense with great patience and equanimity.
Only once in a while does he rouse himself to correct the Company man
on a nominal matter.

"It's Mowgli," he will say, "not Nil."

Smith will agree at once then babble on. He does not place much importance in names. All he wants is assurances that the boy was concerned for
his well-being before running off with his car. On this subject, Grendel
relates the exact truth.

"He himself stopped the flow of blood," he says. "And he instructed me to look after you."

This seems to please Smith no matter how many times he hears it. Often his eyes will brim up and he will reach over to briefly squeeze Grendel's hand with his own sweaty palm. The headache, it appears, has made him sentimental, or soft-brained. For a man robbed of his goods, his car, his future, he seems in remarkably good form.

[2]

Fortunately for Grendel, Smith's compulsive talk is interrupted by lengthy periods of sleep. In these intervals of silence, Grendel sits quietly, listening to the hum of the remaining beetles and for the quiet steps of the ghost. He has been visiting regularly; staying out of sight for the most part, though Grendel has caught a few glimpses of him from afar.

If Mowgli had not told him, Grendel would never have recognised Sebastian Aschenstaedt. The engineer and scientist was still a young man when he helped set off the Second Smoke. Grendel remembers him as excitable and self-absorbed. Now he is a wraith, inside and out, as though his very soul has worn thin. His science has decayed to alchemy, to whispered truth and totem objects: feathers, dead birds, photographs. Grendel understands he stole the latter from Smith; when Grendel last saw him, Aschenstaedt placed one of the photographs on the ground for Grendel to inspect, before disappearing back into the warehouse's shadows. It was, to Grendel's surprise, a picture of Mowgli taken in Grendel's own house. Aschenstaedt himself must have taken it at the time when Mowgli was infected. It appears the wraith has recognised Grendel and wishes to communicate across the chasm of his madness. Grendel does not hurry him. He has taken to walking around armed with a shovel.

This evening Grendel is uneasy, listening to the Company man's quiet snore. Smith got up at lunchtime and walked around. He had to stop after just a few steps, but these are clear signs that he is mending. Soon this service that Grendel is rendering his adoptive son—his one way of proving his love—will come to an end. He himself starts pacing around the warehouse floor and is drawn to the hole in the ground through which one can observe the beetles in their pit. There are not very many now, perhaps five dozen or so, though thousands of new cocoons have since been spun and will soon hatch. Whatever it is the beetles feed on, down there in their room, has mostly disappeared. The pit's walls and floor are curiously clean of Soot as though this, too, has been consumed. Mowgli told him that the beetles carry in them the seed of reason; a world in which our messy needs no longer spill out to pollute our neighbours. Grendel ponders this statement, curious to him given his past relationship with his son.

Then he turns around.

Despite the beetles' hum, he has long heard the shuffle behind him and is not surprised to find Aschenstaedt there, at five or six steps' distance, wearing his long, flapping coat. Grendel speaks unselfconsciously to him. It is like speaking to oneself. Speaks softly, for he does not want Smith to wake and hear.

"It's odd that something so"—he searches for the word—"*primitive* should bring the future. Creepy crawlies from the jungle. But I am sure Mowgli is right." He looks over at Aschenstaedt, cannot tell whether the man follows his words. "Perhaps in a world that does not smoke . . . perhaps he will find me easier to like." Grendel pauses, hoists the shovel to his shoulder, steps closer to Aschenstaedt. "My wife died and he blamed me. And really, he was a spiteful child. Always black with anger. I suppose it makes sense, given what you did to him. I tried to tame him through work, and when he screamed his Smoke at me, I did not react." Grendel shrugs his shoulders in his placid way, his neck crooked, his movements those of an old man. "He hates you, Mr. Aschenstaedt. You killed his people. Not personally, of course, but your men brought in the disease . . ." He stops, close now to the madman, or at any rate, close enough. "I think he wants me to kill you. It'd be another act of love."

Aschenstaedt reacts at last, bending double, before dropping down onto his hands and knees and stretching out his neck, like a feeding cat. For a full minute he holds still, before he grows distracted by a bird carcass sticking out of his coat pocket. He snatches for it, slices the bird open with a penknife he's been holding, then digs around within its entrails, muttering to himself in German. Grendel towers over him, the shovel raised like an axe above his shoulders.

He does not swing it.

"Leave," he says, the same quiet tones. "Don't come back. Disappear."

Aschenstaedt looks up, bird gizzards in his fingers; drops them, rises, shuffles away. Ten yards hence he turns, says something inaudible, then turns again and walks out the warehouse door.

Outside, he crosses the black plain of the docks all the way to the bank of the river. Birds are all around him and they distract him for a while. Then he remembers himself and methodically, folding each divested piece of garment into a neat square, strips naked. The socks—hole-ridden, stiff with Soot—come off last. Without pause Aschenstaedt steps into the water. He takes two or three breaststrokes until he meets the main current, then flips onto his back; stretches out arms and legs and lets himself float. The birds fill the sky above him. Gently, steadily, the Soot-thick Thames begins to flush him east, towards the sea.

Inside the warehouse, Smith wakes on his pallet and asks if there is news from the boy.

(Hilltop)

[1]

On the crest of the hill, the horses stop and will walk no more. They are steaming, a fine, dense mist. It rises out of their mouths and nostrils, from the froth-clotted fur of their necks and flanks. In the failing light it looks just like Smoke. *This is the time when I must whip them on,* thinks Mowgli. *All the way to their deaths.* He raises the stick that has served him as a riding crop. But he can't do it. The horses start shivering, and he slips off the coach box to rub them down. The sweaty froth soon hangs off his rag in fronds.

Ahead, he can make out his destination: the sea, the abandoned port, the pier-bounded basin of the harbour. He sees the hillside dotted with campfires; sees people moving. A lighthouse light has been switched on, facing inward, scooping a section of pier from out the gloom. A crane swings its arm and starts to pull. Mowgli is very close. But what is happening down there is happening right now; and he is on a hilltop, and his horses are spent.

He lost too much time. He did not know where he was going; time and again he had to ask people, many of whom were themselves heading north and west, drawn by a rumour, and just as ignorant about the way. When he entered Cumbria, the land itself wished to slow him, placing mountains in his way, forcing him to follow the irrational flow of the valleys. In his ear, sealed with wax against the racket of the beetles, he hears Smith's voice, lecturing him on Hegel. Mowgli, too, has made the mistake of thinking himself a hero.

He has not slept since he traded car for cart.

As he stands, overcome by his defeat, the wagon starts shaking by his side. At first he thinks it is the horses' shiver, working its way backwards, through harnesses and reins, into the wood and metal axle, until it rattles the boxes that rise from it in a precarious, rope-secured tower. Then he realises it is the beetles themselves that are making the boxes jump. Mowgli digs in his ears, scrapes out the wads of wax that he stuffed there in the hope for quiet. When he takes them out, he realises the beetles' noise has swelled to whole new levels. The air is thick with its drone. He places his palms on the boxes, feels the life inside: impatient, hopping, buzzing life. Shaking the very walls of its prison.

It has been a long drive, this journey north, and lonely. Mowgli used to hate being alone, bereft of a role, and action; afraid of his own Smoke. This time—smokeless; healed in some provisional way by his exposure to Smith, to Eleanor, to the truth about his people, however catastrophic—he used the loneliness to think. His childhood (the time *before*) remains inaccessible, fragmented into words and smells and patterns that are impossible to knit. Reason proved a surer tool to access his past. He has driven the length of England and asked himself what *must have been*.

His people were the first. This point is not important—it might even be wrong—but nonetheless it is impossible to think it without pride. The rock came down (did they see it? or did it predate their coming to the land?) and changed the forest. Say it is a sickness. It killed many of them, then grew into their organs. One day, they started to smoke.

But the forest fought back. The word is wrong—Mowgli knows this—but it is the only way he can think it: the trees whispering to themselves about their enemy; the birds and river fish, the snakes and spiders, pausing their eternal game of eating-being-eaten to hatch a plan of resistance. Just as the Smoke organs had grown in humans, the trees changed their bark; the spiders their webbing. And a beetle—across generations or in one spontaneous act of rebellion—developed its spore. It soothed the Smoke.

He imagines the people did not figure it out all at once. In fact, perhaps his chronology is wrong and the beetles were long in existence when the first humans started to smoke; living quite near to them (though not near enough). At any rate, they figured it out. Perhaps there was a year when the beetle grew overabundant and spread towards the village of his people; a year in which their density was such that the air was thick with their spore. It stopped the village's Smoke. Soon they started keeping the beetles as pets and fashioning them into necklaces; dipped their finger in their liquid discharge. Now the villagers stopped smoking altogether.

Unbeknownst to them, the change went deeper yet: the next generation was born once again without the organs necessary to produce the Smoke. Within a generation or two, Smoke became a story, something sung about in songs or scratched into the face of rocks hauled to the village from afar for the express purpose of turning them into memory. The beetle remained important; not *sacred* (the word is wrong, Mowgli feels, comes from this other world and rings of church bells) but *cherished*. Gestures remained: the wearing of the beetles and the touching of their rumps, the rubbing of the gums. A cultural memory as vague and as fragmented as Mowgli's own. As for the rock, lying there in the depths of the jungle: some part of it must still be there, providing a breeding ground for the beetles, pouring its otherness into the soil.

Beneath Mowgli's hands, a tower of crates chatters as though come to life.

Mowgli pulls a nail and lifts a corner, peeks inside the crate. But it is too dark to see anything. Then beetles start peppering the walls like pellets shot from a child's catapult. What was a buzzing turns into hail. A word rises in him, unpronounceable like so many of the others, a fragment of story, a drawing an elder scraped into the mud.

Mowgli comes to a decision.

He thinks the word means "swarm."

[2]

He opens the crates. It does not take long. All it requires is a single wrench of the crowbar at each of the lids. Then follows a drenching. Beetles: black-horned, fur-adorned, in this, their swarm state, pour out like liquid, rubbing limbs, clapping wing-cases, stretching pale translucent wings. Eight-legged Reason, many-pincered, freed at last. Soon the hilltop is covered in them, gorse and heather turning yellow-black. There may be half a million of them now: they must have bred further in their crates. Cocoon silk is stuck to half of them like tufts of cotton candy. The horses whinny at the sight. Only exhaustion keeps them from raw panic. The noise is exquisite. A smell in the air like rotting leaves.

They fly. There are pioneers: individual beetles who raise their heavy bodies on too-thin wings and hover awkwardly two feet up from the ground, swaying, falling, arresting themselves. Then the whole swarm rises as one. The eye capitulates before their multiplicity; they cease to be beetles and become a dark horizontal smear within the air. Below, in the hard light of the lighthouse, a fuse has been lit, an open flame touched to tar. A Storm unfurls, rooted in the rock; stands in the sky like a line drawn to split in two the far horizon.

Its tilted mirror image—soon as wide as the Storm is high—gathers, hovers, stretches out. Then it flies to meet it with the clumsy speed of airborne chickens, hastening to feed.

[1]

All is hate.

The Storm is a vortex standing in the sky. At its base, anchoring it in a double funnel, are a rock and a child. Even here, at the anchor points, it is rapidly gaining width and has spread to engulf the pier; has disregarded the direction of the wind and jumped from body to body, along connections pre-forged by the child's Gale.

The air is wet with blackest Smoke.

It fills the soldiers' gas masks and overwhelms their crude filters; blinds their goggles, so they rip them off. Most don't bother with their rifles. The rage that grips them has little use for bolts and triggers; calls for tearing limb from limb. Near the rock, one soldier is less picky about his tools. He turns, clutching his rifle barrel like a spear, and jams its bayonet from underneath into the arch of skin formed by his neighbour's jawbone; jams it so deep, it breaks off against the inside of his skull.

[2]

All is hate. The crowd catches it, Eleanor's followers, the children and pilgrims and Miners; the women prisoners turned pirates; the fishermen and farmers who were drawn here by their curiosity. A crone of eighty charges at a soldier, buries weak teeth in the flesh of his cheek; blood spreading on her sunken cheeks like rouge. He rips her off him and—his face gaping—crushes her skull with the heel of one boot. Beside him, a Miner turns a fallen gun into a club, then shoots a hole in his own intestines when his wild swing sets it off. The child next to him is tearing out clumps of her own hair. Her name is Julie.

She is eleven years old.

[3]

All is hate. It chokes Etta May, the placid one, fills her deep-bosomed chest with rage. There she stands, arms wrapped around Balthazar, a smoking gun in their shared fist. When the Storm finds her blood, she bursts into action. A yank and a push send Balthazar sailing across the lip of the pier and down into the black sea.

(Does she do it to preserve him before the Storm swallows the last of her kindness? Or has she remembered that he cannot swim?)

The gun is a hammer-weight in her now solitary fist. In front of her there lies a crippled man whom she will delight to kill.

[4]

Six steps from Etta May (twelve from the soldiers, and twenty from Julie, tearing open her own scalp) stands Eleanor, in the eye of the Storm. She has been here before. Almost. The last time, her gums were rubbed in bee-tle spore—not quite enough to withdraw her from the world of Smoke but enough to shield her, buy her time. Also, that first Storm had already been waning; it had found too little sustenance at sea. Back then she rose to meet it; drank it from the air. In her mind she pictured that internal silo, familiar to her from a thousand childhood self-negations; the place in which she locked up pain. An iron tower, thirty feet high: modelled on the technical drawing of a grain elevator bin that her uncle had amongst his scientific papers. Her child-self seized upon this picture; planted the bin upon a barren field. That's where she led the sea-Storm; shut it in as best she could. The remaining shreds of hate she converted into something else. Mowgli had been there with her, had been raging at her, *wanted* her (was ashamed of it afterwards: of the wanting more so than the rage). She let the Storm unlock some of her own wants. They bit each other in what followed, never hard enough to draw much blood.

Now, too, the Storm is here. There is no Mowgli and no beetle's spore. This time she does not watch it approach from afar, staining the horizon, chasing them across the ocean, the ship engine shivering under her feet. Instead, she stands in the Storm's thickness, in between its twin hearts.

This time, the Storm has a face, a sweet, podgy, big-cheeked face, ten years old and smiling.

Him then. She cannot *drink* this Storm, cannot picture a cup that would be deep enough. But the boy she can see and beckon; she can show him the silo in its winter field. Leather belts have grown, ivy-like, upon the silo's outside; iron buckles; ribs of steel. Its door stands open, though, and in the zero time between two heartbeats (while the gas masks are still filling up with darkness; while a bullet flies between the muzzle of a gun and a smiling Livingstone, warmed as he is by his visions of a future hell), Eleanor tugs him through, the boy, then slams the door shut behind the two of them. It leaves them in the silo's darkness amongst the smell of chaff and fermentation. *Rage in here,* she says or thinks; *fill me up and drown me if you must.* For a moment the child is still, sniffing the moist air.

Then he laughs.

It tears the silo open the way a shell bursts a mud-obstructed barrel, splitting the walls and blowing off its roof. Letting free all that which lay caged.

Now Eleanor, too, is feeding the Storm.

[5]

All is hate. Not far from Eleanor, Anne-Louise, the French engineer turned pirate captain, is fighting with a woman with whom she had shared bread and berth for two whole years. Resentment marked the time, concerning morsels pinched and rations ill divided, and national prejudice so deeply anchored that it now pours out along with ill-remembered childhood hate. They have gone to ground, weaponless; have punched and scratched and bitten. Now Anne-Louise's hands are on the other's throat. She squeezes with her thumbs, trying to press the Adam's apple back against the hard ridge of her spine. Beneath her, her enemy writhes and kicks her knees into Anne-Louise's back, breaking a rib and bruising the flesh above her kidneys.

The kicking will stop only when the woman is dead.

[6]

Farther out in the harbour basin, the waiting warships catch the Storm. On the bridge of the closer of the two, the captain watches its approach. He's an Oxford man, forced into colonial service by family debt. More recent debts, acquired at the racecourse, have turned him into a Company employee. The Storm flicks across the harbour basin. He breathes it in, shudders, then whips around to dash his head against a sharp-edged steel protrusion jutting from the wall. A moment later he detaches himself, backs off, then smashes the burst-open pumpkin of his face once more into the self-same spot now marked for him in gore. Belowdecks, a crazed sailor cuts open a barrel of petroleum, then stills his agitated hands enough to strike a match and drop it in the puddle.

[7]

In the water, at the base of the pier, and ignorant of the impending explosion, floats Balthazar, caught between two kinds of drowning. Whenever the sea closes over his head and his body sinks into the promise of a chilly grave, the bulk of the water insulates him briefly from the hatred of the Storm. As fear replaces hate, he starts a mad thrashing and claws his way back to the surface. Now he breaches, swallows air and rage, and pours it into a mad swing of his fist at the corpse of a soldier freshly rained down from the pier, then sinks entangled in this corpse's deadweight back down beneath the surface of the sea, where the rage is once again leeched from his body and his old legs grow more tired with each struggle up, for air.

[8]

Eleanor is being eaten. The Storm has burst her silo of old pain and emptied it; threaded her into the fabric of its rage. Now it digs deeper, splits open the silo's foundation, there to find a well. And down it dives: consumes her, dredging her, that sea-deep reservoir of all her submerged passions; sucks her up as though with a straw, until all of her is emptied out, absorbed into itself.

All of her?

No, not quite. Ten leagues deep the Storm reaches, down and down. But at eleven leagues there floats a little bottle with a scroll in its corked neck, a scroll that spells out "*I.*" The Storm reaches for it (pudgy child's hands) but it keeps slipping from its grasp. It frustrates the Storm. It rages in her, tears her open sole to soul.

[9]

Hidden from Eleanor by the bulk of their enemy and shelter, Livia and Thomas remain leaned into the rock. Their embrace is intimate. She has stuck her hand into his seeping side: like a murderer with a knife; like Thomas's doubting namesake testing his saviour's flesh; like Adam's Eve trying to claw her way back into that bloody rib. It is as private a touch as any invasion of another's body; connects the pangs of birth to sex to surgery. He stands it coolly, his hands clamped to her skull. He is not crushing bone but holding firm, fingers spread like starfish.

The part of him that's rock is gentler than the man.

[10]

A little boy is the centre of it all. It was his breath that woke the rock. Livingstone saw it as possession: saw the child as a two-legged Storm, an angel turned demon, a thing to march around the world on his avenging leash. Scourging it.

Livingstone was wrong however. The child is not possessed. When Timmy touched the rock, he opened himself up to it the way he has opened himself to everything and everyone since the day he was born in the thick of a Gale. He has spent his entire life without barriers, has never learned to lock the door. The Storm is not occupant but guest.

It is a new situation for both parties. A chance to talk?

[11]

Livia's fist is black with gore. What is it she is rummaging for, down in that open flank rimmed with hard rock-growth? Is she trying to kill the man she loves?

Of course she is. The Storm demands it.

There is something else there, too, however, that she pours into the cut where rock meets Thomas: a raging grief the Storm's made nameless but that retains the image of a waterlogged corpse with copper hair.

The man who once was Thomas receives it, heeds it, feels it spread within his blood.

[12]

Talk?

Surely the word must be a mistake. Rocks do not speak. They have no brains with which to shape concepts; no breath to articulate themselves in sound; no limbs to wave around in order to form signs.

A simile then: old Homer's trick.

The way a fungus grows into stone, fusing with it, dissolving minerals and turning them into itself . . .

The way a tattooist's ink is poured into the skin, staining the pores, one by one, so that ink and skin can no longer be thought apart . . .

The way we eat food, taking it into ourselves, dissolving it into constituent parts through the acid of our stomachs and the filtration system of our bowels, turning it into bone of our bone, flesh of our flesh, while we ourselves serve as food for other (smaller, meaner) mouths . . .

That's how the rock speaks.

[13]

Timmy listens.

While screams and murder spread along the pier; while Balthazar takes his first full gulp of salty water; while a ship goes up in oily flames and Eleanor screams as she is picked apart down in her depths; while Livia holds what is left of the last of her two husbands, in arms that cannot distinguish between love, grief, rage, Timmy listens.

It costs him something, changes him. All talk is contagion. We take into ourselves what is not ours. It reshapes our thoughts and forces reaction; cannot be unheard. Once a message is received, there is no way of going back, to innocence, *before*. All talk is contagion.

Understanding's worse.

The rock is far from home and all alone.

[14]

On the eastern horizon, in the hills, invisible in the night-dark, a cloud is forming. If it weren't for the shouts and screams, one would hear its buzzing. From afar it looks as angry as the Storm.

[15]

A lonely rock. A rock in a strop, abandoned in this pram we call our home, given to tantrums of blind panic.

Is it conscious then? Does it have intelligence? Words fail. If there is an analogy it is not to man or mammal. To a clever fish perhaps, an octopus; a brood of geckos. A bacillus that has gone to school. Not *one,* that's wrong, nor yet quite many. Most certainly not a hive. God might be like that, come to think of it, one and three, flesh-not-flesh. A medieval mystic might have an easier time approaching it than someone from the age of electricity.

The rock is something that we cannot know.

But then of course, the problem is mutual. The rock does not know us either. Its only language is the language of biology. It has no concept of sickness; infection is its mode of speech. It has been sleeping in its bed of Himalayan ice, insinuating itself into the nearly lifeless world around it, converting microorganisms, trapping dust. Imagine its dreamer's joy at the first mushroom springing from its flank; at ice crystals adapting to a chemistry that cannot, must not be; at its own slow transformation.

Adulteration holds no fear for it.

Isolation does.

And then it woke. Timmy roused it. It found itself surrounded by a mob attuned to its speech if unprepared for its volume. For we were already changed: the rock's sister saw to this, that thing in the jungle, along with the laws of conquest and trade that make a (somewhat nasty) village of this world. It had seeded us already; had crept into the part of us most like it, the seat of our wants. We were made ready for its speech.

It woke, raised its voice—in shock, dismay—released the pure cry of its germ speech; then waited (*with bated breath,* though it does not breathe; *with the blush of a bride,* though it knows no gender) for response. For someone to *touch* it. To corrupt it in return.

Instead we started to kill each other.

How was it to know its cry was a blow, its touch a violation; that the words it slipped so eagerly into our blood called forth in us nothing but hate?

[16]

Now, though: the boy. A walking Gale; a conduit for speech.

There's something else, too, just as significant. An irritation, analogous to an itch. Not near the centre (one never itches there) but at the tip of the nose, on the side of a toe: there, at the rock's periphery, at the edge of its being, lies that bit of the world most recently absorbed. It whispered to it in its sea-rocked dreams. The thing that was once a young man—a revolutionary; a hero!—is clinging on to someone he can only half remember. Both are a part of the Storm now; part of its scream.

Still: in their embrace, in their violent, ugly Smoke, there is a flavour running counter to the hatred. The rock feels it, feels it *in itself* (its only realm of knowledge), and paws at it with wonder.

A hesitation, a flicker, runs through the Storm.

[17]

A flicker runs through the Storm.

It is too subtle yet to interrupt the orgy of violence. One would have to retain something, some sense of self, to detect it. Only Eleanor does. From the bottom of the well of her being—eleven leagues deep, a grimy message in a bottle bobbing around her head—she stares up towards the distant disk of sky above and sees it.

Then Timmy is there. He's a good foot shorter than her, and yet the way she sees it he looks down at her, pushing his face and upper body down into her well. He reaches for her, first with Smoke, then with pudgy arms and pudgy fingers. She tries to avoid him, wants to smash his face and rip his hair, wants to punish him for what he's done. He slips down to her, into her well, then reaches clumsily for that bottle with its secret scroll. She wants to throttle him, stomp on his fingers, break his legs. She scoops up the bottle, cradles it against her bosom, finds the harness there, hard as a shell. Then (the lull makes it possible, that hesitation in the Storm) she takes hold of something in the child—a *look,* a puppy-pleading in his Smoke—and suddenly understands what it is he wants. With haste and trembling fingers—before she can think better of it; before the hate returns with all its might—she slips out the cork and lifts up the bottle.

She offers herself: climbs out of the well back onto the pier, away from those childhood pictures in her head, the burst-open silos and sealed messages from *Treasure Island;* opens herself up to the Storm.

And finds she cannot breathe.

[18]

It's the harness that is choking her. Unbeknownst to her, unnoticed in her struggle to hold out against the Storm, blindly marshalling old defences, her fingers have turned over and over the screw that grows from her breast, crushing her ribcage, emptying her lungs. Now she tugs at the screw, fumbling for the little catch that she knows Renfrew's design makes impossible to reach for the harness's wearer, until Timmy draws her hand away and by cleverness or chance presses down on the awkward little lever that offers release.

The next moment—while her lungs gulp air and the Storm reaches for her, a tentativeness now to all its movements—she feels the child tug at her wrist.

She resists him (two tugs, three), then looks past him and comprehends his destination; walks hand in hand with him to where Livia stands cradled in an embrace she shares with Thomas and the rock.

All at once the rock falls silent. The Storm stands pale and frozen in the sky.

In the sudden silence one can move, can think.

[19]

They form a circle. The rock is too large to be surrounded by them but there is no need. Thomas still sticks to it, like a moulting crab dragging its half-discarded shell. He is their centre. Livia won't let go of him, not with the hand stuck in his flank (stemming the bleeding now, not rummaging within the wound). Eleanor wrests free the other hand, threads it through her fingers; takes Timmy's hand and feels his Smoke connect them; and sees his childish hand in turn reach up to Thomas's arm where rock-mould stains his skin. The Storm stands around them water-pale. They grow transparent to one another, each feeling-thought passed around like a bowl of cherries from which everyone must partake.

How stupid, thinks Livia, irate and spent. *Like a bloody game of ring-a-ring-o'roses.*

Thinks Eleanor.

Thinks Thomas.

Ring-a-ring-o'roses! thinks Timmy.

(The rock does not *think*.)

[20]

Out over the pier, the Storm hangs suspended. It does not put an end to all violence, not at once. Every man, woman, and child remains connected, as by a Gale. Wounded and hurting, shocked by what they've seen and done, their Smoke is base and dark. But it is their own anger now, their own shame, not the Storm's unbearable screaming; and threaded through it there are other, subtler passions. Colour erupts, as yet in tender shoots, but undeniably so.

The transformation is faster near the centre of the Storm, where tendrils of calm link the group gathered in a ring to all the others who surround them. It is not insignificant perhaps that this section of the pier remains bathed in a clean circle of light. Even blinkered by rage, the eye recognises a stage when it sees one. Curiosity has a deep hold on our passions. Row by row, attention begins to fasten on that drama played out without gesture or word.

Only at the outer edges of the pier—around the barricades and up the hill—is this focus disrupted by the chitin buzz of an approaching cloud. But even there the crowd turns their backs on the noise and stares inward.

Four actors and a rock.

Shadow-sketched onto the pier.

[21]

An inner drama; it is shared by hundreds, but only in their breasts. Mute and free of gesture. How is one to represent it? Balthazar would enjoy this problem—were he not drowning, salt water in his throat.

So then. *A blank stage painted white.*

Or: *A tiled box of a room, the ceiling too low to stand up straight, the tiles glowing Prussian blue.*

Or: *A stage so cluttered with debris—with furniture and garden waste, industrial tools and marble busts—that one can hardly see the actors for all the junk.*

Or: *A janitor's basement: a worktop and a chair, a mop and bucket, a dirty oilcan; the flicker of an incinerator in one corner. Against the wall, as though left over from an earlier set, a piece of Eleanor's silo, warped and rusting. Rivets one inch wide.*

Yes, that will do.

There, in this cellar, positioned just a little off-centre in deliberate provocation to the audience's need for symmetry, stands a ring of actors, two women and a child, arms spread wide and holding hands. There are ashes in their hair.

(In some productions—those with a taste for the maudlin—there is a third adult, a male, covered in a bedsheet, a piece of pig's lung crumpled in the palm he shares with Livia.)

At the centre of the ring, barely spanned by the outstretched arms, there stands a round ceramic bathtub filled to bathing depth with tar.

And then, coming from somewhere hard to pinpoint, from beneath the stage perhaps or high above it: a voice. Not a general's voice, booming and certain; not the stage whisper of conspiracy. Thomas's voice, calm and normal. Somewhere hiding in it (at the end of words; in the tongue tap of his Ts) some other voice, also his but hoarse from weeks of screaming. Singing ring-a-ring-o'roses; singing it badly, it must be said. The figure of Thomas soon follows the voice, the body clam-studded, a bloom of black-and-sulphur barnacles outlining the swirls of his facial mark. He ducks under the ring of arms and hands, and climbs into the tub. Something strange happens then. The tub must be deeper than it seems, stage magic straining the rules of physics, for despite remaining standing in the tub rather than lying back, Thomas's body disappears up to the neck. The tar is a black collar tucked tight under his chin.

He stops singing, looks around himself, frowns.

Come, he beckons. His hand pats the surface of the tar, raising little ripples of welcome.

It is Livia who reacts first. She gathers up her skirts, steps over the thigh-high rim, almost losing her balance, then sinks in deep on the other side, the tar almost level with her mouth. Now Eleanor climbs in beside her. The addition of another body spills tar across the rim of the tub and forces Livia, shorter than the others, to hold on for support.

Timmy is last. He clambers over the rim as though it were a railing; hops in, arse-first, creating new spillage, then clings to Eleanor lest he sink.

(The ghost, if he's there, climbs in along with them, white sheets growing dark and heavy, pulling him down.)

"Talk to me, please." Again, Thomas's voice, hoarse, uncertain. "Take me in."

This time it is Eleanor who reacts first. She nods, passes Timmy on to Livia, and in a single fluid movement, submerges in the tar. Livia soon follows, then Timmy, then Thomas himself.

Then nothing: the matte oval of a tar-black surface, mocking the audience with its opaque blankness. A bubble rises in it, another, a stream of breath exhaled. The minutes tick past, quite literally so, the sound of a clock projected onto the stage, daring us to hold our breath.

There is no telling what is going on, beneath.

At last a face breaks the surface. It is soon followed by the others. Dipped *in oily black they are indistinguishable, their hair solid cowls of tar, their features blank and smooth.*

Then one face leans back into the liquid, until the small, solid body attached to it rises to the surface and floats, deadman-style, between the others, and from its mouth and chest erupts a sound so powerful that it soon forces its own echo.

All talk is contagion.

There is nothing quite so infectious as a child's untrammelled laugh.

[22]

Out on the pier, the change is both felt and seen. The Storm stands still and colourless, water in a glass. It has turned into pure connective tissue, without content of its own. The intensity of the connection is overwhelming, almost a violence in its own right. Man, woman, and child—attacker and victim; violator and violated; the wounded, the dying—each finds the other embodied in themselves. The sense of loss is just as devastating as what is found.

For a moment longer, the connection carries no trace of the rock. It has withdrawn, negated itself; cancelled any self-expression.

Now it inches slowly from its hole.

Into the colourless Smoke that cloaks the pier like a viscous dome, there threads a colour. It is a new colour, this; *unearthly,* a colour never seen before by human eyes; is passed on glibly by the optic nerve to tease the brain with its impossibility. *Yellow,* perhaps.

But also somehow very blue.

One moment the colour is on the outside: a whisper of rock speech, spreading through the air. The next moment it is on the *inside,* a trace of something strange slipped into one's blood, one's glands, one's flesh. There is disgust and fear within the crowd, as at the discovery of a tumour; the instincts scream to *cut it out.* Dismayed, they—for they are a collective still, entangled in their every need and want—reach for it and, in the very act of plucking at it, open themselves further to its touch. Once touched, a memory flickers, collective and universal, from earliest infancy, to that moment of first abandonment when the newborn reaches for the warmth that should be there beside its skin and finds it gone; to the boundless relief when the child reaches again and finds a body there, a touch, a heartbeat, and a voice.

The whole pier starts to cry.

[23]

(Afterwards, some of the people who were there will swear they saw the rock, too, shed a tear. A weeping god. Postcards will be sold with bad trick-effects, superimposing a misty face onto the sky, tears rolling down its cheek, rich sooty black. Money will be collected for a basalt statue to commemorate the event, and will promptly be embezzled. The statue itself will never be made.)

The whole pier starts to cry.

[24]

And then the beetles are there.

The rock does not flinch from them. If anything, a note of welcome threads through Smoke and crowd. These beetles, after all, are the rock's nieces, a piece of this world altered by the germ-speech of its twin. The note of welcome does not shift even when this cloud of children settles on the rock and starts to feed. And soon—with every bite of every little mandible, and with the spread of airborne spore—the hyper-quickened Smoke connecting those standing on the pier begins to clear. And with it clears the touch of that strangeness that they felt within their skins, until the world is reasonable again and all that remains is the disgusting sight of a mound of beetles eating, copulating, birthing even as they feed.

Within minutes, the weight of all the beetles overbalances the rock. It reels then falls, rolls, suddenly made light, across the pier, and tumbles into the harbour, where it floats under an ever-shifting blanket of ten thousand chitin backs. Some, overgorged, drop away dead or dazed and float upon the harbour waters surrounded by little slicks of black. The birds dive into the water and feast on their plump carcasses.

Just then, a final gunshot rends the silence of the pier.

[25]

The shot is Etta May's. It is not the first that she has fired. In the rage of the Storm she pulled the trigger several times, trying to annihilate that man positioned closest to her, retaining perhaps some understanding that he is her enemy. Livingstone. Her aim was bad, her fist too firm around the gun, her whole arm shaking with hate. Only her first bullet—the one she fired when still sane and Balthazar shared with her the heavy burden of the gun—hit and shattered the man's pelvis.

In the brief moments after the Storm went quiet and she became as one with all the pier, the gun hung forgotten. Livingstone—the only one untouched by the Storm, deaf to the whisper of this visiting god—might have escaped then, or intervened, but the wound was too serious for him to attend to anything other than his pain. Now reason has returned to Etta May and told her there remains a bullet in the pistol's chamber. Her heart is beating in her breast. She, the placid one, wants justice and revenge. She has no eyes just now for the swarm of beetles, feeding, copulating on the rock; treads heedlessly upon gorged and fallen specimens; does not wonder at her lack of Smoke as she places the barrel near Livingstone's head.

He looks up briefly, daring her, but she remembers only the loud bang and then the blood.

Behind her, a wet, bedraggled Balthazar pulls himself up the iron ladder that saved him in the end from drowning. Coughing and spluttering, he clears the lip of the pier where beetles crawl so thickly they cover its stone.

Two hours later, Mowgli walks onto the scene and pushes through the crowd.

He comes as its saviour.

Nobody cheers.

[1]

They are caring for the wounded. Eleanor has taken charge. Who else? Livia is busy with Thomas, who has lost some piece of himself in the past few hours and sits slumped on the ground. Etta May stands arguing with Balthazar, converting the weight of her relief and guilt into bickering. Timmy sits in a circle with some other children, playing with beetles. Everywhere people are standing, staring at one another, digesting the memory of horror and connectedness; of the unearthly sadness of the rock. It all seems distant already. Yesterday's dream. There is no Smoke. All emotion is locked away in individual bodies, separate and unknown. The shock of it has silenced people. It has not registered yet that, from a certain perspective, they might be said to have won.

Anne-Louise is helping Eleanor. Together, they have organised the Company soldiers, some of whom carry rudimentary medical supplies. There is no thought now of skin shades, of hierarchy or sides. They have stood together on this pier. The surviving white officers have ripped off their signs of rank. Together they are stilling bleedings, setting bones. So immersed is Eleanor in her work that she does not at once notice Mowgli standing next to her. He's just another brown face; looking confused. Gaunt with exhaustion. Handsome for all that.

Beetles are perching on his hair.

Then the stare of the soldiers around her urges her to look again. It appears they don't recognise this stranger; he is not one of them. Her heart leaps then, even before she has quite turned her head; the knowledge flooding her that Mowgli is *here*. Anne-Louise senses what is happening and takes the bandages from Eleanor's hands.

"Go."

A moment later Eleanor has risen and drawn him apart, from one crowded section of the pier to another. There is no privacy here. She reaches for his face, then grows conscious of the blood upon her palms and drops them again. He looks older, thinner, sterner. Some of the old shiftiness is gone from his face.

"I am sorry I came too late," he says to her, looking around at all the wounded. And, "Why are you still wearing that damn thing?"

It makes her a little angry, that, and at once makes her wish he could see her anger; could feel it in his blood. "All these beetles—" she says, incoherently.

"They swarmed. I think they will continue swarming, now that they have eaten. Their spore is in the air. It's everywhere. And it'll spread."

He hesitates now, aware perhaps that she won't like the words that come next. "We're free, Eleanor. Smith was right. The Age of Reason."

He does not wait for a reply but steps close instead, the protrusions of her harness digging into his chest.

Eleanor cries as they kiss. Without Smoke she cannot parse whether it's from happiness or grief.

[2]

They return to the Keep. Minetowns is closer, but Eleanor must know whether her uncle remains alive. Balthazar and Etta May accompany them, as does Timmy. It means a parting of ways: Livia and Thomas (turned inward, his face still marked by barnacles, in his side a wound scabbed over with Soot) go west with the Miners. Anne-Louise and many of the women who made up the pirate crew also head to Minetowns, to taste a version of freedom that already belongs to the past. The air is filled with buzzing; everybody is wearing scarfs or caps to keep the beetles out of their hair. It is only fifty miles south that a few of the people who travel with them break into stuttering Smoke. But when they arrive at the Keep, some beetles have beaten them there and are crawling on its walls. Every tree and bush around them is blooming with black silk cocoons.

The Keep is near-abandoned. They find Renfrew alive but in an irresponsive stupor. His body cannot retain enough food. Lady Naylor seems content to nurse him. She accepts the story of the rock as though it were a lie made up by naughty children. Within days, however, she has captured a few beetles and hung them in a birdcage above Renfrew's bed.

"It disquiets him when he soils himself," she explains. "This way he won't."

Eleanor is grateful for Lady Naylor's help but finds it hard to spend time with her; there is an undercurrent of resentment in the aristocrat, at her own insignificance. On Mowgli's urging, Eleanor has finally taken off her harness. Without its armour, she feels smaller somehow, vulnerable. As more and more beetles drift south, eating any dark Soot they can find and in the process cleaning the prison ships in the harbour to an odd shine, their spore once again begins to suppress all Smoke. The water in the bay, meanwhile, is turning darker. Nobody knows why that is.

Within a week Mowgli leaves her again in order to "see what happened to Smith." He returns only a few days later, filled with a sense of mission: he and the Company man will travel east, to India, and deliver them the beetle; his foster father will accompany them. Eleanor has told Mowgli that Miss Cooper, too, has headed east with her store of inoculant. Smith's goal is to "pull the rug from right under her feet," by delivering the product more cheaply. Mowgli's motives for the journey are harder to pinpoint. He has mingled with some of the sepoy soldiers and now wishes to "free the Indian people" from "Empire and Smoke"; and he seems drawn to a place where his skin will no longer mark him out as different. Perhaps he thinks that India can furnish him with a surrogate home, against all the odds. Above all, however, it is Eleanor herself who is driving him away. Both of them are acutely aware of her struggle to accept the smokeless world he has unleashed. Their good-byes are passionate but brief. Smith squeezes her hand in farewell. He vows he will return "her sweetheart" safe and sound, and advises her to plan for a lavish wedding. Then they board the Company warship Smith has somehow contrived to charter and Eleanor is alone once again. One month passes, two. Renfrew is in a coma but continues to live. Finding enough food is a problem, but Eleanor is reluctant to leave the Keep as long as he is alive. One by one, the few dozen people who travelled south with her also leave. They have homes to go to.

Soon only Balthazar, Timmy, and Etta May remain.

[3]

"More letters! Courtesy of the Minetowns International Postal Service. *International,* ha! And will you look at the stamp they have dreamt up? A spade and a hammer crossed on a purple field. If they crawl any farther up their own arses, they will commission a new national anthem, 'In Praise of Toil.'"

"Is it from Livia?"

"Who else? I am surprised she writes to me, not to you."

"You are easier to write to, Balthazar. She and I stood too close, back on the pier. We held hands and communed with a rock. I doubt we will find need to speak ever again . . . So, what does she say?"

"Wait, let me finish it first. God, what a scrawl she has—very aristocratic. And the way she puts things. Clearly but without much poetry. It makes me think of her mother."

"Well?"

"Beetles! Beetles everywhere. They are still swarming, up in the hills. There must be millions of them now. Feeding on every patch of dark Soot they can find. Cleaning up town. Now, she writes, you can see what was Soot and what is just muck. And everyone has stopped smoking. It's put paid to Downtown—there's no point to it anymore—and has killed off half of Minetowns' jokes. If they stop farting, too, the other half will go."

"It's not funny, Balthazar. A lot of people will be desperately confused. And I worry for those children who were born in the Smoke. They must feel utterly lost without it."

"You just wait until they meet the next generation! I wonder how many of them will be born without any Smoke organs. Our tales of Smoke will be fairy tales to them. Until they go somewhere without beetles and get themselves infected."

"Will there be a place without beetles, Balthazar? Somebody has already put some on a ship and brought them to Boston. At least there is a rumour to that effect."

Eleanor pauses, studying the old playwright across from her. They are sitting in her uncle's cell. She has made some half-hearted effort to go through Renfrew's papers but has given up. The business of government is too complex for her, and in any case, she has no right to it. Parliament remains dissolved. It is late summer and Britain is entirely without governmental structure. Anarchy! On a day like today, hot and clear, the word sounds light and liberating. It is unclear, however, for how long it can sweeten the watery porridge they've been eating. It's all they have left.

"You should be on tour," she resumes the conversation. "While you still can, I mean. While there still is Smoke to shape."

"And nurse a dying art?" He prunes his face. "I suppose it's that or go back to writing plays about people who stab each other onstage—like they used to, before the Smoke. Fake blood and onion tears. And long bloody speeches, explaining to the audience what it is the actor feels." He pauses and grows grave, leans forward in his chair. "The truth is, Eleanor, I am ready to go. It's Etta May—she isn't ready. She shot Livingstone and now she thinks she is a danger to the public. A murderer! Timmy's the only one who can make her laugh."

Eleanor looks at him quietly. "If you love someone, Balthazar, you better tell them."

"Hear, hear! You know she almost drowned me, right? And anyway, I have not gotten to the juiciest bit of the letter yet. Livia writes that she and Thomas have 'partaken in the outdated bourgeois ritual of marriage.' They got hitched. The whole of Minetowns will be appalled!"

Balthazar pauses to return Eleanor's smile. Then his smile turns evil, and shrewd.

"You know they have a piece of rock there, don't you? Down in one of the mineshafts. At least that's what Miss Cooper hinted to me. Think about it: a little splinter of God. Unless the beetles got to it already. But if they didn't . . . Perhaps they'll spend their honeymoon there, our newlyweds. It's *in* Thomas, after all. She writes that he's 'quite changed.' And that he 'looked lovely in his dinner jacket.'" Balthazar grimaces at that, as though the phrase itself were painful. "Do you know what a romance is, Eleanor? A romance is a kind of play where you don't know whether to laugh or cry."

[4]

Another month passes. A letter from Mowgli arrives, soon followed by another. Eleanor tells Balthazar all that they contain, though she refrains from reading them to him. This is less because of the professions of tenderness they include (though they do and they are intimate) and more because she does not want the playwright to comment on the poverty of Mowgli's composition (let alone that of his spelling). He and Smith landed in Bombay and had a hard time convincing the native city council that now holds power there not to sink them in the harbour. Nor were the rebels immediately convinced that the beetles were anything more than another tool of colonial rule. The movement was split in any case: along lines of religion, of cast and caste, of money and region. Mowgli cut the Gordian knot by releasing some of the beetles that made up their cargo.

With such misery in the city—producing a great density of Soot, some of it very black—the beetles soon found sustenance. Within a week some of them had spread to the poppy fields and were eating those. It was unclear whether they continued to breed. Miss Cooper, meanwhile, seemed to be active in the very south, where the Company retained some measure of authority. She was selling the inoculant whilst also paying a team of scientists to analyse and attempt to synthetize it.

Mowgli had planned on a speedy return to Britain. Then he heard a story, repeated to him by more than one source, of a northern river pouring black hate into the land—a river that had its source in the mountains of Nepal. So he—Smith and Grendel still in tow—had decided to head north with their remaining cargo of beetles, looking for the parts of the rock still buried in glacial ice. Most of the train lines had been blown up by terrorist activities, so they were travelling with horses and carts. A local maharaja, who up until recently had been one of the Company's many puppet rulers but had now emerged as a leader within the national uprising, lent them an armed escort of fifty men. Given the date of the letter, they may have arrived at their destination by now, though it was unclear whether they would actually be able to cross the Nepalese border.

Balthazar listens to all this without any show of emotion. It is only when Eleanor finishes that he purses his black lips.

"He's quite convinced then, your lover boy. He'll liberate this world! What did he call it? The 'Age of Reason.' Rationality is a bug! I always had my suspicions!" He flares his nostrils, as at a bad smell. "If the beetles find another rock, they will swarm again. Imagine the numbers! It'll be the end of Smoke."

"And the rock, too, will die." Eleanor shudders, the memory of rage running through her, and of the rock's distress, at not being understood. "Perhaps it's for the best. We were not meant to live side by side."

"'Meant'—no. But then what are we really *meant* for, other than to make more of us?" Balthazar makes a crude gesture. "It's strange. I was terrified of the rock. Still am. But to erase it like this—like it's never been here . . ."

"Erase? Not quite, Balthazar. Have you seen the colour the sea takes on some mornings? 'Tar Seas,' that's what the fishermen have started calling it. They come on it in little patches. But they are spreading. Not just here but up north and in the Channel, perhaps farther away than that. Some part of the rock is in *there*. It—"

Eleanor makes to say more, then falls silent, distracted, and cups one hand over her abdomen. Balthazar waits until the inward look on her face has cleared.

"Tar Seas, eh? How poetic! And you? Have you decided on a name yet?"

"*Names,*" she says. "At least I think so."

And then she adds giddily, a girl of eighteen sharing a secret, "Come, Balthazar, put your ear here. Perhaps you can hear."

[5]

What's this? Pregnant? Twins! And when did this happen? In the handful of days after the events on the pier? En route, travelling down from the Lakes, on a woolly blanket rolled out in a private hollow on some hill? Or back in the Keep, on one of those narrow pallets that pass as beds there, fighting for space, half falling off at every rearrangement of their limbs? Was it the day after she shed her harness? Or was she wearing it still and he had to cut her out of it with scissors? Did she smoke and seethe with anger when his body proved unable to respond? Or was it smokeless on both sides, their passion hidden, vouchsafed only by their kisses and their bodies' heat? Or did it happen *before*—in that first Storm, say, out to sea, when it was he who was bound and she drank off his rage like so much spirit, then jumped him drunk on her own lust? Was it ugly then, or beautiful; did it leave a bitter taste?

I know what you are thinking. *We should have been told.*

[6]

And another half year passes filled with letters, conversations, quiet yearning. Renfrew dies and is buried in a simple grave marked only by a wooden cross. Lady Naylor departs for Paris, to see it "cleaned and crawling with black bugs." She leaves Eleanor a purse of money and the keys to two of her estates. Balthazar and Etta May decide to return to North America, taking along Timmy, who has started to talk and now won't shut up, as though words were Smoke and an inner Gale were still blowing inside him, forcing them out in great, unmodulated bursts. Eleanor moves to a nearby village and finds she is not entirely forgotten: a fisherman's family takes her in and dotes on her (their son followed her north, and brought back stories). When her time comes, husband and wife fetch the village midwife and sit downstairs, holding hands like they did when they were courting, listening to Eleanor's cries of pain.

"It will be over soon. A young girl. It goes easy when you are young."

"Shut your mouth," says the wife. "What do you know about childbirth? 'Easy,' he says, like he's an expert in it!"

They sit and listen to her, drinking endless mugs of piping-hot water, wishing it were tea.

[7]

And a story makes the rounds, of a black whale breaching from out of this tar sea, rising to the very root of its tail and standing in the noonday sun like a fist raised in salute—and of its eye, tiny and alive, staring down with cold indifference at the fishermen who saw it—before dropping back beneath the black shroud of the ocean, mourned by a hundred black-and-yellow birds whose cry pierced the air long after it was gone.

"What does it mean?" asks the fisherman's wife, who has come to look to Eleanor for answer to all manner of things as though their ages were inverted.

"It means the world is changing yet again."

She smiles as she says it, for in the air, over one of the cribs if not the other, hangs the faintest plume of Smoke, calling to her with its need.

NACHSPIEL

A blank stage, its only props a single, rectangular table, positioned in such a manner that its long side is parallel with the stalls. The table is split into two halves by a line of chalk. Mowgli and Eleanor sit at the short ends, Mowgli on the right, Eleanor on the left. Mowgli's side of the table is cluttered with decorative knick-knacks, all of them broadly "oriental": a carved elephant statue, representations of a few Hindoo gods, a copper carafe, leather drink coasters, etc. Eleanor's half is entirely empty apart from a sheaf of writing papers and a small photo of Renfrew, positioned at an angle so that the audience can see it.

   Both Eleanor and Mowgli are writing letters. Their movements are precisely synchronised. Now they both write, bent forward. Then they stop, lost for words; look up (not seeing the other but all the same gazing into each other's eyes), then hastily scribble two or three lines; stop again, prop their heads dreamily onto a palm (the right for her, the left for him); write another line, read it to themselves, their lips moving, then quickly cross it out—all at precisely the same time, their faces mirror images, one pale, one brown.

   Now they dig in their respective desk drawers and each retrieve a carefully folded letter; open it; and smile as they read it. They look around themselves, making sure they are not observed, then bring the letters up to their noses and smell them, the way lovers do, for some hint of the writer's scent. Mowgli cries then, a single tear (give the actor an onion to squeeze if he needs it). Eleanor smokes. The fans turn on, carrying her Smoke into the audience, a taste of love: young, lusty, greedy, nervous love.

   The taste of regret in it is only very light.
   BLACK OUT. CURTAIN.
   LIGHTS.

The End

❖ ACKNOWLEDGMENTS ❖

"Human beings fear nothing so much as being touched by something unknown."

So writes Elias Canetti in *Crowds and Power*, a book that apprehends the solitary individualism of modern life and opposes it to the intoxicating and dangerous loss of self that takes place when we accept an indiscriminate "touching" and surrender ourselves to the crowd.

When I set out to write *Soot*, I knew I wanted to write a book about what it means to be touched—about its beauty and its potential for violence; about the long reach that our lives have into those of others, often halfway across the world (a reach facilitated by words and emotions but also by money); about the rootedness offered by community and the oppressions and confinements so often imposed by it; about the crushing loneliness and liberating anonymity of the atomised individuality that characterises so much of twentieth- and twenty-first-century life; and about our continued fear of touching those who come from beyond our borders of understanding.

It should not have surprised me, perhaps, that even as I was engaged in the seemingly so solitary act of writing a novel, I too opened myself up to being touched: by ideas, naturally, but above all by people; by their generosity and enthusiasm, their intelligence and insight. While the touches that are the subject matter of the novel—the multihued tendrils of Smoke that communicate and betray, ensnare and connect—are bittersweet in their implications, those that have reached me in my writer's garret were an unalloyed blessing. They changed me as well as changing the book, and for this I am deeply grateful.

I would like to thank Boyd White, for his sustained engagement with and shrewd insights into the book—I could not have done it without you, my friend. I would also like to thank Dakota White, who I can honestly say was the best possible reader I could have found for a late draft of the book and whose enthusiasm for the adventures of Eleanor, Mowgli, and the dastardly Smith did much to sustain my own faith in them. Thanks also go to the editorial teams at Doubleday, Weidenfeld and Nicolson, and HarperCollins Canada: They provided the tap on the wrist here—and the boot up the backside there—that kept me on course; and to Simon Lipskar at WritersHouse, for being there on my writer's journey and helping me see clearly. Sheeraz Gulsher marshalled the linguistic resources of friends and family to translate a number of sentences into some of the (many) languages of India and Pakistan; I hope my version of the Colonial novel complete with ancient curses and dangerous terrorists (Rider Haggard, eat your heart out!) will give him some pleasure. I also want to thank the many people I spoke to during my travels in India and Nepal, who bore with my many questions and spoke and laughed with me until I no longer felt a stranger. Above all, I wish to thank Chantal, my wonderful wife, for her intelligence and honesty in editorial matters as much as for her patience (the latter was more sorely tried). I would be lost without you, my love.